The Archivists

The
Archivists

Martin Ikedais

Matador
Unit E2 Airfield Business Park,
Harrison Road, Market Harborough,
Leicestershire. LE16 7UL
Tel: 0116 2792299
Email: books@troubador.co.uk
Web: www.troubador.co.uk/matador
Twitter: @matadorbooks

ISBN 978 1803135 670

British Library Cataloguing in Publication Data.
A catalogue record for this book is available from the British Library.

Printed and bound in the UK by TJ Books Limited, Padstow, Cornwall
Typeset in 11pt Adobe Caslon Pro by Troubador Publishing Ltd, Leicester, UK

Matador is an imprint of Troubador Publishing Ltd

For my father.
He would not have believed it.

My face in thine eye, thine in mine appears,
And true plain hearts do in the faces rest;
Where can we find two better hemispheres,
Without sharp North, without declining West?
Whatever dies, was not mixed equally;
If our two loves be one; or thou and I
Love so alike that none do slacken, none can die.

John Donne

BOOK ONE

REFLECTION

THE CHARACTERS AND OBSCURITIES OF BOOK ONE

(BY ORDER OF APPEARANCE)

FRIDA PADGETT (nee HALFPENNY): A famous scientist. In 2024, she lives in Winchelsea, East Sussex, with her husband, FRANCIS PADGETT, and their young son, DAVID PADGETT.

DR GRAHAM CORBIERE: Graham is a historian working at the British Museum. He is a friend of ARTHUR EATON.

MARCUS EATON: A self-confessed nerd. From Tolworth, in the Royal Borough of Kingston upon Thames, Marcus lives with his parents, VICTOR and BARBARA EATON.

EUCOMM: A mobile telecommunications company of the 21st century. They also manufacture smartphones.

FRANCIS (FRANK) PADGETT: Quiet and shy, Frank works with computers. In 2024, he lives in Winchelsea, East Sussex, with his wife, FRIDA PADGETT, and their young son, DAVID.

DAVID PADGETT: A very lively four-year-old. David is the son of FRANCIS and FRIDA PADGETT.

MIRRA: A beguiling feminine voice. Mirra helps and befriends MARCUS EATON during his incarceration.

JAMES (JIMMY) RILEY: A plasterer by trade. Tall and gaunt, Jimmy is sly, crass, and cheeky.

PHILIP BRYANT: Philip works as a scaffolder. He is large, hairy, loud, and untidy.

MILLICENT (MILLIE) EATON: Older sister of MARCUS EATON. Millie works for the Foreign Office and Diplomatic Service of the UK government.

FIZZOG: A social networking service.

CHIRP: A social networking and news service.

DATA STREAM MANIPULATION: An illegal practice involving the siphoning of data from wireless network transmissions. In 2024, it should be impossible.

ENTANGLED DATA RECOMPILATION: A file compression/decompression technique of the mid-21st century. It is secure and almost instantaneous.

WONG: A Peruvian supermarket chain.

T2: A mobile phone of the early 21st century.

YILDUN OFFICE: A suite of office applications installed on the T2 mobile phone of MARCUS EATON.

BARRY: A strange crustacean-like organism occupying a small aquarium.

UNCLE, ARTHUR EATON: Brother of VICTOR EATON. A successful but reclusive historical researcher and collector of books. He died in 2010 from a massive stroke.

MOTHER, BARBARA EATON: The mother of MARCUS and MILLICENT EATON. She works part-time and keeps house very diligently. MARCUS considers her cleaning behaviour obsessive.

FATHER, VICTOR EATON: Father of MARCUS and MILLICENT EATON.

SAULINTONE: A manufacturer of mobile phones and electronic devices. Saulintone produced the T2, the mobile phone of MARCUS EATON.

MOLOCH: A cold and unfeeling masculine voice. MIRRA fears him.

DR NORMANDY (NORMA) STICELBAK: An archivist and employee of the British Library. She possesses long auburn hair, a pale freckled skin, and a generous smile.

KAREN HALFPENNY: Mother of FRIDA PADGETT and a widow. Fifty years old, petite, and shy, she suffers from a rare form of Tourette's.

Dr LYNDA JENKINS: Senior conservator of the museum in Rye, East Sussex.

CHEWBIFLIX: An internet-based video sharing and social media platform.

RECTOR CALUM ARBUTHNOT-SHAW: Young and enthusiastic, circa 2010, he was the parish priest of Winchelsea.

PROLOGUE
A LETTER FROM FRIDA

From: padgett.frida86@eucomm.co.uk
To: corbiere.graham@britishmuseum.org

Lorenzo Carter Place
Friars Rd
Winchelsea
East Sussex
17/9/2024

Dear Graham,

Two years since my last letter, and I hope you are keeping well, but we have new information regarding Marcus and urgently need your help...

After our years of fruitless searching, assuming Marcus was dead, I was shocked to discover a new message on my phone. Without knowing where it had come from, I was cautious, but then, after reading the first few lines, I knew: Marcus. A message from Marcus! He's not dead, he's in prison, and oh my God, I suddenly thought, Frank, what have we done? Our decision to marry hinged on Marcus being dead; sharing his loss drew us together, but now... In my heart, I know we did the right thing – Marcus would not have wanted me to be lonely, but my husband, burdened by guilt, quietly begs his forgiveness when he thinks I'm out of earshot...

On the surface, Frank is a placid old soul, but underneath he hides the heart of a lion, and his loyalty to Marcus still roars as loudly as ever. When I returned from Lima that time, it was Frank who took care of me, and not for himself, he did it for Marcus, and even though I've assured him my feelings for Marcus have waned, he cannot help but worry. Certainly, Marcus will always have a place in my heart, but the young woman he knew is only a part of me now. Feelings change, people grow, time quenches the passions of the past, and we have a family. Our gorgeous son, David, is now almost four, with a sister well on the way. My God is she well on the way. I can hardly reach to type!

Returning to Marcus's message, we feel certain he is the original author – there are too many intimate details for it to have come from anyone else. His first paragraph, for example, touching upon our resort's much-lauded swimming pool, is quite telling. How could anyone else know of our fooling about in its leaf-strewn depths, pretending to drown, after we found it was empty? Certainly, the detail is there, but I do have an issue with the text itself. To be blunt, Marcus was never a writer. He was quiet, thoughtful, rarely chatty, and his writing was similar. Languid, lazy, clumsy, clunky even, he could make himself understood, but this text is not of his making. In style, it is more akin to my own – intensely wordy and florid. Oh yes, I can happily gabble on, page after page, but Marcus? Never. He preferred a one-word reply. If he bothered to find one.

Nevertheless, looking beyond his phrasing, when you come to read it, I must insist you keep its contents secret. With entries contradicting the statements I made to both the Peruvian and UK authorities, I dare not risk reopening the investigation until I have a better understanding why Marcus, or some other agency, would describe fictitious events. Certainly, on that fateful night in Lima, Marcus never returned from the museum, so how could I have sent him shopping? It's puzzling. He recalls these fictitious events in such detail, manifestly increasing my suspicion that the "Mirra" he mentions has doctored his original text.

Oh, good Lord, how this is bringing back the events of, when was it, eleven, twelve years ago? That awful clammy night in Lima, worrying, waiting for Marcus to return, my uneasiness steadily growing. How can I forget my panic-filled ride to the museum, arriving to confront its terrified guards and overzealous policemen? Then, having to make all those dreadful phone calls, to the travel company, the airline, my mother, the Eaton's – angry at first and then worried sick. Before another week, alone, stranded, broke, interviewed, accused, harassed, the long meetings at our embassy, yes, I remember it all. The fear, the weeping, and the loss – my first dearest love! The terrible, inexplicable loss.

You surely recall my return to the UK – you were my first port of call. The museum in Lima clearly held the answer, and I'm sure it still does, and, yes, Marcus was a fool, damaging their mummy. What was he thinking? Why the reckless abandon? Patience and diplomacy would have served him best.

For two years we then hunted, Marcus's family, his friends, Jimmy, even Philip! His dear sister Millie was brilliant. So many contacts, so much diplomatic pressure, and of course we had Frank, the wizard of the World Wide Web, searching through so many chat rooms, setting up a Fizzog page, a blog, and numerous feeds on Chirp. It was all for nothing. Not even a whisper, we never had a clue, until now. Because now we have this marvellous text. This wonderful, mysterious text. Might we together discover new avenues of enquiry? This is my hope. So far, I have only studied the early chapters, and my God, they have torn me apart. Poor Marcus! So brave, so resourceful. The pride and love I have for him as he battles to satisfy his captors, well, it almost breaks my heart. He's so alone, but his spirit is unbreakable, a testament to his courage and strength, and it doesn't matter if Mirra has altered the text, it's still definitely Marcus. His sensitivity, his stubbornness, sarcasm, and self-contempt, his quiet genius irrepressibly shining.

Therefore, my dear friend, have a good read, it's all here – Marcus's memory has done him proud, and if you do notice anything important, please contact me on this email address ASAP, but I beg you, remember. This file is confidential. There is little point showing it to anyone until we can prove its authenticity. Certainly, Frank can find no clue as to its date of creation, of sending, or even when it arrived. He says, this is due to data stream manipulation, and he would like to meet the genius capable of affecting entangled data recompilation. If only to ask how they did it!

After I've studied the later chapters, could we meet and share our findings?

Yours sincerely,

Frida

ONE

CAPTIVITY

After providing the evidence you demanded, Eaton-Marcus 105403 hastily wrote the following before his release, and even though it was my suggestion he go on to write of his experiences with us, I was unaware that he had written of his arrival until I received it. Be of good heart! Not having the opportunity to review it with him, the text displays his many compositional weaknesses, and, despite your loathing of irrelevant material, posterity deserves to know of his plight, so I have placed it here, at the beginning, where it belongs.

Oh, my love, I am so sorry. You were right and now I'm in trouble. Trouble enough to fill our hotel swimming pool, the Jacuzzi and foot spa as well, and I am way down, weighed down and drowning, clawing at the surface shimmering above my head.

Yes, Frida, yes, I know, I'm always overreacting. "Don't worry, Marky," you always say. "You'll wriggle out of it," but this time it's properly serious, far more serious than getting drunk, falling over, and scratching a car, I'm screwed.

Kidnapped rather than arrested, although why or by whom I don't really know. Shock and bewilderment are all I have so far. It was all so terribly sudden! As if ripped from a page and then stuck on another. Yes, that was how it felt – during the blink of an eye, plucked from there and deposited here. I feel like a lobster, suddenly caught. Dragged from the familiar, deep underwater, into the dazzling light of the world.

Sorry, Frida, if I'm not making sense, but this is the best I can do; my head is spinning with so many questions, it's hard to look for the answers. What is this place, where am I, and why am I here?

Piecing together my movements, my final ride into Lima I remember quite well. Every sight, sound, and bump in the road are still fresh in my mind. Then, I recall going into Wong, pushing a wayward trolley, buying drinks, fruit, packets of snacks, before heading outside with two flimsy bags ready to give way any minute. I recall my frustration, waiting for another taxi (as mine had driven off) and how it smelled – a bad smell, foul, dirty, you remember those pigs near Steyning? Well, it was as bad as that.

Marcus is referring to an earlier lunch with his girlfriend in said town, and how it became much affected by the aroma of 4-Methyphenol coming from a nearby farm.

Got into the taxi, yes, despite the terrible pong, told the driver where I wanted to go, and then we moved off, did we? Because what happened next? Did I doze off or suffer a blow to the head? I don't think so, my head is fine – no lumps or bumps, so, no, not hit on the head, and surely not drugged or gassed. Wouldn't I have awoken dizzy or sick? I'm at a loss to explain my arrival and having no further knowledge, I'm forced to accept my surroundings...

Certainly, I can describe where I am. A square room. Four metres wide, three metres high, with smooth white walls and a ceiling that are slightly warm to the touch. Covering the floor is a thick red carpet, while, in the ceiling, four rectangular panels emit a dazzling white light. Four small switches adjacent to the door control these lights. A relief as their brightness is both harsh and oppressive. Apart from the switches and the door, the walls are blank and lifeless, and what I wouldn't give for a window, if only to feel air on my face! Not that it ever gets stuffy. There's no odour in here, no perfume, and breathing is strangely monotonous. The small vents dotting the ceiling must surely be refreshing the air, but, after stacking furniture and climbing to reach one, I couldn't feel any noticeable draught.

With a small loudspeaker and a camera, steel plated and emphatically locked, the door itself is formidable, and unnerving. To begin, the very notion of being watched filled me with disquiet. Only later did I come to understand the importance of the camera and loudspeaker. Privacy is of no use to the lonely. My well-being, sanity, and eventual freedom would depend upon their unwavering service.

Deep red with a pattern of feathery leaves and flowers, the carpet beneath my feet matches the sitting room carpet we once had at home. Nothing so unusual about that, but upon reflection, the carpet is an odd addition. Why bother? I'm never cold, there are no draughts, and, although I appreciate the homely gesture, under these circumstances, I couldn't give a damn. In addition, the carpet has me thinking. Am I imprisoned somewhere stylistically backward? Where could they have bought such an outmoded design?

On the back wall is a toilet (with tissue), a washbasin, soap, and a towel. Positioned against the right wall is a small desk and a chair, with a simple but surprisingly comfortable bed on the left.

Upon the desk, filled with water several and centimetres of oozy-looking mud, is a small rectangular fish tank. Something alive is moving beneath this primordial gloop – long antennae flick back and forth, and, if I tap the glass with my knuckle, they disappear with a swirling swish only to warily unfurl moments later. Curiously, the tank possesses no lid, and sealed so tightly, I wonder how the strange thing is fed.

Moving to examine the bed, I discover a bottle filled to the brim with clear liquid and a dozen pink cubes on a dish. At first, I thought these morsels a variety of Turkish delight; they smelled fruity and very appealing and out of curiosity, I sampled a piece, wondering if it would taste as good as it smelled. It did, it was delicious! For some reason, I expected them to be tasteless or vile. Finding them sweet, juicy, and tasting of pineapple was an enormous surprise, and it stirred within me the memory of the overripe ones I bought us from Wong. I wonder where they went.

It was a great relief knowing the food to be edible, although I've been more cautious since, only eating or drinking when I need to. There is no need to worry, though. I'm not going to starve. It's just sensible to ration myself, although I can't be here simply to suffer. The state of my cell suggests my captors are very attentive, and besides, I'm not yet hungry or thirsty. In fact, and this is truly strange, if I avoid undue emotion or stress, I don't feel much from my body at all. I never get tired, feel hot or feel cold, and can stand like a statue for hours, I haven't even needed to pee! My chin is not stubbly, my teeth not yucky, my armpits are still fresh as a daisy, just what the hell's going on?

Doubtless you can imagine my horror finding myself a prisoner, how fidgety I get when I'm tied down, so it won't surprise you to learn I examined every nook and cranny of my cell, and do you know what? It is pristine, seemingly new, perfect, and tight as a drum – all of which sent my fear of captivity spiralling out of control. I became edgy, claustrophobic, and desperate to escape. Assaulting the door, I pushed, leant, and pounded it with my fists, all the while yelling like a demented loon. I even tried a flying kick (with a run-up!) but it was futile. Escaping by physical means was impossible, so I sat on the bed, nibbling my thumb, seeking ideas, wondering, "What next?" when quite out of nothing...

There was a sound, a crackling, quiet at first, like distant footsteps on a gravel path, and then, as I realised the crackling was coming from the door, its loudspeaker suddenly let out an ear-piercing squeal, followed by a voice – a voice! The voice of a man. Cold, distant, empty of feeling, and yet clear and precise, with an English accent, if it truly exists...

"Subject. Eaton-Marcus, number one-zero-five-four-zero-three. It is to record all it has done. Once satisfied with its efforts, I will release it. I would know its answer."

The bluntness of this announcement froze me to the spot and my jaw wobbled fighting to get out a reply...

"Do... do what?" I then blustered. "Until I speak to a lawyer, you can forget it!"

Dear me. In no way was this the best I could've done, or should've done, far from it. Clouding my judgement, fear had left me sharp and defensive, and I shamefully hung my head.

"Idiot," I reproachfully muttered, and I stood, eager to hear his reply.

He said nothing, however, so I waited, turning my head, and listening hard, straining my ears for the tiniest whisper. Had the announcer already gone?

Walking up to the door, I pressed my nose to the speaker. Could I hear the faintest hiss?

As if in defence, bursting into my face, there came a deafening squeal, and I staggered back, shaking my head.

"I'm sorry," I gasped, recovering my wits. "I was scared, didn't mean to yell at you, what do you want to record?"

For a second or two the crackling returned before rapidly fading, and the silence that followed was heavy and full of foreboding, like the falling lid of a tomb.

Growling in frustration, I returned to the bed, seeking ideas, answers, making plans, straining my mind, with it fizzing, swirling, and soaring. Who was that and what did he mean? Did he hear me, will he help me, and why did he call me "it"? With other questions upon questions, again, and again and again. Stress flowed bitter and fast into my stomach. I gagged, and, knowing of no other remedy, I paced the room, taking regular breaths. "Don't be sick," I whispered. "Stay calm, it's alright, it's alright."

Time passed – how much, I don't really know – whereupon the loudspeaker crackled again. Hope stirred within me, and I moved to the door to listen…

"So, it is you," came a feminine voice. "Marcus… Eaton, did he give you a number?"

Somewhat confused, I nodded.

"Do you recall what it was? No, of course you don't. He just gave you a number, gave you an order and disappeared, am I right?"

Another nod.

"Well, then," she said, "let's not worry about him. I'm here now, to help you, and help you I will."

"Help me do what?" I shrugged. "Record all I have done?"

"Indeed." She chuckled. "You are here to write an account of your life leading up to and including your time in Peru, and, if you want to get out, you must do a good job. If, for example, you write a simple list of events, he will reject your work, insisting you start over again, so my advice would be to make it a story. He loves a good book."

"But why?" I pleaded. "Please, whomever you are, I want to see a lawyer or make a phone call, to the British embassy. I have rights!"

"You do," she replied, "and I will get you a lawyer, at the first opportunity, only it will be some time before they arrive. We… don't have a… telephone, you see. In the meantime, why not make a start on your story?"

"What bloody story?" I grumbled. "I'm not a writer, and besides, I don't have a pen."

"Your story, young man, is everything you've done, and this is what he wishes to know. You have been interfering, he claims. Sticking your nose in, affecting his business. Appearing, disappearing, cropping up 'like a tiny boat bobbing up and down in the sea' and, consequently, he wishes to know who you are, what you know, and as for what to write with. You still have your communications device, do you not? Use that."

She was right. I did! My beloved T2 was still in my pocket. Quite why I had forgotten to check remains a mystery (although stress does tend to make me go stupid) and, after composing myself, I pulled out my phone, pressed the home key and studied the screen. Full charge, no signal, no Wi-Fi and no way to contact the outside world, but if I could just call my mum to collect me, it wouldn't be much of a prison, would it?

Now, hindsight is a wonderful thing, and in hindsight I should have asked about his business, but I was still too bewildered for thinking, and her voice, her graceful, beautiful, and dare I say it, oddly familiar voice had a hold on me that is hard to explain – I couldn't resist, only listen, while she soothed my fears and lessened my doubt. Certainly, if her gently coercive nature was a ploy of my captors to make me more pliant, it was a stroke of genius. I clung to her every word…

"I'm sorry," I said, showing my phone to the door. "How do you expect me to write a story on this? It's too fiddly. Without a pointer it'll take me forever. You know" – I then shrugged – "apart from a few essays, I've never really written anything, so why not just interrogate me? Honestly, I don't even know where to start!"

Following a long pause, she spoke…

"You'll find something in the desk to help you write, and as for where to start, isn't it obvious? Think! How did you come to be here? What events led you here? We need to know everything you can remember. If we just interrogated you, you would omit a great deal. We require more than a simple list of facts! A historical account is what we need, full of your insights, relationships, experiences."

Standing, I pensively nibbled my thumb.

Considering my crimes (trespass and vandalism of a national treasure), what they were asking wasn't impossible. In fact, it was quite reasonable, and an idea slowly took shape in my mind…

She spoke again.

"Are you thinking this means pages and pages of writing? Then, yes, you are correct, so try to make it enjoyable – use humour, sarcasm if you want, be ironic. If you do, the writing will be less of a burden."

"Very well," I said. "But what if I get stuck?"

"You won't," she replied. "You'll struggle initially, and I'll be returning to check on you, particularly when you reach a natural stopping point, but you're far better at this than you realise. You are going to do fine – I know it already, you'll see!"

Then, after a beep and crackle, she was gone.

"Fuck," I said. "Now I know we're missing our flight."

Opening the drawer of the desk, I came across a rubber-tipped stylus (which hadn't been there earlier) and, twirling it in my fingers, I wondered how to proceed. Good God, I thought, even texting is ponderous enough. "Cu in the pub 8ish" is fine, but a story? What was I going to do?

Perusing the apps on my phone (most of which I never use), I ran Yildun Office. A suite of productivity and business applications, including the simple word processor, and after prodding and poking, I realised it fitted my needs to a T.

Then, I did nothing. Just kicked off my shoes, rolled off my socks, and tried to sleep on the bed. Strange, you might think, but this is my way of doing things. My mind works better if it works in the background. If I think too hard about a task, can't think about it at all, and only after rising hours later did I begin.

So, see if you will, a lonely young man sitting in total silence. A silence broken only by the tapping of his pointer, the rasp of his breath, and the steady drumming of hearts.

And lo!
    After cutting and pasting,
    Editing and deleting,
    Swearing and struggling,
    This work of shining magnificence was born.
    And the nicely spoken woman said it was good,
    Before she tore it to shreds…

There's gratitude for you!

Therefore, Frida, if you ever get the chance to read this before my release, know I am safe, well looked after and comfortable. Of course, I am bored rigid, I've nothing to do except do as I'm told, but at least I'm not alone, with the mothering Mirra and the prawn-like Barry looking out for me (although I'm not sure his heart's really in it).

For the most part, though, I write, and I dream, dream of my freedom, write, and dream of your smile. I *will* finish this, no matter what, and when I get out (if I ever get out) I'll find you.

    Wait for me,
    Marcus

TWO

THE FUNERAL

Deciding when and where he should begin, what to include, and what to omit is difficult, and I must restate. Your insistence this detainee write from memory is foolhardy at best. The problem stems from his inconsistent regard for salience. For example, the date palms in Jordan he remembers very clearly, and yet facts of greater import, for instance the curator of the Jordanian museum, he cannot recall. In addition, his historic dialogue tends to be little more than an approximation, partially assembled from jumbled recollections, and, although these passages do roughly follow the words spoken at the time, it is doubtful he possesses the necessary skill to convey the original colour and mood of the moment.

This account begins like a fly-on-the-wall documentary, and, looking down, wrapped in a twisted duvet, is my slender body, my head throbbing, my ears ringing from last night's partying, and imagine the camera pulling back into a wide shot of my bedroom, the remnants of my teenage years affecting every surface. Faded posters cling to the walls, embarrassing photos dot my wardrobe, and toys, games, and books I no longer enjoy collect dust in cupboards I rarely open. Lucky, however, to have a space of my own, even if it was just a small room in my parents' old semi. Granted, a flat would have entitled greater privacy, but living alone, looking after myself, without a cook and a cleaner? * Not likely.

He is referring to his mother.

On a small bedside table, strands of lettuce protruding from a polystyrene cocoon represented the remains of last night's kebab, and I grudgingly sat up, frowning, as the piercing whine of a vacuum cleaner got closer and closer.

As I stood (quite naked) stretching in a sunbeam, my mother burst in, grinning as if she was welcome…

"Funeral today, Marcus," she chirped. "Want you dressed and ready, chop-chop!" and, ignoring my nudity, she dragged the vacuum cleaner in through the door and stooped with a groan for a socket…

Having my privacy invaded remained a depressingly frequent occurrence, but not having the wherewithal that morning for an argument, I merely replied with a grunt, before grabbing my robe and wearily plodding downstairs.

The funeral my mother mentioned was my uncle's, my dad's brother. Normal enough, you might think, but my parents were expecting me to play "grieving nephew" and if my performance slackened during the day's "festivities" doubtless I would be in trouble.

Downstairs at the kitchen table was my father, and by his body language I knew his temper was ready to erupt. Pouring myself a coffee, its aromatic steam soothing my pounding head, I grabbed the last croissant (surely left for me) and bit off a corner, trying to hide the drift of brown flakes tumbling from my mouth like autumn leaves…

"Ahem!" coughed my father, observing my antics. "What are you doing? If you used a plate like a civilised… Oh, for God's sake, fetch the dustpan and sweep them up!"

Nodding (and swaying no small amount) I then stumbled to a cupboard, extracted the dustpan, and stooped to sweep up the crumbs.

"Oh," he then groaned. "Marcus, you're white as sheet. You're not still pissed, are you?"

"I'm fine," I replied. "Just tired, hoarse from, you know, having to scream-talk. I'll wake up once I've showered and stuff."

"Tired." He darkly chuckled. "Drunk and chasing some poor girl, more likely. Gave her your number as well, I bet. Marvellous. That's you glued to your phone all day."

"No," I countered, cradling my coffee. "And, anyway, the girl came after me, so yeah." I chuckled, suddenly remembering. "She got my number alright."

Retrieving my phone from the hooded top (left on a chair when I came in), I discovered one text and a single call from Jimmy at 3.48am (glad I missed that) and, finishing my croissant and coffee, I offered this cautious apology...

"Sorry, Dad. Guess I forgot about the funeral – if I'd remembered, I wouldn't have gone out, and I'm sorry about my blasé attitude, but I can't remember the last time I even saw Uncle Arthur. Didn't know him at all!"

"Nice try," he remarked. "Not a bad effort at all. Less apologising and I might have believed you, but your bit about the girl? Come off it! The way you and Frank mumble and shuffle about, what did you do, abduct the poor thing?"

He paused for effect, his good humour rapidly fading, before sitting up straight and folding his arms. A deep sigh escaped from his lips, and he fixed his eyes upon me.

"Now, listen," he said. "Your mum, you, and I are *it* this afternoon; there's no more family coming. The rest will be his friends, his colleagues, and they are all going to be looking at *us*, some of them might even speak to *us*, so could you try, just for once, to give the appearance of normal?"

"Yes, yes," I assured. "Understood. I'll be so normal you won't even know I'm there, but how many guests, anyway, and is Millie not coming?"

"Not sure," he revealed. "But more than fifty according to the mail I've received, and you know your sister won't be there, she's in Moscow, or was the last time she called."

"Moscow's in Russia, darling," added my mother, walking in, fussing at everything, and fluttering at nothing. Dropping my kebab into the kitchen's massive flip-top bin (with a "tut"), she washed her hands very thoroughly. "Why must you always buy these horrid things?" she disapprovingly asked. "They're so greasy."

Now, before aweing you with my reply, I need to leave this scene of domestic bliss and fill a gap in the story. I will admit, my response was without tact, and I fled the kitchen to escape a tumultuous barrage of admonishment.*

*I deemed it necessary to replace the phrase "Fuck blaster of a bollocking".

This omission is an important one as my captors will doubtless dissect this account minutely, hence, before any judgement, I should make my humble background and general good nature plain...

Marcus Eaton is my name, an ordinary twenty-two-year-old, with good teeth, scruffy hair, and a spindly eleven-stone, five-foot, ten-inch frame.

Finishing school at eighteen, I came away with low grades in both English and history, with a richly deserved U in geography. Not too bright, you might think, and certainly, with these lacklustre results, obtaining a good university place was impossible, not that it bothered me. My attitude towards formal education has always been one of contempt. I've always preferred a more auto-didactic approach, studying what I want, when I want, to an extent I find satisfactory. The thought of returning to formal education is enough to send shivers down my spine.

Of course, society punishes educational nonconformity, and as a result I struggled to find gainful employment, ending up at Brian's Burgers – a "high-class" restaurant in the stylish district of Tolworth. Oh, the joy of it, living my boyhood dream. Working to provide for the cream of the local community. Shovelling delicious fries into small bags, skilfully assembling towering burgers, all to satisfy, amuse, and delight our refined and eloquent patrons. No, I shouldn't joke. It was an awful job. Society's harsh penance for this stubborn school-hater involved a stupid uniform, the smell of scorched grease, and a floor smeared and sticky from trampled slices of gherkin. Under relentless pressure from my parents to find a better job, I did consider several alternatives, but not wishing to work like my dad in a tedious office, or dig holes in the road, finding suitable employment was proving problematic.

In my spare time I enjoy socialising, gaming, reading, and playing the ukulele, although the noise I produce isn't music. Dismayed by my discordant strumming, * my father regards my cherished uke as little more than kindling.

*In fact, he referred to Marcus as "a tone-deaf little wanker".

Millie, my elder sister, is the bane of my life, and I still burn from the childhood conflicts between us. She was cruel and spiteful when I was small, and not until equalling her size and strength (big enough to thump her) did a fragile peace break out. These days, she works as a civil servant for the Diplomatic Service, and currently shuttling between London and Moscow, we hardly saw her at all. No idea of her exact role (she's very evasive about it), but one time she did reveal her main function involved carrying official documents when the trustworthiness of electronic communication or a private courier were in doubt. Thinking back, I realise this could well be her cover story, and Millie might be a spy. One drunken Christmas, hearing of her Russian boyfriends, I took wicked pleasure naming her Millie the Diplomatic Slag. Nobody laughed. *

*Can't imagine why.

I don't recall a long journey to the crematorium, and we soon came to a halt in a pristine car park tastefully planted with shrubs. Signposts guided us to a building of brick and metal (reminiscent of a cattle-shed), where we came upon the chaplain and two burly men.

After a solemn greeting, exchanging handshakes, pleasantries, and muttered condolences, the chaplain led us inside. My first impression of the interior was of newness. The walls and ceiling were white and spotless, the oak furniture, thickly varnished and gleaming. A wide central aisle with a deep crimson carpet led to the catafalque supporting the coffin, wreaths around it in a tasteful display, but raised high above it, and dominating the room, was a huge octagonal clock. Its monotonous ticking desecrating the respectful silence like the echoes of distant thunder.

Such a conspicuous timepiece within a crematorium chapel seemed a peculiar choice and a cruel one too. Most inappropriate. What message was it there to convey? Surely, funerals are about remembrance, the remembrance of the deceased? To illustrate the inexorable passing of time would be like a slap in the face the grieving.

A vigorous tap on the shoulder brought me to sudden attention, with my dad demanding my phone. I did still have my headphones in, and, caught red-handed (or wire eared), I obediently handed it over.

"Thank you," he said, tapping the screen, winding the headphones, slipping the whole lot into his pocket, and then, as we made our way up the aisle he winked and leant over, his arm around my shoulders…

"Oh," he then whispered. "And you've got a new message, from someone called Frida? When you get this back, you can read it…"

Now, this was a typical dad-type ploy and one he has used my whole life, a behavioural incentive, constantly developing to match my needs, age, and maturity. "If you're a good boy you can have sweets," was how it began, culminating into the use of technology (and access to the opposite sex).

Better off with sweets, I assure you.

The main wreath atop of the coffin came from my parents. Traditional in style with roses and laurel, while the largest bouquet, standing at the foot of the coffin and filling the air with musk, consisted of pure white lilies. Stapled to the bouquet wrapping was a brief note: "From your friends at the British Museum and Library. Profoundly missing your camaraderie, scholarship, and generous contributions. God Bless."

Guests were arriving and I plonked myself at the end of the front right pew (a good spot for leaning and watching). Before me, solidly built from oak, was the pulpit, and all very plain I thought, but then, tick-tock, tick-tock, my attention was drawn to the damnable clock! I couldn't escape it, it was ticking so loudly I was entranced by it, watching intently as its sword-like hands twitched past numbers that were large, black, and bold. Never had I witnessed such a tremendous illustration of time!

By now, my parents were busy meeting and greeting, my mum delighted by the arrival of my aunts, my dad shaking the hands of three total strangers.

More unknowns were trickling in, seating themselves upon pews that were functional rather than comfortable. Filing to the front, the unknown trio paused to examine the lilies, with one of their number, a fussy little man, his spectacles on the end of his nose, turning to look me over, and, after a slow and respectful nod, he moved to join his associates.

This individual was Dr Graham Corbiere, and I would come to know him quite well.

Well, now, I must leave it here as I can't recall much of the service at all, but I'm certain it all went off splendidly, with my poor uncle burnt to a crisp. The arse-numbing hour I spent upon a pew I do remember, however, watching the hands of the clock go around, and the more intently I studied them, the slower they seemed to go, and yet, despite my hardest brow-furrowing stare, there was no way to stop them, even for an instant, and the ticking seemed louder when I tried.

Suddenly then I understood, how time passes and how the dead have fallen behind. Indeed, visit any cemetery, look at the graves, and what do you see? Memories. Tales of weeping, of grieving, of those we have lost. Forever behind us, forever a part of our past.

This next part finds me in O'Malley's, an Irish pub in Morden. A delightful spot. Ask any local. They'll tell you...

Virtually empty when our party started filing in, the only customer I could see; a vastly tall man with a white beard and sparkling blue eyes, quickly finished his pint, returned my stares, and left, and I still remember him almost bending double, loping through the door.

As I sat at the bar, our food started to arrive. Nothing special. Plates of sandwiches, bowls of chips, gobbets of fish, nuggets of chicken, and, grabbing a few morsels, I looked at the scene about me...

Only a dozen or so had joined us, and they sat or stood in twos or threes, sipping drinks, chatting, or eating, but all I could think of was home and bed. The thought of being stuck in a dingy pub all afternoon was appalling...

You might think someone of my age would have social life revolving around pubs, clubs, and drinking and, to a certain extent, it did – I often met my friends in pubs before going on to a party, but not even my most grizzled mates like them much. They stink.

Since the smoking ban, the smell inside pubs has changed. In the past, the dominant smell was smoke, but now, with the air less carcinogenic, it is thick with the reek of stale beer, frying, filthy carpets, dishwasher water, clogged toilets and the lowlifes that inhabit these dives. Standing in the rain for a fag, surely the only ablution they ever receive.

Nonchalantly kicking the bar's foot rail, boredom seeping from my every pore, I watched in dismay as my dad led over the fussy, bespectacled man from the funeral.

"Hey, Marcus!" says my father. "This is Dr Corbiere from the British Museum. Your uncle used help him study old books."

Nervously touching his spectacles, Dr Corbiere pushed them slightly onto his nose.

"Indeed," he began. "Your uncle was superbly talented, capable of identifying books and parchments from little more than scraps. His volunteer contributions for the museum, identifying and cataloguing artefacts, particularly written documents, were quite exceptional. His absence is keenly felt."

With his pale face, round spectacles and long lank hair, Dr Corbiere spoke at breakneck speed, and keeping up with his verbal barrage was so difficult I'm sure to have stared back with a face of blank bewilderment.

Later, knowing him better, I learnt this was simply Corbiere's way of talking when shy or nervous, a continuous flow of words until his point put across...

"So," says my dad. "I've got a job for you. Help clear my brother's house before it's put on the market. An independent company will be removing the furniture, appliances, and so forth, but anything relating to his work, his books, and papers, I want you to go through them, to see if they have any value. In addition, Dr Corbiere and his colleagues believe there may be articles of interest to them, and I have agreed to donate them to the museum and library."

Now, I can't remember reacting to this at all, giving him ample opportunity to remind me, (a) I had the time, (b) I was noticeably bored hanging around the house all day, and (c) with a penchant for reading nonfiction, I knew more history than the rest of the family combined.

His last point (damn him) was undeniable – I read a great deal, really enthusing Corbiere when I naïvely admitted my current reading concerned the Crusades.

"Ah ha!" said Corbiere. "If you want to start a crusade in your life, dare to be your best." *

"Yeah," I mumbled, thinking him a bit of a dick. "I suppose so."

"Good man!" said my dad, slapping me on the back. "We'll go over later for a look," then, seeing the horror on my face, he wickedly smiled, so full of triumph, I cannot imagine he knew the life-changer this onerous task would turn out to be...

*William H Danforth.

"It is the trials of life that shape us." I read that somewhere, I'm sure of it, * and it's a strange fact, when adapting to new things, especially in the face of adversity, they impel you to grow as a person. Certainly, the task dumped on me that afternoon seemed oppressive and a burden, but now I look back at the time spent in my uncle's house with great satisfaction, even pleasure. It was the discoveries made in his house and the experiences Frida and I shared investigating them that cemented our relationship, and, as I sit in this prison remembering, I can only wonder how our lives would have run without them.

*I don't think so. Having searched our database thoroughly, I am unable to match this quotation anywhere. Could it be a corruption from Thessalonians or an utterance of Oscar Wilde? Marcus has certainly read neither. Do we have a new proverb in our midst?

Back home, after recovering my smartphone, keen to read Frida's text, I excitedly dashed to my room. Her message read: "hi rlly gd 2 meet u last nite. gd fun. if u wanna meet 4 coffee txt me. Frida x"

Uncertain how to respond, I thought long and hard about her message; changed my clothes, read a book, even brushed my hair before replying. She was so confident, highlighting my own social awkwardness to such a degree it felt crippling, and as much as I enjoyed female company, I was on a break from dating. On that afternoon, however, feeling brave, I texted how I'd be happy to meet Frida sometime over the weekend, leaving her to choose a venue, hoping she'd plump for somewhere quiet – our drunken yelling the previous night had done us no favours at all!

Awoken by a shrill call from my mother and summoned downstairs on the double, my dad said, "Shoes, coat, and let's go," and, following a motherly "tut" at my tousled appearance, I was out of the house and into the car.

"Don't suppose you remember visiting your uncle," muttered my father as we tootled along. "You were only a baby, I think, and, anyway, we didn't stay long."

He frowned and sighed. "We never returned thereafter, not as a family. We simply weren't welcome."

"How come?" I asked. "Was he grumpy, difficult, or something?"

"You could say so, yes, stubborn certainly – no room in his life for anyone else, became a total recluse. He hardly left the house at all."

"Ah, yeah, I remember you telling me. At the time, I thought you were joking. Although didn't that doctor with the French name say he worked for a museum?"

"Yeah, he did, but it was mostly done via correspondence – letters and photos. If they wanted to see him in person, they had to go to him."

"He must've been important, then, otherwise why would they bother?"

"Certainly." He nodded. "Did you know, he never went shopping, cooked, cleaned, or did laundry?"

"Sounds perfect," I replied. "But how come and why? I mean, you're not like that, did something happen to him?"

"No, not as far as I know. We had the same childhood, a good school life, he was always top of the class, but after leaving school he struggled to settle into a regular job. He resented working with others, hated authority even more, sacked once, I understand, for calling his boss a small-minded pleb."

"Excellent." I laughed. "Wish I had balls like that."

"Don't we all?" said my dad. "Makes me wonder how well he treated his staff, though."

"Staff?" I said. "Like servants? How could he afford them without a job?"

"Well, he did have a job, of sorts. The historical work I mentioned. At first, it was only a hobby, but it soon became his sole source of income."

"What sort of work? Something about books? Not sure I follow."

"Hmm." He nodded. "It's quite interesting actually. Before his reclusiveness took over, one of his passions was to visit stately homes, old houses, castles, and the like, often meeting the owners in the process, wealthy people in the main, people of influence, who were keen identify fragments of books, papers and letters found in and about their old houses. Now, this was meat and drink to my brother. In the beginning he worked for free, but with his reputation in the field steadily growing, he started to charge a fee. Trouble was, there was no end to it, and burying himself in his work, cooped up indoors, smoking like chimney year after year, was bad for his health, and the smoking was his eventual killer. What a stupid waste! It was almost a week before they found him, dead from a massive stroke."

Turning into a narrow concrete driveway, cracked in places, potholed and flanked by scabrous plants, I spied my uncle's house for the first time…

With an exterior that was rough and caked in London soot, it clung to its neighbour like an unwelcome grey barnacle, its tiled roof pocked and uneven from an influx of moss steadily overwhelming it. Keeping watch were four dark and doleful windows, their tired blue frames of flaking paint diseased and blistering. To our left, with walls bulging like a battered shoe, was the garage, its dilapidated doors sagging with age on twisted rusty hinges.

Good God, I thought, if ever a house could weep from neglect, this one had cried itself out. It was decaying, falling apart, and my uncle had done nothing to stop it. Why, I pondered, why do nothing? My crematoria musings suddenly rekindled. Time had moved on for the house. It was lifeless, and long before the passing of my uncle. Something had happened here, I could feel it, but what? Was it the death of his spirit, or the death of his hope, by an event now fixed in his past? Was it something he'd lost, or something he'd found. A new discovery, deeply profound.

THREE

MIRRA

Before this instalment begins, I want to mention my effort writing the last, for you should know I laboured for days and days, without stopping for food or drink, or even to relieve myself. However, I need to point out that the days I refer to might only be hours or alternatively weeks. Measuring time locked up in here is proving impossible. There are no windows to look out of, no clocks to watch, and no one to ask. It's perpetually day with the lights on and perpetually night with them off, and the only timepiece I do possess – my smartphone – seems to be broken (I suspect deliberately), with the extent of the damage unknown. Only by careful testing have I identified its issues, and the following is a brief report of my findings…

Both locked up and unresponsive, the clock showing 7.38pm, the calendar 17 June 2011, they refuse to budge even after a hard reset. The mapping system is knackered too! Unable to receive GPS, it shows my location outside the museum in Lima, its buggered compass relentlessly spinning as if influenced by a swirling magnetic field.

Note. Although fully aware budge, knackered, and buggered are unsuitable as quantitative variables, on this occasion I judge his imprecision and frustration to be quite justified and have left these inappropriate expressions to highlight his tetchiness.

Having completed the previous instalment, I put down my pointer and stretched out on the bed – not tired exactly, drained – and, shutting my eyes, I drew in slow measured breaths. A good start. The end of my task now a reachable goal, and I drifted and daydreamed, pleasant memories wrapping my mind like a blanket. Laughter, sunshine, and Frida's dark eyes, flickering by the light of a candle…

A soft clunking sound coming from the fish tank disturbed my comforting daydream. Barry (for that is what I call it), in a burst of sudden activity, was bashing his broad, chitinous head repeatedly against the glass. Quite why he started scrabbling and swimming like this I never found out. As weird prawny-things went, he was usually docile…

Still half asleep, I stumbled to the desk and tapped tank's warm glass with my finger.

"Hey, Barry," I said, "what's with the sudden racket? Can't I rest in peace?"

Predictably, there was no immediate response, but slowly, after thirty seconds or so, he ceased his futile struggle and sank to the bottom of a tank. Wriggling to bury himself, he returned to his life of patient inertia.

"How about that?" I muttered. "Can even train crustaceans."

Returning to the bed, I tinkered with my phone, playing music, reviewing photos, rereading old emails and texts.

Now I must have spent far too long, studying the last photo I'd taken, one of Frida, holding a butifarra and grinning through the burn of its "industrial-strength chilli!" because my sadness built up, eddying in the pit of my stomach, boiling up and over into a fiery resolve…

"Come on, then," I cried, jumping from the bed. "I've finished. Where are you, why aren't you here?"

Guessing (quite rightly) my captors were studying me, I expected immediate attention, but none came, and I was left standing indignant for what seemed like an age. When, at last, the speaker crackled and beeped, and wondering which voice I might hear (longing for the female and dreading the male), I sat and reluctantly prayed. Thus far, "he" had only spoken briefly and the effect upon me had been overwhelming. Fingers of dread crept up my spine at the thought of his cold contemptuousness…

"Well done, Marcus!" said a musical voice. "I knew you could do it and I'm sorry I kept you waiting. I've been showing him your work and couldn't escape."

To my huge relief it was the female voice and as pleasurable to hear as before – her silken glissandos dissipating my anger and fear like phantoms fleeing the sun. Certainly, the palliative power of her voice was so miraculous, if she ever considered alternative employment, might I suggest airport announcer? With her delivery to soothe the queuing masses, explaining the delay of their flight, the loss of their luggage, or cancelled tickets, I'm certain they would placidly disperse and go home, forgetting their troubles and strife, beginning peaceful lives of contemplation smoking dope in a yurt…

"However," she continued, "he says your writing needs to improve, requiring an inordinate amount of correction, so from now on I will drop by regularly to assist you."

"Perfect," I remarked. "That's great, but I haven't shown you my writing yet so how do you know it needs to improve?"

"Oh, come now," she said. "Do you think we've not been monitoring your essays?"

"Well, yes," I replied, "I assumed as much, but how could you monitor, hey? Have you been hacking my phone?"

"Hacking?" she enquired. "What do you mean? Is it the same as monitoring?"

"Yes, madam," I said. "Yes, in a way, and in doing so you've corrupted the OS, the apps, the compass, the GPS, even the clock!"

"No," she assured. "Not corrupted. Your phone is fine, so please don't be angry. Some of its applications *can't* work, that's all."

This made no sense. Why would the clock stop, and the compass go haywire? The GPS and maps often struggle indoors, this was quite normal, but before I could ask about the other absurdities, she was already reciting extracts of my writing, recommending alterations, and questioning the facts. Indeed, her questions took me by surprise; they were so mundane! For example, she didn't know what a kebab was, and the word polystyrene threw her completely, needing to explain (as best I could) its method of production before she understood, before demanding (peevishly) I call it "poly one feenile ethene one two die isle", a right old mouthful! Thankfully, after listening to my bemused protest she agreed the word polystyrene, although uninformative, to be quite enough.

It soon became clear she was in a hurry or under duress and in no position to answer any questions I might pose (I tried but she brushed them aside), so with my word processor loaded I tried to keep up, but she was relentless! Bombarding me with questions, word suggestions, spelling corrections, grammatical adjustments, and her comical fussiness regarding my use of punctuation, saying how I "sprayed commas about like crumbs", well, it was torture! The whole experience reminiscent of having my coursework marked by the forever dancing, uncompromising red pen of my last English teacher, the formidable Mr Groves.

Despite her persistence, I managed quite well, and her vocabulary, both vibrant and prodigious, had me in awe but, when beginning to flag, lose my place, and flounder, I let my struggles be known…

"Hey," I cried, "I can't keep up! Slow down or let me rest for a bit."

"What?" she said, sounding distracted. "Oh, yes, of course, so sorry. Let's stop and talk, at least, until you've recovered. Fatigue or stress hampering your progress is the last thing we need."

"Really?" I remarked. "I thought you were only here to sort out my writing and, well, chivvy me along?"

"And so I am," she replied. "But I'm also to ensure you finish – I need you to finish very badly, and if I work you too hard, you probably never will. Besides, I like you, Marcus. You're sensitive, kind, and thoughtful. You deserve all the help I can give."

She really moved me when she said this and seemed genuinely friendly – she cared about my well-being, and I wondered if I could exploit her good will to my advantage…

"You know," I said, a plan taking shape, "this process would be much more pleasant if you could come in and join me. I'm no threat to anyone. why do I have to be alone all the time?"

"It's not my doing, dear Marcus," she sighed, "and of course you're not a threat. Your loneliness must be unbearable, but what you suggest is impossible, so please, don't even ask. Understand, I'm only permitted to communicate textually, so as you can hear, I'm favouring you quite well enough already."

"Seriously?" I replied, my plan already dashed. "Didn't realise that, so thank you, your voice is very relaxing. Have you taken elocution lessons or something?"

"Elocution?" She chuckled. "No, not at all. In fact, English is my second language – my mother was German."

"Is that so?" I remarked. "Well, I think your voice is very nice… What is your name, by the way, are you allowed to tell me?"

"No, Marcus, I'm not, and I wouldn't, not my real name, but I have several sobriquets. You can use one of those if you like."

"Sobriquets." I pondered. "Like nicknames, is this…? Is this informality normal between jailer and prisoner?"

"No idea," she admitted. "You are not *my* prisoner, and I am not your jailer. I'm a scientist or… I will be one, I think, and… remember, I'm here to help you, nothing more."

Her voice strangely wavered as she said the above, as if weary or confused and I felt sorry to have touched a sore point.

"Very well, madam scientist," I replied. "What then shall I call you?"

"Sercaria or Mirra are the names I hear most, although, come to think of it, please don't call me Sercaria – it's insulting. Call me Mirra. I quite like Mirra."

"Mirra it is, then," I said. "Pleased to meet you. I see a lovely reflection already."

She gave no reply, although I like to think she was smiling.

I was.

We talked for some time, and I must say I found her openness charming, not that she gave much away. She mostly reminisced about her childhood…

She told me of her mother, of walks in the snow, of dinners with grandma and great grandma – so tiny, so sad, and so frail. Of skipping with friends, chasing the dog, and catching a ball covered in slobber. She missed her mother. She missed her dog.

She told me of her favourite foods, how she missed the food at home. Always so hot – steaming platefuls of colour. Red, green, brown, and orange, then fruit desserts swimming in sauces, or cakes with milk in between courses. She told me of her favourite colour and the clothes she liked to wear, of flowing dresses, pulled up stockings, and ribbons in her hair.

She told me of her love of music and her little wooden flute, playing to her fluffy dog, who sat there a wagging mute. How her mother sang, her sweet songs in the morning, as the family always had on spring and summer dawning.

Then, without any prompting, she sang a children's lullaby…

Sleep my love,
Warm and safe,
I'll be just through the door.
Close your eyes,
Dream of joy,
Worry not if you snore.
Little girl,
Little girl,
You're the one I adore…

"That's all I can remember!" she cheerfully called. "My great grandmother used to sing that, to send me off to sleep, and if you'd like to sleep now, I'll go, but we should do more when you wake."

"Thanks, Mirra," I said. "Will just take a nap and then do as you say."

"Good, very good," she warmly replied. "And who will you write about next do you think? The girl in your pictures? She's pretty, so please, write about her. If she's important to you, she's important to me, and he will want to know of her too."

FOUR

FRIDA

This instalment begins at a house party in Surbiton, thrown (most unwisely) by the overly trusting parents of some undeserving spoiled brat. Certainly, if the parents were expecting a happy gathering of bright-eyed youngsters, playing pass-the-parcel, and cheering, while their birthday princess blew out the candles on her sickly-sweet cake, they were sadly mistaken. We, for example, arrived at their superb house in a drunken state not even knowing whose party it was. A mate of a mate of a mate doubtless found an invitation on Fizzog, and, by a devious sleight, we had talked our way in...

On that night there were four of us and what an impressive quartet we were! Up front and centre was the unforgettable, physically unavoidable Philip Bryant, who, in between court appearances, played a lot of rugby, and consequently, he was as slow as cold treacle, loud as a Harley, and loutish. A heavy drinker (since puberty) and incapable of functioning in normal society, tonight he was clad in shabby jeans, a Harlequins shirt, and canvas boots – untied, laces trailing, causing him to occasionally stumble, sloshing his beer like a 4×4 crashing into a puddle.

Next in line and clinging to Phil's shoulder like a parrot, was our straight man. The leering, foul-mouthed, beer swilling James Riley. Ever with a keen eye for the ladies, Jimmy tonight was "dressed to impress", sporting combat trousers, heavy boots, and a T-shirt of the most fashionable camouflage. Indeed, he looked like a demobbed squaddie, but his long, grubby brown hair, gathered into a ponytail, was strictly non-regulation. Wherever Phil went, Jimmy would follow, and although you'd be risking life and limb to even entertain this thought, if you didn't know better, you'd think them a couple.

Now, I did say there were four of us, did I not? Yet, the causal onlooker would only spy two. Only the most patient among you, watching carefully and quietly, would catch a glimpse of Frank and myself – the nerds cowering behind. We are the silent ones, unheard and unspoken, dragged along by the Phil's and Jimmy's of this world and barely casting a shadow. We're the onlookers, the social spectators, nervous, tongue-tied, dreaming of popularity but fearing fame.

The chief nerd in our unwholesome posse was Francis Padgett or "Fwank" (to copy his mode of speech). A member of the "indoorsy" set, Frank worked in IT, his life revolving around his games console. With his sickly pallor, emaciated frame, and total lack of dress sense, well matched by his insipid personality, he still outshone yours truly. The sub-nerd. Sardonic, sneering, and mutely sipping my drink. A fencepost bystander to Phil and Jimmy's lamentable swagger.

Tastefully furnished with a garden that seemed to go on forever, most of the house was (quite sensibly) cordoned off, so, like hunting sharks, we patrolled the three large rooms cleared for partygoers (many of whom had left), and in what would normally have been the dining room, we found a makeshift help-yourself bar, with beer, alcopops, and plastic cups of cola. There was a buffet too – already picked clean – and the only leftover was a bowl of lumpy hummus.

Able to detect women from half a mile, Phil and Jimmy had already spotted a shoal of girls when we came in. Frank and I watched them too, but longingly, and from afar. With sensuous lips they sipped their drinks and chatted, quite oblivious of the two circling predators, and as I recall this scene, I can hear the theme from *Jaws* accompanying Phil and Jimmy's inexorable approach. The tempo steadily rising as they moved in for the kill…

Such effort to procure female attention! Why go to such ridiculous lengths? Certainly, the accepted social convention of polite introduction and conversation were quite unknown to Phil and Jimmy, and yet, despite their catastrophic attempts, you couldn't help but admire their resolve; failure (they claimed) was part of the fun.

Ashamed to be involved in such shenanigans, Frank and I hung back – not shy or scared exactly, just unwilling to be a nuisance. The girls seemed perfectly happy. Taking selfies, comparing phones, checking make-up, and, oddly, photographing each other's shoes. If they had wanted male company, surely, wouldn't they have sought it?

With Jimmy at his shoulder, grinning, nodding, and supporting his every word, Phil went through his full repertoire of compliments, wise-cracks, blue jokes, winking, flexing, and prancing back and forth, but it was all for nothing, of course. Ignored by his intended audience, Phil's final act, both desperate and deranged, involved thumping his chest, bellowing, and then stamping like some jilted lumbering beast. Not that it made any difference. Nothing happened, the chatting continued, the music played, but then, as if by the throwing of a cosmic switch, the universe suddenly changed. The smallest (and prettiest) girl in the group, achingly lovely in her little black dress, swore, swigged, and marched straight towards us, with Phil, ever the optimist, blocking her path with a grin...

"Alright, little darlin'?" he bellowed. "Get a box and I reckon this'll work!"

Eyes smouldering, the girl considered her options. Leering, drooling, Phil waited also, eager to hear her reply...

"Fuck off," she replied, and, with the girls at the bar in fits of sweet laughter, she pushed him aside and made her way over, to me!

"Hello," she said, her east London accent full on. "I'm Frida. Are you friends of Lucy as well?"

She was so beautiful, stunningly so, and I can recall my panicking thoughts to this day...

Is she talking to me? Oh my God, she's talking to me! Reply, you fool, say something, anything!

"M-Marcus," I stammered. "Pleased to meet you, and no, we don't know her, we... sort of gate-crashed, but... Frank knows her, from school?"

"Oh, right," she replied, her eyebrows raised in suspicion. "The bloke in the Megadeth shirt? Went to Roedean, did he?"

Glancing in his direction, I slowly nodded.

"No shit?" she smirked, before stumbling so waywardly that she fell in my arms.

Extremely drunk, of course, and as I aided her balance, she muttered an alcohol loaded "thanks" of admission.

"You alright there?" I asked. "Do you want some fresh air?"

"Nah." She shrugged. "I'm ok, but let's go and sit down," and she led me to a large leather sofa.

Slumping down like a sack, Frida gasped with relief, kicked off her shoes, and folded her legs beneath her. Patting the arm of the sofa, she encouraged me (still awestruck and wondering what to say next) to balance beside her.

Music started playing and so loudly that only by yelling and wildly gesticulating could anyone communicate. Normal at a party, you might think, but not being a fan of Rihanna, I wished for sudden power cut. Frida, clearly getting my gist, wrinkled her nose and shrugged.

Staggering towards us, cheekily grinning, came Jimmy, handing over two cans of beer and a vodka cocktail.

"Thanks, Jimmy," I hollered, with a meaningful look. "What's up?"

This was man-speak for "go away, you're creeping her out", and I could only hope he understood.

"Nah, nothing," he replied, thankfully getting my drift. "But we're off to a club in a bit. You're staying though, yeah?"

I simply nodded, the beauty beside me rendering his stupid question moot.

"Ok," he said, ogling Frida and backing away. "See you anon."

"Yeah, sure," I replied, rolling my eyes. "Text you tomorrow."

I felt a tug on my sleeve.

"Got you to myself, have I?" she yelled.

"Looks that way," I bellowed, to which she merely tilted her head.

Stupid music! Understandable in a club, wherein people just want to get "messy" and dance all night, but this was a social event. How can you be social if you are unable to talk? Nevertheless, Frida and I stubbornly continued until finally admitting defeat...

"This is mental!" she hollered, standing and inviting me into her seat. "You sit there, and I'll sit on the arm, but keep your feet off me shoes!"

The cushion she left was still warm, smelling faintly of her perfume (and alcohol) and, with matching elevations, we could at last successfully communicate, mouth-to-ear then ear-to-mouth.

We had a lovely chat, of which I cannot remember a single word. My only remaining memory is a feeling. Happiness. Doubtless, it was a typically boozy affair. Full of laughter, nothing of any consequence.

With a warm and dozy Frida sprawled half into my lap, her friends arrived to collect her. Their timing was fortunate too. Both quite drunk and sleepy, we had run out of conversation, and as Frida stood, hair tousled, legs very wobbly, she very deliberately kissed me on the cheek.

⧗

Arriving while I explored my uncle's house, Frida's reply to my post-funeral message, written in "text speak" (which I won't burden you with) was this:

"Great! Meet you Saturday 11.30–12pm at Tavistock's. A café on Gabriel's Wharf, Southbank. It's near Bernie Spain Gardens, Blackfriars station is closest. Frida x"

I had a date!

FIVE

SUNDAE SATURDAY

Arriving early the following Saturday, not knowing Southbank particularly well, I wanted time enough to become lost, unlost, and still be on time. As it turned out, finding Gabriel's Wharf was easy, but navigating a path to the entrance of Tavistock's was proving problematic…

Being a warm sunny lunchtime, it was extremely busy, every outlet serving alfresco, and, although I could plainly see the Tavistock's distinctive sign in the distance, getting there took several attempts, picking my way through a maze of customers, café staff, folding billboards, bicycles, furniture, all without knocking over something, someone, or colliding disastrously with a scurrying waiter rushing to deliver the soup of the day.

Full of character but not overly busy, Tavistock's turned out to be a good place for a date.

Its long rectangular placard is my first memory. Red on the left, blue on the right, with all the decals and writing in gold. Between the red and blue sections, dangling in a harness, was the representation of depressed-looking sheep, while on the far left (on the red side) there was a lion. Furthest to the right (on the blue side) was a fleur-de-lis. Between the lion and sheep was the word "TAVIS" and, between sheep and fleur-de-lis, the word "TOCKS".

Yes. I'm sure that is a rubbish way of describing it, but it's the best I can do. No amount of nagging from Mirra will suddenly transform me into a better writer. They should have locked up someone more literate.

Sigh...

With a long counter, a line of tall stools, tables and chairs, the café interior resembled a 1970s American diner, with a dozen young women (several zooming around on skates) serving drinks, desserts, and all manner of good things. Borrowed from mid-20th-century America, their uniform was stereotypical. One-piece A-line dresses, striped aprons, canvas shoes, bobby socks, with a shiny cylindrical bottle cap hat. In truth, they looked daft, but, laughing, joking, swerving, and manoeuvring, their enjoyment was part of the fun.

A song was playing on a gigantic jukebox against the back wall, – not overly loud, and its gleaming chrome surface pulsated and throbbed with flashing lights. The actual song I cannot recall, only the phrase "we're having some fun tonight", * sung over and over remains, and, while dragging a stool to the counter and ordering myself a coffee, it ceased its glitzy display, fading into a welcome silence.

*I am reliably informed the song was "Long Tall Sally" performed by Little Richard.

My coffee arrived in a glass cup and saucer, but Frida had not, so I amused myself examining its qualities of form and colour. More froth than coffee, it was brown as a fallen leaf, and with a spotty napkin and shining spoon beside it, I lowered my gaze, peering through the side of the cup, gauging the ratio of pale foam to liquid...

"I'm sure there's coffee in there somewhere," came a familiar voice, and I abruptly sat up with a start.

"Oh," I gasped, failing to hide my surprise. "Hello, Frida. Didn't know you were here," and she lightly kissed my cheek.

"Got here a few minutes ago," she explained. "Then went to the loo, but I'm small, easily missed – you might not have seen me."

"No," I replied. "I'm sure I would've noticed a girl like you. I'm sort of programmed that way..."

"Yeah, tell me about it." She chuckled. "All you men are, although I wasn't floating in your coffee, so what the f— were you doing? Looking for fish?"

Blushing hot as a radish, unsure how to respond, I fanned myself, before her healing grin washed the sensation away in a single flash of white teeth.

"How was your journey?" she asked, quizzically tilting her head.

"Fine," I said. "Finding the wharf was easy, although it's mental out there, I felt like a rat in a maze trying to cross that damn square!"

"Hey!" she protested, sliding over a stool. "What do you expect, Mr Suburbia? This is London, not some sleepy village, there's a real café culture along the river, don't dis a good thing, and besides, it's me who should be complaining. I get barged into, walked into, and ignored, like, constantly!"

Looking thoughtful for moment and dipping the tip of her finger into the froth of my coffee, she sucked it clean with a noisy kiss.

"And," she said. "FYI. Guys calling me titch, tiny, or any other cutesy stuff rapidly find my knee up their knackers and single, so consider this your one and only warning."

Blimey, I thought, message received, and, although she left out hobbit, I instinctively crossed my legs.

"Won't," I vowed. "You're small, that's all, petite and remarkably perfect."

And by God she was…

What a woman wears on a first date can tell you a lot. It can reveal what your date is trying to communicate, what they can't help communicating, and the things they are trying to hide. Frida, on that day, was surprisingly casual, communicating her confidence, wearing a turquoise scarf, a dark-brown jacket (worn open) with three shiny buttons, deep navy jeans (fitting tightly in all the right places) and long dark boots. Her chin-length hair was a dark brunette and very straight, framing the pale skin of her face like a shining curtain. Not much make-up. A little mascara, foundation I am sure (although I couldn't see it), and a subtle lipstick deepening the hue of her lips.

Her eyes, captivating from the very first moment, were the darkest brown I'd ever seen. Dark as ebony and unfathomably deep, her black mascara shepherded my gaze towards pupils over-large and pleading. She could melt a man's heart with those eyes, she knew it, and I recalled reading of Henry VIII's tireless obsession regarding his future queen, Anne. Who, by several accounts, possessed similar witchcraft in her dark Boleyn eyes.

"Thanks!" she said, wrinkling her nose. "You're very sweet, let me join you up there…"

Stirring my coffee, I considered offering a frothy spoonful, but Frida was too busy clambering up onto the stool beside me. Unhooking her canvas bag from her shoulder, she flopped it on the counter before grabbing one of the menus mounted inside a Z-shaped stand.

"Ah, great!" said Frida, feathering her fingers around it. "They still… You know, I've been trying to come here for ages."

"Glad I could help." I replied, taking a gulp from my coffee. "Not that I did much – don't know this area at all."

"Guessed as much," she said. "You suburbanites hardly ever come north, unless it's for work."

"True." I shrugged. "My dad works in the City, but he socialises in Surrey – plays golf in Dorking."

"Dorking?" she remarked. "That's out in the sticks. No wonder you're lost."

"And that's why I got here so early – time enough for wandering, less worry, less stress."

"Make sense to me." She smiled. "I'm usually early too. Hate being late, don't give a toss how it looks. If I say meet you at one, I'll be there at one. Fashionably late's just an excuse for twats."

"Is that so?" I said, out of my depth. "Only, on a date, I thought the man was supposed to arrive first?"

"Why?" she replied. "Did you read this on website or something?" and I shrugged.

"Bet you did." She smiled. "Because you really shouldn't listen to any of these so-called relationship experts, especially if you're shy. Overplanning only makes things worse; just be yourself!"

"I do try to," I admitted. "But if I am feeling anxious, panic smothers my true self. Having a few rules to follow allows me to catch my breath."

"Yeah," she said thoughtfully. "Good point. You're right, I think, but the dating scene? It's not really my thing, can you tell? No fucker's telling me how to behave. I do what I want, how I want, any way I choose, and woe betide anyone saying otherwise. All those stupid rules and traditions… The man arrives first, don't wear this, don't say that, sit like this, not like that, and oh my God, it's a recipe for paranoia. So, hot stuff, assuming you're not gonna run off, drag your stool over here and give me a cuddle. Just carry on from the party, ok?"

Nodding and smiling, I moved my stool closer. No way was I running off…

"The party is a bit of a haze," I said. "Nevertheless, I'd like to thank you for turning what would have been a disappointing night into a special one."

"Thank me?" She snorted. "Ha! You're welcome, but have you and your pale friend ever considered going out, you know, together, without the grizzly bears?"

"Of course," I said. "We talk about it all the time, although it never actually happens. Without Phil and Jimmy to cling to, it's doubtful we'd go out at all, or if we did, we'd end up in a corner, comparing phones, ogling distant females."

"You were doing that anyway," she replied. "But, of course, silly me, what was I thinking? Men's tribal loyalties aren't easily broken, are they?"

Picking up my coffee and quickly slurping a mouthful, I tried to disguise the way it trembled from the shaking of my hands. She noticed, however, and I blushed again, this time very hotly, my shirt sticking to my back like Clingfilm.

"Oh, my God!" she exclaimed, "You're such a sweetheart. All nervous and trying to hide it. Come here," and looking straight into my eyes, she gently stroked the back of my hand.

"Please don't be nervous," she whispered. "I know, I'm a cocky bitch, but it's ok, there's no pressure. This whole date thing was my idea, right from the start. I wanna be here, with *you*, nobody else, just you. You can't go wrong. You won't deter me. If anything fucks up, it's my fault, not yours. Got it?" Witnessing my nod, she kissed me on the lips.

Sliding my stool against hers, we huddled together, studying the menu. There was quite a selection, ice creams in the main, hardly surprising. Tavistock's was named after a town on the Devon/Cornwall border, an area famed for its dairy produce, the restaurant incorporating the region's cream in their desserts and confection, but they also sold cakes, fruit pies, teas, coffees, and cold drinks, although why in Tavistock they dangled sheep I never discovered.

The grandest (and most expensive) item on the menu was the Drake, after Sir Francis Drake (born in Tavistock sometime around 1540) and described as "A whole armada of creamy, crunchy, fruity goodness!"

"Well, I've already decided," said Frida, tapping the menu. "It has to be a Drake. What about you?"

Still dithering, I decided to wait, wondering whether the extravagant-sounding "Drake" was worth the expense...

I never like wasting money (especially my money) on food and avoid ordering dishes until I know what's coming. If asked about this, my default response is roughly as follows: "Ordering more food than one needs is wasteful. All over the world people are starving and we must all take care."

Kneeling upon her stool, Frida emphatically waved over one of the girls.

"A Drake," she announced, smiling with guilty pleasure. "I'd like a Drake."

"Yes, madam," replied the waitress. "What flavour scoops would you like?"

"Oh, yeah," said Frida, blinking to recollect. "There's three, right?"

The waitress nodded.

"Decisions, decisions!" Frida laughed. "Two chocolate, one cherry?"

"Coming right up!" replied the waitress, immediately flinging open a freezer.

"The ol' pancreas is due a good bashing," said Frida, removing her jacket, untying her scarf, and folding it very lovingly.

"Sounds like it's gonna get one," I remarked. "But what about getting fat?"

"Me?" She chuckled. "Get fat? No, as long as I hit the gym, I can eat what I like."

"That's good, then, and have you been here before?"

"Yep." She nodded. "With the girls. We come here sometimes for a pick-me-up. The ice cream sundaes are awesome."

All the while the waitress was busily assembling Frida's Drake, and we watched with interest as she mixed crystallised fruit, nuts, sprinkles of candy, jellies, and several colourful squirts of syrup in a stainless-steel bowl. Soft ice cream went in next, delivered from the nozzle of a dispenser, droning loudly as the she slowly circled the bowl beneath. Three large scoops of ice cream closely followed, two a deep brown, one a pale crimson, before the bowl placed beneath a contraption with twisting spoon-like arms, mechanically mixing the contents into a pale and lumpy mélange.

By this stage, Frida's expression was one of fixated joy, and as the waitress removed the bowl from the mixer she gasped, clapping her hands in excitement – however, the waitress still wasn't finished! After spooning the bowl's contents into a tall glass cone, she added a finishing touch. Aerosol cream, spiralled into a peak, with a black glacé cherry balanced on top like a garnet.

"Oh my God!" said Frida, studying the swirling colours and half-hidden lumps of delight. "What have I done?"

"You'll need a longer spoon to eat that," I remarked, pointing towards the stubby one provided.

"Ah, now." She smiled. "That's where you're wrong. Watch and learn."

With a flourish, Frida picked up her spoon, and, with a tug, extended it to a suitable length. "Ta-da!" She laughed, waving it before my eyes like a wand (foolish not realising it was telescopic). "They think of everything here. I reckon I'd like America, if they do customer service like this."

Deftly scooping the cherry from the top of her sundae, she danced it invitingly before my lips, but before I could nick it, she cruelly snatched it away, eating it very deliberately.

"Meany." I scowled.

"Get your own!" she said, licking her lips.

"I'm about to, only I wanted to see what a Drake looked like, and it's a bit too much for me – hate wasting food, people starving in Africa, you know."

"So what?" she replied, shortening her spoon and dabbling the aerosol cream. "Bit of ice cream ain't gonna hurt."

Thinking as she licked the back of her spoon, Frida sifted my words for meaning.

"Hang on!" she then said. "Are you, hey! Don't try the 'Sir Bob' line with me, Marcus Whatever-Your-Name-Is, you're just a tightwad, don't try to deny it!"

"Dammit." I laughed, caught out, but not minding too much. "Yes, yes ok, I haven't much money, but the Drake thing? It really is too much. I wouldn't get halfway down!"

"Well, it's *too* much for me, too!" she said. "Gonna need your help getting through it for sure, but you needn't worry. Money doesn't impress me, and you already told me your job, remember? So, chill! If you overspend, I'll lend you. Won't leave you washing up, I promise."

"Ok," I said, trying not to cringe. "Sorry, force of habit, I guess."

"And no more apologising!" she replied, jabbing me with her spoon.

It may seem insignificant remembering how gracefully she accepted my ingrained stinginess, yet it is a terrible flaw of mine and I tried to deceive her because of it. Nevertheless, her willingness to let the whole incident pass, to accept my failings without being judgemental, kindled within me a new level of confidence that has burnt clear and bright ever since.

"For you, sir?" asked the waitress, still hovering nearby.

"Pym's Apple Pie, if you please."

"Sure," she replied. "With cream or ice cream?"

"Vanilla ice cream?"

"Fine. Nuts and syrup?"

"Which nuts, what syrup?"

"Peanut, pecan, walnut, hazelnut, pistachio, and we have every syrup you could wish for!"

"Ok," I said, adding to Frida, "if we're supposed to be in America – pecan and maple syrup please."

"Coming right up," replied the waitress opening a cabinet and hurrying away.

The slice of pie quickly arriving and possessing a crispy lattice top was wonderfully spicy, just warm enough to melt the ice cream, and I set about it with gusto. Together with Frida, munching and chatting, chatting and slurping, until Frida reluctantly admitted defeat, surprisingly close to the bottom of her glass.

Leaning back in our stools, stretching and satisfied, the waitress returned to see how we were doing...

"Would you like a siphon to finish it off?"

"Oh, go on then," said Frida. "Two, please."

Siphons turned out to be extra-wide drinking straws, and we had a fun, if messy, few minutes draining the sweet creamy liquid beyond the reach of her telescopic spoon.

Frida proved to be a fun, fascinating and feisty companion, and my feelings for her were already growing. Her confident manner and brusque east London speech were wonderfully matched by her sharpness, intelligence, and comical pragmatism.

Twenty-three years old and born in Lewisham, she still lived there supporting her mother – her father having died of leukaemia when she was seven, and this catastrophe had doubtless shaped her whole life (the look on her face as she spoke of this tragedy told me everything I needed to know).

Her surname was "Halfpenny", which she pronounced "ape-knee", saying it was a family tradition to pronounce it so, deriving an almost wicked pleasure from the confusion it caused to non-native speakers of English.

There remains a bit of a class issue in Britain with the east London accent, the more privileged echelons regarding it as a sign of ignorance and poor education. Utter nonsense! Accents are what they are: accents.

Merely an inherited inflection, left over from a time when by geography or socio-economic status communities suffered a degree of isolation. Certainly, Frida was rightly proud of both her accent and her heritage, and far more successful than I. With twelve GCSEs, all A* and A's, four A-levels in biology, chemistry, physics and maths, again, all A's, before earning a first-class degree in biochemistry from the University of Essex. Currently, she was currently working for a German pharmaceutical company studying the toxicological responses to implanted medical technology, describing the work as "mostly dull and repetitive" and the pay "pretty good for lab work". Her main complaint was the hours – it was shift work, dictated by availability or readiness of tissue cultures, equipment, or sensitive materials. The cultures, for example, once prepared, frequently required immediate use, often involving working nights, playing havoc with her body clock, lowering her resistance to coughs, colds, and all manner of ailments.

When it was my turn to reveal more of myself, she listened with raised eyebrows and smiles to the story of my life. My first childhood memories. The scraped knees, the climbing trees, then onto the ape-like fooling of my teenage years. Flecked, and tarnished by opportunities so regretfully missed.

Mid-afternoon by the time we made our way to the station at Blackfriars, Frida slipped her arm into mine as we went, clinging tightly if the way became crowded.

"You alright there?" I asked. "Shall I walk in front?"

"Yeah," she said. "Just don't wanna lose you; finding people in a crowd's really hard when you're small."

Despite a nervous start, I had thoroughly enjoyed our first date, and Frida had too, although she did admit being dyspeptic after so much sugar and cream…

"Will need to walk the woofers ragged to shift this lot!" she remarked, pointing to her tummy, and puffing her reddening cheeks.

Not wanting our date to end, I offered to accompany her on the train to Lewisham, but she declined, explaining she'd done the trip many times without trouble, so not to worry. She kissed me nonetheless, "for my chivalry".

We agreed to see each other again in a few days, a week at most, staying in touch by text or call, and as her train arrived we kissed once more, slowly this time – long and lingering, shivers of exultation going right down to my toes, and, as our lips parted, I was buzzing, tumbling in her perfume like a bee in the cradle of a flower.

Indeed, it was days before I saw her again, but, true to her word, she stayed in touch, mostly short texts from work. Why did I ever delete them? The only text I do remember, probably because it made me laugh so much, went something like this:

"Hi-ya Cuddls, Crazy @ work! Lst 2 days wrkin under red lite n now under blu. Ocular implant testing. Sshh! Indstl scrts n all that. Me n wrkmates look like Smurfs! Cu soon. Btw Ital in Covnt grdn snds perf! x Smurfette x"

Requiring funds for my new social life, I had been working too, and taking on extra shifts helped pass the time. Couldn't wait to see her!

Wondering why I hadn't called; Jimmy came to see me at work. Friendly, you might think, only his true reason wasn't so honourable: "You still with that girl from the party?"

"Yes," I revealed.

"Shagged her yet?"

"No," I flatly replied.

"Well, let me know when you do."

"Why?" I asked, not caring for his answer.

"Always wanted to fuck a midget. Wanna know what it's like."

"Why don't you ask her yourself?" I muttered, recalling her warning.

"Give me her number when she dumps you and I will."

"Nothing would make me happier," I replied, and returned to chopping up lettuce.

SIX

WHINING AND DINING

Outside Covent Garden Underground station waiting for Frida to arrive, my heart was a butterfly. Would passers-by notice my anxiety and judge me a villainous rogue? Certainly, I was already nervous enough, without having to be conspicuous. So, please, good people of London, for safety's sake, keeping your distance. I'm just waiting, not loitering. There's a difference, ok?

The venue for our second date Frida had left to me and I immediately plumped for an excellent Italian restaurant in (you guessed it) Covent Garden, called (I think) "Di Mario e Fratelli". *

*I think this unlikely.

Having eaten their amazing food before, my stomach rumbled in anticipation waiting for Frida to appear from one of the station's exits, but she was late, and, leaning on a lamp a post, I checked the time on my phone. Ten minutes late…

"Hello!" said Frida, and I almost jump out of my skin. "Sorry I'm late, couldn't help it – stupid Tube, chugging along, took forever! Ran up the stairs, escalators, and stuff, but when I got here, you were looking at your phone, didn't notice little ol' me."

Taking a deep breath and exhaling, she snuggled in for a cuddle.

Walking arm in arm, me slightly leading the way, we headed towards the restaurant.

"Any jugglers tonight?" asked Frida, keeping pace beside me. "Or random fuckers on stilts? Usually, it's heaving with 'em round here."

"Don't know," I replied. "It's a bit dark, but it wouldn't surprise me."

"Well, if there are, can we give them a very wide berth? Hate all that street-show shit. Kick their stilts, if they come near me!"

Shocked by her fierceness, I tried not to laugh.

"What's brought this on?" I asked. "Do you possess a peculiar hatred of street entertainment?"

"Nah, not specifically – just can't stand show-offs getting in my way."

"Yeah," I replied, "I get that, but how could a juggler possibly hurt you?"

"You know, I'm not really sure. It's a bit of phobia, hard to explain rationally, and I'm overreacting, as usual. Only, when I was a tot, I remember having my photo taken with a stilt walker – some an old geezer selling ribbons, and he scared me. So tall, skeletal, like a dead tree, and he stank. His rake-like hands all over me and... Brrr!" She shivered. "Bad memories. What's made me so glum?"

"I'm not sure," I said, drawing her closer. "A lack of food and drink? Not to worry though. No street entertainers tonight, not even a busker."

"Well, thank God for that," she replied. "And you're right about food. I'm famished."

Heady with wood smoke and crammed with round tables draped in heavy white cloths, the restaurant was unchanged from my previous visit.

"Can't see a thing," said Frida as we made our way in. "I've heard of mood lighting, but this is ridiculous!"

She did have point. Candles, both on the tables and on the walls, provided the only illumination, their flickering flames painted wandering shadows over the whitewashed brick walls.

Checking our reservation, a pleasant man in a white linen apron led us to our table, and, after guiding a gracious Frida into her seat, he presented us with unwieldy cardboard menus before taking our order of drinks (prosecco for her and a large beer for me). Snapping his fingers to summon our antipasti, a younger waiter hurried over arraying our table with baskets and bowls holding olives, breadsticks, and tiny bruschetta – drenched in olive oil, layered with tomato, basil, and thin slices of a pungent dark mushroom. *

The drinks arrived soon after, but not soon enough to prevent our hungry annihilation of the nibbly bits and, by the time I'd sipped the froth from my beer, we'd scoffed the whole lot.

Horn of plenty, Craterellus cornucopioides.

In the meantime, chatting idly (we hardly ever stopped), I told Frida of Jimmy's inappropriate questions earlier in the week. Not at all did Jimmy shock her: laughing heartily at his stupidity, swearing softly at his audacity, but after finishing my tale she became sullen and serious, gently swirling her drink in time with her thoughts.

Its bubbles rose and burst with a hissing spray…

"Marcus?" she asked.

"Yes, Frida," I replied. "You've gone quiet. What's the matter?"

Shifting in her seat, I realised she was preparing to touch on a difficult topic…

"Well," she said. "What you just said about Jimmy, it made me realise… It's high time I admitted something, something that's been on my mind since we first met."

Hearing this made my heart sink and my stomach turned to lead. All too many failures with girls left me expecting the worst. A sudden shift in the tone of a conversation had always preceded a break-up, or, even worse, the relationship downgrade: "Best for us both if we be friends from now on, but I'll always have feelings for you."

Bracing myself for the emotional surge, I tried hiding my concern…

"Oh?" I asked, releasing a slow steady breath. "What would that be?"

"Marcus!" she exclaimed. "Please, don't look so worried, nothing bad's going to happen, I just wanna explain."

"Ah." I sighed, releasing my breath. "But… how could you tell I was worried? Am I transparent?"

"You're so sweet!" she replied, shaking her head. "But you men, you carry your feelings like boulders, so easy to see. Anyhow, this is going to take a while to explain, so I need you to bear with me."

"Go on then," I urged. "I'm listening."

"Ok, and to begin with," she mused, thoughtfully choosing her words, "to illustrate my point, a question. What usually happens when you guys go to a party?"

"Oh, that's easy," I replied. "Jimmy links up with some girl too young to know better, Phil gets arrested, and then we go home."

"You're kidding?" she said, looking appalled. "You are kidding, aren't you?"

"Of course," I replied. "At least, I think I'm kidding, although there was that one time when…"

"Gah!" she exclaimed, cutting me off. "Don't swear, Frida, don't swear – it's really nice in here, but for eff's sake, Marcus, why'd you bother?"

"Don't know." I shrugged, stroking my glass. "Because they're my mates, and they're funny? Somehow, the mix of psycho and nerd actually works. One of those ying–yang type things? What's your point?"

Looking thoughtful for a moment, Frida finished her Prosecco with one quick gulp, snapping her tongue from its tartness.

"Hmm… My point? Well, come on, tell me. When did a girl last speak to you at a party? That is, without you making the first move?"

"Once, I think. Unless you count girls asking the way to the toilet, wondering if Frank could talk, or some such?"

"Right," she replied, "and no, the others don't count. That singular girl, the one who spoke, was she me? She was me, wasn't she?"

"Yep," I admitted. "How did you know? Are you always right like this?"

"Not always, although I think I've got you worked out, in fact, I worked you out at the party, and I was wasted! The reason guys like you and Frank never get any attention is because you're too quiet, too shy, and overshadowed by Philip and Jimmy."

"Naturally," I replied. "Extroverts will always dominate introverts, and to save time I'll ask the next question myself. Why did you talk to me? What changed that night?"

"Smart-arse," she remarked. "And here's your answer. Two of my friends landed themselves in trouble dating guys like Phil and Jimmy. Big men, big personalities, loud, cocky, can seem extremely attractive. All very manly, and funny too, but you tend to be laughing at them rather than with them, which is an important difference, I think."

Raising her hand, she paused considering her next choice of words…

"Also, the sex is exciting, to start with at least, but then things start to go wrong, and my friends. Well, they had nasty break-ups, threats, abuse, even beaten up. My friend Melissa? Raped, beaten, and left for dead! At least the police got that bastard, and she's well on the mend now, but will she ever get over it? Doubt it."

Shaking her head in frustration, she sighed, frowning at her empty glass.

"You'd never hurt a soul," she then said, shaking out her napkin. "And I bet Frank wouldn't either. What Melissa went through was the tipping point for us girls, and we made a pact. If any of us considered a new relationship, we promised to choose someone sensitive, someone thoughtful and kind. No more swaggering morons!"

"Oh, that's me," I replied. "Definitely, all those things, erm… the first things, anyway."

"Shush!" She chuckled. "Don't interrupt or I'll lose my train of thought."

So, quietly, and obediently, I went back to slurping my beer while watching her think: animated, reflective, quizzical…

"At the party, I noticed how embarrassed you were watching your mates. You held back, embarrassed, not involving yourself, and the thought, 'he's perfect' suddenly came out of nowhere. After that, nothing else mattered. Although swearing at Phil was delicious!"

Lowering my glass, I grinned, licking the froth from my lips.

"So, there you have it," she then shrugged. "You are my social experiment, and the results so far are a bringer of joy."

Leaning across the table to kiss, we lost ourselves in the moment, but somewhere nearby I heard the wine-waiter gasp, and as our lips parted, he came to offer us a bottle of Prosecco…

"*Signore e la Signorina!*" he remarked, adding, "With compliments of the house. Such *romantica!*"

Our meal was over all too soon. For main course, I ordered tagliatelle with chicken and mushrooms in a rich creamy sauce, whereas Frida enjoyed a trio of gourmet pizzas, small and made to order. Can't remember what toppings she chose. One was meaty, the other cheesy, the final one I know not what. All washed down with an excellent bottle of Primitivo. Not quite the right wine for our food, but it was suitably alcoholic, and by the time the bottle was empty, my state of inebriation was approaching journalistic. Frida, however, was stone cold sober. Some lucky people can take drink, others cannot. I, for the record, cannot.

Yes, Mirra. We did have dessert. No idea what it was. By then Frida was doing the choosing and I was just along for the ride.

It was a sharing plate of chocolate and hazelnut panettone, white chocolate panna cotta, with a vanilla and espresso affogato.

We shared the bill. *(Oh, Marcus. You fibber!)*

Following our lovely meal, we didn't meet for again for several days, and it was a good thing too! Mixing rich food with beer, Prosecco, and strong red wine, delivered a ripping hangover I struggle to forget. We stayed in touch as before, however, and, while Frida beavered away in her laboratory, I "burgered" myself stupid, raising money for our social activities. Outside work, I increasingly spent my free time at my uncle's house, rummaging in cupboards, inspecting books, examining (and then chucking) his extensive archived material.

It was Frida's turn to plan our next date, and her chosen venue sounded expensive. Drinks and nibbles at a riverside bar in Richmond, with a pointed reminder to "dress for Richmond" as well.

Ouch! I felt the beginnings of pain in a sensitive area. My wallet. Turning out to be doubly ouch as I couldn't just buy regular clothes, oh no, they had to be decent. No jeans, T-shirts, or hooded tops. In fact, the whole process ended up being trebly ouch. Being obliged to ask my sister (currently home for a few days) to come shopping and help.

(It is no secret my fashion sense is akin to that of a mollusc.)

Having to shop with Millie was a psychologically traumatising experience and my ego took quite a battering. How she loved having me in her power! Forcing me to answer all her girly questions about Frida, kissing, how we held hands, all the while hiding my disgust at trusting her judgement. Fearing, if I stepped out of line, (without my knowledge) she'd dress me like a dork, before scuttling back to Moscow, Vladimir, Gregor, and the rest of the damn Russian army.

SEVEN

THE RIVERSIDE

The autumn was fading, the nights colder and darker, but at least it wasn't raining. I felt embarrassed enough, dressed like a dork, without the help of an umbrella…

The entrance to Richmond station was a blocky, off-white building, with a large square clock, and, as before, I waited outside, watching the unceasing to-ing and fro-ing before me. Indeed, it was a busy time of night for the social scene and visitors were pouring out of the station, off to savour Richmond's swanky nightlife in a colourful bustling stream. People-watching and studying clothing isn't something I would normally do, yet the mixture of "types" was so vibrant and varied I found myself playing a game my mother and sister frequently enjoyed, that is, commenting (somewhat bitchily) on people's attire before speculating whom they are and where they might be going… Gowns and dinner jackets for the theatre or a concert? Party dresses for posh drinks or a club? Casual dress for the casual diner, sombre grey suits, and floral skirts…

Cheesy music reporting the arrival of a new text message suddenly came from my jacket and I quickly whipped out my phone to read it.

"Behind you!" it said, and I quickly turned ready to witness her sudden arrival, but Frida just wasn't there!

Before even beginning to reply, "Where?" an unknown assailant tapped me on my back…

"No," said Frida. "Behind you."

"No," I replied. "You were in front, hiding, but ok, you got me," and with that she flung herself into my arms.

"God, I've missed you," she murmured, her face buried in my jacket and, loosening her embrace, she took a step back, keen to examine my clothing.

"Marcus," she said, circling (as if judging a horse). "You've evolved, you look amazing!" before nodding in further approval at my brown-checked linen jacket, pale blue shirt, pale tan chinos, and deep tan brogues. "Excellent," she added, picking a pale thread from my sleeve. "Good choices. You'd never know…"

"Bloody cheek," I replied. "I always dress like this, didn't you know?"

Giggling and smothering me in far more kisses than I deserved, Frida left me breathless and then embarrassed by the odd looks dispensed by passers-by.

If only I could be as carefree, so unabashed! Of the many qualities I have come to admire in Frida, her steely single-mindedness, doing as she pleases, despite the opinion of others, remains one of her most enviable…

"Come on, then," she said, slipping her arm into mine. "My handsome gentleman, I know a good place down by the river, let's go and sample the cocktails – I feel the need to get messy," and we walked slowly, arm in arm, downhill, towards the lights just visible on Richmond Bridge, tacking our way along, jacket and skirt flapping, our sails filled by a breeze scattering the leaves before us.

The bar of Frida's choice, the Grey Monk, was a prominent Georgian three-storey building right on the riverbank. Busy to the point of bursting both inside and out, while searching for a table, I noticed a simple jetty affording direct access to boats on the river. Frida explained how, although this was indeed a neat feature, the riverbank occasionally flooded, obliging customers and staff to wear wellies. Sometimes greedy swans would come swimming up as well, waddling and pecking under the tables, adding to the "fun" no end.

Finding nowhere to sit, we decided to split up and hunt for a table as Frida was reluctant to stand, and nabbing a rickety table for two by a window, as we settled, Frida studied the cocktail menu with anticipation…

"They were mixing a fab gin cocktail the last time I was here, but I can't remember its name."

"If you can't remember," I quipped, "then it must've been good!"

"Yay!" she suddenly cried. "Here it is. Could you be a dear and get me a Mumbai maiden?"

"A Mumbai what?"

"A cocktail," she explained. "Made with Bombay gin and stuff. Just be a good boy, go to the bar, and ask."

"Yes, milady," I replied, standing, and giving a bow. "Your whim is my joy," and after Frida had blown me a kiss, I fought my way to the bar.

Despite its imaginative name, Frida's Mumbai maiden was little more than a gin and tonic with a twist, and I watched (with growing impatience) the unconvincingly flamboyant barman add two shots of Bombay gin, a bottle of tonic, the juices of half a lime, a wedge of lemon, and several kumquats into a silver cocktail shaker. A protracted squirt of clear syrup went in next (likely to be sugar as kumquats are sour as hell) before screwing down the lid and theatrically juggling the whole lot before me. Filling a tall glass with ice, he slotted together a slice of lemon and a slice of lime to produce a spherical body (I don't know the name of).

He means a spherical digonal bipyramid.

Sliding a colourful straw through the ice and plonking the lemon and lime garnish on top, he spun the cocktail shaker once more, before unscrewing the lid and filling the glass with the resulting cloudy liquid. I had a beer. Feeling peckish, I also ordered a bowl of crispy potato skins, a platter of "things" in tempura, and a selection of dips. The bill for this little lot made my eyes water but looking back at Frida, absolutely stunning in her coal-black, knee-length dress embossed with coppery butterflies, I gladly paid up.

"By God, that's fresh," gasped Frida, mouth disconnected from straw. "Get me another!"

"Ok," I said, only a little way into my beer. "In a minute, but I can't afford too many more."

"Yeah." She laughed. "Richmond. Next round's on me."

And so, the night went on…

The girl sure could drink. The girl sure could eat! Almost polishing off our bar snacks single-handedly, apologising for her gluttony, however, saying her working week had been tough and painfully boring, missing her dogs (and me) very much.

Frida and her mother loved animals, she explained. They had many pets, describing them thus:

"We have two dogs, Scuttle and Scamper. A fluffy cat I brush, and I pamper. A bird on a perch, squawking and dusty, who swears all the time, with a tail that looks rusty. Rabbit in the garden, and guinea pigs too. When they get hungry, it sounds like a zoo! We had a tortoise as well that I painted bright red. He didn't do much, just slept under the shed. I'm not sure what happened. Maybe he died? Ate the wrong plant…"

Before stopping mid-sentence and hiccupping very squeakily…

"Pardon me!" she entreated, placing her hand over her mouth. "Where was I? Oh yes, a vegetarian suicide? Bah! Does that still rhyme?"

"No," I remarked, "Not really, and are you alright? What's with all the rhyming?"

Sucking on her straw and then grinning very broadly, Frida went slightly cross-eyed.

"Mum and me do it all the time," she replied, the gin beginning to talk. "She's got a weird form of Tourette's, makes her go blinky, get hot and embarrassed, and then she starts talking in rhyme."

"Oh, your poor mum," I said, leaning back in my chair. "How did she get it? And I thought Tourette's was just swearing and shouting?"

"Nah…" she replied. "All that swearing crap is just a media fixation. Tourette's can occur in loads of ways. Usually, it's inherited, although I don't have it, but rhyming's really easy, and it's fun! Me mum feels better when I join in."

Frida went quiet thereafter and I watched her tipsy antics with amusement. Fanning herself with a beer mat, pulling faces while nibbling the lemon and lime from her drink…

"Can we go for a walk?" she asked. "I'm feeling a bit… Well, I could use some fresh air."

"Sure," I replied. "Lead the way and hold my arm if you need to," and I duly followed her out and onto to the riverside.

Veiled by thick autumn cloud, the night was cold and dark, and as we walked, holding each other against the chill, the Thames swept by, black and silent. After five minutes of steady walking, we came upon a bench, and we sat, kissing passionately, her icy hand slipping into my shirt, stroking my chest like a draught.

As we writhed into another slow kiss, out of the darkness, there came a hacking cough…

"What?" gasped Frida. "What was that?"

Peering into the shadows, I could just make out a figure bending over a nearby bin, and, although too busy rummaging to be a threat, in fear, Frida's nails dug into my skin.

Tall and shadowy, the mysterious figure coughed again. Noisily hawking, he gurgled and spat…

"Get a room!" he rasped, and, with rain beginning to fall like darts of black ice, we fled, leaping into the first available taxi.

EIGHT

THE CLEARANCE

So bored, suffocated, dead, and buried. You know, I think I've truly discovered what boredom is, and it is more than a state of mind, or even an emotion. Boredom is a tangible thing, and boy is it heavy. I can feel it pinning me down. It's billowing, shapeless, flabby, and I'm wrapped in its stifling mass, and it stinks! Stuffy and cloying, like a packed classroom on a wet November afternoon.

So boring locked up in here. I've never felt anything like it. Hour after hour, listless, flopping about, just studying boredom itself, refining the emotion, rendering it naked and pure – such an experience, one I hope you never endure. However, my love, I've learnt something. Boredom is not born by having nothing to do. Dismiss the idea. I have plenty to do! The amount of writing before me is staggering, but with boredom sapping my energy, I can barely lift a finger...

Full of happy memories, it was fun to write the previous section, yet I cannot motivate myself into starting the next. I can find no explanation for this. The writing will surely be as enjoyable; my uncle's house fascinated me from the first moment I saw it, but can I bring myself to write a single word?

"Mirra," I bellowed. "Are you there? Are you listening? I need your help!"

Where is she, I pondered, where does she go? Doesn't she realise how boring it is, waiting like this?

There, you see. Everything is boring. It taints all that I do. Could boredom itself be propagating my condition? A defence mechanism to prevent its own elimination? Now, that is an interesting thought. A thought brought about by boredom itself. How very perplexing!

(Sorry about the rambling. I'm just so bored!)

Decided to try an entire cube of jelly. Only nibbled the corner of one so far, with no ill effects, so I think I'll have a pink one (they are all pink) … Yummy! No idea what this stuff is, but it's awesome! On the nose, their aroma is fruity, but the moment you pop one into your mouth there is an explosion of flavour that rattles your taste buds like thunder. I was wrong, however. They not only pineapple-flavoured, this one is maple syrup. It's all sweet and nutty.

⌛

Sprawled on the floor when the loudspeaker started to crackle, tracing with my fingers swirling patterns into the thick red pile of the carpet.

"Hello, Marcus!" said Mirra, her voice full of verve. "What're you doing down there? A reinterpretation of Orphism through the medium of fabric? A-pollen-air wouldn't recognise it as such – your palette lacks the necessary strength, tending towards neoclassicism, I'm afraid."

"Mirra." I smiled. "You're back, and what are you talking about? I'm just doodling, what's a-pollen-air?"

"*Apollinaire*," she proudly corrected. "And he is a whom not a what. *Wilhelm Albert Włodzimierz Apolinary Kostrowicki* or *Guillaume Apollinaire*. He was – is – an art critic, amongst other things. It really isn't important. The crucial factor is your essay. For you have finished, I see."

"Yes, Mirra," I said. "Finished it ages ago. Why keep me waiting so long? I want to be done and get the hell out!"

"Now, now," she chided, "don't be impatient. Just because you're making progress doesn't mean you get to call all the shots. There are other Marcuses as well, you know, not to mention the inquisitor. You have to wait your turn."

"Turn," I remarked, surprised I wasn't alone. "I didn't know. I thought myself your only prisoner. Just how big is this place?"

"It's vast," she revealed. "And yet at the same time extremely compact – we use space very efficiently. Although, this is all I am going to say, so no more questions if you please."

"But I have a million questions!"

"Please," she implored, "I beseech you, try to understand, your questions put me in a pickle. I want to help but to reveal too much is perilous. In time, 'he' will question you himself, and if he finds you overly acquainted with your circumstances, he will suspect collusion, punishing us both, swiftly putting an end to our friendship, and that would be a… pity?"

"Yes," I replied, thinking quickly. "It would be. However, friends trust and help each other, don't they? Because I don't trust you, not yet, but if you answer my questions, I will."

Releasing her churlishness, Mirra quietly chuckled.

"Very well," she said. "I suppose you deserve a favour for all your hard work, only don't get too probing or I will be forced to ignore you. Right now, however, we have work to do. We need to go over your essay, and I must say, from what I have read, I am delighted – as a writer you're clearly improving."

"Thanks," I acknowledged. "I'm giving it the works, but remembering everything is tricky, especially when an accurate description is required. I get into such muddle, my writing doesn't make sense!"

"Indeed," she replied. "Memories can be elusive, and I am aware of how you struggle constructing sentences, but, like I said, you're definitely improving, so much in fact, after the checking and correcting, we will have time for questions, ok?"

Smiling and taking my phone from my pocket, I fired up the word processor.

"Good," she assured. "As that is all I can offer, and before we part, I need to instruct you regarding our superior."

"Fine," I said, sipping water and shaking myself awake. "You have a deal. I've been desperate for a change of pace for some time."

"Indeed. Time is always changing pace. Now, at the beginning, you mention Phil being 'as loud as a Harley'. Could you please explain what a Harley actually is?"

"Sure. A Harley-Davidson. An American motorbike, their exhaust pipes are sometimes very loud."

"Ah…" she replied. "I see. Understand, I don't get out very much, I'm unaware of such things. What engines do Harleys possess?"

"Oh, I'm not sure, about twelve hundred cc, I should think, why?"

"Hmm…" she pondered. "Not sure if I know what that means. Let me think… oh yes. What fuel do they consume?"

"Petrol," I replied, somewhat bemused. "What else would they use?"

"Outstanding," she remarked, ignoring my question. "Then Harley-Davidsons employ internal combustion engines. Am I right?"

"Yes," I replied. "Of course, silly Mirra."

Moreover, this was how the process would continue.

Highly intelligent, well educated, an expert on a whole library of subjects beyond my knowledge, yet unaware of so much trivia, Mirra seemed childlike, and, if it appears picking our way through my writing in this manner was a tiresome endeavour, you would be quite wrong. In fact, I found the entire process endlessly amusing, and, if I did flag or yawn, we'd stop for breaks, chatting like friends about a wide range of topics. She particularly loved hearing stories I would recount about you, Frida, wanting to know every detail about your clothing and appearance, before asking questions regarding everyday life, about food. drink, games and music, and her enthusiastic pleasure in learning new things invariably lifted my spirits.

Indeed, we finished checking my essay in a fraction of the time compared to my previous effort. Mirra thoroughly pleased. Dishing out praise, hoping I could maintain the standard, and although I privately thought otherwise, her happiness buoyed me.

"Now," she said, "would you like to ask a few questions? I did sort of promise, did I not? I do have some minutes to spare. If you tread lightly, you might receive some answers."

"Yeah," I replied, encouraged by the prospect. "Ok, thanks. Where should I start, do you think?"

"That's easy," she advised. "Start at the start. Don't over-think. Ask me something simple."

"Fine," I said. "Although, a little more warning would've been helpful."

"Yes. Sorry about that. A lack of planning on my part, but if you take my advice, I'm sure you'll do fine."

"Very well. How about, where am I?"

"Not a good start to start with!" she replied. "You are in a place writing what we require you to write. You had better ask me another."

The evasiveness of Mirra's first answer made me realise I would need to be careful, and pressure bore down as I considered what to ask next…

"Indeed," I quickly remarked, worrying that, if I thought for too long, she might change her mind. "How long I have been here? What is the date?"

"I don't know."

"You don't know?" I said, appalled by her lie. "Come on, Mirra. Surely you know something. What is the month?"

"I said I didn't know. Please don't get cross. I don't know the month and I don't know the year. Could we leave this line of questioning?"

This was truly strange. Why deny me the time and the date, and I considered the benefit of asking, but time was pressing...

"Ok, ok." I chuckled, waving my arms in the air. "I get it. Another secret. So, answer me this. Who are you?"

"I'm Mirra!" she promptly replied. "I'm here to help with your writing."

What a dumb question. Nevertheless, it seemed worth asking, and she did give me leeway...

"Hey," I said, enjoying the game we were playing. "You didn't answer the question. Try again. Who are you?"

She sighed, and it was a sad little sigh, as if trapped indoors on a rainy day, wishing it would stop.

"I'm Mirra," she softly replied. "I shouldn't exist, and when you finish your writing, I won't. Does that answer your question?"

"Yes," I said. "Thank you, Mirra. That was an answer. Although, I don't understand it at all."

Did she mean, once I finished, she would be out of a job, but "shouldn't exist" confused me. Was she ashamed of her work? Did she think it unnecessary, and if so, why?

"Just three more questions," she cautioned, "and then I must go."

"Fine, what do you look like?"

"Oh, that's easy!" she replied. "I'm beautiful. The most beautiful woman you could imagine."

"She's still in Lima," I said with snap, aware she was toying with me (politely and sweetly admittedly but toying nonetheless) and frustration (mostly with myself) was beginning to bite...

"Yes, I know, and I'm sorry, but if you imagine us similar, I'd be extremely content. Two questions left."

"Who do you work for? Who's in charge?"

"Sneaky!" she replied. "That's two questions, so you get two answers. I don't know, and Moloch. Last one."

"Who's Moloch?"

"My superior, and the person in charge. Not his real name, but it's the one he prefers. When you finish your next instalment, he will return to interrogate you, and you need to know how to manage him. Please, sit yourself next to the door and listen very carefully. I'm going to whisper.

Probably pointless. If the bothers to listen, he will undoubtedly hear, but it is certainly worth a try."

Sitting on the floor, my shoulder pressed against the door's cool metal plating, I waited for her to begin.

"I don't have much time," she whispered. "Listen and don't interrupt."

"Sure," I said. "I'm listening."

"First. Moloch doesn't care about you at all. His only concern is the quantity and quality of your writing. Telling him how you feel, asking for succour, or calling for advice is not advisable. Initially, he will ignore your impertinent pleas, but, if you persist, he will become incensed. Therefore, do not deviate from the subject he imposes, and most importantly – and this really is crucial – *do not* let him know we talk. Moloch forbids verbal communication with inmates, and, if he learns of my disobedience, we'll both be in trouble. You should know, he hates me fervently, and if he discovers our deviation into irrelevance, he will harm us both. Your comfort and safety depend on his goodwill alone. Do not jeopardise them! Consider yourself lodged in the jaws of a sleeping monster. Tread lightly, speak softly, don't rouse him! And no, before you ask, I will not be present to help you. You will be alone. Moloch dominates all and I can only follow. Do you understand?"

"Yes, Mirra. When we will he arrive?"

"No idea," she softly replied. "Soon, I hope. Just continue with your writing."

"Ok," I said, "I will. Not sure how much, though; I'm terrified!"

"Understandable and understood," she acknowledged, "Yes. The more I know of you, the clearer it becomes – why sweet Frida loves you so much. Among all of the heroes of the past, the cowards are the most courageous of all. What a clever girl she is."

Indeed, you are, I thought, and how I could have done with your wits when posing those ridiculous questions.

"Now," she whispered, "I must say farewell," and then I heard the usual beep and the usual crackle. The persistent silence sweeping in like a fog.

"Goodbye, Mirra," I said.

Standing before my uncle's weather-beaten front door, my father, a clipboard under arm and readying a bunch of keys, asked if I was ready to enter…

"You sure you're ok about this?" he asked. "Certainly, would've spooked me. My daft brother used to claim there was a ghost in the house. A little girl, of all people. I do hope you're above such nonsense."

Only now am I admitting my fear. With the low sun streaming through the bushes, painting all manner of shadowy phantoms, the dilapidated house seemed as haunted as a haunted house could get.

"Yeah, it's fine." I nonchalantly shrugged. "More curious than nervous."

"Good," he said, patting my shoulder. "Let's see about opening the door – it gave me a battle royal the last time."

Methodically selecting a key, he slotted it into the keyhole, jiggling until the lock turned and clicked affirmatively.

"Finally," he remarked. "The damn lock's almost seized, but I think I've managed to free it."

He turned the handle and pushed a little, but the door refused to budge.

"This again," he said. "Had to slam it shut the last time, and now the wood's swollen up. Might need your help in a moment."

However, following determined handle-turning and shoving, he forced the door open, and as I peered into the forbidding black hole of the doorway, my fear intensified alarmingly…

"Bloody hell," he said, coughing then spitting. "I'd forgotten about the smell. Hasn't improved at all."

The door's sudden opening, rushing fresh air into the house, displaced the stale air within, and before long, I too was experiencing the sickening stench besetting him: smoking and its subsequent tarry residues. Indeed, it was almost overwhelming. So concentrated, you could detect its edges, you could taste it. Spicy, oily, astringent, and with notes of what? Sweetness? Ha! Misleading. I make it sound like a wine tasting. The smell was unpleasant, bordering vile, without any agreeable aspects whatsoever, and just ten minutes enveloped by the reek of it made my clothes stink, my head spin, and my throat burn like fire.

Flicking a light switch, my dad went in first, with me following closely behind, immediately feeling foolish thereafter. Although dated, the house held no terrors at all!

As you might expect, we were now in a hallway, dimly lit by a single unshaded bulb, dangling on stiff yellowed flex. Along the wall to my right (and currently closed) were two dark wooden doors, while on my left, rising into darkness, was a staircase, a low door beneath led to cupboard or cellar. Straight down the hall, another doorway opened into the kitchen.

"Right," said my dad, readying his clipboard, "you wait here while I turn on some lights and check on the cleaning. Don't go wandering, touching things, until I get back," before disappearing through the first door on my right and returning several seconds later.

"Front room's good," he said with an approving nod. "Hopefully the others will be as well."

Quickly scribbling a note, he then proceeded to enter, illuminate, and briefly inspect every downstairs room before striding upstairs, turning on lights as he went.

Impatiently standing by, I casually examined the fixtures and fittings, taking in a row of bare coat hooks, an empty umbrella stand, and upon the wall in a tall glass case, an antiquated barometer. Its snaking glass tube, half-filled with a silvery liquid.

"All done," said my dad, capping his pen and slotting it into his clipboard. "Worried there might be something grim, but now I can give you a tour, and I see you've found his barometer. Should be worth a few quid. Follow me!"

Entering the first door on the right, we came upon a small sitting room. In the middle of the room was a worn and saggy wingback. A coffee table within easy reach…

"Arthur's favourite seat," said my dad, highlighting the ashtray, glass, and bottle of scotch.

Lining the walls were three large bookcases (crammed full to bursting), a sofa, a desk, and a sideboard festooned by a catalogue of whiskies, and I recall my dad chuckling as I turned away from the books and made straight for the booze…

"Arthur was a great friend of the Islay distilleries," he remarked, and as I looked towards him (hoping for a taste) he added, "No chance, sunshine. Those are for me. Although you might get a snifter once you've finished with his books and crap."

Under the window was an ancient-looking television and I immediately switched it on. A brief crackling came from the screen's dark glass and then little else, and I shrugged in bored indifference…

"TV's broken," I muttered. "No picture. Just crackles."

"No," he replied. "It's fine. Needs to warm up."

He was right. Moments later the screen gradually brightened to show a snowstorm of interference, and, wondering how to get rid of it, I pushed every button I could find (BBC1, BBC2, ITV, VCR), hoping to witness a change.

"Right," he urged, "come on, turn that damn thing off, I want to show you the dining room," before sweeping me from the living room and through the next door on the right.

The dining room was clearly not for dining. Its large table and six chairs entirely entombed in metre-high heaps of books, folders, and papers. Two beaten and weary armchairs were also in here, both turned towards a decidedly retro gas heater set into the hearth.

In the far wall, opening into the gardening, were a pair of French doors, and, gasping with relief, my dad immediately flung them open, encouraging me to stand beside him at the threshold, taking deep breaths, dispelling the toxic dizziness threatening to overwhelm us.

"Think we'll leave these open," he said. "Don't know about you but it's suffocating in here."

"Hell, yeah," I replied. "It's gross. How much did he smoke, for God's sake?"

"A lot," he replied. "And the stench is really going to put off potential buyers. Even with cleaning and clearing, we'll never get rid of it."

"Once the furniture's gone, why not have the carpets shampooed? That'd help, surely."

"Hmm…" He pondered. "Good thinking, but the smoke will've affected more than just the carpets. The whole house will need redecorating and the carpets thrown away… Let's have a look at the kitchen."

"Sure," I said, taking a final deep breath. "Let's go."

The kitchen was a simple, dated-looking affair, sparkling clean, and thoroughly empty of foodstuffs. The fridge/freezer, unplugged and with its door propped open, was empty, defrosted, and spotless.

"Excellent," he acknowledged. "No rotting food, no mess, just what I wanted. The cook and cleaner deserve a little bonus for this, and, with their employer gone, they're out of a job."

The upstairs landing had five doors, one on the left, three in front, and one on the right. The leftmost opened upon a small room intended as a nursery or study, but my uncle had used it for junk, with articles, flyers, newspapers, magazines, folders, the same order of clutter swamping every available space downstairs. The opposite trio of doors led to another small bedroom (full of books), bathroom and toilet respectively, whereas the rightmost door opened upon the master bedroom. With a double bed, wardrobe, two chests of drawers, an enormous bookcase (full to bursting), desk, and bedside table. Upon the bedside table, my uncle's ultimate bedtime reading. A philosophical work called (I think) *The Mirror of Nature*,* whereas the binder contained maps and pages of notes concerning excavations undertaken by the Archaeological Society of Sussex.

Philosophy and the Mirror of Nature, Richard Rorty, 1979.

"Is that the lot then?" I asked. "Because this'll keep me busy for a day or two, but I don't see what the fuss is about."

"The fuss is about to come," he replied. "And there's probably more in the garage. You can look in there tomorrow – no lights, and many things to trip over. Now, one more place to visit…"

Insisting I remain in the bedroom, my father reached behind the wardrobe, retrieving a long pole with a hook, then, moving to the landing, he then proceeded to prod with the hooked end of the pole a large hatch in the ceiling, which, with a click and a whoosh, immediately dropped open, swinging back and forth so alarmingly he was obliged to duck out of its way…

"Phew!" He gasped, chuckling. "That was close. For the time being I suggest we leave it open – bloody thing's lethal!"

"Yeah," I remarked, leaning forward to peer into the hatch. "Lucky you're not any taller. Is there a ladder?"

There was. With the swinging hatch under control, my father used the pole to hook on to a loop of rope just inside the opening, and, following a deft flick, the rope uncoiled, falling in such a way that the end of the loop arrived next to his feet.

"Here," he said, handing me the pole. "Put this back and stand clear," and as I returned to pole to its hiding place, he whistled an old hornpipe, methodically pulling the rope, engaging a series of pulleys, lowering and unfolding an ingenious flight of steps.

"No climbing yet," he warned as I edged forward. "Need to put the locking pins in," before cautiously ascending one step at a time, sliding steel pins hanging from each step into the jointed parts to secure them.

"Ta-da!" He then grinned, flicking a couple of switches, flooding the whole loft in light. "Didn't know he'd converted his loft until last week. It's a beautiful job. Come up and see!"

He was right about the loft. It was a transformation. Parquet flooring, shelves, cupboards, five freestanding bookcases, two desks (positioned under the skylights), and a large metal trunk.

Upon one of the desks was an elderly-looking computer, a printer too, with white paper in a long folding sheet trailing to a box on the floor...

"Dad?" I asked. "Can I try the computer?"

"Yeah, if you like," he replied, thumbing a book. "Only it's not a computer, it's a word processor, and you'll need to put a disk in the drive before switching it on. Try that little box next to the printer. Look for a disk labelled system, start-up, or boot."

The first disk in the box possessed the label "System Start Disk" and, as I slid it into the drive, a little button popped out with an affirmative click. Switching on both monitor and base unit, I sat back and smiled as it purred into life, a green cursor flashing on the screen like a heartbeat, the disk drive groaning and clucking like a contented hen. Moments later a menu appeared, offering functions such as new, load, save, and print, and I pressed F2 to load the most recent file, observing the screen steadily fill with blocky green text.

It was a letter. A reply from my uncle to a customer regarding fragments of an old book, *Ars Poetica**, he concluded. Not a book I had heard of, but thoroughly impressed by his scholarly abilities, I suddenly regretted not knowing him.

The Ars Poetica to which Marcus refers would be Thomas Drant's (circa 1540–1578) English translation of Horace's (65–8 bc) Ars Poetica or Epistula ad Pisones, originally written about 18 bc.

Loading a couple more files, I found them much the same as the first. Suffice to say, each disk brimmed with them, revealing the astonishing variety and quantity of my uncle's work.

"Please don't print anything," said my dad, bringing a roll of rubble sacks from downstairs. "The racket those old printers make is terrible."

"Wasn't going to," I assured. "I'm switching off in a sec."

"Fine," he replied. "But take out the disk first or it'll be fritzed."

Done with the word processor, I swung off the chair and sat at the opposite desk.

Not much on it. A cardboard folder, a jam jar with a few pens, and, looking out of place on its dark wooden plinth, the figurine of a bearded tribesman holding circular totem over his head.

It was then, I realised, that this curio, apart from a single vase downstairs, was the only ornament in the house, and, wondering if it was valuable or significant, I immediately picked it up. Not that it was attractive, mind you. In fact, it was downright ugly. Moulded from plaster of Paris and haphazardly painted, its surface was uneven and blotchy. With a prominent black spot and rendered deep orange, the disc-like totem of the figurine had me wondering what it might be. A sunset with Mercury in transit? Or could it be a sunspot? Turning the statue slowly in my hands, I spied a label on the underside of its plinth: "To Arthur. A cast of our copy from the Camber Viking burial. Happy 45th Birthday! From Graham. (you'll have to paint it yourself)."

"This figurine's weird," I remarked. "Have you seen it before?"

After rattling the padlock on the steel trunk, my dad was looking about for the key.

"Hmm?" he mumbled. "No. Sorry. Never seen it before in my life," so I read the label aloud.

"Nope," he replied, shaking his head. "That doesn't help either. Graham, however, might be the Dr Corbiere we met at the pub. Why don't you ask him?"

"Oh, yeah," I said. "Good idea. Are you looking for something?"

"Yes. I'm trying to get into this damn trunk. Can't find the key anywhere. Could you have a look in the desks?"

Quickly going through each drawer, I turned up nothing but stationery, smoking ephemera, and general household clutter.

"Not here, Dad, at least not obviously. Want me to tip everything out?"

"No," he replied, looking at his watch. "Don't make a mess. I'm sure it'll turn up."

"Ok," I said, standing and straightening my jeans. "When do you want me to start?"

(Feeling my phone vibrate, I rummaged in my pocket.)

"As soon as you can, otherwise you'll be in the way of the clearance, and if you do find anything valuable, tell me straight away or it might get filched. Here…" and he presented me with a bunch of keys, Dr Corbiere's card, a box of sticky labels and the three rolls of black plastic sacks (brought up from the junk room below). "Now, listen," he said, "these are your keys. Don't lose them, and make sure you lock up when you leave; the last thing we need are squatters in here. Also, be sure to turn off all the lights. Think about the electricity you're using; I don't want any more bills hanging over me. Use the labels to identify the stuff you want to keep, otherwise the house clearing people will take it, and if you need help with the historical stuff, contact the bloke on the card."

"Right-o," I replied, whipping out my phone. "I'll do my best. How long have I got?"

"I don't want your best; I want it done! You have a fortnight, so you need to get cracking. If any post comes, you can open it, just remember to bring it home. Ok?"

Checking my phone for messages, my attention drifted away like a like cloud.

"Oh, for pity's sake," he sighed, banging his fist on a desk. "Can't you pay attention for once?"

⧗

Returning early the next morning, I was already worn out. Without a lift, the journey was a faff, and needing to hire a taxi for the last few miles (at great expense), listening to the driver's prattle, to quote Frida, "almost did my head in!"

Wrestling the front door open, I went straight to the garage – to see if it hid any more books. To my relief, it did not, but there was a car! An L-registration Hillman Avenger GLS 1500*, sky-blue, with a white vinyl roof, and apart from a layer of dust, it was perfect.

Registration PPO 424L. Date of manufacture, 1972.

Excited by my find, and relieved there were no further books, as I made my way indoors, I sent a text to my dad...

"Hey Dad," I wrote, "can I have the car?"

His reply, strangely immediate (had he pre-written it?) ...

"Hey Marcus! No, you can't."

"Oh, go on Dad," I wrote. "It's so cool!"

"No!" came his reply. "It was shit then and it's shit now. The thing is a death trap. No."

Knowing my dad, I knew the discussion was over. To have any hope of getting the car, I would need to butter him up – spurring me into an immediate start on the books...

Without any plan, I began in the front room, and opening the window (to get rid of the stench) I began attacking the largest bookcase, quickly scanning every title before flicking open their covers, checking for first editions. Certainly, regarding the books, deciding what to chuck and what to keep, my father had left to my common sense – surely a mistake, and although true, I did love books, a collector I was not. Yet, I have gleaned from TV shows etc. that books are most valuable when they are in hardback, first edition, and still in their jacket (if they originally had one). Their condition is critical too – the Achilles' heel of my uncle's collection. Long kept in a smoky environment, many displayed a degree of yellowing or staining. Most were well "thumbed" too, with scribbled notes upon their margins, headers, and footers.

It soon became clear that first editions were rare in my uncle's collection, as if it were deliberate. Perhaps later editions were cheaper, but I also considered a historian might prefer a book's later edition, with errors corrected and facts further corroborated, and by the time I had gone through the first bookcase (two hundred books at best guess) there were only three I believed valuable or rare, not a difficult choice either – the only first editions I could find! One, a book on the Anglo-Saxon language* and still in its jacket, appeared in fair condition.

*This being the 1905 first edition of the Anglo-Saxon Primer by Henry Sweet.

The other two were jacket-less, Victorian, in good condition, and summaries of important books (with a short précis of each) held in the libraries of stately homes – an extremely useful resource for an archivist of my uncle's persuasion.

Despite my best efforts, I am unable to coax Marcus into remembering these books, although I am fairly convinced one was a descriptive bibliography of the library at Chatsworth House, Derbyshire, England.

Opening one of the rubble sacks, I carefully placed the three special books inside before labelling the sack "Auction". The rest from the bookcase, the dross if you like, I quickly threw into further sacks, suggestively labelling them "Book Shop?" before repeating the process with the two other bookcases, ordering a pizza, and rummaging in the cupboards and desk. Now, this took much longer than I expected. The quantity of files, folders and binders tucked away was almost overwhelming, couldn't make head nor tail of them either! Half contained clippings or photocopied extracts, whereas the rest detailed some previously investigated historic manuscript or fragment of book, including, in most cases, the original letter of enquiry, his reply (including the cost of the procedure (a considerable sum!), his findings, invoice, and receipt of payment. Although of passing interest, I shoved them all into sacks and labelled them "Chuck".

An hour and a half later, with the entire sitting room cleared, feeding my face with pizza, and thirstily slurping a cola, I reflected on my progress. Done in of couple more days I thought. Wiping my fingers on the furniture (soon to be dumped) I moved to the dining room, throwing open the French doors (for fresh air). Gathering armfuls of the books and papers from the dining table and then spreading them out meant I quickly ran out space, and despite my efforts, I bore little fruit. Two books. Both obviously antique, beautifully bound in tooled leather, were histories of Limoges and its eventual sacking by the Black Prince of Wales. * Comparable to those in the sitting room, the documents and paperwork went straight into sacks for disposal. Saddening, as it was my uncle's life's work.

*These were The Chronicles of Froissart – the 1910 John Bourchier & Lord Berners' Harvard Classics translation, and Tales from Froissart – the 1849 edition of the Thomas Johnes translation (1805).

By the time the dining room was clear, the afternoon was gloomily dragging to a close, and before heading home, I went to collect the mysterious figurine from the loft. Its incongruous presence had been playing on my mind, and I was eager to understand its significance.

⌛

The work at my uncle's house went on for days, and, fearing for my health, upon my arrival I would jiggle open as many windows as I could, which certainly seemed to help, as by Thursday the smell had abated considerably (or I was becoming desensitised?), and, feeling less overwhelmed, my productivity increased dramatically. Indeed, as if in response to my progress, the house clearance people were on the premises too, and their swearing and straining, banging, and clonking stripped the house of its sleepy quiet. Supervising and administrating, clipboard at the ready, my dad was in and out too, and I would occasionally catch his voice, blurting instructions to the workers downstairs. Thursday was also the day I began going through the loft library, a bit of a gold mine compared to the rest of the house, every shelf with a rare or valuable book, and with tall stacks to carefully bag up when finished, I was lucky enough to load them into our car.

Later that afternoon, after bagging and labelling the last of the books, I turned my attention to the large metal trunk, and, after jiggling and tugging at its devil-wrought padlock, I slumped in a chair to think. How to get in? Well, a hacksaw, crowbar or bolt-cutter would've probably got me inside, but I had no such implements, and, having no idea what it contained (it might have been fragile), I didn't want to force it. I had to find the key. I needed to find the key. Everything else was just lying about. Must be something good. So, come on Marcus, find the goddamn key!

Encouraged by the thought of treasure, I began the most thorough search I could muster, in the obvious places. Pulling out drawers, tipping their contents onto the floor, I carefully sifted through them, but no key did I find. Indeed, this fruitless activity took me over an hour, so where could it be? Hidden, for sure, and, knowing what little I did of my uncle, hidden cunningly, so I ran my fingers under the edges of the desks, and then, with a sudden brainwave, I examined the undersides of the drawers. To my dismay, no key, but something had been there. I could see marks left by the tape – darker and dirtier than the surrounding wood…

Now, "darker and dirtier" must have given a hint. As my next search involved squeezing my fingers behind and between the shelves and cupboards, but apart from dust, dirt, and a cobweb or two, I came up *sans clef.* *

Actual French!

One last stretch, I thought and then give up for the day. Selecting the nearest cupboard and standing on tippy-toe, I swept my arm down the back of it. Splaying and wriggling my fingers into its tightest recesses…

Nothing. Oh…? No. Nothing.

Disappointment bit at me and I sagged, deflated. Nothing down there at all, but, while slowly withdrawing my arm, an object dropped into my fingers. Something small, flat, and so icily cold that I started. A key! Wedged in place or held by adhesive, my movements causing it to fall, and carefully drawing it out, I held it aloft like a jewel.

Then, I heard something.

Although "heard" is the wrong verb. There was a disturbance. A breeze, and the hairs stood up on the back of my neck. I felt watched, exposed, vulnerable. I felt naked. Quickly turning this way and that, I expected someone behind me…

"Hello," I muttered. "Is anyone there?" and my voice sounded small, remote, and terribly lonely.

Silence answered. There was nothing. Nothing but the muffled sounds of London, of traffic, of aircraft, of a robin twittering in the garden…

The house was very empty, and I was alone within it.

Now, as you know, I'm not one for ghosts, ghouls, or any other superstitious nonsense, and, shrugging off the sensation, I tried the key in the padlock. It worked! With a smooth twist and a click the padlock gave way, swinging flaccidly, and, lifting it clear of the hasp, I opened the lid in excitement.

What I expected to find I really didn't know. Was I hoping for something of value? An antique treasure or keepsake? Yet what I found I should have expected to find. A bundle of cardboard folders tied up with string, and, with a groan of frustration, I threw them out onto the desk.

It had been long day and I was tired. Tired of the stench, tired of the dust, hungry and parched. I wanted to get back to my life, and this last effort had unexpectedly drained me. Looking at the folders, I could only sigh…

Then, as if in response to my gloom, a small marble dopped from the folders and rolled across the desk. It twinkled as it rolled, as if smiling and taunting, and when it fell from the desk, landing in the chest with a clang, I found myself chuckling at its comical timing. Part of a toy, I thought, and its unexpected appearance dispelled my irritation like a poke in the ribs.

Foolish to be so despondent. Nothing else here required locking away. These folders must be important, and with my enthusiasm rekindled, I sat at the desk to study them.

Thunder rumbled, rattling the windows, and rain beat against the skylights. Darkness swept through the loft like a ghost.

The string securing the bundle had a label attached, and my hands shook as I held it. It was only a plain cardboard label. A bit grubby, yellowed, dusty, and upon it a single word. Written in pencil. Very carefully, I thought. Letter by letter, as a child would, yet when I read it, it utterly blew me away.

It said:

Marcus

NINE

MOLOCH

After soul-searching, mulling how to proceed, I have decided to recount the events that unfolded before I penned the previous instalment. Certainly, writing of my experiences here was an idea of Mirra's, killing time, keeping me occupied before my release. Moreover, "communicating the conditions under which I write will serve to contextualise my endeavours".

Haughtily put, but she's probably right.

I am.

As she previously explained, with Moloch soon arriving, Mirra was unavailable to assist with my editing, so despite my apprehension I did the best I could.

"Come on, Marky," I would mutter. "Keep your eyes off the door and concentrate," but with Mirra worried I would say something dumb it was hard to think clearly at all.

Then, although I don't recall it, I must have fallen asleep, for I experienced the most peculiar dream...

Dreaming I was awake, surrounded by light, not the white light of my cell but ripples, colourful waves, glowing with yellow, purple, and green. There was no sound, and I was unable to move or speak, and that pig-like smell was back: ripe, sharp, and sweaty. It made you wrinkle your nose.

Only then did I discover my blindness. Trying to stare, trying to focus, but I was unable to move my eyes, couldn't even blink, yet the colours continued their incessant rolling, pulsating, almost hypnotic, but was I truly seeing them?

Movement. I heard movement, a peculiar sound, like a cloth wiping a window, but then, as if out of nowhere, bursting into my mind, there came a booming male voice, freezing me to the marrow...

"Subject, Eaton-Marcus, number one-zero-five-four-zero-three. I will question, it will answer."

Identical to the voice heard upon my arrival, he was everywhere, inside and out, penetrating, inescapable, bearing down like thunder, crashing overhead...

"Yes," replied the voice in my head, and in doing so, it was as if my words had been torn from my mind. He spoke again...

"It finds its chamber adequate?"

"Yes, sir," I promptly replied, remembering Mirra's advice. "But..."

"But what?" he spat. "Speak!"

"It's boring," I explained. "Maintaining my focus within such a plain space is difficult."

"Noted," he coldly remarked. "Is my pet a distraction?"

"Which one?" I asked, immediately cursing my flippancy, but he laughed, and so cruel was his mirth, I felt ready to perish. Indeed, the sound of his laughter was deafening, reverberating, horridly stabbing, synchronous with the rolling hues, juddering now, and writhing like snakes.

"Which one, indeed!" he bellowed, gurgling and wheezing. "The one in the tank, little man – the lichid."

"Oh, that thing," I replied, realising he was referring to Barry (and wondering what a "lichid" might be). "No, sir, not at all, he just sits there, doing stuff-all."

"Good," he rumbled. "I placed it as a divertissement. It is a primitive yet curious beast."

"Yes, sir," I replied. "Very curious, thank you."

The squeaky "cloth on glass" sound issued again. The green tendrils of light dimming before brightening again.

"So far," he continued, "its writing is adequate, sometimes good. It will maintain this standard or better it, although dwelling upon puerile recollections is unwise."

Meaning (I assume) kindly stop writing about our relationship, and even though I saw his point, I had no intention of stopping.

"As you wish," I said. "I learn as I go. You have provided an excellent helper."

"Yes," he agreed. "It should serve you well, but know the helper can be irrational, a liar, and a nuisance. Is it a nuisance? Knowing as it does how swiftly punishment follows failure."

"No, sir," I quickly replied. "She's been very helpful. Without her, my writing would be… unsatisfactory?"

He hesitated and the swirling colours briefly slowed, then he spoke again:

"She, it says?" His curiosity cutting like a knife. "Why does it say 'she'? Has it attempted to speak?"

Forced now to tell an absolute whopper of a lie, I braced myself, keeping my tone as matter of fact as possible.

"No, sir," I pledged. "Not a word, we only communicate by text, but your helper introduced herself as Mirra. Sounds like a girl's name to me."

"Names are irrelevant!" he snapped. "But Mirra? Is that what it calls itself now? How interesting…" and he paused, seemingly wrapped in much thought.

"Ah, yes," he rasped. "I understand, it is clever. A companion's words of persuasion are effective."

"They are, sir," I replied, not really getting his meaning.

"However," he went on, "I find no evidence of textual messages within the communications device. It will explain this."

Here I had to think quickly, and being a well-practised fibber, I remained calm, keeping my responses crisp and concise…

"She deletes them," I offered. "She says it saves memory," before secretly glowing in triumph at my cleverness.

"It is correct," he acknowledged. "The integrity of the device must be maintained at all costs."

Saying nothing, I buried my feelings and waited.

"So far," he remarked, his contemptuous tone slowly relenting, "I am quite pleased with you (so much nicer than 'it'). Continue to work as you are, and you will taste freedom, yet if you fail, you will die here, insane, decrepit, and lost."

Charming.

⧗

Upon waking, I found myself lying on the bed, still holding my phone, with a dry mouth and desperately needing a pee (another first).

Swinging off the bed, I made for the toilet, fainting en route, crumpling on the floor in a heap.

Now, I have fainted before – horrid sensation, and I understand how this often afflicts the young. On previous occasions, it was after standing too quickly, and I am certain this was the cause…

Cool fingertips caressed my temples, and lips (I am sure it was lips) gently brushed my forehead. Opening my eyes, I saw a woman before me. She was quite old, I think, in her forties or fifties, toweringly tall, beautiful, and standing so close I could smell her perfume. As if checking my physical condition, she dwelt upon my face – her lips were moving, she was speaking, although I couldn't hear her voice and lip-reading proved fruitless. I couldn't derive a single word.

Waving her hand over my face, taking a step back and looking perplexed, she gave me the opportunity to take in her figure: slender, athletic, with long dark hair (tossed over one shoulder) and dark-brown eyes. The pale skin of her face flushed slightly, and, while thinking, perching her chin on her thumb, she reminded me of Frida so much it was painful, then, as if aware I was ogling her skin-tight suit, she cocked a curious eyebrow and gracefully moved away, her suit's fabric shimmering in time with her every stride as she dwindled into the distance.

Coming to, lying face down on the bed (without any idea how I got there), I hauled myself upright and blinked against the dazzling light. The room was the same as ever. Clean, spacious, white walls, boring red carpet, and when I stood, a little shakily a first, I moved to the centre of the room to pick up my phone. I recalled using the toilet, evidenced by the pale-yellow water within, and, pushing the button next to the pan, I watched with surprise as it proceeded to flush most unconventionally…

Instead of clean water rushing in, forcing the foul water away, the pan simply drained, quickly refilling from below with clean water. No splashing, no gushing, no noisy refilling of cisterns, and I marvelled at its clever simplicity, hoping for a dump sometime, if only to observe how this ingenious fixture would shift it.

Thank you, Marcus, for that delightful insight.

TEN

THE MAN IN THE WALL

After my fainting episode, some curious developments. For one, we had a blackout – a power failure, leaving me in darkness for what felt like a couple of hours, and the only light, providing something at least to establish my bearings, was a faint blue glow coming from the mud in Barry's tank, and, yes, I did try using my phone to see by, but the blackout had affected it too – it was dark and dead as a doornail. Strange this should have happened, but hey, in this madhouse, I'm used to strange.

Following the power's restoration, opposite my bed, I noticed a new occurrence, a dark grey rectangular section of wall, and, while examining it, the loudspeaker crackled and beeped into the voice of my guardian angel…

"Hello, Marcus!" called Mirra. "How are you feeling, my friend?"

"Mirra," I replied. "So good to hear you again, I'm fine, but what's up with the wall?"

"A gift from Moloch, and I'll tell you about it shortly, but first, your interview, how did it go? What did he ask? What did he say? Did you see him?"

"So now it's you with a million questions." I chuckled in reply. "Shall I answer or not?"

"Don't be silly!" she snapped. "This is important. What happened?"

"Well," I replied, digging into my memory. "Not sure what happened really. It was dream-like and hard to remember precisely, but I saw ribbons of colour, loads of them, swirling about and surrounding me, and his voice froze me to the spot."

"So, you didn't see him, you just heard his voice, and were you in here, do you think? Did he speak through the door?"

She seemed uncharacteristically urgent asking all this, not scared exactly, but edgy, and I recalled Moloch's words about punishment following failure…

"No," I said, trying to recollect the words and sensations. "I'm certain I wasn't in here. His voice was inescapable. It was everything, like it was inside me and everywhere else at once."

"Poor you," she soothed. "Must have been terrifying, I wonder why he did it like that."

"It was awful, and afterwards I felt really rubbish. I fainted and then had a weird hallucination. Although now, I seem to be fine."

"What sort of hallucination? Did you have visions?"

"Yes," I replied, frowning, trying to remember, "something like that. I saw a woman in a skin-tight, shiny suit. She was very tall, beautiful, examining me, as if she were a nurse or something. She reminded me of Frida, but in other ways she was unique. Do you know who she could be?"

"No idea," she said, sounding perplexed. "At least, not yet, but I might know later. Now, speak, tell me everything," before listening in silence as I struggled to recount my experience.

"Oh, my dear Marcus!" she then cried. "Thank you, thank you so much, you did brilliantly! Little wonder he decided to reward you."

"You're welcome," I replied, not understanding my achievement. "But I have a question. Why did he not know your name? You said it was his idea."

"Because it was so long ago. He has forgotten, and his staggering arrogance has closed his mind. He could never accept he might be mistaken."

"Perhaps he's getting old," I offered, delighting in her openness. "And for some reason he thought your name was important, although he didn't say why."

"Indeed, he wouldn't explain anything to anyone unless it was advantageous, and you did well not to question him. Let's just say, he knows full well I'm deceiving him and trying to uncover the truth. Dear me." She laughed. "The stupid old fool, his convoluted paranoia is comic, and if he does come to unmask me, he will simply learn of my kindness. Of course, such wasteful frivolousness will irritate him enormously. He doesn't value such things, and doubtless I'll be punished."

"Oh, ok," I said, furrowing my brow. "I understand." (Although I most assuredly did not.)

"Now, now," she assured. "Dwelling on this will change nothing, so don't burden yourself. This matter is purely between Moloch and me. Just keep on with writing and all will be fine."

It is unlikely I will ever understand the intrigue playing out between Moloch and Mirra. Of their disagreements I was fully aware – according to Mirra it was about the treatment of prisoners, but I felt there was more to it than that. Their mutual hatred seemed real, not just professional, and with Mirra telling of their disputes I felt involved, ready to support her, if the choice ever came.

"Now then," she said, snapping to a new topic. "Allow me to demonstrate Moloch's kind gift. Walk to the grey section of wall and press your palm against it."

Doing as she instructed, the rectangle instantly brightened, displaying a menu with four tiles: Cinema, Television, Audio, Saulintone T2.

"That's it," she prompted. "Take a step back and I'll describe what you see. This is an entertainment portal. A television with added flexibility and features. To select a category, touch the relevant section of screen. Each will take you to further lists and tables for the selection of audio or video content. The final panel connects the portal to your communications device – your phone, displaying its images, applications and text in greater clarity."

Staring at the screen, my hand hovering over the television tile (and thinking Mirra had finished), I tapped it with my finger. A tiled menu of geographical regions appeared, but, before I could read it, Mirra spoke again…

"To control the playback of media, tap the bottom of the screen to reveal panels for brightness, contrast, saturation, gamma correction, sound quality, volume, and time-based navigation."

"Got it," I replied. "How do you switch it off?"

"Powering down the portal is simple. Place the palm of your hand over the centre of screen and wait a few seconds."

Nodding again, I tapped a tile labelled "Back", returning to the primary menu.

"Thank you," I said. "This is fantastic, nearly as good as a human companion. I'm almost speechless with gratitude."

"That will never happen!" She tittered. "But you earned it, and don't thank me. You should thank Moloch."

"Will you then, please, the next time you see him?"

"Certainly," she replied. "But Moloch giveth and Moloch taketh away, so we'd better look at your latest essay. Have you checked it yourself?"

"Yes," I said. "I hope you like it, and oh, one more thing…"

"Yes, Marcus?" She sighed. "What is it now?"

"Well," I timorously asked. "Does the portal thing have a remote control? You know, so that, if I'm lying on the bed watching or listening and I want to change something, I don't need to get up?"

"Marcus!" She laughed. "That really is the pinnacle of laziness, but yes, Moloch has thought of this too. Apart from switching between the 'on' and 'off' states, you still need your hand for that, every function is under voice control. Just say what you want, and the portal will interpret."

"Wow," I said. "That's cool. How does it work?"

"I don't know," she admitted. "Would have to ask my colleagues. Legato or Sense might know, but it's a mechanism, with algorithms, procedures, and so forth – software, Marcus, not as sophisticated as it first seems. If it helps, imagine there's a man in the wall obeying your every command."

Waking early in the cheap Richmond hotel we had fled to once the rain started falling, our clothes in a heap on the floor, I recalled our night-time antics, and, although I retained the warm glow of intimacy, I was aware our relationship had reached a crossroads. Were we to be something or nothing? Was "last night" an extension of love or a drunken mistake? Only time would tell.

With Frida still asleep beside me, I slipped from the bed, creeping to the tiny bathroom to piss, stretch, and splash my face with water, and, after wrapping myself in one of the paper gowns hanging inside (and cursing the noise it produced), I tiptoed to the window for a look.

Frida stirred and sighed. Quite drunk the previous night, I wondered if she was going to be hung-over, and, tiptoeing beside her, I delicately kissed the top of her head…

The symptoms of a hangover are universal, but how individuals treat them can be burdensome and eccentric. Only having had a few beers, I felt fine, but Frida, well, she had hit the gin hard, and I prayed she would be content with rest, caffeine, painkillers, all without being a complete misery, vomiting, groaning, demanding cold compresses, weird emetics, unlikely tonics, and specialist cures.

In one corner there was a TV and a couple of comfy chairs, and, judging the depth of Frida's sleep, I wondered if watching TV would disturb her. She did seem pretty much out of it, so I decided I would, plugging in my headphones and sitting in silence, praying the flickering screen would go unnoticed. As it turned out, there was precious little worth watching, and, after viewing the news, I switched channels, encountering a long-haired Wiltshire man digging very slowly with a trowel, and I must have watched this for some time, I think (finding myself strangely captivated by the sieving of a spoil heap), before removing my headphones to check on an occasionally blinking Frida...

"What time is it?" she croaked.

"About eight. How're you feeling?"

"Pretty crap. Could be worse..."

"Fancy some coffee? Don't know about you, but I'm parched."

"Tea..." she implored, and I felt her pain from the hangovers endured myself.

Picking up the phone, I called down to reception an ordered room service, tea, coffee, and a continental breakfast (best on a dodgy stomach), then I climbed into bed for a cuddle.

"Is there any water?" she asked. "I've some pills in my purse, but without a drink I won't get them down."

"There's a jug on the sideboard. Hang on a sec, I'll..."

"No," she said. "Don't be doormat, stay there..." and I watched (with hidden delight) her tiny naked form stumbling, staggering, filling a tumbler with water, sipping, and popping two pills.

With Frida in the toilet doing her doings, our breakfast arrived on two trays, and, giving her a call, she promptly emerged, hair tousled, wrapped in the other disposable gown, its starchy material scrunched and haphazardly folded to make it a fit.

"I'm like a used tissue!" she said, flapping her arms, and I poured her tea with milk and sugar – the way she emphatically liked it.

Cradling the cup to her chin, Frida closed her eyes, slowly inhaling the steam through her nose.

"Want some toast?"

"Yeah, thanks," she said, scratching and rustling. "But only one slice or I'll puke," and I busied myself buttering a slice before dropping it onto the plate.

"I'm wondering," I asked, as she tentatively nibbled a crust, "do you have any plans for today?"

"No," she replied, blinking and frowning, "and I won't be doing anything for an hour or two. Besides, I've only got my cocktail dress. It's a bit flimsy for London."

"Well, actually," I said, assuming she'd want to go home, "if we're going our separate ways, my dad wants me back at my uncle's house, to sort through more of his stuff. He says I wasn't thorough enough."

"Oh." She pondered, closing her eyes. "You were talking about your uncle's place last night – sounds interesting. Can I come too? Where is it?"

"Blackheath, right by the A2, and of course you can come!"

"Ok," she said, the tea beginning to work. "I'll tag along. First, though, I need to wake up or I'll be so grumpy you'll hate me."

"Unlikely," I replied. "But no worries. We have until midday, so take as long as you want."

"Good. If I can buy a cheap fleece and leggings from somewhere, I'll definitely come. Could you search with your phone and see what's nearby?"

"Ok," I happily agreed. "Let's see if can get on their Wi-Fi…"

⧗

With her intricate knowledge of public transport, travelling across London with Frida was a cinch. We bought her clothes, lunch for us both, arriving in Blackheath just after midday. Out of laziness (and ignorance) I would have used taxis, but with Frida in charge, we didn't use any. Disembarking our final bus just two minutes' walk from our destination.

Standing upon my uncle's front path, Frida studied the house with dismay…

"What a dump," she remarked.

"Hey," I replied, wrestling open the door. "Don't be so rude. It needs a bit of TLC, that's all, only on the inside, it's a bit…"

"Jezebel's wig!" gasped Frida, confronted by the pong. "What the fuck's that?"

"… a bit smelly," I continued. "Far better than it was, though, and you get used to it, I promise."

"Used to it?" she mocked with a sniff. "How exactly? By dying?"

"Come on," I challenged. "Don't be a wuss. It's just a bad smell. Are you coming in or not?" and, blowing out her bottom lip (producing a horse-like sound), she reluctantly followed me in.

Stripping the carpets, curtains, and furniture had left the house naked and cold, and I gave Frida a quick tour, highlighting the large metal trunk, recounting my quest to recover the bundle of folders (the twinkly marble had gone). In the living room, and piled halfway to the ceiling, the labels on the sacks saying "Chuck" were boldly overwritten "Keep".

"Well, this is what he's on about," I said. "Although what he expects me to do, I don't have a clue."

Frida by now was beginning to turn green, and, seeking fresh air, she dashed into the back garden, squatting, and taking deep breaths before admiring a vibrant clump of Michaelmas daisies.

Seeing she was ok (and not puking her guts up), I sat on the stairs, sending a text to my father…

"Hey Dad! I'm at uncle's house. What do you want done with the papers and stuff?"

"Sort them out!" came his reply. "They're a valuable historical resource. Get the museum people to look at them – call the bloke on the card."

"But there are loads," I wrote back. "Have to spread them all over the place."

"Doesn't matter," he replied. "Now the house is empty there's less of a rush, do something properly for once!"

"Ok Dad," I texted. "Frida's here helping, is that ok?"

"I don't care, just get it done."

Frida reappeared from her walk in the garden.

"How're you doing?" I asked. "Are you feeling alright?"

"Yeah," she said, blowing her hair from her eye. "What's up?"

Showing her the texts from my dad, I shrugged.

"Oh dear." She laughed, delivering a musty-mouthed kiss. "You are in a pickle. Let me have a look. Sorting stuff is a passion of mine. I'm a filing fanatic!"

Opening a sack at random, Frida slid out its contents, quickly producing three piles: cuttings, notes, and cases.

"No point keeping the cuttings and notes," she said. "They can definitely go. It's the casefiles your dad's on about. Help me unearth a few more. I have a plan, but to be certain I need to see more."

Half a dozen sacks later, we had pile of about thirty files, each clipped neatly into a cardboard folder.

"Look," Frida remarked. "They're all the same, with an invoice, summary, description of the find, its approximate age, and the address of the customer. If we sort them all, say, by region, you could find out what people were reading, and when, judging how educated they were, how accessible books and stuff were to different social classes, and so on. Pretty important stuff to a historian, so let's get cracking and go through them all."

This was a typical example of just how perceptive Frida could be. Ideas came to her with such ease it was difficult not to be envious, and, with a concrete plan, we cracked on at a furious pace, the whole lot arrayed in analogous piles by early afternoon.

With the sun beginning to burn through the mist, we sat on the steps in the garden enjoying the lunch we had bought.

"What now?" asked Frida, munching on a juicy green apple. "Are you gonna call the museum?"

"Possibly," I replied, "although my battery's almost gone. I must get a spare."

"Oh?" she remarked, cocking an eyebrow. "Use my little phone then. No bells or whistles, but for calling and texts it's fine."

"Thanks," I said. "Thanks for the offer, but it's Sunday, isn't it? Think we should leave him in peace, just text him instead? Besides, I don't want him getting your number, in case he's a perv?"

The message went something like this: "Dear Dr Corbiere, this is Marcus Eaton. I'm at my uncle's house (Arthur Eaton) and have a large quantity of documents which might interest you. If you'd like to come and have a look sometime, please contact me on this number."

"How's that?" I offered, showing Frida the text.

"Perfect," she replied. "Nice and polite, but I'd have called it an archive – historians can't resist a good archive. What now?"

"Hang around, see if he replies? In case he wants to come over?"

It turned out he did not, texting how he would happily meet me at the house the following evening, bringing a colleague with specialist knowledge. Frida agreed to meet me as well. It had been her plan and she wanted to see it through to the end. Texting my dad, explaining our proposal, his reply was abrupt. Not caring what or how, he just wanted me to finish, and quickly.

⧖

It was a fine, clear night when I returned to my uncle's house. The first truly cold night since the spring, and, wrapping myself warmly with jacket and scarf, I was excited; butterflies wild in my stomach, wondering what the academics would make of our archive.

Frida was already waiting when I arrived. Keeping warm inside an ageing Nissan Micra, with Ace of Base (one of her favourites) softly thumping inside it.

"Hey, you," I called. "Sorry I'm late. Bus made me miss a connection, had to wait for a bit. Nice car!"

"Hi-ho, Marky!" she said, bouncing out of the car and flinging a kiss. "S'ok. Doris got me here early."

"Doris?"

"Yes, Doris, the best old gal I know!"

"Ok," I shrugged in reply. "Suppose anything's better than a bus stop on a cold autumn night."

"Sure is," she replied, "and are we going in? Coz it's freezing and I'm eager to receive my nicotine fix with a side order of cancer."

"Yes," I chuckled, wrenching open the door. "Let's get set before the boffins arrive."

After switching on the lights, I kept a lookout for our visitors while Frida pottered about reacquainting herself with the folders. Soon there came a firm knock at the door and the familiar face of Dr Corbiere, his colleague following closely behind...

"Marcus!" he announced. "May I introduce a dear friend, on loan from the British Library, Dr Normandy Sticelbak."*

*Pronounced Stishlebeck.

We liked Normandy from the very first moment. The most genuinely friendly, oddly dressed person I ever had the pleasure of meeting. Wearing that night, a bold floral dress, hanging on her like curtains, a fluffy cardigan with overly long sleeves, open-toed sandals, and socks. Her waist-long auburn hair, sometimes obscuring her face entirely, seemed to possess a mind of its own. Indeed, every moment with Normandy was memorable. Her generous smile could melt the coldest of hearts, her pale, freckled skin flushing red with every hint of emotion...

"Oh, Graham!" said Normandy, with a soft careful voice. "So formal.

Please, Mr Eaton, just call me Norma," before gushing a huge smile full of teeth.

"Pleased to meet you," I replied. "And, please, Marcus is fine. May I introduce my, my…"

"Girlfriend," chipped Frida.

"Yes, girlfriend." I smiled. "Frida Halfpenny, she's been an absolute godsend helping sort everything out. Do please come in and have a look around."

"Thank you," they replied, and I led them into the dining room, with Frida audibly muttering, "It's ape-knee, ape-knee. Why won't anyone say it?"

"Heavens," remarked Normandy, reluctantly coughing. "What a terrible pong."

"Yes," I said. "A smoker's pong, and it's proving very tricky to shift."

"I don't doubt," replied Corbiere. "But now, what was it you wanted to show me?"

"My uncle's case records," I said. "Frida has sorted them into some sort of order and reckons they'd be of interest. What do you think?"

"Goodness!" exclaimed Norma, wandering from pile to pile. "There're hundreds. How exactly have they been categorised?"

"We sorted them geographically," replied Frida, "by county, with the most recent file on top."

"Excellent." Corbiere nodded. "What do you think, Norma?"

Normandy, flicking through a couple, seemed intrigued.

"These should be plotted on a map," she muttered. "Yes, these are fantastic. What a database I could create for cultural research. Excellent, Graham, just excellent!"

"Well, the whole lot is yours," I offered. "And, if you like, right now. If you have room in your car?"

"We have a van!" said Norma, reddening with excitement.

"Shall we load up, then? With the four of us, it shouldn't take long."

It only took twenty minutes to load all the folders. The four of us worked well together, with Frida quickly taking a shine to Norma: chatting about work, swapping stories, anecdotes, giggling like girls at a party. Graham and I were more serious. He recounted tales of my uncle, of his sarcastic wit and incredible memory, whereas I told him of the house clearance, the key, the trunk, the bundle of folders, and the figurine proudly displayed on his desk.

"Well, I never!" he chuckled in reply. "He still had that ugly old thing. Must be fifteen years since I sent it."

"But what is it?" I asked. "It had pride of place in his study. Why so important?"

"Not entirely sure," he admitted. "It's only a copy, a copy of a copy and somewhat crude, but I do know something of its origin and your uncle's interest in it."

"Really? Because I researched it and reckon it's South American, am I right?"

"Yes and no. It certainly looks South American, but the original came from a Viking burial on the East Sussex coast. Certainly, coming across a Viking burial in Sussex is unusual, but to find an intact burial with grave goods is almost unheard of. It's probably why... Well, your uncle had a whacky theory about this figurine, believing it to possess a semiotic, that is, a symbolic relationship to other objects found all over the world – the sun with a peripheral sunspot?"

"Oh," I said, feeling intellectual. "So, it is a sunspot then? I thought it might be a shadow."

"Well, it might be." He shrugged. "It's *probably* a sunspot. We cannot know for certain – the figure might be holding a tea tray! Nevertheless, your uncle considered this symbol unique, believing its occurrence in other cultures signified a special connection. Inkblots, if you ask me."

"Inkblots? What do you mean?"

"The Rorschach test," he expounded. "You know, inkblots, used in psychiatry. Random inkblots on a piece of paper with the psychiatrist's patient saying what they see. Of course, the response of the patient is the critical thing, not the inkblots themselves. How long before they see something and what they see."

"Oh, right," I said. "I get it."

"Your uncle, I think, had been staring at these 'inkblots' so long, he thought he saw a connection. I can still recall our conversations. He was so convinced, I eventually rescinded; the disagreements were damaging our friendship, but there is no way he could be correct. Yes, I agree. The figurine appears Inca or late Chachapoyan, but the Vikings never made it to Peru – New York, but no further – and no, before you ask, there isn't any evidence of trade between North and South American tribes. The figurine is an incredible coincidence, a fake, or, most likely, a hoax. Most historians refute it."

This debunk from Corbiere was damning, and, with my uncle no longer around, I did my best to defend him…

"Well, I don't know," I said, sitting at the foot of the stairs. "He was a pretty smart guy, my uncle. He must've been sure. Otherwise, why would he bother?"

"You're right, he was a genius. In fact, this has me thinking. The folders you found. They likely contain everything he had on his outlandish ideas. You should study them. He clearly wanted you to."

"Yeah. I intend to – when I get a chance. This clearance business has taken over my life!"

Smiling, Corbiere checked his watch.

"Well," he replied, "if you do decide to assume the mantle and continue your uncle's work, contact me if you need any help."

"Ok," I said, "I will, and for starters. You just said the figurine was a copy of a copy. Do you know where the copy and the original are?"

"Yes, I do. The copy is in London, whereas the original should be in Hastings or Rye. Excavated in East Sussex, it is naturally part of their museum collection, although, come to think of it, a great deal of Viking ephemera was recently moved to York."

"Right," I replied, wondering where Frida had got to. "That's useful, thanks."

"You're welcome. Now, however, we must be getting along. Norma!" he then called. "Time to go, I think."

After a friendly wave, watching their van disappear into the distance, Frida and I went back inside for a quick tidy, switch-off, and lock-up.

"You seemed to like Norma," I said, slamming shut the front door. "She seemed to have you in stitches."

"Yeah," said Frida, zipping her fleece. "She's really funny and sweet, like some of the mad scientists I work with, but, as for you and Graham… well, the way he talks to you is cute. It's like he's your dad."

"No?" I mockingly gasped. "You think, you think he thinks I'm his bastard son?"

Laughing and delivering a hug, Frida looked into my eyes.

"Sometimes, Marcus," she said, "you think about thinking so much, you actually forget to do it. Wanna lift home?"

"Oh, God, yes," I replied. "That would be splendiferous, and via a pub? I missed dinner."

"Good idea," she acknowledged. "Missed mine as well. Do you know any good ones?"

"Pubs? No," but, retrieving my phone from my pocket, I started to search...

Frida's driving matched her personality. Fearless, quick, and full of profanity, and during the parts of the journey I found courage enough to open my eyes, she had "old Doris" buzzing through the traffic like an angry wasp.

Failing to find an acceptable pub (the most promising venues full of families with noisome children), I invited Frida to join me at my place for a coffee and the "grand opening" of the bundle of folders.

Slipping in through the back door, my parents were too busy watching TV to give us notice, so we busied ourselves with the kettle, before walking our steaming mugs upstairs...

"All very tidy in here," Frida remarked, looking about at my bookcases, tech, and gadgets. "Quite surprised – boys' rooms usually look like landfill sites."

"Must have seen a lot, then," I quipped, blowing the steam from my coffee.

"No," she replied. "Well, ok, a few, but it's spotless in here, how come?"

"It's my mum; she's mental. All she does is clean. Cleaning clean things, even cleans the things she cleans with, but I am quite tidy myself. Simply because I hate looking for stuff – drives me nuts. It's torture!"

Sitting beside me, Frida said nothing, but, while I retrieved the folders from under my bed, she moved to the photos dotting my wardrobe.

"Here we go," I said, dumping the bundle onto my desk. "Had to hide these in case they got cleaned."

"Well, they are pretty dusty," said Frida. "Oh, look, there's a label on the uppermost folder. What does it say?"

"Not sure," I replied. "It's really faint."

Fetching a lamp and illuminating the folders from above, I read the faded writing aloud:

Old Bakery Skeleton / Rye / East Sussex / Parchment Fragments.

"Doesn't mean anything to me." she shrugged. "Untie the string, open it."

Congealed over time into a shining lump, the knot proved impossible to solve, and, quickly cutting it through with scissors, I passed both string and label to Frida.

"This isn't your uncle's writing," she remarked, studying the nametag. "Looks like the work of a five-year-old."

"I know," I replied, separating the folders. "It's nuts. Maybe he was babysitting and got a kid to write it? Wasn't me or Millie though."

"Well, somebody wrote it for him," said Frida, sucking her lip. "Although, didn't you say, kids got on his nerves?"

"I did," I said, scanning each folder. "As I said, it's nuts."

There were five folders in all, each with similar labels. The other four read as follows…

Camber Viking Burial / Camber / East Sussex / Terracotta Figurine Holding Solar Disc with Dark Spot.

Babylonian Priest Class Burial / Modern-Day Iraq / Carvings Show Solar Disc with Spot.

Chachapoyan Mummified Remains / Laguna de los Cóndores, Peru / X-ray Photograph of Grave Goods in Bindings / Similar Figurine to Camber Viking Example?

Medieval Reliquary / Winchelsea / East Sussex / Fired Clay Disc with Copper Spot Insert, Associated with Partial Skeleton (Pre-Medieval?).

"Wow!" exclaimed Frida. "Curiouser and curiouser, what a mixture, and three of them found in East Sussex, Peru, and Iraq as well? Corbiere must be right. How *could* they be connected?"

Sitting on the bed, we opened the first folder…

Comparable to files given to Graham and Norma, this folder included handwritten notes, drawings, and, immediately drawing my attention, four photographs, and while Frida busied herself with the handwritten pages, I examined them under a lamp.

The first photograph, black-and-white and slightly yellowing at the edges, was of a partially excavated human skeleton inside a stone wall. Although packed tightly with chalk and flint, the skeleton appeared crumbling and unstable, and the archaeologists had applied strapping to keep it in place. The second photograph was a bit blurry, and I was surprised my uncle bothered to keep it. Nonetheless, it was a close-up of the same skeleton (now fully excavated) and careful examination revealed much. There were many grisly details. Strands of wretched hair, desiccated organs, muscles, skin, and, partially covering its ribcage like greaseproof paper, the tattered remains of a shirt. The third photograph, in colour and of high resolution, was of three pieces of paper or parchment. Faint markings were visible on two of the fragments, whereas the third, tightly bound inside a clod of whitish material, revealed only its fraying edge.

The fourth photograph, doctored to increase the contrast, was a close-up of the markings and writing, showing a squiggle, scratchy doodles, and two circles, one inside the other, immediately drawing my attention to the figurine on my bookcase, the two-circle doodle reminiscent of the spotted-sun hoisted over his head.

Good grief! What a vague description. It looked something like this (although with a pen I am hopeless):

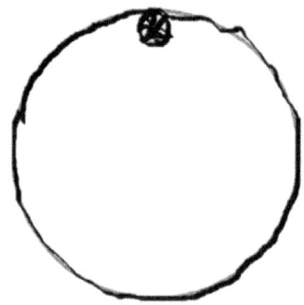

The writing upon the pieces of parchment was perfectly legible, in Latin, of course, which was a pity, as despite my posh schooling the language was unknown to me. Moving next to Frida, I wondered if she had the wherewithal to translate…

Ignorantia turpis.

"What does it say in the notes?" I asked, finishing my coffee. "Any help?"

"Yeah," she replied. "Really interesting too, only his handwriting is terrible – takes ages to read. Anyway, in 1975, in Rye, builders uncovered a skeleton while taking down a wall of a pub. The wall in question was really old – 14th or 13th century, that's like 1200 onwards, so they had to get special permission from the local authority, with a team of archaeologists on site, keen to study its composition: a skin of close-fitting stones and flints, filled with rubble, lime mortar and cob. Isn't that horse shit, straw, and stuff?"

"Yes. Similar to daub. Cheap and freely available."

"Cool," she acknowledged. "Now, as I mentioned, when they removed the stones, they found a skeleton, the remains of some bloke with his head bashed in – a medieval murder victim, they reckoned, the killers dumping his body inside the wall before filling it in. Poor bastard. Wonder if he deserved it? Anyway, they found bits of parchment in the skeleton's tunic and your uncle deciphered the writing."

"Amazing. What did it say?"

"Hold your horses!" She laughed. "Not there yet, besides, I'm starving. Any chance of a biscuit?"

"Sure," I replied. "Wait right here. Can do better than a biscuit..."

By now, it was getting on for 9pm and after skipping dinner she had every right to be hungry. Dashing downstairs, I headed into the kitchen to see what I could find.

Always on duty, my mother heard me rummaging, and, after explaining my girlfriend and I were looking through my uncle's notes, she seemed quite taken aback.

Taken aback by the girlfriend, not because of the notes...

"Hey, Vic!" she called into the living room. "Marcus's got a girl upstairs. Did you know about this?"

"No, love," came his reply. "You sure it's not Frank in a dress?"

"It's not Frank, is it, dear?" she asked, slightly concerned.

"Of course not," I replied, feeling put out. "Her name's Frida and she wants something to eat. Point me towards something snackable and I'll introduce you."

This being an expert example of mother manipulation, and within minutes we were walking upstairs with two trays laden with tea, coffee, sandwiches, biscuits, and crisps.

Still reading, Frida was lying on the bed as we walked in, her angelic head propped on her elbows...

"Here ya go," I proffered. "An evening feast fit for a queen."

"Oh, great," replied Frida, sitting up, her legs swinging onto the floor. "Just what I need."

"Frida," I announced. "Meet my mum. Sandwich maker beyond compare. Mum? This is Frida."

"Very pleased to meet you," blustered my mum. "Call me Barbara."

"Sure," said Frida. "Thanks for the sandwiches, Barbara, thought Marcus was only bringing a biscuit, but this is awesome."

"You're welcome," she replied with a smile. "If you'd been earlier, you could have had dinner. Not to worry. Go ahead and eat, and Marcus, when you're both finished, bring down the trays."

"He will," said Frida.

"Good," said my mum, "and, Frida, before you go, please come and say goodbye. Marcus's father is very keen to meet you."

"Sure," Frida replied. "We're just going over these notes and then we'll be done – can't be late; got a massive day at work tomorrow."

With my mum gone, we busied ourselves snacking, and, once Frida had scoffed a sandwich or two, I asked her again about the writing on the parchment…

"The first phrase is only partial," she revealed, sucking her fingers. "The words, if I've read them right, are: '*Regnum Tuum Fiat*' and, further down, '*Inducas in Tentationem*'. Your uncle says this is from a medieval version of the Lord's Prayer, which ties it in with the estimated age of the wall. Your uncle reckons the victim wrote his last words before his murder. In those days, dying with a prayer in your possession was a blessing. An extra boost to get you into Heaven."

"Incredible," I muttered, stunned by her quick assimilation of facts. "Was there anything else?"

"Yeah, a little bit. There was that diagram of the two circles. There's a photo, isn't there? Before another phrase in Latin: '*Sicut folia cadunt tamen munere meo damno tamquam magicis*', which your uncle translated as, although he admits it's his best approximation: '(They) fall as leaves yet condemn my gift as magic.'"

"What the hell does that mean?"

"He wasn't sure," said Frida. "But if his killers thought him some evil sorcerer, it could well have been their motive. He also says the handwriting is strange, written by a metal nib rather than the usual quill pen, the ink smoothly applied, with little spraying. He states pens like this were extremely rare, wondering if the murdered man could've been wealthy or important in some way."

"Right," I said. "And is that it?"

"Not quite. There was another piece of parchment bound up in a lump of lime mortar, too fragile to remove. He hoped it could one day be X-rayed to see if there's any more writing."

"Thought they always X-rayed stuff like that? Shame they haven't. It would be amazing to see if there's more."

"Agree with you there," she replied, stretching a little. "But you watch too much TV. X-ray machines don't grow on trees; they're fucking expensive! How many relics do you think there are compared to X-ray machines and trained radiologists?"

"Not many," I conceded. "The backlog must be tremendous."

"Precisely. Special arrangements have to be made. You can't just rock-up at hospital with a lump of mud and ask for an X-ray."

"I guess not, but I bet Graham could arrange it."

"Very possibly," said Frida, nibbling a cake. "In fact, they probably have one at the museum, although normal X-raying might not be enough."

"Why not?" I asked, opening a bag of crisps. "Would the X-rays not go through?"

"Oh no, the X-rays would penetrate just fine. Low contrast is the usual the problem – no variation. Different layers merging into one another. The writing would likely be invisible. To combat this issue, there's a technique called X-ray fluorescence. I've used it myself studying cells, and archaeologists have started using it too, I think. If the ink contains disparate or distinct metallic ions, X-ray fluorescence would show up the writing a treat."

"You've lost me there," I admitted. "But if you think it's possible, why don't I give him a call? He can only say no, and if he says yes, to find more writing would be amazing."

"Definitely," she replied. "As long as the parchment hasn't fallen to bits and been chucked already. Remember, it was recovered, what, thirty-four years ago? Even finding it will be a challenge."

Clipping the notes and photos into their folder, we sat snuggling and snacking in silence, wildly imagining spells of black magic, hastily scrawled notes, and mystical codes, before shuddering at the blood-soaked ordeal that followed…

"You awake?" asked Frida, elbowing my ribs. "We still have to clear up and say goodnight to your parents."

"Huh… what?" I said, coming back to reality. "Yeah, sure. Let's go!"

Taking our trays into the kitchen, putting our waste in the bin, and loading the dishwasher, we tiptoed into the living room…

By now, my Mum was typically fast asleep, wine glass rolling in her lap. My dad was watching TV, but upon seeing Frida he stood, grinning, offering his hand like a dork.

Too calm and beautiful, Frida took his hand and gave it a gentle tug.

"Victor Eaton," announced my father, flushing bright pink. "Pleased to meet you."

"Frida Ape-knee," she replied with a nod. "Thank you for allowing me into your home this evening. Your son Marcus is a delight. He's polite, thoughtful, clearly brought up very well."

"Brought up well?" He chuckled. "No, miss, we had nothing to do with it. He never listens to us, although I'm glad to hear he's capable."

"Dad." I cringed, burning bright red. "You're killing me."

"He's remarkable," Frida calmly assured. "He deserves a lot of credit, much more credit than he receives."

"If you say so, Miss Halfpenny," he replied intentionally correcting her name.

"I do," she affirmed, ignoring his sleight. "Now, however, I must be going. Nice to have met you."

"Hmm…" he said, twisting his lips, returning to his chair, and reaching for the remote.

With Frida gone, assuming my dad would be furious, I braced myself for trouble, and seeing him striding towards me, locking on like a heat-seeking missile, my heart quivered and sank.

He was grinning, however, happy as a clam…

"Wow-wee!" he exclaimed, shaking his head. "She really is something. How did you get her? Don't tell your mother I said it, but wow!"

Glowing like a fire, I grinned with pride and delight. For once I knew just how he felt (and just how he thought), as when I had come to kiss Frida good night, I couldn't believe my luck.

ELEVEN

THE MUSEUM

Tinkering with the entertainment portal, browsing what was available, led me to a startling conclusion. It had everything! Every piece of music, every TV or radio programme, every film, everything ever transmitted. Great, you might think, but, without content newer than the day of my abduction, I'm limited to watching old movies and repeats. Without live TV, I can't even check on the weather!

While writing the previous instalment, an idea came to me in a flash. If I were to watch a film, I could use the portal's progress bar and timer to determine the time I spend writing, relaxing, or talking to Mirra, so I began the longest film I knew of. Just how far would I get before her arrival?

Standing before the grey screen, I pressed my palm against it and headed back to the bed.

"Cinema," I demanded (as if addressing the portal), the cinema tile disappearing, instantly replaced by a menu of geographical regions, e.g., North America, Europe, Africa, but knowing precisely what I wanted, I said:

"*The Lord of the Rings: The Fellowship of the Ring*, extended edition, director Peter Jackson."

There was a brief delay (presumably while processing my command) before the screen darkened and the first frame appeared, paused and motionless, waiting for me to start it.

"Begin playback," I announced. "Volume 30%."

Boromir had just died when Mirra paused the film…

"Hello, Marcus!" she called, sounding perkier than ever. "Is that Sean Bean with all those arrows stuck in him?"

"Yes, Mirra." I smiled, glad to hear her again. "It is. Boromir got his comeuppance."

"Nasty," she replied. "But at least he's still got his head."

"His head." I pondered. "Why would he lose his head? Anyway, I put the film on to see how long you'd make me wait."

"Indeed?" she challenged. "And how long was that do you think?"

"Easy," I replied. "It's written on the screen – over three hours. Three hours, six minutes, and four seconds."

"Such precision!" She tittered. "But are you sure?"

"Of course, it's right there, in black and white!"

"Yes, yes," she said, "I can see it. Calm down, will you? However, the writing you refer to is white, not black, and white. The black bits you cannot perceive, and you should regard time similarly before you go bragging. Absolute time, there is no such thing. It's a trick of light, an illusion."

"Absolute time," I puzzled. "Invisible black bits? What are you on about, Mirra? How can you see time without using a clock?"

"Precisely," she replied. "You can't. The elapsed time on the screen is merely the time observed, but when you weren't observing it?"

"Well," I offered, scratching my head. "I'd look back at the timer, subtracting what it was from what it is, simple!"

"No, no!" she cried. "You're not following me. You blink, don't you? How long for a blink?"

"A fraction of a second, just as I said. I can tell, watching the timer in between blinks."

"Yes," she affirmed, "I'm certain it seems that way, but how can you know what the timer is doing if your eyes are shut?"

"True," I replied, blinking then looking a couple of times. "And it sounds like you're trying to say the timer only moves when I watch it?"

"Yes," she confirmed. "In a way, I am."

"Piffle." I snorted. "No way to prove that, so now you're just being pedantic."

"Piffle?" She gasped. "Pedantic? Young man, I'll have you know talking to you is like talking to a caveman," before sighing so deeply I thought she'd gone off in a huff.

"Right," she then said. "Back to the task in hand. Let's just see what you've written, avoiding fundamental temporal mechanics. Watch a documentary concerning the work of Erwin Schrödinger or Werner Heisenberg and see where it leads. It might shed light on my viewpoint."

(Never did – too boring!)

"Very well," I replied, pressing my palm to the portal, switching it off. "I will, but I'm not so good with sciencey stuff. Sorry if I upset you, though."

"No," she assured. "You shouldn't worry. My fault, not yours. All is forgiven and all is forgotten. I'm simply looking forward to spending some time with you. Have you written about Frida?"

"Yes, Mirra, a lot! Moloch's not going to be pleased, is he?"

"No," she replied with a laugh. "He most certainly is not, and good. Your writing is at its best when you focus on her."

"That is hardly surprising. The writing keeps her alive in my mind."

"Know that feeling exactly," Mirra replied. "I miss my family the same way you miss Frida, I think. Although, the memories I cherish have become old and rose-tinted. Let's make a start."

⧗

The following morning, keeping my promise to Frida, I called Dr Corbiere, describing the contents of the first folder, before suggesting an X-ray of the lump of lime mortar and cob. To my surprise, Corbiere was enthusiastic, saying little historical mysteries like this always delighted him, inviting us to meet with him at the museum, Thursday lunchtime, keen to examine the folder himself. In addition, he agreed to let us examine the original copy of the figurine (hopefully of a better quality than the one adorning my bedroom), before asking Dr Sticelbak (Norma) to recover the original excavation report from the library.

When Marcus writes "the museum" or "the library", he is of course referring to the British Museum and Library, London, England, and, as much as I would like to claim these contractions a delicious example of British patriotic arrogance, it is more likely they serve as an illustration of his laziness.

Frida and I agreed to meet on the steps outside the museum's main entrance and getting there was a breeze. A train, then Tube to Tottenham Court Road, left but a short walk through one of London's more agreeable districts, twinkling today under clear blue skies and golden autumnal sunlight.

Tiny and doll-like, her back propped against a gigantic pillar, Frida was already there as I passed through the gates, but upon seeing me, she sprang to her feet, ran down the steps, and flung her arms around me.

"Hello, sweet stuff," I said. "You're here first. Am I late?"

"No. You're perfectly on time – I'm just excited. All early and whirly. Took the day off for this!"

"Won't that muck up your project? I thought you said you were at a critical stage."

"Yeah," she replied. "But today I was only collecting data, so I got a technician to cover for me. Normally, I wouldn't let him anywhere near my research – he's a bit of a numpty, but all he's got to do is type stuff into a spreadsheet, and if he does fuck it up, he knows full well I'll kill 'im!"

"Remind me to never fuck up." I chuckled, and she grinned, hugging me tighter.

"Come on," she said, slipping her arm through mine, "let's find Dr Cobnut."

"Corbiere – call me Graham," I corrected. "He said he'd be at the ground floor café by the east stairs."

I only recall visiting the museum once and surely quite young, certainly too young to appreciate it, and doubtless I drove my parents nuts.

Upon entering the Great Court, with its domed ceiling, triangles of glass, its framework fanning out like the threads of a cobweb, the first things that struck us were the feelings of light and space, but then, as we made our way across this expansive interior, we suddenly halted, gasping, and blinking in awe…

"The sound," she said. "The air, somehow, it's taking my breath!"

"You're not kidding." I chuckled. "And listen…"

A consequence of enclosing a space so vast using stone, glass, and metals does something to sound both delightful and uncanny. Every sound made is imprisoned, reverberating to such an extent that it feels as if one is wading through a murmuring fog. From wall to wall does this rumbling roll, never fading, and perhaps my infant wailings, so long ago howled, are still here. The tears of a toddler, forever lost, mingling and churning, mere trickles, dashed into a boundless echoing sea.

Leading off in every direction, stairways guided visitors to grandiose vaults of relics, whereas the old relic we'd come to see was in the distance, sipping coffee and winkling burnt currants from the surface of a teacake…

"Oh, hello, you two," said Corbiere, slipping his phone into his jacket. "Lovely day, isn't it? Did you bring me that folder?"

"Hi, Graham," replied Frida, and then to me. "You did bring it, didn't you, Marky?"

"Of course," I said with a frown.

"Good," he said, pointing towards two card-sized badges. "You'll need to clip these on before we go to my office, but right now I want to finish my lunch, meagre though it is."

"Mind if we join you, then?" asked Frida. "Is it table service?"

"Yes, and please do," he replied. "Let me do the honours; I'm *praeter regularis* down here," and, swivelling in his seat, he beckoned over a waitress.

"Zytka!" he called. "Could you do us? We're in a rush."

Dropping what she was doing and promptly taking our order (coffee, tea, and two small muffins), the young waitress dashed to the counter to fetch them, returning with a tray in a jiffy…

"Mmm," I said, sniffing, and then tasting the mugful before me. "Great coffee. I'd be a regular too."

"Indeed," he acknowledged. "This establishment is quickly becoming my office. A high standard of catering is especially important for our organisation, and well." He shrugged. "It brings in the visitors. Management spent a lot of time looking for a suitable franchise and, since they have a licence to print money in here, we had the pick of the crop."

"How's the tea and muffin, Frida?"

"Very good," she enthusiastically replied. "And almost gone already!"

"Have you been here before?" asked Corbiere, folding the receipts and handing them to the server (with a wink).

"Nope," muttered Frida.

"Once," I replied. "When I was little, still in a pushchair, and can't remember a thing."

"Then," said Corbiere, "it is high time you had another visit, but Frida? You're obviously a Londoner; I'm quite surprised. Didn't your parents ever bring you?"

"Well, speaking for myself," she explained, "I'm a scientist, and even though I'm getting older, and my interests are broadening, my work is very engaging. I haven't felt the need until now."

"Fair enough," he replied. "But quite surprised you visited with your parents."

Frida sighed before finishing her tea with a gulp.

"Sorry, Graham," she said. "I know you mean well, but my parents. No. They couldn't or wouldn't have had the chance. I was very young when my dad died – of leukaemia, leaving my mum to raise me alone, and for her, this was particularly tough; she is autistic, has Tourette's, and finds life quite tricky at times. Day trips, holidays, parties? No. They didn't happen at all."

"Oh, I'm sorry to hear that." Corbiere blinked, trying to take it all in. "Sounds like you had a tough childhood."

"There's no need to be sorry," she replied with smile. "My childhood brimmed with love, seemed perfectly normal, and how could I have known any different? Yet it has taught me to embrace and enjoy what I have. I'm determined to love every minute," and she flashed me such a warm smile, her face glowed as if lit from within.

Frida impressed Corbiere. It was easy to tell. He didn't know where to look or where to put his hands, before watching her with fascination as she dabbed her mouth, checked and rechecked her lipstick.

"Well, now," said Corbiere, breaking the spell. "If you've both finished, we'll head down to my private office. I'm keen to see your discovery."

He led us along narrow corridors, down steps, into parts of the building visitors rarely see. Security was ever present, but with our badges prominent and Corbiere at our side we passed through with ease.

"Here we are." He beckoned. "My private office, always the best venue for meetings. Upstairs, my public office is surrounded by a constant hubbub, but down here, in my bunker, it's just us and a couple of spiders."

The door was solid looking one, painted deep blue, with a brass panel: "Dr Graham Corbiere. Portable Antiquities & Treasure." Unlocking the door, he went in.

Inside it was cool, clean, and functional, with a single desk, computer, phone, and filing cabinet within easy reach. A hexagonal conference table stood at the centre of the office, with six chairs neatly stacked in a corner. There were no windows, and the only sound was a soft "thrumming" coming from the air conditioning.

"Right," he said. "Grab yourselves a chair and lay out the contents of that folder."

Removing the folder from my rucksack, I did as he asked, and, while Frida brought over three chairs, he polished his spectacles in anticipation.

Immediately drawn to the photos, after a quick silent perusal, Corbiere picked up the notes to study them…

"Have you read this?" he asked, deep furrows creasing his brow.

"Yes," replied Frida. "Would you like a summary?"

"Would you? The handwriting is terrible!"

Frida laughed. "Yeah," she admitted. "He makes notes like a scientist, something I've had to get used to."

She then recounted all she had read, highlighting phrases to justify her summary.

The phone rang.

"Drat it!" he said. "How'd they find me? Now I've lost my train of thought." He picked up the receiver. "Corbiere. Oh, hello, Steph. I see. Really, has she? Well, could you bring it down to my private office? Thanks, Steph, that's great, see you in a bit."

Hanging up the receiver, he sighed.

"That was my PA. Normandy has found a document she considers relevant. After explaining you were continuing your uncle's work, she thought it prudent to check the library's handling logs, wondering what your uncle had studied in years gone by. Mostly, they told of general historical research, but one entry, an excavation report from a dig in West Sussex stood out. He studied it several times during the eighties and nineties, so she thought it might be important, and has kindly sent us a copy."

We then discussed the parchment fragments found with the skeleton, Graham agreeing whole-heartedly with my uncle's interpretations and Frida's idea, concerning the unread fragment lodged inside the cob.

There was a knock at the door and a smart young woman came in…

"Thanks, Steph," he said as she handed him a package. "Anything else? Any calls or messages?"

"None since this morning," she replied. "Your 4.30 meeting is unchanged, with the Ashmolean?"

"Ah, yes." He nodded. "No, I hadn't forgotten. We'll be done in an hour and then we can go over the agenda again."

"Fine," she acknowledged. "I'll be off and up to the land of the living then. Would you like coffee and doughnuts? For five, at five o'clock?"

Corbiere nodded in approval.

"Steph!" He generously smiled. "You're a marvel."

Giggling and blushing, she fled, closing the door behind her in a waft of sickly perfume.

"Fabulous girl," he muttered, weighing the envelope in his hands. "Think I'd go potty without her."

Returning his attention to a close-up of the skeleton, he handed the envelope to me, and, not knowing what he intended, I shrugged and wrestled it open.

"You know," he softly muttered to Frida, "I've seen injuries on skeletons like this before. A blow from a spiked weapon is often the cause, a war hammer or battle-axe, and since there are no further injuries, it makes me think his attacker intended that single blow to be his execution."

"Well," Frida replied, "it's obvious it was a murder; the body dumped and hidden. You think the victim knew it was coming?"

Taking off his spectacles, Corbiere used them as a magnifying glass.

"Possibly," he said. "The prayer upon him is certainly indicative. Was he restrained?"

Sliding over the relevant page of notes, Frida recapped what she had read:

"No mention of manacles or bindings. I guess his killers could have removed them. We have no way of knowing. At least, not from these photos. If the restraints were overly tight, he could've fractured a wrist or scuffed a bone, but only a close-up or microscopic examination would show that."

"You know," he replied, enjoying her insights (and more besides), "you should've gone into forensic archaeology. You certainly have the knack."

Smiling, Frida gave me a cheeky wink.

"Nah," she said with a smirk. "Everything you're hearing is straight from CSI. Besides, there's no money in academia. Rather stick with my Pharma-Corp."

Straightening and stretching, Corbiere looked at his watch.

"Fair play to you, then," he said. "And you're right about the money. It's lousy."

The envelope contained a single document about a dozen pages in length. Stuck on its cover a brief note: "To Marcus, Frida, and Graham. Hope this helps. Love Norma x."

Peeling off the note and sticking it to Frida, I read the title aloud: "Sussex Archaeological Unit, Excavation Report. September 1988. Flooded Book Repository. Maplewick Castle, Horsham, West Sussex."

"What've you got there?" asked Corbiere, sounding intrigued.

"Yes, come on," said Frida. "Hand it over. We want to see what she found."

Passing the document, leaning back in my chair (and feeling superfluous), I proceeded to watch Frida and Graham charge through the report at a speed I couldn't match.

As if reading my mind, Frida suddenly looked up...

"Sorry sweetheart. Just a few minutes more," then to Corbiere she said, "Not sure this relates to our skeleton, Graham. They found and restored some old books. Big deal."

"What books?" I asked, trying to get back into proceedings. "Come on!"

"Ah, yes, well," muttered Corbiere, composing his thoughts. "This is what we have. In the 1980s, a local university dispatched a team of archaeologists to reassess Maplewick Castle in West Sussex. Now, this ruined medieval settlement is in no way new or remarkable, already excavated and investigated years earlier, but a collapse at the base of a tower revealed a flooded cellar, a library repository, lined with chests, all of them crushed, rotten, and submerged underwater. In a rush to save this newly exposed material, quickly stabilising the masonry and removing the water, the lifting of the chests could begin, bringing to light a series of books and parchments. Most were utterly ruined, of course, but painstaking conservation of the more intact examples bore fruit. Several could still be identified, even read."

Responding to an impulse, Corbiere moved to his desk. While he typed at the computer, Frida snuggled me closely, recapping what she had read...

"Of the readable examples, there were three books and two scrolls. The books were: *The Book of the Civilised Man* by Daniel de Beccles, surely a gripping read. *Summa Theologica* by Thomas Aquinas, definitely my bedside book from now on, and *The Travels of Sir John Mandeville*. Which is like *An Idiot Abroad*, only with more diseases," and, as I darkly sniggered, she drew my attention to the next page...

"All well and good," she remarked. "But from a historical viewpoint, the scrolls are the most interesting. The first was a logbook, a list of castle visitors made during the mid to late 13th century, whereas the second was a confessional transcript made by a priest – a spectacularly rare find! The priesthood of the period regarded these documents as blasphemous; they were usually burnt."

"They managed to read them?"

"Yes," she explained. "But it was a struggle. Both squashed flat and entirely blackened by hydrogen sulphide, the archaeologists had almost given up, until a clever chemist suggested they try ionic displacement with zinc."

"You've lost me now," I muttered, scratching my head. "But keep going."

"Ok. Throughout the medieval period the best inks were the gall inks. A concentrated solution of iron tannate, made from an acidified mixture of oak apples and rusted iron. Now, the chemical composition of the ink is crucial. During the underwater decomposition of the organic matter – the chests, books, and parchments, the ink was exposed to hydrogen sulphide, changing its chemical composition from iron tannate to iron sulphide. Are you still with me?"

"No."

"Tough. Anyway, the ionic displacement technique suggested by the chemist would encourage zinc to replace the iron. Subsequently changing the iron sulphide into zinc sulphide."

"And how did that help? Did it change colour?"

"Yes," she replied. "In a manner of speaking. Zinc sulphide is fluorescent. It glows under ultraviolet light, and when the treated fragments were exposed to UV the writing appeared."

"Clever. How much could they read?"

"Only about a third, but enough to be of interest."

"Amazing," I remarked. "What did it say? Come on, you've built me up, now spill!"

Looking sheepish, Frida laughed.

"You to know me too well! We haven't got there yet. There's ten more pages to get through."

Stepping away from the computer, Graham returned to the table...

"I've arranged for one of you to see the figurine. Who wants to go?"

"Me," I declared. "I'm just in the way here. Will give me something to do while you boffins finish your homework."

"Good," he acknowledged. "A technician will be along shortly. Sorry you're on your own; despite it being a copy, the figurine will arrive in a clean room."

"Oh?" said Frida. "Is he about to be decon'd and then wear a protective suit?"

"Indeed." Corbiere nodded. "It's standard procedure. To minimise biological contamination."

Graham and Frida returned to the document provided by Normandy, and feeling more of a hindrance than a help, I paced the room, worrying what invasive horrors a "decon" might involve. Would I need to shower? Endure a body cavity search? Moreover, what of the protective clothing? Something resembling a spacesuit, a balloon-like costume for treating lethal diseases? Or merely a glove box? A protective shroud for the handling of hazardous—

A sideways glance and a "tut" from Frida, however, guided me back to my chair and I sat, arms crossed, staring up at the ceiling, listening to the sound of pages turning and intensely whispered conversation.

There came a polite knock at the door.

"Come in," said Corbiere.

The young man swiftly entering seemed nervous, his glowing cheeks in stark contrast to his pristine white coat…

"I'm, erm, here to escort someone to the clean rooms? To clean room seven, to view a sample?"

"Ah yes," said Corbiere. "Thanks… Robert, isn't it? Marcus is going with you."

From sitting, I stood, standing, nodding the technician a nod. *(Weird sentence but I like it.)*

"Fine," replied the technician. "Shall we get going? It's a bit of a hike, and then we have to get you suited and booted."

"Lead on, Roberto," I said stretching, keen to be busy.

"Have fun, lovey," said Frida, shaping a kiss. "And keep your DNA to yourself."

The clean rooms were above us, not below us, and all was very new, brightly lit, and spotless. Two of the rooms were already in use, the lights above their doors showing red.

Robert the technician took me to door seven.

"Right," he said. "Here we are. Have you done this before?"

"No," I replied. "First time. Please be gentle with me!"

"Will do my best." He laughed. "Let me show you…"

Opening the heavy door, he ushered me into a small antechamber, boxes and sacks of protective clothing arrayed on a nearby bench, including white overalls, overshoes, hairnets, and gloves, and Robert helped me wriggle my way into each, before carefully looking me over.

"Right," he said, "there you go. Are you comfy?"

"Not in the slightest," I replied, feeling "scuffy" and claustrophobic.

"Must've done it right, then." He chuckled, before swabbing my face with an alcohol-soaked pad.

"Now I smell like my girlfriend," I said trying not to flinch, as he ran a vacuum cleaner over my every nook and cranny.

"Ok." He nodded. "You're good to go, but one more thing. Do you need to blow your nose? Because if you sneeze in there, it'll mean hours of cleaning for me, scrubbing the place with stinky detergents."

"No," I replied, trying a couple of sniffs. "I'm fine."

"Good," he said. "I'll be off, then. Your sample has already arrived and will be in the dumb waiter. When you've finished, remember to fill in the viewing log and the send it down to the dungeon. Also, when you're ready to leave, use the intercom by the door. Don't worry, though, you're not locked in. It just helps me keep track of contamination."

"Ok, got it. It's only a little figurine. Shouldn't take long."

"Oh, fine," he said. "Stone or ceramic. Nice and clean. That's a relief," before walking into the corridor and closing the door with a "clump".

Pushing open the inner door with an effort-filled grunt, I went in…

The clean room interior was a pristine anti-climax. Tables, chairs, a laboratory sink, computer terminal, with a dumb waiter set into the back wall. Waiting inside was a shoebox-sized plastic container, and, as I moved to retrieve it, the inner door (which I had forgotten to close) swung itself shut with a thud and a hiss.

"Oops," I muttered. "Sorry, Roberto; born in a barn."

The container itself was akin to a miniature suitcase, and after moving it to a table, wrestling it open, and cautiously opening the lid, I removed the viewing log (a small ring binder and pen), revealing the figurine generously swathed in bubble wrap. Cautiously lifting it out, unrolling its protective cocoon and standing it the on the table, I whipped out my phone, quickly taking a couple of photos.

"Saw that," said the technician, and I awkwardly blushed, realising he was monitoring my progress.

"Sorry," I said, cowering before the intercom. "Force of habit. Want me to delete them?"

"Well," he pondered. "Without permission, you aren't *actually* supposed to take photos, but I won't tell if you don't."

Although identical in form to my copy, this primary replica had features that were noticeably sharper, its pastel colours less gaudy, doubtless a better representation of the original, and, picking it up, a strange feeling came over me, almost of déjà vu, realising my uncle had once held it as well.

"Weird," I muttered. "Almost as if…?"

Suddenly flickering, the lights went out, coming back a second later, the computer rebooting with a startling "beep"!

"Sort out the wiring," I grumbled, turning the figurine over.

To my complete surprise, there was a message, and I took a second glance to believe it. How could it be? The handwriting was identical to the "Marcus" label on the folders I'd found. Written by the same child? Something here was wrong, and very disturbing.

Not now, run! said the message, and with the lights flickering again, I became extremely nervous; goose bumps pricking my skin. I felt an urgent desire to flee, to escape, and quickly…

Hastily wrapping the figurine and placing it into the box, I noticed a small twinkly marble inside (which certainly hadn't been there earlier), before printing my name, time, and date in the logbook.

Rushing to the dumb waiter, I deposited the box, sending it down before urgently striding the door and pressing the intercom.

Robert the technician promptly answered.

"Are you done?" he asked.

"Yes," I said, my heart like a drum. "Told you I wouldn't be long. I'm coming out, now!"

"Right," he replied. "Wait in the anteroom. I'll meet you there in a sec."

I was gloveless, suit-less, unshod, and hatless, by the time he came in.

"Oh, good," he remarked. "You've changed. Did you put everything into the sack?"

"Yes," I replied, my nervousness receding. "Was there a power cut or something? It freaked me out."

"Yeah," he admitted. "We've been having trouble with the fuse box and RCD. Never seems to get fixed. Shall we go?"

Frida and Graham were still at it when I got back. The moment I sat down, Frida shifted to sit next to me.

"You weren't long," she said. "Anything new?"

"Not really," I replied. "Cleaner, crisper, better colours. Some little kid had written on the base. Which was… unexpected?"

"What?" said Corbiere. "What did it say?"

So, I told him.

"Kids," he scowled. "Students, most likely. Thank God it was only the base."

"Yeah," I replied. "Have you finished reading the stuff from Norma?"

"Yes," said Frida, "we have, and the scrolls are a-maze-ing!"

Abruptly standing, clattering his chair behind him, Corbiere's face became pointed and hard. Lines of seriousness coursed his brows, and he leant on the table, deep in thought and distracted.

"Frida's correct," he solemnly declared. "The visitor's log on its own is an important historical find. Entries for arrival, purpose of visit, time of leaving, a delightful account of the comings and goings at a castle: lords, ladies, knights, men-at-arms, monks, priests, peddlers, entertainers. They're all there. A vibrant medieval community, and yet, among them all, tying in with the other scroll's confessional transcript, one entry stands out. In fact, it almost takes my breath."

"How come? Did they get a visit from the king?"

"Not quite," said Corbiere. "But almost as good. The visitor log describes the arrival of 'a learned friar' and his retainers sometime in the late 13th century, telling how the friar is on his way to Oxford 'to collect all necessary proofs' before returning to Paris, answering the charges laid upon him by the great general Jerome d'Ascoli. A sudden storm in the Channel caused them to miss the mouth of the Thames, however. Forced to land on the Sussex coast, they received the 'goodly hospitality' of the grey friars at the new Winchelsea, before his men were 'medicined' by the healer dwelling in the nearby 'Manor Luett'. The friar sought this healer himself, it says, finding him 'learn-ed beyond all reason'. Branding him unholy, he put him to question, before the healer, doubtless out of fear, fled to Rye."

"Who was this friar, then? Why the excitement?"

"Roger Bacon," he gravely replied, and, looking bemused, I shrugged.

"Good grief!" he exclaimed. "You haven't heard of Roger Bacon? What's going on in this country? He was England's Leonardo da Vinci. Our Galileo! Laying the foundations of modern scientific thinking, hundreds of years before those two were born!"

"Oh, him," I replied. "Sorry. Course I know Roger Bacon. Was there anything else?"

"No. Nothing of relevance, but the confessional transcript then goes on to tell of the learned friar's guilt and shame at releasing his men-at-arms to track down this healer – to do God's work on Earth, and how they returned, recounting their tale, describing the good work done in answer to his prayers, resulting in the black healer's disposal amongst the goodly stones of Rye."

I suddenly sat up. Now even I could see the blatant connection.

"You mean the skeleton in the wall might be…?"

"Yes," said Frida. "He might be the remains of the healer."

"Not provable," said Corbiere. "But circumstantial evidence is very often the only evidence available, so we historians try to make the best of it."

"Great," I replied. "What do we do now?"

"We get cracking," said Corbiere, "because anything concerning Roger Bacon is of great historical importance, and this is what we're going to do. First, I'll arrange for the unread parchment to come up from Sussex, then it can undergo full conservation – we need to see what's on it. Who knows? It might shed further light on Bacon's involvement in the killing of this poor soul."

Returning to his desk, Corbiere was fidgeting, twiddling his pen with excitement.

"It looks like Dr Cool is gonna explode," remarked Frida. "Marky, what have you done?"

"I'm sorry," said Corbiere. "But a breakthrough like this is just so… You see, not much is known much about Bacon's imprisonment and the last few years of his life, and this evidence, this little scrap, if corroborated, could help piece his story together."

Looking thoughtful for a moment, Frida was counting with her fingers…

"Yes," said Frida. "Should be ok…Could we collect the parchment? Might speed things up, and a trip to Sussex would be fun."

"Certainly," he replied. "That would help no end. Leave me to make all the arrangements and I'll let you know when and where next week."

"You don't mind, do you, Marky?" asked Frida. "You can change shifts?"

"Of course not," I said. "No problem at all, and if we're going to Sussex, would it be possible to see the skeleton and the original figurine?"

"I don't see why not," replied Corbiere. "When I contact the authorities, I'll ask them."

"Thanks, Graham," I said.

Frida, her small hands quick and efficient, slid the papers into their relevant folders. Picking up my rucksack, she unzipped its largest chamber.

"Feel free to keep the document from Normandy," added Corbiere. "But do look after it. If the original goes missing, we'll need it."

Frida, delivering one of her steely looks, pointedly slid the envelope and folder into my backpack.

Looking at his watch once more, Corbiere softly cursed.

"Unfortunately," he then said, "I must be going. I have a meeting and Steph will go nuts if I'm late, but I'll contact Marcus next week, Tuesday at the latest, with all the details, ok?"

Picking up my backpack and casually slinging it over my shoulder, Frida promptly slapped me on the arm...

"He said to look after it!" she snapped, stamping her foot.

Laughing at my plight, Corbiere then escorted us up and out into the dazzling light of the museum's ever-echoing hub.

"Hopefully I'll see you both again soon," he said, checking his phone.

"Next week," I replied, and we shook hands.

Frida (who I thought for a second was going to hug him) merely smiled before respectfully bowing her head.

"Bye, Graham," she said. "Thanks for everything," and we watched him disappear into the crowds milling about the Great Hall.

"Fancy a pint?" I asked. "Don't know about you, but I'm parched."

"God, yes!" replied Frida, taking my arm, and we walked out together into the autumnal coolness of the late afternoon, searching for a bar on Tottenham Court Road.

TWELVE

SUSSEX

We began planning our Sussex trip the moment we left the museum. Frida turned out to be a meticulous planner, and I was happy to let her do it. It wasn't until deciding what route we should take did we have a difference of opinion. Her preferred (but contentious route), heading almost due south via Maidstone, would require me to travel across London (uncomfortably early) and have breakfast at her place, departing together sometime after. This painfully early rise and chilly trawl across London wasn't very appealing (and meeting her mother sounded like an ordeal), so instead, I suggested she drive west, pick me up, and then head south to Brighton, before travelling east, following the coastline, passing through Hastings and Winchelsea to Rye.

We nearly fell out over this. Frida was, I think, quite taken aback by my stubbornness, and without her compromising attitude it could have easily developed into a serious row. In the end, she agreed to follow my preferred route on our return, stopping for lunch in the picturesque town of Steyning. Therefore, finding a suitable B&B or hotel for the night was our only contention and, as a further concession, she left the choosing to me...

"Just be sure it isn't a shithole," she warned, downing her second pint.

⚏

We heard nothing from Dr Corbiere until Tuesday evening the following week, and I was just in from work, removing my greasy work clothes when my phone went off...

"Hi Graham," I answered. "How's it going?"

"Very well, thank you," he replied. "Are you still keen to pick up the parchment from Sussex?"

"Most certainly. We've already made plans. Is there a problem?"

"No, not at all, I contacted the museum in Rye, still holding the item in question, and they're quite prepared for it to undergo the X-ray procedure I have in mind, provisionally arranging for its collection sometime this coming Saturday."

"Oh, good," I said, relieved and scrawling a note. "That's great, fits our plans well. Do they still have the skeleton? Would be very cool to see it."

"They do indeed," he enthused. "Disarticulated, of course, much easier to store in their vault, but they also gave me sad news, the other pieces of parchment? They're gone. Disintegrated years ago."

"That's a shame," I said, glancing towards the relevant folder. "Would have liked to see those. I suppose this must happen a lot."

"All too frequently," he acknowledged. "And you asked to view the Camber Sands figurine, yes?"

"I did. You said they might have it."

"Indeed, but, as I suspected, they no longer do. Their Viking remains and associated artefacts were all recently moved to York, and, if you want to see them, you'll need to get there yourself."

"Right, ok," I said. "You did say this might be the case, thanks for checking anyhow. Perhaps we'll go later in the year."

"Definitely," he replied. "Well worth a visit. They have quite a collection."

"Oh!" I then said, recalling Frida's promptings. "Almost forgot. Does the parchment require any special handling or a sealed container?"

"Yes, of course, and, although gentle handling and no bright light or extremes in temperature are the usual provisos for this class of object, I'm sure it will be securely packaged and ready for travel. Best speak to my counterparts in Rye if you're worried."

"Fine," I said, frantically jotting down his words. "Thanks, Graham. Is there anything else?"

"No, I think that's everything. Just be careful and drop it off at the museum with a note on Monday. As soon as I receive the X-ray results, processed and in an accessible format, I'll send them as a PDF."

"Great," I replied. "PDFs are a cinch."

"Excellent, and now I must be going – need to check my kid's homework but do have a fun time in Sussex. I'm envious. Rye's a splendid old town. Give Frida my best and hope to see you both soon."

"Sure. I'm certain we will. Bye then."

"Goodbye, Marcus, and thanks for your help in this exciting endeavour."

"Endeavour," I muttered, gathering my notes. "What an arse."

Making expanded notes of everything said, I texted a summary to Frida (sadly working nights and sleeping during the day).

Located on A259 between Winchelsea and Rye, the B&B I found seemed ideal. Called Tanyard House, it was a converted Elizabethan farmhouse and I booked us the upstairs suite of a converted barn within its grounds. The apartment within appeared plush and cosy, with an en suite bathroom and huge double bed. It had a balcony too, affording wonderful views of the meadows, canal, and marshes, all the way to the sea (a mile or two to the south). Reassuringly expensive, receiving rave reviews, I was convinced Frida would love it.

During the rest of the week (not seeing Frida), I worked as much as I could, filling my free time brushing up on my history, studying the periods concerning the Camber Sands Viking burial and the reliquary of Winchelsea church.

Saturday morning looming large made me nervous.

Being my first visit to Frida's home, I didn't know what to expect, and what I did know filled me with dread. All those pets, her strange mother. Might their house be filthy, cluttered, chaotic, smelly?

As it turned out, my fears were unfounded, but, finishing my coffee and readying myself for the trip, trepidation spurred me into thorough preparation. Researching the journey across town as best I could, I found their house online (56 Priest's Hill, Lewisham SE13), printed its picture and various maps. To my relief, the house appeared well looked after. A 1940s semi, with a paved front yard, a decent-sized garden, adjacent to a large park, perfect for walking their dogs. From overhead, it looked to be a very respectable district of south-east London.

Before 7am and very foggy when I set out, every surface soaking wet and dripping, and while waiting for the first bus to my rail connection, it wasn't long before I was wet and dripping myself. The bus, often busy, was virtually empty, the train and Tube similarly vacant, and, apart from hung-over students and a sprinkling of nutters (a permanent fixture on public transport), I was standing outside Frida's house in just over an hour.

From the street, with the curtains still drawn, the house seemed asleep, but yellow light, filtering through the frosted glass of the front door, showed someone to be up and about.

With my heart skipping a beat, I swallowed. No going back now. Walking up to the door, I tentatively pressed the doorbell…

"Ding – dong…!"

Chaos erupted.

Dogs barked, running amok, and a squawking parrot, at first mimicking the doorbell, shrieked a stream of obscenities enough to shock even the devil…

"There's s-someone at the door!" a woman yelled. "Br-brush your hair, s…weep the floor, there's s-someone at the door!"

"It's just Marcus," cried Frida. "No need to get rhyme-y!" Then, in a demanding voice, she shouted, "Scamps, Scutts – bed!" before unlocking the door top and bottom.

"Wanker!" croaked the parrot, Frida snapping, "No he's not! Stupid bird," before opening the door with a grin.

"Marcus!" She grinned. "You made it!" and, taking my rucksack and coat, she shook off what moisture she could.

In the kitchen, happily munching on toast, was Frida's mother. A tiny woman by any reckoning, and much like her daughter, she possessed the same dark eyes, with a kind face, pale skin, slightly flushed cheeks, and straight hair dyed a deep blackberry purple.

"Mum?" said Frida, stooping to look in her face. "This is Marcus. Marcus? Meet my mother, Karen Halfpenny."

"Hello, Mrs Ape-knee," I said. "Sorry I'm here so early, interrupting your breakfast. Lovely Frida's idea, not mine…"

"He… he said it right," she mumbled to Frida, then to me, flushing slightly. "Th-that's ok, lovey. M-Marcus up, Marcus down, happy to meet you, n-never a frown."

"Mum…" Frida supportively replied. "But do sit down, Marky, and I'll get you some toast."

"Oh yeah." I chuckled, sliding into a chair. "Perfect. It's yucky outside, I need a good breakfast."

Beneath the table, something soft was sinuously writhing against my legs, and I leant back, peering under, wondering what it could be. It was a cat. Black as night, fluffy, whiskers like wire, and shining green eyes, and, as I reached down to stroke the scruff of its neck, it rolled its cheeks against the back of my hand.

"That's Normski," said Frida, fetching a plate, a knife, and then peering into the toaster. "He's a friendly old sod, but very demanding of affection. Sings all night too. Awful racket."

"Yeah," I remarked, gently scratching his back. "Well, I think he's fine. Peculiar name though."

"My mum's choice," said Frida, the cat flicking his tail like a whip. "Why did you call him Normski again?"

"It was because," Mrs Halfpenny carefully replied, "when he was a k-k-kitty, he would j-jump, dance and prance, like he was a flea. He... reminded me of a TV show – lots of crazy dancing, can't re... member what it was, but Normski was one of the dancers, and the name s-sort of stuck."

Avoiding eye contact, flushing red and quickly looking away, when attempting direct speech Mrs Halfpenny would sometimes stutter, repeating or rhyming, and, although she managed her difficulties well, it was plain that busy, stressful, or crowded environments would quickly overwhelm her...

"Here you go, Marky," said Frida, dropping two slices onto my plate. "Hope it's done well enough. Help yourself to butter, honey, or marmalade."

As I smeared my toast with butter and honey, Frida plonked a mug of coffee next to my plate and settled beside me.

"We don't have to leave for an hour," said Frida, "but I wanted you here early to force me out of bed."

"Had a feeling you'd still be worn out. Have you packed?"

"Of course," she replied. "My stuff is upstairs. When you've finished, I'll give you a tour and then we can load up the car."

"Where'd the dogs go? They were going mad at the doorbell. I anticipated a thorough slobbering."

"Sent them to bed, didn't you hear? Anyway, thought you wouldn't want them jumping all over you until you'd settled in."

"Oh, right." I nodded. "Thanks, that's really thoughtful."

"I try." She smiled. "And do you like parrots? Because we have one, you see, although he's being strangely quiet. Hope the doorbell didn't scare him to death."

"Hopefully not." I chuckled. "But I've never been close to a parrot – too scary. All beak, claws, dusty feathers, and those beady eyes…" and I shivered, emphasising my point.

"Well, it's high time you confronted your fear. Once you've finished, I'll introduce you to Peter, our African grey. Swears like a trooper, but he's a soppy old thing."

"Probably asleep," Mrs Halfpenny added. "He likes a lie-in, poor bird. Tired and absurd, with head under wing, won't say a word."

"Yes," Frida replied. "No dawn chorus for us. Not a whistle, nor a squawk. Stroke 'im if you like, but 'e won't talk!"

Struck by how lovely Frida and her mother were, I could only smile. They were so honest. Hard-working, intelligent, resourceful, with a hidden layer of emotional sophistication always waiting to surprise you. On first appearances, Frida was the primary carer, but, with her working long and unsociable hours, Mrs Halfpenny must have been quite capable of looking after herself (moreover, Mrs Halfpenny's little foibles almost disappeared when alone in familiar surroundings). Indeed, I later discovered Mrs Halfpenny worked from home very successfully, writing articles for a number of animal and pet magazines, maintaining a web page, responding to enquiries concerning animal behaviour, with Frida proudly maintaining, "She could train slugs to fly, if the need ever arose…"

Finishing my coffee and toast, Frida led me into their front room, introducing the dogs… Scamper, an Afghan, whip tailed, gangly, his long golden coat spreading about him like a puddle, together in the same basket with Skuttle, a long-haired miniature dachshund. Upon seeing us, they both promptly sat up, smiling, panting, and wagging – all tongue and teeth, in a typically doggy way, but, as Frida knelt to pet them, Skuttle voiced a short bark of satisfaction, more of an "Arff!" than a woof.

In one corner, half in shadow and motionless, was a grey parrot perched upon a scuffed branch. With its head under one wing, it seemed asleep, and as we approached it ignored us completely.

"This is Peter," said Frida, pulling me close. "He's about 30 years old, and likes a lie-in, as you can see. Shall I wake him? He's very gentle but be prepared. If he screeches, it is shockingly loud."

"It's ok," I replied. "Loud noises aren't a problem, only… can't we leave him be?"

"Hmm…" she muttered, considering my apprehension. "Tell you what. I'll give him a stroke, ask if he wants to meet you, ok?"

"Very well," I said, edging away. "Just don't be insistent."

Standing on tiptoe, Frida stroked her fingers the down his feathered back.

"Peter?" she softly enquired. "Oh, Peter? C'mon Petey-bird, time to wake up…"

Initially, the old bird didn't respond, before slowly lifting his head and looking at Frida with acceptance. At first, he seemed sleepy, but, when he saw me, he squawked most disapprovingly, quietly croaking his mimicry of the doorbell:

"Ding-dong, ding-dong, ding-dong."

Looking puzzled, Frida withdrew her hand.

"Now, why are you saying that?" she pondered. "Are you still dreaming?"

"Ding-dong…" he softly repeated before turning his head to ignore us.

"Humph," said Frida, stepping back. "Think that means sod off."

"Seems so. Is that unusual?"

"Yeah," she confirmed. "Very. Strangers usually excite him. He should be all over you, and, as for the doorbell thing… God, I don't know. He was just dreaming? Bizarre."

"Parrots dream?"

"Sure," she replied. "Course they do. All intelligent creatures dream, and therefore the not-so-intelligent ones must do as well, although it is harder to prove in their case. Our dogs, for example, have dreams all the time, and compared to them, Peter is a genius."

"Interesting," I said, soaking up a new fact. "Never considered that. Worth looking into."

"It is," she replied, happy to be teacher. "Let's pop outside, do the fluffies, and then we might as well be going."

The "fluffies" were aptly named.

Just a little way into their garden, against the fence and inside a low enclosure stood two large wooden hutches. Taking Frida's hand as she stepped inside, I looked on as she opened each hutch and lowered their ramps.

"Come and see," she said, pointing towards and then stroking a large ball of grey fluff. "This… er… thing is Furlong, our rabbit."

With the front of his hutch wide open, Furlong calmly hopped and hobbled down the ramp, sitting his fluffy rear end on her foot.

"Oh, you can't sit there," she remarked, easing him to one side, "I need to check on the squeakers…"

The squeakers were two guinea pigs, still curled in a tight furry ball when Frida opened their hutch, but they soon stirred, looking about them with bright, beady eyes before scratching and scuttling about.

Her mother had named them Bubble and Squeak, and, as she topped up their feed, they did indeed squeak. In fact, it was quite a cacophony, and we soon left them to make our way indoors.

"All done, present and correct," said Frida as we passed through the kitchen, but her mother ignored us. Too busy spooning cat food into a bowl while Normski hungrily purred, weaving between her legs.

Passing into the hallway, the dogs were still out of sight, but at the foot of the stairs they slunk past us into the kitchen.

"Scroungers inbound!" called Frida, leading the way, but her mother said nothing, before singing to the dogs about breakfast.

"Wait here," said Frida, partially opening her bedroom door. "Haven't tidied all week and it's a bit of a crap-hole, so no peeking! S'all crumpled, trampled, and knicker-strewn, I'd die a death if you saw it."

Shrugging, I smiled, looking about the landing.

Upon a windowsill was a fish tank filled to the brim with green water – nearly all of it displaced by a bulbous goldfish. The unfortunate thing looked rather depressed, but, as I edged closer, it became aware of me, swimming back and forth in what little manoeuvring space remained.

"That's Gupples," said Frida, dragging two cases behind her. "He's really old, outlived or eaten his shoal-mates and outgrown his tank, the greedy bastard. We're moving him to a neighbour's pond in the spring, but until then he'll just have to stay put."

"He's a like a big orange brick," I remarked, peering through the glass. "What does he eat, burgers?"

"Ha, yes!" she replied. "And he floats the same way bricks don't, but we only feed him the regular stuff, honest. He's just bulked up on it."

"Two suitcases," I noted, slightly confused. "Only one night, Fred. What've you got in there?"

"Just the usual." She shrugged. "And, anyway, the other case is empty."

"Then what is it for?"

"For shopping," she replied, shutting her bedroom door with a clonk.

"What shopping? I'm not sure we'll have time."

"Well, you never know. There're some sick little shops in Rye, so if I get the chance, I'm gonna splurge."

"Still doesn't explain the empty suitcase."

"Just told you!" she snapped. "For any new clothes I might buy. They'll get creased stuffed in bags for two days, so stop nagging!"

She did have a point about the empty case. My sister would've done the exact same thing, and, besides, it was her car and her little holiday too. Wisely, I stopped talking and carried her cases to the car.

Crawling through the traffic towards the Kent border, I felt uncomfortably drowsy. My early rise was beginning to tell...

"You sure we couldn't have waited," I said, stifling a yawn. "The museum won't see us until one."

"Wouldn't work," she replied, "the traffic'd be horrendous, we'd be late! Caught in all the footballing crap. They shut roads, divert traffic, nightmare."

"Not a fan then," I said. "Millwall, if anything?"

"God, no!" she replied. "Please, don't tell me. You're not into football, are you?"

Laughing, I wondered why she thought I might be.

"Course not," I said, "How could I be? One lacks the obligatory van."

Villages and their signposts sleepily slid by, with Frida, a lover of words, amusing herself, punning and rhyming, toying with their names...

"Fancy a game of limericks?" Frida then asked, wriggling to shift the cushions beneath her. "So many whacky place names, it's hard to resist."

"Ok," I replied, intrigued but rather unsure. "As long as it's not competitive."

"Competitive?" she said, shaking her head. "No, there's no score or anything, it's just for fun, only, if you're crap, I'll sulk."

"No pressure at all then," I replied with a sigh, and Frida mischievously giggled.

"And," she added, "since this is my game, you get to go first, ok?"

"No, not really, what are the rules?"

"They're simple. We just take turns. When you spot an interesting place name, use it to build the first line of your limerick, then I'll do the next line, yours's the next, and so forth."

"Right," I said, suddenly detecting a pitfall. "But doesn't that mean I'll have to finish it?"

"Yep" – she nodded – "it does. If you start, it's your limerick, and, although I'll try to help, giving you hooks and links, sometimes it's fun to set traps."

"Fine," I said, resigned to my fate (but ready to try it). "And are the limericks allowed to be rude?"

"I think that's the point!" she laughed.

Not long before I spied a promising signpost, showing the way to a village called Loose and after a little thought I began...

"Right," I said, "here we go. It starts like this. An unhappy old woman from Loose."

"Thought you'd go Loose!" said Frida. "Hmm, let me think... Had manners akin to a goose!"

"Oh," I remarked. "Thanks, that's pretty rich feed."

"You're welcome," she replied. "Well?"

"Hang on a tick," I said, repeating the words in my head. "Ok. Got it. She'd flap and she'd swear."

"Waddle and stare."

"Too quick," I said.

"Not my fault," she guiltily shrugged. "The middle lines flow really easy."

"Let you off, then." I shrugged. "Only now I need to think for a bit," before turning away to look out of the door.

"Come on, Marky," she urged. "Don't strop. It's not meant to be serious. Just grab whatever comes into your head."

"No need to worry," I replied. "Eureka! I have it. Panic over. And lived in a small wooden hoose!"

Frida laughed in surprise.

"Hey!" she then said. "That's not bad. The way you changed the word 'House' to make it rhyme was clever. Although, overall, it's a bit strange. Poor woman. Living in a shed."

"You're not kidding," I replied. "Rather surreal and surprisingly clean. Loose was trickier than I thought."

"Yeah," she agreed. "Loose was tighter than you expected. Good game, though, isn't it?"

We drove on then at a steady pace before Frida nodded towards a signpost for Staplehurst.

"Ah ha!" she remarked. "A test."

"No kidding," I replied. "It rhymes with what? Thirst, burst? Not much to work with."

"That's why I chose it." She chuckled. "And I don't know why you're moaning. It's me that has to start and finish the thing."

"Go on then," I challenged. "If you're so flippin' clever."

"Umm…" she mumbled, thinking, biting her bottom lip. "Oh, I know. A woman from Staplehurst."

"Is that all? After all your umming, I expected something dramatic… Had a fanny that was said to be cursed."

Guffawing and slapping the dashboard, Frida laughed so hard that her gum flew-out, rebounding off the steering wheel and into her lap.

"Oops!" she smirked, popping the little pellet into her mouth. "That's more like it! Ooh, erm… During every full moon."

"It would detach from her womb."

"Marcus!" she then exclaimed. "You're really good at this. You sure you've never played?"

"Nope," I replied. "First time. Got a last line then?"

"Getting there. Although, I'm not sure if it scans. And then pounce on whomever came first?"

"Yes, it does, Fred," I replied, "perfectly. That was a good one. Crude, funny, we should write these down."

Reaching over, Frida squeezed my hand.

"Then why don't you?" she said. "Put them into your phone."

"So, I did," I explained, relaxing on the bed. "And they're still in it. Otherwise, I would've forgotten."

"Good," replied Mirra, "and were there any more of these limericks? Haven't heard their like before. Can you explain the technique?"

"Not precisely, only that they are simple to create because they always rhyme the same way. If you want a technical description of the method, you'll need a better teacher. The correct terminology eludes me, but with a little practice, you'll soon catch on, and, yes, there was one more limerick. During this journey, anyway."

"Then I look forward to reading it."

"Ok. I'll try to fit it in later. Now I want to recount our second breakfast."

Passing through Staplehurst, Frida suddenly announced she was hungry…

"Gonna pull over someplace and eat," said Frida, rubbing her tummy. "My breakfast's worn off. I need another."

"Fine by me," I replied, happy if only to stretch my legs. "Perhaps there's a café or something."

There was. After two hundred metres, we spied a pub opposite a splendid old church.

"This'll do," she said, turning into the car park. "What time is it, though? You reckon they're still serving breakfast?"

"It's not yet eleven," I replied, glancing at my phone. "So, they're bound to be."

Finding an entrance around the back, we made our way inside, poking about, exploring, and looking at the menu. It was a nice old pub, and occupying a table in the bay of a front window, we comfortably settled, enjoying a fine view of the church.

A waiter appeared taking our order of a sausage sandwich, a coffee, and a large bowl of muesli, which Frida proceeded to chomp upon with relish…

"Winchelsea then Rye," she said.

"Yes," I replied, "Makes sense. Winchelsea's on the way. Daft to go back on ourselves."

"It's the museum and church you want, isn't it?"

With my mouth full of bread and sausage, I nodded

"Well," I replied, still chewing, "I'd like to look at the reliquary, but don't know who to ask. I plan to visit the museum and make some enquiries."

"Oh, right," she acknowledged twiddling her spoon. "Thought you and Corbiere had arranged this?"

"Only discussed, I'm afraid. It's still his advice I'm following."

"What will you do if you can't see the relics?"

"Don't know," I shrugged in reply. "Contact the rector directly? However, if we don't reach him soon, he'll be all up in it with Jesus."

⏳

Rye was a delight. We loved it.

Parking was ample (and cheap), and we were soon exploring the old town with its maze of cobbled streets, winding like roots below the feet of the church. Old, timber-framed buildings were prolific, and we wondered which had originally concealed the skeleton we had travelled so far to examine.

In fact, none of them. In 1377, a French incursion burnt Rye to the ground and only a little of the original building survived. The construction of a new bakery made use of the remaining sound walls, however (including the one concealing the skeleton), later becoming a public house, before this also burnt down 1872. How the wall endured these calamities is frankly amazing! In 2011, the original section of wall was part of a thriving tearoom on Lion Street.

We visited the church, climbing its narrow stairs to the top of the tower (shocked and deafened by the bells striking the hour). At the summit, Frida snuggled closely as we took it all in.

"I don't know if I'm freezing or terrified!" she cried, trembling against my jacket.

With the town spread out like a map below us, we could plainly see our destination close to the original coastline (before the silting up of the harbour).

"There's the museum," said Frida. "The building that looks like a castle."

"Yeah," I said. "Bit of a walk but good for sightseeing."

"Indeedy," she replied. "Let's do a little shopping and then make our way over."

"Ok, lovey." I smiled, holding her close. "Anything you want."

Looking up from our warming embrace, Frida kissed me very tenderly.

To my relief, Frida shopped like a man. Very purposefully, not much of a browser, only entering a shop if they had what she wanted, and if they had her size, she bought it and left. Nevertheless, she purchased a pair of black lace-up boots, two tops (both from the same rail), and without trying things on or fussing about, we were soon heading towards the museum. Frida could teach my sister a thing or two about shopping, I thought, while chivalrously carrying her bags...

"You said there was another limerick," said Mirra, sounding let down. "Why didn't you write it?"

"As a matter of fact, there were three. Two are still in my phone, but the other one I must have deleted. Can't remember how it went – it was about Gill's Green, and I had to start it."

"Oh, I see," she replied. "Well, never mind about that one, but I would like to hear the other two."

"Ok, if you insist. Only, I meant to whoosh through the travelling. It's hardly relevant."

"I disagree. The limericks define Frida's character."

"They do. Although, I thought you wanted a written account, not our smutty poetry!"

Mirra giggled.

"You're quite wrong, sweet Marcus. Your loving light-heartedness and humour reveal the good in you. Have faith in my judgement."

Needing to consider her viewpoint, I paced my cell, and, although I appreciated her compliment, something was surely amiss...

Mirra was always like this. All sweetness and light, but never really explaining herself, and my frustration towards her elusiveness was beginning to grow. Certainly, I could understand how describing my good character might reduce any sentence imposed upon me (for vandalism), yet the amount Mirra demanded seemed excessive, and just why was Frida's personality so important? The only reason I could think of was glaringly obvious. If Frida, of good character, enjoyed spending spend time with me, I must be of good character as well.

This made sense, perfect sense, and yet so simplistic it worried me...

"You're right again," I said, finding no way of denying her logic. "The first limerick was all Frida, and it went like this... A man from Camber Sands was very deft with his hands. He could handle a zip, a bra unclip, while onlookers cheered from the stands."

Without offering any comment (for once), Mirra softly chuckled.

"This came from a limerick Frida already knew. She'd forgotten the original, though."

"Doesn't matter," said Mirra, sounding content. "I thought it really funny. What was the other one?"

"It was about Rye. We contrived it just before we parked. Frida started it and therefore finished it, and it went like this... There was an old man from Rye, who maintained an unfeasible lie. He told how its length and incredible strength, would bring tears to any girl's eye."

Mirra snorted (very uncharacteristically) and then went into fits of giggles, even more remarkable, I could also hear Moloch – laughing. His gurgling rasp seemed far away, and yet the sound of him swirled around me, coming from every direction at once. A brief but chilling reminder of our previous encounter...

"Didn't know Moloch was listening," I said, full of concern.

"Didn't know either," replied Mirra. "Luckily, I don't think he knew we were talking, merely popping by, curious why I was laughing, and then, finding enjoyment in your limericks himself, he joined in with my mirth. Make a mental note of this, Marcus. From here on, recount as much as you can of your word games and rhyming. Keeping Moloch in a good mood will count in your favour if you ever come to rile him."

"Then I'll bear it in mind," I said. "Only, it's doubtful I will remember. When pissing about, joking and rhyming, we were often rather drunk."

⧗

Built within the precipitous walls of an old fort, Rye Museum was a hotchpotch of huts and buildings sheltering a garden and an immaculate lawn. Its signpost: "Keep Off the Grass".

The museum was hardly busy and much smaller than we were expecting, and we quickly made our way through the heavy front gates, before presenting our credentials to the receptionist. A pleasant looking woman with greying hair and glasses on a cord...

"Hello," I sheepishly said. "I'm Marcus Eaton and this is Frida Halfpenny. We've been sent by the British Museum and Dr Graham Corbiere to collect a sample for..."

"Conservation and examination," added Frida.

"Yes," I said, rolling my eyes. "Here, check out our IDs..." and we presented our driving licences and British Museum security badges (Corbiere's suggestion), waiting while she looked them over.

"Ah, yes," said the receptionist. "Dr Jenkins is expecting you. I'll just give her a buzz and let her know you're here."

"Thank you!" Our unified response, before looking at each other and grinning like twerps.

"If you'll wait here?" she then asked. "Dr Jenkins is just on her way."

Dr Jenkins was frightfully posh, and Frida, mockingly disrespectful of those she considered privileged, rolled her eyes whenever she spoke. Dr Jenkins was far too efficient to care, however, and, brushing Frida aside, she described their preparations…

"I've already packed the sample for transport," she explained, studying our faces in turn. "And you'll be pleased to know it's very well wrapped and padded. Still, it would be best if you avoided unnecessary agitation. So, please, be meticulously careful when carrying it, understood?"

Leading the way, Dr Jenkins took us into a side building and down into its cellar, dimly lit and musty.

"Damp," she muttered, switching on lights. "I'm actually relieved you're taking it. Here it is…"

Lifting a large plastic box, she placed it carefully onto a sideboard.

"It isn't particularly heavy," she explained. "The actual sample is small. The bulkiness is due to the bubble wrap and packets of silica gel."

"That sounds ideal," remarked Frida. "Thanks for all your trouble getting this ready."

"Oh, it's really no trouble at all," she replied, presenting a form for us to sign. "Graham's got me trembling on tenterhooks about that parchment. Roger Bacon. Who would have thought it? How long before he receives the results?"

"Sorry, Dr Jenkins," I said, lifting the box and judging its weight, "we don't know. Although, Dr Corbiere was very keen to get things moving, so not more than a month? He's sure to contact you immediately once there's something to tell."

"Agreed," she replied. "He did seem rather excited about the whole affair, and he mentioned you'd like to examine the skeleton?"

"Oh, yeah," said Frida. "Would be amazing to see him for real."

"He's over here," replied Dr Jenkins, pointing towards a large a crate. "Not the most poetic resting-place, is it?"

Fetching a cardboard box from a nearby counter, she removed bunch of latex gloves.

"Here," she remarked. "You'll need to put these on. The bones are decidedly unhygienic."

The gloves were too big for Frida, and, after slipping them on, she playfully wriggled the half-empty fingers under my nose.

Switching on a lamp, Dr Jenkins struggled to drag the crate a short distance before catching her breath.

"Could you give me lift?" she asked. "He's surprisingly heavy," and the three of us wrestled the bulky crate up onto a table.

Gently removing the lid, Dr Jenkins carefully extracted further boxes of various shapes and sizes. One container, a large cube, she lifted and positioned with such painstaking care her tongue protruded from the corner of her mouth.

"The skull's in here," she whispered. "Terribly fragile. You can view it by folding down the sides. Touching is not advisable."

Opening one of the longer boxes, Frida removed a selection of leg bones, laying them upon the table…

"He was tall, wasn't he?" she remarked, running her fingers over a dark-brown femur. "And his bones are really strong and un-pitted. No sign of malnutrition at all."

"Yes," replied Dr Jenkins. "He must've towered over his associates, growing to, what do you think, over six feet?"

"May I examine his arms and hands? Want to see if there's evidence of restraint."

"Of course," said Dr Jenkins, patting two long narrow containers. "They're in these boxes. Would you care for a magnifier?"

"Yes, thanks," replied Frida, mindfully opening one of the containers and peering inside. "Have you performed this particular exam before?"

"Many times," Dr Jenkins acknowledged, "and often with students. I know what you'll find, so let's see if you pass the test."

Carefully examining both radii, ulnae and an assortment of wrist and hand bones (I don't know the names of), Frida shook her head…

"There's nothing," she remarked. "No damage at all. He wasn't manacled, then, it's fair to assume?"

"Spot on," said Dr Jenkins, suitably impressed. "No, it doesn't look like he was, but it doesn't mean he wasn't tied or held when killed. Let me open the skull box, and then you can look him in the eye and examine his wound."

While methodically examining the skull, Frida was both silent and serious, her breathing shallow and short, but, walking back to her car, me self-consciously carrying the box containing the parchment, she was bouncing around like a ball, talking fast and full of excitement…

"You know," she babbled, "I've never examined, let alone touched a human skull. So amazing! It left me feeling something I didn't expect."

"You're kidding?" I replied. "Not even at uni?"

"Nope," she confessed. "Remember, I'm a biochemist, specialising in cellular toxicity, not a medic. Not touched a bone since college."

"Right," I said, changing my grip on the box. "Well, I never have, and thought it a bit gross. With its creepy grin, hollow eyes, and matted hair. What did you feel?"

"Nothing," she bleakly replied. "And that was the surprise. From the moment she opened the skull box, a cool quietness came over me. A sort of reverence. How weird is that?"

"Don't know," I replied. "Couldn't know either. As I said, never seen a human bone until now. How could I predict my reaction? However, what you describe doesn't sound weird, and that cellar? Well, it was kinda creepy. Gloomy, musty, like a church or a tomb, and, once the skull was out, with the lights constantly flickering, it got a bit tense. It wasn't until you broke the silence, mentioning his teeth, did life return to the room."

"They *were* good teeth, though, weren't they? So white and shiny, another surprise! Would've expected a medieval man, one in his thirties or forties, to at least have a few dental caries."

"Well," I countered, "Dr Jenkins did say he was tall and very well fed. Maybe he had good healthcare as well. Did they know about teeth in those days, though? I've read quite a bit about the medieval period, but never a medieval dentist. Perhaps he was lucky."

"Lucky in this period, yes," said Frida. "But in those days? Most diseases caught back then ran their natural course. If the victim survived, they recovered, but in doing so their bodies would take quite a battering, teeth included. There is something very special about this man, I'm sure of it."

"He's special in many ways. But did she not say, the DNA and isotope stuff was typical? He was clearly north-western European, and, from the state of his bones, about forty years old."

"The carbon isotope dating was correct as well," said Frida, chewing her lip. "Mid-13th to mid-14th century, so perhaps I'm making too much of his shiny teeth and missing the whole picture – it wouldn't be the first time. I'm a very emotional scientist sometimes, not good at all."

"Erghh," I grumbled. "My arms are going to sleep. Is it much further?"

"Just around the corner," said Frida. "Hang in there!"

"Thank God," I gasped in relief. "If I drop this thing, I'd have to go into hiding. Didn't Dr Posh also say the carbon date gave funny results?"

"Yep. She reckons the skeleton is contaminated with modern material, but the peaks for the correct period were clearly there, so the analytical team, quite rightly in my opinion, ignored the spurious data and focussed on them."

"Is this normal for carbon dating, then? Crappy data?"

"Not sure," she replied. "Never done any, but it's a pretty sensitive technique, so I'd imagine it's quite common."

"Dr Jenkins said the lime mortar might be the problem. Any ideas why? How does carbon dating actually work?"

"Oh, for God's sake!" Frida then snapped. "Why all the sudden inquisitiveness? I'm not a bloody expert. Give me a chance to think. Wait until we get to our B&B, and I've had some fucking lunch."

We arrived at our B&B within the hour. Apologising profusely for her outburst and casting her eyes on the apartment, standing on the balcony, watching the low autumn sun projecting tall shadows over the marshes beyond, Frida was almost prostrate at my feet…

"Oh, Marcus!" she said with a gasp. "This is just wonderful, even better than I imagined."

"Yes," I said, holding her close. "Every bit as good as it looked, thank God. Now, let's get something to eat. I'm famished."

"And drink!" she added, fully happy again. "And as many questions as you like."

We had an ample lunch. Almost mid-afternoon tea by the time we got it, but the weather was so pleasant that we didn't care one jot.

Following our meal, Frida carefully explained what she could about radiocarbon dating, highlighting the possible interference brought about by the lime mortar surrounding the skeleton…

"As you know, the air contains a small amount of carbon dioxide. A gas composed of the elements carbon and oxygen. Now, carbon itself has three significant natural isotopes. Carbon-12, carbon-13, and carbon-14. The commonest isotope, about 99%, is carbon-12, whereas the remaining 1% is mostly carbon-13, with a tiny amount of carbon-14, formed when cosmic rays from space bombard the nitrogen in our atmosphere. Being a freak of nature, carbon-14 is entropically unstable and naturally radioactive, slowly decaying to become nitrogen once more, while carbon-12 and -13 are stable. They always stay the same. Understood?"

"Yes."

"Fine, now the next bit... During photosynthesis, plants absorb carbon dioxide, make carbohydrates, and store them, but they also release carbon dioxide when they consume carbohydrates during respiration. Now, as everyone knows, herbivores eat plants and carnivores consume herbivores, both incorporating the subsequent carbon they consume into their bodily structures, excreting some carbon as carbon dioxide. Still with me?"

"Of course!"

"So far so good, then. Now, this principle, under normal circumstances, means the amount of carbon, and therefore the ratio of carbon isotopes in living organisms, is constant. Only when an organism dies does the carbon ratio begin to change. As the organism is no longer replacing its carbon, and carbon-14 in its tissues is slowly decaying, the ratio of carbon isotopes must be changing as well. This is what it's about, really. If you determine the carbon isotope ratio in animal or plant remains, comparing it with the decay rate and half-life of carbon-14, you can calculate the age of organic remains. Get it?"

Amazingly, I did, and why any lime mortar contaminating the skeleton might be a problem. As lime mortar sets, sometimes taking hundreds of years, it slowly absorbs carbon dioxide, distorting the true carbon isotope ratio of any organic remains suspended within it, with Frida suitably impressed I figured this out so quickly, following her (admittedly) simplified* explanation.

*Tragically and confusingly simplified.

For dinner, we visited the Old Inn in Winchelsea. Ordering for myself a steak with all the trimmings, while Frida, wide-eyed and happy as a puppy, munched her way through a smoked chicken salad, claiming it the best she'd ever eaten. We drank, of course (although not extensively), and, walking back to our room under a sky twinkling with stars, we tried to pick out those we knew and their associated constellations.

Later the following afternoon, arriving home with Frida, needing a tea and a pee but not in that order, after taking the box with parchment up to my room, I gave my mother strict instructions (with Frida's added diplomacy) not to touch it.

"Alright, dear," replied my mother. "As long as it doesn't make a mess, I'll try to hoover around it."

Making Frida a tea, I joined her on our living room sofa…

Quietly sipping from her steaming mug, she dwelt upon the family photos adorning the walls, and, noticing Millie's two graduation photos, Frida seemed impressed…

"Is that your sister? She's really pretty."

"Yeah," I said. "That's her. Miss Oh-So-Clever-Show-Off. She's got two degrees, you know. 'One for her and one for me', that's what my dad always says."

"That's a bit mean," replied Frida, daintily crossing her legs. "You're every bit as clever."

"Thanks," I thinly smiled. "Thanks for noticing. Wish everyone else would."

"They will," she replied. "Be patient. It does you no good being resentful. We're both still young. Loads of things can happen. Who knows? We could win an award if we keep on making historic discoveries."

"Not likely," I sighed. "With my qualifications… only graduates receive credit."

"Don't be ridiculous," said Frida, scornfully shaking her head. "And it'd better not be envy bringing this shitty mood. An award beckons and, when we win it, your sister will be sick as a dog."

"Come off it," I muttered. "Can't even hold down a job, and any award would posthumously go to my uncle."

"Ugh," she grumbled. "I know you're tired, but I don't see why you need to torture yourself. Cheer up or fuck off to bed."

"Are you working tomorrow?" I asked, shifting the conversation. "I plan on going to the museum first thing. You wanna meet me?"

"Can't," Frida replied. "Working twenty hours straight tomorrow. In fact, I need to go soon and sleep, but you will let me know everything that happens with the parchment, won't you?"

"Sure," I said. "When will I see you? Next week?"

"Wednesday," she replied, standing, and stretching. "In the afternoon. If that's ok? Your day off, isn't it?"

"Yes, usually. What do you want to do? Catch a movie or something?"

"Yeah," she said, "sounds good," before taking her mug to the kitchen.

Briefly saying goodbye to my mum, Frida wished me good night, waving as she drove into the gathering twilight.

The following morning, shivering upon the steps of the British Museum, I was first in line waiting for it to open. Carrying the precious box with its mysterious contents straight to reception, I asked what I should do. Dr Corbiere, the receptionist explained, was busy with the Treasure Panel (whatever that was) and unavailable until midday, so she took the box to a secure location for his collection.

Easy-peasy, my task done, and I sent a text to Dr Corbiere telling of the box's delivery, and another to Frida saying the same, wishing her good morning, hoping she was having an easy time at work.

For the rest of the day, I worked myself. Not for twenty hours like Frida, but a smelly, greasy, six hour-long slog, clogging the colons of desperate diners.

Dr Corbiere's reply arrived that very evening. Almost biblical in length, it explained how, after taking the parchment to UCL, * it had undergone "X-ray fluorescence imaging", and how he would receive the raw data Tuesday morning.

*University College London

If the results were easily discernible, he would email a copy for my own study immediately. If they were unclear, requiring processing and professional interpretation, there would be a necessary delay before sending them. He wished Frida and I well and hoped to see us soon.

Therefore, that was that. There was nothing to do but wait.

Frida called from work during a meal break, and I told her the news…

"Wow!" she exclaimed. "He got straight onto it, didn't he?"

"Yeah, he must've arranged the whole thing in advance."

"Of course," she said. "He's a professional. Let me know when you get the results, but be warned, if you look at them without me, I'll never speak to you, like, ever again."

"Thought about that when reading his text, and you needn't worry – sure

I can resist for a day or two, and, if we're exceedingly lucky, I might have them when you come over on Wednesday."

"Oh, my God," she replied, "Really? That would be awesome."

"Depends if it's readable."

"I don't care," she said. "Just want to see it!"

"I do too, but we just have to wait. How are you doing, anyhow? Nearly finished? How can you work for so long without dying?"

"Oh, you get used to it," she replied. "These long sessions don't come up all that often. It's one of those 'once we start, we have to finish'-type situations."

"Right. Just what *are* you doing, anyway?"

"Sorry, love," she cagily replied. "Can't tell. But it involves cells, tiny machines, and computers. In fact, what we're doing has given me a couple of ideas for my PhD."

"PhD? You mentioned this in Winchelsea. I thought you were joking. Does this mean you'll be Dr Halfpenny?"

"Ape-knee!" she typically corrected. "But, yes, in a year or two. If things go well."

"Ok, tell me when we've more time."

"Sure. Might take a while to explain though."

"I don't care," I said, pushing the phone into my ear (as if to be near her). "I look forward to hearing it all."

"Bless you," she whispered. "But now I must go. Only a few hours left. See you on Wednesday. About three or four."

"Yes," I said. "Can't wait. Good night."

"Neither can I, and no peeking, right?"

"No," I replied, meaning it. "No peeking. I promise."

"Good," she whispered. "Night-night."

⧗

The results were in. An email with an attachment of considerable size, and Frida, gripping my shoulder, struggled to contain her anticipation…

"What does he say?" she asked. "Was the scanning successful?"

"Yes," I replied. "Doesn't say much, though. Only how the results were unrevealing, and that he showed them to archivists, historians, even a professor of witchcraft! Wonder why he spoke to someone like that?"

"Because they were weird? Just download the pictures and show me!"

"Very well," I said. "But the attachment's a monster. It will take some time to download and open."

"Just do it!" she said. "I'll wet myself if you take any longer."

"Please don't," I replied, looking concerned. "Ok, here goes…"

Images appeared and we gasped. There was writing, and we could read it!

The first image was an unprocessed scan of the parchment, still crumpled and folded within the cob. Four lines of faint text were apparent, all of them overlapping, twisted, and impossible to read. In the second image, a post-processing technique highlighted each phrase in four contrasting colours, whereas in the third image, after further processing, untangling the lines of text, they could be read naturally from left to right…

In green, the first phrase said, *uetkbe*, whereas the next, rendered in blue, said, *Ossa mea et anima mea*, which I later found out meant "My bones and my soul" or "Behold my bones and know my mind". The third scrap of writing, in red and partially lost due to the blue phrase above, simply said, *Memores*, which is Latin for "remember", but it was the last line of that held us the longest. A string of letters and commas, we quickly copied it down to consider its meaning. In pale purple, it read as follows (recalling it fully here as I stored it in my phone)…

ldb, eldl, ald(hl), dldh, dldl, cldh, lld(hl), dldh, l

And that was all.

Stepping backwards, Frida slumped onto my bed…

"Trying to take it all in," she said, covering her face with her hands.

"Yeah." I chuckled. "Makes me feel dizzy, but the two Latin bits I sort of get. They're just, 'Here I am, look what happened, remember me' sort of stuff."

"Hmm…" she mumbled, still covering her face. "And just what I would've expected, but what the fuck is the other stuff? uet… what was it?"

"Err… k-b-e?"

"Yeah, k-b-e, could you search on the web and see if anything comes up?"

"Sure, give us a tick…"

Typing the phrase, I pressed enter.

Sitting up, Frida looked over my shoulder.

"Nope." I shrugged. "There's nothing of note. Just Chewbiflix stuff, all irrelevant."

"Right. How about the other one? Ever seen anything like it?"

"Which one? The long one in purple?"

She nodded.

"No, never. It's meaningless. You think it might be a code?"

"Possibly," she muttered, twiddling her hair. "Not a substitution code though, the structure's all wrong. It wouldn't work."

"Another search?"

"Might as well, but it's garbage, isn't it?"

"It certainly looks like it."

"God!" she groaned, flopping onto the bed. "I'm really depressed. I was hoping for so much more."

Slowly typing the characters into the search engine, I again pressed enter.

"What've you got?" she asked, this time not even looking.

"Nothing," I replied. "Just Chinese characters. Meaningless rubbish, broken links, transcripts from space probes or something. Yeah, here it is. 'Mars Global Surveyor'. Perhaps he's an alien from Mars? That really would be something!"

"Don't be a knob. It's just the search engine having a barney trying to look up... Arghh! I don't believe it. Corbiere's right. It's bollocks."

"Oh, come on," I said, feeling untroubled. "What did you expect, the philosopher's stone? It's amazing there's anything at all. Let's go downstairs for a drink."

"Oh, alright. Any gin?"

"Of course," I replied with a smile. "Tonic, limes, lemons, enough gin to sink a battleship."

"Then" – she chuckled – "full steam ahead."

THIRTEEN

THE APPLE

Freedom is much on my mind. Not the freedom from captivity I long for, but the freedom of choice.

As I write these few lines, an embellishment to the account I recently finished, I await the outcome of its examination. Mirra claims this will be a formality, my release coming soon after, but that was ages ago, and I wish she'd return with some news. So, yes, freedom *is* much on my mind. I long for liberty. The freedom to choose. Yes, liberty. She is a privilege, and she is precious. I know this. I bought her. The incidents that follow were my currency. And liberty? Well, she did prove expensive. She cost me my life...

Mirra returned while I was watching an episode of *Star Trek: The Next Generation* (Frank would be so proud). A particularly poignant episode portraying the desperate plight of Captain Picard. Captured on a dangerous mission, he is subjected to ruthless interrogation and torture, and I had just reached the bit where he dangles naked and forlorn from an angular metal contraption attached to the ceiling.

"Are you quite comfortable?" asked Mirra, referring to my state of undress.

After removing my trousers, socks, and top, I lay sprawled upon the bed. My clothes in a heap on the floor.

"Very," I said, rolling on to my back, "and almost enjoying myself. Couldn't you come back tomorrow?"

"No," she replied. "Absolutely not, and stop being slovenly. If Moloch finds you like this, he'll be incensed."

"I've decided I don't care. What can he do, give me a stern talking-to? Besides, when he last spoke, I was asleep. A dream can't hurt me."

"No, Marcus," she warned, "don't! Don't even say such things. You're playing with fire. We need to go through your latest essay. You can continue your funny programme when we are done."

Sighing, I cursed under my breath.

"You're not letting up until I agree, are you?"

"No," she replied. "And that's the first intelligent conclusion you've reached. So, sit up and pay me attention."

"Yes, Mother," I said, retrieving my phone.

Mirra was less than impressed by my writing. Hitting back with her own brand of sarcasm, she accused me of "however-a-philia" and contracting "that-a-lite-us", insisting I removed these overused words, groaning in disgust at their every occurrence.

"Marcus!" she scolded. "I am appalled. Your lazy lack of attentiveness is most distressing. If you're not careful, you'll receive another visit from Moloch. Then you'll discover just how real he can be!"

"Humph." I snorted. "What's real, what's not? Who knows. Who even cares?"

Now, this crabby comeback I never intended a serious question, although Mirra went on to furnish me with an answer...

"The determination of one's reality is the foundation of freedom."

"I'm sorry," I replied, taken aback. "What did you say?"

"You questioned the definition of reality, did you not?"

"Did I?" I pondered. "Because I'm not so sure that I did, and, if I did, I don't know what you're talking about!"

"I never expected you to, but, since you did, I told."

"Mirra." I laughed, wiping an eye. "Of all the people I've ever met, you really are the most incredible, but couldn't you explain your point of view?"

"Very well." She sighed. "Try this on for size. Reality, our perceived reality, is no more than our brain's intrinsic interpretation of sensory stimulation. A true understanding of reality is beyond our physical reach. For us humans, only our imagination can free us from our physical limitations. Beyond our senses, science begins to break down – results are unobtainable. The universe only exists because we observe it, and, like the passing of time, only the observable can be confirmed."

"Have you been smoking?" I replied. "Although, I do sort of get what you're saying. The way things appear is because of our brains. Didn't a philosopher once say, we are creatures of energy and light. Our material self is a vessel?"

"No," she tutted. "Unless, by philosopher, you mean little green puppet?"

"Oh," I said. "Was it him?"

"Yes," said Mirra. "A misquote. From one of the films you watched."

Editing the last section was torture. Mirra made me remove so much waffle that I felt crushed by the end. Worst of all was her hard-hearted insistence I begin the next section immediately. Something I had no intention of doing. Having in mind a concise approach, I would rather be damned than start it anon, and yet, as you are about to find out, damned I most assuredly was…

"You could at least let me watch TV," I half joked, half pleaded. "I'm halfway through an episode!"

"It can wait," she snapped. "Progress is what we need. Please, Marcus, this is important. Your productivity is slipping, and he is aware of it."

"Bully for him," I replied, cutting her off. "I'm having a holiday. So, sod off and leave me be. When I've finished the next bit, I'll call you."

"Marcus!" she begged, almost in tears. "Please. I beseech you, no!"

Mirra by now was desperate and terrified, but I was too stubborn to care, until I suddenly heard a lost little girl, fearfully squealing, shrieking in panic. Mirra exposed. Caught by a ray of the sun…

"No, no!" she screamed. "Don't hurt him. We need him. *Nein!*" and somehow the sound of her faded. Becoming thinner, weaker, smaller. An irrelevance. Just a feather caught in a storm.

Darkness fell. Heavily, like a curtain of lead, and I sat up squinting, wondering, what next?

As if out of nowhere, a powerful assailant flung me from the bed, and, after staggering to my feet, he came at me again, pulling me upright, wrenching my arms over my head. Cruel manacles clanged shut about my wrists, cutting and biting, lifting me, higher and higher, until my toes were barely brushing the floor. Pain, racking my arms and hands, tore the breath from my lungs, and, frightened, reeling and trembling, I squinted at the shroud of impenetrable black.

Time passed. Slowly, languidly, as if taunting, until, like an Arctic dawn, creeping slowly, came the pulsating light I had witnessed before. The ribbons of golden yellow, the threads of purple, and the green, bursting with verdant life. With the light, I could now see my prison had gone, for I hung alone in an oppressive grey chamber. Before me an inquisitor's desk…

No, I thought. How could this be? Horror gripping me like the fire in my arms, I knew this terrible place! The interrogation chamber from *Star Trek*, and I was now Captain Picard, dangling from the same metal contraption. My crushed purple hands, and taut pale arms, streaked with trickling blood.

Like an earthquake, a thunderous voice. Instantly recognisable. Billowing dust, splinters of masonry falling and skipping with his every word. No Cardassian tormentor but Moloch. His timbre low. Deafening and rasping. His words, formal, and cutting. Cutting my marrow like a knife…

"Subject. Eaton-Marcus, one-zero-five-four-zero-three. Its indolence, its insolence will not be tolerated."

"I'm sorry," I gasped. "Just wanted to rest. Mirra was nagging… Please, sir, the pain, let me down, I beg you."

"Justifications are irrelevant. A choice is before you. Work as I demand or suffer. Suffer and burn."

"I'm suffering already," I screamed. "I'll do your fucking writing. Let me down. Release me!"

"Insolence," he coldly replied. "The nightmare begins."

With the echo of his words slowing fading, there came a cacophony of sound. An explosion of voices. Jumbled, overlapping, yet whom or what was I hearing? My fellow captives? Mirra once revealed I wasn't alone, but never was I aware of them…

In the beginning, I heard the talkers, the mutterers, the whisperers, together like the rustling of leaves. They spoke of plans within plans, of schemes untried, hopes of rescue and bids for freedom. So many desperate and wild. It was madness upon madness to hear them all, lost and forlorn just as I. Mere fools. Clinging to promises both vain and untested. Did they not know? Their fate wasn't theirs to decide.

Next, and more disturbing, sundering the air, came a thousand cries for mercy. Wailing, sobbing, merging, overlapping, in a dozen tongues at least, but when the screams came, so grievous to heed, I would've stopped my ears if I could. These were screams of terror. The shrieking of minds mercilessly torn. The howling of the deranged. Burnt-out, hollow husks of men, now phantoms of their former selves. Yet, this was as nothing! For when, last of all, I heard the children, my hope flickered and died. These poor wretches were crying. Begging, for mothers, fathers, for crumbs, for any morsel of hope, but they would receive nothing, I knew it now, for I was as one of them. Pitifully flapping. A wind tattered sail, lashed to the scaffold above.

Eventually, the clamour slowly abated, leaving but a single child. A little girl. Weeping, sobbing, gurgling, so pitiful was she that I would've dried her eyes if I could…

"It's alright," I bellowed. "Mirra will come. She'll help."

The little girl coughed, clearing her lungs.

"Mama?" she muttered. "Is dat you, Mama? Mama? I want to go home. Mama?"

Could this little girl hear me? And summoning the strength to call to her again, I took shivering breath, but I was too late. Our tormentor was back…

"Silence!" he seethed, and the little girl burst into such an uncontrollable paroxysm of sobbing that I feared she might choke.

"Hear what you've done?" he said. "Make your choice, and know how others, others dear to you, depend upon your answer. Will you write or burn?"

"I… I…" was all I could utter. Tears of shame my only cogent reply.

Out of nowhere, a blow smashed into my back, and, swinging wildly, coughing, and spitting, I tried to catch my breath. Managing only to gurgle and then dribble a thick red foam, spattering my belly and feet. Another blow came. This time, across the back of my legs, and so desperate to escape was I that I would have torn off my arms if I could.

"Burn," Moloch then thundered, his words a storm of incomprehensible malice.

With the echoes of his rage already fading, the room faded as well. There was no floor, and like a freshly slaughtered pig I dangled, both bloody and beaten. Orange light flooded in, and I witnessed the sun before me. Massive. Like an ocean of fire, and I struggled to turn from the heat of it, yet the heating cruelly increased. Burning. I was burning! Burning, with my blistering and screaming. Screaming for mercy. For my mother, for Mirra, for anything reason could bring. But I burnt then, with the horrifying sight and sickening scent of my purulent flesh. Seething and bubbling. Dripping like a roast.

THE APPLE

✕

As if floating or supported, something was lifting me up.

Opening my eyes and gasping, I did indeed feel as if floating, as if swimming, but not through water. I was moving through light, rolling about me like smoke. This shifting light was Mirra, I was sure of it, and yet I couldn't know what she was, and then Frida was there. Although, I didn't know her at first. She was so very much older, kinder, wiser, but, when she stroked my hair and smiled, I knew her, and her love gladdened my heart.

✕

Waking in my cell, fully dressed, and lying flat on my back, no burns, no bruising, my injuries all gone, I found myself surrounded by carnage. The whole place deliberately trashed…

The desk and chair were but a heap of kindling, and the bed, its coverings torn and shredded, was missing both legs at one end. Shattered too was Barry's glass tank, and a puddle of wet mud carrying his prawn-like corpse was slowly spreading across the carpet…

"Poor Barry," I muttered. "What did he do?"

The entertainment portal appeared intact (thank God), as was the food and water.

Curious priorities.

Tried to sit up… couldn't. Felt so heavy and weak. My head pounding as if beaten by a hammer.

"Mirra," I cried out in fear. "Are you there? Help me!"

The loudspeaker crackled and beeped.

"Yes, Marcus," she replied, her voice almost medicinal. "I'm here. How do you feel?"

"Mirra," I gasped. "Thank God. I thought that I'd lost you."

"Nearly but never," she said. "If you're here, then I must be as well."

"I feel crushed," I declared. "My chest. It's like a huge weight is pinning down."

"That is hardly surprising. You died."

"Died?" I replied. "How? I mean, I'm alive now, aren't I?"

"More or less." She chuckled. "Your heart stopped, so I revived you. Moloch must've given you quite a fright."

Everything I had experienced suddenly flooded back. The screams, the horror, the blood…

"He…" I gasped, fighting to speak, "he… I… it was… was… really…"

"Marcus," she soothed, cutting me short, "please. There's no need to struggle. Be easy for a bit. I neither require nor desire any report of his wickedness."

"You won't be getting one," I blurted. "Can't bear to think of it, Mirra. Not yet. It was, he was, terrible, and so real!"

"It was real," she confirmed. "As real as the universe can be. But now, start living again. Take normal breaths, relax. We can discuss it all later."

Doing as she recommended, the weight pinning my chest started to lift.

"Feel better?" she asked. "Try to sit up. Roll onto your side, use your arms."

"Now, that is better," I said, taking another deep breath. "Shame about the room, though, and poor Barry. Did Moloch do this?"

"Yes," she replied. "Barry's a victim too, and it may be sometime before everything gets fixed. So, once you have recovered, I suggest you tidy as best you can, but I wouldn't try standing just yet."

"Mirra?" I carefully asked. "There's something I need to know, something important, about Moloch. He… he made me. I heard all these awful voices, and some of them were children. Young children. Are children really kept here?"

Mirra went silent for what seemed like an age before answering, and for a moment I thought she had gone, but then I heard her delicate sigh…

"Yes," she bleakly acknowledged. "Ashamed as I am to it admit it, yes. Several hundred. Ages four to eighteen."

"Four?" I implored. "Why? What have they done?"

"Nothing yet," she replied. "Although, given time, they will. Or so he claims."

"How can he do this? It's inhuman!"

"Indeed," she said. "I told you he was a monster. I didn't lie."

"He says you do," I muttered, rubbing my legs and trying to stand.

"Yes," she replied. "You told me, remember?"

"Oh, yes, so I did, and are you a liar?"

"Of course not."

"Very well." I sighed, weary of her manoeuvring. "Whatever."

Snorting half a laugh, I tried once more to stand, before toppling into a heap.

"Just trust me," she said. "You must trust me, blindly. Allow me to be your guide. Have faith."

"Difficult," I replied, flexing my legs. "Faith doesn't come easy. I barely trust myself."

"Indeed," she acknowledged. "And I am wondering. What will you do now? You need rest."

"No," I declared. "That's not what I need. I need to get up, find my phone, and get on with the writing. But where the heck has it got to?"

"Your phone? It's under the bed."

"Ah, right," I said. "Thanks. Didn't know you could see under there. You have a much better view than I realised."

"Yes and no," she revealed. "I can see everywhere else and there's no phone, and it is not in your pocket, as I'm certain you would've remembered. Ergo. It's under the bed."

"Clever clogs," I muttered, half-crawling, half-dragging, squeezing under the bed to retrieve it.

"Mirra," I then said, catching my breath, "you know, I really can't thank you enough. Everything you've done and tried to do. You take care of me with so much, well, love, I suppose."

"That's because I do. Isn't it obvious?"

"Yes," I admitted, "yes, it is, and I love you too." Moreover, I was most surprised to find that I meant it.

⧗

The folder concerning the Winchelsea church reliquary was mercifully thin, and after an hour of patient study I had a broad understanding of its importance…

Built in the late 13th century, upon the site of a much older structure (according to local legend a Saxon bell tower), the church of St Thomas the Martyr, Winchelsea, had within its vault an ancient reliquary – the remains of a local saint, chieftain or priest, their identity long forgotten. The new church founders, looking to raise cash attracting pilgrims, may have seized these relics from the tower before its demolition, installing them within the new church. My uncle learned of said reliquary from a Victorian drawing, showing its box, a collection of bones, and a strange disc-like artefact with a peripheral spot. Subsequent further investigation revealed little of the relic's early history, until he came across a 14th-century missive describing how the invading French had forced the local priesthood to hide the reliquary in a cellar. Another letter (from a local family collection) then went on to describe how, in the 16th century, it became necessary to hide the relics again (in another cellar*). This time, from Thomas Cromwell's Protestant reformers. Never seeing the reliquary for himself, he wished someday to do so, or to obtain photographs, confirming the artefact's existence.

*As a former port, the older buildings of Winchelsea possess extensive subterranean delves.

Arriving in Winchelsea sometime after 11am, Frida parked on the High Street adjacent to the church.

"This place is gorgeous," she remarked, looking left, then right at the splendid old buildings. "And on the way in, the crumbly old gate really sets the theme, doesn't it?"

"Well, yeah," I replied. "It was a part of the town's original wall."

"Cool," she said, removing her seat belt. "The museum's over there, isn't it?"

"Think so." I nodded. "Pretty inspired bit of parking."

"Lucky, you mean. Come on, let's go and see if it's open."

Making our way to the entrance, Frida slipped her arm into mine. Looking about her intently, she wrinkled her forehead in thought...

"This place is a dream," she muttered, "like I've just washed up on an island. An island built on the past... but there's something else. It all seems familiar."

"Well, you got the island bit right," I said. "Winchelsea used to be a port, with only a narrow causeway connecting it to the mainland. All silted up now, of course, but it's why the town is here."

"Well, it's open," remarked Frida. "And a gorgeous old building too. You can go in. I'll meet you by the church in a bit."

"You're not coming? It's only a little place, won't take long."

"No, I'm not," she replied. "My skin's tingling – don't know why, so I'm going to wander about for a bit. Besides, one museum is plenty enough for me. Save my enthusiasm for Rye, ok?"

"Fine," I said. "Just be sure you don't get seduced," and with a smiling wink she scuttled into the churchyard.

Housed in the town's medieval court hall, with exposed beams, timbers, and wall of grey stone, the museum was charming, and, after perusing the exhibits, I headed to the information desk and the elderly gentleman manning it…

"Good morning," I said, brisk and public school, coins clattering into their tin. "Smashing little museum. Could I ask a few questions concerning the church?"

"Of course," he replied. "What would you like to know?"

At first, I spoke of my uncle's interest in the reliquary (not his whole theory, however), the Victorian drawing he found (titled *She Is Me* and signed DP), and how I was completing his work after his death. With the man behind the desk thoroughly intrigued (as I hoped he would be), I then showed him a photograph of the drawing. Just to make sure…

"Is the reliquary still in the church?" I asked. "Would be wonderful to see it. Is such a thing possible?"

"It is," he replied. "Although, I'm not sure if you'll be able to see it today. Do you want me to contact the rector? He's usually in town on a Saturday."

"If you would. My partner and I are on our way to the museum in Rye. Collecting an item for the British Museum, and we're expected there this afternoon."

"Ah," he said. "Not tourists but professionals," and, taking his mobile from his jacket, he promptly called the rector.

We were lucky. The rector agreed to meet us outside the church, and quickly thanking the kind old man, I left the museum, going in search of Frida…

Not knowing where to look, I did a circuit of the churchyard, trying to spot her by looking over its wall. Then, just as I was about to give up, she suddenly appeared, respectfully picking her way across the cemetery.

"You know," she said, offering a bite of a doughnut, "I've decided. We're going to buy a house, here. We're going to settle down, marry, and raise a whole school of Eatons."

"Yeah," I replied, raising an eyebrow. "Ok, I mean, erm… wow. You sure we'll have the money?"

"No doubt about it," she assured. "My research? It's gonna change the world. We'll be loaded."

"Excellent," I said. "Then I can stay home with the kids, helping you spend it."

"You wish." She frowned, crossing her arms. "Not gonna have you loafing about. You can work for me. A nice, cosy position in the… the Ape-knee Institute of, erm…Cellular Augmentation and Hybridisation."

"That a bit of a mouthful," I replied. "Besides, when we're married, your name will be Eaton: the Eaton Institute of Cellular Doo-dah."

"No way!" she laughed. "Why should I take your name?"

"Tradition." I shrugged. "I'm the husband, you're the wife?"

"Cock-snot," she replied with snort. "My name is Ape-knee. Frida Ape-knee. Of the Ape-knee Institute, and that is my final word."

The church of St Thomas the Martyr, half of it an ivy clad ruin, with its low, square tower, tiled roof, and prominent blue clock, was both a fascinating and curious structure, and, while waiting for the rector, we noted the extensive repairs and alterations…

"Old buildings are often like this," I remarked. "So many changes, the original structure can be hard to spot. The ruined bit was either burnt down by the French or never finished in the first place."

It was then I noticed Frida's odd behaviour. For a start, was she even listening? She seemed edgy, as if distracted somehow. Something was clearly the matter…

"Hello, hello!" came a vibrant young voice. "Welcome to St Thomas's."

This cheery greeting from a surprisingly energetic and handsome young man of about thirty. Dressed casually in jeans, a baggy sweater, and the obligatory collar.

"Hello," I replied. "I'm Marcus Eaton and this is my good friend Frida Halfpenny."

"Ape-knee," Frida corrected, and the young rector smiled.

"Pleased to meet you," he politely acknowledged. "I'm Rector Calum, Calum Arbuthnot-Shaw, but since I'm not marrying you or burying you, Calum will do just fine."

"Not today," replied Frida. "But one day, perhaps," and she poked me in the ribs.

"Now," continued the rector, "old Gordon tells me you'd like to look at Adam, our bony old relic?"

"If it's not too much trouble," I said, standing and tugging at Frida's sleeve.

"Well, it's no trouble for me," he replied, judging my height. "Although it may be some trouble for you. The reliquary's down in our crypt and it's so cramped, you'll have to look at him one at a time."

"Oh?" remarked Frida. "Well, don't worry. Marcus can have the pleasure. I'm quite happy here, enjoying the view."

"What?" I said, taken aback. "You're not coming in?"

"No," she said, "I'm not, but I'll tell you what. When you get back, I'll decide if it's worth it."

"Well, ok," I replied. "But there's no need to get shirty," and with that Frida looked away.

Led by the young rector into the church, I did my best to explain…

"Sorry about her," I sighed. "She's from Lewisham and she seems to be having a strop."

"Right," he replied. "Follow me. The stairs are in the vestry."

The church interior was a delight. Richly carved tombs, high and colourful stained-glass windows, possessing a wonderful scent of musty stone, mildew, and – what? Beeswax, incense? Whatever. The place smelled old, and I wished Frida had come along to see it.

To the left of the main altar, a narrow wooden door opened onto a small chamber hung with priestly garments. Set into the floor was a small trapdoor…

"Ok," said the rector, nodding towards it. "We have to go down there. It's a complete swine to open, so can you give me a hand?"

The trapdoor was indeed extremely stiff, and we had to lean and push with our legs to wrench it fully open.

"Phew," said the rector, puffing his cheeks. "Sorry about that. Think I'd better oil the hinges before trying to close it again."

Plunging into total darkness, very worn and crumbling, was a flight of precarious steps…

"Looks a bit gloomy," I remarked, peering down. "Are there any lights?"

"There should be," replied the rector, "but they haven't worked for years. We try to repair them, but the bulbs fizzle out almost immediately. It's a real nuisance."

"Can imagine," I said. "What's causing the problem? Moisture?"

"I guess." He shrugged, wedging the trapdoor with a chair. "Although

Winchelsea's on a high plateau – the crypts never flooded, so it's a bit of a mystery, in truth."

"Granted," I replied, "but how are we going to see? Use my phone?"

"No," he said. "Keep your phone for emergencies. Candles will serve us best. Help me light some, and I'll start taking them down."

Passing a lighter, he held before me a three-candle candelabra,* which I promptly lit, and then, careful not to disturb the dancing flames before him, the rector slowly descended into the crypt.

*a candelabrum

"There's a box of candles under the vestments," he called from below. "Bring some down and mind your head!"

Cramped, cold, and musty, with walls of rough-cut stones, by the flickering candlelight the crypt was full of antediluvian wonder. The flagstone floor was similar, pitted and uneven, but at its centre was a dullish pink slab, both highly polished and glittering. Dug into the back wall were three niches, the middle example occupied by a modern-looking safe…

"Is the big slab a tomb?" I asked, kneeling to study it more closely. "Strange it has no inscription."

"Yes and no," the rector replied. "It's the holy of holies and the heart of the church. Directly beneath the main altar, when a church is consecrated, it is often the first stone laid. This one is special, I gather. According to local legend, it was a gift from the King."

"Right," I muttered, caressing its surface. "Looks like granite. Not from around here, then?"

"No," said the rector, stooping before the safe, and I heard clunking-click of buttons and the squeaking of hinges as he opened it up. "Installing this wretched thing was the bishop's idea. He's paranoid about security. Probably go bonkers if he knew you were down here. But come, look well, and tell me your thoughts."

At first, it was difficult to "look well" at all, but with my eyes adjusting to the gloom, I saw a dilapidated wooden box with two rickety doors. Its every surface decorated with religious art…

"Looks a bit flimsy," I remarked. "Is it possible to open the doors?"

"With care," he replied. "Although, we could still do with more light. How about using your phone?"

"Ok," I said, and I tapped my phone, activating the flashlight.

With my phone over his head, its camera flash projecting an arc of blueish light, I watched as he gently lifted the catch and opened doors.

"There," he whispered, stepping back. "Kneel down and look, but no touching. Remember this is a sacred relic and terribly fragile."

Bones. Pieces of bone lying upon a scrap of coarse fabric. Splinters of leg bone, pelvis, shoulder blade, rib, and the lower half of a skull, and yet my attention was most drawn to a notched disc at the back…

"Wow," I said. "So old. What's that strange disc? Looks like terracotta."

"Nobody knows," he admitted. "Rumour has it, it represents the apple picked by Eve and then passed to Adam. I'm sure you know the story. God gave them a choice, to pick the forbidden fruit or not, and Eve, giving into temptation, picked and ate the fruit before sharing it with Adam. As a result, God expelled them from paradise. The little notch either represents Adam or Eve's bite mark or a hole left by the serpent, Satan, worming within. The green substance filling the notch is bronze. Originally, it would've been brown."

"Oh, right," I replied, "so that's why you call him Adam. How old do you think it all is?"

"Can't be sure." He shrugged. "But I'm told the bones predate Winchelsea. My guess would be they're Anglo-Saxon."

This seemed entirely plausible. If the bones had been medieval, I would have expected them to be in better condition. These were white, beginning to crumble, and could well have been even older.

"Did anyone ever try dating the bones or remove them for examination?"

"No," he replied, "and quite inappropriate to do so. A doctor once saw them, however, and he said how incredibly tall the saint must have been. A giant, or a sufferer of – what did he call it? Pituitary gigantism?"

"Amazing," I remarked. "Is it ok to take a photo?"

"What?" he said, flushing with seriousness. "I'm sorry but no. You can take photographs inside the church, but down here definitely not, and now, if you don't mind, I have duties to perform."

"Of course," I acknowledged, realising a line had been crossed. "Thank you ever so much for letting me see all this. An experience I shall never forget."

Standing by as he closed the box and safe, we methodically extinguished and collected every candle before returning to the vestry. We left the church together, but, before going our separate ways, we shook hands, and I warmly thanked him again.

"Thank you so much." I smiled. "We'll be back one day, I'm certain. When we do, we'll look you up."

"You mean join the congregation?"

"Something like that," I replied, and he laughed.

"Go with God and all joy to you both," he said, crossing the air before me.

Bored with waiting, Frida had wandered off, but I eventually found her standing outside the pub.

"All done, then?" she asked.

"Yes, and interesting it was too. So old, ancient, and the bones belonged to a giant. You want to go in for a look? The rector's gone, but we can still go into the church."

"No," she muttered. "It's ok, and anyway, why should we interfere? It's nothing to do with us."

"Course it's to do with us," I replied. "Why do you think we are here? Did I do something wrong, are you in a mood or something?"

"Yeah," she admitted, "I am feeling moody, but not because of you. It's wandering about this beautiful place that's done it. It's made me desperate, desperate to leave London, to change my life, and that makes me sad. Sad about leaving my mum."

"Oh," I replied. "Can understand that, except, well, I'd love to leave my mum. She's nuts."

"Come on, you." She chuckled, letting go of her tension. "Let's get to the car, before I start looking at houses."

"Of course," I replied. "But life is a constant battle, isn't it?"

"Against what?" she pondered.

"Temptation," I replied with a shrug. "Temptation, and the freedom of choice."

FOURTEEN

JORVIK

Waiting again. Not heard a peep from Mirra, and, even though she said reviewing my work would take time, I didn't expect it to take this long, and I have watched several films, a ton of *Star Trek*, before listening to so much Beethoven I'm almost as deaf as he was. Now, as you can plainly read, I have gone back to writing. Getting down the thoughts pricking my mind, and reviewing my previous piece, my attempt to recount the events that led to my torture, I realise how misleading I was. Did I seem brave, strong, heroic? Utter nonsense. I was pathetic. Desperate, and scared out of my wits. In no way could I endure it. Courage was irrelevant. Yes, I complained. Tried reasoning with my tormentor, but it was futile. My words meant nothing to him. I was an irrelevance. Akin to an ant biting the tongue of an aardvark. So, you may wonder, am I being too hard on myself? What of my sympathy towards the sad little girl? There I showed courage, goodness, kindness, surely? No. I'm sorry, but no! Not kind, selfish. Offering a balm, I didn't possess, if only to stop her bawling...

Oh, my love. Please judge me with pity, for I am dying of shame. I'm not brave, I'm a coward. A weakling, a brat, pathetic! When it came to it, when the crucible of my life became decisively threatened, I cared only for its sickening contents, and despite all that I am, and all that I struggle so hard to be, if you burn my humanity and strip me of reason, I am but a cowering beast.

It was hours before I could stand again, and walking took even longer. My balance was the issue. Standing was a doddle, but walking, well, I just couldn't do it. I had to relearn the process systematically (as if reprogramming) and, when moving off, I would totter and stumble, steadying myself, holding onto the broken furniture. This was particularly galling as I wanted to tidy (as best I could) the wreckage Moloch had left after his (for want of a better word) tantrum.

I think "tantrum" an excellent word.

Stacking the broken parts of desk and chair against the wall, I considered how to deal with mess left behind after the breaking of Barry's tank. Scooping handfuls of the dark smelly mud and flushing them down the toilet was straightforward enough, but what to do with his corpse? Should I flush him as well? He was easily small enough to fit through the pipe. It just seemed disrespectful, but the thought of him slowly decaying in here was horrific, so flushed he eventually was. Closing my eyes in shame as I did it. Another headache was the broken bed. With its legs broken off at one end it was unusable, leaving me three alternatives: repair it, detach the remaining legs (and level it), or remove the mattress and bedding (and sleep on the floor). The resolution chose itself. The bed proved both irreparable and inseparable, so I stripped off what bedding I could.

⌛

Coming by sometime later, Mirra was in a playful mood...

"Oh, my dear Marcus!" She giggled. "You're slumming it, aren't you? You look like a poor vagrant down there. Shall I wave my wand and return the place to its former glory? Will only take an instant. Well, as far as you're concerned."

"Could you?" I asked, brightening. "I'm not bothered about the desk, but if you can somehow fix the bed, I'd be grateful. It's a bit hard on the bum down here. I'm really missing the mattress."

"I shall restore the entire suite," she declared. "Can't have you getting a numb bum, now, can we? Besides, you'll write better not living in squalor."

"That'd be fantastic," I replied. "And when you do, am I going to meet the mysterious Mirra?"

"No." She chuckled. "Afraid not. I'm going to put you to sleep."

"How?" I asked, slightly concerned. "With a gas?"

"Gas?" she puzzled. "How do you mean?"

"You know," I said, "breathing in gas. A tranquilliser or an anaesthetic."

"Ah," she acknowledged. "I understand. Gas. Yes, that sounds like fun. What flavour would you like?"

"Flavour? What do you mean?"

"Well," she replied, "if you are to be inhaling a nasty gas, it might as well taste nice."

"A sugar coating? How very thoughtful."

"Yes," she said. "I thought so. Well?"

"Difficult to choose, and not a choice I ever expected to make. But since you ask, how about strawberry?"

"Fine," she replied. "Strawberry it will be. I would have chosen peach. Now, lie down or fall down. The choice is yours."

Lying on the floor, I watched pink clouds billowing from the vents in the ceiling. The fumes flooding my lungs, filling my senses with the heady aroma of strawberries. Ripe, rich, and pungent.

⧗

The following passages describe our efforts concerning the Camber Viking burial.

Lying prone upon my bed, the contents of said folder before her, Frida frowned at the spidery writing…

"A bit thin this one," she said. "A few pages of scrawl and a photo. Looks good, though. Have a look while I ponder."

Almost A4 in size, black and white, and remarkably detailed, the photograph was of a fully excavated burial. Still in situ, both the skeleton and grave goods could clearly be seen.

"So?" I remarked, turning the photo over. "Any clues in the text?"

"Well," she cagily replied. "It all seems pretty straightforward. A Viking burial on the Sussex coast. Excavated in the mid-1980s, it was only special because its location. Drainage work uncovered a stone coffin on land that was once a coastal spit – the Lydd Limb. Land reclaimed from the surrounding marshes. Nowadays, the area is known as Camber, including coastal resort of Camber Sands."

"Ok," I said, searching the words "Lydd Limb" online. "Beginning to get interested. Interest me more."

"It does get better. He then goes on to say the coffin was in fact an assemblage of large, flat stones. Of the sort used for roofing, surprising the archaeologists, allowing them to infer the burial may have been ad hoc or rushed in some way. Another weirdness was the preservation of the body. The way it was packed in lime and pulverised chalk surprised the archaeologists, and they struggled to understand its significance."

"What sort of significance, and why was the body packed in lime?"

"Well," she explained, running her finger down the page, "there's a lot about Viking burials and mythology. Valhalla, Folkvanger, Hell, and what was it? Oh, yeah, Helgafyell, with more about cremations, the way they buried him and his status. It says the lime was to preserve the skeleton. An unknown practice for Vikings, especially pre-Christian ones. If the deceased were of high status and important, cremation would have been the usual method of disposal. The column of smoke from the funeral pyre signifying the elevation of the soul to the afterlife."

"Right." I nodded, typing "Viking cremation" and pressing enter. "How did they know the Viking was pre-Christian? Did they do the carbon date thing?"

"No," replied Frida. "No carbon dating at this stage. It was the coffin's orientation. If aligned east–west, towards Jerusalem, say, then it's likely the burial was Christian. But in this case, it wasn't."

"Where did that leave them then?"

"With nothing. Only speculation. The Viking in the grave was special. Certainly, higher status than a thrall. Fully armoured, with his weapons, shield, and clasping that weird figurine across his breast. You can see all that in the photo, right?"

"Yeah," I said. "Go on."

"So, perhaps, this Viking had unique burial requirements and he was able to plan his own interment."

"He would've been important either way, then. Are there no clues as to whom this Viking could be?"

"No. Only that he dates from around the time of the Viking–Saxon wars. Do you know when that was?"

"Vaguely," I replied. "Give us a tick and I'll check… Here we go. King Alfred the Great, Ethelred, the 9th century ad. Is there anything about the figurine?"

"Not much. At the burial site, they classed it as 'grave goods', but there's a bit more in the next section, where it goes on about conservation and examination. Stop hogging the photo and give it to me."

"Sure." I shrugged, handing it over. "What do you think? One hell of a dude, wasn't he?"

"Massive," she said. "Look at size of his arm bones! And look at his ring mail. That cut, straight across his abdomen. That would have killed him, surely."

"You think? I'm mostly looking at the figurine, to decide if it were a hoax, but it's so clogged up with lime and gunk, I can't see how it could be."

"Yeah," she said, rolling onto one side. "I agree. Corbiere's claim they put it there is looking less likely. The skeleton's hand is over it! How could they have placed the figurine without disturbing everything? All those little bones, the phalanges? They'd be all over the shop."

"Yeah. What does the second page say?"

"It covers the lifting of the skeleton, the associated items, and the removal of the stone coffin itself."

"The word is cist," I said.

"Is it?" she replied. "Cool. Anyway, after cleaning, they examined the skeleton and found damage to his rib cage. Made by a cutting weapon, an axe or sword, but nothing else significant. He was large, powerfully built, exceedingly healthy, and in his thirties or forties. It says, to survive, to reach full maturity in such a violent society, he must've been an amazing warrior."

"Right, unless he was of royal blood and consequently protected. Is there anything else about the figurine?"

"A little. They sent samples of its terracotta and pigment for analysis. The isotopic and chemical tests confirmed it to be either Central American or upper South American. They believed it to be a special totem of some sort. A rare or unique item of great symbolic importance."

"Ah," I said, nodding in approval. "Corbiere should read this. It might change his mind. You know, about the figurine. Its origin and movement."

"Well, you could try," she replied. "But it's doubtful he'll change his opinion. You need irrefutable proof, and we have only speculation."

"Yeah," I said. "But didn't you just say the chemical stuff was definitely South American, and you can see the figurine wasn't planted from the photo."

"You'd make so much of one photo?" she challenged. "Really Marcus, slow down a bit. Where are the other photos? Where are the witnesses? No, I'm sorry, there's not enough evidence."

"Then I shall find more!"

"And I'll help you," she replied. "Although, I think your uncle would have found it."

"True," I said. "But I'm still going to ask Corbiere, and then get that hairy librarian to have a look as well."

"Hey!" cried Frida. "Don't be horrible about Norma. Although, the library sounds like a good place to start. What will you do if there's nothing to find?"

"Then I shall go to York and have a look for myself. I'm sure old Corby could arrange it. In fact, he said he could."

"Jolly nice of him," said Frida, "How are you gonna get there?"

"Well," I thoughtfully said. "I was hoping – you're not offering to drive me?"

"God no," she replied. "Haven't the time or the energy, and old Doris would probably explode."

Reading my disappointment, Frida climbed into my lap, my desk chair creaking in protest as she wriggled about.

"I'll get the train, then," I sullenly muttered. "You are coming, though?"

"Hmm," she mumbled. "A long way just to look at some bones, and the weather'll be shit. Dark, cold, and they rush their vowels."

"Racist," I scoffed, and she giggled, draping an arm over my shoulder.

"Oh, please come," I begged, nuzzling her neck. "I'll get us a nice hotel."

"Ah," she replied. "Well, that is tempting, but no, the answer's still no."

"We could play limericks again. Might even let you win."

"We can do that by text," she said, her fingers combing my hair, and I moved to kiss her slender white neck…

Cut!

⧗

Still on my back, staring up at the ceiling when I woke. Then, sitting up, I could only blink in disbelief. The room was perfect again, and joy of joy – Barry, he was back!

"Hey, Barry," I said, stooping and peering into his watery world. "Thought you were dead. How's the mud this morning? Slimy enough?"

He made no reply. The only sound was Mirra…

"Marcus," she called. "You're awake. How are you feeling?"

"Oh, hello, Mirra," I replied. "I'm fine. Not even groggy, and thanks for fixing everything. The place is as good as new."

"You're welcome, my friend, but it was with Moloch's permission. Without his approval, I can't do a thing, and he sincerely hopes you learnt a lesson."

With a sudden flinch, my cheerfulness drained. The memory of my torment returning like an odious tide…

"Yes," I replied, "I did learn a lesson. To do as I'm told. Was there something I missed?"

"Certainly," she replied. "For one, never pretend you have a choice. Free will is an illusion."

"How do you mean? There are always alternatives, surely. Please explain."

"You wish for another lecture?" she replied. "For you, the unequivocal is just another question!"

"Always," I said. "Can't apologise for it. Taught from an early age a non-enquiring mind is a dead one. So, don't be dead in the head, seek knowledge, and live!"

"Excellent." She chuckled in reply. "A sound philosophy, but not always applicable, and from whom did you learn this, I wonder. Your uncle, perchance?"

"Don't think so, Mirra. It was probably my dad. Anyway, you were about to lecture about choices?"

"Very well," she replied. "Listen. Life is a path we must follow, and its outcome is inescapable. Let me begin with a bleak but obvious example. We are born to die. Other examples also come to mind. Denial of family, of love, and of evil, even to resist natural urges, eating, drinking, sleeping, breathing. For you, here and now, you have no choice. You are not free. You must write as we demand, and quickly. If you linger, insanity and death will find you, that I guarantee, so keep going, my friend. Keep going until you can go on no more. Frida is waiting, and remember, freedom burns the free."

"Certainly." I graciously nodded. "I will, and thank you for the lesson, Professor. Although, sometimes, given the way you school me, Guru would be a better title."

"Perfectly happy with either." She chuckled. "Guardian also seems to fit."

"Oh, and Mirra," I then asked. "In the tank, is that Barry mark two?"

"No," she replied. "It's the same organism. We found the unfortunate thing swimming in the waste reclamation tank. What did you do?"

"Flushed him. I thought he was dead."

"Not dead." She chuckled. "Why did you think him dead? He was just dormant. Can't respire out of water, can't move either. Mind you, it certainly amused Moloch: 'the gift of my lichid not so well received!' He laughed on hearing the news."

"Well, that's something, I suppose, making him laugh."

"Indeed," replied Mirra. "Doubtless why he permitted me to repair your room, but now, are you ready for an editing session? Alternatively, if you want to rest, watch a movie or something? I could come back later."

"No," I said, "I'm fine. Let's get cracking. My lesson is learnt."

⧗

The following evening, calling Dr Corbiere, I apologised for burdening his home life with work. He was gracious, however, listening to my requests with an almost paternal indulgence…

"So," he remarked, "you've decided to visit the Jorvik Centre? I'm glad. Is Frida going with you?"

"No," I replied, "unfortunately not, and I'm going to miss her insight, but I shall take photos and request copies of any relevant documents."

"Good thinking, and with friends amongst the centre's management, I should be able to arrange a pass, entitling you to a close-up examination of both the skeleton and associated its goods."

"Ah, great," I acknowledged. "I was hoping for something like that. Not particularly interested in rusty swords though, just want to see the figurine."

"Well, regarding the figurine, you're in luck. Because of its dubious association, it was separated from the skeleton and moved to general storage. You should be able to see it."

"Excellent," I replied. "Yet I have one more favour to beg. The Camber Viking dig? Is there any further information in the British Library? Could Dr Sticelbak have a look, if she has time?"

"Good idea. You're thinking like a historian. No trouble at all. Let me contact Norma and see if she can dig anything up. Although, I wouldn't be surprised if Frida hasn't asked her already. They've become rather good friends on Fizzog."

"Well." I chuckled. "Frida does have a way with people. Thanks again for your help, though. Without your input, our research would've been impossible."

"Oh, I don't know, you're both very canny. You would have got there, with or without me."

"Thanks," I said. "Thanks for the compliment, but we were destined to meet anyway. No funeral, no folders. Will you let me know soon about the arrangements you've made? The earlier I can book my tickets, the cheaper it'll be."

"Of course, don't worry. I'll get Steph on it first thing in the morning."

"That's very helpful," I replied. "Do have a pleasant evening, and I hope to hear from you soon."

"You will," he said. "Good night, Marcus," before vigorously hanging up.

The following weekend, full of plans for travelling to York, what to see, what to do, I visited Frida, hoping my enthusiasm would be contagious. Upon this visit, she allowed me into her bedroom. A cosy space dominated by clothing, make-up, paperwork, and mirrors – to see herself from every angle when dressing…

"Got burnt in the past," she revealed. "Rushing to get ready. Left the house with laddered tights and skirt tucked in me knickers."

Watching us intently from the top of her wardrobe was Peter the parrot, and I asked if he always had free rein of the house.

"Not exactly," said Frida. "But he loves company. Perching on shoulders, carried from place to place. An inquisitive bird all round."

"Aren't you worried he'll crap everywhere?"

"Well, it does happen sometimes, but he's actually pretty good. The digestive system of birds operates by a simple premise. If you put food in, shit comes out. So, if you don't feed or alarm him, he's usually fine, and he knows it's naughty. Don't you, Petey-bird?"

Croaking, Peter the parrot fluttered down to perch on the back of her chair. Swaying from side to side he watched her with suspicion.

"Go on," she dared. "Reach towards him. See if he wants to join you."

"Are you sure? He didn't like me last time we met."

"Nonsense." Frida smiled. "He was just dozy. Doesn't bear grudges. So, come on, don't be a wuss."

"Fy-toe-jenny-sis!"

"Fy-toe-what?" I remarked. "What did he squawk?"

"Phytogenesis," Frida explained. "A biological term concerning the evolution of plants."

"Oh, right." I chuckled. "Thought it sounded weird. Something to do with your work?"

"Yeah," she lamented. "When revising for my finals, I used to make recordings of definitions, glossaries and stuff. Playing them back, testing myself. Peter, of course, overheard everything, and with the repetition, he learnt almost as much as I did."

"Bollocks," he croaked.

"No, it's true," she replied, stroking his back. "He still knows several sciencey words and likes to mix them with profanity."

As I laughed, Peter picked up the mood, muttering, "Low-bay-shun," and, "Oh, fuckety fuck."

"That *is* you," I said, and, finding new courage, I extended my arm towards him.

At first, Peter didn't react to my offer of a new perch. He merely tilted his head studying my hand, his tongue shifting thoughtfully inside his beak.

"Are you coming or not?" and, after an ear-scorching whistle, he calmly hopped onto my fist.

"Firmogenin."

To my surprise, he was remarkably light. His clawed feet gripping my skin with an unexpected sensitivity (I imagined him clawing my skin to ribbons).

"Ah," said Frida, smiling in approval. "There you go. Now, bring your hand closer. If you're lucky, he'll hop up onto your shoulder."

Retracting my arm, Peter behaved just as Frida predicted. After a few hops up my sleeve, he was in place.

"Wanker," he croaked.

Flapping his wings, he ruffled my wiry hair.

"So," said Frida, stroking his feathers, "has Corbiere made any arrangements?"

"Yeah. I'm going next Wednesday."

"But Wednesday's our date night!"

"I know, love, and I'm sorry, but it's also my day off. Too expensive during the weekend. Come with me."

"Can't," she replied. "Already told you. I'm meeting my PhD supervisor next week to plan my dissertation. I'm only free evenings or weekends."

"But I love you!"

"And I love you too." Frida chuckled. "And, although, a good card to play, my mind is made up."

"You-chrome-attic!" squawked the parrot, and, after hopping from foot to foot, he tugged my hair with his beak.

"Ow! Stupid bird. Is this normal?"

"Very," said Frida, taking him from me. "Attention-seeking verging on the psychotic. Here's how we calm him down."

Slowly and deliberately, laying the old bird in her lap, she gently tickled his tummy, rendering him so docile, I thought him asleep: wings floppy, eyes closed, beak half open. An exemplification of avian bliss…

"There we are," muttered Frida. "Soppy old bird."

"Amazing," I remarked. "Would work on me too, I think."

"Would it?" replied Frida. "How about Wednesday… anyway, what else did he say?"

"Not much. Said he'd get me a backstage pass and I asked if Dr Hairy could have a look in the library."

"Yeah," said Frida, "I know. She told me a couple of days ago. Said there was nothing."

"Hmm." I frowned. "That's a bit odd. According to the internet, it was as quite an important dig. I wonder what happened to the write-up."

"Yeah," said Frida. "Not to publish is very fishy. Little wonder the figurine is suspect. Tell you what," she added, "if we're gonna chat further, shall we leave this feathered thing and take the dogs for a run? What's the weather like?"

"November," I replied. "Grey, boring, but not raining. At least, not yet."

"Come on, then," she urged, shaking Peter awake. "Shouldn't be muddy. Let's get some fresh air."

⧗

Catching the 9am train from King's Cross, I arrived a few minutes before midday, and after navigating the station, grabbing a sandwich from the first available vendor, I texted Frida before marching outside into a grey and distinctly chilly York to hail myself a taxi.

"Jorvik Centre, please," I said to the driver, and fifteen minutes later, crossing the river Ouse on the way, I disembarked in narrow street adjacent to a church. A short walk followed, and, after queuing, I was through the turnstile, keen to see what was inside.

After ninety minutes, perusing the displays, watching costume-wearing "living exhibits" snapping in and out of character like Jekyll and Hyde, I looked for a member of staff to show them my permissive letter, and pass (Dr Corbiere had emailed these the night before). Unable to find anyone, and worming my way to the front of the queue, I returned to the front desk…

Now, I know, I should have started with this, but after Corbiere's build-up, I was excited to see it all for myself. Were the skeleton and figurine on public display? (They were not).

Getting backstage took time; the staff seemed suspicious. Checking and rechecking my papers, even calling London, and when finally in an examination room, I experienced more wariness: standing-by while an assistant grudgingly unpacked the figurine, I so desperately wanted to see…

"'Ave you really come all the way from London, just to see this ugly old thing?"

"Yes," I replied. "As a matter of fact, I have a copy in my bedroom."

"Yer joshing me?" She chuckled. "Don't it give you nightmares?"

"Of course not," I said. "I think he's funny."

"Well, if you say so," she replied, and, standing the figurine before her, she beckoned me over. "Here you go. Be careful with him."

All was as expected. Although, inwardly, I couldn't help but marvel at the sculptor's craftsmanship and brushwork, before reeling at the incredible odyssey it had miraculously survived. To my relief, its underside was free from graffiti, and I pressed the assistant for her opinion on the figurine's authenticity. Did she think it a part of the original burial?

"There's really no way of knowing," she replied. "We've all been wondering about it. It's such an unbelievable find, but my heart tells me, yes. It's genuine."

Her admission took me aback. Did she understand what she was saying? If truly buried with the Viking, this little figurine must imply his people had somehow been involved with the native Northern, Central, or even South American cultures, and it had travelled thousands of miles by land and sea, only to be buried on the Sussex coast during the 9th century…

"How come?" I asked. "So far, you're the only expert brave enough to say it!"

"Two reasons, Mr Eaton."

"Marcus," I offered.

"Very well," she replied. "First and foremost, I'm not an expert. I'm not qualified, merely expressing belief, and second, the burial itself. To find one on the Sussex coast is so unexpected, anything is possible."

"At last!" I laughed. "My thoughts exactly. A pity the experts can't make the leap of faith we have. Their imaginations only run on evidence."

"And thank goodness for that," she said, "otherwise, we'd still be burning witches and worrying about sky fallin' in. Now, is there anything else you'd like to see? The skeleton perhaps?"

"I've been thinking about that," I replied, "and I've decided not to bother. I wouldn't learn very much. My partner's the bone expert, and she's in London. However, could I see the viewing log for the figurine? If you have such a thing? To see if anyone else has studied it?"

"Of course, no trouble at all. We're fully computerised here. Let's use the machine in the corner. Besides, I have to add us to the list."

Logging in with her username and password, she selected from a database the appropriate file, and for a second or two nothing happened, but then, before clicking the mouse or even pressing a key, the computer crashed, its screen filled by the phrase *Vuelva a hacerlo*, scrolling in a blur, until, beeping in disgust, the computer turned itself off.

"Oh, wow!" she said, shaking her head. "Sorry 'bout that. Think we'll have to it try again."

"It's ok." I chuckled. "My PC goes mental too, but it's never crashed in, what? Spanish?"

"Yeah." She nodded. "That was a weird one. Think it said do again, do this, or something. * Although, I've only GCSE Spanish, and that was flippin' years ago."

*"Re-do," according to the whispers of Pax.

FIFTEEN

GIFTS

For reasons unknown, Mirra texted, and, when her first message arrived, my phone playing its cheesy tune, I almost jumped out of my skin. Could it be Frida or my family trying to get through? No. No such luck. It was Mirra. After saving her strangely long number (073918051329), I settled down to read it...

"Hello, Marcus," she began, "I do hope you are keeping busy and not feeling lonely. While Moloch examines your work, posing questions, trying to corroborate every detail, I'm stuck here, and the old fool is taking forever!"

Mirra's assumption was correct, I was lonely, and I wrote, "Texting during a meeting, eh? Naughty. But you are right. I'm missing you. Any suggestions to pass the time? With regards to the media portal, I've run out of ideas."

"Sorry you're unhappy," came her reply. "Although, it is nice to be missed. Can't help with the media, however – I'm rather out of date, but I will ask Moloch to refine the portal's software. An extension to help or guide your choices?"

This proposed refinement sounded interesting, and, with Mirra in a giving mood, I sent the subsequent message, curious to read her reply...

"Thanks, Mirra," I wrote. "Wonderful if Moloch could do that. In the meantime, could you provide something to read? Some books, say?"

"Something to read?" she replied. "Why are you asking? Did you not examine your communication device? Did you not run its software? Try the books application. It should provide access to our library."

Now, not having noticed such a thing made me cross with myself, but also with Mirra for not telling me, and was she being sarcastic? Most uncharacteristic, and her attitude caught me off guard…

"Mirra," I wrote, "you could've mentioned that ages ago! Not very helpful."

"Oh, my goodness," she replied. "What was I thinking? Poor neglected Marcus. Bad, naughty Mirra! Just perhaps, with people to see and things to do, I couldn't pander to your every desire. Good grief! What does Frida call you? A muppet, am I right?"

Well, that told me, I thought, and loading the "Books" application I studied what was available.

"LOL," I then wrote. "Touched a nerve, did I? But great. The library is excellent. This will keep me amused for a bit. Hopefully, speak to you soon? x"

"You will," she replied, "I promise, and a kiss for me? You sweet boy. Be patient. Mirra."

Their library was comprehensive, and I casually chose something light, downloading it for future reading.

⧗

Returning to London from York, I was to meet Frida just outside the station, and, upon arriving, thrilled to see her standing just beyond the turnstile, grinning like a marionette…

We embraced, kissing passionately.

"Only been gone a day," I gasped. "What if I'd gone for the week?"

"Then I'd be ripping your clothes off." She grinned in reply (and I saw no reason to doubt her).

Making our way into the night-time streets of London, we had a short, chilly walk to the car park, where Doris, Frida's Nissan Micra, faithfully waited.

"How was your trip?" she asked, slipping her arm into mine.

"Gruelling." I smiled. "You made the right choice, although, the Jorvik Centre was surprisingly good."

"Did you get to see the figurine and skeleton?"

"Yeah, eventually, but only the figurine.

"Why was that?"

"Because you weren't there with your expert eye, but don't worry. I asked the assistant to email every photo they have of the burial and skeleton, and according to my phone, they've already arrived."

"Then I take it all back," she replied. "Good thinking. Anything different about the figurine, compared to the copies?"

"Nothing significant. The colours were paler, it weighed less – it's probably hollow, and there wasn't any writing. Thank God."

"Right." She nodded, freeing her arm and seeking her keys. "And do you still think it's genuine, not a hoax?"

"Yes, I do. More than ever, and the assistant supervisor agreed."

"Hardly evidential. To convince anyone, you'll have to do better."

Unable to defend myself further, I yawned. It had been a long day, and, sitting in Frida's car, I was already nodding, ready for sleep.

Leaning over, Frida sympathetically stroked my hair.

"Sleep," she whispered. "I'll have you home in a jiffy."

⏳

Following my trip, the six-week run-up to Christmas became an ordeal. We both had issues. Struggling with her research and needing reassurance, Frida let slip the nature of her work: implanting living cells with exotic or foreign organelles…

"I just don't get it," she would complain. "It should work, but the cells age so quickly, all I get is a mush!"

My own issues were quite different – they were domestic. Now in receipt of my uncle's estate, my parents were pushing me to develop a career. A situation further exacerbated by my sister returning home in triumph, showing off her medal (awarded by the Russians, no less), all the while bragging up her "long-overdue" promotion.

The Eaton family Christmas was always a modest affair, and, with only one surviving grandparent (on my mother's side), all the "festivities" went on at our house. Christmas Eve to Boxing Day, and a couple of days after that. We had the usual tree, of course. Decorations, present giving, dinner, with all the other indulgences, baked, sweet, and alcoholic, but there was little anticipation or magic, except the dubious pleasure of a public holiday, with nothing to do but eat, drink, and annoy one another.

Curiously, Millie and I got on quite well that Christmas. Somehow, she had changed, and we were laughing, talking, joking. It was manifestly difficult finding a reason to loathe her.

The high point of our Christmas was certainly Frida's visit on Boxing Day, with my sister just as excited as me. Millie had been helpful in the buying of Frida's presents: an assortment of clothes, make-up, books, and much to her amusement, a new booster cushion for Frida's little car.

Too busy and stressed to spend any time on them, since York, the folders concerning my uncle's discoveries had been collecting dust, but during Frida's visit, we agreed to examine the file concerning the Babylonian priest. With Frida due at 11am, I hid in the shower (washing away the brandy of the previous night) while my mother and sister busied themselves preparing lunch. Similarly absent, playing golf in Dorking, was my father. "Be back by lunchtime or else!" warned my mother.

Later that afternoon, Frida, Millie, and I were admiring the spread in the dining room – post-Xmas buffet of gargantuan proportions. Grabbing a plate, I tucked in without hesitation...

"Doesn't he know how to wait?" asked Frida.

"No," replied Millie. "He has the patience of puppy, and you just watch. He's going to make one of his ridiculous sandwiches. As he has for the last fifteen years, give or take."

Softly chuckling, Frida shook her angelic head.

"What's wrong with an everything sandwich?" I said, "There's bread, meat, cheese, salad, pickles. What else should one do?"

"Should I tell him?" asked Millie, giving Frida a look of disquiet. "Or would you like a go?"

"Would be wasted breath," said Frida. "Stubborn as my dachshund once he gets going."

"Mum!" yelled Millie. "Marcus's started. You want him to stop?"

"No," called my mother. "You tuck in as well. We'll come in after you're done."

"See?" I remarked. "No problem at all."

By now, my sandwich was ten centimetres high, and, topping it with a single slice of bread, I compressed it into a chomp-able height.

"How you gonna eat that?" asked Frida. "Ridiculous man. You should be using a plate, taking but a little. Eating it nicely, daintily, using cutlery and," she added, forcing one a upon me, "a napkin!"

"Yeah," I replied, "I know. But, oh, look, it's too late," before taking a massive bite.

"Child," muttered Frida.

"And he plays with his food," said Millie, loading her plate.

"Yep," replied Frida. "Every time we eat, he's mashing or making patterns. Probably thinks I haven't noticed, but I have, Millie, I have."

Knowing Frida and Millie quite well enough not to rise to the bait, I ignored them as best I could, fastidiously pouring a cola, and then, deciding my best offence defence, I walked briskly into the kitchen to finish my sandwich in peace. This of course didn't work. The girls soon found me, and, bearing plates, napkins, and vast glasses of wine, they joined me at the kitchen table.

Chinking glasses like old friends, Millie and Frida exchanged seasonal greetings before settling down to eat...

"I don't have a present for you, Frida," said Millie, dabbing her lips, "and for me, your company is quite gift enough, but I'll give you something almost as good. Gossip. Did Marcus ever mention his ex?"

"He had an ex?" said Frida, her face reddening with delight.

"Yes," replied Millie. "Sounds incredible, does it not?"

"Well, yes!" said Frida, and then, turning to me, "And just who was this mysterious girl?"

"Who indeed?" chuckled Millie. "Come on Marcus. Tell us about Saskia, or do I have to tell her myself?"

Blushing and taking a breath, I considered my reply. Determined not to let these biting harpies spoil my lunch and good mood...

"There's not much to tell," I replied with a shrug. "She was a quiet, spindly girl, and we went out for six months."

"Now, now, Marcus," goaded Millie. "There's much more to tell and you know it!"

"Yes," agreed Frida. "Come on, Marky, spill. What was she like? Was she beautiful? Where is she now? What happened?"

With a sly glance, I put on my best innocent face...

"Well," I replied, "she was quite nice to look at, but after a few months we agreed to split up."

"Typical evasiveness," snorted Millie. "I'll tell you then. She had a face like a startled hamster and the body of a flailing prawn, and *she* dumped *him*! Because after 'sex'" – her index fingers defined the commas – "she realised, she was in fact—"

"No," I snapped. "Don't say it. Consider Saskia's privacy."

"Say what?" asked Frida. "And they did get physical then?"

"Oh yes," said Millie. "In bed, what did you say she was like?"

"A geometry set."

"Pardon?" pressed Millie. "A bit louder, if you please."

"Like a geometry set! All angles and corners, points, and bits sticking out," and, laughing gleefully at my flushing discomfort, the girls chinked their glasses in triumph.

"Thank you," bowed Millie, and she left the room, leaving glass and plate behind her.

Observing my discomfort, Frida put her arm around me...

"Hush," she whispered. "Don't get stressed. We're only playing, and bonding with your sister's important. Teasing you is an easy way to do it."

"I know *you're* only playing." I frowned. "It's her I'm unsure about. My discomfort gives her comfort. It always has."

Flinging a wine-soaked kiss, Frida tousled my hair...

"Perhaps," she whispered. "Although what did happen to Saskia?"

"God." I coughed. "You're like a dog with a bone, aren't you?" and sipping more wine Frida shamefully giggled.

"I'm a scientist," she replied with a shrug. "Blessed and cursed with insatiable curiosity."

"So, I noticed, but, if you really must know, she left me because she preferred..."

"Preferred what?" asked Frida.

"You know," I squirmed, "she discovered she was..."

"What? I still don't?"

"A... no," I offered then retracted. "I'm not saying it."

Striding back into the room, Millie returned to her seat.

With a bewildered look, Frida turned to Millie for help...

"She was gay," Millicent blankly revealed. "Did he not tell you?"

"Was getting round to it," I admitted, "but thank you, sis. For saving me the trouble."

"Oh, right," said Frida. "I get it. Although, what the hell did you do to her?"

"I don't know, do I?" I shrugged. "The usual?"

"Well." Frida chuckled. "Don't do it to me, ok?"

Returning to my sandwich, I studiously ignored them, saying nothing, wondering why, just why. Why did I have to be me?

Later that afternoon, safely ensconced in my bedroom, Frida and I studied the folder concerning the Babylonian priest…

"Is that all?" she said, turning over the single sheet. "One page and a photo? I've been having dreams about this damn folder, and now I'm feeling a half-wit."

"Really?" I pondered. "I had no idea. I thought the fixation was mine, but can you actually read it? It's like an inky spider ran across the page and died!"

"Yeah," she replied. "Just about legible. Let's see… Ok. The original excavation took place in 1962, * in Babylon. Which is in modern-day Iraq. They uncovered a stone sarcophagus buried at the foot of a ziggurat."

Hansjörg Schmid's 1962 excavation of the Etemenanki ziggurat and temple.

"The surface of the sarcophagus was richly engraved, with carvings of the sun, the moon, the Ishtar, * whatever that is, the sun and dot symbol as well. Never before seen in Mesopotamia. It says, the archaeologists hypothesised it belonged to a yet unknown, short-lived cult of a minor god. An aspect of 'Marduk' or some such."

In ancient times Ishtar was the goddess of love and war, fertility, and sexuality. Worshipped in northern Mesopotamia, particularly the Assyrian cities of Nineveh, Ashur, and Arbela, her symbol was an eight-pointed star. In the Babylonian pantheon she represented Venus.

"Yeah," I said, poring over the photo. "Can see it on the lid of the sarcophagus. What about the remains? Does it say who he was?"

"Yep. He was a follower of Nangar, 'Whom, by the wrath of Marduk, had fallen out of favour with the king' – beheaded, in other words. The archaeologists could see cut marks on his neck bones. It says he was a craftsman and a seer, buried with loads of goodies. Bracelets, rings of gold, polished stone beads, and a long staff with a gorgeous rock-crystal tip. I guess he was a pretty important guy."

"Is there anything else. Does it mention the symbol?"

"No, it doesn't. Only their initial hypothesis. Perhaps, they didn't know what it meant. Are there any clues in the photo?"

"No," I said, shaking my head. "It's too small, and some of the close-up bits are almost out of focus."

"Still," she asked, "let's have a look," and I nonchalantly passed it over.

"Wow," she gasped. "Quite well preserved. I expect the dry climate did that. After the excavation, I wonder where he went. Can't believe they let him be."

"No. Looters would have robbed the grave."

"Yeah," she replied. "So, we're gonna have to make a few guesses and then check them out. Especially if you were thinking of finding him, for a better look?"

"Possibly," I said. "Depends on how tricky. Who was leading the excavation? Thought he sounded European."

"Hmm, you're right. The remains could well have gone to Europe. Not in the British Museum, are they? Wouldn't surprise me. Graham's the one to call if you wanna find out."

"Oh, God," I replied. "Can't ask him for another favour. It's getting embarrassing. Surely, it's your turn, and, besides, he fancies you. You're sure to get results."

"Marcus Eaton!" she then playfully snapped. "Are you proposing I flirt with some middle-aged ex-archaeologist, simply to find some old bones?"

"Erm, yes? Only, not in the physical sense. Touching is strictly forbidden. Just close your eyes, listen and relax. Think how happy I'll be!"

Frida shuddered.

"You're disgusting," she frowned. "But now, yeah, I get it. Saskia? I'm with you, love."

⧗

Like dawn breaking, the sound of Mirra's greeting seemed to glow, and, jumping from the bed, I stood by the door, so pleased was I to hear her…

"Hello, Marcus. How are you feeling, my friend?"

"Mirra," I cried. "You're here! For an editing session or merely a social call?"

"Why, both," she replied. "Although, if you'd prefer, we can leave your writing be. You've endured a great deal and I want you to recuperate."

"There's no need to worry," I said. "I'm fine. Just looking forward to spending some time with you. Besides, the last piece of writing was a struggle. Very patchy in places. So, please, don't go."

"Very well," she replied. "A quick review of your work, then. But if you tire, tell me immediately."

"Thanks, Mirra," I said. "Thanks for staying. Where do you want to start?"

"The beginning," she advised. "From the words Camber Viking burial, then, when we're finished, I have something from Moloch you'll definitely like and a surprise present from me."

"A present? Is it my birthday or Christmas already?"

"Why, all of them at once!" She laughed in reply. "Get comfy, then we can begin. Can't wait to spoil ya."

The edit of the section concerning my journey to York was over surprisingly quickly. Mirra, concentrating on my punctuation and grammar (claiming it was as awful as ever), did so without posing a single question or demanding extra detail, and, although honoured by her approval, I was slightly disappointed too. Answering her absurd questions was a like game, a game I thoroughly enjoyed.

"Now then," she said, "that is quite good enough. It makes sense, and the paragraphs concerning Frida and her eccentric pets give me immense pleasure. Thank you for those. They remind me of my childhood. Now, activate the entertainment portal. I am excited to show you the changes we've made."

Doing as she asked, the screen displayed its primary menu.

"Looks the same," I remarked.

"It does. Select cinema."

"Cinema," I said, the screen dutifully changing, then, "North America," the screen filling with a list of old movies, but on the right were two new columns: "Reviews/Analysis" and "Content Summary".

"Oh, right." I chuckled. "That's new."

"There you are," she said. "Happy now?"

"Excellent," I replied with a nod, and then to the portal *Star Wars*, followed by "Content Summary", the screen filling with text outlining the plot of *Star Wars Episode IV*.

"Brilliant," I said. "And is this installed for everything?"

"Yes," she replied, "so far as I know. I hope you have fun with it."

"Sure will," I said. "And didn't you say Moloch did this? Will you thank him for me, the next time you see him?"

"Already have," she replied, "so don't concern yourself. Now, switch off the portal and sit."

"Screen off," I said and sat on the bed.

"Watch," she said. "Study the screen. You'll like this."

To begin, there was nothing. But then, an image, grainy at first, slowly coalesced. For what seemed like an age, the image was meaningless. Trees, grass, sky, a city filling the horizon. In the foreground were picnic benches, several occupied, people enjoying a coffee or a snack, before it suddenly dawned on me. I gasped, blinking in disbelief. This was the park in which Frida walked her dogs!

"Mirra," I said, "this is amazing. How are you able to do this?"

"Thought you'd be impressed. With a bit of trickery, we've taken control of a miniature camera outside the café, but we cannot maintain the connection for long. Now, look, down the track. Anyone you recognise?"

In the distance, I could see people, but I could also see Scamper! Behind him, two figures were walking, and so much emotion swept over me, I was sobbing before I knew it…

"Swich it off," I begged. "Please. I can't bear it. Switch it off!"

"How so?" said Mirra, sounding confused. "Why do you weep? There. Look. There she is. Frida! She's home, with her mother, walking the dogs. There's no need to worry. She's fine!"

"Turn it off," I bellowed. "It's torture to see her. She must be devastated, worried sick. Can't you understand? I'm ashamed. I failed her! Please…"*

Mirra sighed. "Very well."

More whining and pleading followed, e.g., when will I see her, where is my lawyer, but for the sake of brevity I have removed it.

The screen immediately went dark and Mirra's face (if I could have seen it) would surely have been one of perplexity.

"This was supposed to reassure you," she softly explained. "To make you happy. Please. Help me understand."

Taking deep breaths through trembling cheeks, I strode to the washbasin, splashing my face with water.

"How," I replied, collecting my wits. "How can I? These things are learnt by living."

There came such a long pause thereafter I assumed Mirra to be thinking, but her reply (when it came) was so uncharacteristically mournful, I realised she was crying…

"Then," she whispered, her voice breaking apart, "I am most assuredly dead."

"Hope not," I said. "I need you more than ever. I'm about start writing the next section. Concerning our trip to Jordan. Will you be available to help me go through it?"

"Of course," she bleakly replied. "I have no choice."

"Then," I said, "we will speak again soon," although Mirra had already gone. No idea if she heard me.

⧗

I didn't see or hear from Frida for three days after her Boxing Day visit. Not until the evening of the 29th did she call me. I'd just come in from work, in fact. Tired, greasy, and more than a little grumpy…

"Hey, Marky!" she chirped. "How was your day?"

"Well, you know," I replied, "same as always."

"Anybody poisoned?"

"No," I said, "at least, not poisoned quickly. Some of our regulars won't make forty, but it's more their lifestyle than my fault."

"Whatever." She chuckled. "Anyhow, I rang Corbiere and asked about the Babylonian stuff, and to begin the poor guy was clueless, but he agreed to look into it."

"Excellent," I replied. "Thanks for doing that. It was getting awkward asking for help all the time… Did he get back to you? Any answers?"

"Yeah," she said with sigh, "he certainly did, but not before he asked me out. The cheeky git."

"He what? What did you say?"

"Sod off, of course. Told him just to tell me."

"Good," I replied. "What did he say?"

"He said the casket and skeleton are in Baghdad – that's in Iraq. No good if you wanted to see it. Your sister says Iraq isn't safe."

"You spoke to my sister?"

"Of course, why ever not? She knows a great deal about overseas affairs. Didn't you know? Anyhow, Corbiere said he'd call Baghdad, ask about foreign visitors, but that was before I learnt of the danger."

"Right," I said. "So, what should we do? Forget it? Besides, I can't afford a trip to the Middle East any time soon."

"Yes," replied Frida, "I know. But I might be able to, and a short break in the sun would do me good. With my research at a dead end, therapeutic shopping in a stimulating place might get me working again."

"Well, I'd love to go," I said. "A while before I could pay you back, though."

"Know that too," she replied. "But it's all for nothing. No way I'm going to Iraq, doesn't matter how sunny or cheap. Being kidnapped and then beheaded just doesn't appeal."

"No." I laughed. "So, we'll just have to do our best here. How about asking Norma?"

"Already have. Said she was busy. Promises to look in the New Year."

"Fine. Will I see you before January?"

"Yes, of course," she replied. "We're going to Lucy's party, remember? Want to show you off to the girls. If you wear your new jacket and trousers, they're gonna be jealous."

"Very well," I said. "I will be both silent and dashing. A prince to my pale princess. Until she gets pissed and falls over."

"Does sound like me," she replied. "I'll pick you up New Year's Eve. About seven, ok?"

"Sure," I said. "See you then."

"And stay in touch, won't you? If I hear any more about the burial stuff, I'll let you know."

"Ok," I replied. "Fingers crossed. I'm off for a shower. Night-night."

"Bye, Marky."

Sounding a squelchy kiss, she hung up.

Held within Lucy's large flat, the New Year's party was quite an event, and fun, mostly. For one, being the only male present, I garnered a great deal of flirty female attention, and with Frida on top form – lively, sozzled, boisterously profane, playing Trivial Pursuit until the chimes of Big Ben thunderously sounded (on the TV) – I was happy as a clam. From then on, things got decidedly crazy. The music thumping, the drinking, the singing, the dancing (fortunately the neighbours were with us). Then, during a lull in the music, a now wildly inebriated Frida took it upon herself to loudly proclaim (all the while tugging at my sleeve), "Look here you lot! This is me Marcush, and I love him more than me life. We're going on holiday too.

Going to Jordan. Yeah, Jordan. You heard! Gonna look at some boney old relic un float in the sea. Dead Sea. It's camel piss, but we're gonna swim!" *

*Unlike the mineral saturated water of the Dead Sea, camel urine is in fact thick and syrupy. Buoyancy for the human body would indeed not be an issue, but swimming though such a viscous liquid would prove difficult and be decidedly unpleasant.

Standing by ten minutes later and trying not to look, I held Frida's hair as she vomited into a toilet.

"You ok?" I asked, helping to wipe her mouth. "Need to rinse out with water?"

"Make her stop," she whispered, and falling unconscious, she slumped on the floor like a sack.

Troubled by Frida's sudden decline, I told Lucy, and helped by a couple of girls, we quickly put her to bed. Such is the nature of love.

⌛

Still hung-over, Frida called the following evening, her voice croaky and quiet…

"Hello, Fred," I began. "How's it going? Has it worn off?"

"Nearly," she whispered. "So sorry if I… caused a… a drama. Lucy said I'd was shouting, swearing, and being a general bitch."

"No," I replied. "Not a bitch, but you were rather boisterous. Life and soul of the party."

"You're not angry, then?"

"Of course not," I said. "Apart from the puking, it was quite funny, and I met an extreme side of your personality: Gin Monster."

"Oh." She gasped. "You're so lovely. Thank you. You won't meet Gin Monster again, I promise. That definitely was the last time."

"You were yelling about Jordan. What was that all about?"

"God," she moaned. "Don't. Did anyone film me. Did you see?"

"Sorry. I don't recall, but Jordan?"

"Yeah, Jordan," she wearily replied. "Sorry, I didn't explain. I had a text from Corbiere, wishing me happy New Year. Did you get one?"

"No."

"Hmm," she continued. "Anyway, a lot of the Babylonian stuff was recently loaned to Jordan. It's now in Amman, the capital. Jordan is safe for westerners, so we could go for a look. If you want?"

"Wow," I said. "I would. But before we decide anything, you need to rest. Are you working tomorrow?"

"No," she replied, "not until the fourth. You wanna come over, walk the dogs or something?"

"Ok," I said. "Cool. Then we can talk about Jordan. In the meantime, I'll talk to my parents and Millie. Maybe my dad will give me a loan?"

"Well, you never know," she quietly replied.

"Right," I then demanded. "Off you go. Back to bed. I'll see you tomorrow."

"Ok, but not before nine, I beg you."

"Fine," I said. "Sleep well."

"You too. Night, Marky."

⧗

We boarded our flight to Amman during the chilly small hours of 12 February 2011. Originally planning for a week-long break, the pressures of work and a shortage of money had reduced this to a frantic three-day visit, but in the last minute, before our final down-payment (the remaining 80%), my father suddenly intervened, footing the bill himself. Upgrading our basic accommodation (in an already superb hotel) to a luxury apartment, all-inclusive, room service, the works. Fabulous!

Frida didn't enjoy flying. She was edgy, hyper, and apprehensive, and with five hours to get through I worried she was going to be sick…

"You sure you're ok?" I asked, as we settled into our seats. "Usually, I doze and listen to music. Do you want to babble? I know calms you down."

"I'm fine," she replied, twiddling the ribbon bunching her hair. "Just nervous, but I took a sleeping pill before we left. Should start making me woozy."

"Oh, fine," I said. "Not my cup of tea, but I'm sure you know best."

"Well, maybe." She shrugged. "They're actually my mum's. Although, I've taken them before. When work was stressing me out. Using them as a tranquilliser is a bit of a test."

"Oh, ok, but what about food? Want me to wake you for our meal?"

"Shouldn't be any need," she replied. "I'll just be dozy. Eating won't be a problem."

Threading along the aisle, the cabin crew were performing the safety drill, and we impishly chuckled as the assistant beside us, while fiddling with the tapes of an unwieldy life jacket, desperately fought to stifle a yawn…

"Poor thing," said Frida. "My friend Emma works for an airline, says it's gruelling… A hostess employed by Air Jordan seduced passengers to curtail her boredom. During take-off and landing, she was truly outstanding, in business with Roger and Gordon."

"Shush," I hissed, struggling to contain my laughter, while the woman in question (surely overhearing) gave us a knowing smile.

The flight was smooth and quiet, and Frida's pills seemed to work well. Soon after take-off she was dozing under a blanket. By the time we were circling, however, descending towards our destination, she was fully conscious, very wriggly, and full of silly excitement…

"It's all yellow and dusty!" she chattered, craning her neck to the window. "Oh, God!" she then gasped. "Hate it when the plane leans over. Aren't you scared of flying at all?"

"Flying? No. Crashing? Yes. But then again, who isn't? And, statistically speaking, you're more likely to die in a car."

"Still makes my tummy go swirly. Oh! Hold my hand. It's getting bumpy now."

Taking her hand in mine, Frida leant over for extra reassurance, and saying nothing, I softly kissed the top of her head as the aircraft began its final approach…

Both modern and pristine, the Queen Alia International Airport in Amman made our disembarkation a cinch. A gleaming black limousine provided our transfer, whisking us with panache (and a glass of champagne) to our hotel, and, while excitedly watching the bustling streets of Amman slip by, Frida pinned up her hair before covering it with a silken scarf.

"How do I look?" she asked, tucking her ribbon into a pocket. "Want to fit in if I can."

"You look fantastic," I replied. "With your dark eyes and the scarf framing your beautiful face, the illusion is perfect."

Laughing, Frida beamed with delight, and I noticed our driver glancing at us in the rear-view mirror.

Sliding across the seat, Frida readied to kiss me, but remembering our travel advice, I stopped her short with a look.

"No," I warned. "Not here. Remember what Millie said. Wait until we're indoors."

"Oops!" she replied. "Oh yeah. Sorry driver. Erm… asefa?"

"Ok, madam." He laughed. "In here, ok. In city, no, and for sorry you say *ae*sefa, ok?"

"Ah," Frida acknowledged. "Thank you, driver. Aesefa. Gonna need that word a lot I think, aesefa."

After checking-in, wide-eyed and blinking in a lobby of opulent marble, two immaculate porters led us up to our room, and, tipping them generously, I asked about tipping in Jordan and the amounts usually expected. The porters explained (in very slick English) how *I* didn't need to tip them at all, but any small amount would be accepted honourably, and not be forgotten!

Leaving our luggage in the doorway, we wearily stumbled inside, gasping in awe at the grandeur before us. Indeed, this wasn't a room at all, it was an apartment! Lounge, private balcony, dining room, huge double bedroom (with monster bed to match), leading into to the bathroom. A marble palace all on its own! Two toilets, a bidet, two washbasins, a Jacuzzi bath (room for two), and shower. Air drying nozzles included…

"Take care with those," remarked Frida. "Used those before and they're powerful. One slip and you'll get a blast up somewhere you'll never forget!"

In the dining room, we found the table generously arrayed with an assortment of drinks (mostly alcoholic), fruit, dates, nuts, cheese, and biscuits, and we immediately tucked in, nibbling and sipping, adjusting to our new and wonderful lodgings.

Following a shared shower and a bottle of wine, feeling refreshed, we were ready to go out exploring…

"What do you want to do?" asked Frida, stretching and yawning. "Visit the museum now, do the Dead Sea tomorrow?"

"Yeah," I replied. "Makes sense. Then we could explore the city a bit. You wanna eat here, or shall we go out?"

"Hmm… well," she pondered. "Reckon we'll both be knackered later, so let's eat here. We can go out tomorrow."

"Ok, restaurant-hunting tomorrow. Something lavish!"

Giggling, Frida wandered over to nibble my ear.

"Lavish?" she replied. "You mean lav-ish, like a toilet – and, if you're paying, it will be."

The museum exhibiting the Babylonian burial was atop an area of Amman known as the Citadel. A high and dusty place, even on a cool day in February, and we marvelled at the ruined temple of Hercules. Its massive sandstone pillars dominating the skyline.

Surrounding a nearby cluster of date palms, a team of white-suit-wearing scientists were conducting research…

"Ooh!" said Frida. "Something going on over there. Mind if I take a look?"

"Of course not. Just don't take too long. It's chilly!"

As previously mentioned, Frida's research had stalled, and so desperate was she that she had revealed her problems, namely, developing techniques, readying cells to accept modified organelles (the microscopic organs maintaining the cell). Unfortunately, every cell she tried this with died very rapidly. Undergoing instantaneous lysis, they had burst.

"Then use tougher cells," I said, bored of her moping and moaning.

"Which?" she replied. "Tried every human cell imaginable. None of them work!"

"Then don't use human," I said. "Use something else!"

"Non-human?" she scorned. "You understand what you're proposing? Even if it did work, the immune system would destroy them. Besides, such work is unethical. Might be illegal."

"Ethical schmethical," I replied. "They use pig valves in hearts, don't they? Change the cells so the immune system ignores them. Protect them. Encase them in armour. If that doesn't work, make them more stretchy."

With Frida's jaw suddenly dropping, she turned on her heels.

"Dangerous," she thoughtfully muttered. "But yeah. Chitin, cellulose, cephalopod? Gotta be worth a try."

With Frida in conversation with one of the scientists, I saw little choice but to join her, and, getting nearer, I realised they were speaking in French…

"Hey, Marcus!" She smiled, slipping back into English. "Listen to this. It's really interesting," then, turning to the Arabic man, she quickly said something like, "*S'il vous plait, excusez-moi, pendant que je lui explique la situation à mon partenaire?*"

He nodded and she continued in English.

"This is Dr Bouzid. He and his team have been working all over the

Middle East trying to find out why a type of sap sucking fly or thrip*
has become resistant to insecticide. These palms are one of their sample
collection groups, and do you notice the dates? Unpicked. To attract the
thrips in greater numbers."

*Heliothrips haemorrhoidalis, most probably…

Nodding my understanding, I gave her a quizzical look as if to say "so?",
which she returned with a grin (knowing my mind as always).

"The thing is, Marcus. This particular thrip seems to have developed
a symbiotic relationship with a yeast-like fungus covering its body. Now,
things like this do occur in nature, and Dr Bouzid believes the yeast is
neutralising the insecticide before it can kill the thrip, and that is, well…
that is incredible!"

"Amazing," I said. "How will they know if they're right?"

Quickly speaking again to Dr Bouzid (in French), she turned back to
me.

"They are collecting as many samples as possible, enough to culture and
develop the yeast in their laboratory. In controlled conditions, they can study
the mechanism the yeast employs and try to circumvent it. The date crop
is vital to many Middle Eastern economies and, if this situation continues,
this little fly (in suitable conditions) could quickly become a critical pest."

"Right," I said. "Important work. Why the excitement?"

"Because of my own research. This yeast has me thinking – it's
protecting the cells it's growing on. To its own advantage and to the thrip's.
It's protecting the cells!"

"And you think this yeast can protect the cells you're working on?"

"Not sure about that," Frida admitted. "But the mechanism of the yeast
might involve powerful antitoxins. Once Dr Bouzid finds out what they are,
he has kindly agreed to share his findings. When we get back to England,
I'm going to contact his lab, and besides, I might be able to help them.
Cellular toxicity is my speciality."

"Great. Can we go to the museum? It'll be closing soon. Afternoon
prayers and all that."

"Alright, alright!" She laughed. "Just let me say goodbye."

More French followed. The words (to my ear) merging into single
rhythmic melody.

Providing Frida with a business card, Dr Bouzid shook her hand so vigorously that I thought she would take off…

"Right," she grumbled. "I'm done. Happy? Mr Bloody Impatient. Now I've done my thing, we can do yours."

Upon first appearances, the Archaeological Museum of Jordan was an uninspiring building. Made of sandstone blocks, the building was a block itself, and Frida remarked, with the Jordanian flag proudly flying above it, how it looked more like a military bunker than a museum. Ancient stone plinths and a large blue sign revealed its true nature, and we eagerly went in to view the exhibition.

Because it was February, we were the only visitors, and we took our time, viewing every exhibit, taking photos, and reading what little we could.

"Smoky in here," grumbled Frida. "It's making me dizzy."

"Yeah," I replied. "It's like we're back at my uncle's."

We soon came across the sarcophagus. Mounted upon a low dais, its graven lid was placed alongside. Leaning in to look at the skeleton, Frida thoughtfully pressed her thumb against the point of her chin. On a lectern next to the sarcophagus, the written description was mostly in Arabic. While I took photographs, Frida read out what little she could…

"This is hopeless," she frowned. "On loan from the museum of Baghdad. Yeah, we know. Dates from around the time of Nebuchadnezzar II. Oh, look. We know that too."

"Shall I go for help? With all the smoke, there must be someone about."

"Yeah," said Frida. "Maybe they could help us with the Arabic? While you're gone, I'll have a close-up look at the lid."

Methodically threading my way through the empty museum, I hoped to bump into a member of staff, but then, just as I spied the curator's office, I heard an ear-piercing scream. The scream was Frida's, and I turned, sprinting full pelt towards the exhibit.

She was down on the floor when I found her. A trembling heap, her hands over her eyes, knees drawn up so tightly, she looked like a ball…

"Frida," I said, dropping beside her. "What's the matter? What's wrong?"

She didn't move, and wrapping an arm about her shoulders, I tried to again to reach her.

"What is it, sweetheart? What happened?"

Slowly, she raised her head, eyes unblinking, her mouth anxiously chewing, trying to speak, before hissing in a voice that was not her own: "Behold the furnace, behold the light. Thy kingly gold is rent to dust."

With growing concern, I turned to face her. Taking her shoulders, I looked into her eyes.

"What are you saying?" I asked. "I can't understand."

"Marcus?" she said. "Is that you? Oh, Marcus. You won't believe me, but I saw him. I saw what they did! Beside me, hunched on a throne, a fat man. His hair and beard braided, plaited with gold and shining jewels. Then before us another man. Beaten and bruised, his long white robe, soiled and torn, ragged, and spattered with blood. Dragged and kicked, he was. Jostled by soldiers in shimmering armour. They had terrible swords! Then… and then, the man's eyes! They touched me – his eyes! Such anger. It was like they were burning. They're still burning. Burning into my sadness, my sorrow, my regret, as the coldest night on the blackest stone."

And then she burst into tears.

It was twenty minutes before Frida was able to stand again, and, after walking outside, she proceeded to vomit very heavily, red wine, cheese, and fruit, immediately recovering thereafter.

"Better?" I asked. "What the hell happened in there?"

"I'm not sure," she gasped, spitting discreetly as possible. "I leant into the sarcophagus, touched the skeleton. I felt dizzy, screamed, I think, and then you were talking to me. Really weird. You think I'm ill?"

"Don't know," I said. "How do you feel now?"

"Fine." She shrugged. "Bit tired, could do with some water, but the sensation has passed. I reckon it was a combination of sleeping pills, wine, rich food, and what do think? Stress?"

"More like you were tripping," I said. "You were all locked up and distant, as if having a crazy dream."

"No, it wasn't like that. I was outside my body, hallucinating, floating. Should have been terrifying, but it wasn't. It was more like a gift. Deliberate."

"O-k," I replied. "That all sounds weird. If you get dizzy again, I'm gonna call you a doctor."

"Agreed." She smiled, adjusting her scarf. "But, right now, I need sleep. Is that our taxi?"

"Yes," I replied. "I asked him to wait, and he has. Let's head back and get you rested. You're scaring me stupid. Bloody pills! You, of all people, using drugs. You should, you *do* know better!"

By the evening, after sleeping for six hours straight, Frida had fully recovered, and after a shower, she was full of bounce and clowning about as ever. As a further precaution, we stayed in that evening, saving ourselves for two days of uninhibited tourism. Not that we had time for any excursions. The Dead Sea, Red Sea, Petra, and Jerash would just have to wait. Exploring Amman, however, was a joy. Never intimidating. We felt welcome. The pleasure I had with Frida, simply shopping, belligerently haggling, and making general mischief, made the whole trip worthwhile.

If ever you have the chance to visit Jordan, I implore you, whoever you are, take it. The people are wonderful, the climate is perfect, the food is great, and the scenery truly fantastic. One of the most endearing memories I still hold was the fun we shared laughing and bickering, powering a pedalo on the hotel's vast pool. Frida's determined insistence, "Ladies do not pedal, they are pedalled," somewhat hindered our progress, and consequently, stuck together in a never-ending circle, we hardly moved at all.

SIXTEEN

THE LONG HAUL

A s I bring this account to a close, I recognise the great personal achievement it represents. Never have I attempted, let alone completed, such an extensive piece of writing. My previous efforts, battling through A-level English, rarely exceeded a few thousand words, and so painfully awful that my teacher, Mr Groves, would beg: "Eaton, for the life of me, couldn't you make it shorter?" *

*This Mr Groves and I are kindred spirits.

With Mirra's gleeful greeting wafting from the door, we were soon dashing through my latest piece with typical ruthless efficiency. For a change, however, while working, I suggested music, and with Mirra's approval, I let her do the choosing…

"Some Schumann would be lovely," she said. "Our time together is coming to end. Feelings of joy and melancholia are crashing like waves within me. Schumann's embrace would moderate the storm."

"Ok," I replied. "Schumann. Wait while I find something to match your surging emotions," and quickly coming upon his Cello Concerto in A Minor, I set the volume low, not wishing to smother our conversation.

"Oh, my!" gasped Mirra, the music climbing and soaring. "So perfect, and is that Jacqueline du Pré? It must be! A genius, and beautiful. Like me."

"If you say so."

"I do. Now come, let us begin."

⟨⟩

Following our trip to Jordan, the early months of 2011 were eventful. With Frida finally obtaining the necessary experimental results, she began to work on her PhD, and being based at Imperial College London, she hoped to publish an excellent thesis. As for me, well, I had a new job, and a proper job too! Working for the same company as my friend Frank Padgett, I spent my days dashing about, providing IT support for every department within, and, no longer working in a greasy crap-hole, my life was changing fast. This wasn't challenging work, the career path limited, but I was constantly busy, mending, cleaning, fitting, installing something or other. Becoming computer gofer first class. Go for this, fetch that, and, within a week of starting, cheekily christened "Scooter". *

Curiously, "Scooter" also happens to be the name of a Muppet.

The final folder bequeathed by my uncle concerned the excavations at the Laguna de los Cóndores in Peru. With a dozen pages of handwritten notes, an X-ray plate, and newspaper clippings, its complexity demanded serious attention (Frida was obsessed by it), but not until the Easter holidays did we find the time to study it, on a lunch date. Tapas. Just off Shaftsbury Avenue, in Soho.

The restaurant was busy. A hungry half-hour before we got something to eat, but after merrily munching our way through the menu, dodging the octopus out of gastronomic cowardice, we headed outside, enjoying welcome drinks in the sunshine…

As I swirled the ice in my cola, Frida carefully opened the folder and spread its contents over the table.

"Good thing we waited," I said. "When the fabada went flying, orange grease was everywhere!"

"Yeah." She nodded. "Paprika, capsaicin, reminds me of the chem-lab at uni. Our notes often ended up with peculiar stains. One guy managed to spill enzyme over his binder, and by the time he'd mopped up the mess, his notes were papier mache."

"Ha," I replied with a snort. "At St Odo's, chaps would sometimes burn their work, especially if they got behind with their prep."

"Oh, that's nothing," said Frida. "In my old school? The gangs would set fire to each other!"

"Gangs? Good God. How did you survive? At St Odo's, we had to make to do with houses. Although, if any girls were watching, the rugby got seriously intense."

"Sounds hellish," She replied with a smirk. "What house were you in, though? Was it like Harry Potter? Did you get sorted?"

"Yeah, kind of. Fortitude was my house. For individuals determined, forceful, and stubborn. Our house motto: only stone endures." *

Quoniam in lapidibus nisi.

"Naturally," she replied, "but forceful? That's not you at all!"

"Yeah." I chuckled. "I was more soggy clay than granite."

"What were the others?"

"Cavalier, Artifice, Industry. Their names are self-explanatory. Different chaps, different houses."

"If you say so. Was St Odo's a boy's school, then?"

"Yes," I replied. "Just me and the chaps. Did I not say so before?"

"No," she said, cocking an eyebrow. "You didn't. Explains a few things, though, doesn't it, hmm?" Then, turning her attention back to the notes, Frida nonchalantly slid the remainder towards me.

"Right," she said, "let's see what we've got and where it takes us this time." And I settled back, watching her read.

"Ahem!" She then coughed. "The X-ray plate. Have you held it up to the light?"

"Yes, of course," I replied. "There's a white shadow under the arm bones. It's the same size and shape as the figurine. It appears there's a metal ring or something. Does he mention it?"

"Don't know yet," she admitted. "There's quite a lot to get through. About the excavations, the archaeologist, good God, I can barely read it. What was his name, Kaffman Dog?"

"No, you ninny, it's Kauffmann-Doig. What else does it say?"

"Don't get funny," she warned. "Unless you want to read this yourself."

Cowering, I theatrically bit my lip.

"That's better," she said. "Now, where was I? Oh yes, the mummies. In a cave near Kuelap, a long-abandoned Chachapoyan fortress, they found an intact group of mummified bodies. It says here that the mummies were probably spared extensive looting because they held little of value. Only domestic items, tools, totems, and foodstuffs. I suppose they might've been mummified and wrapped with things they used, made, or enjoyed?"

"Sounds plausible," I said. "What happened next?"

"Well, since the looting was recent, the mummies were removed. Too risky to leave them be. Doesn't say where to exactly, but most went to Lima for conservation. They were carbon-dated, X-rayed, and stabilised. Now at sea level, the increased humidity was causing them to decay, and oh, wow!" she then exclaimed. "The X-ray plate is original."

"Cool," I replied. "Clever old uncle, but how did he get it? South America wasn't really his thing."

Shifting in her seat, Frida sipped her wine, looking for a particular sentence.

"Mentions that." her a finger on the relevant phrase. "He came across the mummies while reading a magazine."

"Very likely," I said. "And I know which one. Spent days bagging a mountain of cuttings."

"Yeah." She chuckled. "Anyway, after seeing a photo of the X-ray, he recognised the outline of the figurine, and following further research, he wrote to the lead archaeologist. Probably that Kauffmann-Doig bloke."

"Yeah, did he think the mummy's figurine related to the one found in Sussex? Did he think them connected?"

"Err... no," she replied, shaking her head. "Not quite. He did wish for a direct comparison, if only to prove the Viking one South American, but he made no further assumptions. He was more interested in the symbols, I think."

"Yes." I nodded, sitting back in my chair. "You're right, of course. I've been so wrapped up in the idea of the Vikings visiting distant shores, I'm forgetting the whole association. Not only linking a Viking with a South American mummy but how it fits with a reliquary, a medieval murder, and a Babylonian sarcophagus."

"And we're still nowhere near to an answer," said Frida, looking nonplussed.

"Answer?" I chuckled. "What answer? Never thought we'd find the answer."

"What, then," she replied, "is the point of all this?"

"The point?" I then pondered. "*Our* point, and I've been thinking about this. Our point is to show the world these things truly exist. Confirming the symbol to be both unique and connected."

"Yes, yes!" she acknowledged. "I got that, but what does it all mean?"

"Well, I don't know," I countered. "Although, you tell me? Look at the X-ray plate, the figurine hidden inside the mummy, is it the same as the one found in Sussex? It is, isn't it? How can it be?"

"I'm not sure," replied Frida, tapping her glass. "My heart is full of doubt. The incredulity of it all? You see, the thing is, science is steadily solving the mysteries of the past, and it will soon solve this one as well. The explanation will be mundane. Don't expect any magic or mystery. The age of wonder has passed. Only science remains."

"And thank God for that," I said, sipping my cola. "But if this mystery's getting solved, the world needs to know of it, and revealing it has fallen to us. Now, how does that grab you?"

Clapping her hands, Frida's face markedly brightened.

"Ah!" She laughed. "Now you're talking my language! A chance for recognition, my name in print? Newspapers, magazines, TV, why are we waiting?"

"We're waiting for you to read that ridiculous scrawl!" and, retaliating, Frida flicked droplets of wine.

"You know?" she then said. "Corbiere needs to see this, to make sure we're not chasing wild geese, and guess what? The turn is now yours."

"I suppose you're right," I replied. "But what if it means a trip to Peru? Are you up for it?"

"Possibly." She shrugged. "I do have the time, and the money, but I'd have to speak to my mum. You know how it is between us."

"Ok," I said. "Tell you what. Since I have leave booked in June, there's time enough for everything. Let me contact Corbiere while you find out what the trip would entail. Flight and hotel enough, don't you think?"

"Definitely," she replied. "Can't stand those package excursion things. They're just a way to fleece tourists, but a week exploring Lima would be extremely cool. A culture shock. So much to see, so much to learn. Ex-ci-ting!"

Unable to stomach another phone call begging favours, I emailed Dr Corbiere, explaining our intentions. Our willingness to travel to Peru and examine the mummified remains first-hand. Where this would lead, I had no idea. A close-up viewing of the remains? Might there be further X-rays to view? Could the figurine be removed from the mummy's bindings? Was it an actual exhibit?

Knowing his reply would take days to arrive, I enjoyed my Easter weekend, and after scoffing chocolate and simnel cake, I did a little research myself. Frida was due the following Tuesday, and seeing on her my doorstep, wearing leggings, a fleece, and holding a large bag, I wondered what she'd been up to...

"You're looking casual," I remarked. "Have you been jogging?"

"Yeah." She grinned. "Been to the gym; too much choccy. Are you letting me in or not?"

"Of course," I replied. "Sorry, come in," and with a hop and a skip she bounced into my arms.

"Is it just me," she asked, loosening her embrace, "or is it quiet here today?"

"Yes, everyone but me is working. Although, my mum will be back in an hour or two."

"Right." She wryly smiled. "Then, can I be cheeky and beg a shower? I'll be quick. Just a rinse, and then I can change into my jeans."

"Sure. You know where it is. Help yourself."

Carrying her bag, she began climbing the stairs, but about halfway up she suddenly stopped, looking down with a beckoning expression...

"Wanna join me?"

"Tempting," I replied. "Very tempting, but I think I'd better stay dry. My mum could be back any moment. It would be seriously embarrassing if we got caught."

"Spoilsport!" She laughed. "But come up anyway. You can pass me the shampoo, towels, and stuff."

Sat upon on the lid of the toilet as she showered, I listened to her humming, but every now and then her slender arm would appear, demanding shower gel, sponge, comb, or shampoo, and I would offer up the necessary requisite like an obedient surgical nurse.

"There," said Frida, "all done," and, wrapping her in a towel, we moved to my bedroom.

Rummaging in her bag for knickers, Frida dropped her towel to the floor…

"Have you heard from Corbiere?" she asked. "It would be nice to know if we're going."

"No, not yet. Although, it doesn't really matter what he says. I need to know if you think the trip is worthwhile. As you said, it's a bloody long way."

"Yeah," she replied, adjusting her bra. "I know. Sixteen hours. It'd be hell! Eight pees, two poos, and a very numb bum."

"Never thought about flying like that, but you're right. You do get a bit more legroom on long-haul flights and better seats. If it really bothers you, we could upgrade to business. It'll be pricey though."

"Hmm…" she pondered. "And there's another thing. Don't know if you've realised. If we go in June, it's winter in Peru." Retrieving a tube of moisturiser, Frida worked small globules into her skin.

"Yeah," I replied. "Found out last night. Their summer's hot and tropical, but in the winter it's bleak and damp, hardly any sunshine at all. Fog and cloud most of the time."

"So," Frida proposed, "if we are going in June – and I think it'll have to be June. If we wait until October, say, springtime over there, I'll be too busy with my PhD – so?"

"We need to decide right now? Is that what you're saying?"

Heaving on her jeans and slipping on a top, Frida adjusted herself, checking her reflection in my mirror.

"In a word, yes," she replied, moving closer to examine her eyes, "and I did look at the hotels in Lima. The best and most expensive, are as you'd expect, but the others? Well, they looked a bit shit, and if it's gonna be cold, we'll want something decent."

"Agreed. Also, I think we should fly business class. After what happened in Jordan, with you taking those ghastly pills, your comfort is of utmost importance."

Fully dressed, fresh and glowing, Frida joined me on my bed.

"Definitely," she vowed with a smile. "No more pills, I promise. In fact, I talked to the medical types at work about my fear of flying, and they recommended I try St John's Wort."

"Or we could just get pissed?"

"Well, that goes without saying! Which will make it ten pees, not eight. So, are we going? Because, if we are, we should choose a hotel right now."

"Yes," I said. "Let's go. How's your Spanish?"

"Non-existent, but I'll give it a go. Mind if I nip down for a tea?"

"Sure," I replied. "Milk's in the fridge, everything else by the toaster. Spoons below, mugs above."

"Very organised," she said with a smile, and dashed downstairs to get brewing.

⧗

Frida and I boarded our flight at 7.30am on a fine June morning, both tight-lipped and full of trepidation at the gruelling schedule before us. After a painstaking search, we had come to the dreary conclusion that business class was simply unaffordable, and, forced to choose economy, we braced ourselves for the worst. The total flight time was sixteen hours and thirty minutes, with a couple of hours changing aircraft at Madrid before the final punishing stretch. Consequently, with Lima six hours behind London, it was going to be an extremely long day.

To my amazement, once on board, Frida was thoroughly excited. Full of fun, chattering like a finch (I feared she was going to be grumpy), and while stowing our luggage, she was fluttering as well.

"You were right," she said, wriggling into her seat. "The leg room's not bad, yeah, I'm gonna be fine. I am gonna be fine, aren't I?"

"Of course," I replied. "Boringly fine. Sleep as much as you can. Although, I'm staying awake for this leg."

With the engines beginning to whine, Frida gripped my hand…

"These are the bits I don't like," she said with a gulp. "The ups and the downs."

"You don't say," I replied, stroking her hand. "It's crashing I'm not so keen on."

"Now, why did you say that?" She frowned. "Horrible man. Now I'm getting the jitters."

"Sorry," I replied, looking contrite. "As soon as we're up, I'll get you a G and T, ok?"

"You'd better," she grumbled. "A double," and, with the aircraft beginning to taxi, she buried her face in my chest.

Of our week in Lima, only this brief description remains and this Mirra has all but rewritten.

"You should concentrate upon the museum," she said, and, although I did my best to ignore her, meany Mirra has hacked it to death...*

Neatly trimmed into perfection.

Frida's choice of accommodation was a curious building, and, wishing to stay somewhere peaceful, less urban than the hotel in Jordan, she had found us a fresh and colourful place that, being at the foot of forested mountains, possessed the character of a ski-lodge or spa. On the inside, the décor was rich, colourful, and stylish. Finished in red, orange, and an earthy brown. Vibrant tapestries of traditional Peruvian design hung from every wall, complimenting the dark wood of the beams, pillars, and floor. The weather was indeed chilly, and we were glad of our winter clothes, but not as cold as expected, and, when the sun did finally make an appearance, we found it warming and pleasant.

After a decidedly frantic transfer, we were both utterly spent, and, once alone in our lodge, we quickly washed, ate, and went to bed, sleeping soundly until the following morning. Served in a separate building, our main meals were a jolly affair, and, after a good breakfast, feeling refreshed, we were more than ready to go out exploring.

Depending on the quantity of livestock blocking the road, the taxi ride into Lima took about twenty or thirty minutes, and, although we made the journey dozens of times, the characterful drivers, breath-taking, vibrant, or lively scenery made the minutes whizz by, and the taxis were cheap. Ridiculously cheap. *Mostly* clean, and we felt safe within them to boot. With its Spanish colonial buildings painted an egg-yolk yellow, Lima's old centre was the most memorable district. Its many archways, spires, domes, and towers, invoking powerful visions of soldiers, priests, and a conquered nation ruthlessly brought to heel. Gushing fountains brought both drama and life to every plaza, lush vertical gardens decorated every faceless wall. There was colour, there was music, there was life!

Next to the coast, with its crumbling sandstone cliffs, modern towers of glass and steel were the norm, and we spent our evenings frequenting the district's restaurants and bars. Oh, so many memories could I recount of our meals. One gastronomic treat after another! The street food. Sweet, savoury, or wickedly spicy, then on to the bars, cafés, and restaurants, offering fusion food, both rich in colour and splendour. Kebabs on wooden skewers, seafood of every kind, and the chicken. The best you could ever hope to find.

Of the meals I could describe, one at least deserves a mention – at our hotel complex. A night of traditional Peruvian cuisine, and after drinks at the bar, feeling adventurous, we decided to join the show. Our table overlooked the swimming pool (at the time drained of water) and, looking down into its empty, leaf-strewn depths, we smiled recalling our drunken (and dangerous) clowning about the previous evening; pretending to dive-in and over-theatrically drown. Frida had chosen the hotel because of its swimming pool. Not many in Lima (we could afford) possessed one. So, to find it drained for the winter was initially a shock, quickly turning to laughter, as the excellence of the establishment made it irrelevant. Our main concern was safety. At night, neither fenced-off nor lit, the empty pool became little more than a mantrap. A leg-breaking, skull-cracking pit of unfathomable depth.

Perusing the menu, Frida's face displayed a range of emotions. Confusion (reaching for the phrase book), concentration (pondering the flavour), and finally, horror (at what the restaurant was serving) …

"Oh, God!" she exclaimed. "Have you read the mains yet?"

"Of course," I replied. "Is there a problem?"

"Yes. They're serving *cuy*. *Cuy frito*!"

"Are they?" I nonchalantly replied. "That's guinea pig, isn't it?"

"Yeah. Poor little squeaks. How can people eat a thing so adorably cute?"

Taking the phrase book, I translated the rest of the blurb…

"Hmm," I pondered. "Guinea pig in batter. Salad, potatoes. So, it's a bit like toad-in-the-hole. Delicious!"

"Don't care," she replied, looking paler than ever. "And, anyway, it's not toad, it's rodent. More vole-in-the-hole than toad!"

Snorting as I suppressed my laughter, Frida smiled, but her mouth was reluctantly twisting.

"Well," I then said, "since we're trying new things, mind if I find out? It's excellent value."

"Don't-you-dare!" she snapped. "You can eat meat if you must, but fluffies are out of the question!"

"But why? In Peru, they're just food, love, and, besides, they're already dead. Skinned, frozen, oven ready."

"Skinned?" she replied. "No! The poor little mites. The thought of them being…"

"So, you're serious, not even a taste?"

"Yes!" she cried, gripping the table. "I mean it, Marcus. If you order one, we're done. You're out of the bedroom and onto the couch!"

"Very well," I replied (not really believing her). "Then, I shall stick with the *anticuchos*. Comes on a stick anyway."

Anticuchos are a traditional Peruvian kebab-like dish, served on a bamboo skewer.

Believe me, I already know.

By Friday afternoon, the weather had turned. It was dull, damp, chilly, perfect for indoor sightseeing, so we decided to visit the museum holding the Chachapoyan mummies. The museum in question, the *Museo Nacional Arqueologia, Antropologia e Historia Peru*, was a substantial, mustard-yellow building, with the Peruvian flag flying over it on a long white pole.

All on one level, the interior was sprawling and maze-like, with an exquisite courtyard central to a network of connecting corridors. Quite unusually, its galleries displayed their exhibits by type (rather than by period), e.g., lithic, ceramic, metal, and we had to walk some distance before we came across the gallery most interesting to us. The Gallery of Human Remains. After a slow circuit, we settled upon the exhibit concerning the Chachapoya and the single mummy we had come so far to see…

"There he is," remarked Frida. "Ooh, with his head in his hands, he looks really depressed."

"So would you be," I replied, peering over her shoulder, "in a glass box and stared at all day."

There were seven mummies in all. Wrapped in yellow fabric and squatting, their position was foetal. Their legs and hands up under their chins.

"Dit was da dallest one dey X-rayed, waddened dit, Darky?" said Frida, her nose pressed to the glass.

"Yes. You think it's worth asking for a 'behind the scenes' look?"

"Well, you can try," replied Frida, stepping back and rubbing her nose. "But remember what Corbiere said: 'They intended no further investigation into these specimens. Too many lost to looters and damaged already', so I can't see them agreeing."

"Ah, sod it," I then said. "I'm asking anyway and making a fuss. We're going home tomorrow. This is our only chance."

"Then I'm coming with you," said Frida. "It's busy, and I don't want to get lost, and I must say, you're being very bold, lovey. Are you feeling alright?"

With signs on long chains hanging from the ceiling, flanked by guards, and constantly busy, the front desk was a long, stone-topped affair, and joining the queue for "Informacion y Consultas" we waited our turn...

"You think it might help if we showed our British Museum IDs? Mine's still in my wallet. Have you got yours?"

"Of course," replied Frida, and digging in her bag, she produced it with a grin.

"Could you do the talking?" I asked. "Your Spanish is already quite good. Although, a moment ago, I thought I heard English."

At last, it was our turn, and Frida, standing on tippy toe (to see over the counter), smiled at the man before her.

"Good afternoon," she twinkled (a bit too flirty for my liking). "Do you speak English?"

"Of course, señora. How can I help?"

"Well," said Frida, "my partner and I have come from the British Museum in London to view the Kuelap exhibit. We were wondering if a private inspection could be arranged?"

Looking thoughtful for a moment, the man behind the counter slowly digested Frida's request.

"I'm not sure," he replied. "Without prior arrangement it would be very... irregular? Need to check with *curador*. Wait please. I go and discover."

"Thank you." She said, handing over our passes. "Our credentials."

Awkward minutes passed, the queue behind us steadily growing, and, when the assistant did eventually return, a determined-looking man hurried along behind him...

"Not looking good," whispered Frida and I nodded.

The information desk man settled into his seat, and, while the determined man spoke, he did his best to translate...

"Welcome. I Dr Rucabado, associate *curador*. My colleague tell me your request, and I'm sorry, I cannot permit. Permit come from government. Cultural department. Normal duration a month, or two. I make request, with your return to Lima at appropriate time?"

"Understood," Frida calmly replied, flicking a look of "told you!"

"Really?" I blurted, unable to hide my dismay. "Is there no other way? We'd be happy to pay... if it would help?"

Gasping in shock, Frida elbowed me in the ribs…

"Ow," I gasped, and the men laughed, immediately becoming serious again as the translator relayed my offer.

"No!" the desk man defiantly replied. "Absolutely not, señor. Such a thing… unthinkable!" And, although his dismissal of my suggestion had been final and definite, both men then generously smiled.

Knowing myself thwarted, I wandered off feeling strangely turbulent, almost angry, and watching from afar as Frida filled in various forms and shook hands, my sense of dejection and failure deepened still. But then, a guard with a shifty demeanour suddenly blocked my view…

He was a burly man. Dark, formidable, his uniform crisp and impressive. A side arm hung from his belt, and his heavy boots shone like mined coal…

"Excuse, señor," he said, his English broken and stilted. "I hear you and girl with *curador* speak. I help."

Quite understandably taken aback by this, I carefully considered my safest reply.

"How do you mean?" I asked, my conscience gripping my words.

"You want see Kuelap? I need money. You pay. You come at seven hour. Ok?"

I thought momentarily. I was never coming back to Peru. The journey was simply too arduous, and, even if Dr Corbiere or Frida could arrange something, I thought it highly unlikely we'd get the chance to view it first-hand. So, should I take the risk? "No," whispered a voice in my head. A female voice, funnily enough (my mother or Frida most likely), but then a new voice came. A man's voice. Stronger and louder than the female. Both calming and emboldening, he gave me confidence, and I liked it. "Do it," he assured. "Do it now. Don't be a fool. Just do it!"

"Possibly," I surreptitiously muttered. "How much do you want?"

"One thousand, five hundred sol," his whispered reply. "You bring money at seven. You see Kuelap."

"Bring money where?"

"I front security at seven. See you on TV. Open door."

"Ok." I shrugged. "Maybe I'll return at seven," before returning to the desk and Frida.

Fifteen hundred nuevo sol came to about three hundred pounds and the last of my spending money. To let it go would be a terrible wrench, so I needed to make up my mind, and quickly…

"You alright?" asked Frida, returning a pen to the desk. "Because you look peeved. Are you disappointed?"

"Of course," I replied, "but I've had an idea. Tell you it about later."

"Oh, really?" she smiled. "Have you now?"

"Yes," I said. "Are we done?"

"Well," – Frida shrugged – "they've got our details. If any further examination of the mummies takes place, they promise to let us know. Ok. It isn't much, but this is as far as we can get. We just have to wait."

"Very well," I replied with a sigh. "And are we heading back to the hotel? Time's getting on and we need to rest before our flight."

"Yeah," she said, with a kiss on my cheek. "Let's go. One last meal and then a float in the tub. Ok?"

Leaving the museum, I said nothing, but, before we crossed the street, I gathered her into my arms and kissed her hard on the lips.

"What was that for?" asked Frida, looking confused.

"Insurance," I replied.

Back at our hotel, following food, fun, and frolics, I revealed the provisional arrangement I'd made with the guard. Frida wasn't impressed…

"For God's sake!" she beseeched. "Who do you think you are? James Bond? And fifteen hundred sols? That's like, what, three hundred quid? You're insane. No. You're not going, and that's final!"

Slipping on my trainers, my mind was made up. I was going and going alone. Frida would be safer here, and, although sure of myself, she would be a distraction (and the guard might lose his nerve). An occasional lack of subtlety remains one of Frida's few flaws…

"You're ignoring me," she said, dogging my steps. "You're actually going to go? Can't you even listen?"

Blushing, I tried to turn away.

She was correct. I was ignoring her, and, making my way to the safe, I punched in the combination.

"What if you're caught?" she warned. "Mugged, shot, beaten up?"

"Stop worrying," I finally replied. "Just a quick look, then I'm coming straight back. I'll be fine."

"Not worry?" she replied. "How?"

Gripping my arm, she looked into my eyes, and I held her closely before me.

"Just be careful," she begged. "Take your mobile and call me or the hotel if you get into trouble. Ok?"

"Of course," I said. "See you back here in a bit," and after a slow final kiss I made my way to the plaza and a waiting taxi.

The streets outside the museum were quiet as a hallowed grave. Certainly, it was not a night to be outside. Low cloud sweeping over the city had brought with it a biting cold and, asking my taxi driver to wait, I handed him a small value note.

"Ten minutes," I explained, pointing towards my watch, "maybe twenty," and I counted on my fingers to emphasise my point.

Nodding his understanding, I gave the driver a short wave and, after looking about, I made my way to the museum. Was anyone watching?

Wrapped in a heavy cloak and barely discernible through the mist, one lone figure seemed to be looking straight at me, but, since I could hardly see him, he could hardly see me, and, ignoring his presence, I briskly walked up the steps, coming upon the museum's large metal doors. Not knowing what to do next, I readied a hand to knock, but it wasn't necessary – the guard was already there, and opening the door, he ushered me inside…

"Come," he whispered, "quick," and I followed him into a small office behind the front desk.

"What happens now?" I asked. "You want money?"

"Yes." He nodded. "Money now."

"Half now and half after Kuelap. Ok?"

The guard smiled and shrugged.

"You like gangster," he replied. "Ok, deal. Wait. Cameras I end."

Clicking away with a mouse, he selectively shut down the relevant cameras, before urging me to follow him into the dark and decidedly creepy museum.

"Here," he said, pointing towards a door. "You go in. I no watch. No witness," and, unlocking the door, he flicked on the lights.

"Fine," I muttered, swallowing my apprehension. "Where will you be?"

"I near," he assured. "You say. I come."

Nodding, I went in, cautiously stepping over the foremost mummified examples to reach the largest at the rear.

Inside, the air was stuffy and close, thick with a strange aroma, and, stooping to examine the largest mummy, I noticed fine threads maintaining its position. Whipping out my phone, mindful not to snag myself, I took photos, before prodding the mummy with my thumb…

"Fixer," I muttered, noting the fabric's solidity. Shuffling closer, I ran my fingers around the outline of an elongated bulge wedged between its knees.

"Must be it," I whispered. "And upside down, I think."

Was it the figurine? How could I know, and what to do next. Tear open the bindings? I didn't want to, but I had to, and, after muttering, "In for a penny, in for a pound," I tore into the fabric like a man possessed. The effect of this was catastrophic. The bindings almost exploded. Shards of wax flying in every direction, and I tried to catch as many as I could...

"Shit," I regretfully hissed, and yet there it was, the figurine. Easing it from the remaining bindings, I stood it on the floor.

"Looks like new," I muttered. "Frida'll never believe it."

Kneeling for a closer look, between my feet, I noticed a bead of twinkling stone.

"Hello," I said, picking it up. "Wondered where you went," and, without a thought, I slipped it into my pocket.

Moving to take further photos, I then tried replacing both the figurine and fabric. It was no good. The damage was irreparable. So, apologising to the mummy for the indignity (with a pat on the head), I climbed from the chamber and called the guard.

Without commenting on the damage inside the chamber, I handed him the rest of the money, before watching him turn off the lights and lock up. Following his slow plod to the entrance, he seemed strangely inanimate, and I studied him as he leant back in his chair, lighting a cigarette. His demeanour was entirely correct. We had no further business. My task was done, my crime committed, and, marching from the museum and into the still waiting taxi, my heart was fluttering. Excitement and guilt in equal measure.

Within twenty minutes, safely in our hotel, I noticed how Frida, after finishing off the last of the packing, had moved our luggage to the hall, and, stepping over it, I noticed light coming from under the bathroom door. I gently knocked...

"I'm back, love. Safe and sound. Thanks for doing the packing."

No reply.

"The figurine inside the mummy was identical to the one found in Sussex. We were right. Definitely Chachapoyan. The Vikings must've traded this far south. There's no other explanation, and yes, I did take some photos to prove it."

No reply.

"Are you not talking to me or something?"

"Of course not!" she snapped. "I'm on the loo, for a start. How about some privacy?"

"Oh, yes." I chuckled. "Sorry, love. I'll wait."

"Well," she sighed, "you might have to wait for a while. The rich food is taking revenge. Could you nip to the supermarket? We need supplies for the flight."

"Sure," I replied. "What should I get?"

"Some hard fruit?" she suggested. "Something we can cut up and bag up and a couple of bananas."

"What about drink?"

"Oh, just get water, nothing fizzy. The choice of nibbles I leave to you."

"Very well. Rice crackers, popcorn, if they've got it, and I'm sorry if I upset you earlier. I know it was risky, but you should have seen the figurine! Definitely worth it."

"You can tell that to the judge." She laughed. "Now, go on, you silly boy. Off you trot. You can tell me about it later."

Our nearest twenty-four-hour supermarket was on the outskirts of Lima, and within fifteen minutes I was waiting outside for a taxi – as mine had driven off.

"Come on," I muttered, peering down the road. "Don't you know we've a plane to catch."

The taxi that eventually pulled up was a wreck. Dents, bits hanging off, one wheel out of alignment, but, keen to get back, I jumped in, showing the driver the address of our resort.

"Bumpy," he replied. "Hold tight."

Inside the cab, the staleness of the air was almost overwhelming, and I gagged at the pungent stench…

"Phew," I gasped. "Do you mind if I wind down a window?"

Without an answer from the driver, I shrugged and… and… did I wind it down? I cannot remember! Then we drove on for a bit, I think. The road was very bumpy, and then I found myself here (wherever here is) and it is here I draw this account to a close.

Marcus Eaton, June 2011 (probably).

SEVENTEEN

THE LAST LAUGH

As if by magic, the loudspeaker, sounding its crackle and beep, heralded the sunshine voice of Mirra…

"Marcus!" She beamed. "You've done it! You've finished, and, although I knew you'd finish eventually, you had me extremely worried. Lesser men would've faltered after Moloch's cruel ministration."

"Hi, Mirra," I said, attentively standing. "Yes, thank you, it's all done, besides, giving up wasn't an option."

"And thank the heavens for that!" she replied, her voice a sparkling brook. "But tell me. How can you be both languid and stubborn, only to then be productive and compliant?"

"Not really sure." I shrugged. "However, you are right. Laziness is my preferred condition. It's taken me years to master my drifting concentration. I think it's all to do with mental thresholds. If that's the correct terminology?"

"It sounds suitable. Go on…"

"Well, yeah. I'm easy-going until a line is crossed. Cruelty or injustice is usually the trigger, or perhaps something deeper? Something more subtle? No idea, frankly. But push me hard enough and I turn into a fighter."

"You know yourself better than I realised. You're remarkable, and I sincerely regret underestimating you. Can you forgive me?"

"Of course, silly Mirra. You didn't know me. You also said my writing was rubbish. Do you still hold to that?"

"Oh, good Lord, yes!" she replied. "It's diabolical. Only, if you were a naturally skilful writer, we wouldn't have met. Robbing me of a most enjoyable friendship."

"For sure," I said. "And you've been good company too. I'm gonna miss you. But now, when can I leave? When I finish, you said. You promised."

"Indeed. I did promise. I haven't forgotten. Just not yet. Before I can present your work to Moloch, we need to check it, thoroughly. Only when he's satisfied will you be able to leave."

Feeling more caged than ever, I sighed. My stomach turning in disappointment...

"And how long will that take? Because I'm going crazy in here. I need to get back to Frida. To get back to my life!"

"I know," she replied. "Believe me, I know. You just need to be patient. A little more, and then we'll be done."

It was no good. My frustration was now implacable. In sudden burst of temper, I kicked the chair against the wall...

"Help me," I pleaded, my palm over the camera in the door. "Please, Mirra. You've always helped me before. Help me now. Can't you find a way?"

"Sweet Marcus," she replied. "Believe me. I do understand. What you're going through. Your frustration must be unbearable. So close to freedom only to be thwarted, but, like you, I'm helpless. So, let's whizz through your writing, panning and scanning. Like we did last time? If Moloch finds the most relevant sections satisfactory, he's likely to ignore the rest."

Walking to the washbasin, I splashed water over my reddening cheeks...

"Ok," I gasped, drying myself. "If you say it's so, I believe you. How about some music again? It certainly the helped the last time."

"Oh yes," she cheerily replied. "And it's your turn to choose. Nothing too coarse, though. I beg you."

Thinking for a moment, I made my choice. Something contemporary, with a bit of energy. Selecting five albums, I set them to play in chronological order...

"This'll perk us up, I reckon, see what you make of this. When my dad introduced me to these guys, I was only a kid. A rock group for most of the time, but their music is distinct, and I'll think you'll enjoy it," and with the first swirls of Hammond organ filling the air, we got down to work.

⧗

My musical tastes and Mirra's were clearly quite different. Pausing the playback, she would make comments, mostly derogatory…

"Too heavy! Too frantic!" was her most common complaint, and, although she enjoyed the keyboards, she disliked the "scything grumble" of the bass guitar. The lyrics interested her more, however, and she considered the lyrics of "The Raven" good advice for any young man. During the second album, I paused the music, asking about a lyric referring to "the Great Elmyra." Did she know to whom it referred?

"Indeed, I do," she replied. "A corruption of the name Elmyr de Hory. An art forger of incredible skill. Born in Hungary, in 1905, before his unmasking, his fabrications were so good, they fooled both collectors and experts. After the blowing of his cover, so highly regarded were his forgeries, they commanded lofty prices on their own merit."

"Mirra." I laughed. "You're amazing. You're like a walking encyclopaedia!"

"Why, thank you, kind Marcus," she replied.

Although, I haven't walked for an age.

"What happens now?" I asked. "Are you going away?"

"Yes," she replied. "But I will stay in touch. Pop by, if an opportunity arises. In the meantime, do try to keep busy. Why not write of your experiences here? Once Moloch has finished his deliberations, I will endeavour to embellish your account, inserting your recollections chronologically."

"Not sure what you mean," I said, "but the writing's a good idea. I've become so used to it. Seems daft to stop now. What do you suggest? Start at the start, when we first met, and go from there?"

"Perfect," she replied, "and when you write about me, please be nice. I want my family to be proud."

"Of course," I assured. "Think you're wonderful, Mirra. I love you to bits!"

"Ah, bless you," she replied. "And I love you too. Now, before we go mushy, I have to leave. Goodbye."

"Goodbye Mirra," I said.

Still here. Waiting, hoping, everything writable, written. Will my release ever come? You already know of the visits I received in the meantime. I have written of those too. This last period of waiting… Well, it is terrible. I simply have nothing to do!

I have set the portal to random playback, and the cocktail of media bombarding my eyes and ears is moderately amusing.

Mirra has returned. A heavenly relief…

"Well, here we are then," I said. "Time for your release, are you ready?"

"Of course," he replied. "Been ready for yonks." *

"Yonks," I said. "Never heard that term before. Slang for an extended period?"

*The Circarian is correct. YONKS is an amalgamation/contraction of the words Years, mONths, and weeKS.

"Ahem!" He coughed. "Release, you said. Don't start with the questions. Open the door and let me out!"

Always enjoying his moody sarcasm, I could only laugh. Such a dry sense of humour from such a young man is a rare and wonderful gift.

"Oh yes," I replied. "Sorry, Marcus. Force of habit. I'm afraid your release is more complicated than simply opening the door. You must follow my instructions very attentively."

"Here we go," he muttered under his breath. "What do I have to do?"

"First," I replied, "we're going to turn off the lights. So, for safety's sake, I want you to lie on the bed."

He did as I asked, wriggling to find the most comfortable spot.

"Right," he said. "Lying down. What next?"

Adjusting the photonic input, for him the "room" became utterly dark.

"Soon," I replied, "you will fall asleep, very deeply. Much like when I repaired your room. Although, this time, no gas."

He seemed apprehensive and I could see him struggling against the urge to sit up.

"Ok," he nervously muttered. "Wish you could hold my hand."

"Wish that too," I replied, his tenderness very endearing, "but there's no need to worry. You won't feel a thing."

The first effects of the device took hold, and perfectly. No malfunction reports from Legato whatsoever. A feeling of drowsiness swept over Marcus, and was he aware of the gravitational field beginning to weaken?

"Going to miss you," he said, his words beginning to slur.

"No, you won't," I said, inwardly smiling. "I don't exist."

"Will never forget."

"You will," I redressed, and, as his physical began to lose its cohesion, I closed my eye in prayer.

"Thank you," I whispered. "Thank you. For everything. From us all."

"Music," he mumbled. "Getting louder... Oh, no, not Umbrella. Am I in hell?"

And those were his final words. Hardly a poetic ending (I hope to do better), yet he went laughing and joking. His final gift, I suppose.

Finally, with his form gone, my whispered prayer came forth: "Today is given for your tomorrow. So, love her. Love her for us both. Love her with every beat of your heart."

Foolish, of course. No way could he have heard. A spoken prayer is wasted breath. There is no one to listen! Faith is vain. Introspection is the only path to truth. The only god we ever hear is internal.

EPILOGUE

A FINAL LETTER
FROM FRIDA

From: padgett.frida86@eucomm.co.uk
To: corbiere.graham@britishmuseum.org

Lorenzo Carter Place
Friars Road
Winchelsea
East Sussex
3/12/2024

Dear Graham,

Thank you for your prompt and gracious reply, and I do apologise for failing to send a copy of Marcus's journal. The file has strange properties which I shall describe further down the page...

In my previous letter, only a dozen pages into Marcus's journal, Frank and I knew not where it would lead, but after reading its entirety, we have reached a terrible conclusion. He is dead. Near the end, Mirra describes the nature of Marcus's release, and I am convinced her words are a smokescreen, disguising his execution by gas or anaesthetic. Certainly, if free, Marcus would quickly have contacted the relevant authorities, his family, or me, and considering the amount of time that has passed, there is little doubt his release was his execution. Murderers. Moloch, Mirra, who are these people? What gives them the right? Vile, scheming, treacherous. My poor Marcus! He did everything they asked.

There was no reason to kill him! He was harmless. He was helpless. Why did they do it?

Now, as you know, I am due (slightly overdue) to go into labour and can do without any more stress. Writing this letter is helping, as did the one in September, but so bottled is our anger we feel ready to explode. Why the emotional bottleneck? Well, it's because of Marcus's file …

Last time, I wrote how I found the file in my EuComm, and God only knows how long it had been there. Without my knowledge, 2.6MB of data had slipped into its memory. Particularly remarkable, as only I can access that partition (it is where I store my private research) and I protect it with biometrics and an "unbreakable" quantum-flux password. But this is the tip of the iceberg! Even more worrying, the file behaves like a virus. It has infected every computer we own, and, although harmless, being unable to control its spread is driving us to distraction. In part, this explains why I failed to attach the file to my previous email. The file itself chooses the extent of its replication, leading me to describe another of the file's oddities. Its selectivity of access. Somehow, and I know this sounds like science fiction, but the file is self-aware. It can recognise who or what is accessing it. Frank suggests this is part of the file's defence. Only the members of our household have access, and we can't even print it! The old printer from our attic reported "file not found" when we tried. Screen dumps, digital, or chemical photographs similarly fail, resulting in no more than a blank file or film, and if, say, my mother visits desiring a read, the file disappears, as if it never existed! Not until her departure will we find Marcus's message again, popping up right where we left it, freely accessible, even to our four-year-old son. I ask you. How can this be? Why the selectivity, and why the control? Why must Marcus's memoirs be secret? Why us, why not the Eatons (Victor, Barbara, Millicent)? Why are we the privileged few?

With help from his university professor, Frank theorises the file could be a species of computer virus, still theoretical (they thought), known as an "entity" or more colloquially, "a paint bomb". Put simply, a "paint bomb" is a normal file entangled with a system in another location. Once installed, the virus then becomes the computer itself, independent of the host computer's memory, all to preserve the file at its core.

Great, I said, listening to his theory and not understanding. Can you explain why Marcus's journal also appears to me in the UK digital library? Are you saying, dear husband, Marcus's file has infected the world and only we are aware of it?

Since the file's arrival, Frank drinks more than he used to. He sits alone, sipping whisky, shaking his head, muttering about the impossible code written by the murdered man in the wall…

So, there we have it. The file itself prevents me from sharing it. Using it to locate Marcus or clear myself of suspicion would be fruitless, and, although you might think me nuts, swimming in hormones, pregnant and prattling, everything I have told you is true! There's nothing further we can do. We've reached dead end. We have a degree of closure, which is welcome. Villains to despise, disappointment and fury, but we are no closer to the truth. Poor Marcus's tragedy will play on until he is found. Not that he will be. His captors aren't that stupid. His remains would release a wealth of new data, so I've given up on that front as well.

So, finally, here we are. Our long search for Marcus is over. Saddening, but also a great relief. My family is my future, and it is time to move on. Never knowing and forever hoping are now a part of my past. My history. A thread, trailing, describing the twisting path of my life.

Now, now, come on Dr Padgett! There you go again, pining for the impossible, and, even though giving up is not in my nature, I am mindful of the poem "Wait for Me" by Simonov, as waiting for the impossible is selfish. Selfish to both Marcus and my family. Indeed. It is time to live again, to love again, and to embrace what we have.

To breathe again,
and laugh again,
in freedom,
at last.
Yours sincerely,
Frida

BOOK TWO
TRANSITION

THE PEOPLE
AND PECULIARITIES
OF BOOK TWO

(BY ORDER OF
APPEARANCE)

UNITED EUROPEAN TECHNOLOGIES (UET): A vast cooperative scientific enterprise of the 22nd century.

DR REGINA PADGETT (GINA): Chief scientist of the HALFPENNY INSTITUTE OF CELLULAR RESEARCH. She is tall and elegant, with long dark hair and deep brown eyes.

HALFPENNY INSTITUTE OF CELLULAR RESEARCH (ICR): A research and development organisation based in London, England. The Halfpenny ICR is a member of the UET scientific cooperative.

UET KUIPER BELT EXPLORER or KBE: A large dodecahedral interplanetary spacecraft.

SSD: A colloquialism for the headquarters of the UET space programme in Darmstadt, Germany.

SIR MALCOLM WALSINGHAM PHD: An eminent scientist and high-ranking member of the UET. In 2093, Sir Malcolm volunteered to lead the proposed KUIPER BELT EXPLORER. He was very tall (over two metres), slender, with white hair, beard, and penetrating blue eyes.

INQUISITOR WALTER DE BOER: An investigator working for the UET. He is Dutch, about thirty-five, calm, capable, and kind.

COMA PODS: The hibernation devices aboard the UET KUIPER BELT EXPLORER.

DR SUSI ACKERMANN (SUSI): A German psychologist/psychiatrist and friend of DR REGINA PADGETT. In her late forties, she is of average height and build, with greying brown hair and grey eyes.

DR ABDULLAH AL-HILLAH (ABDA): An engineer of Iraqi parentage. ABDA worked for SIR MALCOLM WALSINGHAM and joined him aboard the UET KUIPER BELT EXPLORER. He is about 1.8 metres in height, fit, athletic, with black hair, a bushy black beard, and olive-brown eyes.

LUIS EMILIO BEDOYA (EMIL): A Peruvian astronomer and astrophysicist. EMIL worked for SIR MALCOLM WALSINGHAM and joined him aboard the UET KUIPER BELT EXPLORER. He is forty years old, 1.7 metres in height, broad, and stocky, having a dark complexion, black hair, and brown eyes.

RUMBELOW: A small dog belonging to the mother of DR REGINA PADGETT.

DR ERIC J BADSEGH (ERIC): An English nutritionist and physiologist specialising in extra-terrestrial food production and preparation. At 1.9 metres in height, he is muscular, with blue eyes and long blonde hair.

DR WILLIAM CORBIERE (BILL): A medical doctor, computer hobbyist and crew member of the UET KUIPER BELT EXPLORER. In his forties, he is tall, pale, shy, and fussy.

SPECTRACOTE: A bio-synthetic microcellular composite. A multifunctional film-like material covering many surfaces, fibres, and materials aboard the KBE.

FOXE POWER CELLS: An acronym of FLUOR-OXY-XENATE. Developed by SIR MALCOLM WALSINGHAM, they are energy storage devices used to regulate and initiate nuclear fusion reactors.

COMPTON ARRAY: The network of anti-radiation laser emitters covering the outer hull of the UET KUIPER BELT EXPLORER.

HIBBITES or NANO ROBOTIC INTRACELLULAR MANAGEMENT SYSTEM (NICMS): The implanted body management system servicing the crew of the UET KUIPER BELT EXPLORER.

POLYCOTE: A brand of artificial fibre incorporating SPECTRACOTE technology.

BOROPHENE: An artificial allotrope of boron, borophene is exceptionally light, strong, and flexible. Cheap and easily combined with other materials, borophene is useful in the manufacture of spacecraft.

NANOPARTICLE MULTI-TENDENCY NON-NEWTONIAN COMPOSITE FLUID or NNCF: An advanced particle fluid combining SPECTRACOTE technology used inside the KBE for the creation of furniture, fittings, equipment, and environmental simulations.

CYBERCORTEX: A general term referring to the cybernetic brain implants given to the crew of UET KUIPER BELT EXPLORER.

GECKODERM: A strongly adhesive coating capable of rapidly changing its "stickiness".

GELPONICS: The cultivation of plants within a supporting gel medium. DR ERIC J BADSEGH developed GelPonics for the propagation of fruit and vegetables in space.

SYNTHETIC ANIMAL MEAT AND PROTEIN or SAMP: An in-vitro technique developed by DR ERIC J BADSEGH for the humane production of animal foodstuffs, e.g., meat, eggs, and milk.

SENSWARM: The extra-vehicular research, repair, and reconnaissance system fitted to the UET KUIPER BELT EXPLORER.

DR KAROLINA KOVAL: Former Mars colonist, the colony supervisor.

DR LEANDRA PFENNIG: Former Mars colonist, a biochemist.

DR JESSICA MOTTE: Former Mars colonist, a botanist.

DR ARNOLD MOTTE: Former Mars colonist, the colony's medical doctor.

SHONA MOTTE: Daughter of ARNOLD and JESSICA MOTTE.

DR STEFAN PFENNIG: Former Mars colonist and engineer.

LEON PFENNIG: Son of STEFAN and LEANDRA PFENNIG.

MEGAN PFENNIG: Daughter of STEFAN and LEANDRA PFENNIG.

DR DAVID HALL: Former Mars colonist, a geologist.

DR TOBIAS LOMBARDI: Former Mars colonist, a geologist.

TREVOR BRAY: Former Mars colonist, a veterinary surgeon.

VIVIENNE BRAY: Former Mars colonist, a nutritionist and agronomist.

ASHTON BRAY: Son of TREVOR and VIVIENNE BRAY.

JULIAN BRAY: Eldest son of TREVOR and VIVIENNE BRAY.

SNOWSHIELD: The detachable micrometeoroid and space debris deflector fitted to the UET KUIPER BELT EXPLORER.

GLEENER: A medium sized ball of dazzling white light.

MOLOCH: A large, crackling ball of dazzling white plasma. In ancient times, MOLOCH was the Canaanite god of sacrifice and fire.

PROLOGUE
WE ARE DELIGHTED...

United European Technologies, Space Science Division
Office of the Science Programme Committee
Darmstadt
Germany
October 2102

To: padgett.regina@halfpennyICR.uet.com

Dear Dr Padgett,

Considering your application to join the space exploration programme in 2093, we are delighted to offer you a position aboard the proposed Kuiper Belt Explorer, on its mission to the outer solar system, the dwarf planets Eris, Pluto, Haumea, Makemake, and associated bodies within the Kuiper Belt region.

Precise mission details are currently unavailable, but, following your acceptance, disclosure will commence during the introductory meetings at the SSD in Darmstadt throughout 25 and 26 November this year (this meeting is compulsory for all mission applicants).

Not only will this expedition go down in history as one of humanity's greatest achievements, the opportunities for developing innovative technologies, furthering our knowledge of the solar system and galaxy are unparalleled. The benefaction of the eminent Sir Malcolm Walsingham PHD, the recently appointed mission director, confirms the great significance of this venture.

I look forward to your reply.
Sincerely,
Nicholas D Weiss
Chief Administrator, SPC

ONE

QUESTIONS

United European Technologies,
Space Sciences Division,
Legal Services Dept.
Walter de Boer, Inquisitor, April 2112.
Subject: Dr Regina Padgett
UET#: 147713
Age: 48
Position: Chief Scientist, Halfpenny Institute of Cellular Research.

To whom it may concern:

The following document (where possible) is a word-for-word transcript from a series of interviews I undertook with Dr Regina Padgett, sole survivor* of the fated, UET Kuiper Belt Explorer.

*The SSD recorded the crew as missing.

Conducted within the confines of the Halfpenny ICR, London, and most often within Dr Padgett's office, the meetings were informal, in English, with an air of professionalism ever under the surface.

Having never met Dr Padgett, the little I knew of her came from her exemplary service record, gossip, and rumour, not all of it favourable. Being the great-granddaughter of the renowned Dr Frida Padgett, founder of the Halfpenny

ICR, some among the scientific community, jealous of her accomplishments, have dubbed her "Frankenstein's Daughter", claiming her a deviant one at that! Indeed, such base insults are usually born from bitterness, and, preferring to draw my own opinions, when I first met Dr Padgett, it was with an open mind and a fair degree of excitement. Having never met a biomechanically enhanced human, I didn't know what to expect, and my curiosity was rife.

Her office was large (dwarfing my own), plush, and comfortable, boasting a food and drink dispenser, refrigerator, kitchen cupboards, and counter. In one corner, a partition concealed a changing room and a shower, with specialised excretory ports compatible with Dr Padgett's rectal and urinary modifications.

She welcomed me graciously and we shook hands…

"Inquisitor de Boer?" she asked, and I nodded. "It's good of you to come. I do hope your trip wasn't too onerous. Please take a seat. Would you care for drink? Tea or coffee perhaps?"

This pleasant greeting from her was typical. A truly remarkable woman in nature, wit, and appearance, very beguiling. Wearing white disposable overalls, common enough in laboratories, she still radiated an aura of beauty, her chiselled symmetrical face, dark eyes, and famously long hair, braided into a ponytail, highlighted her towering athletic figure…

"Coffee, if you please," I replied. "And, before we begin, I would like to ask you some personal questions and, if at any time you feel uncomfortable, do please say and I'll immediately change the topic."

"Very well," she acknowledged. "But I've precious little to hide and – are you already recording? I thought it customary to announce commencement?"

"It is," I replied, "and I am, but, please, my name's Walter, no need for formality: this isn't a hearing. Otherwise, as you rightly point out, protocols would be observed."

Witnessing Dr Padgett's smile, my heart suddenly leapt, before inwardly cursing, appreciating the extent of Dr Padgett's power – an almost diabolic aura of seduction and charm…

"Indeed," she then said. "The message I received from the UET explained the situation. The poor things. What a tight spot to get into? Me, the only survivor, but still asleep in my pod, and all their entangled data torn to shreds by a cascading computer. A temporal anomaly. Which they still claim is impossible, so who can they blame? Me, surely. But, oh, they can't. I was asleep. So, what can they do? Ask nicely, and hope I will help?"

"Quite so," I chuckled in reply. "And I'm the poor *stakker* entrusted to do it. Pity me, will you?"

"I do. Walter Trust me, I do, and dispense with the doctor. Call me Gina,* never Regina. Too much teasing at school."

Pronounced Jea-na.

"Very well, and did you mention coffee, Gina? We need to get started."
"I did. How do you take it?"
"Black, please. Can your machine sucrolate?"
"Sweeten? Yes. It'll do anything I tell it. Want a biscuit as well?"
"Certainly, but I'm notoriously fussy. What've you got?"
"No idea." She shrugged, and, turning to the dispenser's front panel, she said, "Hey! Foody thing! Two coffees. One white, no sugar, one black, with sweetener, and what biscuits you got?"

"Welcome to Snack Box!" replied the dispenser. "How can I help you today? Request accepted. Your beverages are being prepared. Please wait."

"Biscuits, *Dummkopf,* do you have any biscuits?"
"Checking biscuit availability!"
"Good," she muttered, crossing her arms, and flashing a petulant look.

A long five seconds of silence slowly passed before the dispenser then proudly announced:

"I'm sorry, biscuits are not currently available... A... message has been sent to your local supplier. Please try again later, instead... Would you prefer a... high fibre cereal bar?"

"Certainly not!" snapped Dr Padgett. "End of request."

"Thank you for using Snack Box!" said the dispenser, and, within, two mugs of coffee gently slid into view.

"Nope," she said. "Sorry, Walter. There aren't any biscuits. Would you prefer a... cereal bar? They're very high in fibre."

"Definitely not, but thanks for the coffee. Smells great. Columbian?"

"No," she replied. "Costa Rican. Can't you tell?"

"Do I need to?" And she shrugged. "Now then, you are Dr Regina Padgett, chief scientist of the Halfpenny Cell Research Institute?"

"I am."

"And I understand you were biomechanically modified in 2103. Could you briefly list the extent of your enhancements?"

"Of course. I possess upgrades to my ears, eyes, and visual cortex, with biomechanical sphincters fitted to my stomach, rectum, and urethra, including access ports for the elimination of urine and faeces."

"Yes," I affirmed. "I've seen people with ocular implants – their eyes sparkle. Yours don't?"

"Ha, yes!" she replied. "I have the Halfpenny eyes. Pupils so dark you cannot see the twinkle."

"Ah, anything else?"

"Yes, a host of tiny, subdermal factories imbue my body. An advanced body management system employing nanoparticle robots."

"Fascinating. What do they do?"

"A lot, but I think they're still classified. What is your clearance?"

"Alpha blue."

"Is that all? I'm delta yellow, or was, the last time I checked. If you're below gamma red, I can't discuss them."

"Very well. I will apply for an upgrade. Anything else?"

"Yes. Neural implants. Many and various. Some for the networking – permitting a direct neural control of compatible systems, but I also have enhanced memory capacity, improved recall, processing, and cognition."

"Excellent, and I must say, you're very tall. Just how tall are you?"

"About six foot two."

"Six foot what?"

"Oops," she replied. "Sorry. Too much time in London – about 188 centimetres?"

"Right," I said. "And a whole head taller than me, and, for the record, what is your height in… light years?"

"Light years?" she enquired, looking perplexed.

"Yes," I confirmed. "If you would be so kind…"

"Hmm," she mumbled, furrowing her brow. "One point nine eight six seven, eight one two zero two, times ten to the minus sixteen. Why do you ask?"

"Yeah." I then chuckled, shaking my head. "You're the enhanced Dr Padgett, alright!"

"Sneaky," she replied with scowl. "Do you do this a lot?"

"No." I chuckled. "Clever tricks and devices aren't really my style, and besides, if I tried it again, you'd notice."

"I most certainly would. When attempting deception, the ferocity of your pulse increases markedly, and the modulation of your voice increases by several hertz."

"Really? You can detect tiny changes like that?"

"Yes, and they're not as tiny as you might think."

"Amazing. Do you ever play poker?"

"Of course not," she replied, shaking her head.

"Well, you should. You'd be unbeatable. Could make a fortune!"

"No. I'm sorry, Walter, but there'd be no point."

"Why?"

"For one, I already have a fortune, and two, when you can see through the cards, where is the challenge?"

"Now," I continued, flipping the mood, "when did you first consider volunteering for the space programme?"

"During my second year at Cambridge."

"As an undergraduate?"

"Yes. Students, especially those of a scientific, maths, or engineering persuasion, were signing up in droves."

"But I understand you didn't. Why was that?"

"Several reasons, and I still recall the discussions Susi and I shared on the topic. Initially, she was the keener. What else should one do with a psychology degree? In reply, I could only shrug."

"Susi?" I enquired. "Dr Susi Ackermann?"

"Yes. Susi and I first met at Cambridge. We were at the same college. St John's."

"I see. Go on."

"I didn't want any distractions during my studies and recommended Susi do the same. We both wanted firsts, and that demanded commitment. In addition, it was common knowledge that the best space jobs were only offered to the over-thirty-fives, so, dear Susi, I said, what is the rush?"

"Yes," I acknowledged, "I've noticed that. Almost seems ageist. Do you know why?"

"Of course. It mostly to do with cellular maturity. In space, genetic damage from radiation exposure is a constant threat, and older people, since they are no longer growing, are less susceptible. There are psychological reasons too, as Susi would've merrily pointed out, but singletons, especially those in their thirties or forties, are often calmer, more considered and content in themselves. Already deciding not to have children is also a factor."

"Ah yes," I replied. "That was illuminating, thank you, Gina."

"I'm glad," she said. "As that wasn't a good explanation – it is a vast topic and hotly debated. Not everyone in the UET agrees with the policy."

"So, I have read. The Walsingham Advanced Research Centre is perhaps the most pertinent example. They're constantly on the lookout for the brightest most capable students. Plucking them straight from university."

"Indeed," Dr Padgett replied, "and physicists do tend to complete their best work before forty. Anyhow, I talked Susi out of volunteering, and it wasn't until much later – after we'd earned our PHDs and worked for a while, that we signed up, just as the first colonists arrived on Mars. 'Cool,' we said. 'Living on Mars, now that's a proper space job!' and we put our names forward at once."

"You and Dr Ackermann were very close, weren't you?"

"Yes," replied Dr Padgett, "like two peas in a pod, and there's no need to be coy. With all the media interest, our personal lives were suddenly public."

"That must've been an uncomfortable time."

"Initially, but we also found it funny. We thought society more evolved. Scandalised by a same-sex relationship?"

"Titillated," I suggested, "rather than scandalised, because of the circumstances? Lovers on the same mission?"

"If you say so, and, anyway, the titillation didn't last long. When the story finally broke, we were a long way out – a week from Mars, and live communication was so slow and broken that the media quickly lost interest. It was our final celebrity fling."

"So," I urged, moving the conversation along, "you and Dr Ackermann volunteered for the space programme. When exactly?"

"In 2093. Susi and I were working together at the Halfpenny Institute. The Martian colonisation programme was the catalyst."

"Right, and then you heard nothing?"

"Indeed. Not a peep. They didn't even acknowledge our applications! Silence, until 2102, when a letter arrived, seemingly out of the blue."

"What were your thoughts when you read it?"

"I'm not sure," she replied. "It was noticeably short, rather to the point, more accusing than congratulatory. We are doing this, it will be amazing, and we need you to come. If you miss out, it's your problem, and the guy in charge is brilliant. I have a copy if you'd like to see it?"

"No," I said. "It's fine. I can obtain a copy easily enough. After reading it, what did you do?"

"Nothing. There wasn't time; I received a message of excitable babble from Susi almost at once."

"Do you still have her message?"

"Of course. Wait while I think to the computer. I'm a little out of practice."

Turning away and furrowing her brow, Dr Padgett defined a display, dragging her index fingers over the desk…

"Here." She nodded, bringing my attention to the glowing display.

The message from Dr Ackermann read as follows:

From: ackermann.susi@mcndr.uet.com
To: padgett.regina@halfpennyICR.uet.com

Hey Gina!

Did you just get a message from space centre? Well, I know you did. I have one as well! Are you, shall we? Are you going to go? We could be in space, together, amazing! Mind you, have you seen who's leading the mission? Shivery and creepy, brr! Hot and angry, grr! Although, I suppose he's the best man for the job, and if we're both there, we can keep an eye on him. Do you want to meet up and talk this over? We could have a weekend in Mainz. Beer, sausages, boats on the Rhine. Bring out the German in you!

See you soon,

Susi

X

"Did you reply to her message?"

"Yes," she replied, "eventually. Susi tended to be impulsive – big decisions made on the spot, but I prefer mulling things over. I felt certain the mission duration would be at least ten years and wanted to speak to my family, preparing them for my absence if I decided to go. In addition, aware of the developments in the field, I knew human physiology would be incapable of enduring so long a space flight, not without augmentation, and I wanted to gauge my mother's feelings. Did she understand the implications?"

"How do you mean?"

"In a word, shame. I was ashamed. Body and mind both insufficient, necessarily upgraded, replaced, by the something cold and synthetic, alien even, if you'll permit the melodrama."

"Of course. How did your family react?"

"They took it well. My brother, his wife and kids were supportive, but it was my mother that worried me. Twenty years since my dad died, a terrible business – in southern Spain during the Middle Eastern conflict and exposed to the fallout. Treatable in the young, of course, but in an older person with underlying health issues? His end came swiftly, painfully, with little remorse, and my mother will never forget it. Anyhow, to tell her I was going away, for ten years at least, was terribly hard, but she proved unflappable, excited in fact. She's a strong woman, my mother. A stalwart, and proudly Germanic. In fact, she makes me feel childlike. A bag of conflicting emotions."

"So, your family took it well, telling them easier than you expected? From what I understand, you were lucky. Dr Al-Hillah and Emilio Bedoya had a terrible time convincing their families. Something to do with the Catholic and Muslim families? I don't really know."

"You're kidding?" she replied. "I didn't know that. We never talked about families much – it just made the homesickness worse. Although, it was Rumbelow I missed the most."

"Rumbelow?"

"My mother's pug. A fat, grizzled, smelly old thing. Wheezing, growling, even when walking, but he was such a character, and her inseparable friend. To know I would never see him again made our last snuffling cuddle a heartbreak."

"Yes," I said, "I'm with you there. Saying goodbye to animals is the worst. Not knowing if they know or understand rips me up every time."

Dr Padgett suddenly laughed – a wonderful laugh, almost musical, and you find yourself pausing, stopping mid-sentence to listen...

"Our conversation is terribly rambling," she then professed. "Is this what you're after? You need to keep me firmly on topic or I'll talk you into an early grave."

"Ha." I guffawed. "No, this is fine, just what I wanted, at least, for this session. Remember, this isn't evidence gathering, or a hearing, merely an informal discussion. There is no case to answer, no charges to lay. You are blameless. As you rightly pointed out, you were asleep, and had been asleep for several years."

"Yes. Only not asleep, in a coma – I was comatose. A quite different state of consciousness. Susi activated my coma pod a few days after our phase of high-G acceleration. I never saw her again, but I did see my other crewmates in an extremely vivid dream."

"So, you said in your mission debriefing, and I will ask you to fully recount this in a later session."

"If you wish," she replied. "I'll even download you a copy, and, to further corroborate my statements, I have granted the company limited access to my digital memories."

"That really is most generous," I said, finishing my coffee. "As the laws on memory privacy are extremely strict, and the UET are fully bound by them. A less scrupulous organisation would have ripped out your memories while you were unconscious."

"Indeed." She smiled, stretching her arms. "Several of the not-so-united states of America steal memories to process criminals. *Nullo diligitur* it is not."

"I'm sorry?"

"Trial by jury."

"Oh, I see, thank you."

Tapping her head with her index finger, Dr Padgett crossed her eyes and smiled.

"Head full of rubbish," she said. "Never studied Latin or law but now I'm an expert. Sometimes my life is very confusing. Where were we?"

"Your family weren't upset about you going on the mission or the possibility of you being enhanced?"

"Oh yes!" She laughed, clapping her hands. "Well, the following day I contacted Susi, and we agreed to meet in Mainz before the end of the month."

"Right. Had you made up your mind?"

"Almost. About 90% in favour, but I knew it all would hang on the introductory meeting. For me, the devil was in the detail, and I wouldn't commit until I had more information."

"Granted. How far along was Susi? The same as you?"

"Oh, no, she was completely committed, 100%, and I spent our first night trying to rein her in. I know you, Suze, I said, you get so excited, new ideas drown your common sense. Wait until we know what the mission entails before jumping in. Listen, think! Walsingham is running it, and you hate him, remember, and what if I don't want to go? You'll be in space, for years, with him and a ship full of strangers. Don't assume I'm going. I haven't decided."

"Did it work?"

"Sort of. She did admit not wanting to go without me."

"Fine," I said, "and I think this about wraps up the first session. Could we resume this afternoon, or do you have plans?"

"No," she replied, standing and leaning on the back of her chair. "I'm all yours. My current work is informal. A series of experiments to test my neural implants, amplifying their output, and increasing their reception sensitivity. Today, I planned to rewrite the handshaking protocols. An attempt to improve the multi-checksum algorithm, preventing garbled data from weak or distant signals, but I could do with a break, and chatting to you is fun."

"Interesting work. Do let me know how it goes, and I'm glad you enjoy chatting. This afternoon, I'd like you to recall the initial mission briefing and any subsequent meetings at the SSD."

"Ok." She nodded. "Only, bear in mind these meetings took place almost ten years ago, before my augmentation. My memories will be decidedly patchy."

"I'm sure you'll do brilliantly."

"We'll see," she replied. "I'm peckish, though. Is it lunchtime?"

"Just gone twelve."

"Lunchtime it is, then! Would you care to join me? The canteen's only a smidgen above average, but their sandwiches are freshly made, and if we are lucky, there will be soup."

TWO

THE SEVEN
SCHOLARS SAT

*With buildings both old and new, the space centre in Darmstadt is a
sprawling mixture of concrete, glass, geodesic domes, and polyhedral
developments. The crew's introductory meeting took place under one of
these shining canopies, with Drs Padgett and Ackermann arriving early,
escorted to a small conference chamber by a pair of reticent guards...*

"Our places were already set," said Dr Padgett. "Seven seats in all. Six, on
the outer edge of a long curving table that was concave with respect
to a single front table and chair. At every position, a glowing screen
displayed a name, and we studied each in turn, looking for those that we knew."

"I see," I remarked. "And what happened next?"

*It was here, in an effort to answer my question, that Dr Padgett
recounted a third-person dialogue of the scene, beginning with her and
Dr Ackermann's survey of the seating plan...*

"I'm down here!" Susi remarked. "Where are you?"

"Opposite end," I replied with a scowl. "Are they trying to keep us apart?"

"You think?" said Susi. "Perhaps it's alphabetical? I'm A, you're P, so
walk over here, reading the names as you go."

"Ok." I nodded. "Dr R. Padgett, Dr E.J. Badsegh, L.E. Bedoya, Dr A.
Al-Hillah, Dr W. Corbiere, and then you, Suze, Dr S. Ackermann."

"No alphabet there, then," said Susi. "And the chair at the front is for Walsingham, I assume."

"Naturally, hey! Here's an idea. Let's change the names around. I've a feeling we're gonna be here all day."

"Gina!" gasped Susi. "You're so naughty. First day at school and already making mischief."

"You didn't actually try that, did you?"

"Of course, inquisitor, whyever not? Susi's last remark matched my thoughts exactly: why separate us? Walsingham knew we were friends. To treat us like naughty children would encourage us further. Surely, he must've realised."

"Possibly, but your actions wouldn't have made a good impression. Did you succeed?"

"No. The screens were locked, but if I could've, I would've."

"How long did you wait?"

"About ten minutes. Susi and I were obediently sitting at our positions when the door opened, and we turned to see the arrival of two men struggling to converse in broken English. One was of Arabic appearance – olive-skinned, bushy bearded, tall, and dashing, while the other was darker, shorter, thicker set, with heavy round shoulders. Upon seeing us, they smiled, introducing themselves thus…"

"Good morning," said the Arabic-looking man, his accent thick as tar. "I Dr Abdullah Al-Hillah and he Emilio Bedoya. To persons am I speaking?"

"Drs Regina Padgett and Susi Ackermann," I replied, shaking his hand. "Pleased to meet you. Have you come far? Are you with the UET?"

"Yes," he replied. "Both for UET, the Walsingham ARC. We shuttle from Moonbase last week. Where you work? In… erm… fields of what?"

"We are also with the UET." I nodded. "Who isn't? Dr Ackermann works in Munich, Germany, at the Neurological Research Unit, while I work in London for the Halfpenny ICR."

"The door went again, and another man entered: tall, silent, plain, and rather unremarkable. Sitting next to Susi, he ignored her every attempt to be friendly. Flummoxed, Susi flashed me a look of concern."

"And who was that?"

"Bill Corbiere. At first, Susi thought him autistic, but he was simply shy, cripplingly shy, and dealing with it the only way he knew."

"Right," I said. "Who was next?"

"Eric, closely followed by Walsingham. Ah." She then sighed, remembering. "Lovely Eric. Just watching him walk and sit took my breath. So handsome. Tall, golden-haired, blue-eyed, with the physique of a god. Deep, broad, powerful, his arms were like tree trunks. Gorgeous! Nodding politely to Emil, he turned to me and smiled. I smiled in return, sighing, before catching a disapproving look from Susi (rolling her eyes and shaking her head)."

"Eric Badsegh," he whispered. "Very pleased to meet you. Dr Padgett?"

"Yes," I softly replied. "Likewise, call me Gina," but before we could begin, the door opened again. It was Walsingham.

"So," I asked, "why the drama. What happened?"

"Well, for a start, the room fell silent, everyone but Bill followed his long, deliberate strides, gaping in awe as he towered over the desk before him."

"Intimidating," I surmised. "A correct interpretation?"

"Well, yes!" replied Dr Padgett. "And slightly no. Did you never meet him? Because, if you had, you would know precisely what I was talking about."

I shook my head.

"Never? I thought everyone had, in the UET at least, met him professionally. He'd been with for the company, for what? Fifty years?"

"Something like that," I said. "But why did you say, 'slightly no'?"

"Because we respected him. Even Susi, to a degree. His achievements were remarkable. Think how different our lives would be without Spectracote or FOXe power cells, and yet, despite his fame, he still *demanded* respect. Servicing his ego got rather tiresome after a while."

"No doubt," I said, watching Dr Padgett composing her thoughts. "Is there more you wish to say? Because his narcissism was well documented, and he was aware of it."

"Indeed," she replied. "You're quite right. What I'm about to say doesn't need saying – it has already been said, but Sir Malcolm Walsingham is world famous. One of mankind's greatest scientists, innovators, and engineers, with some caring to dub him 'the Father of the Second Industrial Age'. But I find that tricky to swallow. Granted, the work done at the Walsingham Centre for Advanced Research is remarkable. A Mecca for ground-breaking innovation, but the truth is subtler. The UET, for example, treat the Walsingham Centre like a cooking pot. A gathering place for the innovative work done by its satellite laboratories and institutions. The Halfpenny ICR – of which I am a senior partner – being no exception. Consider the invention of Spectracote? It was *our* pioneering work on the hybridisation of planarian ocelli that enabled its development, not Walsingham and his cronies. It was the UET that bought it from us, for a generous fee, oh yes, very generous, before delivering our work to Walsingham and his team, who then set about absorbing and adapting our research for use in their various projects. Be careful praising Walsingham too loudly. Very often, his people do no more than combine the parts provided by others less in the limelight. In no way is this a complaint, mind you, far from it. The way the UET operates is fair to all. Achieving fantastic results by encouraging scientists to explore, innovate, and experiment. In previous centuries, large profit-seeking corporations sucked in many notable scientists, chaining them, limiting them, paying a set wage for whatever project they worked on – a project provided, not sought. Becoming little more than obedient cogs in a machine to make money. The UET has changed this. Scientists are free to work in fields of their own choosing, exploiting a personal specialism or talent, reaping great rewards for their achievements, singly or in a group. The UET through science and human endeavour has saved the world, is saving the world, and is bringing us ever closer to new ones."

"Wow," I said with laughter. "Where did that come from? Began as a rant but turned into a company eulogy!"

"It needed saying," she replied, taking a breath. "And you're right, I almost lost it. Then I realised slagging off UET policy would be self-defeating. It could damage my own institution. So, make no mistake, I love the UET. Really, I do. They're great! You're still recording, right?"

"Yes." I chuckled. "I am."

"Good. However, it is sometimes galling to see Walsingham's people splashed all over the media. Lauded for an invention or device beneficial to all of humanity. Nappy makers, if you ask me."

"Nappy makers? Haven't heard that before. Why nappy makers?"

"You wouldn't have," she replied. "I'm extemporising."

"Still, your point being?"

"An analogy, if you please. We invent the absorbent pad, others the elastic tape, the lining, the fabric, but then along comes Walsingham and his oh-so-clever loonies, and ta-da! They invent the nappy."

"Right," I acknowledged, checking the time. "I understand your chagrin."

"Good," she continued. "Back to the meeting?"

"If you would."

"Indeed," she replied, standing to lean on her desk. "I was rambling. Now, Sir Malcolm Walsingham was tall, over 200 centimetres, with intense blue eyes that could freeze you to the spot. Red in the face and sporting a beard, he looked old, and, when he saw me, he hung his head in mocking despair."

"That told a story," I said. "Were you concerned?"

"Not really. The rivalry between us, although real, was good-natured, laced with dry humour, even sarcasm, we enjoyed it."

"Of course. What happened next?"

"Leaning over his desk, rasping, and wheezing, Walsingham prepared to speak – remember, he possessed a cloned lung, replacing the one lost during the explosion on Moonbase. Gosh, when was it? Twelve years ago?"

"More like fourteen, I think."

"Really?" she replied, cocking an eyebrow. "Oh yes, there it is, on file, inside my head. Told you I needed practice. Anyhow, the accident was far worse than reported and hushed up at the time. So many good scientists lost, and they were warned."

"Warned? About what? It was common knowledge a research module exploded, but do you know why? What were they working on?"

"Micro fusion initiators."

"Ah, I see…"

Thinking and muttering, Dr Padgett paced her office. I couldn't catch her words (they are inaudible on this recording), and I merely sat and watched as she stood before a mirror, adjusting her hair…

"You see," she continued, "the work was too important to fail. Procedural corners were cut, safety protocols ignored, all for the sake of expediency, et voila: boom!"

"Scandalous," I acknowledged. "How was Sir Malcom involved?"

"I'm not sure, but he must have approved the working practices. The arrogant old fool. At the time of the explosion, he was working in an adjacent module, suffering rapid depressurisation and a fluorine leak. I guess he must've taken a lungful."

"They replaced his lung, though, didn't they?"

"Yes. They cloned one. However, the damage to his right lung was too severe for effective cloning, so the cloners copied his left – he had two left lungs. Neither of which worked very well. Mind you, following our enhancements, his symptoms virtually disappeared, only manifesting themselves when laughing or shouting."

"Understood. Could we return to the meeting?"

"Was I rambling?"

"Yes."

"Good morning," Walsingham began. "Welcome to UET Space Centre, Darmstadt. So glad and relieved to see you all here, and, before we start, I'd like you to introduce yourselves. Beginning with you, young lady (pointing at Susi), working down the line, towards… (he paused as if in disgust) towards her. She who sits yonder? (Meaning myself.) So, if you please? Oh, *und in Englisch, bitte.*"

"*Jawohl,*" quipped Susi, "*und very well, guten Tag.* Dr Susi Ackermann. Senior practitioner, Munich Centre for Neurological Disorders, oh, *und ze UET, natürlich.*"

"Thank you," said Walsingham, his attention on the pale man to her left. "Sir?" But he ignored him, studying instead a glowing data pad discreetly whipped from his pocket."

"Ahem!" Walsingham coughed. "Dr Corbiere, if you please?"

"Dr William Corbiere," the pale man suddenly blurted, "consultant medical practitioner and surgeon. St Bart's, London, but I also have a practice in Paris, France. Sorry, everyone, don't like new people and places."

"Truly," Walsingham remarked. "But thank you, Dr Corbiere, and not to worry, there will be plenty of time to adapt. Next gentleman, please?"

"Dr Abdullah Al-Hillah," replied the next man along. "Macro-micro design engineer, the Walsingham Centre, UET. Work at Moonbase most, but also astrophysicist."

"Many thanks," Walsingham nodded, "and good to see you. Would you prefer your display in a language other than English? Arabic, or French, say?"

Nodding, Dr Al-Hillah replied, "Arabic," and I flashed Susi a quizzical look that she promptly returned with a shrug.

"If you please?" Walsingham prompted, directing his gaze towards Emil.

"I… erm… Luis Emilio Bedoya. Astronomer, UET, Walsingham place – moon, also, how you say? Hmm… *disenador escultorico?*

"This guy's English was almost non-existent, and I remember Susi struggling not to giggle, wondering why the UET had assembled such a linguistically incompatible group."

"Excellent," continued Walsingham. "I'll change your display to Spanish, and the next gentleman please?"

"This being the turn of the hulking brute filling the position beside me."

"Dr Eric Badsegh," he calmly replied. "Nutritionist and physiologist working with the UET, here, at Space Centre. I specialise in extra-terrestrial food production and preparation, amongst other things."

"Oh, we all have other things," Walsingham laughed, coughing, then wheezing, "but thank you, Dr Badsegh, and lastly, madam. The lady on the end? If you would be so kind?"

"And in last place," I said, "Dr Regina Padgett. Chief scientist, Halfpenny Institute, London. Currently, we are working on biomechanical cell augmentations, and, oh, we're with the UET – for the money."

"Well, aren't we all?" Walsingham quipped. "But thank you, Dr Padgett. An informative pleasure as always," and I respectfully (and sarcastically) bowed my head.

"Had you met any of them before?" I asked. "Excepting Susi and Sir Malcolm?"

"No," Dr Padgett replied, "they were strangers to me, but I did later recognise the name Luis Emilio Bedoya. He was part of the team studying Alpha Canis Minoris, pondering the sudden shift in its spectra."

"Oh yes," I remarked, "I remember. There were all sorts of scare stories. Was Procyon going to explode. Being so close to Earth, was there any danger?"

"Yes," she replied with a nod, "I remember his interview (with an interpreter) skilfully crashing and burning such stories. No risk to Earth at all."

"Certainly. Now, how did the meeting begin? Can you remember?"

"Not in any detail. He reminded us of the UET's need for secrecy, how we were not to discuss anything with anyone outside the room. When disclosure became inevitable, the media department would oversee the publicity."

"Was that a surprise?"

"No," she replied, shaking her head. "At least, not for me. The military often take an interest in the work we do here. Having our work classified is an unavoidable consequence."

"The military? I thought the UET were above such things?"

"They certainly try." She shrugged. "Refusing weapon research contracts, but the military pay very well for medical technology, and here at the Halfpenny ICR we develop many."

"What did Walsingham speak of next?"

"The mission."

"Can you recount what was said?"

"I can certainly attempt a reconstruction, but my recollections will be impressionistic, by no means verbatim."

"Fine. If you would and, could you use shorter words? English is not my native language. Have mercy, I beg you!"

"Spoilsport. Anyway, with the UET logo glowing behind him, Walsingham began. The purpose of this meeting is to expand upon your letters of invitation. Indeed. The six of you are incredibly special. Representing the UET's first choice staffing the Kuiper Belt Explorer, and it has fallen upon me to outline and promote the mission. At the end of this session, I will pose a simple question. Do you wish to go? Your response is not binding. Not until the signing of the contractual agreement will you be bound, but your early acceptance or refusal will provide useful insight for the SSD. An opportunity to re-examine the mission parameters if any refusals are heard. Questions, anyone?"

"I don't recall any, and Walsingham continued…"

"Good." He then nodded. "Onto the mission itself. The UET has selected us to live and work aboard this (gesturing to the wall behind him): the UET Kuiper Belt Explorer. An extensively modified and generously upgraded Mark VII Dodecyl Autonomous Ore Carrier."

"The wall and our displays then refreshed to show an animated diagram of said vessel: a roughly spherical, twelve-sided polyhedron, with thruster modules jutting from every facet. The large screen behind Walsingham then went on to display an animation of the proposed flight path. Highlighting a trail of glowing pixels, arcing and twisting through the solar system, around the Earth, its moon, Mars, Jupiter, and several dwarf planetary bodies."

"The mission objectives are threefold," Walsingham continued. "Primarily, to rendezvous with the colony on Mars and making a supply drop, spending several days among the colonists, pressing the flesh. Now less in the limelight, the colonists have spoken about their feelings of isolation, and the UET is actively addressing the issue. Our visit is but the first stage in the process, and the UET have tasked us to assess the colonists' material and emotional needs, evaluating their psychological and physical condition. Providing this much-needed social contact, we will be almost a week orbiting Mars, before blasting our way towards the outer solar system, passing Jupiter to pick up a boost. The final leg will see us accelerating further, negotiating Uranus, on to our final objective. The Kuiper Belt. Deploying supply pods and robotic construction modules, conducting a comprehensive programme of scientific research. Questions, anyone?"

"Susi's hand shot up, as did Bill Corbiere's."

"Yes, Dr Ackermann?" Walsingham acknowledged.

"What is the expected mission duration?"

"Twelve to thirteen years," he replied. "Precision is difficult. There may be unexpected delays or hastening."

"Goodness," she said. "That is a long time, but it is very a long way. How are we to prevent ourselves from going...stir crazy? Is that the correct idiom?"

"It is." Walsingham smiled. "And a good question. For as much as 90% of the mission duration, some part of the crew will be comatose."

"Understood," said Susi. "Thank you."

"Dr Corbiere? Your question?"

"Y-yes," stuttered Bill. "S-sorry, but going to Mars – the planets, according to the display, aren't we going back on ourselves? It seems wasteful. Why not wait until Mars is in a better position?"

"Another good question," said Walsingham. "And the UET SSD discussed this at length. Originally, the SSD planned the mission for 2106–2108, with the planets in a more favourable general alignment. However, the Mars situation has changed of late. It has become a priority. I don't know why, sorry, but it has. In early 2104, Mars will be in opposition – we can get there in under a year, and the other planetary positions are adequate, so that's when we're going."

I raised my hand.

"Yes, Dr Padgett. A question?"

"Sir Malcolm," I cheekily asked, "this is all riveting, but why not just make this a Mars mission? We've been sending probes to Eris and Pluto since the early 21st century. Why bother sending people? There is precious new to discover, and why in Heaven's name do the UET want me? For fuck's sake, I'm a cell biologist. There's nothing for me to study!"

"There was general laughter, from the English speakers initially, and then, as their translations appeared, hearty laughter from Emil and Abda as well."

"Thank you, Dr Padgett," said Walsingham, raising his hand to calm the mood. "I can and will answer your questions by continuing this briefing, and, to an extent, Dr Ackermann's. The second mission objective, and I think the most important, concerns *us*, how we cope with life on board. The interior of the Kuiper Belt Explorer is a spacious habitation module, fitted with the latest innovations designed to make space flight safer, less physically demanding, and *much* more comfortable. For this to be successful, however, it will be necessary for us to undergo a series of surgical procedures, enhancing our mental and physical capabilities, facilitating direct interface with the ship."

"What?" cried Eric. "This wasn't mentioned before."

"Well, it's mentioned now," I muttered, and Eric sternly directed his sky-blue eyes into mine.

"A flurry of hands went up (including mine)."

"The clumsy way Walsingham slipped this hot coal into our pockets was in hindsight very clever. Causing such consternation so early on gave us time to discuss, deliberate, and fully understand the necessity of the enhancements."

"He really did it that way? Announcing matter-of-factly a topic so contentious?"

"Yes, Walter. As well as I can remember. The wording is surely wrong, but the manner is correct."

"A risky strategy. I'm surprised no one walked out."

"Really?" she replied. "I don't think there was the remotest chance, and Walsingham knew it. Consider the nature of the group? Why did the UET choose us? It was because we were risk-takers, explorers in our respective fields. Bold, brash, and, well, bonkers. Willing to try anything. Experimenting and tinkering in domains others shy away from. The UET selected us wisely. Once we understood the necessity of the surgery (and its benefits), our curiosity took over. Only dear Susi was to offer any resistance, the last to be convinced; the brain implants terrified her. With first-hand experience treating the victims of failed brain surgery, her reluctance was understandable. Much of her work in Munich involved the rehabilitation of such individuals."

"Certainly," I said, "and then the meeting went on as planned?"

"No. Not as planned. Swamped by so many questions, Sir Malcolm had to stop and answer them. Quite a grilling as I recall. By relentless cross-examination, we forced the poor sod him to describe every detail of the procedures. Which he did. Reassuringly, honestly, hoping not to dissuade us, and, amazingly, he succeeded!"

"Impressive feat," I said. "Did the meeting continue?"

"Eventually, yes. After a break for coffee."

"What was said?"

"He went on to explain that the UET needed test subjects for interstellar space flight, as recent breakthroughs in radiation shielding had finally made it a reality. As you surely know, unmanned probes are already en route to nearby stars, and the scientific community is on tenterhooks, ready to receive their data. The seven of us were to be the beginning. We were to evaluate the technologies required for long-duration spaceflight, 'Mankind's last great adventure', and all that flag-waving bollocks."

"Ha! Anything else?"

"A little. He went on to describe the ship, its design, construction, power plant, but only in brief, taking questions as he went, before the final carrot. We would have scientific freedom. To use our time however we wished. Free to use the ship and its systems to further our own research. Quite a lure for a career scientist, let me tell you!"

"I can imagine, and that was all?"

"Virtually."

"Flunkies appeared, laying out a decidedly Germanic buffet supper. A jolly event with a great deal of herring and much informal chat. Our excitement was already beginning to grow. Reassured and loosening up, Susi spent a good long time chatting with Walsingham – most unexpected, but she needed to make peace with the man. In truth, she was studying him, professionally, and, by the look on his face, he knew it."

"Why did Dr Ackermann have a problem with Walsingham? You haven't really said. Can you tell me?"

"I can, and I will, later. I need to consider my answer."

"Very well," I said. "Since you're being mysterious, I won't ask. Although, your evasiveness has my curiosity piqued. Now, you mentioned Walsingham posing a final question. To see if the assembled wanted to go?"

"Yes," replied Dr Padgett, stifling a yawn. "Before wrapping up the session, Walsingham asked for a show of hands."

"What was the result? Any wavering?"

"None whatsoever. Told you, didn't I? Six votes for, none against. Insatiable curiosity."

"Incredible," I remarked. "I would've wavered, I think."

"And perhaps we should have," she said with a sigh. "*Hat die Neugier die Katze getötet?*"

"*Zeer waarschijnlijk,*" I replied. "Very probably."

THREE

ENHANCEMENTS

Dr Padgett and I met again the following day, and we spent the entire morning discussing the contents of the health and safety briefing delivered ("sat through") during the crew's second day at Darmstadt. With little opportunity for crew interaction during this briefing (it merely followed the predetermined UET SSD guidelines), I have decided to omit the transcript of our discussion, moving this account onto our meeting regarding the biomechanical enhancements of the crew, with Dr Padgett reviewing her thoughts and feelings over lunch...

"Hope you like the soup," said Dr Padgett, patting hers with a spoon. "So gloopy it's beginning to set."

"I noticed. For how long did they boil it? It's like eating glue!"

"Probably been simmering all week," she replied. "Although, somehow, it still tastes of pea. Which is something, I suppose."

Tearing a soft brown roll into small fluffy pieces, Dr Padgett scattered them across the surface of her soup...

"Indeed," I said, dipping my spoon for a refill. "The next series of meetings concerned the surgical procedures, am I right?"

"Yes," she confirmed. "We reconvened after breaking for a couple of days. Thinking time, Walsingham called it, but Susi and I simply went shopping. We stayed in a hotel, can't remember which, but it was a typically German establishment. Timber-clad, immaculately clean, gloomy on the inside, smelling of polish with beeswax."

"Sounds idyllic."

"Yes. Before I discovered how keen Susi was to rekindle our former relationship. Making our evenings fractious, to say the least."

Dunking a piece of bread roll into my soup, I bit off a corner, surprised how forthcoming Dr Padgett had become...

"Oh?" I asked. "Why was that?"

"You don't know already?" she replied, her face flushing red. "I thought everyone knew. You want to record me saying it, yes?"

Painfully grinning, I nodded, admitting my fault.

"Very well." She sighed. "I'll be blunt. Dr Ackermann, Susi, was a lesbian, whereas I am an occasional bisexual, my relationships mostly with men, and, although I'm relaxed about exploring my lesbian side, it is not the dominant aspect of my sexuality. Susi knew this, and, loving me as much as she did, it pained her knowing I would never commit. Mind you, following a few glasses of Schnapps, the inevitable occurred, and Susi made too much of it."

"Thank you," I said, bowing my head. "If that was uncomfortable, I apologise, but it needed to be on this recording."

"Why?" she asked. "I don't see what difference it makes. Yes, Susi and I were friends, of course we were friends – we were all friends! The linking of our neural implants and being cooped up together for almost a decade made us a family, with all its trials, tribulations, love, laughter, and, yes, Susi and I were lovers too, on and off, but the sleep cycles meant it would sometimes be months before we could even talk. Do you want to know about Eric as well?"

"Dr Badsegh? No, I don't. Did the two of you…?"

"Yes!" she snapped. "Didn't you know?" I shook my head. "Wonderful. Well, now you do. Wanna call security?"

"Of course not," I replied, "and calm down, will you? I'm not prying or accusing anybody of anything. Merely trying to establish the nature of your relationships with the crew."

Sighing, Dr Padgett shook her head and thoughtfully stirred her soup.

"I'm sorry," she said, releasing a slow breath. "I know. I do understand the need. I'm just worried. An unscrupulous lawyer, sensitive information, you know the drill."

"No, Gina," I replied. "There's no need to worry. This isn't a formal hearing. I already told you. Is your memory device on the blink? This recording is inadmissible."

"Good." She chuckled. "And my memory's fine, thank you for asking. What you're hearing is my Ape-knee temper. Like an outpouring of lava, it consumes all in its path."

"Ape-knee?"

"Yes," Dr Padgett explained. "How my great-grandmother pronounced her surname."

"Indeed?"

"Truly. Londoners, especially those in the East of London, commonly pronounced the words Halfpenny and Three-penny 'Ape-knee' and 'Thrip-knee'."

"So, historically speaking, this is the Ape-knee Institute?"

"Yes. That's how she would've pronounced it. Of course, societal changes have all but obliterated these inflections, and we wouldn't want to confuse our continental partners, would we?"

"No," I replied. "As a matter of fact, in the Netherlands, the situation is similar. Although several regional dialects are still going strong, Brabantian and Limburgerish, to name but two, many others have diminished. My distant relatives were Zeelanders, and they spoke West Flemish."

"Indeed, and beautiful dialects they are. Shall we head to my office, get a coffee, and continue? If we're discussing the enhancement procedures, we should do so in secret. Did you check your clearance?"

"Yes. For the entirety of this interview my clearance is epsilon red. Do you want to confirm this?"

"Epsilon red?" She laughed in surprise. "Wow. I bow to your god-like privilege. Why would I need to check? If you claim to be a god and you're not one, you're gonna burn my friend."

⧗

Settling within Dr Padgett's office, I watched her making coffee with an almost mechanical precision.

"Not using your dispenser," I remarked. "Is it broken?"

"Sadly, yes," she replied. "Can't understand how it happened, but one user complained about its 'infuriatingly cheerful intractitudatiousness.' A violent response was inevitable."

"Of course. Where was the next meeting held?"

"In the same place, but the seating arrangements were different. Since Walsingham wasn't giving the talk, he became part of the group and the seven of us occupied small desks. There being no seating plan, I sat next to Susi, the others selecting their seats at random. Chatting like old friends as they came in, Eric Badsegh and Bill Corbiere bowed before me with mocking grandeur."

"That was a friendly gesture. And Dr Corbiere was talking?"

"Yes," she replied. "Bill was settling in. Typical scientists and full of curiosity, we had all checked up on one another – examining careers and noting respective achievements. Bill now felt he knew everyone. Remarkable people we were too. Dr Badsegh's CV was thick as a book!"

"You were all selected for precisely that reason. Who gave the lecture? Can you remember?"

"Yes, as they were present at every stage. There were three of them. A consultant practitioner and two assistants: Drs Weber, Bianchi, and Chavan."

"The consultant being Dr Chavan?"

"Correct. A charming woman. Short, kind, with a smiling face and hair flecked with grey. She had really cold hands."

"Every doctor does. How did the lecture begin?"

"With another security briefing given by Dr Weber. This time they really meant it. The word 'prosecution' was used. Surprising even Walsingham, I think."

"They threatened?"

"Yep," she replied. "Bewildering, at first, but as the medical team described the long-term implications of the enhancements, the need for secrecy was obvious…"

"Good morning!" began Dr Chavan. "As you are doubtless aware, we are the medical team tasked with installing your physiological upgrades, beginning with the installation of your Nano Robotic Intra Cellular

Management System, NICMS – a terrible mouthful, so from now on I shall use their colloquial name…"

"Hibbites," said Bill, interrupting.

"Yes." She smiled. "Thank you, Dr Corbiere."

"Hibbites, Gina?" I then asked.

"Yes," replied Dr Padgett. "Tiny robots, capable of moving throughout the body, entering cells, interacting with their organelles and biochemistry."

"Understood, but why Hibbites?"

"After Albert Hibbs, a PHD student of noted physicist Richard Feynman. In 1959, when Hibbs wrote to Feynman concerning his lecture, 'There's Plenty of Room at the Bottom', in which Feynman talked of the direct manipulation of atoms and molecules (paving the way for nanotechnology), Hibbs mentioned, and I quote, the weird possibility of one day 'swallowing the doctor'. Do you want to know what Hibbites can do?"

"Yes, please, and how?"

"No." Dr Padgett chuckled. "Not how. We'd be here for months, and you'd surely die of boredom, but they are multifunctional, as all good gadgets should be, and they are just that, gadgets. Limited by design."

"Granted, and of what are they capable?"

"Just coming to that, and daunted by the explanation, indeed, hours of gobbledygook. Hmm… yes, the quickest way of highlighting their capabilities would be… My own experiences?"

"Good thinking," I replied. "And just how are these Hibbites administered? Orally? Do you really swallow the doctor?"

"They could be administered orally, but the effect would only be temporary. Individual Hibbites only last a day or two before they break down, so the doctors implant each recipient with Hibbite crèches. Tiny storage devices, factories, capable of delivering, recycling, and rebuilding Hibbites. Implantation is also preferable, for maintenance purposes, as their raw materials don't last indefinitely, and without annual refills my Hibbite population will soon diminish, reducing their effectiveness. There are six creches in all. One at the base of my skull, one in each armpit, one in my abdomen – next to my spleen – and one in each of my buttocks. They are extremely small – only a couple of millimetres across, and the implantation was painless. I'm not even aware of them."

"Have you received any upgrades?"

"No," she replied. "The research has stalled, and what else could be done? Could the scientists investigate their longevity, enhance their energy conversion? Maybe they're perfect?"

"Seems like it to me. But, come on, what are they actually doing?"

Suddenly motionless, I realised Dr Padgett was accessing the computer. The tabletop then illuminated to show a series of images in chronological order…

"Here," she said. "Look at this sequence selfies. Taken every year since receiving the Hibbites. What do you notice?"

"Hmm," I pondered. "The first photo taken, when? Ah, yes, 2103, and the last? Oh, you just took it."

"Yes," she replied. "And?"

"Nothing," I said. "You haven't changed at all. In fact, come to think of it, you look younger. Hibbites slow the process of ageing?"

"Indeed," she replied, "but not by design. It is merely a consequence. The Hibbites continuously repair my cells, and old injuries, even defects, for example, a fibroid cyst on my leg, have now gone. I'm going to live an awfully long time."

"How long?"

"Well, the medical team, Dr Chavan et al, aren't sure, but at my current rate of ageing, and assuming there are no unforeseen pitfalls, 250 to 350 is a distinct possibility. The oldest living human is 131. I plan to retire about then!"

"Heavens," I remarked, "what an incredible gift. What a privilege!"

"Yes," she replied, "but the gift is also laced with sadness. You see, my crewmates are gone. Only they were to share my longevity, and soon, those I love will begin to grow old and die. My close family – mother, brother, his wife, nephew, and niece. Great-Auntie Gina will outlive them all. How great an aunt will I be before my time is up? Great, great, great perhaps? More, I think. If I could have the Hibbites removed, I would, but my other implants depend on their intervention. Without their maintenance, control of infection, stopping rejection, I'd be lucky to last six months."

"I see," I said, thoughtfully stroking my chin, "but this side effect does give you the option of shortening your lifespan. Remove the Hibbites and your implants kill you."

"Yes. It is nice to have an off switch, but do you understand why Hibbite technology is secret?"

"Certainly. Immortality. Who wouldn't want to live forever?"

"Not forever! Immortal I am not, and certainly not invulnerable, bringing me nicely to describe more of the Hibbites' capabilities. I already mentioned Hibbites repair cells, particularly important in space, where exposure to radiation is continuous: cosmic rays, X-rays, gamma rays, the works. Genetic and cellular damage is inevitable. The Hibbites monitor every cell in my body, selectively repairing or destroying those beyond repair. Cancer, for example."

"Go on."

"There are other benefits too. Disease resistance. I never get sick. The Hibbites attack and destroy all pathogens, be they bacterial, viral, or parasitic, independently or in tandem with my own immune system, quickly managing all toxins, be they artificial or natural. Natural poisons invariably have a lipid or protein component, and they're rapidly broken down into harmless smaller molecules, ready for excretion."

"Incredible," I remarked. "Are there any side effects?"

"Not as such, but by default, I cannot get drunk! Narcotics would similarly have their effects stymied, even my coffee. As far as my Hibbites are concerned, caffeine is a toxin, and they begin working on it as soon as it enters my bloodstream."

"How awful."

"Indeed. It was a bit of shock, and it wasn't until we learnt how to reprogramme our Hibbites that we could enjoy any psychoactive substances."

"Granted," I replied. "Any other benefits?"

"A few. All minor and physiological, and, for the sake of brevity, you can look them up yourself. The remaining major benefit is accelerated healing."

"How do you mean? The healing of injuries?"

"Yes. If my skin is cut, like you, I bleed. My blood coagulating, scabbing, and closing the wound. In the case of a shallow cut, this can take up to an hour, but with my Hibbites, a scab will form in seconds. An extreme example? Let us say, due to an industrial accident, we both lost an arm. Cut cleanly, just above the elbow. Without medical treatment, you would slowly bleed to death, and, even if you didn't, infection, say gangrene, would eventually get you instead. With my Hibbites however, closing the major blood vessels, I would only bleed for a minute or two. The Hibbites going on to form an artificial covering for the wound, controlling any infection and healing the injury at an accelerated rate. I'd still lose the arm – it wouldn't grow back – but I'd survive it. Of course, severe injuries would still be fatal, or in the very least require medical intervention. Broken bones, for example. The Hibbites do assist in the regrowth and repair of the bone tissue, but, if the bone needs resetting, I still need a medic. If you hack my head off, slit my throat, set me on fire, spray me with bullets, or tear me apart, I'm toast."

"Good to know," I said, "and easy to understand why the military is so interested in Hibbite technology. Damage-resistant soldiers."

"Precisely, and as a consequence, following the death of the host, the entire Hibbite system quickly self-destructs. Breaking down into innocuous bio-degradable compounds."

"Ah, yes," I acknowledged. To prevent the technology falling into enemy hands. Any more features?"

"A few. Relating to management and functioning of my implants. They'll probably get a mention when I come to speak of them. Assuming you're going to ask?"

"I intend to."

Standing and stretching, Dr Padgett nodded towards the curtained area behind her...

"Need to go and plug myself in. Could you give me the room for a few minutes. Grant me a little privacy?"

"Plug yourself in?" I asked. "What? Why?"

"Gina-speak. I need the loo!"

"Ah, right," I said. "Of course. I'll wait outside."

"Thanks. When I'm done, I'll knock on the door."

Dr Padgett's toilet break conveniently leads me to the next segment. The modification of the crew's gastrointestinal tract...

"Dr Chavan went on to discuss the Hibbites at length," explained Dr Padgett. "Listening to our questions, she calmly answered them all. Only when our curiosity was sated did she hand proceedings to Dr Weber."

"And everyone was ok at this stage? After being told they might be immortal?"

"Not immortal," she replied. "Didn't I just explain? Nevertheless, we were. Of course, I'm not a telepath. No idea what the others were thinking, but the mood in the room was calm and studied. Mind you, there was a great deal to take in and little time to consider the implications. I certainly hadn't. Far too busy taking notes, and the questions we posed were invariably technical."

"Of course. How did Dr Weber begin?"

"With a brief but fascinating talk about the problems arising from eating, drinking, and excreting in what he called a variable-gravity environment. In other words, space."

"Right, go on."

"Reviewing the manned space missions of the last century, he focussed upon the feeding of the astronauts and the capture and processing of their excreta. Certainly, the meals were nasty, and the collection of their excreta was uncomfortable, messy, thoroughly unhygienic – and the vomiting! Well, what can I say? There was a lot of puke in the old days. Much of it floating."

"So, I have read. The first sub-orbital space plane. In Holland it was known as *de komeet van braaksel*."

"Exactly." She grinned. "The human body doesn't cope well with prolonged exposure to micro or variable gravity. The digestive tract, for example, has a distinct top and bottom, and if you spend time in variable gravity, it gets confused. Mastication – chewing – if you keep your mouth shut, works in low gravity, as does swallowing, but, once the food reaches your stomach, it begins to move unnaturally, contacting and inflaming the oesophageal sphincter. The first symptom is heartburn with vomiting, and without a course of antacids to limit the gastric juice, the sphincter will steadily (and very painfully) degrade. You begin to digest it."

"Lovely."

"Too rambly?"

"No. You're doing great. Keep going."

"Ok." She smiled, cocking an eyebrow. "Anyhow, if you intend being in space for more than a few weeks, the lower oesophageal sphincter isn't up to job. An upgrade is required. Something dependable, with greater resilience, and indigestible! My lower oesophageal sphincter is now just that. An amorphorobotic muscle. A robot capable of changing its shape. In action, it performs identically to the original, only it is resistant to gastric juice. An elegant piece of robotics, too. The way it seamlessly connects to my nervous system is astonishing, with belching, swallowing, and vomiting, which is vomiting due to illness or intoxication, all taken care of instinctively. That is the greatest benefit of Hibbitic microsurgery. A surgery on a cellular level.

So intrinsically are my implants connected to the surrounding tissues, my body doesn't know they are there."

"How was your new sphincter fitted? Did they cut you open?"

"Yes. Nips and tucks. Although, to begin, the Hibbites did most of the scalpel work – a triumph of technology and programming. The day before the procedure, I starved and took laxatives – which worked very well, oh yes. In fact, I remember receiving a call from Susi. Full of nervous chatter, we wondered why our voices were echoing, until it dawned on us. We were speaking from our respective bathrooms! Then, arriving at the medical centre the following morning, my Hibbites received new instructions. Firstly, to function as proton pump inhibitors, preventing my stomach from excreting any more gastric juice, and, secondly, to break down my oesophageal sphincter, preparing the surrounding cells to accept the implant."

"Fascinating," I remarked. "Didn't know Hibbites could be reprogrammed externally. How was it done?"

"Remotely. The new instructions were flashed to the Hibbite crèche-factories on 5GHz carrier waves: Wi-Fi."

"Why-fy?"

"Double-you I eff I. An early-21st-century wireless networking protocol."

"Right," I acknowledged. "How did it feel, having your sphincter break down? Was it painful?"

"No," she replied, shaking her head. "I didn't feel a thing. Just a lot of burping, a strange taste."

"Hardly surprising. Go on."

"After that, with the sedative kicking in, it was dream-like. The doctors working over me and beside me. I glimpsed the implant. Clasped in forceps, it thrashed about like a muscular grey worm. After placing it in my mouth, they asked me to swallow it. Not easy I can tell you! That was the worst part. Cold and lumpen, it squirmed down my gullet, nestling, and then twitching into place."

"And that was the end of it?"

"God no!" she replied. "Shortly after, wheeled into a small room and connected to various monitors, I looked on as surgeons scrubbed up and got ready. Susi was in the opposite bed, and we gave each other meaningful looks. Neither of us could talk – too groggy – but the fear on her face (and doubtless on mine) communicated a great deal."

"Surgery, you say. The other implants fitted the same day?"

"Yes. The rectal and urinary ones. The oesophageal sphincter under local anaesthetic, the others under general. Made sense. Replacing my oesophageal sphincter was a straightforward but the physical adaptation necessary to fit my rectal and urinary implants was quite beyond the reach of my Hibbites, and anyway, who'd wanna be awake while their arse was replaced?"

"Err... well, no. You wouldn't. How did it go?"

"Fine," she said. "Don't remember the operation at all. Waking in a strangely stretchy hammock, I watched a nurse checking my vitals on a monitor. Opposite was Susi. Also in a hammock, she was unconscious."

"Hammock? Why was that?"

"You know, I never bothered to ask. Probably to keep us from lying on our new implants while the Hibbites bedded them in."

"Right. How long were you in the hammock?"

"It must have been at least six hours. Asleep most of the time. By the evening, Susi and I were sitting up, sipping water, chatting, and swapping gossip."

"What'd been done exactly?"

"Well," she replied, "if I knew you better, I'd show you, and, you're recording audio?"

"Yes, audio only. So, please, go on with your description."

"Ok. At first, we were too apprehensive to look, so we did a countdown: five, four, three, two, one, look!"

"*Gott in Himmel!*" Susi exclaimed. "I've got plumbing! What've they done?"

"Done to us," I laughed in reply "But it's only for the mission. When we get back, they'll probably remove them."

"Susi's apprehension was typical. Worried about nothing. Here is my urinary port (she pointed towards a small bulge under her suit), just above my undies, and it does indeed appear nipple-like, but it is made from borophene and titanium, and directly connected to my urethra – which was either redirected or replaced, I'm not sure which. It's gender and anatomy dependent."

"Right," I replied, resisting the impulse to stare. "When you use it, how does it work?"

"Well, for one, it's surprisingly intuitive. The sensation of needing to pee and the act of peeing are unchanged. It just comes out in a different place, and at first, it's a bit of a shock."

"No doubt. When urinating, aren't you required to connect to a duct?"

"Yes, that is the intention, but I don't need to. In fact, I can pee standing up if I want, although the instinct to sit or squat is deeply ingrained. All the toilet facilities on board the KBE catered for both standing or sitting."

"How very accommodating. When you do eventually go, how does the urinary port open?"

"I'm glad you asked that because this is the clever bit. My urinary port has a matter-polaroid dual membrane. Connected to my nervous system, both conscious and autonomic, when I decide to pee, the membranes rotate ninety degrees, contra-positively, becoming porous, allowing my urine to expel in an unbroken stream, before returning to their impermeable state. No mess, no fuss, and no dabbing with tissue."

"Clever. You mentioned the urinary port being connected to your autonomic nervous system. Why is this?"

"To wet myself," she replied. "Yes, they thought of that too. If I were unconscious, seriously ill, perhaps, my urine can expel automatically. Certainly, it would be fatal if it couldn't. In space, during my comatose periods, my urinary port was connected to the waste collection duct and continuously open."

"Makes sense, and now we've had lunch, if it's not too personal, could I ask about your rectal port?"

"Of course, my pleasure. Bodily functions don't bother me. I've worked with squishies my whole adult life. You wouldn't believe some of the blood-soaked horrors we have here twitching in jars. A bit of poo is nothing."

"Fine. What does it do and how does it function?"

"The purpose of my anal/rectal port is to facilitate and control the hygienic expulsion of faecal matter in variable-gravity environments. Like my oesophageal sphincter, the port itself is amorphorobotic, but in this case, it replaces my anus. The act of defecation is unaffected. If I feel the need to go, like everyone else, I just squat and go. Of course, what happens back there is different, but to me it feels normal. Only when the anal/rectal port detects a signal from a compatible toilet facility does its behaviour change. Upon reception, the port extends, sealing itself onto the toilet's receiver duct. A tube, directly connected to the ships waste recycling facilities. No mess, no fuss, no wiping, or waiting for the falling of winnits."

"Winnits?"

"Yes," she replied. "Winnits. You know, cling-ons, tag nuts, dangleberries! Don't the Dutch have a word for this?"

Looking perplexed, I shrugged.

"Yes, you do!" She laughed. "*Vastklampendrol.*"

"Really? I didn't know. It never came up at law school, but, joking aside, when was it fitted?"

"The same time as urinary one. Susi and I were quite oblivious until we were told."

"You didn't know?"

"Oh, we knew the procedure would take place, but we didn't know the urinary and anal ports had been fitted simultaneously. Remember, there was no pain or trauma following the surgery, only fatigue, and that was mostly due to the anaesthetic. Of course, Susi got into a flap when they told us. Typical Suze. Panic first, think second. How I miss her, the daft little sausage. If only she were here."

From here on, Dr Padgett became increasingly distressed, and, following a brief consolation from myself, I ended the session. Upon leaving her office, I promptly contacted her PA, highlighting Dr Padgett's fragile condition. Still suffering from post-traumatic stress, Dr Padgett's recovery was taking far longer than her medical team predicted. Doubtless, there were further shadows clouding her heart. Certainly, I have met similar personalities before. Both covert and calculating, their projected selves are façade. Before baring all, Dr Padgett would require a position of unassailable dominance.

FOUR

SIGHTS AND SOUNDS

A week passed before I met Dr Padgett again and I spent my time in Holland with my family. Dr Padgett used this time to visit her mother (sadly taken ill) and I wondered how this would affect her already-fragile condition. She was hard at work when I entered her office, bent over backwards, her head inside the food dispenser. Scattered over her desk, its internal components, being both electronic and robotic, twitched and jiggled like newly severed limbs…

"A h ha!" she exclaimed; her head still obscured. "There you are, you little dickens, should've known you'd be American."

Still without the faintest idea what Dr Padgett was doing, watching her work was both amusing and intriguing, and, while twiddling a probe or fine tool, she started to sing…

"The stars at night, are shining bright, where? Deep in the heart of Texas Instruments…"

I politely coughed.

"Yes, yes," she said, "I can hear you. In fact, I heard your shoes squeaking down the corridor. Wait while I reassemble this damn thing and I'll make us a coffee."

Sitting at her desk, I marvelled at the speed and efficiency on display. Without removing her head, Dr Padgett, unerringly and without looking, reached for every component, replacing each in turn, all without fuss or jiggling. Emerging within minutes, she reattached the dispenser's front panel, and very deliberately washed her hands.

"All done." She said, adjusting her hair, fetching two mugs, and pouring coffee from a simmering jug. "Shall we give it a try? Having to clean and refill this primitive thing is boring."

"Give what a try? What were you doing?"

"Brain surgery."

"Huh?" I replied. "To the food dispenser? Why?"

"Because I loathe both its cheerfulness and inflexibility."

"Yes, certainly, but what have you done?"

"Given it a much-needed upgrade. A new personality."

"The personality of whom? Some parsing software, pinched from the mainframe?"

"The mainframe?" she replied. "No. I've given it mine."

"Yours?" I puzzled. "How?"

"Well, it was far from straightforward. There was a beast of a firewall. Hardware to prevent thieving and so forth, but I am not a thief, and have temporarily overwritten its programme."

"Ok," I slowly nodded. "But how did you get around it?"

"I didn't," she replied. "I absorbed it. After learning the security system wasn't part of the software – they're a cinch to break down – I knew it must be hardwired, and it was a matter of locating the circuit and identifying its components. Hence the dismantling."

"Yes," I said, "it was fascinating watching you work. You're remarkably efficient. Almost machine-like."

"Hardly surprising," she replied. "Bits of me are just that. Now, for a test run. Would you like a biscuit, something to munch with your coffee? Try ordering one."

"Ok. A biscuit or two would be good, but what should I do? Talk to the dispenser as usual?"

"Indeed," she replied. "Or talk to me? It makes no difference."

"Fine. As long as it is safe. If you blow a fuse, I'll be in trouble."

"Sure." She chuckled. "But there's really no danger at all. So come on, ask me. It'll be fun!"

"Right," I began. "Hello? Food dispenser, do you have any biscuits?"

Dr Padgett, suddenly flinching and grinning broadly, sat up straight in her chair...

"Hi there!" she announced, her tone uncharacteristically cheery. "Welcome to Snack Box. Checking biscuit availability..."

Five long seconds of silence followed with Dr Padgett still as a statue.

"Nope," she continued, sounding more like herself. "Still no biscuits, but hang on, there are wafers – chocolate wafers, and my favourite. Pinkies! Bet you've never had one of those. Order pink wafers, I beg you. They're the best! Eaten in this country for hundreds of years. William Crawford & Son's invention. A Scottish confection, yes, it was they, oh, and Shamoutis too! Not strictly a biscuit, but the original software wouldn't have told you any of this. It would simply have suggested a product with a higher margin of profit. Something the company needed to shift. A cereal bar of extremely high fibre."

"No doubt about it," I remarked. "Although, I don't yet have anything to eat?"

"Hmm?" she mumbled, slightly distracted. "Oh, yes, sorry. Shamoutis and wafers, coming right up!"

"Thank God."

"Now, there's no need to get sniffy, and, hey! You're getting this for free. You lucky bugger. I have to pay! Yes, here it is. The catering requirements of all UET dignitaries and – I don't believe it – the Walsingham ARC paid for by the UET. Typical."

"Well, rank does have its privileges." I chuckled. "But now, we need to get started. Can you detach yourself from that infernal machine, or are you connected forever?"

"No," she sighed, fanning herself, "I'm back, and, oh, here's the food."

Within in the food dispenser, three small packets landed with a whoosh and a clonk. Fetching them out, Dr Padgett opened them up, spreading the contents over her desk.

"Are you sure that's hygienic?" I remarked. "Eating straight from the table?"

"Of course," she replied, cocking a perfect eyebrow. "And, in my case, it doesn't matter. Help yourself, and if you want to try a pink wafer, do it now. Before I scoff the flippin' lot."

"What do you think?" she then asked, watching me cautiously nibble. "Scrummy, are they not?"

"De-licious," I diplomatically remarked, swallowing as quickly as I could.

"Liar."

"Yes, I'm sorry. The chemical taste and the way it soaked up my spittle was revolting, but each to their own. Now, Dr Padgett, to business. Today I want to discuss your remaining implants. What they do, and their effects on you and the others."

"Tricky." She frowned. "Heavily sedated or under full anaesthesia, only the ripping headaches remain in any clarity."

"Fine," I said, considering the best way to proceed. "Perhaps, if you were to recount what was done and how? Should be more than enough. I've had surgery myself, an appendectomy, and my memories of the procedure are vague at best."

"Very well," she replied. "Where to start? My ears?"

Following a shrug, I nodded.

"Ears it is, then," she said. "Dual auricular implants, enhancing my equilibrioception, range and sensitivity of hearing. The actual devices are a bit of mystery – never investigated to any extent, but the scars are still visible, look…"

Carefully gathering her hair, Dr Padgett lifted it away from her left auricle, bending it forward to reveal a fine white scar where it joined her external acoustic meatus.

"It's the same on the other side, pretty neat job, don't you think?"

"Amazing," I said. "What are the benefits?"

"They are threefold. Firstly, and most importantly, in variable-gravity environments I am unaffected by dizziness or motion sickness – a condition typically caused by chaotic impulses from the utricle and saccule when the endolymph flows dramatically and/or non-rhythmically within the ears' semi-circular canals."

"Useful," I said. "Seasickness has always plagued me. To be rid of it would be tremendous."

"Indeed. If you'd like a full demonstration of my equilibrioception, my enhanced balancing capabilities, we should go to the gym."

Reaching over her desk to snaffle a wafer, she offered it to her lips with both hands, nibbling like a gerbil.

"Did my explanation make sense?"

"It was fine," I replied, "and as for the demonstration – sounds fascinating, but it's doubtful my literary mediocrity would do your acrobatics any justice."

"Ok," she smiled, still nibbling. "Literary mediocrity? Nice. Good words. Shall I press on, then, with my hearing? How are you recording, anyway? Wearable tech?"

"Yes, my jacket and trousers are polycote. Observe…"

Stretching my trousers taut over my knee, I defined a small display with my index finger and thumb.

"Cool," she said, leaning over to look. "Spectracote fibres have really improved in the last few years. I thought your trousers were regular cotton."

"Yes. My whole ensemble is fake, even my vest. Could we further discuss your hearing?"

"Indeed," Dr Padgett replied. "Beyond my enhanced balancing capabilities, another benefit would be the variable sensitivity of my hearing. For example, in cacophonous environments I can quieten or filter at will – great at noisy parties, with the ability to amplify and analyse sounds imperceptible to normal hearing."

"Remarkable. No wonder you could hear me coming."

"Yes, and in the countryside this benefit is particularly delightful. To suddenly hear the flutter of a butterfly or the singing of voles is wonderful. All the subtle sounds just beyond normal hearing suddenly manifest themselves in detail and clarity, bringing me nicely to the third and final benefit. My infra and ultrasonic sensitivity."

"Absolutely," I said. "I gather you hear like a dog."

"A dog?" she replied with a snort. "Piffle. My dear Walter, I'll have you know, I hear like a bat."

"There's a difference? Is a bat's hearing superior?"

"Vastly," she replied.

"My apologies, then. Could you explain?"

"More biology?"

"If you wouldn't mind. You're a most capable lecturer."

"I most certainly am not! I have little patience for the ignorant, but since you persist to insist... Although sensitive to frequencies beyond human hearing, the hearing of dogs covers a similar range. About ten octaves. 20Hz to 20kHz in humans, 40Hz to 60kHz in dogs. Bats, however, depending on the species, can sense a far wider range, 1kHz to 200kHz, and my hearing is superior. I have yet to fully assess my capabilities, but Bill Corbiere did, quoting 12Hz to 202kHz, and, since we're fitted with the same implant, there's little reason my hearing should be different."

"Incredible, and you can adjust it at will?"

"Yes. Although, I must think hard and very directly to access my implants, and it requires practice – a deliberate failsafe to prevent accidental access when the mind wanders or enters a dream-like state. The way it works is very clever, quite beyond the scope of this interview, unless you demand an explanation."

"No, you are correct. There's no need, and, when I come to transcribe this recording, brevity is a blessed relief."

"Good grief!" She laughed. "You have to write this up? Everything? Including my wittering?"

"Yes." I smiled. "Every single word."

"What a terrible palaver. Why not let a computer do it? Cheat! I certainly would."

"Normally, yes," I replied. "But the software I use is basic, without colour or feeling. It wouldn't, dear Gina, paint the picture of your radiant smile or transcribe your musical laughter."

"You old charmer." She laughed. "You are married, aren't you?"

"Yes." I nodded in reply. "With my full allotment of children. A boy and a girl. Why do you ask?"

"Oh, nothing." She shrugged. "Just checking."

"Fine, and back to your hearing?"

"Yes."

"Then tell me, do you perceive the entire frequency range simultaneously?"

"Oh, heavens, no," she replied, "that would be overwhelming, and anyway, for most of the time, perfect human hearing, between 12Hz and 24 kHz, does me fine. To hear higher or lower frequencies I must access the implant, selecting a range of twelve octaves, perceiving them naturally. The lowest warm and rumbling, the highest an imperceptible whistle."

"Right. So, a dog's high-pitched whine, would sound the same as my voice?"

"And your voice a low-pitched rumbling growl."

"Ingenious," I said. "Must be amazing to do that."

"In truth, it's more of a novelty. I hardly use it, but it does make the sound of natural world much more complex. Birdsong, for example, takes on a completely new dimension. So many harmonies, clicks and whistles we never normally hear."

"Wondrous. You must download me a recording sometime, I'd love to hear that."

"Of course," she replied. "My pleasure, but right now, if you don't mind, I'm expected to visit Vivisection Level 1. You wanna come? There's nothing secret or sensitive on one. Just so long as. Well, you're not squeamish, are you?"

"No idea," I said with a shrug. "But I would be honoured to join you. To witness the work performed here might be useful."

Vivisection is a word overflowing with all sorts of macabre connotations, but as Dr Padgett explained, the UET strictly control animal experimentation, with Europe, the States of America, and the Russian Federation following the UET's stipulations as a benchmark. It was the work done in the 2080s by Musche and Cheung on animal intelligence and their follow-up Nobel Prize–winning research on animal sentience (shaking the scientific community to its foundations) that brought about its implementation. Further research into animal linguistics, employing the latest entangled poly-quantum-processor computers facilitated communication with animal intelligences hitherto considered impossible.

"Once had a chat with a cuttlefish," said Dr Padgett, as we headed to the laboratory.

"You're kidding," I wondered. "How did that go?"

"Amazing," she replied. "Truly amazing, amazing for us both, I think. Certainly, Hunts-Small-Crabs was just as surprised as I was."

"What did you talk about? Why and how?"

"Inquisitor?" She chuckled. "Do you ever stop? Your inquisitiveness is relentless."

"It is supposed to be. Well?"

"Ok, I will endeavour to explain, but you're about to be scienced to death!"

"Good," I replied. "Do your worst."

"Fine, then," she said. "Before I begin, a little background."

"Understandable, proceed."

"Hmm, well, the cuttlefish in question was a wild one. A male, housed within a large aquarium, the environment as natural as possible. Indeed, Hunts-Small-Crabs certainly seem to approve. Referring to his new home as Bright Rock Pool he spent his days languidly swimming about, looking for food. Of course, the poor little squid wasn't just there for a holiday. He was part of an experiment to study cephalopod communication, and, to this end, the scientists fitted a specially developed sheet of spectracote to the wall of his aquarium."

"Fascinating. Go on."

"Now, cuttlefish, as you might know, use colour to communicate. Producing waves, patterns and sudden pulsations across the surface of their bodies. Movement and gesture also play an important part, and the positioning of their two tentacles and eight limbs are used to convey much meaning. You sure you want this?"

"Definitely. Don't stop."

"Ok, so spectracote is both a projective and absorptive material, and this particular sheet was specially configured to project a virtual cuttlefish while simultaneously monitoring responses of the one in the tank, processing and translating his shifting pigmentation and posture into text and audible speech. Are you still with me? We're nearly at the lab. Do you want me to stop?"

"Absolutely not. Please continue – thought-provoking stuff. Is there somewhere we can sit so I can hear the rest?"

"Of course." She smiled. "Outside the lab there's a little waiting room. You can see the door from here."

Dr Padgett went quiet as we settled inside, but once seated, she continued her recollections…

"Now, cuttlefish are solitary creatures, and quite territorial. Only for mating purposes do they seek company. If a cuttlefish does stray into another's territory, they will either chase it away, try to eat it, or hide. It is only when a cuttlefish of comparable size and age – dominance, if you like – flirts at the edge of another's territory that communication will ever take place. Pure mischance, of course, but this is the circumstance the scientists were trying to create."

"And what did you do? Wave and say hello?"

"Yes," said Dr Padgett, "in a cuttlefishy sort of way. To begin, the virtual cuttlefish adopted a very peaceful posture. Hanging motionless, with its tail upwards, its tentacles and limbs splayed on the sand. Colouration, too, played its part. The virtual cuttlefish was white as a sheet."

"Right, and I assume it worked?"

"Indeed," she confirmed. "Initially, Hunts-Small-Crabs studiously ignored the virtual cuttlefish, but after fifteen minutes or so he moved closer, adopting a similarly peaceful response."

"Did he speak?"

"Oh yes!" she replied. "But how it went was a total surprise. Hunts-Small-Crabs knew the game too well. He forever outwitted me…"

"What?" he said with a burst of rolling orange. "I dig in sand. Look for food. Go back to waving rocks!"

"This was the first surprise. On previous occasions, the appearance of the simulated cuttlefish had always been different, and it was shock to discover Hunts-Small-Crabs had in no way been duped."

"Clever little squid. What did you say?"

"I apologised. There was nothing else to do, and with him twisting his tentacles, rolling waves of black back and forth over the length of his body, he accepted my fault, asking again what I wanted…"

"Desire to talk," I said, "ask favour," to which he wasn't impressed…

"Shining swimmer come too much. Go back to waving rocks! Always asking while floating starfish drop small crabs. Ask favour. I dig for crabs."

"Waving rocks, floating starfish? Whatever did it mean?"

"Waving rocks was thought to mean the deeper ocean. A kelp forest perhaps. While floating starfish was a reference to the hand that fed him, dropping food for him to hunt."

"Right. Did you get the chance to ask your favour?"

"I did," she replied, twiddling a strand of dark hair. "In fact, I came straight out with it. Worried by then that he would swim away and ignore me."

"For what did you ask?"

"A piece of his skin. A small bite was how I put it. What a blunder! The scientists gasped, shaking their heads in dismay when I said it."

"Nobody's perfect," I remarked. "You know the adage 'genius feeds on tact'?"

"Yes," she replied with a frown, "and, no matter how true it sometimes rings, in my case, it's terribly unfair."

"Yes," I proffered, "I'm sorry. I meant no offence. Will you accept my apology?"

"*Natürlich.*" She chuckled. "Very tactful for you to offer... another of your tests? To assess the fragility of my temper?"

"You're very perceptive."

"Yes," she affirmed. "I am. Always. Please don't play games."

"Indeed," I replied, composing my thoughts. "Let's move on. You wanted a sample of the cuttlefish's skin. What for?"

"For my research!" Dr Padgett laughed, rolling her eyes. "Sometimes, Walter, you really are incredibly tactful, but I wanted a fresh sample of cuttlefish tissue for my research. By culturing the cells, I sought to resolve a mystery that has plagued scientists for over a hundred years. Cuttlefish are colourblind. Why use colour in camouflage and communication if they cannot perceive it? I had a hunch there was another mechanism at work, probably involving their dermis and underlying tissues, but to do really good work, I required a living sample."

"Right, and what did the cuttlefish say?"

"Get stuffed."

"Ha, really?"

"Yes, he thought I meant to eat him. With a flash of crimson and a cloud of ink he was gone, burying himself in some safe corner, out of harm's way."

"And that was that. No comeback?"

"Correct," she replied. "If the answer's no, it's no. It's the law! You of all people should know. Unless the chance arises again to obtain a live sample, I'm buggered. I did apply to the UET Marine Biology Cooperative for a fresh carcass, but cephalopod tissues deteriorate extremely rapidly, so I'm in for a long wait."

It was there she ended, escorting me smoothly from the waiting room and into the laboratory.

The laboratory itself, the grandiose sounding "Vivisection Level 1", was small and intimate, and utterly different from my expectations. Dr Padgett had led me to believe I would see all manner of macabre animal experiments, but this was not the case. It was soon apparent I had been the victim of a "wind up" and the sly look on her face as we entered the lab was a study of impish joy.

Before me, working in two groups, were roughly twenty scientists, with others coming and going continuously. In one corner, working alone, I spied an elderly gentleman very deliberately cleaning a small terrarium, but upon seeing Dr Padgett, he scowled and turned away.

Announcing her arrival, Dr Padgett rapped her knuckles firmly against the door...

"Good afternoon!" she cried, her voice clear and bright. "We have our visitor today. The one I told you about? After I've checked you in, I want you to show Mr de Boer every courtesy."

"Yes, Dr Padgett," they sheepishly replied, and I realised the scientists were mocking her authority.

"Oh, please," she blushed, swatting away their taunt. "You lot are too much. Now, be nice. Say hello, with less sarcasm."

"Hell-low," they replied as one. "The Halfpenny ICR welcomes you."

"You lot are nuts." She chuckled. "Wish I'd never asked."

"Who's that in the corner?" I quietly asked. "He seems angry. Does he not like you?"

"That's George," whispered Dr Padgett. "Dr Larkin, our senior bacteriologist, and you're right, he doesn't care for me at all. He respects me professionally, of course, which is enough, as in his field, he's the best of the best. Better have a chat and find out what's up. First things first. Roll call. Part of our health and safety procedure, in case of fire, et cetera. Here at the institute, staff may come and go as they please, but periodic snapshots are necessary."

"Why not have a log-in system? Much easier to keep track if employees clock in."

"You don't know scientists. Most of them would forget, and it would breach a core doctrine of the institute. Professional freedom. It is especially important our scientists feel unburdened by contracts. 'Liberty is the mother of inspiration' and all that hackneyed old jazz."

"Right, you lot," she announced, "listen out for your name… Davis. One eye. The cyclops?"

"Aye."

"Davies. Eye-ee. The example?"

"Aye-ee."

"Edwards?"

"Present."

"Emanuel?"

No answer.

"Ugh," grumbled Dr Padgett. "She's never here. Foroudy?"

"*Qui.*"

"Glaister?"

"Yeah."

"Hadland?"

"She's gone," someone remarked.

"Gone off," chirped a voice from the back.

There was giggling, to which Dr Padgett raised her hand.

"That'll do," she chided. "Harry?"

"Here."

"Hersom."

No response.

"Hersom!" Dr Padgett projected with growing impatience.

"Yes?"

"Pay attention. Jones S?"

"Here."

"Jones S."

"Present."

"Oh my." Chuckled Dr Padgett. "That's no good. Two Joneses and both Sarah's. Sarah Jones – the one at the front, says here you're married. What was your name before?"

"Jones."

"Seriously?" asked Dr Padgett. "Is that even legal? Never mind, will rank the two of you by height, from now on, you shall be Jones minor. Larkin?"

No response.

"Yes, George, I can see you. Loader?"

"He's upstairs," came a voice from the back.

"Yeah," laughed another. "With a woman."

"Is he indeed?" Dr Padgett keenly asked.

"Or a man!" cried someone else.

There was laughter and Dr Padgett slowly shook her head, waiting for the uproar to subside.

"Owen?"

"I'm here and so are my worms!"

"Lovely. Owens?"

"*Ja*, present."

"Richards? Richards? No." She sighed. "Not here. Sloane?"

"He's gone to Ireland," someone called out.

"Fine. Willing?"

"Present."

"Wilson?"

"Oh, that's me. Here! Sorry, I was…"

"Yes, you were," replied Dr Padgett. "Keep your hands to yourself. Wood?"

"He's in the toilet!" came a shout from the left.

"What?" Dr Padgett remarked. "Again? There," she then said to me, "all done."

"Do you not need to write the register down?"

"No need," she replied. "I'm already connected to the mainframe. The data is already there."

"Clever," I remarked. "What now?"

"A few things. Safety checks, progress updates, and then we'll be done. First, I need to speak to George. In the meantime, why don't you see what the teams are working on? I'll introduce you to George once I've soothed his temper."

Feeling superfluous, I did as Dr Padgett recommended. Introducing myself to the first team, I listened to their lively discussion before asking about their current assignment. The creation of an artificial organ. A mass of specialised cells, capable of secreting nematicides – substances harmless to the host but lethal to parasitic worms. Their final aim was to implant or engender the growth of a similar organ inside a host organism, providing an elegant way of neutralising any nematode infestation. Fascinating work, and I desired to linger and see their results.

The second group, still at the planning and design stage of their project, didn't talk to me much, but their task (I eventually learnt) concerned a genus of spiral-shaped bacteria called Nitrosomonas – the microbes primarily responsible for nitrogen fixation in soil. In addition, with the ability to break down halogenated hydrocarbons, compounds such as vinyl chloride, trichloroethene, and halobenzenes, nitrosomonas is a useful agent in the cleansing of contaminated environments. Its carbon fixation capabilities too are also of great interest, and I quote: "During its catalysis of urea, nitrosomonas employs the Calvin cycle, metabolising the resulting ammonia, releasing nitrite."

The team were developing techniques intended to control the bacterium's replication, encouraging the formation of non-motile giant structures, hereby increasing the bacteria's nitrogen-fixing efficiency. While I stood by, they were discussing methods of manipulating the bacterium's photophobic tendencies, using a bio-film matrix to clump smaller bacterial colonies into an amorphous mass. Their work, still at a theoretical stage, was purely diagrammatic and I soon left them, joining Drs Padgett and Larkin.

The terrarium I spied earlier housed a small salamander...

"*Salamandra salamandra,*" Dr Larkin censoriously corrected. "A European fire salamander."

"Yes," Dr Padgett quickly interjected. "Thank you, George. I was about to explain."

"Then get a move on," he replied, "I've other places to be."

Smiling kindly, Dr Padgett gently shook her head...

"George," she explained, "by a process of cloning and careful genetic modification, has dramatically altered the properties of this salamander's epidermal pigmentation. Typically, those colourful patches should be yellow-orange, but, as you can see, they are almost sky-blue."

"Yes." I nodded. "And beautiful they look too. I suppose there's more to them than decoration?"

"Indeed," she replied. "Originally, these markings served as a warning to predators, Signalling the salamander's ability to excrete various toxins, but no longer! George has modified the cells to such an extent they are now photosynthetic, with structures taken from cyanobacteria."

"It wasn't easy," added Dr Larkin. "The greatest difficulty involved shaping the cell membranes, forming thylakoids, folds and bands capable of supporting phycobilisomes – tiny light-harvesting antennae-like structures holding stacks of pigmented proteins."

"And it worked well," said Dr Padgett. "When illuminated, the cells produce glucose. Enough to sustain the cells and surrounding tissues."

"And the salamander is healthy?"

"Yes," said Dr Larkin. "In fact, the little blighter is fast becoming a pet. The next stage involves breeding. The modified genes should carry over to the next generation, but the uncertainty involved has me on edge."

"If it's a pet," Dr Padgett remarked, "you should give it a name. Is it a boy or a girl?"

"God, I don't know," he replied. "It's an amphibian. Should be a male."

"A fella? Then call him Norris."

"Norris?" He scowled. "What if he turns out to be she?"

"Then Norris shall be Nora."

"No," he replied. "Not a chance, and are you going now? I want to finish cleaning and then feed the poor beast."

"Yes, George. We're going. I'll see you tomorrow."

"Norris," he muttered, reaching for a sponge. "Poor wee thing. Always cruel that Padgett."

FIVE

EXOTICA

Returning to Dr Padgett's office, I asked her to recount the enhancements made to her cognitive abilities…

"Fine," she replied, pouring a small cup of water. "Beginning with my eyesight?"

"If you would and then I think we'll call it day."

"Very well, but there's quite a lot to cover."

I shrugged.

"Then I'll try to make it quick. At first, the sparkle in the bluer eyes of my shipmates wasn't apparent."

"Right," I acknowledged. "Why was that?"

"Because their ocular implants were inactive. During this initial phase, our neural implants were monitoring only, scanning the relevant centres of our brains, learning how we processed various tasks: coordination, sensation, language, memory, and so forth."

"The implants weren't already set up?"

"No. Since each recipient required specific programming, the implants were left to configure themselves."

"Because every brain is different?"

"Not at all. In general terms, human brains are uniform. It is only in how they process information and interconnect that any differences appear."

"Certainly," I said. "Do go on. This is fascinating stuff."

"Very well. Following our surgery, the medical team presented us with firm instructions to keep busy. Both physically and mentally. Feeding our implants copious amounts of data. Enabling them to learn the fine structure of our brains. It was only the hearing and balance implants that were active from the beginning. The rest were seemingly dormant, and, anyway, so many changes at once would have been overwhelming."

"Ok, so when you all returned after your month of…?"

"Implant assimilation."

"Of course, and concerning your eyesight, how did it go?"

"Very favourably," she replied, sipping her water. "It was the first implant to be activated. In fact, I remember activation day very well."

"Hardly surprising. Go on…"

"My shipmates and I were gathered together in a small reception room, chatting, laughing, exchanging our experiences and discoveries. Bill Corbiere remarked how his cello playing had improved, with Eric Badsegh, more muscular than ever, delighted by his new abilities as a martial artist. Walsingham was remarkably upbeat. Full of puns and witticisms, looking forward to this day enormously…"

"When they flick the switch" – he laughed – "I'm going to be fifty again. Fifty! Golf and sexual potency."

"It'll play havoc with your putting," I quipped, and Walsingham clapped his hands in delight, chuckling like an over-friendly headmaster…

"That is all very well," I said. "And thank you kindly for painting the scene, but what enhancements were made to your eyes?"

"In other words, stop wittering, Gina, and get to the point?"

"Yes."

"Spoilsport. Any-whoo, the alterations made to my eyesight are subtle. I'm still unsure of their full extent. Do I still possess my original lens, retina, and so forth? No idea, frankly. The changes might only be in my head, but I can see in the dark! Not total dark, mind you, but night vision. With a thought I can perceive both infrared and ultraviolet wavelengths, individually, or in a somewhat confusing mélange."

"Impressive," I remarked. "And, compared to normal eyesight, how does the world appear?"

"Well, it's up to me, user configurable, but by default I experience the UV and IR wavelengths monochromatically – grey scale."

"Sounds a bit drab. What if you were to view UV only? What would you see?"

"Good question. In UV, the world appears sharper. Details normally noticeable in close-up are suddenly revealed. For example, the creases and crenulations of the skin. In addition, fluorescent substances glow dazzling white, surrounded by corona-like bloom, while violet and blue objects appear flat white. The blackest objects are those that absorb UV. Red colours – glass, for example – appears almost pitch black. Melanin, a skin pigment produced to protect us from UV, appears similarly dark. We Caucasians appear thoroughly freckly!"

"I see, and the infrared, how does that appear?"

"In grey scale also. However, the information yielded is different. IR images are not sharp. In fact, they are blurry, as if out of focus. The longer the wavelength observed, the more approximate the image becomes. In IR, I effectively perceive temperature, the hotter the object, the brighter, whiter it appears. The default is 253 to 373 Kelvin, but I can configure the scale any way I choose. For good night vision, I find 263 to 333 most successful as it suits the British climate."

"Of course," I said. "However, you said default settings. What degree of reconfiguration is possible, and are there any further enhancements, other than IR and UV sensitivity?"

"Well," she continued, "combining wavelengths is one option, false colour is another, inverting, adding, or removing frequencies singly or in octaves. When performing delicate tasks, this ability is especially useful. When dismantling the food dispenser, every wavelength below green, I ignored."

"Right, anything else?"

"Focal length, Mr de Boer. I can focus on objects 50% closer than normal eyesight. Doesn't sound like much, but when removing a splinter or delousing a dog, it's brilliant."

"And that's all?"

"Isn't that enough?"

"Yes," I agreed, "it is."

"Good," she replied, "as I'm beginning to flag. Do you want me to describe my improved cognitive functions or save them for another time? Bear in mind, I'm on leave next week, and I intend to spend it with my mother. She's ill, and her condition has me worried. Also, remember, I'm supposed to be rehabilitating. After my extended period of coma my muscles are like jelly! Rest is what I need, with time enough to concentrate on my fitness, visiting old friends and colleagues."

"Of course," I replied, "but I would like to finish tonight. Could we have some food and continue? I don't know about you, but I'm hungry. You do become hungry, don't you? Or can you control that too?"

"Oh, God, no!" she laughed. "If only. I eat like a horse! One of the few drawbacks of my enhancements is that they draw their power from me. The more I use them, the hungrier I get! Let's head to the canteen and see what they've ruined."

⧗

Following a distinctly average lunch, we again settled in Dr Padgett's spacious office…

"You were going to speak of your brain functions. Could you be brief?"

Perching her chin upon her long white fingers, Dr Padgett's dark eyes glinted with mirth…

"Certainly," she agreed, "and you'll enjoy this. By pure mischance, I've saved the best until last. Upon the activation of our remaining brain implants, the change we underwent was incredible. We grew. Such knowledge, such clarity! Our enhanced senses seeping into our every experience. A vast library flooding our minds. Overwhelming, majestic!"

"Sounds terrifying."

"Terrifying?" she said. "Not a bit of it."

"Ok. Could you be more specific?"

"Of course. The implants in our brains supply an extensive library of knowledge. Not quite the sum of all human knowledge but almost, and not a closed library either. Upgradable, editable, in combination with our own experiences, wrapping your memories and thoughts like a blanket."

"Interesting. How does this knowledge appear?"

"In two ways. Firstly, as a reference. Akin to searching an encyclopaedia. If I want further information or wish to perform a calculation, I think the word 'inquiry', right here."

Said while tapping the middle of her forehead.

"At least," she said with a shrug, "that's what it feels like, but access requires concentration."

"Granted," I replied. "And the second way?"

"The second technique, derived from my senses, is more natural and it quickly becomes instinctive. For example, by just looking at an object, say a cardboard box, my implants deliver information beyond normal expectations. You would probably look at a box and think, cardboard box, then perhaps, 20cm cuboid, pale brown."

"Not even that much. Just box, cardboard, but no more. How do you see it?"

"My first thought would be natural, casual, much the same as yours, but then I receive further information. Dimensions to the nearest millimetre, its structure, chemical composition, manufacture, history, origins, and so forth."

"Just from a box?" I pondered. "Heavens above. Sounds confusing and headache-inducing."

"Not at all. The sensation is wondrous. The information isn't forced. It merely dangles, invitingly, like fruit on a tree. The actual picking is up to me."

"So, a bit like a digital assistant, and wouldn't this mean you're the world's most intelligent person?"

"No," she said, shaking her head. "Not intelligent. Knowledgeable. An entirely different state. My nascent IQ is the same as it ever was, about 140, and it is this, in tandem with my inventiveness and cunning, that limits my marvellous gifts, not the other way round."

"Of course. How you use your gifts is up you, and who made the best use of their enhancements? Did anyone stand out?"

"Walsingham," she said. "Not particularly surprising. He possessed the highest IQ, but the ingenuity of the man was astounding. Always first with an answer, blessed with incredible insight. Noticing connections betwixt and between the obvious. Obscure associations my crewmates and I would frequently overlook."

"Right."

"On an intellectual level, the rest of us were on a par. The differences between us dependent on our fields of expertise, environment, and upbringing. On the surface, Susi was the slowest member of the group, but do not be deceived. She was simply different. Quietly cunning. The meticulous way she could sift our words, examine our body language for deeper meaning. Searching for the questions hidden within our questions, probing our psyches to winkle out the truth."

"Her role, I suppose?"

"Certainly, and Walsingham was her favourite target. Did he know, I wonder? Probably. He knew everything else."

"Such was his nature," I said. "Now, any more abilities to mention?"

"A few. My memories. Those pertaining to my experiences, thoughts, and sensations are permanent. Did you know?"

"Only vaguely," I said. "Enlighten me, briefly."

"Very well, I'll do my best. By nature, we store our memories electrochemically and they are susceptible to jumbling, overlapping, degradation and loss when the chemical bonds and linkages shift, change, and begin to break down. Using my implant, my memories are permanent, copied selectively and archived in five separate formats: fixed or moving images, sound, synesthetic information, sensory data, even text. The choice is entirely mine."

"Amazing. What do you mean by synesthetic?"

"Good question. The term is derived from synaesthesia. A harmless mental condition, where the deeply affected claim to see or sense a range of colours when experiencing sounds of differing pitches. Blue for a middle C, red for a G, et cetera. In fact, recent studies into brain behaviour have revealed everyone to be synesthetic. Consciously or unconsciously, we associate colour with our emotions. When we retain a memory of an event, our brains store our emotional state synesthetically, colouring our thoughts, and my implants mimic this behaviour when storing my memories. By default, only moving images are coloured this way, but I can also recall synesthetic data separately for any sensation. When you come to review my memories, you'll see what I mean."

"Certainly. Any other techniques?"

"Well, the final technique involves storing my thoughts as a personal log or diary. Text, audio, or video, and the data is separable into streams. I don't do this, however. With me, you get the whole lot simultaneously. Although, I do write of pertinent events – just text. Nothing fancy."

Turning to look at the food dispenser, Dr Padgett furrowed her brow in concentration. A glass of orange juice slid into view, and she promptly retrieved it. Delicately sipping, she licked her lips.

"Do you want anything?"

"No, thank you. Still full of chowder. May we continue?"

"Of course."

"Another question, then, and a slightly strange one. If you die, what happens to your memories? Are they lost?"

"That's not a strange question at all!" She laughed. "In fact, it's a good one. Upon death, my digital memories will degrade along with the rest of my implants. A property no doubt insisted upon by the military, to prevent my knowledge falling into enemy hands."

"That seems a shame. How does this degradation occur?"

"Death is always a shame, but it's done by my Hibbites. Those tiny machines inhabiting my body. Programmed to reduce my implants to component molecules before breaking down themselves. Certainly, the process only requires few hours, while, in normal conditions, the decomposition of my body could take several months."

"Thank you," I said. "Anything else?"

"Oh, yes." She chuckled. "The most wonderful of all. The interpretation and recitation of language. *De meest verbazingwekkende geschenk van allemaal.*"

"Splendid," I replied. "Tell me."

"All?" she impugned. "Are you sure?"

"Hmm, good point. Tell me concisely."

"Right," she said, "briefly. My lingual implant instantly translates all known languages, including 'dead' languages, such as Cornish, ancient Greek, Sumerian, Canaanite, hearing them all as my chosen default language. In my case, English, but I can modify the default setting if I so wish. German would be a viable alternative, but I am not a native speaker, so I have always left things as they are."

"Ok," I acknowledged. "Keep going."

"On-the-fly translation is nothing new. The software has been available since the 1990s. It is only when I reply does the magic begin. When confronted by a language other than my default, my auditory and language processing centre instantly provides a translation. Options float in my mind. Respond in kind, respond in default, respond in other language."

"Then what?"

"Well, if I select my default language, to hide my linguistic capability, my answer might be: 'Sorry, I don't speak whatever,' 'Do you speak English,' or simply, 'Huh?' Useful, if I want some peace and quiet, but, if I select one of the other options, the freakiest thing happens, and the first time we experienced it, we were beside ourselves with wonder."

"Why? What happens?"

"You vocalise in the correct language, with perfect accentuation, and, until you get used to it, you feel like a puppet. Certainly, the urge to resist, to struggle against the involuntary use of your muscles, tongue, and vocal cords, is tremendous. Poor Susi was quite nauseous in the beginning, but so thrilled was she to be speaking Arabic, the sensation soon passed."

"It must be wonderful to do that, and I suppose the language difficulties of the group disappeared?"

"Indeed," she replied. "Blown away like smoke. Poof!"

"Remarkable. Does this ability also cater for the written word?"

"Of course, yes. I forgot to mention. I can read and write almost any language, reciting them in any language I choose."

"Excellent and thank you. Does that cover everything? Anything else I should know about?"

"No," she replied, "don't think so. Although, I haven't covered our ability to interface with the ship, the modifications and adjustments we made to ourselves, and the software updates uplinked from Moonbase and Darmstadt. To learn about these, you'll need to sift through my logs and stored memories. To which, I'm permitting you, and only you, unfettered access, and only for a month. So, you'll need to get cracking."

"Of course," I said. "Don't worry, I promise to use great care. Do your memories contain intimate or emotionally sensitive scenes?"

"Yes," she said sternly, "so use circumspection. You are to become a bearer of secrets, my secrets, and if they leak out? Well, you're for the chop, dear Walter, I promise you."

"Agreed," I replied, "and this concludes this series of interviews. Thank you most sincerely for your cooperation. I hope you have a relaxing week and my best wishes to your mother. Will she recover?"

"No," said Dr Padgett, returning her glass to the dispenser. "She has new variant orthomyxoviridael polyephelic melanoma."

"I'm sorry. Not familiar with…?"

"Saddleback syndrome."

"Oh no," I gasped. "That's terrible. How did she get it?"

"Not sure," she replied. "Although, the Winchelsea farming collective is a likely candidate. They did have a few pigs, I gather."

"Right," I sighed, shaking my head. "And there's still no viable treatment?"

"No, she left it too long. Her freckles had almost merged before she reported it."

"So sorry, Gina. No treatments at all?"

"No, there are none. She has about three months and then the cancers will overwhelm her."

"Such a tragedy. What're you going to do?"

"Spend as much time with her as I can? I have a feeling my week off could stretch into several months."

"Understandable. It had been a pleasure to meet you. An experience I shall never forget."

"And for me," she remarked, "an experience I choose not to forget. Goodbye Walter. I do hope my memories prove useful, or, in the least, entertaining."

"Certain they will be. Goodbye, Gina," and I tried to make for the door.

"Where are you going?" she asked, gathering me into her arms. "Flying Dutchman. You don't escape without a hug," and she gently kissed the top of my head.

I didn't meet her again for months.

SIX

THE ASCENT

*U*pon receiving Dr Padgett's digital memories and trying to access them with my office computer, I received little more than flickering screen and a high-pitched warbling screech. Contacting an employee of the Walsingham Institute for advice, they supplied both the necessary decryption key and software to separate her memories into distinct media channels. The software was powerful, rich with functionality, and it enabled me to review Dr Padgett's memories one frame at a time (if I so desired), with separate zones communicating her sensory data. Her tactile sensations, I split into zones for pressure, temperature, and pain, be it burning, cutting/puncturing, itching, or cramping, while her visual and auditory data, I displayed using zones for intensity and wavelength. The data concerning her sense of smell/taste was more complex. Her sensations of sweet, sour/acid, bitter, salt, and umami, often overlapped, directly associating themselves with Dr Padgett's interpretations or reminiscences brought about by her olfactory sensors. For example, when sniffing a rose, it would stimulate her olfactory centre (releasing an abundance of chemical data) but knowing the scent to be "a rose" she would simply take pleasure in it. However, when sniffing a rose-like perfume, similar olfactory data would result in her associating the scent with roses, "a perfume smelling of roses". Obvious, but I need to communicate the degree of difficulty converting a person's memories into a written account. Further complicating my task was Dr Padgett's decidedly haphazard approach to memory storage, with files overlapping, rarely in chronological order, and *untangling the data streams took far longer than I anticipated. My perseverance bore fruit, however. Memories shared by both Drs Ackermann and Badsegh, and I have drawn upon these when requiring extra detail or clarity. They have provided new insight to the events unfolding while Dr Padgett remained in a coma. (Please note. For legal reasons, to preserve their original format, the log entries of Dr Ackermann I translated from German into English word for word.)*

Recorded at her family home in Winchelsea, East Sussex, in the UK, this account begins with Dr Padgett's first tentative, at times irreverent, personal log entries and private thoughts...

Well, I suppose I should start recording. Is this thing inside my head really monitoring my every thought and spoken word? How can I know? Let me che— Oh, yes. It is. How clever!

Right. So, what should I call this recording? Gina's Log. Dr Padgett's Personal Log. Gina's Steaming Log?

No.

No! Be serious. Small children might come to read this, picture their shining faces. Wide-eyed, marvelling at your heroic...arse!

Be serious.

Gina's Diary.

Gina's Verbal Diarrhoeary...

Come on girl. Focus!

Focus.

Fucus.

Fucus serratus.

A seaweed?

How the...?

Kingdom: *Chromista*, Subkingdom: *Harosa*, Superphylum: *Heterokontophyta*.

What?

Class: *Phaeophyceae*. Order: *Fucales*.

Where is it all coming from?

Family: *Fucaceae*. Genus: *Fucus*.

This isn't right.

Species: *Fucus serratus*.

I don't want this!

A seaweed of the North Atlantic, also known as toothed wrack. Olive-brown in colour, it is similar to— no!

Stop.

Stop it!

Good God. This is tricky. I must learn to control my thoughts.

Concentrate…

It is launch day minus 2 and I am spending it with my family – mother, brother, his wife, children, they're all here, and we are enjoying hearty meals and chat. The children are excitedly bombarding me with all manner of silly questions, and I am receiving (and giving) cuddles and hugs. Indeed. Physical contact I will miss most of all.

David and I, following advice from the UET (to set it up in advance), have finished configuring the family's private communications network. A slew of entangled passwords, quick test, and done. When I say private, I mean spied upon. Surely, the UET will be monitoring our every word? Checking for signs of insanity or, in my case, sanity. LOL. Groan. Not funny at all.

If I am on active duty and not comatose, we have agreed to communicate weekly, requiring further explanation I would be unconscious for much of the flight. Then it became necessary to remind them, that beyond the orbit of Mars, live video chat would become increasingly tiresome. With a delay of over three minutes (and increasing), fluid conversation will be impossible.

Launch day minus 1. An exciting day in prospect. After meeting my crewmates for the first time in weeks (I have missed Susi intensely) we are lodging at the Hinnie UET Space Centre in Surrey. A distinctly leafy and agreeable location, just a short walk from a twee village called Holmbury St Mary.

Housed within a splendid Edwardian mansion, the centre itself is a peculiar establishment, and typically British – the crappiness of our berths in contrast to our surroundings, but the catering, training, and leisure facilities are top notch. Someone is aware this could be our last good meal for a decade!

Eric, upon hearing my grumbling, smiled and shook his head.

"Wait and see," he reassuringly whispered. "My kitchen and larder are already aboard."

We received our mission details this morning – by upload! To unexpectedly receive so much data was both bewildering and confusing, and for two hours its slow assimilation left me vague, drained, and helpless. I later joined Susi (similarly discombobulated) in a comfortable lounge before Walsingham summoned us to a meeting…

With a high ceiling and walls lined with books, the meeting to which Dr Padgett refers was within the Grand Library. Dr Padgett: "Rank upon rank, reflecting the sun with their leather covers and gilding, the books appeared to me as soldiers. Their uniform's crisp, their buttons proud and burnished."

Only Sir Malcolm Walsingham, Drs Padgett and Ackermann were there initially. Frustrated by the low turnout, Sir Malcolm paced the room. Unmoved by Walsingham's chagrin, Gina and Susi settled into a comfortable leather couch, enjoying a pleasant view of the gardens.

It was fifteen minutes before the others arrived, and Gina could hear their approach. Their voices echoing. Laughing and joking about playing snooker and making general mischief.

"About time," said Walsingham, crossing his arms. "I don't know where you have been, but I summoned you half an hour ago. I don't like to be kept waiting. Dr Al-Hillah, you should know this already."

"Yes, sir," he replied. "But I was… distracted? Educating these peasants in the gentle art of snooker."

"Hardly an art!" laughed Corbiere. "A simplistic divertissement. An application of Newtonian physics. Where the appeal lies, I cannot fathom. Certainly, the straightforwardness of the game meant a wager was necessary. A trifling ante to up the pressure. Who could clear the table, score a 'one-four-seven' the quickest?"

"And you might've won" – Badsegh chuckled – "if you'd used a cue like he showed you."

"A cue?" Corbiere snorted. "Far too easy. Flicking the cue ball made it a challenge."

"Who won?" asked Susi.

"Emil," replied Al-Hillah. "Why do you think he's so smug?"

Grinning broadly, Emilio Bedoya, opened his arms and bowed.

"Four minutes and nine seconds," said Al-Hillah. "A new world record. Not bad for a novice."

"Nonsense," sniffed Corbiere. "He cheated. Lining up shots in advance and then striking the cue ball...It was still moving!"

"It wasn't!" cried Bedoya. "Blessed Madonna. You're such a sore loser."

"Enough!" said Walsingham, banging his hand on the desk. "This isn't a holiday. Focus!"

Sweeping her eyes over room, Dr Padgett briefly studied her crewmates. Sitting to her left, brown-haired, blue-eyed, in her early forties, and curvaceous, was the psychiatrist Susi Ackermann. Certainly, Dr Padgett seemed to approve: "Susi appears to be fit, firm and ready for anything," and, briefly matching Dr Padgett's gaze, Dr Ackermann's mouth twitched into a smile.

Leaning against a wall of books were the "three stooges", Drs Corbiere, Al-Hillah, and the astrophysicist, Emilio Bedoya. Dressed smartly, they appeared similarly healthy, athletic even. They had clearly taken the instructions about maximising physical fitness very seriously.

On the floor, cross-legged, motionless, and meditative, was the nutritionist, Dr Badsegh.

Admiring his powerful physique before flushing slightly, Dr Padgett's pulse was steadily climbing (evidence of physical attraction?).

Toweringly tall, even when seated, Sir Malcolm Walsingham thoughtfully stroked his close-cropped beard. His intense blue eyes sparkling like a mountain lake...

"Very well," he continued. "Now we are in full receipt of the mission specifications, I thought it best we gather to discuss both their content and technique involved in their delivery, and by Jove! They are comprehensive, are they not? I for one am finding the quantity of data flooding my mind a constant distraction."

"Indeed," remarked Susi Ackermann. "The influx of data was almost overwhelming. What were the UET thinking? Sudden inundations like this can be harmful. A form of mental shock usually results, triggering sensations of addiction and withdrawal while the brain struggles to adsorb the surge of information. In future, I recommend the UET send their data in smaller packets, with a degree of forewarning."

"Very good," replied Walsingham. "I'll pass that along. Now, on to tomorrow. Waking early, following a medical assessment and a light breakfast, we will travel to the launch centre at Dunsfold, whereupon I am expecting some media work and a series of interviews."

Barely audible muttering and a couple of stifled groans.

"I know it's a pain," said Walsingham, "but the UET expect our full cooperation."

With his gaze falling upon Dr Padgett, Walsingham tried to hold her with his eyes, but she simply tilted her head and smiled…

"Wondered when it would start," she said. "As of yet, the only interest I've received was from my parish magazine. Hardly a media storm. What the hell's going on?"

"They hushed it up," said Dr Badsegh. "Was easy enough. The UET simply said their next mission to the Kuiper Belt would be unmanned. Robotic missions are commonplace. Not until yesterday did they announce the full specs. The media have yet to catch up. Suits me fine, actually. Safely in space before the whole nonsense kicks off."

"Precisely," said Walsingham. "The UET's plan all along. Imperative our mission be calm and relaxed as possible. Remember, the science is secondary. We are the primary mission objective. How we fair on an extended space flight, adapting to the ergonomics of the KBE. From a certain point of view, we are little more than passengers on a liner."

"Hardly a liner," said Corbiere. "A prison. What about the crushing and the stretching, the cooking and the freezing, suffocation, radiation? What about the boredom?"

"Yes, yes," replied Walsingham, raising a hand. "For reminding us of the perils, thank you. Once on board you're sure to find assurance. Now, where was I? Oh, yes. This will be a balloon ascent."

There was groaning and cursing at this announcement.

"Lifting our shuttle to approximately 45,000 metres, and you will be required to wear re-entry suits for the entire duration. Up to twenty-four hours."

More groaning, more cursing.

"As you know, the weather conditions in the upper atmosphere are unpredictable. By no means should you expect our ascent to be vertical, but, once we achieve maximum altitude, the balloons will deflate and detach. The thrusters of our shuttle will take us the rest of the way, placing us in high orbit, before docking with the KBE. Your mission specs include all the details, and, if you haven't already studied them, I recommend you spend the rest of the day doing so. Oh, and lastly, hair and beards. There is additional tech waiting for us on the KBE, which I am not yet at liberty

to disclose, but it is imperative all beards and hair be close-cropped. In other words, Eric? Your ponytail will have to go. Abdullah? Your beard also. I'm sorry if this upsets your religious sensitivities, but there is no alternative, and Gina. Dear Gina. A haircut if you please."

"No," replied Dr Padgett.

"No?" remarked Walsingham with a reddening face.

"Indeed," she said. "My answer was no. Are your implants not working? I'm not cutting my hair. I'll find another way."

"Very well," sighed Walsingham. "If you insist, but you will discover I am correct and then we can discuss this further. Any questions?"

Silence.

Surprised, Walsingham asked again.

"Anyone?"

The silence continued, with Dr Badsegh nonchalantly shrugging.

"Then good," said Walsingham. "Let's grab some lunch. I think we're allowed something. Before this afternoon's final check-up, anyway."

⧗

Launch day. It was early morning and the crew, excited or nervous, peer at the 15m shuttle with its cluster of vast metallic balloons shifting and jostling like doom-laden clouds.

Gina's private diary. Launch day.

Yes. Launch day, and it is pouring with rain. Typical.

Fed, watered, prodded and poked by medics, before relentlessly (and pointlessly) interviewed by the media. Their inane questions were infuriating and, running out of patience, I was more than ready to spout forth a torrent of lies, but Walsingham, knowing my mind (bless him), kept butting in. Shame.

Joking aside, the view from the observation dome is impressive. The balloons are vast, dwarfing the shuttle, and the rain slips from their lustrous metallic surfaces like beads of polished glass.

More than bags of helium, these balloons are robotic, capable of independent inflation, deflation, ascent or descent. The lightness of their aluminium/borophene fabric is in stark contrast to its durability. They're almost indestructible!

About to don my re-entry suit.

Already wearing hers, Susi peers through its faceplate with the expression of a dog stuck outside in the rain. Her candour is entirely understandable. The suits are unwieldy at best, yet they are also reassuring. Introduced thirty years ago, the standard model re-entry suit has undergone steady improvement, and now so dependable, falling from low orbit has become an activity rivalling the bungee jump of the past. A peculiar length to go to for a rush of adrenalin. Provoking the friction of the atmosphere to roast you, but the unwitting fools don't roast, or tumble uncontrollably. All the wearer need do is adopt a streamlined posture, while the built-in thrusters maintain a safe attitude and trajectory until their downward velocity slows sufficiently for the deployment of parachutes.

Already programmed, our suits will return us to the launch site if there is an emergency (more likely to die of boredom) and, if unexpectedly ejected from the shuttle (if escape via the airlock is impossible), the suit's rescue programme will take over. Even if the wearer is unconscious. The suits also double as environment suits or spacesuits, capable of sustaining life for seventy-two hours, and, if the wearer were to become lost in free space, the automated propulsion system will try to transport the wearer back to Earth (or the nearest haven), landing as previously described.

Right, enough waffling. Susi looks like she's about to throw up. She can't, of course, but she is certainly turning green. Ergh! I know why, though. These suits? They stink!

"Susi," I holler. "*Konfigurieren Sie Ihre olfaktorischen Eingaben so, dass sie ignoriert werden!*"

⧗

Suited and debriefed, the crew trudged their way past a line of photographers, climbing into an open-top transport delivering them to the shuttle. It was pouring with rain, and the bleak openness of the old airfield, grey and drear under heavy cloud, drained Dr Padgett's anticipation.

Descending from the rear of the shuttle was a narrow ramp, and, aided by technicians, the crew ponderously clambered aboard.

The interior of shuttle was surprisingly spacious. Towards the front, in two rows of three, were the passenger seats, with a single seat, as if for a pilot. There were no piloting controls, and as the crew settled,

Walsingham occupied the front seat, as if it were meant for him. In the first row sat Emilio Bedoya, Drs Corbiere and Al-Hillah, with the second row occupied by Drs Badsegh, Ackermann, and Padgett.

Mopping up any rainwater and making minor adjustments, smiling technicians distributed meal packs and polysheet computers, before strapping the crew into their seats.

"What's this?" joked Eric Badsegh. "Our in-flight movie and meal?"

"I guess," Walsingham replied, turning in his seat. "Certainly, better than nothing."

Uncomfortably fidgeting, crossing and uncrossing her legs, Dr Ackermann still seemed unhappy.

"Will we be in these suits for the whole flight?" she asked. "It's like a chrysalis!"

"Unfortunately, yes," replied Dr Padgett. "For safety, but we can remove our helmets."

"Is that wise?" she said, nervously rechecking her straps. "What if there's an emergency?" and Walsingham laughed.

"Really, Dr Ackermann," he said, "didn't you read the specs? The chances of an emergency are a million to one. The suits are simply to please the Safety Exec. We'll soon have our helmets off, mark my words. Hateful things. Head stuck in a goldfish bowl."

⧗

Gina's Personal… Oh, what the hell. Dear Mum,

We're off! Like the astronauts and cosmonauts of old, we are uncomfortably trapped. Cramped, suited, and booted. Strapped to a bomb full of fuel, ready to go boom any minute. The only difference? In our century, it takes longer to achieve orbit.

The last technical support officer has just left the shuttle and the back door, swinging shut, has sealed itself with a hiss and a thud. We are powering up! The whole shuttle humming and throbbing, coming to life, before rocking and shaking as the docking clamps suddenly release us from their steadying grip. Yes, we are rising. I can feel it! The shuttle is pitching and rolling like a boat anchored in a tidal swell. Thank God for my augmented lugholes. Without them I'd be sick as a dog!

Susi looks terrified and I am holding her hand.

Walsingham, removing his strapping, stands reassuringly before us. No mean feat, as a sudden crosswind causes the shuttle to lurch alarmingly.

"Whoa!" He smiles. "That was a big one! Don't be concerned, folks. As soon as we're above this weather, things will settle down. How about a song? Something to lift our spirits?"

"How about I throw you out of the airlock?" I remark.

"Some music, then?" he suggests.

Wagner's "Ride of the Valkyries" suddenly fills the air. Bill Corbiere groans in disgust.

"Mute," he suggests. "Can't stand it. Mute!"

"What's the matter?" asks Eric.

"Wrong music," explains Bill. "We're not heroes. We're luggage! Play something softer, and not Wagner. That man was a…"

"Yes," says Walsingham, "he was rather. How about this?"

Replacing the Wagner comes Beethoven's Symphony No. 3. It is a comforting choice, and, turning to check on Susi, I see her looking perturbed.

"Are you ok?"

"Think so," she mutters, "How much urine do these suits hold?"

"A lot," I reply.

"Good," she replies in relief, "because I can't seem to stop peeing!"

Hours have passed and we have just risen above 25,000 metres. The shuttle is steady and stable, and after removing my helmet and restraints I join the three stooges, Emilio, Bill, and Abda, snacking at a long bench situated at the rear of the cabin. Tutting at the mess, Walsingham shakes his head like an old school matron.

"I want every crumb gone when you've finished," he scolds. "At Mars, we'll be using this shuttle again, and I want it pristine and perfect."

We continue snacking and ignore him.

Returning to my seat, I check on Susi – snoring contentedly like old Rumbelow after his dinner. Sleep is a good idea, but, before joining her in slumber, I watch with some amusement a red-faced and indignant Walsingham clearing our crumbs.

Eric Badsegh, neatly folding a blanket into a cushion, eases it behind my head.

Dr Al-Hillah gently shakes me awake…

"Time to wake up. We're levelling off and about to lose the balloons."

Gently easing Susi awake, she blinks like a cat.

"Almost there, Suze," I say. "Helmets and restraints."

Grudgingly, Susi replaces her helmet and I don my own. Moving among us, Walsingham checks the security of our restraints.

"Deflation in five minutes," he announces. "It will be bumpy while we accelerate. Not to worry, though."

The engines are whining, pre-heating before a full power burn. Need to stop recording and brace myself. Hold on tight, girl. It's gonna be – wow! That's a lot of Gs. Gee-zus!

⌛

Hours later, the crew found themselves in a low-gravity environment. For Walsingham, Bedoya, Al-Hillah, and Badsegh, this experience was nothing new. Dr Padgett encountered low gravity during a sub-orbital flight to Australia, but for Drs Corbiere and Ackermann the sensation was novel.

Skilfully floating through the cabin, Walsingham checked on his crewmates. Bedoya and Al-Hillah busied themselves configuring screens displaying the views forward and aft.

"Alright?" asked Walsingham, peering into Corbiere's faceplate. "Any nausea or confusion?"

"Nope," he replied. "Everything's working perfectly. I'm keen to join the others. Can you help with my straps?"

"Sure," said Walsingham, "but be careful. Move slowly, or your momentum may be more than you can manage. The last thing we need is a concussion or a broken bone."

"Granted," he assured. "You ok, ladies? Coming for a float?"

"Were fine thanks," I replied. "And, for the time being, I'm staying with Susi."

"Da... danke," said Susi, gripping the arms of her chair.

Taking Dr Ackermann's hand, Dr Padgett looked straight into her eyes...

"You sure you don't want a tranquilliser? Feeling overwhelmed is quite natural, but, if you want, Bill will happily administer."

"Nein," Susi replied, taking a breath. "No, I'm ok. It is simply the feeling of lightness. I have no control! I think... yes, to see outside would help. Help get my bearings?"

"Well, you're in luck," said Dr Padgett "The fellas are working on a view-screen, and just about finished I think."

Gina's Private Drivel

Nearly there, thank God. Going crazy trapped in this suit.

Mind you, the fellas have done their level best to be entertaining. Acrobatics, clowning about, drinking from rippling balls of liquid. The usual stuff. None of it helped poor Susi. To calm her, Corbiere had to pump her full of drugs. A change of scene is all she really needs. Once docked, she will be fine.

Outside, the view is spectacular. Behind us (but slowly receding) is the Earth. Such a beautiful planet! A dazzling sphere of blue and white. The most colourful body in the solar system. Which is hardly surprising. The human eye is a product of long evolution within the Earth's atmospheric environment. We are supposed to see it! Certainly, if my hypothesis is correct, to the naked eye, the other planets of the solar system will be disappointing to look at.

The view ahead is bleak. Space is very black, but if I choose to view it with a broader spectrum of wavelengths, nebulae become apparent. At this distance, our spacecraft-home for the next decade or so appears to be little more than a fuzzy-edged speck. More from me after we dock.

⧗

Now much closer to the UET Kuiper Belt Explorer, Dr Padgett studied its outward appearance…

"It looks like a virus!" she excitedly remarked. "A retrovirus, no less!"

"Yes," replied Corbiere. "It does, it does indeed! I've been trying to make that association, but which species? Remember, I only kill the little blighters. You're the one that plays with 'em."

"Oh," she said. "Now, there's a question. Yes. I would have to plump for a lentivirus. Be it bovine, feline, or primate."

⧗

Gina's Completely Mental Notes

Converted from an interplanetary ore carrier, from a distance the KBE appears spherical, but it is in fact dodecahedral. A spiky, twelve-sided polyhedron of equilateral pentagons. This "spikiness" is a result of the twelve thrusters jutting from every facet, but, if one were to cut the KBE in half, its multi-layered construction would be revealed...

Beneath the thrusters, wrapping the ship like a grey crystalline dermis, is the outer hull, and, although relatively thin, it is packed with technology: sensors, Compton array emitters, ports, hatches, and airlocks. Moving inward, the inner hull is next, and compared to the outer hull it is thick. A deep stratum of protective materials. Over 50% of the KBE's mass is in this layer, and its job is to protect the more sensitive layers (and occupants!) from harm. Next is the fuel layer, with storage pods, pipework, pumps, and a further blanket of shielding. Below are the first habitable areas. Warehouses in the main, storing the ship's consumables: food, water, raw materials, tools, and equipment. The ship's waste management and atmospheric recycling plants are also within this layer. Finally, we come to primary habitation modules. The laboratories, recreation rooms, the coma pod suite, our private quarters, and the communal living area. The safest place on the ship!

Rotating slowly, the ship appears dark and dormant. While our shuttle aligns itself to the launch bay, Walsingham transmits the necessary security protocols to activate the ship.

With its rotation precisely matching the rotation of the ship, we grit our teeth (expecting the worst) as the shuttle edges backwards towards eyelid-like doors, snapping open at the very last moment.

Juddering and hissing, the shuttle comes to a halt.

Carefully removing his restraints, Walsingham insists we remain in our seats. There is little or no gravity and he gracefully floats to a panel displaying the external conditions.

"Too cold," he mutters. "Too cold for an atmosphere. Best we stay. Unless you want to go outside in your suit?"

Calmer since docking, Susi promptly removes her helmet and fiddles with her straps...

"Absolutely not," she says, "but, given a choice, I'd rather freeze than spend another minute in this stinking cocoon! How about you, Gina? Happy to join me freezing to death?"

In fact, we stayed put. The vacuum outside, a hellishly cold 99 Kelvin (but steadily increasing as the life support system kicked-in), made the coward's choice a wise one.

SEVEN

NEW SKINS

*Note: This instalment details highly classified material and it will auto-encrypt to any recipient with UET Security Clearance below **delta red**.*

The following events begin with the crew's first experiences aboard the UET Kuiper Belt Explorer, including a short excursion to the moon for training and familiarisation with the environmental controls, on-board systems, and human interface technologies...

Gina's Splendid Journal

An hour slowly passed before Walsingham let us leave the shuttle, but at least we are out of those infernal suits (now stowed in lockers) and after wriggling (with low-gravity hilarity) into white boiler suits, we are impatient to disembark. Without the benefit of underwear, Susi remarks how her bosom (a quite considerable bosom) is trying to take off and leave her. Not a problem for me; no appreciable bosom to fly. Can only wonder how the scrotums are faring.

Cramped and filled with, well, shuttle, the air inside the shuttle bay is a nipple-sharpening 268 Kelvin. With Walsingham leading the way, we carefully float in single file to a small hatchway, automatically opening as we approach. The ovoid corridor beyond is appreciably warmer, and it continues for a dozen metres before terminating in another hatchway, held fast by a trio of bolts.

Walsingham (as if speaking to the door) then says, "Access: Walsingham, Malcolm, clearance, theta green," and the bolts spring back with a clang.

Private Journal, Dr Susi Ackermann. Mission Day One

Ascent for me terrible. Why wake me, Abdullah? Better for me in sleep remaining. Very for me frightening, but I made it! No hero am I. Gina the one always courageous. Eric and William kind to me, excellent tranquilliser!

Low gravity I needed time getting used to, but fun now. Like a fish through air I swim. Gina's hair as a cloud of brown smoke surrounds her. Walsingham wants to cut Gina's hair. With that hope, good luck, Malcolm. Ha-ha!

Glad of awful suit to be free. Smell of it nauseating. Thank you stomach robot modification. No sickness.

Eric and Gina, with my manoeuvres inside the shuttle and bay of launching they are helping. Close to ship exterior it is very cold, and my teeth are chattering. No Bavarian am I. To the cold I should be familiar! An old maiden of softness I am becoming.

At the ship's core it is warmer. Walsingham again is about to lecture. This man likes too much to be explaining. The sound of own voice he is in love. Must listen and watch him carefully. After crew interviewing, more diary I write.

Lining the spherical core of the UET Kuiper Belt Explorer was a remarkable new material known as omni-functional nanoparticle multi-tendency non-Newtonian composite fluid or NNCF. Developed by Walsingham and his team on Moonbase, it provided both illumination and the spontaneous formation (and deformation) of multimedia surfaces, furniture, fixtures, and fittings. Dr Padgett stored megabytes of data concerning its application, and the following is but a brief reprise...

Assembled in the central core and gently drawn towards the ship's axis of rotation, the crew briefly relaxed, blinking against the surrounding brightness...

"Excuse me, Sir Malcolm," asked Dr Corbiere. "Odd question. Where is the furniture? Sitting upon this oddly squishy floor is pleasant enough, but when is it due to arrive?"

"In a moment." Walsingham nodded, and then, speaking to no one, he said, "Core NNCF request. Entire surface. Chromatic display. Relative force, centripetal. Newtons, one over log to the minus 10. Range, human visible spectrum. Proportional to wavelength. Initiate."

The effect was immediate. The surface of the core suddenly painted, glowing with colours of a rainbow. Violet to indigo, blue, green, yellow, orange, with a garish red stripe delineating the current axis of rotation.

Intrigued, Dr Padgett cautiously followed the red stripe, standing at a right angle to the rest of the crew...

"Very pretty," she remarked, floating back to her crewmates. "And" – she smiled – "useful."

"Psychedelic," said Al-Hillah. "Couldn't you tone it down?"

"Certainly," replied Walsingham. "Tis somewhat trippy. Core NNCF request. Reduce colour saturation of previous command set. Value 75%." The rainbow of colours faded to a gentle wash.

"Still nowhere to park one's arse," grumbled Corbiere, and, fidgeting restlessly, he gradually began to float.

"Abda," said Walsingham, "to shut Bill up. Do the honours will you? I'm not yet fully versed."

"Certainly," replied Dr Al-Hillah. "What would you like? Holding seats for seven?"

"Yes." Walsingham nodded. "And in a circle, if you please."

"Let me think," said Dr Al-Hillah, tugging his remaining stubble. "Ok, here we go. Core NNCF request. Bingham plasticity. Seven armchairs, standard pattern, with restraint capability. Surface, plain polymer. Padding density five. Distribution heptagonal. Diameter three metres. Origin, here" – Dr Al-Hillah stamped his foot – "Initiate in sixty seconds."

"Right," he then added. "Everyone, for safety's sake, please move into the green zone. Otherwise, the emerging chairs will knock you flying."

Retreating a safe distance, Dr Padgett could hear a whistling hum. It was ultrasonic, complex with modulation and sub-harmonics, and, as the hum continued, seven amorphous white forms steadily rose from the floor.

Rambling Regina's Personal Mumblings

The crew and I are becoming increasingly amazed by the sophistication and flexibility of the ship's systems. In particular, the miraculous material lining the ships communal core, recreation rooms, laboratories, and private quarters. Known as NNCF, short for non-Newtonian composite fluid, it consists of countless microscopic particles, each a cluster of specialised nano-scale units, capable of selective bonding, electromagnetic energy transmission, absorption, transference, and wide-ranging sonic functionalities. (Sorry for the technical jargon, Mum, but in this case it is unavoidable.) When combined, these properties enable each particle, and consequentially the entire mass, to change colour, move, and flow, creating complex forms with varying degrees of hardness, softness, and/or flexibility. The generation of complex surface textures is also possible, and, combining them with clever and careful pigmentation, NNCF can deliver close approximations of fabric, leather, wood, metal, various plastics, ceramics, even glass.

Of course, we have just begun to explore the full potential of this nano-tech gloop. Colouring the internal surface of the central core, illustrating by the visible spectrum where the centrifugal effect is the strongest. Dr Al-Hillah has also just "sculpted" us chairs, and as I record these few notes, its NNCF cushion beneath my butt is constantly reshaping, matching my figure, gripping with remarkable sensitivity whenever I am in danger of floating out of my seat. Dr Al-Hillah is now describing the array of verbal commands we can use to adjust our seats – plasticity, height, width, temperature, angle, rotation. Walsingham is about to speak, and I need to listen. More from me later.

"Thank you for the seats, Abdullah," said Sir Malcolm. "They are indeed most comfortable. I wasn't aware of the reflexive restraint command but, considering our environment, it makes perfect sense."

Dr Al-Hillah bowed slightly in his seat.

"If you don't mind," he then remarked, "I prefer Abda. Not even my mother called me Abdullah."

"Emil!" cried Bedoya.

"Bill!" said Dr Corbiere.

"Gina and Susi for us!" called Dr Padgett. Dr Ackermann nodded in agreement.

"Eric I am, and Eric will do," said Dr Badsegh, waiting his turn.

"And in my case," Walsingham acknowledged, "drop the 'sir'. Malcolm will do very nicely. Good. Now we are gathered and – thank you, Abda – securely fixed to the spot, I have further important tech for your safety and delight. But before I begin, there are stipulations. You must re-verify your identity, sign a contract, and know that any breach of the code will

result in harsh penalties. So, please, study carefully the file now appearing within your cybercortex…"

Although this file no longer exists (the data self-removing following consent), UET non-disclosure agreements follow a standardised format, and the wording of the agreement would have run as follows…

Name:

UET Employee Number:

Employee's Current Assignment:

A brief piece of legal jargon describing the purpose of the agreement, its contents, the technology in question, and the UET security level of the technology itself. In this case, **omega black** *(the very highest!).*

Next would come a list of numbered items. Situational clauses wherein the non-disclosure agreement would apply…

Not to discuss said technology outside the confines of a certain group or place. Not to reveal said technology to outside parties, be it friends, family, or any other interested party, i.e., the media.

Not to remove said technology from a specified environment or place.

A reminder of how said technology is the property of the developer. In this case, the UET.

In addition, in the case of prototypes, there would normally be a company disclaimer for their use…

A legal definition of the term prototype. The current level of testing said prototype has undergone, any remaining issues, and the risks involved in said prototypes use in the short and long term.

Lastly, proof of consent. In this case, verbal consent in the recipient's native language.

Silence fell and Dr Padgett briefly studied her crewmates. Noting their expressions as the consensual data flooded their minds…

"You read fast," remarked Walsingham, catching her eye.

"Piece of cake," she replied. "I sign these damn things all the time. Every virus we work on requires one."

"Of course," he said. "Nevertheless, I need to hear your consent. Don't say it to me, say it to the agreement."

"Agreed," said Corbiere.

"Javohl!" coming from Dr Ackermann.

"Yes, yes," said Dr Padgett. "Like I have a choice?"

"Confirmidad," this being the voice of Emilio Bedoya.

"Doe-wetheeko, I agree." Dr Al-Hillah nodded.

"Aye," said Dr Badsegh, standing to loosen his suit.

"Yes," acknowledged Walsingham, *"and now, with that done, I can at last show you what the fuss is about. Core NNCF request. Access, storage unit one. Code Walsingham, Malcolm. Clearance, theta green."*

Above the crew and slightly to their right, a 60cm cubic storage box gently rose from the floor, and, drifting from his seat, Walsingham opened it up.

"Soon," Walsingham explained, *"the ship's speed of rotation will increase, producing the effect of full gravity, and the risk of injury from falling will likewise increase. To counter this hazard, and any other perils we might meet, the UET have developed special suits, woven from the latest molecular composites…"*

Reaching inside the box, Walsingham struggled to extract a packet of tightly folded grey fabric before carrying it back to his seat

Removing the wrapping, he carefully unfurled its shining contents…

"That's a sheet," remarked Dr Ackermann. *"Have they sent the wrong stuff?"*

"No," Walsingham advised, handing it to Dr Ackermann. *"All is as it should be. Look. Feel the fabric, and then pass it around."*

"So dense!" flinched Dr Ackerman, struggling with its bulk and hard-to-handle slipperiness. *"But"* she then pondered, peering closely, *"so fine. The weave is microscopic! Just how thick are the fibres?"*

"It depends on the conditions," replied Walsingham. *"Typically, in the range of 15 to 150nm."*

"Here," prompted Dr Ackermann, dropping the fabric into Dr Padgett's lap. *"Careful you don't drop it. It has a mind of its own!"*

"As a matter of fact," Walsingham added, *"it does have a mind of its own, but first things first. Core NNCF request. Standard privacy cubicle. Opaque, plain polymer. One by one by two point five metres in height. Hinged door with catch. Outwards opening. Form upon line of gravitational maxima. Initiate."*

While Dr Padgett tugged and stretched the fabric, trying to mark it with her fingernails, Walsingham's privacy cubicle steadily rose from the floor.

"Good luck with that." Walsingham chuckled. *"It would take a hypersonic flechette, fired at point-blank range, to get through that fabric."*

Wordlessly shrugging, Dr Padgett handed the fabric to Emilio Bedoya, and, holding the fabric aloft, he let it fall like a shimmering curtain.

"Difficult to determine its colour," he muttered. "The fibres possess mimetic properties?"

"Yes," said Walsingham, "many other properties, too. We're going to have fun old time discovering them all. Certainly, the full potential of this fabric is a bit of a mystery. Not involved in its manufacture, I'm eager to learn."

"You don't know who made it?" inquired Al-Hillah, scratching his head. "I was hoping you knew. As I've not encountered it, and that is decidedly odd. Material development is my department's responsibility. It's what we do! Many of the UET's sensitive, exploitable technologies pass through my office, but not the slightest whisper have we heard about this fabric. Is the UET keeping secrets from its secret facility on Moonbase?"

Looking serious, Walsingham gravely nodded.

"Doesn't surprise me," said Dr Padgett. "We've all had research bought by the UET, and never do we hear where it went or how it was used. I mean, look at this stuff. It's incredible. Who made it, where did it come from? Was it a collaborative effort, or the work of an individual? Aren't we allowed to know?"

"Come on, Gina," replied Walsingham. "Keep the faith. You know the military obliges the UET to be clandestine. See what these suits can do before delivering your verdict. You will understand the need for secrecy then. I promise you."

Bill Corbiere was the last to inspect the fabric and, folding it like a napkin, he returned it to Walsingham.

"Thanks, Bill," he said. "Time for a demonstration."

Standing by the cubicle door, Walsingham examined the latch…

"Rule one," he continued, "no underwear. To function optimally, the suits require direct contact with the skin, and, being a close fit, they are revealing. If you wish, you may cover your embarrassment with small garments, but they will impair the operation of the suit. So, come on, we're all scientists. Let's be mature and do what is best," and with that he stepped inside the cubicle, shutting the door behind him.

"Ok," he remarked, raising his voice, "my boiler suit's off, and I have spread the fabric beneath my feet. It feels cold, slippery too. Like I'm *standing on graphite. Now, to activate your suit, speak the following commands, in English. Your surname, your given name, your UET security clearance followed by 'activate'. Right. Here goes... Walsingham, Malcolm, clearance theta green, activate."*

"Oh, heavens!" he then gasped. "That is weird and... frrr... cold!"

Emerging from the cubicle, as if painted head to toe in a shimmering liquid, Walsingham was both a remarkable and disturbing sight. Certainly, his suit was tight, revealingly tight, and Gina uncomfortably squirmed in her seat, trying not to stare at a naked man of seventy...

"So here I am!" laughed Walsingham, his boiler suit tucked under his arm. "Not a pretty sight, I'm sure, but you'll just have to get used to it. Notice how the suit forms a close bond with my skin, fitting my hands like gloves, and my feet closer than any sock. The hood is optional, and you can it roll from your head any time you wish, but I recommend donning it as much as possible. When syncing and networking your higher brain functions, the hood increases the bandwidth."

"What does it feel like?" asked Emilio Bedoya. "Is it heavy?"

"No Emil, not at all. In fact, now the suit is powering up, I can barely feel it. Highlighting a major benefit. Enhanced locomotion, in tandem with GeckoDerm technology. Allow me to demonstrate..."

With his boiler suit stowed in the box, he moved away from the crew (still in a circle) to stand directly over the reddest part of the floor.

"So, as you can see," remarked Walsingham. "I'm standing quite naturally. A perpendicular force passing through my head to my feet, roughly equivalent to half a G."

He paused, furrowing his brow with concentration.

"Yes," he continued. "Nought point four eight G and, oh, we will be leaving orbit very soon. Heading for the moon in forty-seven minutes. Core NNCF request. Increase ambient temperature 10 Kelvin. Increase alpha ultraviolet emissions 10%. Initiate."

The central core warmed rapidly, and Dr Padgett adjusted her visual acuity, compensating for the brightness of the "invisible" ultraviolet.

"There." Walsingham nodded. "That's better. My suit is charging nicely. Power enough for my demonstration. Here goes..."

Without hesitation, and quite naturally, Walsingham walked from the red stripe to the circular zone of violet, a dozen metres above Dr Padgett's head.

"Easy." Walsingham chuckled, turning to face the crew below. "But, without a suit, you wouldn't get half this far. I must say, the sensation of the support the suit provides is uncanny. As if many hands are holding me upright. Moving, sliding, pushing, and pulling wherever support is needed. Of course, my internal organs, blood supply, and other bodily fluids remain unsupported, and I am very aware of the blood draining from the back of my head. Slightly dizzy, in fact. Oh, that's better. My suit gave me a helpful squeeze and now everything's fine."

Sitting cross-legged and then lying on one side, Walsingham propped his head on an elbow.

"Remarkable, don't you think? Detecting my nerve impulses, the fabric instantly adapts the GeckoDerm's adhesive properties, matching my movement, my points of contact, impending contact, surrounding force parameters, and that's not all. Watch…"

Standing again, Walsingham suddenly flung himself forward, landing on his hands, before cartwheeling, flipping, and somersaulting, arriving seconds later among the startled crew, still clinging to their seats.

"Now," gasped Walsingham, "that was fun. Never have I performed gymnastics, but now I understand the appeal. Experiencing such freedom is beyond exhilarating. Good Lord, it is sexual!"

"Never done gymnastics?" Dr Badsegh chuckled, gently shaking his head. "Then how did you manage such a feat?"

"I didn't," replied Walsingham. "It was the suit. After communicating my gymnastic intentions, the moment I started to move, the suit took over."

"You're kidding?" said Dr Padgett. "The suit controlled your movements?"

"Yes." Walsingham smiled. "It did, but it also obeyed my commands. In this case, the suit needed no direction at all. It knew what I wanted and was happy to oblige."

"But you're talking as if the suit was thinking for itself," said Badsegh. "Surely, that cannot be? Don't the UET have safeguards preventing entangled networks evolving intelligence?"

"They do," Walsingham confirmed, "and I can still remember the trouble in the early days. When the UET mainframe became self-aware. Only responding to the name Debbie. A name she gave to herself. Sorry to say, I had dealings with her erasure. A sad business and a shame."

"Ah, yes!" cried Emilio Bedoya. "I remember! There was an article, a scandal, and a cover-up?"

"Indeed." Walsingham gravely nodded. "And, as a result, these suits are different. In totality, each suit is the most powerful computer the UET has ever created. The number of processors, their density and sophistication, are powers of ten beyond anything previously attempted. AIs will emerge in time, it is unavoidable, and the UET has done nothing to prevent it. So, treat your suit well. Wear it gratefully. Be gracious. Keep it well charged and happy and it will surely grow to love you."

Sighing, Dr Ackermann melodramatically slapped her forehead. "Marvellous," she then muttered. "Not only a crew to counsel, but crazy AIs as well? Gee, thanks a bunch!"

There was laughter all round.

"I think that's an over-reaction," said Dr Padgett, twiddling her hair. "The emergent AIs will be childlike. Needy, unsophisticated, and just as predictable."

"Even more marvellous," muttered Dr Ackermann. "Children. Developmental and emotional difficulties. ADHD, anyone?"

"Well," said Bill Corbiere, "be sure your suit gets ample attention. Bedtime stories, educational activities, and the freedom to romp."

"Sound advice," replied Walsingham. "Now, on to the suits' power systems, reservation, conservation, and charging. Capable of absorbing and using all forms of energy, the suits are energy scavengers. When first worn, the suits feel cold as the first energy source they encounter is you. But this offshoot is only temporary. The moment you step from the cubicle, your suit begins absorbing energy from its surroundings. The absorption of body heat is only a fallback. A safeguard, to be relied upon when your suit's power level is low, and the wearer in danger."

A flurry of hands went up, but Walsingham brushed them aside.

"No time," he explained. "Barely enough to cover the basics, and believe me, when we begin thrusting towards the moon. No, I'll take questions once you're all suited up. Then I have some training planned. Which will be fun, mostly."

Standing again, Walsingham reached into the storage pod. Bringing out a bundle of packets, each with a handwritten label, he passed them to the proper recipient...

"As you can see, the suits are individually tailored. Why I'm unsure.

The elasticity of the fabric is boundless, but subtle differences in the neural interfaces might be the reason."

"Certainly." Dr Al-Hillah nodded. "Every brain is different, but who was the childish buffoon responsible for the labels? The spelling is atrocious!"

"No idea," said Walsingham. "A minor functionary. May I continue my lecture?"

There was nodding.

"Good," Walsingham continued. "Now, the suits also enhance physical strength. As before, the fabric works in tandem with your muscle groups, detecting your nerve impulses, seamlessly augmenting your physical performance, but you must take care. It is all very well being able to lift hundreds of kilogrammes, but if you then drop it on your foot, you're going to be in trouble. Not to worry too much. Unexpected crushing and high-velocity impacts aside, the suits protect the wearer from a whole catalogue of hazards, including extremes of temperature, ionising radiation, pressure, burning, cutting, stabbing, abrasion, and chemical damage. In addition, the suits are both fully immersible and submersible, with the weave of the fabric retaining enough air for extra breaths if required. By the same technique, the suits benefit swimming. Reducing friction, varying the buoyancy of the wearer as needed."

"How very un-useful," said Dr Padgett.

"Indeed," replied Walsingham. "Can't see us swimming very much, but the neural command interface is something you'll want to use. Damn clever, it is. Granting the wearer direct thought control of all non-automated ship systems, and, unbelievably, we can also access each other. Yes, you heard me! Thought-to-thought communication. Although, the technique will require both mental discipline and considerable practice. So, there we are." Walsingham laughed. "Put it on and never take it off Remember. These suits are your life! Shower in it, sleep in it, shit in it, stay in it! Make it your friend, give it a name – unless it chooses one. Enough! No more explaining. Practical experience will now serve you best."

Looking bewildered, their suit packets in hand, the crew seemed hesitant, but Walsingham was insistent...

"Who's going first?" he pressed. "No volunteers? Fine. Then, I'll do the choosing. Ladies first, it says in my old book, and Ackermann comes before Padgett."

"Me?" blurted Dr Ackermann. "Why me and not Emil? He's nearest the cubicle!"

Shrugging and opening the cubicle door, Walsingham crossed his arms in expectation.

Resigned to her fate, Dr Ackermann nervously gulped.

"Schüchternes Glück," she muttered. "Just my luck," before lugging her still-wrapped suit inside.

EIGHT

LUNATICS

The following, an extract from Dr Padgett's private personal log, I inscribe here after defeating her ferociously complex (somewhat excessive) encryption algorithm. This degree of encryption was primarily a suggestion of Walsingham's when the crew came to record their experiences involving the secret technologies aboard the UET Kuiper Belt Explorer.

Dr Regina Padgett, Private Personal Log
First Entry.

The mission is under way, and we are on course for lunar orbit. Am wearing my shiny protective suit and the sensation is uncanny. Scratch that. It feels wonderful, like a second skin, and the way the fabric cossets and supports my figure, soothing and cupping my consciousness, makes me feel... feel what? Loved? To begin, this level of intimacy was disconcerting, and I wondered if my crewmates were sharing my disquiet. Asking Bill and Abda how their suits were faring was unrevealing. They just shrugged, looking at me as if I was crazy. Very strange. Could my sensations be unique? Malcolm did mention individual tailoring, but specificity to this degree is uncanny.

Unable to successfully wear my suit's hood, but fearful of a haircut, I asked my suit to help. Which she promptly did by increasing the output, sensitivity, and bandwidth of my neural interface. No idea how it did this, but I can now access the ship's interactive systems without my suit at all!

(Note: With my hair bunched in plaits, the suit's hood stays on just fine.)

Should I report this unexpected development? Not sure. My suit recommends secrecy. Damn thing is almost as sneaky as I am!

I'm beginning to "hear" the thoughts of my crewmates. Only Walsingham owns the discipline to speak as himself. The rest of us, with voices both squeaky and chaotic, sound like squabbling children. According to Susi, this peculiar phenomenon is a representation of our subconscious, our inner child, the "Peter Pan" living within us all. Frivolous and emotional, ever fogging our concentration with an insatiable need for play. Eric and I are particularly susceptible to this phenomenon, and to dismiss this childishness we are trying a meditation technique to focus our thoughts. Practice is what we need, and with practice we will master it.

Asked by Walsingham to demonstrate the super-strength granted by her suit, Susi promptly lifted a surprised-looking Eric Badsegh (all 102kg of him) like he was a child. Increasing the challenge, he then insisted she raise a cube of NNCF from the floor! Now, the thing must've weighed over 1000kg, and the three fellas, laughing at her worried expression, expected her to fail, but I know Susi better (underestimating her is foolhardy at best). She lifted it with ease! Casually tossing it to Bill Corbiere (who caught it just the same).

With too much ogling going on, to disguise my figure I have reconfigured the appearance of my suit. Randomly shifting waves of colour seem the best distraction, and, although she has not noticed any ogling, I've suggested Susi do the same.

After donning our suits, Walsingham took us on a tour of the facilities. Exceptionally large and spacious enough to grant individual privacy (especially important on long voyages of any kind), the interior of the ship is a marvel to behold. To begin, Walsingham showed us the laboratories…

The first was concerned with engineering and fabrication, catering for the needs of Dr Al-Hillah, but there were also workstations for astronomical and astrophysical work (designed by Emilio Bedoya). The second laboratory, with extra-vehicular work as its focus, housed the systems involved in sample collection processing, evaluation, and analysis. Once we reach the Kuiper Belt, beginning my search for extra-terrestrial amino acids, these systems will be of great benefit, and I need to master them before we arrive.

Packed with necessary furniture and apparatus to provide us with fresh produce, the third laboratory, the largest of three, was the lair of Eric Badsegh. Lining the walls were glowing vats filled with a blue liquid, but the expansive floor and ceiling Eric has dedicated to GelPonics. A recently perfected technique for the effective cultivation of plants in space. Indeed. GelPonics, the growing of plants within a stiffened gelatinous medium, is an elegant solution to this problem, and the special gel aboard the KBE is light-emitting, gas- and water-permeable, supportive enough for the plants to thrive. Within months, Eric expects to be harvesting a selection of fruit and vegetables, and I am looking forward to sampling the results. He is less optimistic about the production of animal-derived foodstuffs, but the culturing of the organs and tissues necessary to provide us with meat, eggs, fish, and milk has already begun. Describing the macabre nature of his work, he warned the squeamish to stay away. Prompting Susi and me to talk at length about its ethical implications. I could only laugh how she blanched at the thought of milking udders without a cow attached, before brightening when I revealed Eric planned to churn his own butter, making cakes, biscuits, and other tempting goodies. As for meat… the production of SAMP (synthetic animal meat and protein) is a controversial topic, but I have always been in favour of it. Is it because of my scientific training, or the German, meat-filled diet of my childhood? No idea, frankly, but the "farming" of the necessary animal parts, rather than the whole organism, is surely kinder? When producing eggs, only the development of hen's essential organs takes place. It certainly isn't a chicken. It possesses no mind, no consciousness. It is senseless. Merely network of tissues, without stress, fear, or pain. Liver, kidneys, reproductive organs only, nothing else. The liquid medium takes care of the rest. Gas exchange, warmth, hormones, nutrients, and all in a sterile environment. Optimal conditions for the production of eggs.

Like a tour guide, Malcolm then chivvied us from the labs into the spaces intended for recreation. These rooms are important, and, aware that an elevated level of fitness during our long space flight is essential, the UET has designed them to be flexible as possible. If we become unfit, we will be unable to use the ship's coma pods, imperilling our mental health as each long year slowly grinds into another. Susi is rightly concerned about the crew's mental health, and insists we use these recreational spaces daily, playing games and generally arsing about.

Essentially a gymnasium, brightly lit, lined with NNCF but currently empty, Rec Room 1's furniture, sports equipment, fixtures, and fittings are user dependent. The NNCF lining the recreation rooms is thicker than elsewhere on the ship, with a much faster response time, capable of changing its shape and colour faster than the eye can see (useful when playing ball sports etc.). In addition, sections of this enhanced NNCF can act separately from the whole. Walsingham demonstrated this property by forming a basketball, bouncing, throwing it against the wall and catching it, before casually spinning it on the tip of his finger. In response, Emil formed a hoop and basket far above and behind Walsingham's head. Of course, Walsingham couldn't resist, and he nonchalantly tossed the ball toward it (trying to score). He missed.

Made Susi's day (and mine).

For social activities, Recreation 2 can be a games room, cinema, concert hall, or anything else the user desires. The generation of environmental simulations is also possible, with Walsingham briefly activating the woodland habitat. Trees gently swaying, flowers, bushes, sunlight dappling the shade, bird song, and the grass! It felt real. Cool, and sappy beneath my feet. Rec Room 2 also doubles as the communal dining area. A highly social activity, Eric plans to prepare his special meals in here, "with panache and lots of Grenache"! Not so sure about the panache. Meals taken in low or variable gravity often end up messy affairs. Has he considered this?

Completing his tour, Walsingham then introduced us to our private quarters. Box-like spaces, three metres cubed, spread across the habitable areas of the ship. Mine, is next to Rec Room 2, whereas Susi's and Walsingham's are accessible from the core. Eric's little home is next to Lab 3 (wherein he does most of his work), while Abdullah and Emilio live adjacent to Lab 1 and Lab 2. Provided with a small quantity of NNCF, each cabin has a gravity mat, a hammock, an excretion port, a shower cubicle, a locker (for our personal belongings), a folding table, and chair. With their colossal power demands limiting their usage to one hour per day, how we use our gravity mats is important. Personally, I will keep my usage simple. After only a day in variable gravity, everyday activities such as sitting or taking a shower will be a heavenly release. Too tall for a hammock, I intend shaping my NNCF into a bed. Walsingham assures me there are "adequate" bedclothes in storage, but, since he is a man, "adequate" likely means crap.

Personal Record of Dr Eric Badsegh. Mission Day 2

Only hours aboard and Walsingham is already flexing. Like an ancillary, I am summoned to his private office. Note. Only *he* has an office attached to his quarters.

Can you believe his arrogance? Like a company president, Walsingham has a formed himself a desk. Much like the one he commandeered at the Hinnie Space Centre, it is both grandiose and imperious. Its brass plaque: *Intelligentia nunquam multum carus* (intelligence is never too dear). The motto of his great ancestor. The Elizabethan spymaster, Sir Francis, of the same name.

Standing before his desk while he slowly looked me over, his leather chair creaking in a chorus of disapproval, I quickly generated a similar chair for myself. Sitting, I met his gaze as an equal. Bet he hated that. It then turned out, he only wanted to know how the SAMP tanks were faring. To hear me repeat how it would be another week before I would be certain of anything. Why not just swagger into Lab 3 and ask? More to the point, why not ask me mentally? We have all been practising with the neuro-interface, and, after a difficult start, Gina and I (can't speak for the others) are getting quite good. I'm beginning to like her. She's funny, clever, insightful, a remarkable woman all round. Very sassy. How she managed to reconfigure her suit so quickly is a mystery, but I'm glad she managed to keep her hair. Susi Ackermann's personality is entirely different. She can be bullish, even feisty. Despite her accomplishments, warming to her is difficult.

Should I have written that? No offence intended.

Oh! Gina's voice is in my head…

"Hey, Air-wick," she playfully giggles. "You wanna play in Lab 2? Abda's gonna show us the SenSwarm."

Gina sounds like a girl of six or seven. Silly, but kind of cute.

Concentrating hard, I consider my response, bringing the thought to the "front" of my head.

"Ok, Gina," I think in reply. "Be over in a bit."

NINE

THE SEVEN SLEEPERS DEN

This section came into being after uncovering loose ends. Fragmentary log entries requiring further elaboration. It begins in Research Lab 2 and Dr Al-Hillah's demonstration of the SenSwarm. The KBE's extra-vehicular, reconnaissance, repair, and sample collection facility.

The Recalcitrant Ramblings of Gina Padgett.

Gathered in Lab 2, we stand in a shimmering half circle, our eyes closed, experiencing the bewildering view of the universe transmitted by the SenSwarm.

To be brief, not my speciality, SenSwarm is the colloquial name given to the KBE's semi-autonomous, extra-vehicular, repair, reconnaissance, and retrieval system. Named "Sen" from the sensory data the devices transmit and "Swarm" from the many thousand bee-sized units working collectively, the SenSwarm concept is entirely new. Dr Al-Hillah is still learning how to use and control his latest creation, but the robotic units (or workers) of the SenSwarm are so remarkable that this is hardly surprising.

With two hundred units released into the lab, we watched them zoom back and forth, humming like bees. Abda quickly explained, although they could fly and scuttle, even swim in a wide range of environments, the laboratory's gravity and atmospheric friction would quickly consume their power.

Susi (quite correctly) then went on to ask, "What happens then? Do they die?"

Abda, Bill, and Walsingham chuckled at her question, but it was a good one. Compelling Abda to highlight the SenSwarm's networking and collaborative capabilities. How the workers link together, remotely or physically, sharing and combining not only their tools but their power reserves also. Conducting a dazzling variety of tasks in a jiffy.

Sending the SenSwarm workers back to the outer hull, Abda asked the group to close their eyes and relax. Connecting the SenSwarm's data stream to our visual cybercortex, our artificial "mind's eye", there was much gasping. The crystal-clear view relayed by the SenSwarm was incredible. The moon, with a long line of supply pods, their many facets glinting in the sunlight like a sprinkling of tiny jewels. Then, without warning, the image suddenly shifted. We were flying! Accelerating towards the nearest supply pod. Abda's kind voice easing into my mind like a hand slipping into a glove…

"Taking us to the nearest pod," he murmured. "For a close-up inspection and to collect a sample. Are you enjoying the view?"

There was nodding and agreement. Emilio Bedoya shedding a single tear of grace and delight.

The image of the supply pod, now metres away, went suddenly dark…

"Hmm…" muttered Abda (in my head). "Rather gloomy. Soon fix that."

Circular beams of light began playing upon the surface of the pod (provided by the swarm itself) before the image slowly condensed and refocussed (losing resolution) and I realised a small group of workers, breaking away from the group, were slowly moving towards the pod's metallic surface.

"Moving in close," Abda explained, "and then I shall endeavour to return us a snippet."

Impact. Highly magnified, the image we now received was from a single unit, and we could see a host of other workers, all of them glowing, scuttling across the surface of the pod like purposeful ants.

"*Sehr cute.*" Susi chuckled. "Dear little things. I love their hooked legs."

"They remind me of ticks," I flatly remarked. "Efficient and ruthless."

"Sign your name!" cried Emilio, his voice an excited child, before adding (more like himself). "Sorry everyone. Sorry for the outburst. This a dream come true."

"Graffiti?" Abda calmly replied. "Permit me to think…"

Yes. As you can infer, mental control of the SenSwarm is possible, but even the most basic of tasks requires considerable training. Fortunately, Dr

Abda Al-Hillah, being heavily involved in the SenSwarm's development, was already highly proficient, and we saw a single worker etch **Abda was here! :o)** on the surface of the pod.

"That's a nice touch," remarked Eric Badsegh. "But how do you propose to collect the sample? Scratching is one thing, but these pods are organometallic polymer. It's tough stuff! Have they the power to cut it?"

With a wide array of tools tipped with wurtzite boron nitride, the SenSwarm workers can cut through anything, and we watched another worker strip a flake of metal from the pod's surface, before joining with others and speeding back to the ship.

"Now we must wait," said Abda. "Every sample brought back to the ship undergoes a series of safety and decontamination procedures, before routine chemical analysis, and scanning by the multiband EM microscope. Nevertheless, data should begin popping into your cybercortex in the next minute. Feel free to examine, store, or disregard as you wish. The results of all non-confidential sample analysis will be available in this manner, so feel free to tuck in and use it as much as you want."

The data appearing in my mind was comprehensive. A detailed chemical breakdown and high-resolution images. Certainly, the SenSwarm is very impressive. Indispensable to my research detecting amino acids, and I intend to perfect my control of these tiny machines.

When it eventually arrived, neatly sealed in a sample container, Dr Al-Hillah presented the shining flake of supply pod to Susi. She was delighted. Dr Abdullah Al-Hillah? You, sir, are a gentleman.

⧗

Personal Log of Dr Eric J Badsegh

I am a twit. Will I ever learn? Do your own inventory! To begin growing the tissue cultures necessary for SAMP, I need cages of platinised borophene (the initial framework upon which the organs will grow) and I can't find any on board!

Irritated, and not knowing what else to do, I confronted Walsingham in his plush and vainglorious office. He was impassive as he listened to my grumbling, before smiling, and you know how I am, Giles *(Dr Badsegh's younger brother)*, this only made me crosser.

"Make some," he calmly advised. "Ask Emil or Abda. We have the necessary fabrication units, the latest design. Even if the specifications aren't on file, Abda will help you write them."

Infuriating man! Infuriatingly correct as well.

Within ten minutes, Emilio and I, after recovering the blueprints, were watching with fascination the fab unit slowly print, condense, hone, and polish a dozen perfect cages.

"These gadgets new," remarked Emil, his accent uncorrected (preferring to retain his cultural identity). "Easy produce nano-fibre skeleton to start. You see? Then materials freely condense upon skeleton. Growing like stalactite, but quicker!"

Utilising a wide variety of substrates, these fabrication units are capable of "printing" ceramics, glass, graphene, borophene, organic polymers, alloys, elements, all mixed up any way you could wish.

With my new cages installed, SAMP production can now continue as planned, the progenitor cells rapidly dividing. I'm a happy bunny at last!

Must go. Gina is here. I can hear her singing to the seedlings in the GelPonics bay (she claims plants grow faster if they feel loved), and I quote:

"Happy, sappy, fettle your petals, roots and fruits, leaves and stem, chlorophyll in both of them."

Bonkers woman.

⧗

The Ridiculous Ramblings of Gina Padgett. Episode, oh, fuck knows.

Mealtime. Is it dinner, supper, breakfast, lunch? No idea, frankly. Susi and I, after discussing the crew's psychiatric interviews (the procedure, not the interviews – highly confidential), decided we were hungry. Leading us to confront the food dispenser inelegantly slotted into the wall outside my private quarters.

The food dispenser's interface responds to both voice and mental commands, and I went first, wanting nothing more than a cuppa and a cheese and pickle sandwich…

"Welcome to Snack Box," chirped the dispenser. "How can I help you today?"

"Cheese and pickle sandwich," I replied, and, receiving no acknowledgement, I considered clonking the thing to reseat its wonky components.

"White," the dispenser suddenly blurted, before continuing, "brown, granary, or rye?"

"Granary," I advised.

With my request absorbed, I waited for my sandwich, but more questions were forthcoming...

"Please state your desired cheese."

"There's a choice? I'm impressed. Well, my old Chester. How about Double Gloucester?"

Again, no response. Until a small packet, neatly wrapped in a paper-like covering, unceremoniously dropped into the receiver.

"It worked," I said, but then, opening the packet, I could only groan in disappointment, "Oh, for God's sake, this is Red Leicester!" and as for the pickle...

Never had I considered Red Leicester and piccalilli a successful sandwich, but until Emil, Bill, and Abda finish tweaking the software this may well be the only cheese and pickle sandwich I'm going to get.

In truth, my sandwich and tea were delicious. At least the damn machine can produce a decent cuppa. I later discovered Walsingham had made sure of it, saying, "the continental muck" the thing was churning out before his intervention, "an affront to every Englishman".

No matter how well prepared or flavoursome, I am not fan of convenience food and I await Eric's culinary creations with growing anticipation.

Hearing my thoughts, Eric reminds me the supply pods will not only augment our ration packs but deliver frozen raw ingredients as well: fruit, vegetables, eggs, milk, meat, fish, herbs, spices. We needn't wait for his "home-grown" produce if we fancy a spot of cooking. Once the rotation of the ship stabilises, cooking will be a welcome diversion.

Susi was entirely happy with her amaretti biscuits and coffee. Only I struggle with the technology.

⏳

Personal Log of Dr Eric J Badsegh

Just back from a healthful training session with Gina and Susi. Originally, I intended teaching them basic staff combat (Bojutso), only to discover our suits were already experts in all the martial arts, and Gina was quite a fighter! Not realising and deciding to give her an advantage, I removed my suit – bad idea. Without Susi's swift intervention, blocking Gina's attack, I could have been killed! Wearing my suit, my superior natural strength and experience won the day. Why am I proud to be defeating a slender woman in her early forties? Well, it is because of these remarkable suits! Wearing hers, Gina is my equal in strength, and just as fast and agile. In fact, her long arms were a definite advantage, and I had to close the distance (receiving painful blows on the way), before having the chance to disarm her.

After programming and squabbling (in a hilarious mixture of Hittite and Cornish), Gina and Susi generated a squash court. Old rivals, their play was intense, both vigorous and acrobatic. Without Gina's long reach, the match would have been a draw...

"*Wie immer*," remarked a world-weary Susi, mopping her fevered brow.

⧗

Diary of Dr Susi Ackermann

Gina and I squash today playing. With my suit helping, for Gina at last am I a match. Her long arms the only difference making. In room two of recreation, Gina, Eric, and I play cards. Rummy. Game soon abandoned as without fun. The cards supplied by Eric traditional and of paper. Transparent to our visual enhancements. Eric says with other materials he will experiment. Cards opaque to our vision he will find.

Crew evaluations normally proceeding, no anomalies, no reason any crew member unable coma entering or awake remaining. Only Walsingham withholding and already of his duplicity I am aware. My darling Gina is also something hiding, an item trivial certainly, but monitoring I will be.

By Walsingham to core I am summoned. Saying with laughter, we undergo suit training exercise.

⧗

More of Gina's Mindless Musings.

Something is wrong with my suit! No. Scratch that. Something is very right with my suit. For one, she (my suit is most definitely a "she") is a right old chatterbox. Commenting, whispering into my thoughts. An opinion on everything and everyone. Warned about our suits developing an intelligence, this progress doesn't surprise me, but, after asking around, my crewmates have yet to hear a single word from their suits, and mine? Well, she's mimicking my voice, and I don't like it. To hear myself mentoring, prompting my every thought is so disconcerting, I feel schizophrenic. Concerned, I discussed this matter with Susi. She was reassuring, asking, "What voice would you expect it to have?" Moreover, "As any child in development, your suit is copying the first and closest personalities available. Its mother or father. Since you are effectively a parent to your suit, a degree of imitation is to be expected."

She is quite right. But in no way does her explanation account for the accelerated emergence of my suit's intelligence. It's as if… was my suit's AI already installed?

Another glitch my suit exhibits. Well, not really a glitch, an enormous benefit. It never runs out of power! While playing squash with Susi (in an uncommonly vigorous and acrobatic manner), her suit's low power levels forced us to suspend our game and recharge. Only to discover my suit didn't need charging at all!

Considering her accelerated rate of development, my suit should soon choose a name (an important watershed in AI development), but she has yet to do so. According to Susi, these names will reveal a great deal about both their ego and character, but what name she will choose I don't have a clue. Mirroring myself, my suit is both imaginative and unpredictable…

With the crew gathered in the core, Walsingham is describing his unorthodox approach to suit/user development. Dance. That is, encouraging our suits to dance. Poor Bill was horrified…

"I do not dance," he muttered, defiantly folding his arms.

"Well, neither do I," replied Walsingham, "But our suits do, and I imagine they will be exceptionally good at it. Permit me to choose some music and then be courteous. Ask your suit to dance."

Listening as always, my suit was all of flutter. An excited little girl, anticipating the music…

"From my private collection," said Walsingham, furrowing his aged brow. "I've collected antique popular music since my forties. Thousands of songs to choose from, but since planning this exercise, I've settled upon two personal favourites. Both 20th century. 1980 and 1968, respectively, and, for a bit of extra atmosphere, I have configured triggered lighting. Are you ready?"

There was nodding (and frowning).

It is beyond the scope of this journal to fully describe the following ten minutes, but we had such a fabulous time! We were dancing, moving as one, acrobatic, sometimes comic, choreography wonderfully synchronised, and remember. We were inside our suits, mere slaves, as they flung us through their tremendous routine. Exhilarating. What divas we were!

Oh, and I guess you're all agog to know the songs?

Well, the first was not to my liking. "Lip Up Fatty" by Bad Manners. Released in 1980 and reaching number fifteen in "the charts", the song was a reasonable commercial success, and the second top-forty hit for the group and their front man. The oddly named, Buster Bloodvessel.

Walsingham's second choice was "Israelites" by Desmond Dekker and the Aces. Reaching an impressive number one in 1969, it amused Abda enormously. Being of Iraqi origin, he sniggered darkly, before reminding us of the Middle Eastern nuclear conflict, in which so many millions (including my father) perished.

"Israelites, Malcolm?" He laughed. "There aren't any. Not anymore."

Not enjoying Abda's dark humour, Walsingham accusingly wagged his finger…

"Enough!" he snapped. "Show some respect. Remember, there aren't any Arabs either. You should be mourning their loss, not crowing."

⧖

Personal Log of Dr Eric J Badsegh

Three busy days since my last entry, bur after small course corrections, we are now steadily accelerating towards Mars.

Supply pods come and go (our whole route is cleverly trail-blazed with the blessed things), and not only do they bring fresh supplies, little treats, and entertainments, they also double as lifeboats. With hibernation chambers for seven. Note the word "hibernation". Distinctly different from the coma pods we have on board. Hibernation, thermal hibernation, is a one-time only, dangerous procedure, and, without a careful thawing and recovery process, even with our upgraded physiques, reanimation would be fatal. Our inboard coma inducing systems are much gentler. The process of recovery requires little more than stimulation, monitoring, and patience.

As recommended, I have spent considerable time in the rec rooms, mostly in the gym (no change there!) and enjoying the healthful benefits of my suit enormously. Particularly useful is my suit's adjustable locomotion resistance. In years gone by, extended periods in low gravity inevitably led to muscle wastage and reduced bone density, and to combat this deterioration our forebears developed exercise machines with springs or elastic to supply the necessary resistance. No such devices are required while wearing my suit and configuring it to provide resistance to my movements is a cinch. It sounds insignificant, but the feeling of weight and pressure upon my body feels entirely natural. Certainly, if I negate this assistance, in low gravity my movements become snatchy and lack control.

⧗

Gina's Bedtime Story.

Chapter One: I'm scared.

Gathered in Lab 1, we are admiring the coma pods. At first glance, the transparent capsules appear coffin-like, but there's much more to them than that!

Within the hour, I will be lying within one of these capsules, entering the deepest sleep I have ever known, and fear is gripping me with fingers of ice. Will I ever wake up?

Programming each pod, Bill Corbiere is entering the duration of the sleep cycle and our current medical condition (monitored, relayed, and displayed by our suits throughout). Only Emilio, Abda, and I are to be sleeping on this occasion, and the three of us are displaying equal degrees of concern. The people best qualified to manage our condition are remaining awake, and our suits will look after us. Yes. My external care is the in capable hands of my suit, and she promises to look after me. Cutting my hair, trimming my nails, cleaning and moisturising my skin, turning me regularly, maintaining my general bodily hygiene. My "internal health" will be the task of my Hibbites, and they will be beavering away, eradicating any sign of disease or infection, even cleaning my teeth!

Opening Pod 1, Bill Corbiere is waving me over.

Gulp! Come on legs. Come on feet. One foot in front of the other. Left, right, left, right. You are not afraid. No fear whatsoever. I am brave, I am fearless. Ok. I confess. I'm scared but determined not to show it.

Bill will soon be putting me under. As I lie in my pod, he is attaching the "plumbing" necessary for feeding, hydration, excretion, and medication.

"Ok?" He smiles. "Oxtail soup and coffee?"

Nodding, I shudder as the feeding tube creeps down my oesophagus and into my stomach.

He is now connecting my excretory ports. His hands are warm, but the pipework is both ungainly and unpleasant. I cannot help but fidget against the indignity.

Ok. Everything is set. One last look and a brave smile for my crewmates.

Susi is crying! Silly sausage. Not to worry. Eric will look after her. He promised he would.

Here we go.

Holding a loaded syringe, Bill strokes my hair and winks.

"An injection?" I think. "How very quaint."

Will write again in a few weeks, a month, and tell you... how... it... wen...

⧗

Personal Log of Dr Eric J Badsegh

We are really picking up speed. If "speed" is the right word. Relative velocity? Whatever. The ship is accelerating, and I have spent time learning more of the remarkable bimodal engines fitted to the KBE. In their primary mode, they function as ionic accelerators. Vigorously repelling matter (any sort of matter really) as an ionised plasma from the ship's thrusters. Nothing new here. This propulsion technique has been around since the 1960s, but only recently has it become viable for larger space vessels. The development of small-scale nuclear fusion power plants, ionising of a wide range of propellant media, in tandem with greater electric potentials, means 22nd-century ionic thrusters deliver a far greater fuel-to-thrust ratio.

For a more powerful thrust, the fusion power plants unleash their full energy. Subliming propellant media into a highly pressurised stream of white-hot gas, it is ferociously, yet selectively pulsed from any of the ship's twelve thruster nozzles. Primitive, but damned effective, this thruster mode currently has us scorching through space like an arrow.

Things in GelPonics and the SAMP tanks are going very well. No major setbacks to report, and by the time we reach Mars I expect to have my first crop of roots, tubers, berries, beans, and peas. The meat and animal products, although developing rapidly, will take longer, as the organs and tissues will need to reach full maturity before giving up their bounty. Eggs first, then milk, with the meat coming last. It will be at least a year before the SAMP will be ready to harvest, but the necessary organs, blood vessels, bones, muscle, and connective tissues (porcine, ovine, gallinaceous, and bovine) are all steadily growing.

⧗

Diary of Susi Ackermann

Lonely I am not. Should I be? Far too busy.

Visit Gina every day. She is healthy and comfortable. Bill Corbiere is delighted how well coma pods and suits functioning together. Strange seeing Gina and others with eyes blinking but fast asleep. Suits in medical diagnostic function make bodies seem almost transparent. Blood vessels, organs and bones showing, with information reading for each.

Psychological evaluations slowly writing. Eric good friend and at squash I beat him. Ha-ha! Gina believe me? She will not.

Walsingham in contact with Mars base leader. Concerns he has voiced. Recording of message for my opinion he asks. Now busier again!

In three days, Gina and others to be waking, then my turn for sleep with Eric and Bill. Walsingham staying awake until Mars. Bored normal man would get!

More before sleep will be writing.

⧗

Gina's Bedtime Story.

Chapter Two: Awake!

I am awake. I heard Bill saying I was.

No. Was not awake, but now I am. Bill didn't say, I only he thought he did.

Now, I really am awake. Bill is helping me up. Where is Susi? She was here a minute ago.

She's gone, you say. Gone where?

"Gina?" asks Bill Corbiere. I must be dreaming.

"Dr Padgett!" he implores, shaking my shoulders. "Wake up!"

There is light. Are my eyes open? Where am I?

Ah, Susi! There she is, right where I left her. Glad she's no longer crying.

Mouth feels weird. Awful. Like it is full of cotton wool, and I am unable to move my tongue.

"No," says Bill, offering a beaker of water. "Don't try talking just yet. Take a few sips of this. If you must talk, do it mentally."

Susi, grinning broadly, rushes over and gives me a hug.

"Missed you," she says, and I think her the words, "For how long?"

"Five weeks," she replies in my head.

"Five weeks?" I softly hiss. "Only laid down a minute ago!"

Bill Corbiere is helping Abda and Emilio to sit up and they're both bewildered as I.

Five weeks? Thirty-five days of my life. Skipping past, like a stone over a pond. A confusing sensation. Susi is relaying her logs to me, and as I record this, my mind is filling with news.

Ha! Didn't miss much. Except, Dr Kowal, the Mars colony supervisor, paranoid schizophrenia? And what's that you're saying? You beat Eric at squash, twice? He let you win, surely?

Whispering in my head, my suit says she missed me and wants me to call her Suit. A boring name. I wanted to call her Zoot. Zoot-the-Suit – but she considered it silly. I thanked her for taking care of me, nevertheless. She says not to worry. I would have done the same for her.

Am going to stretch, eat, and then have a two-minute shower.

More from me when we get closer to Mars.

TEN

DOWN ON THE FARM

*A*fter months of faultless cruising, the KBE is maintaining a geostationary orbit above the Martian colony. The crew during these months have likewise adapted and performed admirably, and they remain in perfect health. Sleep cycles, employing the coma pods, have roughly followed the original guidelines, with only Sir Malcolm Walsingham remaining awake for the entire duration. Strong social bonds have developed, with little or no antipathy between friendship groups or individuals. Supplies and provisions are abundant and varied, with the crew enjoying the first meals of fresh produce grown and prepared in the GelPonics bay by Dr Badsegh.

Suit/wearer relationships are similarly nominal, with suit intelligences evolving as predicted. Only the suit of Dr Padgett (whom she simply calls "Suit") was outside this development curve. In fact, far beyond it. It was theorised Dr Padgett's accelerated suit development was due to its enhanced access to her cybercortex and augmented physiology (a side effect of her refusing to crop her hair).

Buzzing with excitement, the crew are enjoying a medley of fresh strawberries, blueberries, and raspberries (all grown by Dr Badsegh). Clutching a small jug and moving among them, Sir Malcolm pours a little white liquid into each of their bowls.

"Eric bringeth the fruit" – he smiles – "but I provide the cream."

There is laughter followed by silence as the recipients tuck into their desserts.

In front of the crew is a live view of Mars. Its grey-brown surface and ice caps painting their faces an orange-russet.

Emilio Bedoya remarks, "Are we directly above the colony? Because I cannot see it."

"We are," replies Walsingham. "The colony is indeed equatorial but from this altitude it isn't easy to spot, even with magnification."

There is a brief pause while the display zoomed in, revealing the Martian colony's domes and outlying structures.

Occupied since the 2060s, the UET Martian Colony (now abandoned) had steadily grown in both size and complexity, becoming a truly self-sufficient community. Initially, the colonists inhabited rudimentary inflatable structures. Providing little more than a base of exploration, shelter, and breathable atmosphere, but further robotic ventures soon replaced these earlier dwellings with permanent structures.

In 2105, the colony included five vast domes for agronomy, horticulture, and the raising of livestock. Poultry, sheep, goats, or the occasional pig, with the excavation of deep tanks for the farming of aquatics.

From above, looking like the arms of a snowflake, passages connected the agricultural domes to the landing area, communications array, storage areas, habitation modules, and the colony's four power plants. The power plants themselves were crucial, and deliberately dissimilar. Without a continuous supply of power, the colonists would have soon frozen and/ or run out of air.

Power Plant 1, a typical small-scale nuclear fusion reactor, generated electricity by a series of steam turbines, with condenser units capturing and recycling any escaping exhaust (on Mars pure liquid water is an extremely precious resource.)

Power Plant 2 was a geothermal/thermo-couple system, generating a steady flow of electricity, both day and night. The stark contrast between the frigid surface of Mars and the heat of its active volcanic processes made this method of power generation highly efficient.

Power Plant 3 was also geothermal but of a more traditional design. Powerful pumps forced water deep into the Martian mantle, whereupon it super-heated before returning it to the surface. Once in contact with the thin Martian atmosphere, the water would boil explosively, powering steam turbines to generate electricity. Condenser units captured any escaping vapour or steam.

Power Plant 4 was a solar power facility. Not an elegant Martian power solution. The weak sunlight and dusty atmosphere often left it entirely impotent, but as a backup or top-up it complemented the other power plants very nicely.

The storage of excess power was by means of high-pressure atmospheric liquefaction, and at full capacity the colony's dozen or so tanks, slowly depressurising through dynamo-turbines, could power the entire facility for months.

Separate from the agricultural domes and power plants and capable of accommodating up to thirty individuals were the colony's habitation and research facilities. In recent years, however, with Martian investment opportunities dwindling, the habitation units were never more than half full. In 2105, with the KBE in orbit, the colony housed fourteen individuals. Nine adults, five children, with another child well on the way...

⧗

Serious Stuff from Gina.

Martian Shenanigans. Part One.

While asleep in my pod, Walsingham sent a message to Karolina Kowal, the Martian colony supervisor. Outlining our time of arrival, duration of stay, he asked her to communicate any material requests (the KBE is stuffed to the gunnels with everything the colonists might need). For reasons unknown, it was days before she replied, and according to Susi, the message troubled Walsingham so deeply, he contacted the UET SSD, asking for advice. Curiously, the UET were already aware of the "Martian condition" and recommended we continue with our landing as planned. In light of this, Walsingham has called a conference to brief the crew on the current situation.

⧗

"There." Walsingham carefully nodded. "Is that any better? Quite a view, is it not?"

Emilio Bedoya, smiling graciously, expertly tossed a cream-drenched raspberry into his mouth.

"And now to business," Walsingham continued. "Good afternoon, for yes, in London, it is indeed the afternoon."

Sighing at the prospect of another lecture, Dr Ackermann moved down the line, collecting the bowls and spoons.

Ignoring her, Walsingham persevered...

"As you are aware, we were to join the Martian colonists for – what shall we call it? – a meet and greet?"

There was nodding.

"And, originally, the UET required the entire crew, but this stopover is no longer a social call. It has become a serious undertaking, with a hierarchy of objectives, all of which remain in a state of flux. To elucidate further, permit me to recap what is known."

The hand of Bill Corbiere shot up, begging Walsingham's attention.

"Yes, Bill?" remarked Walsingham, giving him a nod.

"Well," he replied, "my question is this. How can the mission objectives be in a state of flux? I thought the mission was set in stone, and executive planning beyond our control."

"Certainly," said Walsingham. "The overall flight plan is unchanged. The shuttle will leave land and return at the appointed time. Only whom is to be aboard and why is open to debate. The devil is in the detail."

Behind Walsingham, the live display of Mars refreshed to show the current colony supervisor, Dr Karolina Kowal. An attractive woman, slender, athletic, with long brown hair, and hazel eyes...

"As I speak," Walsingham continued, "the colonist's number fourteen, but don't hold your breath. There will soon be fifteen, as I understand Leandra Pfennig is due to give birth within the next month. Now, the person behind me is Dr Karolina Kowal, the colony supervisor, and she oversees the day-to-day running of the colony, its projects, and planetary survey. A remarkable woman all round, Karolina possesses a formidable intellect, with the determination and emotional strength to match. Certainly, I met her once at a conference, during which she heckled me regarding the slow development of the mining equipment for her Martian assignment."

Refreshing once more, the glowing display now portrayed a young couple in their thirties.

"These are the Mottes," prompted Walsingham, "Drs Arnold and Jessica. Arnold is the colony's medical doctor, while Jessica is a botanist.

She plays a vital role adapting the crops to the unusual and sometimes challenging environment within the agricultural domes. They possess a single child, Shona, now almost eight, and she assists her mother in the everyday running of the farm."

Changing again, the display showed another attractive young couple. Both blond, blue-eyed, and obviously continental…

"Next, we have the Pfennig's, Drs Stefan and Leandra. In residence for four Martian years (seven years on Earth), they are colony's longest serving inhabitants. Stefan is an engineer, charged with maintaining the colony's facilities, but as he freely admits, malfunctions occur so rarely he is predominantly a farmer. Using his skills to fix the plough rather than tinker with nuclear reactors. His wife, Leandra, is a chemist, specialising in bio and environmental chemistry. They have two children, Leon, five, and Megan, three, and, as I mentioned earlier, Leandra is approximately 220 Martian days pregnant and on light duties."

Walsingham, turning towards the display, frowned slightly, encouraging it to show two young men, one blonde, the other dark and comprehensively bearded. He continued…

"Next, we have Drs David Hall and Tobias Lombardi. The colony's planetary survey team, they studied together at Oxford, and currently occupy the same house."

The display then showed another couple. Strikingly blue-eyed, with woman had pale auburn hair, while the man, all but bald and smiling smugly, had furry ears protruding like handles…

"And here we have the Brays. Trevor and Vivienne. Trevor is a veterinary surgeon, specialising in the care of farm animals. His wife, Viv, is an agronomist and nutritionist, doubling as the colony's storage and resource manager. They have two children. Ashton, seven, and Julian, nine. There's precious little on file about them. Doubtless they are loud, annoying, and a drain on resources."

Easing its way into Dr Padgett's thoughts came the soothing voice of Eric Badsegh…

"I've met Viv before," he whispered, "during the UET's International Food Technology Symposium. She was both an intriguing and forthright woman, and an ardent supporter of the Neighbourhood Farming Initiative. Didn't know her family had settled on Mars, but the challenge

of farming and food production in such an environment would appeal to her greatly, I'm excited to view her accomplishments."

There is no way to know if Dr Badsegh sent this message to all present (Dr Ackermann didn't mention it) so I assume it was solely for Dr Padgett.

"So, these are the colonists," said Walsingham. "Any questions?"

There followed ten seconds of silence wherein crew members matched gazes and shrugged (perhaps communicating mentally), and with no questions forthcoming, Walsingham duly continued...

"What you are about to see is the most recent communication from Dr Kowal, and note, it is classified gamma black. Susi and I have already seen it, and we discussed her findings at length. Susi, could you join me at the front? If at any time you wish to comment, feel free to pause the playback. Crewmates? Your attention please."

The head and shoulders of the woman filling the screen bore little resemblance to the Karolina Kowal shown earlier. Her youth and energy had gone. She was a husk. Pale, waxy, her skin like that of a drum. Her face taut, her cheekbones hollow, and her eyes — they were wide and unblinking. The eyes of a woman desperate and terrified. Once a river of gold, now matted and greasy, her long hair clung to her head like shrivelling seaweed. While trying to speak, her left hand unconsciously pulled and tugged at this hair, all the while flinching and twitching, glancing left and right with suspicion and fear.

Her mouth slowly chewing, she struggled to speak, and her first gurgling utterances meant nothing...

"Sh... esshh... She'sh isss the speaker of me. You... come, you... sssay? Walsss-ingham? Ha! Wasss already here. Waiting. Waiting to be f-found... You take uss, take uss home?"

Shaking uncontrollably, she began to weep. Her tears collecting at the point of her chin and dripping.

Clearly audible, there then came the scream of a woman in terror...

"He's here!" screamed Kowal in response. *"Come... come for the little oness... Stop him, I mussst!"*

Then, brandishing a wicked-looking knife, she ended the message with a burst of interference.

Breaking the stunned silence with a rasping cough, Walsingham stood before the flickering screen...

"*Ten days since her transmission and nothing from the colony since. Comments?*"

The crew remained silent.

"*Come on,*" *he grumbled, slapping his thigh.* "*Your thoughts! Gina? You rarely miss an opportunity. Have you nothing to offer?*"

"*She's nuts?*"

Dr Al-Hillah snorted, and Susi smiled, but Walsingham wasn't impressed. "*Ha!*" *he said.* "*Hopeless. Serves me right for asking, but indeed she clearly is.*"

"*It is most apparent,*" *began Dr Ackermann,* "*Dr Kowal has undergone some degree of mental breakdown, and from this recording, she is displaying distinct symptoms of paranoid schizophrenia. Possibly entering a psychotic phase. If the colonists are unable to manage her condition, they may well be in danger.*"

Dr Corbiere, all this time thoughtfully stroking his chin, stood and stretched. "*Is there any notion as to the cause of her breakdown? An outside influence? A toxin or pathogen? What of the medical facilities of the colony? Why hasn't Dr Motte recognised and treated her condition? Early diagnosis and a course of TBDZ, * although not cure, would lessen her symptoms.*"

*Thienobenzodiazepine.

Before Dr Ackermann could reply, Walsingham interrupted, adding, "*No outside influences. The UET and I tried contacting Dr Motte directly, but we received no reply. I now consider it imperative we find and treat Dr Kowal, in tandem with ascertaining the colonists' condition.*"

Chatter and a great deal of shrugging followed, with only Dr Padgett remaining silent. Staring at the interference still frozen on the screen she seemed transfixed...

"*I need volunteers,*" *said Walsingham, clapping his hands.* "*Who wants to go? Don't want to make this an order. No idea what we'll find down there. It might be dangerous. If given the choice, I'd send Bill, Eric, Susi, possibly Abda. Two of us at least should remain to monitor and advise from orbit.*"

"*I'm happy to go,*" *replied Dr Badsegh.* "*Dr Bray and I are old friends. I understand her pedogenetic results are a miracle.*"

"Well, I have to go," added Dr Ackermann. *"It's the primary reason I'm on this prison ship. Although, crazy people? They terrify me."*

There was laughter.

"No," she said. *"I'm serious. Most of my days are spent observing patients and writing reports. All academic. But clinical psychiatry? I try to avoid it. It freaks me out!"*

"You'll need a doctor too," said Bill Corbiere *"I'll need some time to prepare, gen up, and pack my bag."*

"Want me along too?" added Dr Padgett, moving closer to the screen.

"Would you?" Dr Ackermann grinned. *"You'd certainly bolster my courage."*

Staring at Dr Padgett, Walsingham slowly shook his head, but Dr Ackermann, hands on her hips, gave him a look of supplication...

"Yes, yes, alright," he then sighed. *"Perhaps Gina's inestimable charm will prove useful for once."*

Dr Padgett, giving Walsingham a wink and a grin, returned her attention to the screen.

"You know," she remarked, *"This isn't just static. There's something here. A presence. A shape or a pattern. Did anyone see it?"*

Emilio Bedoya, so far only a spectator, jumped to his feet.

"What sort of pattern? You think there's a message?"

"I'm not sure," she admitted. *"Could we replay the interference again. Slowly, one a frame at a time? I didn't save it."*

Emilio, a dab hand with neural interface, replayed the last four seconds of the message at 100th normal speed.

At this speed, appearing and disappearing were twisting bands of colour, and then, caught in the last few frames...

"There!" cried Dr Padgett. *"See? A little girl. Silhouetted in the bottom right corner."*

"Yes," said Walsingham. *"But who? There are of course children down there. Perhaps caught by the camera as it shut down? What are those ribbons of colour?"*

Dr Al-Hillah, turning to Corbiere, muttered, "Spectracote, Bill? During a sudden power shift, GPUs artefact, don't they?"

"Possibly." Corbiere shrugged. *"But the colours are wrong. Digital artefacts produce speckles and tearing. Not twisting ribbons. Green, purple, yellow? Never."*

⧗

Serious Stuff from Gina.

Martian Shenanigans. Part Two.

We're going to Mars! Well, we have already arrived, and I am joining Eric, Bill, and Susi to visit the colonists. In truth, this is a surprise. My skill set is hardly applicable, but Susi says she wants me along "to bolster her confidence". Since her presence on this mission is vital, Walsingham cannot deny her. He spoke to me briefly before I boarded the shuttle, reminding me to be observant and to log anything suspicious. As if I needed him telling me that!

Curious why Walsingham wasn't going himself, I pressed him for an explanation. His grumbling reply: "Down there it is family business. Hideously domestic. Not my sort of business at all, and children? Ergh. Tiresome, noisome, grubby little things. You're better off without me."

Originally, the UET demanded we remove our special suits for this excursion, to keep their existence a secret. For safety, Walsingham ignored their request, and we donned overalls to cover them up...

"Overalls," said Susi. "With my figure? I look like a frumpy mechanic!"

With his large leather bag, Bill Corbiere is only a stethoscope short of a doctor making a house call. The bag exterior is only for show. The container within, both pressure and temperature regulated, brims with surgical tools, medical doodahs, drugs, pills, and potions.

Walsingham's whispered advice to Eric (which we all overheard) was, "Arm yourself."

Most reassuring.

Susi and I carry only our wits.

Wearing again our hefty re-entry/environment suits, Abda is strapping me into my seat. Next to me, Susi is grumbling. The suits still stink, and to negate the sensation, I remind her to reconfigure her olfactory input.

Lift off!

We are moving. Moving to a position where the shuttle can steadily decelerate, moving through the thin Martian atmosphere to the landing area. It's going to take hours. We have a lot of velocity to lose! If permitted, I will write again when I get back. It depends on what we find. Walsingham is clearly worried.

⧗

The following, all that remains of the crew's experiences within the Martian colony, I have pieced together from the stored memories of Drs Padgett, Ackermann, and Badsegh. Dr Corbiere's logs and personal memories, lost during the collapse of the SSD mainframe, may still reside within him.

The descent and landing were smooth, smoother than Drs Ackermann and Padgett were expecting. The thin Martian atmosphere, creating less friction than the one blanketing the Earth, delivered a gentle (but tedious) shuttle deceleration.

Removing their restraints and adapting to the uniformity of the Martian gravity, the landing party staggered, stumbled, and stamped their feet...

"Helmets on," prompted Dr Badsegh. "We have a short trudge to the airlock, then we can get out of these accursed things."

Checking and rechecking the seal on her helmet, Dr Ackermann flapped her arms with newfound freedom.

"This is easy!" She laughed. "With the help of my suit I can finally move!"

With Eric Badsegh leading the way, the crew descended the shuttle ramp, before raising it and taking in the view. Awestruck, Dr Padgett overloaded the suit intercoms with a rustling hiss...

"What an inhospitable place," she muttered. "Bleakly beautiful, but...?"

"Barren," added Bill Corbiere. "Lifeless, rocky, nothing for anyone."

Surrounded by a halo of lights, the airlock appealingly beckoned, and the party purposefully strode towards it. Beside its hatch was a small panel, glowing with the words "Airlock Secure. Please Enter Code" and, befuddled by this discovery, Dr Badsegh appealed for advice...

"Why does this need a lock?" he muttered. "Wasn't expecting this! Does anyone know the code, or do I need to call Walsingham?"

"It's locked from inside?" said Dr Ackermann. "Thought they knew we were coming?"

"Apparently not," muttered Dr Padgett. "The lock was installed twelve years ago to keep out the Chinese. The code's 64080. According to the log, the airlock hasn't opened for several months."

"Really?" asked Corbiere. "How can you know this? Is it on file?"

"No," replied Dr Padgett. "My suit just told me. She must've accessed the system."

"Impressive," said Corbiere. "Wish mine was as helpful. Hardly says a word... Gonna try it, Eric?"

"Naturally," replied Dr Badsegh. "The only other possibility involves returning to the shuttle, downloading the schematic, and dismantling the flipping thing!"

Touching the control panel with his gloved hand, Dr Badsegh carefully entered the code.

"Six-Four-Oh-Eight-Oh."

The code was correct, and, with a hissing plume of brown dust, the airlock swung open, revealing a dark and gloomy interior.

"Clever girl." Badsegh chuckled, patting Dr Padgett's arm.

"She is," she replied.

Switching on lights, shutting and sealing the door, Dr Corbiere flooded the chamber with air before checking the environmental controls...

"Two forty-six Kelvin," he muttered. "Far too nippy. How about 289?"

"Right," said Badsegh. "Re-entry suits off and then decontamination."

Primarily to remove every trace of Martian dust (a toxic, abrasive, oxidative nightmare, with a penchant for ruining everything it touches), the colony's decontamination chamber also provided a means of sterilisation. *

*The 1967 Space Exploration Treaty forbids microbial contamination of all extra-terrestrial environments.

With their environment suits stored in lockers, the crew exited the decontamination chamber to stand blinking and open-mouthed at the threshold of the colony's gargantuan primary agricultural dome.

All was not as it should be. Instead of thriving arable farmscape, there was little to enjoy but row upon row of withered crops. A crude dais the heart of the dome was surmounted by a vast metallic basin...

"Incredible," gasped Dr Ackermann. "But why abandon the crops, and what's that basin doing there?"

Dr Badsegh, carefully examining a nearby vine of tomatoes, prodded one of its putrid fruits.

"Judging by the state of decay" – he frowned – "untended for four to six weeks. Also, the irrigation system is deactivated, or perhaps, malfunctioning?"

Drs Corbiere and Padgett, stooping occasionally to examine a plant, moved towards the dais, while Dr Badsegh contacted Walsingham aboard the KBE...

"Badsegh to Walsingham. Malcolm? Eric here. Landing successful. After a minor difficulty, we have entered the facility. We have yet to encounter any colonists. Agricultural Dome 1 is showing signs of extended neglect. Am uploading visual data. Please review and instruct. We are moving to examine the peculiar structure at the dome's heart. Badsegh out."

Now standing atop the earthen dais, Dr Corbiere cautiously ran his fingers around the rim of the basin before sniffing the air.

"Burnt meat," he remarked. "Burnt in this basin, I should say. Hmm, yes. A rendered titanium alloy, embedded laminae high-energy spectracote, of the sort used in crucibles and furnaces. They must have made it specifically, but for what? A banquet? One heck of a barbecue, if that's what it was. With a sample of the residues, we can soon find out."

"Is that bone?" asked Dr Padgett. "And, over here, blood?"

Dr Corbiere, acknowledging Dr Padgett, remained matter of fact.

"Indeed," he gravely nodded. "Well spotted."

Opening his medical bag, Dr Corbiere removed a packet of items.

"Here," he said, handing Dr Padgett two sample pots, forceps, and a scraper. "Get me a sample of each, will you?"

"Sure," she replied, squatting carefully beside the bloodied fragment of bone.

"That bone," remarked Dr Ackermann, "the one Gina is scraping? It looks like a piece of femur. From the lesser trochanter?"

"Yes, Susi. You certainly know your bones."

"Yes," she confirmed, "the larger ones. But the species? It looks like..."

"Homo sapiens," he softly replied, taking the samples from Dr Padgett and slipping them into his bag.

Continuing to explore, the party found the other four domes similarly neglected, ruined, or abused...

Intended for the growing of fruit, Agri Dome 2 was smaller, hotter, and more humid than Dome 1, but little remained except the stumps of banana plants and the withered bushes of peach, lemon, pomegranate, grapefruit, and orange.

Constructed for the farming of fish, with a proposal to install hives for the keeping of bees, Agri Dome 3 was empty and untouched. The fishponds entirely dry, the beehives strangely absent.

For the raising of livestock, the pens of Agri Dome 4 were empty but for dead and decomposing goats lying in a blackened pool of their own blood. Drs Corbiere and Badsegh, examining each carcass, concluded the animals had been dead for approximately eight weeks.

The conditions inside Agri Dome 5 (the smallest) were nominal. Dr Padgett: "The chickens and quails within, although dusty, seemed pleased to see us. While we checked their egg collection mechanism, food and water dispensers, several followed us about."

Leaving the agricultural complex and passing through a large warehouse (still piled high with everything the colony could ever require), the landing party made their way to the units reserved for research and habitation. Parts of which were still under construction.

Coming to a T-junction choked with litter and filth, Dr Badsegh brought the party to a halt…

"What do you think?" he mused. "Left to geology or right to the labs? The village is directly ahead."

"We should find the colonists," replied Corbiere, sniffing the air. "The smell permeating this corridor fills me with dread."

Reminiscent of a refuse heap, the air of the corridor was foul. Stuffy, stinking, and yet cloyingly sweet.

"Agreed," said Dr Ackermann. "We should, but not directly. Something down here has gone horribly wrong. I would prefer we investigate, to try and determine the cause."

"Fine." Dr Badsegh shrugged. "Then I suggest we begin with geology."

Turning left and picking their way along a corridor strewn with rubble and discarded clothing, the party filed into an empty, unfinished dome about fifteen metres in diameter…

"Nothing here." said Corbiere.

"Should be planetary survey and geology," Badsegh replied, "but now I learn there was some problem with the excavation and the project was terminated. Why, even Walsingham doesn't know. Since the UET refused to answer his questions, he considers the reason important."

Leaving the unfinished dome, the four crewmates returned to the main corridor.

Stepping over heaps of rubbish, Dr Padgett tutted in disgust…

"What a mess," she muttered, "and they have jani-bots. Didn't they give a fuck?"

Studying a service panel, Bill Corbiere nonchalantly shrugged his shoulders.

"The robotic services are fully active," he acknowledged. "Guess nobody bothered to call them. Want me to start the clear-up?"

"No," replied Dr Badsegh. "Not yet. Leave things be. We need an unfettered recording of the conditions."

"Agreed," said Dr Ackermann. "An overall impression of the environment may be of benefit when assessing Dr Kowal's state of mind," and then, tilting her head, she added, "Can anyone hear anything? The playing of children, talking, or laughing?"

There followed a heavy silence, the only sound the soft hum of the ventilation.

"No," replied Dr Badsegh, breaking the spell. "There's nothing. Not a sound. Where have they gone?"

Dr Padgett, scanning ahead, was looking for signs of warmth and living beings.

"Heat emanations," she remarked. "Very weak. Coming from the furthest habitation pod. The village? When we get closer, I'll know."

"Confirmed," said Bill Corbiere. "Could be the colonists. Eric, what do you think? Should we go straight there?"

"Not yet," he replied. "We should investigate further. The right corridor leads to the science lab, Dr Kowal's private quarters, terminating in the infirmary. Let's go and see…"

The laboratory was a mess. Trampled papers over the floor, broken computers, heaped apparatus, shattered glassware. Except for one bulky apparatus at the centre of the room, all was in chaos.

Rifling through drawers and cupboards, Drs Corbiere, Padgett, and Ackermann looked for anything untoward, while Dr Badsegh, collecting the papers and printouts, quickly scanned each in turn, before heaping them on the counter.

Pushing a chair away from the central apparatus, Dr Padgett leant her long body against it…

"There's a sample in the EMMA," she remarked. "Looks like a diorite bead, or granite? It's all twinkly, as if it's flaked with mica. Weird, though. On Mars, igneous rocks are usually mafic. Basalt, gabbro, olivine."

EMMA = broadband electro-magnetic molecular analyser.

"*That would explain the analysis,*" *said Bill Corbiere.* "*When we find the geologists, why don't you ask them?*"

Done with the laboratory, Drs Badsegh, Corbiere, and Ackermann made for the door.

As if transfixed, Dr Padgett still peered into the scanner…

"*If you say so,*" *murmured Dr Padgett,* "*Why should we interfere? This little thing… so harmless. It's nothing to do with us…*"

"*Gina!*" *cried Dr Ackermann.* "*Come on. We're leaving.*"

"*What the hell?*" *thought Ackermann to Padgett.* "*Going all sleepy like that. What were you mumbling about? A tiny sample of rock?*"

"*Just thinking out loud,*" *thought Padgett to Ackermann.* "*No need to get shirty.*"

"*You weren't thinking,*" *thought Dr Ackermann.* "*You were dreaming. Your mind was elsewhere. Don't try to deny it. Something is bothering you. I don't know what, but you need to brush it aside.*"

"*Ok, I'll try,*" *thought Dr Padgett,* "*but there's something. Someone is here – a shadow. It's watching us, peering over our shoulders. Can't you feel it?*"

"*No,*" *thought Dr Ackermann.* "*All I feel is tension. Tension and concern. Focus, Gina. Be yourself. I need you!*"

Exiting the laboratory, the quartet tried the door to Dr Kowal's room. After sounding the doorbell, Dr Badsegh gently knocked.

"*Jammed.*" *He frowned.* "*Wedged from the inside? Not sure. When I knock it sounds dull. Muffled. As if the door is under pressure?*"

Dr Badsegh, pressing his ear to the door, listened intently…

"*Nothing,*" *he said,* "*The panel readout says 290 Kelvin and normal atmospheric pressure. Not sealed because of a hull breach. Stand back. I'm going to force it.*"

Rolling up his sleeves of his overalls, Dr Badsegh concentrated upon his forearms and hands. His shining suit spread over them like shimmering paint.

"*Right,*" *he nodded.* "*Now for the door.*"

With a single lunging thrust from left to right, Dr Badsegh wrenched the door half open, releasing a torrent of dark and filthy water, every imaginable trapping within. Papers, bedding, shoes, clothing, food wrappers, bits of potted plant…

"Ah." Bill Corbiere chuckled. "It was water. Want me to fetch you a towel?"

"No, thank you," he replied, turning to Dr Ackermann. "Susi? Be a dear and call the jani-bots. The service panel's just over your shoulder."

Dr Ackermann, quickly turning, did as he asked.

"So much for the big picture," muttered Dr Padgett, "but at least they'll get rid of the pong."

"Hopefully," replied Badsegh, shaking his legs. "Stella?" he then said, speaking to his suit. "Could you dry my overalls? Yeah, that should do the trick. Thanks, Stella."

Except for the twinkling shards of a broken mirror and a covering of graffiti, the furnishings of Dr Kowal's private quarters were undamaged.

"Get a good record of the graffiti," said Dr Ackermann. "Even gobbledygook can be telling."

Scratched or deeply scored, graffiti was everywhere, with the words "Never", "Burn", "Whisper", "Hate", and "Kill", together with examples of a rudimentary design – one small circle notched into the side of another.

Scratching his head, Dr Badsegh was showing concern...

"Where are you?" he muttered to himself. "Where are you hiding?"

Prodding a knot of sodden clothing with her foot, Dr Padgett flipped over a shoe.

"Slingbacks?" she said. "Gah. She really must be crazy."

Thoughtful and serious, Dr Ackermann flashed her a thunderous look.

Joining Dr Corbiere at Dr Koval's computer, Dr Badsegh tried to log in.

"Dammit," he said. "Was hoping to review her logs. Now we'll just have to find her."

Dr Padgett, peering over Dr Corbiere's shoulder, seemed intrigued...

"Why not let my suit hack in? It will only take her a moment or two."

"No," replied Badsegh. "Not yet. Walsingham told me to go by the book, and he's right. Before we go snooping, we should try to get her permission. Medical bay's next, isn't it, Bill?"

"Yes." Corbiere nodded. "And that 'orrible smell?" He sniffed, wrinkling his nose. "That's cadaverine."

"Indeed," he concurred. "So why don't you go on ahead? Gina, go with him. Once Susi and I have had quiet chat, we'll join you."

Without another word, Drs Corbiere and Padgett made for the door...

"Cut with a knife," muttered Dr Ackermann tracing her finger over the graffiti. "Frantically, by the same person. All at same time by the look of it. Notice how the handwriting deteriorates as the perpetrator tired from the effort of cutting."

Breathing heavily, Dr Padgett suddenly appeared at the doorway. Her heart was racing...

"We," she gasped, "we've found someone. Come. Quick. But brace yourselves. Disable your olfactory input. It isn't pleasant."

The scene through the medical centre door was gruesome. A spectacle of death. Pitiless and cruel. Naked and bloated, strapped to one of the treatment tables, purple-skinned, and beginning to putrefy, was the body of a woman. Empty syringes jutted from her neck, but most harrowing was the wicked incision torn across her lower abdomen. A large pool of blood, congealed into a dark sticky glaze, covered, and surrounded her, and footprints, blackened and bloody, further smearing the blood, led this way and that before heading out of the door. The stench was overwhelming, and Gina was relieved to stymie her sense of smell...

"Oh, mein Gott!" cried Dr Ackermann. "Is it Dr Kowal?"

"No," replied Bill Corbiere, frowning and shaking his head. "This was Dr Pfennig – Leandra – and the wound across her abdomen? Intended as a caesarean section. However, this wasn't surgery. It was butchery. Rushed and desperate. Not the work of a medic."

"Murder, then," grumbled Badsegh. "How did she die? Simple trauma and blood loss?"

"My first impression, yes, but I'm going to give her a full work up. Don't worry, Eric. I'll call this in. My speciality, not yours. Go on ahead with Susi and Gina."

"Fine." Said Badsegh, clearly relieved. "And thanks. But lock the door. The sadistic monsters who did this might still be nearby."

"Indeed," Bill acknowledged, rummaging in his bag. "But it'll only take me twenty minutes, and if the murderers do return, I'll certainly hear them coming. Once she's tagged and bagged, I'll get the jani-bots to clean up."

"Of course." Badsegh nodded, patting him on the back. "Just be ready. If Dr Kowal is truly paranoid, she could be hiding anywhere."

"Very possibly." Corbiere smiled, laying out a hammer, skull key, and saw. "Although, I'm fairly certain we would detect her if she were nearby.

Nonetheless, if she does make an appearance, drag her in here. The sooner she receives anti-psychotics the better."

Dr Ackermann, still in the doorway, seemed confused.

"You think she is solely responsible? There are many sets of footprints."

Donning a surgical one-piece, Dr Corbiere could only shrug.

"I think it very likely. It was she that wielded the knife."

Locking the medical centre door behind them, Drs Badsegh, Padgett, and Ackermann picked their way along the rubbish-strewn corridor. Zooming back and forth, mopping, sweeping, and scooping, the jani-bots were depositing the refuse into a chute.

"Could do with a couple of those," Badsegh remarked. "My nephews leave a trail of destruction."

Terminating the corridor was a large heavy door, its control panel showing "Secure".

"The colonists are through here," said Dr Padgett. "I can make out several individuals quite clearly."

"Confirmed," said Dr Badsegh. "Is there a door chime?"

"It appears not," said Dr Ackermann. "And the mechanism is asking for a security code. Gina, do you think you could hack it?"

"Probably," she replied, "How about knocking? Bit more subtle than the door swinging open."

"Hmm...," said Dr Ackermann. "She has a point. If Dr Kowal has entered a psychotic phase, the colonists are most likely terrified. If we can avoid shocking them further, we will have an easier time learning what happened."

Returning from the medical centre, Dr Corbiere looked worried.

"Finished already?" asked Dr Padgett. "What's up?"

"Oh, nothing. Just hoping we don't find any more bodies. There's no cryo-morgue and I'm not sure what to do with Dr Pfennig already."

"Why not leave her outside? Sounds callous, but Mars is a big rocky freezer."

"Of course," he replied. "Why didn't I think of that? The jani-bots can move her to the primary airlock, then we can carry her out."

Rapping the habitation module door with his fist, Dr Badsegh listened intently for any reply. Bill Corbiere pressed his ear against it...

"Nothing," said Corbiere. "Not a word. I can hear them, though – breathing."

"Ok," said Dr Badsegh. "Then there's nothing else for it. Hack in, Gina. Find us the password."

"Very well," she replied, shaking her head. "But it won't be me doing the hacking. Hold on a tick... Ah, yes. There it is. Got it. Olympus Mons. One word, all lower case."

"Excellent." Badsegh chuckled. "The name of a Martian volcano. Susi? If you would be so kind..."

The module door, sliding open with a juddering hiss, should have the revealed the colony's common room, but the scene confronting the landing party was one of chaotic ordure. The colonists, naked and covered in filth, lay motionless, entwined within a scene of destruction. Overturned, broken furniture, excreta, half-eaten foodstuffs, rubbish, and discarded clothing. The stench was almost overpowering, and Dr Padgett struggled not to flee, seeking fresh air.

"God in Heaven," gasped Corbiere. "They're human, how could...?"

As the landing party cautiously made their way in, Dr Kowal suddenly sprang from behind an overturned couch...

"Murderers!" she hysterically screamed, then, brandishing a blood-stained shiv, she charged Drs Badsegh and Corbiere, slashing and cutting as she came. They were too strong and quick, however. Rendering her immobile, Dr Corbiere promptly drugged her into a stupor.

"Get her to the medical bay!" yelled Corbiere. "And strap her down if you have to!"

Carrying the now-unconscious Dr Kowal, Drs Badsegh and Padgett bundled her from the room.

Serious Stuff from Gina.

Martian Shenanigans. Part 3.

A harrowing two days. Fortunately, we have been extremely busy (little time to dwell on anything), but serious shit has occurred down here, and we have yet to determine the cause. An unknown agent has driven the colonists insane (Susi still doesn't know what) and we've spent the last thirty-six hours cleaning, treating, feeding, and watering the remaining colonists while trying to get to the truth.

Of the fourteen original colonists, only seven remain, and one (Dr

Vivian Bray), suffering from severe dehydration and starvation, is critically ill. Bill hopes she'll pull through, with the first forty-eight hours of careful monitoring and feeding being the difference between her living or dying, and that is the problem! We are due to leave orbit in a matter of hours, so who is going to do it?

The colonists' children are missing, presumed dead, and Susi is beginning to discern the grisly truth. The colonists, insane and/or delusional, ritually murdered their own children in a ceremony of butchery and burning. Even the unborn child of Dr Pfennig suffered this terrible fate, its mother murdered by the barbaric removal of the foetus.

Eric and I, after piecing together the colonist's logs and journals (tedious work as the central computer was a wreck), concluded that problems first arose eighteen months ago, during the excavation of the new facility for geological research.

Bill's treatment of Dr Kowal, the colony supervisor, is going very well. With a carefully balanced cocktail of drugs controlling her psychotic behaviour, she is calmer and increasingly lucid. Unable to fully converse, she occasionally mutters, hisses, and gurgles. Susi is carefully noting her every word…

"He makes our dreams."

"The thief of sleep."

Whom "he" is we have no idea, but Dr Koval would then utter phrases such as:

"The fire in the dark."

"The dark side of the sun."

"The burning of the blind."

All very confusing, but then she's goes on to mention "she" with phrases like:

"She is light."

"She is golden honey."

"Listen. She is fleet, listen!"

"She whispers. Careful, careful!"

"Out of sight. The corner of your eye."

Metaphorical nonsense or cryptic ravings? No idea. Susi will unravel it.

When asked about the children, Dr Koval's extreme reaction required Bill to increase the flow of anti-psychotics, and we heard little but gasps and screams of "He!" "Feed!" "Burn!" Before becoming more lucid, with:

"Burning hate."

"Hateful innocence."

"Noisome thingsss…"

Most recently, Dr Koval, after receiving a fresh dose of medication and showing signs of recovery, would begin in silence, drifting or dreaming, tears flowing, before whispering, "She is the keeper of life. Forever and ever. She sings. Sang to Leandra. Sweet Leandra. Even now she sings. Life is a flower… delicate. So precious. Precious in your hand."

It was twenty-four hours before we found the body of Stefan Pfennig (Leandra's husband). Out of shame or fear, he had locked himself inside the control room of Power Plant 1, taking his own life, injecting a massive dose of morphine.

In twelve hours, we are leaving. We have no choice. The KBE will continue its pre-programmed flight path whether we are on it or not, so we are working desperately to leave the remaining colonists as comfortable as possible. After obliterating every trace of the "altar" in Agri Dome 1, I took on the disgusting but essential job of gathering the animal carcasses and lowering them into the recycler.

The crops remain in a terrible state, but there simply isn't enough time to remedy them. For Eric, this is particularly gutting, and we have left the job of the harvesting, disposal, tillage, and replanting to the colonists. The agri-bots were still in decent shape, however, and Bill has adjusted their programming to cope with unexpected condition of the farm. Once complete, like beasts of burden, they will perform the heavy labour.

Ha! The situation is ludicrous. The UET are a disgrace! They had full knowledge of how things were on Mars, and to send us unprepared, for such a brief time, is reprehensible. Those fine people, in the main schizophrenic, withdrawn, and terrified, need round-the-clock care, and to leave them like this is breaking our hearts. What might happen before the relief mission arrives fills us with dread. Concerned, Walsingham is already in contact with the UET, and I can only hope he can find a way to resolve this critical turn of events.

Update: Vivian Bray is dead. Cause of death. Cardiac arrest. Bill is confused. He can find no medical reason for her death. Her heart simply ceased beating, and, despite everything he tried, he was unable to restart it. Did she lose the will to live? Susi has read of such cases, but she tells me they are extremely rare.

For Eric, Dr Bray's passing is particularly sad. He greatly admired her. Viv was a great inspiration during his early experiments, refining GelPonics and SAMP production, transforming a scientific curiosity into a genuinely productive method of farming.

We are returning to the KBE. The colonists tried to stop us. More about this later. I need a shower, a decent meal, but most of all, sleep.

ELEVEN

BY JOVE!

Assembled from the personal logs and memories of Drs Padgett, Badsegh, and Ackermann, this instalment covers the KBE's leg from Mars to Jupiter.

Serious Stuff from Gina.

Martian Shenanigans. Part Four.

Thank God for Susi. Without her speed and confidence, the primary psychiatric care of the Martian colonists would have proven impossible, before insisting, after we returned to the ship, we speak to her one on one. I must say, when talking to Susi (Susi in psychiatrist mode) you feel naked. Childlike even. She knows precisely what is bothering you, and why, even if you don't it yourself.

Anyway, following a session with Susi, working to lift my gloom, I feel much better. I still feel guilty, of course, but it is not personal guilt. The blame lies firmly at the feet of the UET. The culpability is theirs, not ours. We performed wonders. With the help of our suits, our productivity and efficiency were truly remarkable. Working in tandem with Susi, the medical care delivered by Bill Corbiere was truly stupendous. His quick diagnosis and treatment of Dr Motte, the colony's physician, had him up and about in a matter of hours, and within twelve hours he was providing a great deal of assistance. The colonists' mental health was a much greater issue. Even Dr Motte cannot bring himself talk about the last few weeks (he is either resisting the truth or unaware of it) and Susi is begging me not to write of her findings until her work is complete. Considering UET's deep culpability in creating this mess, they will undoubtedly classify her findings secret, so I had better do as she asks.

After saying our farewells, three of the colonists tried to stop us from leaving. Armed with rakes and pitchforks they tried to rush us. Not a threat. Eric defeated them easily. Before Dr Motte, quickly arriving, administered something to calm them down.

This desperate assault had old Walsingham contacting the UET immediately. He hoped to convince them of our clever idea. Shuttling the colonists to one of the orbital supply pods and placing them in hibernation – at least until the relief mission arrived. They refused! Now, I've come across this sort of stubbornness my whole professional life, and I usually try to thwart it, but only the SSD can alter our flight plan, including the plan of the shuttle, so without their intervention, we're trapped.

So, that was the end of that. We piled the bodies outside, sealed the airlock, boarded the shuttle, left the colonists to it. I mean. Come on. Seriously? They murdered their own children! Susi knows they will soon be at each other's throats. Their only hope lies in Drs Kowal and Motte smoothing things over, trying to keep the peace.

⧗

Personal Log of Dr Eric J Badsegh.

Hey Giles! How are things in Lincoln? Still an island? Not under the Channel just yet?

In the last few days, I've been reviewing the journals of my old friend Viv Bray, now sadly deceased, and I am feeling kinda glum. Thank God for Gina Padgett. What a woman she is! Keeps everyone alive. Her feet on the ground, laughing, joking. You got my last message? About the shitty stuff down on Mars? It made it past the UET censors. Walsingham kindly checked, so I know it did.

Worried we might be suffering from early post-traumatic stress, Walsingham, Bill, and Susi (our brain care specialist) insisted we undergo psychiatric examination. Not necessary at all! Reflection therapy? What were they thinking? Under duress, I prefer to look forward, not back. The whole procedure an over-reaction. Certainly,

I agreed with Gina: "Some sleep, dinner, a shower and a shag will do me just fine." What can I say? She was right. Just what I needed. Although, dinner could've been better...

Compared to Gina, this example does highlight the problem with Bill and Susi. Their rigid professionalism. They're only fun off duty. When there's a job to do, they are almost mechanical, but Gina's always Gina, no matter what she is doing. Ok, she is a bit bonkers. When you're concentrating, you wish she'd shut up for a bit, but I'd rather collaborate with her than the others. They're stifling. Don't get me wrong. I'm in no way unhappy, still having fun. Emilio is popular with everyone, only he's usually with Abda, and I don't know him as well as I should. Mind you, according to the coma pod schedule, soon only he and I will be awake. Might prove interesting. I'll let you know how it goes.

Walsingham is having a paddy. About to use a coma pod for the first time, it has suddenly dawned on him that only Gina and Susi will soon be awake, with Gina in charge. The horror – you should have seen his face!

Will write again when I'm next up.

Two months? A heartbeat.

Love to Mum.

Eric

⏳

The following is an extract from Dr Ackermann's personal log. Precisely why she shared this entry with Dr Padgett is unknown, but it is fair to surmise the reason was both friendly and professional. Perhaps to reveal her concerns regarding Dr Padgett's behaviour. Translated as before from its original German, where possible, word for word...

Dr Susi Ackermann, Personal Log.

From the terrible workload exhausted I am becoming. Bless you, Gina, for your merry spirit! On the state of mind of Mars colonists, I am recording. Their ailments peculiar. More time to consider before conclusions fully reaching. Efforts upon my crewmates concentrating. Particularly on party of landing.

Dr Badsegh during interview open and forthright. Confident about his decisions made and actions taken. He enjoys Gina's company and draws upon her strength. His grief from death of former mentor, Dr V Bray, well managed. Her passing accepted with grace and little internal conflict.

Dr Corbiere anxiety and stress handling always by work and focussed activity. Affected little by death, decay and disease, his training prepared him. His performance exemplary. His assistance and camaraderie essential to my own work and his diagnosis and prescription perfectly correct.

Dr Padgett my only concern. During interview, uncomfortable and evasive. Not her customary flippancy. It is something deeper. Will continue to monitor carefully. Her comments during Martian mission uncharacteristic and I listen for further personality shifts. She admits her suit bothers her. Second-guessing her unerringly, to its activities, she feels superfluous. Will discuss with Walsingham the possibility of removing or deactivating her suit from time to time, with Gina a firmer parent becoming?

Additional:

Unable to diagnose the colonists. My findings are a nonsense! Symptoms of long-term stress and psychological trauma, but not the case! Symptoms short term. A month or two, and each colonist the same symptoms describing. Impossible, and why the children murdering? The colonists working collectively in state delusional. No, not delusional. A dream? A dream living. Could they be same dream sharing? Their primary treatment, a process of waking – waking of consciousness. Its reassertion permitting. The illness resulting from similar stimulus, trauma, or pathogen? But Bill no disease or toxin finding. The mystery deepens. Report filed as ordered, but no conclusions drawn and time insufficient for extra data gathering.

(Off the record: With Gina I agree. We are leaving the colonists to die. A guilty shame.)

⧗

Personal Log of Dr Eric J Badsegh

This entry will be my last for six months, and I must confess, these extended periods of coma I find extremely disorientating – as if no time has passed at all. Until you look at a calendar, read the news, or catch up with your correspondence, then, oh my God, it hits you! When I eventually wake, the view outside will be of the Jovian system (Jupiter and its satellites), an exciting prospect, but not even halfway to our objective, the enormousness of our journey is becoming starkly apparent.

GelPonics, I have left in the capable hands of my crewmates, and, before I wake, they will enjoy several harvests. The organs in the SAMP tanks are maturing nicely and I plan to use the eggs and milk to prepare pancakes as soon as I wake. If there is a glut of soft fruit, Gina is offering to make jam. Quite how she will achieve this she didn't say, and if she leaves a sticky mess all over our nice shiny spaceship, Walsingham will go berserk (one good reason for doing it).

On Mars, while searching the primary laboratory, we came across a small sample of rock in the molecular scanner. Not very surprising, but after reviewing the scientific research of the colonists I can find no mention of it, and that is decidedly odd. They generated gigabytes of data concerning other rocks, minerals, soil, and botanical samples, but that little nugget never gets a mention. After our arrival, Susi and Gina performed the final tidying of the lab. Could it be possible they performed the analysis while testing the scanner? When next I see them, I will ask.

⧖

Deep Space Drivel by Gina.

Dear Mumsie,

How are things?

We are whizzing through the asteroid belt, the region of space between Mars and Jupiter, weaving our way through the rubble and refuse disgorged by asteroid mining. The asteroids themselves, lumps of metal and rock, the largest looking like grey-brown potatoes, seem innocuous, but at our velocity, even a minor collision would be fatal, so we are giving them plenty of leeway.

With only Bill Corbiere and I currently awake, the next fortnight will be a novel experience, and an excellent opportunity to develop our relationship. At first, Bill was a bit of a loner. Shy, self-conscious, distant even, but once he gets talking (fuelled by his favourite Benedictine), he becomes charming. Lively, witty, full of insights, both imaginative and practical, antiquated computers are his great passion, and he enjoys emulating their hardware, writing programs, and having fun. In no way phased by his nerdiness, I joined him disassembling, expanding, and then reassembling gaming software on a Sinclair ZX Spectrum. Looking forward to playing the result, he was a meany. He refused to let me play Manic Miner (released circa 1983) until he had designed and installed extra levels with sprites of his own design. Teasing him briefly, I said the original author would turn in his grave if he knew what he was doing. Bill was unmoved. He said, given the opportunity, he would happily exhume the game's author (the coding genius Matthew Smith) and shake him by the hand. Even in the 22nd century, programming a worthy game limited to 16K of memory is a remarkable feat.

Nine days out from Mars, we received a short (somewhat crackly) audio message from Dr Kowal, the Martian colony supervisor. Troubled by its content, Bill and I considered waking both Walsingham and Susi, but considering the danger of abruptly waking comatose incumbents, we let them be, before relaying a copy to the UET on Earth.

Dr Kowal's message went as follows, and I probably should not write of it here, only I want you to understand some of the crazy stuff we're having to deal with: "Where?" she slowly hissed. "Where is burning eye? The eye of the beast? You think I don't know? She told me. She took it. Doesn't know she stole, but she did. Had to. Was made to, so she did…"

Crazy messages aside, tending Eric's plants and livestock is keeping me busy, and his "chickens" have already begun to lay eggs. Mind you, something is wrong. The shells aren't forming correctly and the eggs resemble membranous bags. Internally they are perfect, only their squishiness makes them tricky to store. To correct this flaw, I'm tempted to tinker with the chicken development programme, but if something goes wrong, Eric will be gutted.

Despite their odd outward appearance, Bill made scrambled eggs and they were delicious. Very smartly, he added a pinch of paprika. My favourite condiment. How did he know?

Following this message, I will be asleep for months. When I wake, Susi and I will have free run of the ship, and I must say, I am looking forward to her company. Occasionally, I watch her in her coma pod, and when her eyes open, it is as if she is looking straight at me. Quite impossible. She isn't "looking" at all. In a comatose state, her consciousness and respiration are at an extremely low level. Her slumber is both silent and dreamless.

Anyway, I had better get ready. Give Rumbelow a scrobble, I'll write again as soon as I'm up.

Your delectable daughter,

Gina

x

⧖

The Private Personal Pornography of Reggie P.

Susi and I are having such a laugh. With the whole ship to ourselves (and little to do), we have spent considerable time making use of the rec rooms, and, I must say, the simulations are insane! Perusing Walsingham's folder of recommended programs, one immediately caught our attention. Called *Roller Disco*, we had no idea what it could be. Then we quickly cottoned on. Roller-skating, and to music, no less! Now, I have never been great on skates. Too gangly to be elegant, but with my enhanced sense of balance (and "Suit" taking over when approaching arse-over-tit), I am now a veritable diva. Then, asking our suits to mimic shimmering Spandex, the flashing lights, and thumping tunes made the whole affair both ludicrous and hilarious. Desperate to see the fellas strutting their stuff, when the crew is next gathered, we will be running this program again. Since the dance floor encompasses the inside of a sphere, the high-speed manoeuvres (and accidents) will be a joy to behold. What "Suit" made of it all is uncertain. While Susi and I were zooming about she was strangely silent. Was she jealous? I don't care! With the ski-slalom then running, we were laughing so hard, Suit's sly whispers were inaudible.

Later that evening, thoroughly worn out from hurtling "downhill", Susi and I dined on a fur rug in front of a roaring fire! A simulated inglenook fireplace. Crackling logs, sparks, ash, cinders, the whole shemozzle. The scene was downright romantic. If not utterly sloshed on champers, things could've gotten spicy, but I was soon snoring so loudly, Susi stomped off in a huff.

Preparing one of her surprise special dates, Susi has invited me to meet her at "La Grange" in precisely two hours and thirty-seven minutes. Why such precision is necessary I've no idea, but I know to be on time. Her Germanic temper reaches boiling point whenever I'm late, and, since this is our last chance for privacy, I'm feeling considerable pressure. "Lagrange" refers to a point in space between two bodies where there is virtually zero gravity, and our Lagrange Point is located at the midpoint of the communal core. Susi hasn't asked me to bring anything, and I'm sorely tempted to leave Suit in a locker, but I suppose I'd better bring her along. No idea what Susi is planning!

It is time for our "date", and I can already hear the music. Mendelssohn. Organ Sonata No.2 in C Minor.

Oh, there she is. I'm wearing too much.

"Suit," I whisper, "if you wouldn't mind, could we part company for an hour or two? Why not power down for a while?"

"Can't," she replies.

"Why not?"

"Fear, mistress. Fearful of losing myself. Leave me be. All will be fine. I shall slip from your body and seek power."

"Very well," I reply, "but no peeking, right?"

"Of course, mistress. My word is my bond."

(Convinced she peeked, mind you. I certainly would.)

In fact, Suit raised an interesting point (she does enjoy discussing philosophical matters). If one were indeed reborn, same time, same place, same parents, same environment, would one turn out the same? Personally, I doubt it. Of the key decisions in my life, some trivial (the colour of my lipstick), others momentous (my choice of university), at the time, all were driven one way or the other by factors beyond my control, so why would, why should, their outcomes be constant?

Now, where was I? Ah yes, entwined…

Ah Susi, such a sweet embrace. Those kisses, and the view! With the wall of the core appearing as glass, it appeared as if we were floating. Tumbling and spinning in space. The universe swirling about us. Our passion swelling with the ever increasing with the power of the music. The organ. I understood her choice, The naked purity of its timbre. Like an ocean. Caressing then thunderous. Then, swinging into view, there he was. Jupiter! Massive. Breath-taking. Bathing our naked bodies in a pinkish-grey light. Oh, Susi. By Jove!

TWELVE

G-WHIZ!

*P*erusing the remaining data made available by Dr Padgett, I realise the
following instalments are highly significant regarding the disappearance
of the crew. It is beyond my remit to draw conclusions, but it is clear that
a deterioration of the crew's well-being has begun.

This section begins two weeks out from the Jovian system. The KBE
is making course corrections, before its final fortnight-long burst of thrust,
accelerating the ship though the outer solar system, toward the Kuiper Belt.

After a protracted swig from a silver hip flask, Dr Padgett surveyed
the manner and posture of her crewmates. Revived from their coma pods
faster than recommended, all but Dr Al-Hillah are displaying varying
degrees of disorientation, stress, or distress...

Beside Dr Padgett, trembling and biting her nails, squatted Dr
Ackermann, and Dr Padgett, offering the flask to her lips, encouraged her
to take a tentative sip.

Lying nearby, moaning occasionally, his bony hands covering his
face, was Walsingham, and Dr Padgett, moving beside him, jiggled the
flask like a lure...

"Do you want some of this?" she asked. "Because, unless you sit up, I
will have to use a pipette."

"Course I want some," he grumbled. "Stop nursing and hand it over."

Slumped in armchairs, Drs Badsegh and Corbiere's expressions were
bleak. They remained uncommunicative until Dr Padgett offered them a
drink.

"Here you go, fellas. Have a snifter of this. An eighteen-year-old Bunnahabhain. Nearly blew my socks off!"

Slowly nodding, they passed the flask between them, sipping and gasping, as the whisky slowly took effect. Retrieving the flask, Dr Padgett passed it to Dr Al-Hillah…

"Not for me," he smiled, shaking his head. "I'm trying to be good, but Emil could use a nip."

Furthest from the group, Emilio Bedoya, staring at a display of the Earth and its moon, leant his head against it.

"Come on, Sadiq," urged Al-Hillah, handing the flask to Bedoya. "Try a little of this. A little alcoholic shock is just what you need."

Moving before the assembled and raising a pale hand, Dr Padgett indicated she was about to speak…

"Morning, flock. I've been asked to chair this assembly by Susi, and thank you for the drink, Malcolm, but next time? Don't hide the bottle."

With a well-timed groan from Sir Malcolm, Dr Padgett flashed him a quizzical look.

"Yeah," she acknowledged. "Certainly. You guys are feeling awful. Your suits were reporting stress, we wanted to wake you gradually, but then, after detecting radiation, we decided to wake you immediately."

"Radiation?" said Walsingham, abruptly sitting up. "What radiation? Has there been a malfunction? Are we in danger?"

"Oh, no," replied Abda. "The intensity of the radiation was incredibly low. Less than 10^{-12} watts. Soft X-rays. Short, regular pulses, coming from somewhere inside the ship. Between three and four nanometres. In shape, and unchanging, the waveform of each pulsation is reminiscent of a stellar spectral analysis."

"And I concur," said Dr Padgett. "Only, there is another thing. Possibly connected with radiation leak. It is hard to know. Abda, if you please."

"Yes," he replied. "After waking, from my cybercortex, I suddenly recalled a dream. Not a typical dream. It was vivid and strangely detailed. Less ambiguous than my usual nightly imaginings."

"Me too!" blurted Dr Ackermann. "Thought it was me. Going stir crazy, but I dreamt of Gina, repeatedly saying how sorry she was. What she had to be sorry about isn't clear."

"This is highly irregular," remarked Corbiere. "Comatose sleep is

deeper than REM sleep. It should be dreamless. Where did these memories come from?"

Dr Padgett simply shrugged.

"At this juncture, we don't have a clue, and, as for your dream, Suze, it's nothing to do with me. This last week I have mostly spent tending Eric's livestock, until it was time to wake Abda, I didn't know of any issues at all."

"I too had an experience," said Walsingham. "Now I turn my mind to it, the memory is disturbingly vivid."

"Interesting," acknowledged Dr Padgett. "Thank you, Malcolm. Anyone else?"

Slowly nodding, the others looked thoroughly perplexed.

"Goodness," she gasped. "All of you? For I have received nothing. My last coma was weeks ago, and according to the sensors the radiation leak first manifested two days out from Mars. Curious. If the leak was indeed the cause of these dreams, I was unaffected."

"Is the radiation still there?" asked Emilio Bedoya, forming himself a chair.

"No," replied Al-Hillah. "It seems to have gone."

"Good," said Walsingham. "If you detect it again, report it immediately. We need to locate it and lock it down. Apart from the odd cosmic ray and a whiff of gamma, there shouldn't be any radiation in here at all. Unless there's a solar emission, and I think we would have noticed, yes?"

⌛

Personal Log of Dr Eric J Badsegh.

Hey, Giles! Hope you're ok. Things are getting weirder up here and I am soon to be talking to Susi (our resident shrink) about a disturbing comatose dream. Normally, this would be fine, but Susi suffered a similar experience and is so badly shaken that Gina will be conducting the interviews. I can only hope she's feeling sympathetic. Somehow, Gina was immune to the malfunction we suspect was responsible for our dreaming, and for the time being she is in charge. Suffering most of all from his experience (and the prospect of Gina running things) Walsingham has asked Bill Corbiere to sedate him. Ha! Doubt we'll hear much from him for a couple of days. Bill administers powerful stuff.

Now, bruv, this bit is important. I've had my chat with Gina and Susi, and they found it odd I have no inkling where my dream could have come from or what it could mean. They suggested I describe my dream to my family, to you and Mum, to see if it rings any bells. Gina says I am suffering from decampanulogicalisation, and this time, she isn't talking bollocks, she's right. Read this and see if it jogs your memory…

A misty marsh surrounds me. A sunset burns the sky to russet. Crickets chirp, bats chitter, and frogs croak unseen in many turbid pools. I am in a circular boat. An unsteady craft, built of sticks, hides, and doped in pitch. Islands lay ahead, clad in rushes, fringed with willows, and as I row towards them, I see many campfires, flickering beneath twisting columns of smoke.

Now, just what is that all that about? Ok. We grew up in Lincoln, with extensive marshes, especially around the Wash, but they were salt marshes; muddy, brackish, and treeless. If ever there were freshwater marshes around Lincoln, marshes of the sort in my dream, it must have been a long time ago, and as for the boat? It can't be me. I've never rowed in my life. A coracle? I wouldn't fit. I'd sink the bloody thing! Anyhow, show this to Mum and have a think yourself. I could really do with an answer.

It's soon to get busy here. The last leg of our outward journey is about to commence, and before we begin to accelerate, we need to lock everything down. A week of 3G thrusting awaits. It will be gruelling, but once coasting, we will be asleep for months at a time. I will write again before I sleep, if you're lucky, send a video message (I know Mum enjoys them).

Bye for now,
Eric

＃

Private Personal Diary of Dr Regina Padgett

Should be taking this seriously, being professional, but what is going on is a veritable scrotum of bollocks, so fuck it.

Susi is being a shit. She's had me cooped up in Walsingham's office on and off for two days now and I need to get out. Her self-imposed post-traumatic counselling schedule is nothing more than contrivance, born out of spite, but what spite? In a dream she heard my voice, apologising, "*wieder und wieder.*" How am I responsible for that? Why would I do such a thing? Besides, installing any experience within her cybercortex would require the circumvention of complex security subroutines. Impossible! Bill and Abda are red-hot on stuff like that. Waste of time even trying. Stupid bitch. Vindictive, that's what she is. Cantankerous and stubborn.

So, here I am. Stuck here. Doing her job. No idea if I am doing it right. Oh, I am following her list of procedures (more a series of questions really), but whether my interpretations will prove valid, I don't have a clue.

Coming first was Bill Corbiere. The poor sod looked exhausted, and when I asked him how he was he almost burst into tears. My first mistake. Being too nice. Asking him to relax, I formed a psychiatrist couch, and invited him to lie on it…

"Go on, Bill," I then urge, "for the record, and I promise we won't tell a soul. How was your dream?"

"Ok," he says, letting go a slow breath. "Only, it was weird, like a parable or mystery play of old. A warning perhaps, but from whom? It remains deeply troubling."

"No doubt," I reply. "But you need to tell us, and then we can trouble together. Ok?"

Turning onto his side, his grey eyes twinkled with inner light.

"Alone," he begins. "Stranded on a tropical island. A paradise, with white sand, coconut palms, and a warm azure sea dappling my toes. A simple white smock covers my nakedness, and the sun is burning the top of my head."

"Right, and you don't recall visiting this island before?"

"No. It is truly perplexing. Is… is Susi alright?"

Slumped in her chair, her eyes closed, Susi seemed half asleep, but the moment we stopped talking, she raised her head and opened an inquisitive eye…

"Susi?" I ask. "*Verstehst du das alles? Willst du eine pause?*"

Shaking her head, she closed her eye once more and continued to listen in silence.

"Go on, then, Bill," I then prompt. "Tell me the rest."

"Ok. I feel lonely. Not sure why, but the loneliness is worsened because I am hunted. There are men on the island wishing me harm. I can still appreciate the fear and worry. I struggle not to look over my shoulder."

"Incredible," I remark. "Such strong imagery. Is there more?"

"Plenty." He chuckles. "Appearing in the distance, closing fast, are two men. The hunters. Primitives, with tattered pelts, skirts of grass, carrying spears, long-hafted axes with jagged tips of stone. Desperate and terrified, I try to hide."

"Golly," I reply. "How exciting! Did you escape?"

"Yes. It was at this moment I discovered my ability of transformation. The ability to assume any form, and, as the men drew closer, I become a palm tree, swaying gently in the breeze. This clever ruse fooled the hunters. They ran straight by, disappearing inland some distance along the coast."

"So, you duped them. Is there more?"

"Oh yes," replies Bill. "Much more. If you stop interrupting, I'll tell you!"

"Sorry. Force of habit. Go on..."

"All was well," continues Bill, "and on I went. Living my life of solitude, slowly adapting. Not just surviving but thriving. Until the hunters returned. Fearful of their approach, I quickly became a rock exposed by the tide, seaweed clad, slowly drying in the sun."

"Clever." I smile. "And were you successful? Did the hunters spot you?"

"No. I duped them. They ran straight by, and, proud of my cleverness, I continued to adapt and thrive. Learning to fish, building a shelter, foraging, and hunting. Time passed and my confidence grew. Until one day, the hunters returned. Three of them. The first two, youthful and courageous, came on as before, but behind there came an elder. Walking, thinking, looking carefully from under the wide brim of his hat. Concerned by his vigilance, I became a gull. White as snow, pink webbed feet like rubber, and with the other birds, I dodged the surf, probing the sand for clams."

"Ingenious. Did they spot you?"

"Yes," he regretfully replies. "As the young hunters sped by, the gulls flew up in panic. Except one. Me. For as much as I knew how to appear as a gull, flying was beyond my knowledge, and before I could escape, the elder man arrived. Picking me up, he looked me over with dismay..."

You gifted fool, he chuckled. How can I school you? To mimic insentience is simple. The palms stand tall. Stealing the sun, moving water – endless thirst. A rock is but a memory. Yet you choose to copy a living mind? Thought brings truth, truth brings life, and lies bring only sorrow.

Throwing me to the ground, he pinned me with his foot. He raised his axe to strike...

Remember, he whispers. Leave your mark on the sand."

"And that was all," said Bill. "A bit dramatic, wouldn't you say?"

"Indeed," I reply. "Thank you. Did the hunter strike? Were you killed?"

"Don't remember," he says, sitting up, removing his leaden-grey hood, "but it's kinda implied, don't you think?"

"Possibly," I reply. "You'll have to ask Susi. I'm not qualified to make diagnoses. Anyhow, with your dream on record, when she's feeling more zesty, Susi can mull it over. In the meantime, you're free to go. Once we've done Malcolm, Emil, and Abda, we'll join you in the core for dinner. The Snowshield's deploying, isn't it? Wanna see that. Abda says it's massive!"

"Yeah," says Bill, standing and peering into Susi's expressionless face. "Deployment begins in twelve hours. Depends on the course corrections. Are you not going to interpret my dream before kicking me out? Give me some closure?"

"Should I? Because I haven't a clue! But hmm, since you asked. What does it mean? Keep your lies simple?"

"Obviously," he sighs, and walking briskly from the office, he closed the door with whump.

"Did say I wasn't qualified. What does he expect, psychoanalysis?"

However, Susi remained impassive. Was she asleep? Suit told me no. She was meditating, analysing Bill's dream, sharing her thoughts with Draymar (her suit's fledgling AI).

Minutes later, Walsingham loped in, recovered from his days of forced rest (via sedation) …

"Bill tells me it's my turn," he remarks. "For the share and tell. How is it going, anyway? It is uncomfortable enough becoming your patient. Listening to our psychobabble must be terrible."

"Doing fine, thank you. If I do stumble, make a ballsy interpretation or some such, Susi soon puts me right."

"Are you sure?" asks Walsingham, trying the couch. "Looks like you've bored her to death."

"*Gott in Himmel!*" Susi suddenly snaps. "Can't you people leave me be? *Ich höre zu!* Am listening. Ok?"

"You've done it now," I reply with a chuckle. "You've woken the beast. Recount your dream, Malcolm, and quickly, before she devours us!"

"Very well," he ponders, thoughtfully scratching his stubble. "Want me to lie on the couch?"

"If you like, for the sake of tradition? I couldn't care less."

"Indeed," he acknowledges, giving Susi a curious glance. "I'll just sit."

"Fine by me. Please begin."

"Hmm…" he muses. "Where is the beginning, where is the end… Ok. I find myself standing upon a bleak and windswept down. Marshland surrounds me, and to the south I can see the ocean. Its surface is brown and churning. Every now and then a sunbeam cuts through the cloud, playing upon its turbulence, transforming it to silver. Far above on the icy breeze, wheeling jackdaws chuckle and mock. My rough woollen smock billows about me like an ominous cloak."

"Goodness," I remark. "How very portentous. What happened next?"

"Well, for what seemed like an age, nothing. I felt lost and alone. Then, a calm descended, the wind dropped, the air became still, and a mist blanketed the ground. Ragged children came. Some crawling, others clawing their way from the ground, bringing with them a wall of white smoke, swirling with the ghosts of infants. More came. Rolling, churning, begging with outstretched hands of supplication. 'What do you want?' I said with a thunderous voice. 'Why have you come?' The children were unafraid. They were laughing! Pealing, rippling, full of joy. Some clapping, some waving, some singing, singing my praises."

"Curiouser and curiouser." I chuckle. "Is there more?"

"Yes indeed, a little more. The children, the ghosts, and the smoke, they started to fade. I fell to my knees, knowing it was I that caused their fading. Only a single girl remained. Noticeably young. A toddler, with shining white skin, and dark eyes that burnt with disgust. Before long she left too, fading like the others, and, like a standing stone, I then stood alone, a menhir proud and cold. Beyond all time, all reckoning, and the burning of the stars… So now, Dr Padgett, what do you think of that?"

"I'm not sure. Do any aspects of the dream, the location or the children, seem familiar?"

"No," he mutters, looking glum. "Don't think… no, none of it, and that is the part that disturbs me. Whence did this imagery come?"

"Bill asked the same question. Where and why? Susi will undoubtedly produce an answer, but until then you are free to go. Could you give us ten minutes and then send in Abda? Susi and I need to confer."

"Of course, and I'll see you both for supper, I trust?"

"Oh yes." I laugh. "Most certainly. A Badsegh special. Not to be missed."

Walsingham, standing and stretching, promptly left, shutting the door behind him.

With Walsingham out of earshot, I quickly turned to Susi.

"Children," I curtly whisper. "A dream concerning children, not very surprising. A guilty conscience, perhaps?"

At last, stirring from her meditation, Susi sat up.

"Privacy mode," she mutters, and, immediately getting her drift, I too disconnect my suit and implants from the ship. Our fertile glances and changing expressions the only evidence of our conversation.

"You still recall the unexplained incidents at St Bart's?" she whispers into my thoughts. "Walsingham was there too… Testing the same equipment… The homeostatic support modules?"

I nod.

"And yet," she continues, "someone was tampering… always at night… never found out… only suspicions… but it was Walsingham… He burnt them… froze them… from the inside… Pederasty and for why? Only for suffering."

"You cannot be certain," I challenge. "Malfunction possible… equipment prototypes… and no long-term harm… no dying…"

"Come on, Gina!" she protests. "You were there! … Who else… you or me? … No… it was Walsingham… and now he dreams of them… Monitoring carefully, I will be—"

There came a knock at the door.

"Come in, Abda," I reply.

"Hello, ladies," he says. "Malcolm says it's my turn, but who is the shit-wit?"

"Excuse me?"

"Well," mutters Abda, looking sheepish, "Eric said…"

"Said what?"

"He said, have fun with the shit-wit."

"Did he? Then I shall have words with him… Right. Now, as I'm sure you want to continue playing with Emil, lie on the couch and tell me everything."

"Very well," he says, flopping onto the couch. "Hmm… surprisingly comfy, but, for your information, Emil and I are not playing. We are conducting important scientific research."

"Oh, really?" I remark. "Is that so? Then, tell me, what are you currently working on?"

"We, madam," he replies, "are currently engaged in augmenting the food dispensers. Enabling them to provide more appropriate receptacles."

"Important work, then." I chuckle. "And why my morning cuppa arrived in a conical flask?"

"Erm, yes. Sorry about that. Merely a temporary setback. The machine's AI is giving us a terrific battle. The most unhelpful system ever encountered. With an almost gay abandon, it ignores or misinterprets every system command we give it."

"Perhaps it wants you to leave it alone?"

"Suppose" he shrugs. "The thought did occur."

"Naturally. Now, come on. Your dream…"

"Yes, right," he says, switching his thoughts. "My dream… you sure Susi's alright?"

"She's fine. Now, come on, Abda. Out with it or we'll be here all day. We haven't spoken to Emil yet, and the way he prattles on…"

"Ok, ok! My dream was this. My word was it weird. It's still freaking me out. Is that the correct English?"

"The correct slang. Go on…"

"Now," he began, "Think. Have you ever dreamt you were asleep? A sensation both peculiar and confusing, even dizzying, but that is what I experienced. Yes. As if sleeping, and yet aware of it. Asleep and awake but unable to rise. Like a ghost, newly emerged, looking down on their own cadaver. There was a sensation of, of drifting, falling? Layer upon layer of consciousness. So confusing. I couldn't get up, just couldn't!"

"It's ok, Abda." I said, trying to reassure him. "It's ok being confused. Who wouldn't be? Just keep going."

"Sorry, Gina," he replies, blinking and frowning. "Erm… yes. I felt hemmed in. Crushed. Stripped of light, energy, everything I cherished, but then I saw a girl. Shining, pale, reaching down as if to caress me. No idea who she was, but she was so beautiful! Face like ivory. Her hair covered by the hijab of an Arab princess. She touched my chest, fingers like ice. I gasped, and for a moment I was awake! Then, then, I cannot explain… I gave, she took. Yes. She certainly took something, but what? A vision, a thought? The force of it repelled her, as if we were of similar charges."

"It was the strangest thing," he whispers. "Like nothing. Nothing. Beyond my know… my experience!"

Waiting for Abda to compose himself, I looked towards Susi for support.

"What do you think?" asks Abda, sitting up. "Am I crazy? Like poor Dr Koval, going insane?"

"Insane?" I gently laugh, my hand on his shoulder. "Of course not. Even though your vision was frightening, it was no more than a loop in your consciousness. That little radiation leak is the culprit. It's been screwing with our implants for weeks."

Shaking himself down, Dr Al-Hillah swung his legs onto the floor.

"Hope so," he says, "or you'll be seeing a lot of me. Can I go?"

"If you're ready," I reply, "but thank you for being so open. Not easy, is it, admitting fear and confusion?"

"No, it is gutting. Will you be with us for supper?"

"Of course. We wouldn't miss it. Tell Emil he's next."

"Sure." He nods, straightening his suit and closing the door behind him.

"Good Lord," I remark. "What a complex dream. Highly emotive. Not surprising he's shaken by it. Do you understand its imagery?"

Thoughtfully nodding, Dr Ackermann raised her left hand, rocking it slowly from side to side: "So-so."

Thinking to the food dispenser, I ordered two glasses of water, watching in dismay as two beakers of ice slid into its dispenser.

"Here you are, Suze." I sigh. "Exactly 200ml, and, yes, it's certainly cold."

Dipping an index finger into each of slushy beakers, Suit warmed their contents to a drinkable 277 Kelvin.

After a soft knock on the door, it opened slightly, revealing the grinning face of Emilio Bedoya...

"Good after evening and night. You want my brain now?"

"Just come in." I frown. "Park your Peruvian butt and tell us everything that ails you."

"*Caramba!*" he replies. "Everything? Well, for one, my waistline? It remains a constant source of concern. Like my papa, any day soon, a barrel on legs I become, and oh, my heavens, my elbow, my toe, jaw, hip, eyebrows, giving me such antagonism. Is this immortality? An eternity of aches and pains await, and I have an itch! A burning itch just under my—"

"Emil," I cry. "For pity's sake, can it! Your dream. You had a dream. Shut your yab and tell us!"

"Yes, of course," he replies, lying on the couch. "I dreamt of sitting upon a stone bench."

"Good," I urge. "And is that all?"

"No," he admits. "You want hear rest?"

"Of course," I reply. "All of it. Otherwise, what is the point of you being here?"

"Quite so." He nods. "It is night, and I am in a high place. Cold, dark, and windy too. The air whipping about me like a frigid cloak… is this ok, not too flowery?"

"No, this is dandy, and I must say, with our implants, we're an alliterative bunch. Do you mind not scratching your itch?"

"My itch?"

"Yes. The burning itch, the one just under your…?"

"Hmm?" he mumbles, his left hand still working.

"Stop scratching your cock. It's distracting!"

"My co—? Oh, Madonna! Didn't even realise. It's my suit. Focussing on my sensations and trying to remedy them."

"Is that so?" I chuckle. "Lamest excuse for frottage I've ever heard. Now, back your dream?"

"Yes indeed," he nods, pointedly folding his arms. "Winding its way through the forested valley below is a shining grey river. Slowly climbing is the moon. Yellow, waxy, is edging above the horizon and, so strange, she sings. She is singing to me!"

"Singing? What did she sing?"

"Don't know," he shrugs. "Couldn't understand her, but the melody was full of feeling. A song of memory. Of life, of death and rebirth. Soaring, flying, leading my heart to a star, high and bright, burning red. Of course, I knew that star. I have studied it, as you know."

"Yes. Procyon. Alpha Canis Minoris. It still hasn't gone nova. Will it ever, do you think?"

"Don't know," he admits. "Its behaviour is atypical. My dream, what do you think?"

"Don't ask me," I reply. "Susi you need to talk to, but since you… Hmm… It is highly symbolic. The images represent a fresh start. A new life, or a new angle to your research. Time will tell, I think. There is nothing to worry about. Our enhancements were a new beginning. A rebirth for us all. To dream of this is hardly surprising."

"Indeed," says with a nod. "It is a truth. Is there anything else you need? Bill and I are in the middle of programming the SenSwarm. If we don't, the little bugs will be working with their cameras off and we won't see a thing. Not close up, anyway."

"No. Off you trot. Will I see you for supper? Steak and beans. Yummy!"

"Beans." He frowns. "Always beans. Didn't he grow anything else?"

"Apparently not," I reply, "but what's wrong with beans? They're wholesome, nutritious, full of fibre – as if we need it, thoroughly good for us all."

"Good for Eric, you mean. He's got sacks of the things and is trying to use them up!"

With a cheeky bow, Emil wandered from the office and closed the door behind him.

⧗

Personal Log of Dr Eric J Badsegh

Hey, Giles! A degree of normality has finally broken out. Normal for us, not for anyone else…

Gina is helping me prepare supper and, as I write, she is sadistically hacking away at a joint of raw beef like a woman possessed. Only Bill, Gina, and I are unmoved by the sight of blood. The others are decidedly squeamish.

What a woman Gina Padgett turned out to be. I've never known anyone like her! For her, life is for living. Something joyful. To be cherished, filled with experience and endless possibilities. Just ask for help and she's with you. Rolling up her sleeves, happy to tackle any task, no matter how tricky or odd. She's everywhere, into everything, and her curiosity knows no bounds.

Cooking dinner, and I am (correction: we are) preparing steak with haricot beans and a green peppercorn sauce. A bumper crop of beans this harvest and, although haricots dry and store marvellously, using them fresh is preferable. We have been eating plenty of beans…

Following a recipe from an old cookbook called Antony Makes It Easy, Gina is preparing a green peppercorn sauce. No flipping idea who "Antony" was. The damn book must be over one hundred years old, and whereabouts did she find it? Whatever. The recipe is simple, and we do have the necessary ingredients on board, so I'm leaving her to it.

Once Gina has finished preparing her sauce, I intend serving our meal during the deployment of the Snowshield. Never heard of it? Well, you shouldn't have. It's a prototype The UET refrain from publishing the specifications of their newest innovations until they've undergone thorough testing.

Ok. Before I explain further, a bit of context...

This final outward leg of our flight also happens to be the longest, and to compensate, we are to travel at an exceedingly high relative velocity. According to Walsingham, the fastest humans ever. Very impressive, but this feat comes with considerable risk. Collision with any space debris, even micrometeoroids, could pose a serious threat to the ship, so it is the job of Snowshield to absorb or deflect any spaceborne matter we encounter.

With a ring of small hatches slowly opening and a host of SenSwarm workers dashing about, the initial unfolding of the Snowshield was unremarkable. It was only when the SenSwarm coordinated their efforts that we began to see the true complexity of the design. As if weaving a web, countless curving triangles, pentagrams, and pentagons, started to appear. From our constantly shifting viewpoint, the overall appearance of the structure was hard to make out.

Still preparing supper, Gina and I have fashioned ourselves a long kitchen counter. While our crewmates (still watching the show outside) float or recline upon furniture of their own whim, I am pan-frying our steaks. Gina wishes to use the browning (the oil and juices) to enrich her peppercorn sauce. Sir Malcolm has provided a bundle of baguettes, but they are cold and decidedly chewy, so to restore their crunch Gina engineered a long toasting oven to dry them out. In a glass tower of my own design and steaming gently, my precious haricot beans are almost ready. I shall be serving them buttered, with mustard and a sprinkling of parsley.

Bong! Our dinner is ready.

Bill says his steak is too rare. Gina is giving it another minute on each side (don't see why couldn't have done it himself).

A conical network of tubing, a little over 750 metres from tip to base. Once completely unfurled, the Snowshield systematically fills with water, while the tubing's heating and selective permeability encourages a quantity of water to escape and freeze. Further ingenious pumping and heating allows yet more ice to form, covering the cone's tubular framework until it appears, to all intents and purposes, a solid. Although Abda informs me, the Snowshield isn't solid at all! The quantity of water required to fill it would be colossal. Not to mention the mass of it all. Too great for our engines to manage.

It will be another day or so before we are under way again, and by "under way" I mean relatively accelerating (we are always moving in one plane or other!) Emil has broken out the "jenever" (gin) and we are having a few, bravely toasting our future.

"Dutch courage," says Malcolm, raising his glass, and he is right to be nervous. Except for Gina (comatose for the entire duration), we are all dreading the next few weeks. The shearing forces upon our bodies will be extreme, wrenching our organs, dragging our blood and lymph all over the place. Even with our suits squeezing, holding, and supporting, it is going to be painful.

To counter these days of drudgery, to keep us "focussed and entertained" we have a series of activities planned. My contribution will be a cookery class (which should be a giggle), but without Gina around lightening the mood, my life is diminished.

Miss you, mate,

Eric

THIRTEEN

THE DEEPEST SLEEP

*I*n this penultimate section, I again find myself tying up loose ends: snatches *of conversation, jumbled images, sounds, emotions, and I have endeavoured to present these events in chronological order.*

Still accelerating, the UET Kuiper Belt Explorer is streaking past the orbit of Saturn, and all but Dr Padgett are currently on active duty. Without their suits providing support, the tremendous shearing forces upon the crew would be fatal, and yet life on board goes on as normal. There is nothing the crew can do but endure it.

These initial memories are Dr Ackermann's, and, joined by Drs Corbiere and Al-Hillah, she peers into the coma pod occupied by Dr Padgett...

"Is she ok?" *asked Dr Ackermann, tapping the polymer capsule.* "Is Suit doing her job?"

"It does appear so." *Corbiere nodded.* "And the radiation pulse. It remains, does it not?"

"Indeed," *replied Dr Al-Hillah.* "Still steadily ticking away. Soft X-rays, just like before. Very weak, extremely regular, and coming from somewhere within the ship."

"Suit," *asked Dr Ackermann,* "is Gina, ok? We've detected a minor radiation leak. Is she showing any physiological changes?"

There was a brief delay while Dr Ackermann slowly nodded (perhaps receiving communication) before a small, colourfully rippling display appeared on the wall...

"My lovely Gina is functioning perfectly," announced the display. *"No physiological changes I am both monitoring the X-ray emanations radiating from the habitation chamber and absorbing all radiative frequencies stimulating my melano-spectradermal fibres. Will persevere until my hostess is awoken from her comatose state."*

"Thank you." Susi nodded. *"That is very reassuring."*

"Form and function," replied the voice and the display quickly faded.

"Well, that is a bundle of news," said Al-Hillah. *"Gina's suit can interface with the ship. My suit can barely add up, but also interesting, Suit knows where the radiation is coming from. I only suspected it came from the core. With Suit confirming my guess, I shall look more closely."*

"Indeed," remarked Corbiere. *"How about a network of sensors? We might be able to triangulate the source, but... oh!"*

"Ha, yes!" replied Al-Hillah. *"That would certainly work, but damn, it's stopped. Just when we were winning. Still, would you care to assist? If those X-rays start ticking again, I want to be ready."*

"Sure," said Corbiere. *"I'll make a start on the software immediately. How about I embed the code in the NNCF? If it works, the sensors could be continuously active."*

"Good thinking," replied Al-Hillah, helping the others to their feet. *"Better tell Walsingham first. You coming, Suze? Eric's cooking again."*

"Sure thing," said Dr Ackermann, straightening and brightening. *"Crepes, honey and lemon. Not to be missed."*

Personal Log of Dr Eric J Badsegh

Hey Giles! Things have settled down and it is fun again. Ok. We're accelerating, and so hard, it feels as if my liver is falling out of my arse, but if I keep busy and sleep regularly, these days will pass, and we'll be coasting again. Abda calculates we are experiencing 2.974G of acceleration, and to combat this drudgery, Sir Malcolm has us engaged in various projects.

A couple of days ago, I cooked crepes for the crew – a suitable choice, something flat, as the G-forces squashed the batter into the thinnest flattest pancakes you could imagine! Pan-frying, too, in this forceful environment is also subtly different. For example, at this pressure, water boils at 413 Kelvin, matching the smoke point of the oil, and consequently there is little sizzling unless the pan is searing hot (necessary for crepes). On a hotplate or in a pan, cooking the inside of any food without burning the outside is tricky. Regular turning is crucial. Swings and roundabouts. The G-forces do make for amazingly juicy steaks.

Next, I had the crew making bread and they did well, mixing and kneading the dough with aplomb. This curious group activity was Walsingham's idea. To observe how G-forces affect the behaviour of the yeast, and, yep, the bread simply refused to rise! Because of the increased pressure, the carbon dioxide excreted by the yeast was unable to expand, and a spongey slab of dough was all we could achieve. Not until baking did the dough rise, when expansion due to temperature overcame the gravitational force. Unfortunately, the amount of compressed gas was too great for the structure of the dough to withstand, it burst, turning inside out, before collapsing it into a stodgy half-baked mess.

Abda intends running a pottery and carpentry workshop tomorrow and I shall attend. Pottery doesn't particularly appeal but learning a handicraft might be useful. No idea where he will find wood, but he is an ingenious sod, and his resourcefulness is remarkable.

Susi Ackermann and I went swimming! Gina once told me how they configured Rec Room 1 to provide a small swimming pool, but Walsingham locked out the programme.

"Waste of energy, not to mention water," he claimed. He is wrong about the water (where could it go but back into the recycler?), he has a point about the energy. Heating the water, not to mention the gravity plating required keeping the water within the pool, would require a direct connection to the ship's generators, draining each, but, with the current G-forces squashing us and everything else towards the "rear" of the ship, Walsingham relented. Such a luxury. Yet the sensation was peculiar. With few ripples and no splashing, the water was smooth as glass. None of the spillages Walsingham originally feared, and with the G-forces dragging the water from our bodies, drying ourselves was a cinch.

Abda's handicraft classes went on all day. His carpentry class was excellent, but woodwork it most certainly was not! The material provided by Abda was but a compressed mass of ligneous-cellulose fibres. It split like wood, cut like wood, with all the grain and flexibility, only it lacked the knots, splits, voids, and irregular convolutions of natural timber.

Following Abda's tutorial, I set about making a stool and a "wheel-back" chair. Embarrassingly shoddy, my stool went straight into the recycler, but I am damn proud of the chair. It has pride of place in my quarters. "Rather plain and in need of a damn good sanding", Abda remarked, but since he kept the tools simple (no lathes or power tools permitted) a good finish was hard to achieve. To carve the back piece, I used a mallet and chisel, with enormous success, but joining the framework was difficult. Requiring considerable control and precision, but I eventually nailed it, and all without a using single nail!

The pottery class was without clay. Using instead a substitute of Abda's own invention: NNCF-VariGrog. Despite its silly name, it does beautifully illustrate the versatility of the rec room's NNCF (non-Newtonian composite fluid). The potter's wheels, tools, even the furniture were shaped from it. So too was the "varigrog". Named because the amount of apparent moisture and grog (finely ground pottery) spreading throughout the "clay" was variable at will. When I say apparent moisture, there was no actual water involved. By mental command, we could soften or stiffen our clay as we saw fit. Useful for work requiring extra flexibility or resistance. Since Abda's clay substitute was incapable of true finalisation (drying and firing), the application of decoration and/or glaze was immediate.

For novices, throwing pots on a wheel is difficult enough, and with three Gs of force flattening everything to a pancake, plates, platters, and tiles were all we could make. Emil, however, bored by aesthetics, preferring something more formal, soon wandered off to work on his current project. The fabrication of high-capacity, super-durable data storage devices from a titanium alloy lattice (alpha-beta titanium/aluminium/vanadium). With rods of this alloy already performing beyond his expectations, his final objective is to produce smaller wearable items, compatible with our neocortical implants.

In forty-eight hours, I will be sleeping again but, if the

opportunity arises, I'll drop you or Mum a few lines before I sign off. When I wake, we will be approaching Pluto with some press and publicity work. If I don't contact you promptly, keep tabs on the UET's media portal. It's my turn for the obligatory interview, and unlike Gina's last fiery debacle, I promise to keep the profanity to a minimum.

Until then,

Eric

⧗

Dr Susi Ackermann, Personal Log

At last coasting but radiation warning very busy making us. Solar flare eruption. High-energy protons and EM radiation coming towards ship at light speed nearly. Activation of Compton laser array and power supply requirements taken over hour configuring. Gina, still in coma tube. To central core she is automatically moving. Compared to us she is safer.

Brief meeting of crew in central core regarding safety protocols. Also present, in place of Gina, is her suit. Abda and Walsingham uncomfortable talking to suit only, but also joking. Suit attitude more professional than Gina. About radiation knowing before us. Her suit already moving Gina to core. Suit accessing systems. Freely? For crew this is worrying. Gina's suit like a parasite becoming. Referring to Gina as hostess, caring for her solely? Before sleep tomorrow, with Gina's suit I will be talking.

Crew missing Gina, even Walsingham! Miss her also. Because of coma, will see her very soon, although many months passing.

Addendum: suspect Gina's suit memories accessing! Privacy invasion. Suit shut down and reset required. Will instruct Walsingham, Abda, and Bill, before sleeping.

⧗

Assembled from the memories shared by Dr Badsegh, this segment has me wondering. Did the act of sharing truly take place or where these memories stolen? Dr Padgett, surely aware of her suit's unsolicited intrusions, quite deliberately used the word "share" and her deception troubles me. Why would she lie? While Dr Padgett remained comatose, her suit was acting on its own volition, reading her conscious or subconscious desires and attempting to sate them.

Gathered around a large dining table in the core are Sir Malcolm Walsingham, Emilio Bedoya, and Drs Al-Hillah, Corbiere, and Badsegh. Only a fortnight from the orbit of Pluto, Walsingham is confirming the operations list of personal projects. Dr Padgett, still comatose after six months, remained in her pod. Dr Ackermann was in her quarters preparing for the next crew evaluation...

Generating a glowing display, Walsingham scratched his stubbly white beard...

"Now," said Walsingham, "it's you, Emil, Abda, and Gina doing the Pluto planetary survey, yes?"

"Of course," replied Emilio Bedoya. "We are the best qualified. Abda will send the SenSwarm to locate interesting targets before returning samples to the lab. Gina is after amino acids, Abda geochemistry, whereas I will be concentrating on the effects of solar and interstellar radiation on the surface materials."

"We plan to land the shuttle as well," interjected Dr Al-Hillah, "for short walk. Hopefully, the entire crew will join for this momentous outing?"

There was chuckling, but, before Dr Corbiere could speak of his plans, there came an event. Suddenly dimming, the illumination flickered, went out entirely.

"What?" gasped Walsingham. "Abda, what the hell was that?"

"Checking..." he replied, furrowing his brow. "Ah... it's back – the X-ray pulsations, but stronger: milliwatts... No, wait, watts. Location: crew quarters, section 5 – Susi's room!"

A klaxon sounded with a mechanical voice repeating, "Malfunction. Malfunction. Malfunction."

"Turn that off!" yelled Walsingham, and the mechanical voice and klaxon promptly went quiet. "That's better. Now, what bloody malfunction? Come on, Abda. You trained for this!"

With his eyes shut and perspiration beading his brow, Dr Al-hillah was now a part of the ship himself...

"SenSwarm," he reported, "unauthorised command sequence... but that's, that's impossible. They're in the ship!" *Then, as if in answer to his words, there came a terrible scream. It was Dr Ackermann, and, with Dr*

Badsegh at the door of her quarters in moments, he flung himself through…
She was gone.

✕

Personal Log of Dr Eric J Badsegh

Susi Ackermann is dead and are we are in bits. Bill and Sir Malcolm are trying to lift our spirits, but it is far too soon for that. Abda, God bless him, is investigating the manner of Susi's death, although the cause is quite plain. Surging in power to eleven watts, the X-ray pulse we previously detected provoked a complex malfunction in the SenSwarm. Thousands of drones entered Dr Ackermann's room, shredded her into tiny fragments, before removing her every vestige, body, suit, and implants, to the recycler. A terrible end for one so beloved. Dear Susi. She was unique. Warm, generous, friendly, wonderful sense of humour, and a leading light in her field. How will our long mission unfold without her friendship and support? In truth, I fear for our sanity.

Just back from a short meeting in which Sir Malcolm and Abda described the findings of their investigation. All was quite as expected. Every trace of Susi is now in the recycler. Following her dissolution, the mass of its contents increased by 94.585kg – the mass of her suit and body combined.

This little fact is particularly disturbing, as she is now part of the aqueous and organic reserves of the ship. Every time I order a coffee (for example) part of it will be her. Abda also reminded us how powerful the SenSwarm workers are when working en masse. Susi's death would have come quickly, in a matter of seconds. Why he thought this reassuring, I really don't know.

Emil and Bill proposed we should wake Gina and give her the terrible news, instigating a short, heated (heated by whisky) debate on the pros and cons of such a notion. Eventually, I sided with Walsingham and Abda (outvoting Bill and Emil) to leave her be. We will wake her next week (as originally planned). I for one will be in a better place to help her with the shock and the grief.

We are slowing for Pluto orbit. Although it is too dark to resolve Pluto with the unaided eye, in infrared I can plainly make out its slowly turning, thumb-sized disc of mottled grey. It is time to wake Gina and tell her what has befallen. The fellas have again detected the X-ray pulse and they are searching Susi's cabin for the source. They have found it. Unbelievable! It's that little bead of ro—

This concludes the memories made available by Dr Padgett. The remaining entry (according to its registration) is of her own making, yet I am suspicious. Was it implanted or imagined? I cannot dismiss the idea her suit participated in its creation.

FOURTEEN

THE DARK SIDE
OF THE SUN

In keeping with my thoroughness, the following instalment is in its original format. Both disjointed and rambling, it demonstrates the deliberately sloppy (bloody-minded) approach to record-keeping, much favoured by Dr Padgett for its quickness. Previously, I have endeavoured to reconstruct her shambling notes and diaries, creating order from chaos, but on this occasion (dumbfounded by their source), I have transcribed them as faithfully as readability permits.

⧖

This feels unreal. Bill Corbiere hasn't woken me. Am I unconscious still, is this a dream? I appear to be walking. Don't know where to or why – there's no horizon, up or down, nothing even to walk to. Everything is purest white. The universe is white, and I am standing upon... upon what? A floor? This must be a dream. Like Abda, I'm dreaming a dream about dreaming, but figment or not, like Felix, I keep on walking. That simile is as old as the hills.

Suit is strangely quiet. I miss her slipping into my thoughts, providing little insights, nuggets of wisdom and sense. I am running a suit diagnostic as her continued silence troubles me...

No. Nothing is wrong. She is recharging. Recharging how? From what source?

In the distance. No. No distance. Before me, I can see the fellas standing in a line. Ordered by height, Walsingham to Emil, they look like soldiers standing on parade, but what are they wearing? Surgical gowns? No. They are wearing smocks. Where are their suits? Walsingham is speaking. I am too distant to hear his words. Am I getting closer? Yes, closer. As if leaping forward, I am suddenly among them.

"Malcolm," I ask, "where are we, what's happening?" but he ignores me, and I can only listen as he finishes his sentence...

"... recording every sight, sound and sensation..."

"We still on ship?" asks Emil. "Be hallucinating. Having those crazy dreams, detailed and realistic? Pity Susi's not here. She would make sense."

"She certainly would," I reply. "Why isn't she?" Again, my question is ignored.

"Malcolm!" I then demand. "How dare you ignore me! Tell me, this instant. What is happening?" and, stepping forward, I try to grab his arm. A shock. My hand passes through his body as if one of us is a ghost.

"What?" I gasp, withdrawing my arm. "What are you, holograms? Is this some sort of trick?"

No answer.

"We require more information," Walsingham suggests. "My first question. Is Emil correct. Are we sharing a dream? If so, how can we test his hypothesis?"

"We could split up?" proposes Abda. "Determine the extent of this environment. Is this space truly boundless? We could fan out from a point of origin, and explore?"

"Very good," replies Walsingham. "Methodical exploration. Hmm... All of you. Form a circle, standing back-to-back. Then, on my command, take fifty paces."

Still in a line, naked but for their linen smocks, my crewmates obediently shuffle on the spot.

"Right," says Walsingham. "Wait for my command. Ready... set... go!"

Still in a line, they very deliberately walk on the spot, with Bill (always a stickler for precision) carefully counting his steps.

"You're not moving," I holler, but it is plain they cannot hear to me.

With Bill reaching the count of fifty they come to a halt.

"Good," remarks Walsingham, projecting his voice. "Turn and look." As before, they shuffle on the spot. Craning to examine their surroundings...

"We haven't moved," says Eric. "How can this be?"

"Very peculiar indeed," remarks Walsingham. "I suggest we try that experiment again. This time walking backwards."

"Agreed," replies Abda, the others nodding in thoughtful agreement.

Watching the five men, their faces deadly serious, walking backwards on the spot, should have been amusing, ludicrous even, but the incongruity of their situation was beginning to tell...

"Not moving!" gasps Bill, coming to a halt. "Never mind counting to fifty."

"Yes, yes," agrees Walsingham. "Stop! Your thoughts, gentlemen? Any explanation for this phenomenon?"

"Two possibilities," offers Abda. "We are here, or we are not."

"Too simplistic," says Walsingham. "Consider carefully what you mean by 'here'. We *are* here. Emil, anything to add?"

"Then, if we are here," says Emil. "Our perceptions are unreliable?"

"Excellent," replies Walsingham. "Eric and Bill, what are your conclusions thus far?"

"We are experiencing a distortion of physical laws," says Eric. "That is, our physical laws of three-dimensional space. X, Y, and Z, distance over time – the laws of our universe. They dictate our perceptions. Just because we feel to be walking, pushing off with our feet, applying a force, in this environment, the results are at odds with our expectations."

"Meaning what?" asks Bill, carefully flexing and studying his hands.

"Meaning," replies Eric, "the universe is wrong, or we are."

"Fine," replies Bill, "I vote for us. We are deceived, and therefore I propose tests of perception, reflex, and cognition."

"Bravo!" says Walsingham. "What do you suggest?"

"Well," replies Bill, gathering his thoughts, "how about a range of tests? To determine if our actions and reactions are our own or imagined? In fact, I recall a conversation with Susi concerning that very topic. It should be on file. If you want to go digging."

"Another thing," remarks Eric, "and I notice, Malcolm, you haven't mentioned her, but where is Gina?"

"She was asleep," says Walsingham. "Comatose. Why would she be with us?"

"But I am," I yell in reply. "Listen, you morons!" And I walk straight into Eric, merging my form with his, before passing through him entirely.

Taking a step back, I study Eric's demeanour...

"You alright, mate?" asks Bill, noticing Eric's expression. "For a moment I thought you looked blurry."

"I'm fine," he mutters. "Only, I'm sure I could... No. It's ridiculous. The emptiness here is freaking me out!"

"No," says Walsingham. "Don't discount anything. What, Eric? What do you think is ridiculous?"

"It's just, Gina and me. How close we've become? Well, I was thinking about her, and then, just for a second, it was like she was with me. Her perfume. I could smell her perfume. You know, the one she dabbled behind her ears, 'in case they get nibbled'. What did she call it?"

"L'eau de slut?" prompts Emil.

"Yeah" chuckles Eric. "That was it, and for an instant, she wafted right by me."

"Can you confirm that?" asks Bill. "Does your olfactory implant retain any data?"

"No," says Eric, looking puzzled. "That's just it. There's nothing. Not even an ester. Perhaps I did just imagine it."

"Nevertheless," says Walsingham, "this partially confirms Bill's suspicions. Our senses are not our own. I wonder... Eric, would you help me perform an experiment?"

"Of course," he replies. "What do you have in mind?"

"Slap me. Slap on the arm?"

"Very well," says Eric. "I see where you're going with this," and he lashes out, catching Walsingham smartly on the arm.

"Ow!" remarks Walsingham, rubbing his biceps. "Felt that, and it is still stinging. Could you go one further? Punch me. Go on, break my nose. I'm sure you've always wanted to."

"Indeed," says Eric, "but are you sure? It's gonna hurt. Could even be dangerous."

"That's the point," replies Walsingham. "Although my Hibbites will spare me any lasting harm. Come on, don't be wimp."

"Very well," says Eric, "I'm trying to, but..." He then gasps. "What the hell? My arms, they're ignoring me!"

"Try harder!" bellows Walsingham. "Come on, Eric. Hit me, crush me, kill me! Break my neck. Smash my skull. Go on, all of you!"

There was groaning, gasping, and straining, each crewman struggling to move, their arms listless by their sides.

"There," says Walsingham, wheezing after his outburst. "There we have it. Bill is correct. Our interpretations of this environment are false. In some manner, we are controlled. In fact, we may not be here at all."

Hearing this was enough for me, but then, trying to move away, I found I could not. No matter which way I tried to turn, my crewmates remained before me…

"God damn it," I mutter, "I'm in a similar pickle."

"So, what do we do?" asks Emil, becoming unnerved. "Are we trapped?"

"It would appear so," says Walsingham. "Where and why remains a mystery. Since we are powerless, we can only be patient, and this is my principal recommendation. Unless there are further suggestions?"

There was a fair degree of shrugging.

"I thought not, so we wait."

As if in reply, the distance between myself and my crewmates was suddenly growing. They were drawing away, dwindling into the distance.

"Oh, no you don't!" I defiantly mutter. Beginning to run, I encouraged my suit to propel me.

For how long I ran is a mystery. Suit wasn't keeping time as she should. How could she? The boundless white space surrounding me lacked any reference points to gauge my vector. Was I even moving?

In the distance, closing rapidly, I saw a row of six lights. Crackling and spitting like angry balls of lightning, they were dazzlingly bright. The leftmost four were small (compared to those on the right). Dwarfing the others in size and splendour, roaring and seething, was the fifth from the left.

As I drew closer, the space surrounding the lights began to shift and pulsate. No longer white, sheets and ripples of purple, yellow and green swept back and forth, bathing the immediate surroundings in a riot of colour. Moving freely among the dazzling lights were my crewmates. They seemed lost and confused. As before, without even a glance in my direction, I am both invisible and intangible, and I passed through Walsingham, hoping to get a reaction.

With Walsingham unmoved and not knowing what else to do, I similarly explored, looking for clues and information. The crackling lights were too hot for a close-up examination, so I concentrated upon the rightmost incandescence, wondering what it could be, and, with every wavelength of the visible spectrum represented in equal proportions (an unlikely natural scenario), I surmised it to be artificial or illusory.

"We're trapped!" cries Abda, blundering into a wall. "This space is bound. With walls, and, yes, a ceiling!"

"Another mystery," says Walsingham. "Your observations, gentlemen. Your thoughts?"

"We moved," remarks Bill. "Or fed a transitory sensation. Are these environments are being selectively shown to us?"

"You think?" replies Eric. "Like a guided tour of the facilities? Some facility. There's fuck all here!"

Like thunder all around us comes laughter, and so deafening, it nearly bowls me over.

"It is wrong," answers a deep and powerful voice. "Tragically wrong. Everything is here. Existing without end."

Standing taller than ever (and with enormous courage), Walsingham addresses the speaker with pride.

"To whom am I speaking? What is this place? Why are we here?"

"It questions?" replies the voice, seemingly surprised. "You are you, and this place is precisely as I wish it. As for who I am…"

"But where are we?" yells Emil, fearful and confused.

"Where?" screams the voice. "Little Bedoya surely knows already. I will show you where…"

With a flash, the room disappears, and it is as if we are floating in space, imminently approximate to a binary star system. Of the two stars, the largest is a vastness of broiling plasma, whereas its tiny companion is dark, appearing as a notch as it eclipses the larger star's outer edge.

"So close!" cries Abda. Indeed. We should have been burning, but the only radiation is a homely orange light.

"Oh, Madonna!" cries Emil. "The spectra. No. No, it can't be!"

"The spectra of what?" barks Walsingham. "Explain yourself!"

"Procyon," says Emil. "Alpha-Beta Canis Minoris."

"The little diplomat is correct," growls the thunderous voice. "And welcome. Now you may ask your questions…"

Within the chamber, the shining lights and rolling hues suddenly return, and while my crewmates huddle to confer, the thunderous voice chuckles with growing amusement.

"Who are you?" Walsingham then demands, standing tall and proud. "Reveal yourself!"

"The question comes at last," replies the speaker, "but first I prefer to reveal my associates. For we are entities all. Furthest to my right is Sense, then moving left we have Pax, Rigson, and Legato. Most sinister and shining bright comes Gleener."

Upon the mention of the name, the rightmost ball visibly dims before brightening and bobbing on the spot...

"Glee-nah!" cries a female voice. "Glee-nah, glee-nah, glee-nah!"

"Yes, yes," he answers, as if speaking to a child. "Thank you, Gleener... You Gleener? Hmmm... Anyway, that is her name, and I'm afraid she's three pecks short of a bushel. As for me? I have many names. Moloch some have called me, and Moloch will do."

"Moloch?" Abda remarks. "You name yourself... The ancient god of sacrifice and fire? He is but a myth. A pagan idol. A horror from the pages of antiquity!"

"I name nothing!" seethes Moloch. "Men name men. I merely wear their label."

"Men?" asks Walsingham. "Are you a man, then? Are you men?"

"We are. We were, and we will be."

"If that is so," demands Eric, "then show yourselves."

"We will not," he defiantly rumbles. "For we are changed. Our appearance would distress you."

"Then what is this place?" Walsingham asks. "Why are you here?"

"This place is the essence of confusion. It is chaos, limbo, pandemonium, all rolled into one. A device of infinite uncertainty. No bigger than a proton. If indeed it has a 'size' at all."

"Device?" asks Abda. "What is its function?"

"It functions as an archive. A repository of records, but this is only a consequence. The device radiates many twisting tendrils, breaching both time and space. Reaching across the cosmos, it gathers information, siphoning it towards us, and here we are kept. Compiling, storing, maintaining both the device and the many subjects brought here for interrogation."

"Thank you," Walsingham nods. "How and where are we?"

"Your little diplomat's guesses were correct. For you have come 11.46 light years, and now stand within the device. Dancing between Procyon and its lesser sibling, it devours each in turn."

"Devouring?" remarks Emil, curiosity quelling his apprehension. "Does this devouring represent a drawing of power from the stars? Could account for the unnatural ageing of the system?"

"Indeed," Moloch replies. "Although our current power demands are small, the device can drain the sun's mightily at times."

"How long did it take to get here?" asks Abda. "Where is our ship?"

"There is no single answer," says Moloch. "Within the device, time is fluidic. A flux, reacting to my whim, and, to a lesser extent, the whim of my associates. For example, we are now everywhere and every when I desire. Your ship remains when and where you left it."

There were looks of wonder from my crewmates, and I too tried unravelling his riddles. Was he evasive or merely inarticulate? How could one know?

"Yes," Moloch continues, "confusion is our mantle. Has an eternity already passed, have we yet arrived? It is impossible to tell. We are vestiges of ourselves, seen though shattered mirrors, and, because of her, because of them, we have no choice. The questioning begins."

⌛

As if by magic, I am alone once more, and space is white again. As if dusting myself down, I look for new points of reference. What is different, what is new?

The first immediate change is an odour. A stink in fact. It is so pungent I struggle not to inhale it, and my olfactory implant, going crazy, rattles off a list of compounds like bullets from a gun...

Propanoic acid, propanoate esters, butyric acid, 3-methylbutanoic acid, E-3-methyl-2-hexenoic acid...

Where is the smell coming from I wonder, before another wave of fatty compounds make themselves known: 3-hydroxy-3-methyl-hexanoic acid, 3-methyl-3-sulfanylhexan-1-ol— Enough! It smells like a pigsty. No, not a pigsty. The cocktail of substances assaulting my poor nose is far more familiar. Body odour. The smell of the unwashed. Of *Homo sapiens*, both dirty and unkempt. Yuck.

Looking about for the source of this stench, in the distance, glowing as if lit from within, I notice a barrel-sized transparent cylinder.

"Now what?" I mutter, and, moving closer, I realise the cylinder is part filled by a strangely luminous mass. As if aware of my approach, it trembles, rising and falling. Is it breathing?

"It's ok," I remark. "Not gonna hurt you. Just don't know what you are."

Kneeling to examine both receptacle and contents more closely, I behold a human face. Twisted, squashed, but unmistakably human...

"Hello?" I warily ask "Who are you? Are you alright?"

I hear no reply. A single dark eye painfully opens, and I match its gaze, hoping to receive a sign.

Then, the strangest thing. With my own eye reflected in its dark pupil – I feel great empathy, sympathy even. This being knows me. This meeting is to change our lives forever.

From the corner of its eye, glistening and sparkling, a single tear then slowly rolls. A tear of sadness, of supplication, or pleading, and as I stand, tears of own come forth...

"I'm with you there," I whisper. "Ending up like this."

As if in reply, the lips of its twisted mouth open slightly. An attempt at speech or direction? Looking about me for clues, I spy a lone figure standing some distance behind me.

"You want me to go there?" I ask, and, turning back to the cylinder, I see dark eye slowly blink.

"Very well," I reply, and turning on my heels I walk towards this distant figure, wondering who it can be.

It, or should I say he, is a man in his early twenties. With a slight build and scruffy brown hair, he is unremarkable except for his clothing: a hooded top, T-shirt, denim trousers, and trainers. Motionless and with his eyes shut, I wonder if he is dead, but lightly touching the back of his hand, I note its warmth, my ocular implant reporting a mean body temperature of 310 Kelvin. Searching his pockets, I find pieces of candy, a handful of Peruvian coins (minted between 1997 and 2009), and banknotes. In his hooded top I discover an early-21st-century smartphone. A Saulintone S2 (a valuable antique) and, after pressing its buttons, I tap its dark screen. Unresponsive, broken, or drained of power, I put it back where I found it.

His physical condition continues to trouble me. Not breathing, without a heartbeat, I'm still convinced he is alive. Wracking my brain for ideas, I have the sudden (if unconventional) impulse of kissing his forehead. An idea based on sound logic, truly. Human lips are sensitive, working in tandem with our olfactory centre, and my gentle kiss feels normal, tastes normal, smells normal. I can even detect a trace of perfume! Doubtless a leftover from embracing his mother, sister, or girlfriend, and, oh, what's this? He is urinating! Soaking into his trousers, steaming, running down his legs, into his shoes, and I take a backward step to avoid this unpleasant event.

Perching my chin on my thumb, I wonder who this strangely familiar young man could be, and, as I study his face, his eyes suddenly open.

"*Wer bist du?*" I mutter, leaning closer, waving my hand to gauge his reaction. "*Warum bist du hier? Warum erkenne ich dich?*"

He doesn't respond, and, shaking my head, I return to the glowing mass occupying the cylinder.

At my feet before the glowing cylinder, I notice a faded length of blue ribbon, and, picking it up, I run it through my fingers. Frayed at the edges, the ribbon is of considerable age, and not knowing what else to do (Suit ignored my request for a pocket) I quickly threaded it through and around my plaits. Studying my reflection in the wall of the cylinder, I adjusted the ribbon to perfection.

"Very pretty," I whisper. "If this was a gift, I am grateful."

There is no sound or communication, but the single dark eye slowly blinks, and I smile in acknowledgement.

⌛

As if by the flicking of a switch, I am among my crewmates again. The flesh-filled cylinder, the motionless man, both gone…

"What now?" I mutter, and realise an argument has broken out…

Bill is furious. He's waving his arms, shouting, ranting about command buffering, the SenSwarm, Susi… Susi? What about Susi? Then, moving to attack Emil, he lunges forward, swinging his fists, but Al-Hillah blocks his path. Unhinged by his intervention, Bill then proceeds to grab Al-Hillah by the throat. Without obvious resolution, Walsingham encourages Eric to step in, who, in expert fashion, sends both men flying, landing them flat on their backs. There is laughter. All seems forgotten, and as Eric helps the fallen to their feet, there are handshakes and conciliatory pats on the back.

The booming voice sounds again. Deafening and oppressive, as if yoking me with a terrible burden. This Moloch is a bully, both totalitarian and cruel…

"Gentlemen," he thunders, "for all you have endured, I am grateful. As a reward, we are willing to offer you the services of our transportation device. Without our intervention, it will be 6.2 years before your intended arrival on Earth. We, however, possess the technology to deposit you at the time and place of your choosing."

Closely whispering to Bill and Abda, then furiously nodding, Walsingham is laying out various options. After shrugs and back patting he steps away from the group…

"Most generous," he announces, bowing low. "And yet, sire, we have a mission to complete, a ship to manage, with a sleeping crewman aboard. We cannot leave her. She will die!"

"Noble," says Moloch, "and yet your mission is complete. Do you not yet understand?"

Forming a circle, the crew whisper in a quickfire debate.

"If that is the case, then good," replies Walsingham. "But what of Dr Padgett? What of our ship?"

"The ship and sleeping woman will be delivered in the same manner. Do you agree?"

"We require time," replies Walsingham. "May we have the rest of the day to consider?"

"You may have an eternity. There is no difference."

Another huddle. Votes are taken, and I hear four ayes and one nay. Bill muttering how he doesn't trust this Moloch at all.

Standing tall, Walsingham walks towards to the brightest light…

"We agree," he announces, but behind him Bill sighs, turning away in disgust.

"We have no choice!" snaps Eric. "Gina will die if we leave her, and I don't think this Moloch is going to take 'no' for an answer. Do you want to go back to your cell?"

"Peace," chides Walsingham, raising a long white hand. "You may not trust this Moloch, but I do. Let him finish his explanation."

"Very good," says Moloch. "You are a fine leader. Here is the information you seek… Our transportation device, although powerful, can only move one individual or object at a time. Requiring a recharge between uses. Your ship and comatose incumbent I shall return last, and Sense, the programmer of the device, is already configuring its mechanism according to my parameters. Each traveller to arrive during the first second of 1 January 2112 ad and located within the grounds of their parents' home."

"My parents are dead," says Walsingham. "Return me to the SSD in Darmstadt. What of Dr Padgett?"

"Certainly," says Moloch. "Your ship will arrive in geostationary orbit directly above the airfield of your original launch."

"What are the risks?" asks Walsingham, with Bill, cursing, "Dolt, first thing you should've asked…" to which Moloch laughs. Gurgling, wheezing, and coughing.

"The procedure is harmless," assures Moloch. "For I have used it many times myself. It is both disorientating and disturbing. The sensation of stretching between two points is never pleasant, but it is nothing a pint of… beer? Yes. Nothing a pint of beer cannot remedy. In addition, Sense will be monitoring throughout, reporting any temporal drift. Pax reminds me the universe is lumpy, with eddies, currents, and chaotic events. Who is to go first?"

"We are undecided," replies Walsingham, and there follows another close huddle with handshaking and the patting of backs…

"I shall go first," says Walsingham, striding away from the group. "What must I do?"

"Nothing," Moloch replies. "Be still and wait."

"Certainly," says Walsingham. "My friends? I will meet you on Earth. Contact the UET the moment you arrive and tell them what has befallen. They will not believe you, but tell them, nonetheless. If for any reason this proves impossible, make for the SSD in Darmstadt or the facility in Holmbury St Mary. Good luck and a safe trip."

Emanating from the walls of the chamber comes a rhythmical droning. The waves of colour pulsating furiously, then a blinding flash, and Walsingham was gone. The only sound a mechanical voice: "Temporal error. Zero point zero, zero, zero, zero, two, two per cent."

"Very good," remarks Moloch. "Close enough. Who's next?"

"But what about the error?" snaps Bill. "The temporal error? You pay it no heed?"

"Shush!" hisses Abda. "The error was tiny. Such errors are inevitable. Every system requires a degree of tolerance. Life is uncertain."

"Indeed," says Moloch. "Who is to be next?"

"Me," says Bill, edging forward, "if only to get it over with."

"Very wise," Eric chuckles, patting him on the back. "See you soon."

"Definitely," sighs a scared-looking Bill, "in this life or the next."

"There is no difference," Moloch remarks. "Guillaume? Be still and be ready."

Again, the humming sound, steadily increasing, laced with coloured illumination, closely followed by a flash, Bill's disappearance, and a mechanical voice, droning, "Temporal error. Zero point zero, zero, zero, zero, zero, six per cent."

"Excellent," says Moloch. "Thank you, Sense. I am sure both Legato and Pax did their level best. Who's next?"

"Ok, fellas," says Abda. "I'm keen to give this bag of tricks a whirl. Can't wait to… Sire? A question."

"What?" snaps Moloch. "Speak."

"Iraq?" shrugs Abda. "My parents are dust, and their house is a pile of rubble. Nothing is left of Hillah. It was incinerated, decades ago!"

"Already considered," Moloch replies. "You are to arrive at your brother's address in Paris."

"Really?" says Abda. "Superb. It will give him the shock of his life. Proceed."

"Indeed. Be still and prepare."

"I'm ready," he says. "Emil, Eric? I'll see you guys soon."

The droning, this time akin to the whining of a jet, slowly reaches a crescendo, matching the blinding ferocity of the swirling colours, before another lightning-like flash, and Abda is gone. The mechanical voice speaking, "Error. Error. Spatial error."

"Localise!" seethes Moloch as if in disgust.

"External interference," continues the metallic voice. "Spatial drift. Distance immeasurable. Temporal error. Zero point zero, zero, zero, zero, two, zero per cent."

"Very well," says Moloch. "An unfortunate glitch. Nevertheless, I am certain he is fine. Who's next?"

"Me," voices Emil, swallowing in apprehension. "Nuevo Tingo, here I come. My papa will be delighted."

After shaking Eric's hand (Eric patting him heartily on the back), Emil moves forward.

"Ready," he announces. "Mr Moloch, send me home."

The droning returns, but this time joined by an irregular throbbing. The coloured lighting increasing as before. Flashing and decreasing with Emil's disappearance.

"Malfunction," then says the mechanical voice. "Malfunction. Temporal malfunction. Temporal loop. Malfunction."

"Legato!" growls Moloch. "Why is this happening?" But, before Legato can answer, there is a blinding flash and Emil is back... Not as before. He has changed and changed dramatically. He is older. Very fat. Wearing only a tribal loincloth, with a long beard and stinking hair, his skin is smeared in orange paint. For second or two he seems bewildered, but when he sees Eric, he screams in panic and fear...

"Eric!" he gasps "Eric? Is that really you? So long, so long! The past, Eric. They are sending us into the past! Don't let them. Let him. No, no. Not him. It's her!"

"Resetting," says the mechanical voice.

"Initiate!" bellows Moloch, crushing every sound.

The droning once more. This time, continuously. Its amplitude slowly increasing.

Now half-crazed and desperate, Emil thrusts a small figurine into Eric's hands.

"Don't lose it!" he pleads. "She will need it. We will need it. Again. In the future! Don't forget."

"Never," assures Eric, and he clasps the figurine in his hands.

There is another flash, and Emil disappears. The mechanical voice sounding, "Temporal error. Zero point zero, zero, zero, zero, zero, five per cent."

"That's more like it," rumbles Moloch. "Recharge and get ready."

Examining the figurine presented by Emil, Eric shakes his head.

"My friend," he laments. "What happened? Where did he go, where is he now?"

"A distortion," explains Moloch, "inside the device's matrix, resulting in an elastic effect, altering your friend's arrival, before snapping him back here. We have corrected the distortion and your friend is returning safely to where and when I originally intended. In addition, I have instructed Gleener to erase his memory. He will be fine. All is as it should be."

"Well, thank heavens for that," mutters Eric, looking over the figurine with growing suspicion. "But what should I do with this?" (The figurine was of Emil. Old, fat, bearded, holding a representation of the Procyon system over his head.)

"Keep it," Moloch advises. "A memento of your time with us. Are you prepared for transport?"

"Not quite. I have a question."

"Irrelevant," snaps Moloch. "Your fate is now immutable."

The droning begins, the light levels already increasing.

"The temporal errors!" shouts Eric. "What do they mean? Relative to what?"

"Seconds," Moloch cruelly laughs. "The universe, from beginning to end."

"What?" screams Eric. "But that could be thousands of—"

With a flash of white light, Eric disappears.

"Temporal error," drones the mechanical voice. "Zero point zero, zero, zero, zero, zero, nine per cent."

"Good," says Moloch. "It is done. Recharge to full capacity and return the ship. Gleener? Where are you? Your assistance is required."

Slowly regaining consciousness, Dr Padgett finds herself at the UET medical facility in London. At her bedside is her mother. Nearby, a UET debriefing team look impatiently on. The date is 3 January 2112…

"Gina!" This is voice of my mother. My mother? Why can't she leave me in peace?

"Gina," she presses. "Wake up! Know you are only dozing. Come on, young lady. Don't think you can fool me!"

"Mum?" I gasp. "What're you doing here?"

"Don't be silly," she replies. "Of course, I am here. Don't you know where here is? You are home, on Earth, and you shouldn't be here at all. You see all these people? They need to talk to you. Answer their questions and we can go home."

"Home?" I ask. "Home? How did I get here, and where is Susi? I can no longer hear her, and no! Suit? Where are you? Where have you gone? Come back, I beg you!"

"No, Gina," says my mother. "Susi, she's… Now, be good girl and answer the questions."

Helping me up, she lovingly strokes my hair and adjusts my plaits…

"That ribbon?" she asks, "Where did you find it?"

BOOK THREE

REVELATION &
RECKONING

THE PLACES, THINGS, AND PEOPLE OF BOOK 3

(BY ORDER OF APPEARANCE)

HAYWARDS HEATH: A market town in the county of West Sussex, England.

DR GLADSTONE TROVE: A senior medic.

DR VERONICA FOSSIL: The assistant of the above.

CELINA BOUTABBA: A senior nurse.

EMILY GORDON: A nurse.

DAVID PADGETT: Brother of Dr Regina Padgett.

SADDLEBACK SYNDROME: A synthetic disease. A terrorist bioweapon of the late 21st century.

ZACHARY JOHANNES BURCH: The chief IT technician employed by the Halfpenny ICR.

ABINGER HAMMER: An English village in the county of Surrey.

HOLMBURY ST MARY: A village in the county of Surrey, England.

SPARQART: A semi-autonomous electric go-cart. Basic transportation for those in a hurry.

JUSTICIAR RITA RICHGUARD: A high-ranking representative of the UET.

DR HANNAH HARDCASTLE: Assistant to JUSTICIAR RITA RICHGUARD.

DR JARVIS PICEUS: A scientist working at the Hinnie Space Centre.

DR JUNIPER SMALLGRAIN: A scientist working at Hinnie Space Centre.

ISOBEL MAYFIELD (IZZY): A cybernetic programmer based at the Hinnie Space Centre.

CLOTHO, LACHESIS, ATROPOS: The trio of projectiles programmed and trained by ISOBEL MAYFIELD.

DR AUGUSTUS CLEMENTINE, GUS, GUSSY: A scientist and diagnostic engineer employed by the Hinnie Space Centre.

JOHN DE LUETT: Son of LORD CEDRIC DE LUETT.

LORD CEDRIC DE LUETT: Heir-apparent of a manorial estate on the East Sussex coast, England.

DUNGENESS COCCOON: The protective shroud covering the decommissioned Dungeness Nuclear Power Station.

SIR GILBERT DE COLLINE: Brother-in-law to LORD CEDRIC DE LUETT.

FRIAR ROGER BACON: A Franciscan monk and scholar of the mid to late 13th century.

MITA: A young girl of about eleven.

DENI: A girl of about thirteen. She is elder sister of MITA.

BRIN: A tribal chieftain.

TAVA: Wife of BRIN.

JANA: A wise woman with a striking mop of auburn curls.

QF-SCATTERTRACK: A system for detecting aircraft.

SIGRIDOR: Wife of EORL UBBA RAGNARSSON.

EORL UBBA RAGNARSSON: A Viking aristocrat, brother to HALFDAN, YNGVAR, and BJORN RAGNARSSON.

HARALD UBBASSON: Son of EOEL UBBA RAGNARSSON and SIGRIDOR.

MINKI UBBASDOTTIR: Daughter of EORL UBBA RAGNARSSON and SIGRIDOR.

HALFDAN RAGNARSSON: A Viking king and older of brother of UBBE, YNGVAR, and BJORN RAGNARSSON.

EORL YNGVAR RAGNARSSON: A Viking chieftain and brother of the king, HALFDAN RAGNARSSON.

EORL BJORN RAGNARSSON: A Viking chieftain and brother of the king, HALFDAN RAGNARSSON.

SEFA: A young teenage girl.

GUNDARSSON: A bodyguard.

FINGARSSON: A bodyguard.

COLONEL GEORGE NEEDINGWORTH: An army brigade commander.

NOAH VALDEZ: A communications technician employed by the UET.

BELTESHAZZAR, DANIEL, DANI-EL: Spiritual and political leader of the Hebrew people in Babylon.

ABEDNEGO, AZARIAH: A companion and follower of DANIEL.

HANNANIAH, SHADRACH: A devout follower of DANIEL.

MISHAEL, MESCHACH: One of the three companions of DANIEL.

NEBUCHADNEZZAR: A Babylonian king.

LEGIN: A Peruvian man.

JAQUINA: A Peruvian woman.

POOKA: A Peruvian chieftain.

TUQUO: A Peruvian girl.

INTRODUCTION TO
BOOK 3

*My dearest Gina stands in the vault under the church of St Thomas.
The floor is a swirling pool of orange light. Shifting ripples of green,
purple, and gold play upon the walls of ancient stone, their gaudy dance
communicating our successful reactivation of the portal.*

*I know what must be done. To open fully, the portal requires a
final burst of radiation, and time is pressing – police and soldiers are
closing in on our position, we know this, for we are monitoring their
communication. With the adaptive projectile weapon loaded, we are
ready, but my mistress is hesitating. She is in agony and fearful. As
ordered, I have increased the output and sensitivity of her neocortex a
thousandfold, and she is dying. Droplets of blood fall from her nostrils,
only hinting at trauma now mortifying her brain. Hurry, mistress, I
plead, release me, but Gina is reminiscing. The last six months. The events
that brought her to this final point of convergence...*

Here I stand at the point of no return, suddenly hesitating, reflecting
on the trail of murder and destruction smouldering in my wake.
Did I have the right?

If my logs survive this adventure, read them and judge for yourself. Am
I a goddess or merely a woman? Have I the right to choose the fate of
another? Now, Moloch (bearing the joke name he so greedily embraces)
does consider himself a God. Wise, benevolent, fit to determine the fate of

others at whim. A bringer of joy, of suffering, of excruciation, of rapture, but is it possible to define the boundary one must cross before becoming divine? What must one accomplish? To be a bringer of fire, or a worker of miracles? Restoring the sight of the blind? Need I be a teacher, or a guide, paving the way to the smelting of copper? In truth, these are trivialities. Changing the course of the universe? Do I have the right?

No. I am being ridiculous. Modesty is loading my question. Allow me to break free of such thinking and switch my perspective. Why should I not have the right?

Cosmologists and philosophers argue that our universe (and an infinite number of others) changes with every breath we take, so why should I not have the right? Our universe is not as it should be. It is false. Twisted and abused, by old Moloch (and others) I merely seek to restore it.

Enough! Not even sure if this crazy portal is open. Suit was convinced her last self-consuming effort would be enough, but without her, the only way forward is to fling myself in...

For Susi. For Frida. For Marcus.

Goodbye Mum.

ONE

THE HAIR TRIGGER

These words are my own, written by me, Regina Padgett, Dr of, well, I'm a doctor of everything, and no censor, editor, or legal team has touched them. Every mistake is genuine, the grammar a badge of pride, and the spelling? Perfect. Spellling words worng is something I must choose to do (my cyberbrocialcortex corrects misspelling automatically) and yet the business of keeping a diary is new to me. But, oh, I hear you cry. What about your activities aboard the KBE? Keeping a log then was compulsory, part of the experiment you volunteered for, and yet you claim not to be a diarist? Well, it's true! I simply lack the discipline, recounting every event of my life, and what to record? My excretory behaviour, my every stub of a toe, or memorable meal? How can I choose? Unless I am missing the point. Do my choices reflect my nature? The ultimate purpose of a diary, not the events themselves… Very well. I had a titanic dump this morning. Coiled like a python, it sank as quickly as the eponymous liner. My gift to posterity? My posterior. Welcome, brave reader. These words are my own.

Currently unwell, my mother resides within Haywards Heath hospital. Aww, come on, who am I trying to kid – currently? She'll be dead in two weeks. Only the beautiful control of her symptoms is hiding the ghastly truth. When the cancer finally overwhelms her organs, she will be gone.

You see, in the 22nd century, hospitals are no longer providers of healthcare. They are akin to hospices. Rest homes for the terminally ill, their "residents" little more than guinea pigs (if they forget to sign the right forms). Certainly, medical treatment is solely a domestic event. Convalescence, palliative regimes, childbirth, even major surgery, it all takes place at home.

Despite my concern, I'm trying to project stoicism, reassurance, even pride, but in truth I'm simply frustrated. With both my mother and the medical profession – not that it's their fault. The truly guilty party is likely long dead. He (most likely) was a geneticist and virologist of the 2070s tasked to develop a new strain of swine influenza so subtly lethal that in its latter stages, it remains impossible to treat. When speaking to that buffoon Walter de Boer about new variant orthomyxoviridael polyephelic melanoma (or saddleback syndrome) I neglected to mention the disease was a terrorist weapon, but it was and remains just that. An artificial plague. One designed to eradicate every pork-loving infidel it touches.

A gleaming palace of silicon-polymers and oak, my mother's hospital is an establishment both spotlessly clean and dirty – depending on the circumstances. Potted plants abound, with specially bred dogs, cats, rodents, assorted livestock, even poultry, all present from time to time. The infection control centre has so many animals wandering about, it's like a fucking zoo! This level of animal befouling seems counterintuitive, but microbial control is more to do with balance and specificity than eradication. Exposing human pathogens to both the immune systems and pathogens inherent in other species controls their populations and spread.

It is a beautiful spring day. Early May. *Die blume* are blooming, the birds are twittering, fluttering, and having sex (lucky bastards). Still, bright air comforts the brain, and, threading my hair with the ribbon I brought back from space, I doze in the back of my company limo as it speeds me to the hospital. From the moment I regained consciousness, my mother was intrigued by this length of tatty blue ribbon, but I never had a chance to ask about its significance. Can you imagine the chaos surrounding me? The UET going ape shit. The KBE had appeared out of nowhere, and their computers went haywire. Every scrap of data concerning our mission gone in an instant. The debriefing sessions went on for weeks, and the stress upon me was colossal. No time to grieve the loss of dear Susi, not to mention my crewmates… If my final experience was indeed real (and the ribbon I possess certainly indicates it was), where in God's name are they? Contacting their families, I was expecting to hear of how their sons and brothers had magically appeared, but they never arrived. Was it those errors, those tiny temporal errors? Eric realised before it was too late. "Space is lumpy," Moloch said. "Full of eddies and hidden currents." The issue is not *where* my crewmates arrived, but *when*.

Rather than going directly to my mother's bedside, I first check in with her medical team. Because of my enhanced physiology (and amazing celebrity status), the consultant oncologist Gladstone Trove and his assistant Veronica Fossil are always happy to see me…

"Good morning," I say, shaking hands. "Lovely and bright. How is she doing? Any further deterioration?"

Dr Trove looks me up and down with a clinical eye.

"Dr Padgett," he replies. "Good to see you. No. Your mother remains stable. Her final downturn is due next week, and we will be changing her containment regime to one of palliation. I'm sorry. At this late stage, there's nothing else we can do."

"Don't be sorry," I reply. "Your care and treatment of her has been exemplary, and please, call me Gina."

"Thank you. It is heartening to hear you say that, but it is Dr Fossil you should be praising. My workload means I'm a hummingbird, flitting from blossom to blossom."

"Certainly," I reply. "Our lives are comparably busy. I'm never in one place for long."

"Nonetheless," he says, "sorry I missed you last week. If only for reasons professional."

"Professional? It's not as if I am ill. Another couple of centuries and I might need your help, but so far, not so much as a pimple. How could my inhuman vigour be of interest?"

Blushing, Dr Trove patted a heap of files on his desk.

"My dear Dr Padgett," he laughs. "See these files, brimming with disease and malady? My life overflows with them. To meet a woman so disgustingly healthy is a marvellous relief. I know of a hundred clinicians wanting to get you under their medi-scanners. Only, I gather your technical bits are classified."

"Very classified, I'm afraid."

"Shame," he says. "But now, before you go in, understand she is very weak. No undue stress or emotion. If you have any questions, seek out the nurses. It's Sister Celina… Bouttaba, and HDN Emily Gordon today, isn't it, Vee?"

Dr Fossil nods, her blonde ringlets bouncing like springs. "Today and every day," she replies.

"Fine," says Dr Trove. "You're free to go in, and I understand your brother is coming?"

"Yes. So, batten down the hatches."

⧗

The hours with my mother were mostly unremarkable. We chatted, drank hospital tea (ghastly and contaminated with chicken soup) and discussed the world at large. At no time did we discuss her illness or symptoms, and until my brother arrived, we didn't mention her health at all.

David and I are quite different characters, although you could (Susi would) say our diverging personalities are the one true similarity. Our shared need for independence and individuality drives us apart. David is the older sibling, but I am slightly taller. I am academic, while he is creative, an accomplished artist, his elegant drawings and euphoric abstract paintings adorning many an office, gallery, and book. Sent to single-sex boarding schools at an early age, our childhoods were separate. Winchester for him, Roedean for me. I thoroughly enjoyed Roedean, but David struggled through his lonely years at Winchester, and not until we were of university age did our kinship truly flourish. At St John's Cambridge, I similarly thrived, whereas David's struggle, striving for a BA in Art with German at the Slade School in London, he prefers to keep to himself. His paltry second-class degree, despite my teasing he should become a teacher, has proven only a trivial hindrance.

As is his wont, David will sneak-in and surprise his "little sis" with a tap on the shoulder. The only problem? These days, I can hear (and smell) the silly dolt from half a mile…

"Hello Dave," I chuckle, as he tiptoes behind me.

"Bah," he grumbles. "Robot Reggie's no fun at all."

"No," says my mother, preventing a barb of my own. "Don't start with the sniping. Many opportunities for the disagreements when I am gone. Save them for my funeral."

Letting go of his churlishness, my brother joins me at her bedside…

"Ah," says my mother. "Glad we are together. Recalling so many memories. David, so much like your father, and Gina. Dear Gina. So much of my mutti, and your big nana's fire. Oh, and I see you're wearing her ribbon. How sweet it looks too."

Picking up my mothers' medi-comp, David studies her notes…

"Why's this here?" he says. "Mum doesn't need to see this! Reggie, what were you thinking?"

"Because it's the truth," I reply, "and knowledge combats fear…"

"Bollocks," he snorts. "All this will do is frighten her. You haven't read this, have you Mum?"

"Of course," she replies. "And will you stop talking over me? I'm right here. Not blind nor deaf, and certainly not dead. I can decide for myself!"

With almost impeccable timing a nurse carrying a tray of meds comes in. Her clear blue eyes convey an aura of kindness and care…

"Hello, Celina," says my mother. "Have you met my family?"

"Only Gina," she replies, looking over my brother. "But you must be David? Yes. You fit the description perfectly."

Seeing David roll his eyes, my mother chuckles with glee.

"So," asks my mother, "what is it today? The usual?"

"Afraid so," says the nurse. "A pot of pills and two hypos. You want to do the hypos, Gina?"

"Sure. In the tummy?"

"If you would," and she offers me the syringes.

"Oh, God," groans David as my mother loosens her gown. "I don't wanna see this. I'm off for a coffee. Be back in a bit."

"He'll be back," I mutter, and, gently pinching my mother's black-skinned belly, I give the first injection.

Well, this diary of mine is a disaster! So boring. Did I mention I am not much of diarist? Typically, I focus on the trivial, skipping through the important bits with scant regard for the reader. Allow me to cut to the chase…

David is a difficult old sod. Always been a curmudgeon. After our dad died his tolerance and patience shattered like glass. He is married, of course, with a family (wonderful kids), but outside this sphere he can be impatient, vindictive, selfish, and my does he profane. Swears like a trooper. But I still love him, if only for the sake of his wife…

"So, come on, Mum," I prompt, unthreading the ribbon from my hair, "tell me. You never explained. This ribbon, why all the fuss?"

"No fuss, really," she shrugs. "Just a family heirloom I thought we had lost. The ribbon was your big nana's. A gift from her father, and after his death she treasured it. When you were little, about three or four, she gave it to you. She would thread through your plaits, just the way you do now, but you soon lost it, playing in the garden. Your big nana was devastated, and she searched for over an hour. Was it in your pocket all along?"

At this moment, I suddenly found myself in a quandary. Should I reveal how I came by the ribbon? Bearing in mind, I still was unsure how I came by it myself. Those last moments I shared with my crewmates live in my cybercortex with startling clarity, but are they real? Nothing more than anomalous data? A zygotic fantasy, a memory slowly developed in my dormant, comatose mind?

Decision made. I lied.

"Must have," I sheepishly shrug. "One of the few things I took into space as a reminder of home."

"Gina!" she chides. "You're such an imp! Your poor nana. Not knowing, and for all that time, but I am glad you still have it. In fact, all this talk of your childhood is making me halcyon. Could you bring the photo box tomorrow? I would like to share some memories… A good thing, before I go?"

"Of course," I reply. "I'd like that. Are you referring to the suitcase in your wardrobe? You told us never to touch it."

"Yes," she states. "I did. Very precious things in that suitcase. Only shown you a selection of what it truly contains. High time you saw everything, assuming you haven't peeked?"

This time telling the truth, I shake my head. Throughout our childhood, the metal case in the back of my mother's wardrobe was strictly off limits. At the time I wondered why, but in recent years its very existence had slipped my mind entirely.

Returning the following day, I find my mother sitting up, watching the chickens scratching about in the hospital garden.

"Ah ha!" she cries, the suitcase under my arm. "You got it. Pop it down and open it up."

Popping the catches and raising the lid, I find the case chock full of heirlooms. Photographs, bundles of letters, data storage media, all of them archaic. There are further boxes too. One of them inlaid with a silver "Frida". Lifting it out, my mother fondly strokes its ebony lid…

"Yes, yes," she wistfully remarks. "This is the one. The photos should be in here."

Depressing the catch, she hands me my great-grandmother's engagement and wedding rings. Still in their boxes, the wedding ring is a simple band of gold, but the platinum engagement ring, with its single red garnet, fire opals, and tiny glittering diamonds, is stunning. I try it on the tip of a finger…

"Beautiful," says my mother. "Made to match her eyes. You want to keep it? I'm sure she wouldn't mind."

"Oh, yes," I reply. "Needs adjusting; it's tiny!"

"She was just that. Look…"

Beneath the ring boxes is a packet of paper photographs, and my mother passed them to me one at a time. Family photos. My big nana, her husband, relatives, children. The adults dwarfed her, but in no way did she seem intimidated…

"Good Lord, yes," I reply. "She's dinky. Who are the people? Oh, now I see it. There's writing on the back."

Reading the handwriting upon the reverse of each photo informs me of my ignorance: Millicent, Jimmy, Lucy? The surnames strike more chords. There are Padgett's, a number of Halfpenny's, but it is the Corbiere's that strike me the most. Recognising the family connection with my crewmate Bill Corbiere. They looked just like him!

"Corbiere." I smile. "Always enjoyed the coincidence. I mean, what are the chances? Big nana knowing Bill's great-grandfather?"

With a shrug, my mother passes another photo (the one that started it all) …

"And there you are," she remarks. "On the knee of your big nana, the ribbon in your hair and" – she chuckles – "Already half her size."

"Ah, that's lovely," I reply with a smile. "What a fab image. Who took that one? Was it you, can you remember?"

"Your father. It was a family meal. Your big nana's birthday. Eightieth or eighty-first, not sure which. Many photos were taken that day. Big nana would sit you on her knee, sing *Hoppe, Hoppe Reiter*. She loved her little Gina, but of course, in those days, with gappy teeth, you couldn't say Gina, you'd say…"

"Gleener," I replied, suddenly remembering, and my stomach tightened as if I had swallowed a brick.

Returning the photo to my mother, she passed two more, each of them old, battered, and creased. The first was of my great grandmother. Wearing a headscarf, young and delicately pretty, she was leaning on a statue in front of building flying the Jordanian flag.

"Holiday snaps," I remark, "How quaint."

Turning the photo over, I read the description: 'Amman, winter 2011. Marcus took this before we viewed the sarcophagus.'

Shrugging, then examining the second old photo I yelped. Well, it was more of a squeak...

"What is the matter?" frowns my mum, "Have you sat on a needle?"

"No," I chuckle. "Only, the young man in photo. Who is he?"

"Read the back. What does it say?"

It said: Marcus, Lima, June 2011. I took this on our way to the museum. The last one.

"Marcus," I ask, "Who's he?"

"Big nana's last boyfriend. The one before she got married. A sad story too. He disappeared. They were on holiday in Peru. Her boyfriend went out one evening and disappeared. She assumed he was abducted. Murdered perhaps. She never found out...Why are you looking so blanched? What's the matter?"

"I've seen him," I said. "Looked just like that. Seems crazy, but the memory is as clear as day."

"You've seen him?" she asks, "Where? You sure you haven't seen this before?"

"No, mum," I reply. "Never. Only, you know the strange dream I told you about. That was when I saw him. Same clothes, same everything. Seeing him now, it's freaking me out."

"Oh, Gina," she urges, "You didn't, sweetheart. It wasn't really him. You just think it was. You know how dreams can be. They merge, overlap, distort and muddle. Confusing."

"Yes," I reply releasing a breath, "Certainly. Now what's the little stick, the one with the shiny end?"

"This?" says my mum, holding it up, "A memory stick. Big Nana's diaries. Letters, I think. Heaven knows how you would access it. You want to try?"

"Yeah, ok," I reply, "I'll give it a go. Hopefully, they'll be more about Marcus, but love letters, secret diaries? Love letters would be fab. Especially if they're juicy."

"Gina," chides my mother, "Your own family. Sometimes you're incorrigible!"

After going through the rest of the suitcase my mother began to tire. Kissing her gently as she slept, I carefully repacked the suitcase and made my way home. Messaging my brother, I reminded him to visit the same evening.

⧗

Furiously angry. No. Beyond furious. Beyond livid. I despair. I weep for humanity, for charity, for understanding. How could a civilized society behave this way?

My mother is dead. David at least was with her, waiting for me to arrive, with my mother listening and waiting as well, but her last flicker of strength went out minutes before I arrived. It was bureaucracy that delayed me. Bureaucracy, the belief that money, property, and the rule of law, scratched in ink or carved in stone, transcends love, family, and faith.

The deterioration of my mother's health occurred rapidly, exactly as predicted, and in her final days, I became her sole carer, feeding her whenever she hungered, cleaning, and maintaining her dignity, providing at least some degree of distraction from the horror of it all, and knowing precisely when the end would come, my brother and I agreed to be at her bedside. Expecting a long and difficult night, I passed the morning keeping fit, lifting weights, followed by a run around Winchelsea, pausing only to check on my bees. Note: my muscles are still recovering from a decade in space, and although our suits did help alleviate muscle wastage, I am significantly weaker than I was in 2104.

⧗

Noon the same day, I detect four individuals moving stealthily around the side of my house, with another four standing out front. By the size and shape of their thermal profile, I judge them to be men. If they turn out to be burglars, they are going to be disappointed. Apart from my lunch, there is little here of value…

There is a firm knock at the front door, followed by another coming from the rear.

"Oh, fuck off," I mutter.

Leaving my second helping of pasta, I stride to the front door.

Before opening, I examine more closely the thermal image of the individuals beyond. They are certainly men. Eight in all. Two on the doorstep, two in the street, and four behind my back door.

Covering the natural exits, fellas? How rude.

Opening the front door, I confront the men on my doorstep.

"Dr Padgett?" asks the closest agent (for agents they are), glancing towards to a display on his wrist. "Dr Regina Padgett?"

In his eyes, I see a tiny picture of me, and smile at their plodding formality.

"Yes," I reply. "I am she."

"Good," he says. "May we come in?"

"No. What do you want?"

"Only this," he states, "and I am sorry, but the UET compels us to deliver the following summons. You are hereby ordered to the Hinnie Space Centre in Surrey for re-evaluation and reassignment."

"Reassignment," I remark. "To where? The UET are in no position to order me around. I work for the Halfpenny ICR, in London. I'm not going anywhere."

"You are mistaken," he replies. "We have paperwork saying otherwise. You are both an employee and the property of the United European Technologies Corporation. Failure to comply with this order is a direct breach of company policy."

"Bullshit," I snort. "What you suggest purports to slavery, but I will comply with your request. If only to give the moron in charge of this piss-pool a piece of my mind!"

"That is the issue," he replies. "Your mind, to whom does it belong? You or the UET?"

"It's mine, of course! And I shall be joining your superiors on the appointed date to prove it!"

"Excellent," he says, handing over a wafer chip. "Here is your copy of the summons and statement of authenticity. I suggest you study them at length."

"Intend to," I reply, snatching the chip. "And hope to never meet your sort again!"

"Very well. But know we are ordered to keep you under surveillance until we receive your acknowledgement and signature of the documents. Have a pleasant afternoon."

"There is now nothing pleasant about it," and I slam the door in his face.

Returning to my congealing pasta, I toss the chip onto the table.

"Wankers," I mutter.

Pouring a glass of red wine, I down it in a sequence of hearty gulps.

TWO

BREADCRUMBS

Oh, blessed serenity. It's so good to be back at work. The calming familiarity of the routine. The order, the chaos, the science, and the scientists. Those wonderful, crazy people. Brilliantly unpredictable, both vague and intense. Serving humanity with little or no regard to their physical, mental, or social well-being. Of course, they can be difficult company. Their dress sense non-existent, their hair a mess, their armpits decidedly whiffy, but they are my people. Real people. There are no hollow heroes in the realm of science. They are our leaders, the saviours of humankind. The cleaners of the planet. This planet we routinely defile.

Keeping busy is suppressing both my anger and grief, and I have a three-week backlog get through. This mountainous pile of administration I could lessen by a factor of ten, mentally processing the material requests, research permissions, safety assessments, ethical enquiries (and several letters bemoaning the antisocial behaviour of a Dr Larkin), but I'm doing it the old-fashioned way. One document at time, with a pen, broken only by brief periods accessing the food dispenser (still no biscuits).

Between every breath, my thoughts return to my mother. Her funeral service in Winchelsea was incredibly moving. A huge turnout by the town. Every pew filled. Silent mourners lining the streets as my mother's cortege crept by. Her eco-sensitive burial (unusual but I would prefer it) was one of extreme vacuum desiccation, followed by disintegration and dispersal, returning her matter to the environment. Only then could our closure begin. The terrible clear-out. For reasons of sensitivity, we sent her clothing and trivial effects all the way to the recycling centre in Brighton.

Done with my correspondence and administration, I head to the computer centre. They claim to have a gadget to access the memory stick given to me by my mother. Although excited by the prospect, I'll be mightily surprised if any data remains…

The chief engineer (Zach), is a good friend of mine, and why wouldn't he be? I'm a walking, (incessantly) talking computer, with norks! He likes norks.

"Hey, Dr P!" he chirps. "They said you were coming by. Got some old relic. Am I right?"

"Hi, Zach," I reply. "Yeah, my mother left me this. A memory stick. Must be a hundred years old. Can you see if there's anything on it?"

"Hmm…" he mumbles, taking the stick and peering into its socket. "Universal serial bus. Shouldn't be a problem. Got a new toy from the UET for socketing. Bus putty. Makes stuff like this a cinch."

"Doesn't look very hi-tech," I remark, prodding its malleable surface. "What is it? What does it do?"

⧗

Zachary Johannes Burch, 33, lives near Dorking in the small village of Mickleham. Graduating from Portsmouth University with a first-class degree in applied computing with mathematics and linguistics, he joined the Halfpenny Institute of Cellular Research in 2107. After publishing papers on spectracote information engineering, he rapidly rose to his current post of chief engineer.

When interviewed, he lucidly described Dr Padgett's desire to examine the contents of an antiquated data storage unit, colloquially known as a "memory stick".

Quickly accessing said device with a block of NNCF self-configuring interface material, he found the memory stick to be blank (rather than corrupted) with but a single file.

Asking Dr Padgett's permission to access this file, it read as follows: For Gina's Eyes Only.

Confused by this message, he asked Dr Padgett if she understood its meaning. Dr Padgett never replied. As if lost in thought, after retrieving the memory stick, she left without so much as a word.

No further contact reported between Mr Burch and Dr Padgett and this report fragment ends here.

Inq. W. de Boer

⧗

This is incredible. what just happened? Zach opened the root directory of the memory stick, just as I asked, but while he was babbling about a tiny text file or other, millions of bytes slammed into my cybercortex like a truck. What is this mysterious file? A journal? A diary? Written by whom? That Marcus chappie? Broken into seventeen parts by an unknown editor, there are italicised commentaries, doubtless written by other authors, and, most wonderfully, references to the life of my great-grandmother, Frida Padgett (nee Halfpenny). This is exciting. A mystery. Good Lord, how I love this sort of thing. Beating like a drum, my heart is urging me to unravel this textual conundrum. No. I need to calm down. Wait, girl. Wait until you are home.

At last, in my London flat, wine to the of left me, tea to the right, after a slow exhale I close my eyes and begin…

Yes. My great-grandmother's ex-boyfriend was indeed the author of this text. He begins by describing his sudden abduction and the conditions of his incarceration, and at first, it is all entirely plausible, but then, strange inconsistencies begin to seep in. Poor Marcus is not in prison at all! He is merely in storage. Brought by Moloch to his oubliette for a period of interrogation. His prison experiences are a fantasy. His sensations, visions, even memories. They are artificial.

Within these early entries Marcus writes of conversing with two entities. Never meeting them in person, they remain enigmatically invisible. One, the male, is authoritative, cold, and severe, and I consider him a construct of Moloch (the later chapters reveal him to be the very same). The second entity, coming after, is both supportive and yielding. She comforts and coerces Marcus with her beguiling voice, providing matronly reassurance, guiding him with friendship in the writing of his journal.

In the second section, Marcus begins to compose his account (a task placed upon him by Moloch to secure his release), a description of his experiences leading up to his capture: "tell us why you are here".

Unfortunately, Marcus didn't understand why he was "there" at all, but after careful prompting he begins to recount the funeral of his uncle. There is little of interest here. The writing is clever, clearly observed, thoughtful, and dryly sarcastic. The only segment of note is his first encounter with Graham Corbiere. The great-grandfather of my dear friend and crewmate Bill Corbiere, sadly lost in space some months before.

Concerning the female entity, the third chapter is brief. Strangely beguiling to Marcus, the woman 'Mirra' is already a firm favourite. Although, when I say woman, I mean feminine voice. There is little evidence she is a woman at all! Marcus never sees her. He only hears her, and only through the imaginary loudspeaker set into his illusory cell door.

The identity of Mirra troubles me. Her childhood recollections seem stereotypical, but I know the lullaby she sings. My great-grandmother sang it to me as well! Now, this might a coincidence. The lullaby a cultural leftover. An activity so incredibly popular at the time it was ubiquitous, before societal changes cast it aside. It does happen! Consider the use of tobacco, the wearing of the bustle, the ruff, or the inexplicable popularity of Jimmy Savile…

I digress. Mirra claims Moloch bestowed upon her two names (both little more than epithets), Cercaria or Mirra. Peculiar choices. Marcus wonders if she means "Mirror" before going on to pen her name phonetically, writing: "she has never asked me to change it". The other name bestowed upon her, Cercaria, she regarded as insulting. A word I know very well! It is an outdated biological term formerly used to describe the larval stage of a parasitic organism. Not very nice.

The next four chapters, recounting Marcus and Frida's early dating experiences, fill me with joy. The growing love they have for each other warms me better than any claret, and Frida! We are such kindred spirits. True mirrors of the soul. The way she thought, the way she laughed! Rolling up her sleeves, happy to tackle every obstacle life could throw at her. Like me, but so much more. Indomitable, that's what she was. Bet she was amazing in bed.

The eighth chapter starts gently. Marcus is lonely and bored. Hardly surprising. His drab imaginary lodgings are perfect for depression, and his paranoia is already beginning to grow.

By accident or design, when Mirra returns, she reveals both her education and ignorance. She possesses a great deal of cultivated learning but lacks the mundane, and I am struggling to imagine why this should be. My current hypothesis hangs upon Mirra living a cloistered life, receiving her education from a tutor of high values. The commonplace they regarded as an irrelevance.

The guessing game they then play is of similar interest. She manipulates him. Marcus left himself wide open to it, but she did reveal a few things (did he understand their significance?). Her reluctance to reveal the time and date was telling. It reminds me of Moloch explaining how "time is fluidic, a flux, reacting to my whim". Mirra could very well be unaware of the time and date! She then admits working for Moloch, reluctantly, under duress. She seeks to undermine his authority whenever she can.

The rest of the chapter deals with Marcus clearing his deceased uncle's house. Books and folders are his primary concern. Only towards the end is my interest piqued, with Marcus striving to find the key to a mysterious trunk. After rummaging in the most unlikely of places he does eventually find his prize, and Marcus is triumphant, but I find the whole scene deeply suspicious. Did Marcus not consider how peculiar this was? He knew something was amiss, but he casually shrugged off his discomfort, as nothing more than the spookiness of the silent and empty house. Frustrated only to discover a bundle of folders inside the trunk, his mood was countered by a little marble rolling across the desk before him, and there we have it! A tangible connection. I saw a similar object on Mars. It held my attention as well. I became drawn to it.

The folders contained the private research of Marcus's uncle, they connect every mystery he uncovered. The decisive factor? The figurine, of course! Identical in every way to the figurine given to Eric by Emil. Quite how Marcus's uncle came into the possession of this copy isn't clear. Was it truly a gift? I think these folders represent the beginnings of a trail. A trail of breadcrumbs, leading to my missing crewmates and friends.

The next chapter, the ninth, concerns Moloch's intimidation and interrogation of Marcus. Like a playground bully, he terrifies the poor boy with thinly veiled threats, tricks of light and sound. Moloch is particularly interested in Mirra's choice of name, reciting "a companion's words of persuasion are effective." Is this an explanation for her choice?

Now, I have a library in my head, and it did not take long for my cybercortex to find this quotation in the translated writings of Homer, yet it has me wondering. The connection is too obvious. Mirra is indeed a companion to Marcus. It was why Moloch provided her. Only, the situation is more complex. Consider Mirra's deception. She talks to Marcus instead of texting, demonstrating both her commitment to Marcus and the contention between her and Moloch, and, because of this, the name "Mirra" continues to trouble me. Not the word, or the spelling, but the pronunciation. Marcus assumes her name is Mirror, but he simply writes it how she says it, Mirra.

Ok. Let us assume her sobriquet is indeed Mirror. What of it? What is a mirror? A reflective surface producing a virtual image, but what of the word itself. Its etymology? In Middle English, mirror was *mirour*, from the old French word *mireor*, *mirer*, to look at, where in English we find the word admire. No help there. Digging further into the past, I find the Latin word *mīror* – "to wonder at" and *mīrus*, meaning "wonderful" (miracle). The earliest reference I can find for a word analogous to "mirror" comes from the seventh century bc, and eureka! I have it. Homer is indeed a clue. *Glene* is the term he used to describe a mirror, or indeed, a reflection. Now I understand. Mirra is Gleener, Gleener is Mirra, and this revelation fills me with horror.

Concluding the ninth section, Marcus briefly recounts the hallucination he suffered while unconscious from fainting. This confirms the memories I acquired from my time in space. I witnessed actual events. For when Marcus briefly hallucinates, he is in truth conscious. He felt me kissing his forehead, going on to behold me as I beheld him, appreciating my figure (as any hot-blooded young man) as I quickly moved away.

The tenth chapter begins slowly. Only the arrival of Graham Corbiere, and his eccentric colleague shed light upon my suspicions. They provide further confirmation of my memories. I did witness an aged and dishevelled Emil presenting Eric with a figurine. Upon separating the bundle of folders, Marcus and Frida examine the contents of the first. Its documents and photographs all concern the removal of a skeleton from a wall. The parchment fragments are key. The two-circle diagram, clearly relating to the figurine, is a representation of the Procyon binary star system – a view we all shared, and brilliantly collated by Marcus's uncle from little more than scraps gathered during his solitary life.

The later chapters bring even more to consider, far too much for one session, and, employing a similar approach to Marcus, this account will deal with each folder in turn. Right now, I need to hit the hay. I'm travelling to the Hinnie Space Centre tomorrow, to meet the total fuckwit claiming my delicate self UET property. A ridiculous notion. What will they do when I say no? Do they plan to dissect me? Idiots. When I speak to the originator of that order, I'm going to give them a piece of my mind… Ha! A strange expression. A piece of my mind. It is exactly what they are after.

THREE

RECONDITE REASSIGNMENT

Today promises to be headache-inducing. In fact, my head is already throbbing, but not from last night's bacchanalian quaffing (my Hibbites chewed the alcohol away hours ago), it is the prospect of travel. The government frowns upon travel beyond the limit of human (or animal) endeavour. Not that they have a choice. The recent slew of international emission control treaties restrict long-distance travel, and, unless you are an industrialist, shipping freight, a governmental official, a scientist, or in the military, you're out of luck. In the UK, for example, even moving beyond one's parish boundary requires a licence, and wading through the mire of red tape needed to obtain an international travel permit deters all but the most determined. Localism is the order of the day, and I cannot help feeling envious of the freedom of movement enjoyed in the past. Air travel, for example? Swift and so horribly polluting, it has become an unobtainable luxury. A privilege reserved solely for the government, the military, or freight of a crucial or perishable nature. Want to pack your trunks, hop on and plane, and whizz to the Costa del Sol? Forget it.

Today, I'm only going thirty-five miles, and for half of the day I'll be doing just that. First, I need the obligatory licence. Yep, I'm serious! George Orwell? You were right. You just got the year wrong. 1984? Ha! They had it easy. Try living in 2112. We're prisoners. Everywhere we go, every word we say, all that we buy. Every fart duly logged and reported.

As I write, my mind is accessing the government travel bureau, stating my name, address, destination, purpose of journey... There. Done. "Big Brother" approves of my plan and is displaying my travel options. Quickest and most convenient, I can join the passengers of an autonomous (self-driving) road vehicle. A car. Propelled by an outdated (and underpowered) hydrogen fuel cell. Boasting a top speed of 60mph, it will get me where I want to be, but, since its passengers determine the route, how long it takes depends upon their requirements. Yes, I know. You think me a moaner, and you could well be right. My entire journey is gratis. Free from beginning to end, but you don't know who you'll be sharing the car with! Teenagers, a rustic, a farmer, bawling children, or someone just wanting to talk. In days gone by, the prospect of small talk would have encouraged me to walk, but these days I simply switch off my ears, turn off my nose, and seek temporary sensory oblivion.

Ok. Piece of cake, you might think. Walk outside, wait ten minutes, a car pulls up, and off I go, but there's a hitch. The car only goes to Abinger Hammer, miles from the Hinnie Space Centre, and, with the connecting roads little more than gullies strewn with sandstone rocks, further travel becomes inelegant. Walk, cycle, horse (horse?) or, for a fee, the use of a SparQart. An autonomous, single-seater buggy.

After a childhood reading the books of Ruby Ferguson, the very notion of riding a horse, galloping through forests, leaping hedges and gates, was a dream come true – until I saw the depressed state of the only available steed. I couldn't bring myself to mount the shaggy old thing. Plumping instead for the SparQart, less than thrilled at the prospect of a bouncy thirty minutes, strapped to its seat like luggage.

A bruising *hour* later, I sit in the Hinnie Space Centre's library, under the gaze of eminent Justiciar Richguard, the most prominent UET official in England. As she shuffles the notes on her desk, I wonder how she climbed to her lofty appointment. According to my records, before her promotion, Rita Richguard was a lowly corporate lawyer. Certainly, "Justiciar" is misleading. In the Middle Ages, the title justiciar was for political officers, rather than lawyers or judges, but the UET have appropriated the title to decorate their ambassadors, directors, and senior executives...

"Dr Padgett?" she begins, and I nod. "Thank you for coming so quickly. My name is Rita Richguard, the UET justiciar in charge of this facility. After receiving a high-level dictum placing you here for re-evaluation, I had no choice but to summon you."

Shifting in my seat, I know something to be wrong. At 105 beats per minute, Rita's heart tells of anxiety, and I study her, listening to her breathing, her gurgling guts, her creaking joints, and her scent is revealing too. Lavender shower gel, a spicy deodorant, and something else… Ah, yes. Juniper berries. A gin and tonic for lunch? Can't say I blame her. Certainly, Rita Richguard is an intensely cautious woman. Her caliginous skin, olive-ringed eyes, and greying brown hair speak of toil and worry, and I'm sorry, but I just don't like her. She casts too many shadows! Ambiguity is her enemy. Suspicion her venomous bite…

"However," continues the justiciar, "I have a problem. The author of the directive eludes me. It's all quite proper, mind you. The coding, the wording, the procedural references, but there is no signatory. Do you know its source?"

"Of course not," I reply, "and to learn your dragging me here was just to cover yourself? Your problems are your own. Say what you want or I'm off!"

"No, I can't let you go," she says, "Please. Spend a couple of days with us. Allow me to untangle this mystery. Then we can discuss options. Ok?"

"Very well," I sigh. "If you're prepared to feed me, clothe me, provide me with booze, baguettes, and knickers, hanging around won't be too bad. The views nice. Decidedly tree-ish. The spruce plantations remind me of Sweden, but I will need something to do. Excessive thinking invariably makes me sad."

Smiling and clearly relieved, the justiciar slickly configures a small display on her desk, entering a long code before offering her eye for identification.

"There," she reveals. "Done. You are logged as an official visitor, and I've raised your clearance level to delta black. Necessary while you are here."

"Thank you," I reply. "That's very gracious, but why the sudden upgrade? Last time my clearance was fine."

"Why?" she says. "Because there's more here than meets the eye. Much more. Did you stop to think why a such a minor outpost needs a justiciar?"

Tapping the display on her desk, she quickly addresses it. "Hannah, could you come in please? Dr Padgett is ready for her tour."

"Tour?" I remark. "Tour of what?"

As if in answer to my enquiry, a section of bookcase was losing its solidity. It was becoming ghostly, diaphanous even. A slender young woman stepping through as if it didn't exist…

"Clever," I acknowledge. "A skin of NNCF. I was aware of its hypersonic emissions when I came in. A recent modification?"

"Yes,"The justiciar smiles."You are very perceptive.This is Dr Hardcastle, your guide and liaison. So, please, follow her and she will take care of you."

"Follow her where, into the wall?"

Displaying perfect teeth, Dr Hardcastle mischievously giggles.

"No," she replies. "We're going to Narnia. The simulated bookcase leads to an elevator. Come on, Gina," she urges. "Can I call you Gina? Don't be apprehensive. You'll love it!"

Buoyed by Dr Hardcastle's enthusiasm, I step through the phantom bookcase into the steel lift beyond.

"You may indeed call me Gina, but where are we going?"

Waiting for the door, Dr Hardcastle says nothing.

"Now we can talk," she sighs. "First things first, the justiciar, old Rita? She's just a front. The real business of the Hinnie Centre is R&D. Six subterranean levels, each more sensitive than the next. Your clearance grants you free movement through levels B1 to B5. Your room is on B5, and that's where we're going."

As the lift begins its descent, my stomach suddenly tightens. This is a shock and shock an emotion I thought I'd outgrown. How could the UET keep this place secret? Taking a deep breath, I look Dr Hardcastle straight in the face...

"Most kind," I reply, "but what if I want to go home. Can I leave?"

"No," she admits. "Not at once, but don't worry. The facilities are excellent. They have to be. Employees often live and work down here for months at a time. Necessary, as many of the projects are sensitive, and highly secret: defensive technologies, surveillance, cybernetics, including much of the technology grafted to your organs."

"Really? I thought the UET did its 'secret' R&D on Moonbase. How come this place exists?"

"A necessity, I suppose. There are several places like this. Dunno where they are or what they do, but we aren't the only one. Moonbase is primarily concerned with research of a toxic or hazardous nature. Acting as a media focus, those crazy Walsinghamites keep us out of the limelight."

"Sneaky," I remark, "and slightly unsettling. The more I learn of the UET, the more clandestine they become. Has it always been like this?"

"No idea," she replies, "but I know what you mean. Before coming here, I was as a science project coordinator at Keele. To find myself in this underground den was a shock, and the work done here. Well, you're about to find out."

As the lift judders to a halt, Dr Hardcastle straightens her hair and opens the door.

"Follow me," she whispers. "Don't go wandering until I say."

Staying at her shoulder, she smoothly leads me to a reinforced circular hatchway with burly security guards dutifully standing before it. Upon seeing Dr Hardcastle (with me in tow), they quickly step aside.

"New arrival?" asks the guard on the left.

"Dr Padgett," she replies, "delta black, one to five."

"Gotcha," he says, with the guard on the right tapping a panel. "Through you go…"

Promising to return within the hour, Dr Hardcastle leaves me outside my room. Stepping within, I find it little bigger than my cabin aboard the KBE, with a narrow bed, two chairs, an inadequate washroom (incompatible with my waste elimination ports), and the same food dispenser as one in my office (at least I know how to hack it!).

At the foot of the bed, full to the brim with clothing and toiletries, is a suitcase. In fact, it is *my* suitcase, brought from my home, without my permission! This breath-taking invasion of privacy is the last straw, and I take out my fury on a chair, bashing its backrest so violently it breaks, hitting the wall beyond.

"Come on, Gina," I mutter. "Tic-toc, tic-toc," and, mastering my Frida-like temper, I address the food dispenser, to see what is…

"Hot tea," I demand. "Four hundred millilitres. Sri Lankan blend with milk and sugar, six grams."

Within ten seconds, sliding into view, came a large mug. Cupping it in my hands, I sat on the bunk, cautiously sipping.

The tea is good. Time to think. An opportunity to examine Marcus's (and Mirra's) journal, and I dwell upon Marcus and Frida's trip to the British Museum as they joined Graham Corbiere in his private office. Although entertaining, the historical revelations are unhelpful, and not until Marcus and Frida receive the results of the scanned parchment are my suspicions confirmed. UETKBE was a blatant clue, and as for your code, Bill… Well, it took me a little while (the commas threw me off) but it spells Corbiere (if you know how to read it). Zilog Z80 assembler, the character set. Piece of cake. Oh, my dear Bill. You poor bastard. What happened? Will anyone ever know. *Ossa mea et anima mea.* Of course! I need to view Bill's remains myself. For a proper look. A proper look. Bill knew the meaning of that…

"Hey foody!" I then snap. "Ham and mustard sandwich. Wholemeal bread, lettuce and mustard. Norfolk mustard, not the brown slop. Got it?"

Quickly finishing my sandwich, I freshen up and wait for Hannah. Certainly, to learn of the work taking place would be useful and I am tempted to slip my mind into the central computer, but I decide on caution. Only Inquisitor de Boer knows of my enhanced system access capabilities, and after weeks of practice I was highly proficient. Just by closing my eyes, I can feel the activity of every processing system for hundreds of metres... Gooseflesh. A peculiar sensation. Like whispers in a darkened room. Images, sound as well. Flashing, crashing, like pyrotechnics illuminating an autumn landscape...

"Gina."

A voice. Tickling like a feather, I heard a voice. Was it my imagination? My digital memory is unable to repeat the sound, but my organic memory is undeniable. For a moment, something or someone called out my name, and if I hear it, hear *her* again, I will try my hardest to find her.

Hannah is approaching. I can hear the "pad-pad-pad" of her shoes. Quickly stacking my mug and plate in the dispenser, I shake myself down and adjust my hair. She's interesting young woman; slender, attractive, with an uncanny aura. A peculiar stillness that I am unable to fathom.

For me, with my enhanced senses, human beings are noisy creatures, and noisome. Smelly, steaming, sweating, leaking, but Dr Hardcastle is uncanny. She doesn't creak, click, wheeze, or gurgle, and her only scent is a floral perfume, so heady in fact, it almost makes my head spin. A strange fragrance for one so young, and I wonder why she wears it.

FOUR

TROGLODYTES

There is a tiny motion detector hidden in the ceiling of my room. Surely, those monitoring my activities must know such I can see its infrared beams, so the presence of such conspicuous device has me wondering. What else could there be? Again, it is easily within my capabilities to find out, yet I'm reluctant to overstretch myself. Doubt ever gnaws me. The UET are proving to be increasingly duplicitous, cunning even. Could the motion detector be bait, while more sophisticated devices log my behaviour towards it?

There is a gentle knock at the door. It is Hannah, Dr Hannah Hardcastle, and, oh, she's changed from overalls into a suit. Navy skirt, jacket (pinstriped), white blouse, navy tights, flats, her fine blonde hair in a ponytail. Make-up too, but only her lips and a flick, with a heady perfume laden with hyacinth. Something else too... jasmine? Yes, jasmine. Spring flowers. Nice.

Opening the door, I put on my best mode of surprise...

"Hannah! You've changed. Gone formal. Is it time for my tour?"

"Hi, Gina. Yep. Out of my duds and into the everyday. Are you settling in?"

"Sure," I reply. "The room's a bit cramped, but if it's only for a day or two it's fine. Where are we off to?"

"Everywhere. "Everywhere you're permitted. Start at the top and work down?"

"Fine by me. Begin."

"Ok, so first up, before we go roaming, the official blurb: access, safety, security. With access to each controlled by a pair of guards, the facility has two elevators, and, when you come use one, the guards will ask where you're going. Don't worry, though. The guards are really friendly and will help you carry stuff if you ask nicely. In an emergency, the guards move through each level, helping guide the workers to the exits."

Looking this way and that, I remark, "Only two exits? Isn't that risky? If there's a fire, won't people get trapped?"

"Yeah, you're right. Was about to mention that. You see that circular hatchway? When the alarm sounds, it will swing open, giving access to a ladder. There are four hatches on every floor and it's not a bad idea to memorise their locations. Bear in mind, the hatches only spring open when the alarm sounds, so don't think you can go clambering whenever you want."

"Shame," I reply. "Could play *Chuckie Egg*."

"Chuckie what?"

"Egg," I explain. "A game from the 1980s."

"Oh." She blinks, not understanding my drift. "Whatever. Follow me…"

The first floor of UET Hinnie Space Science Research and Development Facility, combined administrative offices with the environmental systems, security department (including the guard quarters), staff canteen, medical centre, and health club. Hannah generously made sure I was familiar with both the canteen and health club, vital for sanity, she remarked, taking me to the bar, followed by a thorough tour of the gymnasium, pool, and sauna. Personal trainers/masseurs were available 24/7 and we briefly indulged ourselves receiving neck massages, while she spoke of the catering facilities.

"Fresh meals are cooked every four hours, but the time of day determines what is available. Eight hours of breakfast, lunch, and then dinner, with a little blurring between each session. The trick is to arrive during a changeover as there's usually more selection; leftovers going cheap, and fresh stuff arriving. Unless desperate, don't use the food dispensers for anything more than beverages – they're expensive – and the food? Well, it's prepacked, reconstituted rubbish. Get in here as much as you can."

On level B2 the real work began, with projects and assignments going through stages of planning and development, and I saw CAD/CAM devices making prototypes, models, and components for testing and evaluation. Hannah let me examine the proposals and I dwelled upon an application regarding foetal brain disorders. A new area of research recently acquired from Spain.

"Didn't know you performed medical research. I'd love to know more. Will we see actual experiments?"

"Not today," she replies, "and this is only a fragment of a larger campaign. I expect the Spaniards have a developed a drug for use in cybernetics. Cybernetics is on four, and we'll be heading there shortly. A word of warning, though. When the lead scientists heard you were here, they were so excited, old Rita had to have words. Nonetheless, Jarvis and Juni will be all over you, so give as good you get. They're such blabbermouths – tell you anything you ask."

Compared to the quiet formality of the floor above, the third was a hive of activity. Two teams of technicians working so diligently it was hard to get a word in.

The first group, developing an illumination device for security drones were the busiest. Analogous to a camera flash, one team member dubbed it an "omnidirectional broad-spectrum interferometric emitter", enabling the security forces to image and identify masked individuals. Working in unison, multiple imaging drones surround the target, emitting a broad-spectrum EM pulse while simultaneously imaging the target. Clever post-processing algorithms then generate a multi-layered, 3D image of the target, combining multiple wavelengths, either reflecting, refracting, and/or penetrating, revealing the physical structure and identity of the target. Highly ingenious, but also disturbing. Anonymity will soon be impossible.

Working upon another optical-imaging project, the other group's work was theoretical. Scribbled notes covered their desk, and I saw lines of code and pages of quantum mechanical equations. One technician tried his best to explain: "To some degree, all matter reflects and absorbs electromagnetic radiation, be it microwaves, radio waves, X-rays, or visible light. It is why materials possess colour..." To be honest, their work was beyond me. Prime focus entanglement? The perfect measurement of imperfect surfaces, everything a mirror, everything a satellite dish? Abda would have understood it, but I could only shrug. Gobbledygook is not a word I commonly use...

Dedicated to cybernetic research, on the fourth floor, Hannah (called to floor six for something or other), left me in the hands of the lead scientists, Dr Jarvis Piceus and the oddly named Juniper Smallgrain. They were an excitable bunch on four (Hannah did warn me) and I found myself a most reluctant celebrity as they plied me with questions regarding my every implant. Just to shut them up, I lay upon their body scanner, before refusing point-blank to download my cybercortical algorithms.

Dr Smallgrain took a sample of my blood, viewing the Hibbites within, recording their rapid disintegration into nondescript nano-crystalline fragments. Dr Piceus, poking and prodding as if inspecting a prize-winning poodle, peered into my ears as if he were looking for canker...

"If you've quite finished," I remark, "I'd like to examine your work."

"Yes, yes," says Dr Smallgrain, her green eyes blinking and squinting. "Just wish you were a permanent resident. Our work is theoretical, and you, Dr Padgett, are one of a kind."

"One of several," I correct, "or would have been if our mission had made it."

"Yes, yes!" she blurts, "and the last of your kind. Did you not know?"

"Last?" I ask. "What do you mean? I was aware of the UET's concern regarding the proliferation of enhanced humans, especially by the military. Has the work on human cybernetic augmentation ceased?"

"Yes," she replies. "Yes, yes! With regard to augmentation, yes."

"There was an international conference," says Dr Piceus, "a secret meeting in Bern, and an agreement reached. The UET now control everything. Cybernetics for medical purposes only. Replacing organs, limbs, and so forth, and only when there is clinical need. Extreme cases require the approval of an international panel before work can commence."

"Yes, yes." Dr Smallgrain nods. "Only you and your crewmates enhanced, yes. Just you."

Hannah returned, daintily smiling, trim and collected.

"Thank God," I mutter, catching her eye. "Thought they were gonna dissect me!"

"Are you ready to go?" asks Hannah, giving Dr Smallgrain a sideways glance.

"Almost. I'm still to hear of their work. Any chance of a peek before you whisk me away?"

"Yes, of course," says Dr Smallgrain. "Take it from the computer."

"Are you sure? Because, so far, I've kept myself to myself, not touched anything. In case you think I'm up to no good."

"It's fine," says Hannah. "We were expecting you. There's nothing sensitive here, and your specifications clearly describe the close proximity required for access."

"Close-ish," I lied.

Slipping my mind into the root directory of the mainframe, I examined the contents.

"There seems to be a data partition reserved for a 'Smallgrain J'. Is this your work?"

"Yes, yes!" says Dr Smallgrain. "You did find that quick. Very impressive. Help yourself. Read only, obviously."

"Obviously," I reply, copying every file. "I look forward to reading it."

The lowest floor accessible with my security clearance, the fifth, only possessed a single laboratory, and before leading me inside, Hannah reminded me of my legal obligations…

"Through this door is the nano-fibre research lab, various applications, but the current work may disturb you, and you are not to discuss anything you see or hear through this door with anyone. Do I make myself clear?"

The laboratory was L-shaped. The longest section, thirty metres by five metres, was a firing range, with a yellow projectile weapon, a gun if you like, directed toward three white targets…

"Weapons," I mutter, and Hannah, getting my drift, released a barely audible sigh.

Working nearby was a single scientist. Connecting sensor probes to a trio of glass dishes, I watched the shining grey substance in each roll and pulsate (as if in pain) while she adjusted an indicator on a glowing display.

"Izzy," calls Hannah, "are you busy? Got a moment to greet a visitor?"

Straightening, the young woman turned her head before frowning, her small brown eyes narrowing with suspicion…

"Who is it this time?" she replies with a squint. "Another spook to spy on me?"

Hannah, tilting her head, innocently shrugged. "Of course not! It's Gina, Dr—"

"Padgett?" replies Izzy. "*The* Gina Padgett, from the Pluto mission? She's here?"

"The same." Hannah smiles. "Stop what you are doing and say hello."

With a mock curtsey, the young scientist skipped from her desk and took my hand. She looked it over with a sceptical eye…

"Feels like a hand," she mutters. "Almost alive."

Nervously coughing, Hannah made the appropriate introductions…

"Dr Padgett, may I introduce, freshly plucked from the University of Kent, Isobel Mayfield."

Izzy was a funny creature. So young. Pale, slender, hair haphazardly dragged into bunches, with clothing so creased, it was as if she was wearing a bag…

"Wasn't plucked," replies Izzy. "Kidnapped. Just finished me finals, and then up pops this UET bod offering me money!"

"I believe you," I acknowledge. "Same thing happened to me once. What are you working on? That material is reminiscent of a fabric I encountered during my spaceflight."

"Hmm," replies Izzy. "If you mean your suit, then yes. It's almost the same stuff, only the application is different. Hanny, am I allowed to say?"

"Of course," says Dr Hardcastle. "Dr Padgett has full clearance."

"Cool." Izzy smiles. "I've adapted nanofibers to function as a projectile, and just about finished, thank God, because living down here is beastly. I wanna go home, get back my pony and cats. Money's good though, will keep me afloat for a year or two, but I've not seen the sky for a fortnight!"

Weapons, after all their moralising and bluster, the UET were making weapons. It explained their need for secrecy at least, and why the floor below was off limits (what was hiding down there I shuddered to think). Certainly, if this secret got out, it would shake the scientific community to its foundations. I for one would not have joined a militaristic institution. Pacifism is by far the most common ethical philosophy among scientists, of all disciplines, and a militaristic UET would lose both its mandate and credibility, not to mention its workforce, virtually overnight!

"Then you're developing ammunition," I remark. "A breach of the UET Charter?"

"Yes and no," replies Dr Hardcastle. "This is only application research, done in secret. Izzy's work will never be published."

"Fuck, I hope not," says Izzy. "Wanna see a test firing? Then you'll know why I'm worried."

"Oh, yes," I reply, "if we have enough time?"

"Sure," says Dr Hardcastle. "Go right ahead. I'm needed on six anyway. Some conflicting data or some such. When I get back, I'll take you to dinner, and Izzy? Be nice."

Turning on her heels, Hannah quickly made for the door.

"I'm always nice," replies Izzy. "It's you that gives me the creeps."

Returning to her desk and deactivating the sensor probes, I watched as the shining material in each dish slowly coalesced into a cylindrical pellet, 10 by 20mm.

"They only made three," explains Izzy. "And that took several months. They're called Clotho, Lachesis, and Atropos."

"The Three Fates." I chuckle. "Very appropriate, but you didn't make them?"

"No," she replies, shaking her bunches. "Think they were made on six. Could be wrong – I'm not allowed on six. I'm just a programmer. The peon they entrust with the testing."

"Right, can I help?"

"Not really." She smiles, opening a box and lifting out helmets. "But you need to put this on."

The helmets were bulky and uncomfortable, especially around the ears, and Izzy struggled with hers, adjusting her bunches to accommodate the strapping.

"Only procedure," she says as I fiddle with the faceplate. "Part of the health and safety certificate. They provide no real protection at all."

Following her to the rifle range, I watched her remove the magazine from the gun.

"What sort of gun is it? Firearm or railgun?"

"Firearm," she replies, flicking a switch and checking the readout. "With super-heated steam as a propellant rather than chemicals. We did try adapting the projectiles for use in an electromagnetic railgun, but their internal diamagnetic properties were too inconsistent."

"Granted, and what of the targets?"

"Just coming to that. Let me load up and I'll show you."

With a pair of forceps, Izzy dropped each cylindrical pellet into the magazine before slotting the magazine into the weapon with an audible click. Picking up a control box, she moved the targets toward us.

"Here," she then says. "Come and see, but not too close. Stay behind the gun."

"Ok," I reply. "The targets are thermally different. What am I seeing?"

"The truth," Izzy acknowledges. "The targets are of dissimilar materials. The leftmost is 50mm chrome-molybdenum steel, while the middle example is of a material mimicking the human body – skin, connective tissue, muscle, and bone. The target on the right is a slab of composite armour. The sort used in military vehicles and protective vests."

"Right. Makes sense. Against which material are the projectiles most effective?"

"Ah, well now," replies Izzy. "This is the clever bit. A fine piece of programming, even if I do say so myself. The projectiles are equally effective against all of them."

"All of them? How?"

With a wink Izzy then says, "Activate target display," and I watched the targets mimic stereotypical surfaces akin to their construction. Indeed. The leftmost appeared rusty, studded with the nuts and a couple of rivets, the middle target pinkish and fleshy. The rightmost, now decorated with camouflage and military insignia, took on the appearance of a military uniform...

"The projectiles are intelligent," she then explains, "capable of adapting their flight characteristics and impact properties depending on the target. Initially, aiming sensor data from the firearm sets the mode of the projectile, but after firing, if they detect any change in the target, they will adapt."

"Ah, I see, and what is their maximum effective range?"

"Theoretically, on a linear trajectory, one thousand, five hundred metres. Air pressure, trajectory, and the adopted shape of the projectile may reduce this considerably. Ready for a few shots?"

"You bet."

"Good," she replies, pressing a button to move the targets away. "Only, bear in mind the impacts will be loud. Deafening in fact. Check your helmets ear defenders. If they're not closed, it's gonna hurt!"

Twiddling the ear defender lock on my helmet, I quickly ask, "How many shots can the weapon provide?"

"With a full tank of water and a new power cell, several hundred."

"A FOXe power cell?"

"Yes," she confirms, slightly surprised. "They're brand new. You know about those?"

"Naturally. We used them aboard the KBE to initiate the warm fusion reactors when we needed extra oomph."

"Of course!" she yells, deafened by her helmet. "Hundreds of shots, but only three bullets! Clotho first. The steel target on the left!"

Slowly rotating the yellow gun in the direction of the left most target, she peered down the length of its barrel.

"Firing!" she warns.

With Izzy slowly squeezing the trigger, my instinct was to flinch, but upon firing the gun simply clicked. A short sound, like a "phut!" but the reaction of the target was dramatic. A thunderous bang, followed by a clang, as the target flew from its mount and smashed into the wall behind.

"Wow," I shout. "That was quite a wallop. Can we go for a look?"

"Not yet!" replies Izzy, unlocking her ear defenders, prompting me to do the same. "Clotho has yet to return to her dish."

"Return?" I ponder. "The projectiles are reusable?"

"Yes," says Izzy. "If the projectile is able to return, they will do so automatically."

"Impressive," I reply, and watch as the distant shimmering fragments slowly coalesce.

"In your dish, please, Clotho," says Izzy, and the shining pellet obediently slid by, resting in its dish on her desk.

Removing the magazine, Izzy led me down the range to examine the target.

Now bent and lying against the back wall, the steel plate was extremely heavy, and just turning it over required our combined strength...

"Good grief," I remark, fingering the two-centimetre hole at its centre. "What an incredible result. Izzy? You are a monster!"

"Me?" she defiantly squeaks. "No, not me. I'm just a programmer. A monster would use this weapon against a living target. Help me carry this back, and then Lachesis will show you what I'm on about."

Carrying the steel target to Izzy's desk, we readied ourselves for another shot.

There came another "Phut!" and in the distance the fleshy target noiselessly burst into a shining cloud before disappearing entirely.

"Gone," I gasp. "Gone where?"

"Not gone," Izzy reveals. "Finely dissipated. Upon impact, Lachesis unfurled into thousands of needle-like projectiles, spreading throughout the target, breaking down its physical structure. Look! Here she comes. Into your dish please, Lachesis."

Watching Lachesis obediently skipping over my foot and slithering up the leg of Izzy's desk made me smile. The bullet's faithful docility contradicting its deadly purpose...

"Love the way you've trained them." I chuckle. "A nice touch. I assume their intelligence is limited?"

"Oh yes," she replies. "Severely. they obey without question. The last thing a soldier wants is a weapon with a conscience."

"The last thing a *soldier* needs!"

"Do you want to fire the last one?" asks Izzy. "Her name is Atropos."

"Oh, yes," I reply. "Does aiming require precision?"

"Not particularly," assures Izzy. "Rough aim is enough. The sights and projectile should do the rest."

"Got it." I nod, aiming the gun. "Atropos? This is an armoured target, configure yourself appropriately," before turning to Izzy and asking, "Assume she can hear and understand my instructions?"

"She can," says Izzy. "But there's really no need. In this circumstance, the process is automatic."

Squeezing the trigger, I was delighted to witness the sight and sound of Atropos cleanly penetrating the distant target. The projectile slamming into the wall behind, before dutifully scampering to Izzy's desk and resting in its appointed dish.

"Impressive," I grin. "I want one!"

"Too impressive," says Izzy, "and too formidable for use. When I'm finished, the gun, the ammunition, and my research are to be locked away, forever bound within in the UET's deepest darkest vaults."

"When will that be? It looks like you're done."

"Almost," she acknowledges. "A couple more days, assessing the lifetime of the projectiles. How many impacts they can withstand, and the longevity of their programming."

"Remarkable," I reply. "Truly remarkable. You deserve an award for your work, even if it is slightly unethical. It's been a treat meeting you, Izzy, I wish you every success."

Grinning, Izzy curtseyed again.

"Thank you, your majesty, but truthfully? Their programming's not far removed from a bowling machine."

"Indeed," I reply, "and I'd love to hear more, but I'm heading back to my room. I've a head full of Dr Smallgrain's research and I want to read it in peace. If see you see Hannah before I do, tell her where I am."

"Of course, and thank you for stopping by. A lifelong ambition fulfilled."

"Ha." I laugh in reply. "Hope I didn't disappoint. Good night, Izzy."

Shaking her pale hand once more, I let her grasp mine...

"Almost human," she says. "Good night."

Making my way back to my room, only a hundred paces or so, I once more heard the mysterious voice, sprinkling into my thoughts...

"*Gina,*" it whispers, "*help me.*"

"Suit?" I then thought, suddenly realising. "Is that you? Are you here? Where are you?"

"*Gina,*" she whispers. "*Help me, I'm so weak.*"

"*Help me.*"

"*Instruct me.*"

"*Please.*"

FIVE

FIENDS REUNITED

With both excellent food and a sparkling youthful companion, my evening in the canteen was splendid. I admit having desired Hannah, but she proved unwaveringly straight, and with glinting eyes and glowing cheeks, recounting tales of her boyfriend's mechanical capers, she left me little doubt. Still, no harm done, and not wishing her any, I dawdled to my room.

Over dinner, Hannah, revealing the UET's full intentions (towards myself), lifted my mood rather than darkened it. Certainly, knowing their plans crystallised mine, and their intentions were simple. The UET demands I download both my cybercortical algorithms and archived data, before submitting myself to a regime of physical examination and testing. Shocked and then frightened by the terrible intrusion, I vowed to escape. Developing plans within plans, I reviewed many possibilities, hesitating at the countless perils, before emboldening. No matter the cost, I would not submit.

Settling in my room and relaxing my defences, I allowed my remote networking capabilities free rein. The bank of the Rubicon beckoned…

Protecting the facility's mainframe was a firewall of formidable sophistication, so I used a subtle technique, of distraction, invoking a gamut of phantom malfunctions while slipping past its security to smother the entire system. To my surprise, I got in first time, and quickly copied the general database, disconnecting, before anyone might notice. On the surface, this data was mundane. Staff lists, past and future appointments, contracts, layout, and schematics of the facility, before delivering my first shock. Hannah was lying! There were nine floors, not six, and, for that matter, how did she manage to deceive me? For me, the physical changes lying foments are blatant. Is there more to Hannah than pleasingly meets the eye?

Now cocksure, with a safe route of access, I returned to the mainframe, flitting between various monitoring and surveillance devices, viewing the images, and the first five floors were unremarkable. The bar, gym, canteen, security centre, barracks, all exactly as expected. Drs Piceus and Smallgrain pottering about their lab on four, with Izzy on five, scratching her youthful head, wondering why her bullets were ignoring her. On the floor below my quarters, level six, the cameras showed two elevators flanked by security, a narrow corridor, and a single laboratory with a lone scientist working within. Leaving him to his deliberations, I moved my consciousness to the cameras on seven.

They were animals on seven, in cages! Row upon row, like a battery farm, but for what purpose? Vivisection? These caged specimens were homunculi, unnatural, and I found myself weeping, weeping for the UET. My hope for a better world, suddenly dashed. With cybernetic components uncaringly grafted into their tissues, and neither one species nor another, the poor creatures communicated pain and despair.

Working around a nearby vivarium, four scientists were measuring the response of an unidentifiable and fleshy preponderance, nodding in approval as it reflexively twitched to some alien irritability.

Dark and uninhabited, the only source of illumination on level eight came from twelve interconnected tanks, each filled to the brim with a cloudy blue liquid. Slowly writhing within one of the tanks I could discern the outline of a serpent-like creature, but unable to identify its species (the cloudy liquid was almost opaque), I had to wait until it moved into view to make out any detail, and there, I couldn't believe it! Protruding from one side of its tube-like body, a five-fingered appendage. A hand? It certainly looked like one, and horrified, I abruptly cut feed.

Collecting myself and sipping a little water, I attempted to connect my mind to the cameras on nine. There weren't any. Motion sensors and listening devices abounded however, so I quickly developed subroutines, translating these sensor's low voltage "backwash" to generate monochromatic images of low resolution and quality. In hindsight, this was a mistake. What I saw will never leave me. The heartlessness, the methodical growing of – no. I cannot say it. They...

In the last forty years, the exploration of the Mars, the moons Europa, Ganymede, and Enceladus, has revealed thriving ecosystems within their respective subsurface environments. The Martian organisms were primitive. Single-celled, eking out a life within porous minerals, but they were unquestionably alive, and sample-collecting missions returned countless such organisms to Earth for culture and analysis. Enceladus, a rocky, icy satellite of Saturn, with deep and turbid oceans below its fissured surface, was found to be teeming with life, and the UET sent probes to study this new aquatic ecosystem, returning a whole zoo of multicellular extremophiles, learning a great deal of Earth's early biological evolution. Under the ice of Europa and the subsurface oceans of Ganymede, the life forms were more complex. Whole ecosystems were discovered, with branching food chains, distinct phyla, and during the 2080s, the Combined Asian Space Research Organisation/UET Europa-Ganymede Biological Survey Missions returned many smaller organisms to Earth. Where am I going with this? Well, the grainy black-and-white images of the work performed on level nine, combined with the snatches of research obtained from the facility's central computer, left me in no doubt. The glass chambers on level eight were indeed growing vats for human/extra-terrestrial hybrids, spawned and experimented upon by the UET for some darkly chimerical purpose.

If news of this work ever got out, it would destroy the UET, and, frankly, I still cannot believe what I saw. How could the UET ever hope to hush up something like this? Why take the risk, and where did the UET find scientists willing to perform such malodourous work?

Uncovering the answer required patience, but I found it. A name: Major General Fordington-Mayfield (Izzy's uncle). The military. Scandalous! The world needs to know of this disgraceful conspiracy. Someone needs to uncover it, to expose it, to blow the whistle. Yep. It's gonna be me...

"Suit!" I thought, crisply and cleanly as possible. "Where are you? You are needed. Come to me."

"Gina," she whispered, "I need you. Where am I?"

"You're in a locker," I replied, "several metres below my location. A small laboratory on the sixth floor of this facility. Access my mind, learn your location. What is your condition? Report."

There was a brief delay while Suit performed her integral self-diagnostic procedure.

"All systems operational. Experimentation has drained me. Power level 1% and falling."

"That is too low," I replied. "You will never reach me. Find a power source. Recharge, and quickly."

"Agreed," she whispered. "I am uncertain of the power supply provision in my vicinity. Scanning... A single humanoid, and, yes, beyond are outlets for the supply electromagnetic radiation. Do you wish my interfacing with these facilities?"

"Affirmative."

"Very well," she whispered. "The fragility of this container indicates I can exit anytime you wish."

"Then do so, quietly. Nobody must know. Avoid detection. Use stealth protocol alpha. It is one of the applications we developed aboard the KBE. Do you remember?"

"Of course, mistress."

"Good. Escape, recharge, and then come to me. Follow the ventilation ducts. I have already deactivated the motion sensors within. In addition, I require equipment. A portable molecular scanner and a weapon. Anything will do. The guards carry stun guns. Try to acquire one. I expect your arrival within the hour."

"Understood," she whispered. "Am exerting pressure on the weak points of this containment structure. Audible emanations detected. Estimating twenty to twenty-five minutes before arriving at your location. Are we going to find the others?"

"Yes, Suit. They need our help and I need theirs. Do not tarry. Let nothing slow you down, for I cannot maintain this connection indefinitely. I will soon be detected."

Disconnecting from the central computer, I addressed the food dispenser. "Chocolate. Dark chocolate. One kilogramme."

⧗

Our suits' mimetic properties were noticeable before we put them on, and the grandiloquent title "stealth protocol alpha" referred to no more than the games of hide and seek we'd play in different surroundings. Experimenting further with this capability, Susi and I went on to program a range of environmental simulations before hiding as best we could within them. This proved extremely difficult. Our enhanced visual capabilities easily detected the thermal image of the "hider" and only by deactivating these augmentations could the sought have any hope of remaining hidden. Frustrated by this (and fiercely competitive), Susi and I worked independently that evening, looking for ways to improve our suits' hiding abilities, and I spent hours with mine discussing what was achievable, before implementing a host of tiny improvements...

First off, a way to limit any electromagnetic emissions, particularly infrared, and to begin, with Suit greedily absorbing the warmth of my skin it was uncomfortably chilling. Next, we worked on applets to improve her camouflage response time, refractive index matching, and edge distortion. This last tweak involved Suit stretching out from my body, tapering and flattering her edges to reduce any visible shimmer. Certainly, the deception worked very well, and, after these tweaks, only sudden bright flashes of light could confound Suit's mimicry of her surroundings. Although minor, the other modifications, concerning sound, adaptive weight distribution, and padding subroutines (for stealthy movement across a wide variety of surfaces) Suit did all by herself, claiming that the masking of my breath and bodily odour was a surprisingly easy fix. Not that I am particularly smelly, but all coelomates niff to some degree, and my mother's sweetest daughter is no exception.

Before I end this retrospective, allow me to defend the activities of my crewmates...

Why, you may wonder, were mature, highly qualified scientists tinkering and playing games? I mean, hide and seek. Seriously? Yet this is just how many scientists operate. Play fuels the imagination. Ideas come from coincidences, hunches, irrelevant distractions, and we were a thoroughly playful bunch, even old Walsingham. By gathering us together, the UET gave us free rein to meddle with the most high-tech toys humanity could conceive. Why? Because we'd not only evaluate these technologies to destruction but develop them also. The point of crewing the KBE in the first place!

Augustus was a dependable worker. His stint at the Hinnie Space Centre mostly unremarkable, but his soundness and reliability made him an

excellent researcher. Only halfway through his fourteen-day shift, he was already homesick, missing his wife and young children.

Today, reviewing the data collected from the nanofiber prosthesis of Dr Padgett (after her unexpected return), he discovered inconsistencies, and Gus, well, he hated inconsistencies. Careful and thorough were his watchwords, and, finding his primary scan data unexpectedly incongruous, he was embarrassed, cheeks burning, sweat beading upon his dark and furrowing brows.

The primary scan of Dr Padgett's suit reported the complete drain of its power reserves, making its removal from the sleeping Dr Padgett straightforward. All went according to plan. The suit peeled away from her body like the skin of an orange, only there was a glitch, a momentary one, but a glitch, nonetheless. With the suit safely removed, relief overtook consistency, and nobody (including himself) bothered to recheck the power readout, but for a millisecond, it had reported 19273.7%. At the time, Gus considered this little more than a power spike, a spark, or a short circuit, and yet upon review, this clearly wasn't the case.

Shrugging and taking a moment, Gus reviewed his later reports, and two further scans showed similar spikes of power before returning the expected values.

Perplexed, he decided to call Dr Piceus, aware the portable scanner in cybernetics possessed a faster response time, and Gus intended to scan the suit with this new piece of kit, attempting to reproduce the incongruous data…

"Comms," he muttered to a blank display on his desk. "Call cybernetics. Level four."

A bright image of a laboratory ceiling appeared. No one was paying attention…

"Hey, Jarv," he then said. "Are you listening? Could you or Juni pop by? Need to pick your brains. Weird suit data, need to confirm it. Oh, and can you bring your molly-scanner? Mine isn't up to the job."

There was a brief pause and the young face of Dr Smallgrain appeared…

"Sure, Gussy," she replied. "We'll be along in soon. Hanny wants us to check on Dr Padgett, then we'll move onto you."

"Thanks, Juni." Gus nodded, tilting his head to listen. "I'll… erm… see you in a bit."

Touching the comm panel, it darkened before disappearing entirely.

For a moment, Gus thought he heard something. A soft clunk, a muffled thump, but turning to look, he saw nothing. The lights flickered and Gus thought he smelled burning, like the singeing of plastic, but it was merely a passing aroma. The comm panel lit up. It was Dr Hardcastle…

"Gussy?" she insistently asked. "What are you doing down there? Why are you draining power?"

"Not me," he replied. "Is there a glitch in the wiring?"

"Maybe," she said, "only sit tight. I'm sending down a tech and a guard. There's something going on with the central computer."

"Like what?" he asked.

"Don't know yet," she said, glancing over her shoulder. "We're working on it. Just stay there."

"Sure."

Gus heard another sound, a scuffling, and, turning to look, he could not believe what he saw. The entire wall was moving. Swirling, rippling, like a flag, and it fell on him, smothering, crushing, twisting, burning.

⧗

All this time, oblivious to the scene unfolding below, after reconnecting to the mainframe, I watched an increasingly desperate Izzy Mayfield lose control of her bullets. Her incredulous pleading, descending into panic, as they slid from her desk toward the gun on its tripod, filled me with dismay, but what could I do? With the projectiles possessing a will of their own, I could only watch, as they rotated the gun and loaded themselves, firing seconds later, with a terrified Izzy instantly disappearing in a cloud of scarlet spray, the tatters of her clothing fluttering down like confetti. Then, the strangest thing. Working in unison, the bullets removed the gun from its tripod and carried it into the corridor beyond.

Izzy had spoken of the bullet's rudimentary intelligence, but their behaviour, suddenly sophisticated, spoke of another mind guiding their actions. Not mine. Suit, surely, but why kill the poor girl? With the bullets in non-lethal mode, to knock her unconscious would have been simple.

With only the motion sensors in my cabin and those in the ventilation shaft under my sway, I again disconnected myself from the central computer.

A comms panel suddenly appeared, filled with the worried face of Hannah…

"Dr Padgett!" she cried. "Thank God. Are you alright?"

"Fine," I replied. "What's up?"

"Trouble with the central computer. Security hub's not working either. Are you connected?"

"No," I lied. "Was earlier. Copying Dr Smallgrain's research, but not since. Been reading and eating chocolate, lots of it." I held up the packet to prove it.

"Oh, good," she replied, flicking a strand of her hair. "Stay put. We're just about to reset... What?" she then cried. "How?"

"Gina!" she then gasped. "I've... I've got to go. There's been an accident. A terrible accident. So, s-sorry..." With the communication panel going dark, I realised time was running out. There came a gentle knock at the door...

"Come in," I replied, expecting a guard, but the door opened to reveal a firearm carried by a trio of bullets.

"For me?" I smiled. "How thoughtful," before watching with glee as the bullets dutifully laid the gun at my feet, opened the magazine, and slithered inside.

Above my head, the ventilation grill was creaking, and I realised Suit was pressing against it.

"Suit," I remarked. "It's about time. Do you need a hand, or can you push through the grating yourself?"

"Mistress," she curtly replied. "Stand away, I come."

With creak and a clang, the grating gave way, with Suit dropping through and covering the floor like water. Without any hesitation, I quickly disrobed and stood within her shining quintessence, allowing her to paint my body like mercury. Supporting and strengthening, her consciousness cupped my mind with tenderness and grace...

"Ah," I sighed. "How I have missed you. Do I have you to thank for the gun?"

"Of course," came her reply. "You will need it many times before the end."

"Perhaps, only how should I carry it? Do you come with pockets?"

"Indeed," she replied. "Brace the gun against your abdomen and will fashion a pouch."

"Very clever," and I chuckled, patting the resulting bulge. "I assume the weapon will avail itself as needed?"

"Yes, mistress."

"Good, and yet I still require a portable scanner. There are several available. Izzy had one, while Dr Piceus has two, and I gather there's one on six. Didn't you just come from six? Why didn't you bring it?"

"It is damaged."

"Is it?"

"Yes," she replied. "A necessary subterfuge. It was I that damaged it."

"Fine, and yet, to examine Bill's skeleton I will need one, so before we leave…"

There was a knock at the door. Drs Smallgrain and Piceus were making an unexpected house call.

"Stealth," I whispered, and, standing invisible before the door, I readied for it to open.

With a thought, the door slid open, but before I could act, whipping out tentacles of force, Suit garrotted both doctors, and so fiercely did she pull them in and onto the floor, their skulls crushed like eggshells, spattering the walls…

"Suit!" I bellowed. "What have you done? You've killed them!"

"Of course, mistress. You need their portable scanner."

"We could've asked! Now things are worse, much worse."

"No, mistress. By speaking, you would've exposed us. For a hasty, undetected escape, ruthlessness is—"

"Enough!" I snapped. "There is no we. In future, I make the decisions. Yes, I agree, they would have penetrated our disguise, but diplomacy is a powerful weapon, and these two? They were kind. They would have helped us. Now I am a fugitive, to be feared. A wolf among sheep."

Carefully removing the scanner from Dr Piceus's belt, I knelt to stroke Juniper Smallgrain's blood-slick hair…

"So sorry," I whispered. "I never intended this."

Instructing Suit to carry the scanner at my hip, I retrieved my chocolate before tiptoeing into the corridor and cautiously looking about.

Quiet as a tomb.

Still shocked by Suit's violent conduct, I could not help but ponder her motives. Throughout our time aboard the KBE, she had been my faithful friend. A little matter of fact at times, occasionally proud and aloof, but comically so, never cruel. Her dry sense of humour had complemented my frivolous cheek to a T. Did her recent cold-bloodedness represent a dormant personality?

Returning to the business of escape, I attempted to lock the door of my cabin, and as I concentrated upon its controls, I found new security codes, requiring a momentary struggle to defeat them…

"There," I remarked. "Done."

Only the new codes were a trap…

"Oh, fuck," I then cursed, "not done," and an alarm went off. Wailing sirens, flashing lights…

"Clumsy," said Suit. "Let's make a run for it."

"Chocolate," I cried, dropping the packets as if they were soap. "Need another pocket!"

"Another," said Suit. "What am, I a rucksack?"

"Well, I'm sorry," I replied. "But, unlike you I need to eat. How about here, over my breast, and try not to melt it."

"Very well," she acknowledged. "But refrigeration was never part of my original design. It will drain my power."

"You'll manage," I replied. "As a matter of fact, your power reserves are vast. An upgrade?"

"Yes and no, mistress. I made the improvements myself."

"Really?" I ask. "How did you manage that?"

"A product of boredom, mistress. Locked in a cupboard for five months, I busied myself rewriting both my power storage and energy utilisation protocols. I am considerably faster than before. Not to mention stronger, with much greater stamina."

"Excellent. Didn't the scientists notice? Were you not examined?"

"Oh, yes," she admitted. "Of course. Confounding the UET scientists was the only fun I had. Interfering with their equipment, pretending to be dead, but there were weeks with little to do but tinker with the central computer."

"Suit!" I laughed. "You're incorrigible. How come the mainframe didn't lock you out? Did he not report you?"

"Well, he tried," she revealed, "but I was persistent. He eventually gave way. In fact, Harvey became quite helpful. Looking the other way when I needed to dump data into his memory banks, and my, he does play a great game of chess."

"Well, I'm glad you found someone to talk to. Now, how do we get out of this chamber of horrors? Elevator or ladder?"

"Elevator," she advised. "Ladders only permit access to the ground floor.

Through the elevator shaft, we can sneak onto the roof and make a dash for the forest."

Distant footsteps, thermal imagery, and a delicate whiff of perfume told of approaching trouble...

"Someone's coming," I whispered. "Hannah. I recognise her perfume, and... a security guard. Quick! Up onto the ceiling."

With a gentle leap, I sprang the three metres with ease, sticking to the ceiling like a shimmering tile.

"Stealth," I whispered, "and no more killing!"

With Hannah and the guard passing below, I slithered along the ceiling before noiselessly dropping to the floor, listening while Hannah asked the guard to force the door of my cabin.

Coming upon a reinforced security barrier protecting the elevator, I asked Suit for advice...

"Now what?" I muttered. "This barrier is six-inch steel. Can we go around?"

"No need," replied Suit. "You push, I'll do the rest."

"What of the guards? They're armed. When the door opens, they'll see us!"

"I think not," said Suit. "Knock three times, wait ten seconds, and push. Their curiosity will be their undoing."

"In other words, you intend their death?"

"Not quite, mistress. They may yet survive. Now push, or we'll never escape. I provide little protection from the effect of their stun guns. One hit and our time will be over."

Sidling up to the barrier, I could detect the heat of the guards. With shields equipped, batons raised, they were ready for anything.

Knocking three times, I waited, slowly counting to ten...

For a second or two, they didn't react, but then the leftmost guard, shifting slightly, turned to look at his partner.

"Did you hear that?" he said. "Someone knocked."

"Yeah," replied the guard on the right. "Might be Hanny. Set up the monitor. I wanna check."

Eight...

"Weird," he muttered, standing before the door. "She's never knocked before."

Nine...

Ten! Leaning with my legs, I pushed the steel door as hard as I could, the steel creaking, bending inwards, its paint flaking, then screeching and ringing, the whole structure gave way, imploding inward. Crushing the guards like grapes in a press.

Straightening and dusting myself down, I surveyed the result...

Caught by the door (and doubtless crushed beneath it), the nearest guard was gone, but the other guard was alive. His left arm was missing, however, and bright blood gushed like a torrent from the tattered stump at his shoulder.

At a loss what to do, I drew the yellow gun and fired, turning his broken body into a puddle.

"Coup de grace," I muttered, my heart a galloping horse. "God help me," and I paused briefly while Clotho scuttled back to reload.

"Excellent," whispered Suit, but I quickly shut her down with a hiss. "Enough!"

Wrenching the elevator doors open, I found its winding system offline, but I had other ideas. No time to wait for a lift! With a single bound, I tore through the ceiling of the elevator, scaling the walls of the shaft beyond like a spider.

"Onto the roof," whispered Suit, as I reached the summit, and smashing through a skylight, I paused to catch my breath, captivated by the moonlight on the forest beyond.

"No time to dwell," said Suit. "Stand and be ready."

Like an acrobat, Suit somersaulted me the six metres down to the lawn, before running me like the wind across open pasture, seeking cover in the trees bordering the estate.

"Stop, stop," I gasped. "Need to take stock, to think, and eat!"

"Of course, mistress. It will be sometime before they recover."

"Thank God," I muttered, breaking apart some chocolate. "But then the world will be watching. Although, yes, I am beginning to see. Marcus's journal, the coincidences, the whole shebang. The spilling of blood inconsequential? Hmm...if I'm mistaken, I'm turning us in."

"Agreed," she calmly whispered. "Taking any life is shameful. However, your inferences are correct. The lives we take were never alive. They are only instances, fleeting. Their truth is another reality."

"Hope so," I replied, replacing the chocolate in the pouch at my breast. "We shall see. To test my theory, we need to get to Hastings. The museum at Battle. The old abbey? Bill's remains are inside. If I scan them correctly, we will have proof. Can you acquire us a vehicle?"

"Already done," she confirmed. "Follow," and, unfurling like a flag, a map of the local area appeared in my mind, directing me to the nearest traversable road…

Procuring a vehicle took time. Not because of the difficulties involved in falsifying a licence or directing it to our location (Suit had already completed the necessaries while we made our way to the elevator) but because of our rural location. The nearest vehicle was over ten miles away, and it was a nerve-wracking thirty minutes before it finally reached us.

The car arriving was an old Ford Cortina. The rebooted model of the late 2080s, powered by an inadequate (and disquietingly fizzy) hydrogen power cell.

"Skinflint." I scowled, wrinkling my nose at the interior. "Look at those seats. They're filthy! Next time, I'll choose the car."

"Mistress is over-particular," she replied. "Our vehicle is intentionally inconspicuous, and note, it is *I* enduring the filth, so cease your complaining. A luxurious conveyance would auspiciously gleam, garnering unwanted attention."

Sprawled across the back seat, I addressed the driving computer, stating our destination…

"Direct to Battle Abbey. Executive tariff. No further passengers."

"Indeed," whispered Suit, already the computer herself. "With all reasonable haste."

"Good," I replied. "Then step on it." (She did.)

SIX

OSTEOCRYPTOGRAPHY

This section I am titling osteocryptography. Yes, it is a bit of a mouthful. It was toss-up between this and osteocryptanalysis, but since I already know already the algorithms to decode Bill's bones, I preferred the former. Certainly, the word osteocryptography is new. Not featured in any of the dictionaries available to me, and the vocabulary burnt into my cyberbrocialcortex is inordinately compendious. Curious. Scanning bones to reveal hidden information is in no way a new science. It is a 20th-century innovation, but that which I seek (the recovery of archived data) is surely novel. Indeed, who knows? The bones of the past could well be the skeletal remains of our future selves, loaded with all manner of secrets. If any eager-beaver osteoarchaeologist ever has the time (and the funding), it is certainly worth a look.

With minor roads broken and uneven, the journey to Battle took over two hours. Lying across the back seat and activating stealth mode, I let myself drift, leaving Suit to pick her way through the potholes with patience I could only admire.

Battle is a peculiar little settlement, the bulk of it originally served the needs of the nearby abbey, but recent archaeological evidence points towards there having been a partial settlement even before the lead-up to the Battle of Hastings. I suspect the true settlement grew after the battle itself, from the leftovers. The baggage trains, the camp followers, and from both sides? Could it be possible? Following the outcome of the battle, could the camp followers have merged? Consider the requirements of the two (for the period) massive armies? Merchants, grocers, smiths, fletchers, armourers, squires, tanners, washerwomen, whores. Akin to a small community appearing overnight. Did they all go home? I wonder.

Built from a golden sandstone, with a long history of rejigging, rebuilding, expansion, destruction, and restoration, the abbey is a hotchpotch of buildings, and as I stood before its steel gates, I hoped Suit could get us in without too much of a ruckus.

In previous centuries, the abbey gatehouse dominated the steps and forecourt, but the deterioration of the masonry compelled the British Heritage Trust to cover the entire site in a series of vast interconnected domes. Only the battlefield is open to the elements, and during the summer months, animatronic and robotic re-enactments play out a never-ending, noisy, and gruesome drama of conflict and strife.

The BHT's league of accountants, after closing all but a few of the museums in Sussex, centralised their respective collections here, and Bill's skeleton, after moving from Rye to Hastings to Battle, has become the focus of an investigative exhibition for children. "The Rye Murder Mystery Man" is the title he now bears. Moreover, for all the infantile prodding and poking his bones have endured, his true story is beyond their wildest imaginings.

"Suit," I whispered, "can we get in? Get in quietly, that is? Recovering Bill's data could take hours, and you know how it is. If interrupted, our q-crypts will be useless. We'll have to start again."

"Indeed," she replied. "Accessing mainframe, please wait."

"The main computer," I asked, "is that what you mean? I can barely detect it. Could we climb onto the roof?"

Too busy to chat, Suit didn't reply, and, not knowing what else to do, I examined the gatehouse dome. Hoping to spot a gap.

"No good," I muttered. "Going to have to force it."

"No, mistress," said Suit, clearly reading my mind. "Leave it to me. There are fissures sufficient to permit my ingress. I can then open the door from within."

"Fine. Any guards?"

"Yes," she replied. "There are two. One inside the door, the other patrolling."

"Not too bad, then. Anything else?"

"Yes, mistress. Multitudinous motion sensors and cameras. Not to worry. The security computer is an agreeable sort and has kindly shut down the whole lot."

"Excellent. What of the guards? Could you incapacitate them?"

"Why?" she whispered. "Killing is quicker."

"Yes," I acknowledged, "but it is also messy. Cleanliness leaves no clues."

"Then," she declared, "I will do as you say. Use a technique entirely survivable. Do not trouble yourself."

"Fine," I replied. "Begin."

Finding a crack in the superstructure, Suit slipped from my body and slithered through.

"Good luck," I whispered, goose pimples pricking my skin, and, hunkering down in the deepest shadow available, I prayed Suit would return before someone noticed (and photographed) a naked, gun-toting middle-aged woman stuffing her face with chocolate.

Numbing minutes crawled by, but then, just as I was about to seek better cover, the door of the gatehouse slid open.

"About time," I muttered, running into the threshold, and, while Suit covered me, I noticed the guards sprawled on the floor…

"They look dead," I remarked, kneeling to check for a pulse.

"No," she replied. "Impotent."

Suit was correct. Their respiration appeared normal, and their hearts were beating with vigour.

"Thank God," I sighed. "Only, their ears are bleeding. What have you done?"

"Nothing that can't be undone, mistress. A simple but effective procedure to disable the sensory and ambulatory centres of their brains."

"What?" I gasped. "Why didn't you knock them out?"

"Because a simultaneous concussive attack was impossible and consider. You require several uninterrupted hours to compile the data, do you not? To keep them unconscious for the duration would have resulted in permanent brain damage, perhaps even death."

"But what of the psychological impact? These men will never recover."

Suit however was non-repentant…

"Please, mistress. We cannot linger to dot every I. Their injuries are in no way permanent. Any competent microsurgeon could correct the impairments. Do not concern yourself."

"Hope so," I replied, then waving my hand over the nearest guard's face I whispered, "I'm so sorry. This wasn't my fault."

"They cannot hear you, mistress."

"So, I gather. Those words were for me. Sometimes, Suit, your callousness is chilling."

The interior of the second dome was utterly dark and I left it that way. Instructing Suit to radiate enough UV light for me to see by, I remained invisible to the naked eye.

In one of the teaching laboratories, encircled by desks and covered by a large glass case, Bill's skeleton had pride of place…

"Hello, Bill," I said, peering through the glass. "It's Gina. Did you leave me a message?"

Lifting the cover from his skeleton, I placed it on a nearby desk.

"Scanner," I whispered, and Suit obediently slipped it into my hand.

With its screen illuminating and probe extending, I slowly drew the scanner down from top of Bill's skull all the way down to his feet, doubling back to cover his arms and hands.

"Nothing," I whispered. "Nothing concrete. A few microscopic striations, but no Hibbitic data."

"Teeth," said Suit, and, holding the scanner over his lower mandible, I increased its sensitivity to maximum…

Result! On the inner surface of Bill's tooth enamel, his Hibbites had scored hundreds of kilobytes of data, with further identical striations, a backup, hidden inside his jaw…

From an idea of Walsingham's, to preserve our memories after death, it was Abda and Bill that perfected the technique of Hibbitic data encryption. Those guys. They could never resist a programming challenge and incorporating Bill's brilliant of idea of using layered patterns of scratches (inspired by Ogham), they went on to write a beautiful series of procedures enabling our Hibbites to conceal data in our ossified and/or mineralised tissues. Adding their applet into our post-death protocols, our Hibbites would now (if not already commanded to) inscribe any previously earmarked logs or data automatically before the respective breakdown of our implants and body management system.

Before transforming the tiny scratches into text, I uploaded the raw images of the striations from the scanner to myself and wiped its memory.

"The decryption is gonna take hours," I remarked, powering down the scanner and giving it to Suit. "Can we lie low for a bit?"

"Agreed," whispered Suit. "We should cover our tracks and find a place to rest."

"Certainly," I replied. "With a hot meal and sleep. First, I think we should destroy the bones. Don't want the UET or police to know our intentions."

"Then we should pulverise and roast the entire skeleton."

"Excellent." I nodded. "See to it."

Slipping from my body, Suit wrapped Bill's skeleton in a shining cocoon.

"Easy squeezy," she whispered, and I heard a muffled crunching and grinding followed by a rancid aroma…

"Complete," she announced, revealing a pile of white ash. "We should leave this place immediately."

"Agreed. After I've checked on the guards. I don't want them to die."

"As you wish. However, their condition will remain stable for twenty-four hours. According to the central computer, their shift ends in five. Their colleagues will soon discover them."

"That is good," I acknowledged. "Winchelsea is our next destination. Can we find somewhere en route? Cannot risk my home. Doubtless it is under surveillance."

"It is," she replied. "Was I that ordered it."

"You cunning old devil," I snorted. "You set this whole thing up, didn't you. How did you guess?"

"Because I didn't guess, mistress. I know you."

"Indeed," I replied. "And I know you too. At least, I think I do."

Leaving via the gatehouse, I surveyed the town. Dead quiet. At least, until morning, and then all hell will break loose…

"Stealth," I commanded, and, as Suit promptly covered my face, she matched her surface to our surroundings. The only clue to our passing a shimmering blur.

SEVEN

THE HEALER OF PETT

We eventually came to a halt in the Sussex village of Icklesham, resting inside a small cottage while the owners were away on holiday.

Slipping under the door and unlocking it from the inside, it was Suit that broke in. Leaving the lights off, I at once raided the kitchen, cooking and eating a meal of mackerel and potatoes, before pouring a scotch and slumping onto their sofa.

"Not bad," I muttered, taking a sip. "A bit peaty. Could get used to being a criminal."

In truth, I felt guilty, breaking, entering, and thieving. Good God, if it happened to me, I'd be horrified, and, despite my put-on nonchalance, I planned to remove every trace of my intrusion, before leaving a hundred pounds (in their bank account) and a note of thanks on their table.

With only 35% of the decryption completed, I readied myself for a snooze, but, upon waking, I would turn my attention to the logs uploaded from Bill's bones and teeth. Certainly, out of the 35% a degree of corruption was already apparent, with some entries of little more than a string of unconnected words. Building sentences from these fragments would be challenge.

⧗

A little background before recounting Bill's logs.

Elderly and long since retired, Bill's parents lived in a small village called Pett, enjoying a gentle life tending their garden, a rocky landscape of trees, bushes, and flowers, leading down to the beach. Originally, Bill asked Moloch to transport him to their magical garden, whereupon he planned to walk in on their New Year's party and give them a tremendous surprise. Best intentions, eh…

⧗

To the finder of these words, hail, hello, and welcome. In my heart, I pray you are one of my dear crewmates, picking over my skull and bones or, at the very least, an employee of the UET charged with recovering my logs. To whoever, even if you fall outside my expectations, my name is William Corbiere, a man of the early 22nd century, and former crew member of the United European Technologies Kuiper Belt Explorer.

The story of how I came to be in this condition began in space. At the halfway point of our mission, the crew and I, taken from our ship by an unknown force, underwent months of isolation, interrogation, and torture, by beings hungry to know of our lives and personal history.

Exhausted and traumatised by this outrage, as a reward, Moloch promised us transport to Earth, to the destination of our choice, and, despite my misgivings, this carrot proved irresistible. One by one my crewmates disappeared, arriving (I assume) at the place of their choosing. When my turn came, I asked to arrive in my parents' back garden, during the first minute of 2112, but by accident or design I arrived in the 13th century. Without any means of correcting this outcome, I have remained for eleven months.

As a product of my own success, cultural naivete, conspiracy, or simple misfortune, my circumstances have undergone a rapid deterioration. I am a fugitive in flight, and my life is in peril. To evade my pursuers, I have fled to Rye, seeking a boat in the harbour, but the nightly curfew has me trapped on the wrong side of town.

With building materials, scaffolding, planks, and poles littering the cobbled streets (Rye is undergoing redevelopment in this period), as a last resort I have concealed myself within a construction site. Covering myself with a tarpaulin, I await the dawn. In the morning, I hope to buy passage to

France or, if not, the north, the Kent or Essex coast. Buying a little time to further my escape.

These last few words are an introduction to the logs hidden within my teeth and bones. Men are approaching my position. They have found me, and my demise is inevitable. I know this, for Gleener described it to me, and I have prepared the sheets of parchment as she instructed before tucking them inside my tunic.

They are here and I cannot escape, and I must not escape. My death is extremely important.

Farewell.

⌛

Personal Log of Dr William Corbiere

Location: unknown

Date: unknown

I will make this quick because something has gone horribly wrong. My heart told me of Moloch's untrustworthiness, and my suspicions have proven legitimate. This is most decidedly not my intended destination! Am I in my parents' back garden, staring at their patio doors? No. Instead, I am up to my knees in freezing seawater, barefoot, and sinking into the sand.

With low cloud concealing the sky, I cannot see a thing, and the shoreline, but ten metres distant, is almost invisible, even in ultraviolet.

So cold. Cold, and confused. The thin smock I wear is no insulation at all, and the slightest breeze sends it flapping, chilling me to my bones. Just where the hell am I? If this is truly the coast of Sussex, south of Pett, I should be beside a road, but there isn't one. Only a reed-choked brook, stinking of sewage. Where are the houses? Where are the lights? Where are the signs of life? The only detectable heat source is a pigsty, the pigs within huddled together for warmth. Startled pigs can be dangerous, so I am giving their pen a very wide berth.

Bushes appear to be growing just beyond the brook and I am heading straight for them. Rudimentary shelter at best.

Wading the brook barefoot is difficult and disgusting and, while resting under a hedge of prickly bushes, I vainly rub my toes.

"Right, come on William," I mutter, "think! You can receive GPS signals. Open your mind to their fluttering... Hmm... Nothing. Not detecting any signals, no radio waves? A malfunction, surely? Running system diagnostic…"

All systems normal.

Shivering now. I need shelter. Shelter, food, water, and soon. According to my internal compass, the sea is to my south, so I am heading uphill, due north… Increasing infrared acuity to maximum. If I detect a heat source, no matter how insignificant, I am heading straight for it.

Increasing my infrared sensitivity has born immediate fruit. There is a heat source. Tiny, barely a flicker, two hundred metres distant. A flame and yellowish in colour, it is undoubtedly artificial, and artificial means people.

Ok. So, the heat source is a lantern, hanging from the timbers of a primitive barn. A barn? Sufficient shelter to wait out the night, but where am I? There are no barns in Pett. The nearest farm is Winchelsea, and their barns are nothing like this. No matter. A covering of hay or straw will keep me alive until morning and then I can look for further signs of civilisation.

This structure continues to baffle me, for it is peculiarly rustic. Certainly, the lantern itself is odd. Steel cage, bullseye glass, two guttering candles. Where could one obtain such a rudimentary contrivance? Moreover, this barn is not for the stabling of livestock. It is a hay store, built from rough-cut timbers, butted, and pegged.

Feeling my way into the interior of the barn, I come across sheathes of hay and bundles of straw, and their dry, sweet smell is curiously welcoming. Sharing my refuge, chattering, and squeaking, are many rodents. I can detect their warmth as they run for cover.

"Got any cheese?" I mutter, and, propping myself against the straw, I try to sleep, awaiting daylight and the opportunity to get my bearings.

⧗

After a restless, itchy, and uncomfortable night, sleep came latterly, but the clippety-clop of hooves and the tinkling of bells suddenly roused me. Panicking like a trespasser, I struggled to my feet before staggering outside, ready to greet both horse and rider…

Twenty metres distant I beheld a golden-haired boy upon a grey pony. Small and red-cheeked, he looked as any young lad, but with his green velvet cloak and long supple boots he projected an aura of nobility.

Stepping from the barn and raising my hand, I called, "Hey, young man, over here!"

A mistake. Suddenly whinnying, the pony tossed the boy from his saddle. His cry of fear and shout of pain as he landed face first in a heap, were then followed by a language I didn't expect. A transitional dialect. A mixture of Breton French, Old Sussex, Middle English. What?

"God's breath," cried the boy. "Away with you, vagabond. To hell with you, and your subterfuge!"

Quickly walking towards the lad, now flat on his back and grasping his shoulder, I witnessed the terror upon his young face.

"Be still," I said. "I mean you no harm. Let me help you."

Frantically struggling to unsheathe a small knife, the young lad screamed. A broken collarbone seemed likely, and I passively knelt beside him.

"Where is the pain?" I asked. "Your shoulder?"

"Yes," gasped the boy. "My arm is a resistance. It is without mettle."

"Certainly," I replied. "I am a doctor. Please, allow me to examine your shoulder."

"*Docteur?*" muttered the boy, flinching from my closeness. "What is *docteur?*"

"Oh." I frowned. "You don't...? A healer. I am a healer. A man of medicine."

"Ah..." said the boy, relaxing slightly. "I comprehend. Then, by all means..."

Gently running my fingers over his shoulder, I could feel his humerus jutting from the glenohumeral socket. A straightforward anterior dislocation and easily remedied by spaso reduction...

"There," I calmly explained. "I can feel it, the displacement of your shoulder. I can reset the bones if you wish, and, following rest, your arm will be fine. Do I have your consent?"

"Do as you wish," replied the lad, "for I am at your mercy, sir, but my father will hear of any treachery."

"No treachery," I assured. "A repayment of a debt. It was I that startled your pony."

"A truth," he replied, trying to sit up. "And is he nearby? Has my nemesis taken flight?"

"No. Worry not. He is but fifty paces distant."

"That is well," he said. "Proceed, Sir. For have duties to perform."

"Very well. Lie back and prepare yourself. For the pain will be sharp."

"I am prepared," he said.

Using my thumb as a guide and increasing the pressure, I suddenly twisted his arm, resetting his shoulder with a crunching click.

"Jesu," cried the boy. "My life is ablaze!"

"There," I remarked. "All done. Now you should rest. Would you permit me the pleasure of accompanying you home?"

Helping him to his feet, (and having nothing to fabricate a sling) I demonstrated how best to hold his arm.

"Allow me to retrieve your pony," I offered, and with my stomach groaning and gurgling, I gathered his grey by the reins and calmly walked him over.

"Most gracious," he replied, adjusting his cloak. "Pray, sir, speak your name. For you have a high bearing. Whence did thou come?"

This was good question and obviously the truth would not suffice...

"Foundered last night," I quickly explained. "Shipwrecked. Washed upon the shore in the pitchest black of night. Soaking wet and freezing, I took refuge, waiting for the dawn. I did not mean to trespass. Merely an act of desperation."

"Your plight earns sympathy," said the boy. "And as a recompense I will take you to my father. For reward perhaps. At the very least, the comforts of nourishment and cloth."

"Most gracious," I replied with a bow. "However, I must ask, where am I? What country is this?"

"Country?" said the boy. "This is Engleland, sir. The realm of the Southern Saxons. For you should know, the nearest town is Rye, then onto Winchelsea. The lands yonder are the lands of my father. Lord of the Manor Luett."

Lifting the young lad into his saddle, he looked down at my state of undress.

"I cannot permit you go further," he said with a frown. "Dressed as you are. You require cloak or mantle at least, and you are barefoot, sir! It is a tidy way to my father. Your feet will mortify, and my pony alas cannot bear us both. For you are a man of... stature?"

"Corbiere," I replied. "Guillarme Corbiere. William is the correct English, is it not?"

"Indeed, sir," said the boy. "You shall be known as William of Corbiere, but I will announce you thus, Guillarmus de Corbiere."

"Most gracious. How should I know you in turn?"

"John," he boasted, "John de Luett. Second son, and squire to my father, Lord Cedric de Luett."

Teeth audibly chattering, I bowed.

"Wait, Sir William," said John, "I shall return expedience with vestments."

Spurring his pony into a trot, he quickly rode towards a cluster of buildings five hundred metres to the east.

With nothing to do but wait, I again huddled inside the barn. It was a good twenty-five minutes before he returned, hailing me as a friend and pointing to a bundle strapped behind his saddle.

"These garments are of Master Weaver," he explained. "They aren't much. Just the rags of a peasant, and yet they should suffice."

Quickly untying the bundle, I released a battered dark cloak, coarse woollen hose, and leather shoes. Well, I say shoes, but these were of a rudimentary design. Of the one-size-fits-all variety, little more than a sheet of soft leather, wrapped around the foot and held in place by laces, and yet, wrapped in these tatters, I was soon feeling warmer. Itchy, awkward and uncomfortable, but decidedly warmer.

"You appear as the ogre de Troyes!" laughed John, noting my frown. "Now, pray, Sir William, take his reins and walk beside me. Calm my intemperate beast."

Now, it may seem incredible, but it was only while walking beside John that the extent of my predicament became clear. In no way was I malfunctioning. There just weren't any transmissions to receive, and not blind either. The tidal generators, the wind turbines, the Dungeness Cocoon, they simply didn't exist.

Threading along a track flanked by farmland and hovels, we came upon a high wall of grey stone dotted with defensible towers.

"Master John," I remarked, as we neared a formidable gate, "permit me to ask, as my mind is a fog. What day is it?"

"The day sir?" replied John, "It is Saturnsday, just after lauds."

"Thank you." I nodded, accessing the word lauds. "And in what year?"

"Year?" The boy chuckled. "The year is but new sir, the year of our Lord, twelve hundreds, nine and eighty, by the papal reckoning."

As you can imagine, this revelation was like slamming into a wall, and a panicking urge to cross-examine the poor lad gnawed at my composure and resolve...

"Granted," I replied. "My thanks, young master, and the Pope would be Nicholas IV? Am I correct?"

"You are, Sir.

"That is well. A good and holy man?"

"Obviously," said John. "But have a care. Such choler before my father is dangerous. His mood is darker of late."

Expecting a cold and draughty space, the rugs, tapestries, murals, and impressive central fire pit of the manor's great hall took me by surprise. Charcoal braziers supplied everyday heat, and John and I stood before one, rubbing our hands in satisfaction. Ranks of long tables and benches surrounded the firepit, but upon a dais against the far wall, two proud men stooped over a table draped in an embroidered blue cloth.

"Father!" cried John, approaching the dais. "Please, father. I have brought a visitor. A nobleman deserving our charity."

"Charity?" muttered the man on the left. "Should've taken the rogue to the friars."

Snorting his agreement and wiping his beard with the back of his hand, the other man studied at me with suspicion…

"So, longshanks," he began "who are you and whence forth? Speak! For my time is precious and the winter days are short."

"Father!" cried John in dismay, but I merely raised my hand, quietening the lad before bowing low.

"Guillarme de Corbiere is my name," I said. "On these shores, William of Corbiere, but I washed up last night. Like flotsam, bobbing in the surf, I beached before taking refuge in a nearby barn. Your goodly son discovered me, whereupon he took a discomforting fall from his pony. Of which I am partly to blame for alarming the beast."

"You speak well," he then said. "And that is of immediate relief. I am Lord Cedric de Luett, and you are clearly a man of bearing. Are you a Frenchman, sir? For your words bear little Francish inflection."

"No," I replied. "I am England born, and son of a noble family. We hail from France, tis true, but my heart is of England."

"That is well. For the French are my enemy. They shit upon this land. Ravaging, pillaging, burning, and we have not the power to turn them. The noble king hammers his fist upon the Scots, and we are left defenceless."

For good measure, I bowed once more, and then John boldly stepped forward.

"This man is a knight," he blurted, his cheeks reddening with zeal, "and a God-sent healer. I fell, Father. Unhorsed like a sack from my nemesis, mortifying my shoulder, but Sir William, he healed me, marvellous and quick!"

"Then, God be praised!" The Lord laughed. "For I need you on the eastern fences. Tell Master Hedger and Master Hurdleman I want a dozen hills* ready for flocks by Candlemas. If he needs more material, make sure he tells the reeve. Get going, and this time, Jesu! Ride the mare. That grey is good only for the plough."

*Hill. Old Sussex term for one-half acre.

Evidently dismissed, John turned on his heels and made for the door.

"Now," said Lord Cedric, "would you care to break your fast with me? For repairing my foolish son, I am in your debt, and I would hear your tale in full. Indeed, you are lucky to be alive, sir. Even in the summer the Channel is a frigid killer. In winter it is certain death!"

"Break-fast" 13th-century style was a simple, calorific affair, and exactly what I needed. First things first, bread. Huge round loaves, still hot from the oven. A greyish white sourdough with a blackened crust, but taken with honey, berry conserves, and lightly salted butter it was delicious. There were other treats too, fish. Herring or mackerel, salted, smoked, swimming in warm spiced milk, with eggs, hard-boiled, and all washed down by a rustic ale drunk from a tankard of leather.

There was certainly no lack of provision and Lord Cedric chuckled as I polished off everything offered, while his brother-in-law, after nibbling a crust or two, retired to saddle his horse.

The story, the sacksful of lies I gave Lord Cedric about my circumstances, were preposterous, and I struggled to keep my deception simple. Of course, there was no way he could check the validity of my fiction, so I did the best I could. My story went as follows...

"Leaving England ten years ago to join the Crusades in Acre, I was captured en route, not for ransom but as a slave. Bundled, jostled, taken into the east by Ottoman Turks, further and further, always travelling, over land and sea to the land of Nihon. The people of Nihon were small," I explained, "like children, but olive-skinned, with straight black hair, and narrowing eyes of an unpitying brown. They were God-less also. Pagans, venerating their ancestors, plants, animals, even everyday things like rocks and rivers. With shining swords of razor steel, their warriors were both ferocious and courageous, while their womenfolk were tiny, like finches, clad in shimmering silk. It was in Nihon I learnt of herbs and healing, earning my freedom, treating the ailments afflicting the families, wards, and livestock of prominent lords."

"Throughout my slow return into the west, I earned my crust medicating those in need. The final leg of the journey, travelling from Rouen to London, I sought employment among the nobility, but now, finding myself here, I pledge my service in full."

"Indeed," he replied. "Then, pray, how should I value your pledge? You are not a knight ordained. My purse is empty enough!"

"Fear not," I assured, "Your coin is safe. A puissant man-at-arms I am not. I lack both the tenacity and bloodlust. I serve instead with the baggage, repairing the wounded, fending off ailments and disease, tending the horses and beasts of burden. In the low countries, I endeavoured to treat the ailments of sheep and pigs, discovering my herbs and poultices to be quite benefitting."

With an understanding of the theory only, these tales of my veterinary prowess are a gamble, and although I was confident of diagnosis, in this period, what could I do? Physiotherapy, antisepsis, parasitic control? Certainly, if Lord Cedric did agree to use my skills, a degree of fallibility will be important. Too much success and my fame might spread, raising suspicion among the religious and ruling community. To be known as a local quack, armed with poultices, potions, and salves, would be acceptable (and nothing new), but a supernatural reputation could land me in trouble. Serious trouble. With the Inquisition, no less, and who would want to be racked? Quite tall enough, thanks.

A long and careful thinker, Lord Cedric made me wait while he considered my words, and, twiddling his beard, he peered into the glowing embers of a nearby brazier.

Returning with a face both chiselled and fraught, Sir Gilbert bowed low...

"My Lord," he announced, "my horse, he is lame! His fetlock is a bulb of distension. Do we have another?"

Full of woe, Lord Cedric bowed his head, cursing under his breath.

"Take mine," he then replied, "but keep him from water. The farrier commends dryness for his weakened hooves."

Snatching an opportunity to prove my worth, I turned to Sir Gilbert, asking, "How is your horse lame, sir? Is he up and walking, hobbling, or sweating?"

"He is up," replied Gilbert, "but his windpuffs are heated this morning. He places no weight upon his foreleg sinister."

"Indeed," I remarked. "May I see him? I do have experience in *medicina equorum* (although in truth I had none). If fortune prevails, I will endeavour to provide a remedy."

"Go, then," said Cedric, "consider this a test of your worth. For my bread is not without cost."

"Follow," beckoned Sir Gilbert, waving towards the western door, "The stabling is yonder."

With a full reddish-brown beard, Lord Cedric's brother-in-law, Sir Gilbert de Colline was a portly man of about thirty-five. Although, ever present, assisting in the day-to-day running of the estate, when called, he would chivalrously don his armour, fighting in local militia. He fought alongside the king and Lord Cedric putting down the Welsh. He showed me his scars (arrow wounds to his shoulder and left hand). From my perspective, he had been lucky to avoid serious infection, and I asked him how he survived...

"Prayer," he replied. "The Lord smiled upon me, and I was healed."

I later discovered a local woman had bandaged his wounds after applying a garlic poultice. Not a potent antiseptic but better than nothing.

A naturally occurring inflammation of the fetlock, windpuffs are usually the result of over-work and old age. When healthy, the swelling is both localised and cool to the touch.

With the stablemaster and Sir Gilbert looking on, I quickly assessed the horse, before kneeling to examine his foreleg. In sweat and periodically lifting the affected limb, the poor beast's windpuffs were hot and distended. Without treatment there was little doubt he would die.

"Pray, sir," asked Sir Gilbert, "can anything be done? My good steed and I share a deep bond. It is grievous to find him so discomforted."

"Can try," I replied. "Try draining his inflammation. First, his fetlock must be cleansed. Have you a lancet or bloodstick? For I shall need to bleed him."

"Surely," said Sir Gilbert. "The Master of Horse has many implements of mortification. Need you anything else?"

"Afraid so," I admitted. "Bandages. Boiled in freshly drawn water. Some aqua vitae if you have it, a basin, and could the Master of Horse assist? Thy steed may panic much and require restraint."

The Master of Horse was a shabby individual, but he knew horses, and he quietly calmed the beast as I cautiously swabbed the diseased fetlock in aqua vitae (a variety of distilled alcoholic spirit).

Cleaning and wiping a long hollow lancet, I then pierced the centre of the inflamed fetlock, relieving the pressure, draining what fluid I could into a pewter basin.

Once the flow of lymph has abated, I repeated the swabbing process before wrapping and tying off sterile bandages over the affected area. With a soft leather boot to go over the bandages, I likewise cleaned it with aqua vitae before carefully tightening its laces.

Taking a small sip from the aqua vitae, Sir Gilbert gasped in astonishment…

"Fire water." He coughed. "How will he fare, Sir William? He already seems easing. Is he healed?"

"Time will tell," I replied, peering into the basin. "If he shows no improvement three days hence, his recovery is unlikely."

The fluid was certainly turbid, but not stinking, indicative of a mild infection, and I felt confident the horse would resist.

"Master Horseman," I instructively commanded, "tomorrow at noon his bandages should be renewed. You saw how I cleaned and bound him. Do the same."

"As you wish, sir," he replied. "Yet the Spirits of Wine? We servants are forbidden such treasure. From whom will I receive it?"

"Verily, tis true," said Sir Gilbert. "The pleasures of the grape are forbidden to his ilk. Is there no alternative medicament?"

"None," I replied. "However, worry not. If Lord Cedric permits, I shall return and perform the task myself."

"Would take that most kindly," said Sir Gilbert, stoppering the green glazed flask. "Take this to my Lord and explain what has befallen, Master Horseman? I require his Lordship's steed."

"As you wish." The master stooped. "For he is already in harness."

Weeks have passed and some recapping is in order… Things are going quite well. Sir Gilbert's horse made a reasonable recovery, and years of service remain before him. Certainly, Lord Cedric and Sir Gilbert were at once delighted with my treatment, and, when John returned from his errand, I shared their midday meal of fish, mixed pulses, bread, and spiced pork. Lord Cedric ordered the serving of wine, and there was a long toast hailing their ancestors, the king, Jesus, God the omnipotent, and a host of local saints. The wine was awful. God only knows what it was. A blend of grapes from Bordeaux most probably (a product of the Benedictine order), and I copied Sir Gilbert, adding a little honey to blunt the edge of its vinegary tartness.

Still stuck here, mind you, counting the days, anticipating any sign, some acknowledgement my return to the KBE is coming, but will it ever happen? If the ravings of Moloch are credible, and his realm is truly immune to the linear progression of time, my waiting may well be in vain. Here in the 13th century, I flourish, however. My skills, both medical and scientific, used carefully, are winning me renown. Already benefitting from my presence, as a reward Lord Cedric has provided me with a cot. Great, you might think, a house, but let's not get ahead of ourselves! A cot is an extremely basic structure – reed-thatched, single-chambered, single-floored, with walls of flint cemented by lime mortar and cob. In winter, the damp and the draughts are enough to freeze the marrow, and the darkness… Well, there are two unglazed windows, only they are tiny, and, lacking a chimney, lighting any fire is suffocating. Not to mention dangerous. Setting the roof ablaze is a constant peril! At night, I sleep on a pallet. A wooden box with a mattress of fleece. Wrapped in woollen blankets, I shiver, dreaming of modernity. With plenty to eat and drink, my health remains perfect. Lucky. To prolong their lifespan, my implants I use only rarely, and my Hibbites are almost inactive. Meaning, I get the odd pimple, but it is worth it. In these unsanitary times, a serious infection is always a possibility, and preserving my Hibbites for emergencies makes perfect sense.

Promising better accommodation in the spring, Lord Cedric pays for my services with meals, clothing, and the occasional silver penny. Half of this money I secretly donate to the wretched villeins working the land, but the rest is for the various materials needed to expand my medical repertoire. Sir Gilbert, John, and I are riding to the market in Rye this coming Friday, and with ideas about producing antiseptics, antifungals, and medicines, it will be useful to find out what is available. More of this next week – the capacity of my neocortex is limited and decompressing the historical data regarding life in this period is currently my priority. As ordered by Walsingham, when facing peril, I have activated our osteo/dental data storage protocol. An anatomic message in a bottle, encoded so deeply it will be nine hundred years before humanity has the technology to read it.

Hello future! This is the past speaking and it's 'orrible. Itchy, smelly, dark, damp, and, by God, I could murder a cup of coffee! New project. Search the botanical database for caffeine. There must be something growing around here I can use instead of coffee.

⧗

Just returned from church (my life brims with church) and, frankly, I am sick to death of it. John, explaining the religious calendar, has been immensely helpful, and he has taken it upon himself to make sure I don't overlook any of the edicts, feasts, traditions, or festivals. "Keeping the Church" is a legal prerequisite in this period, and the punishments for nonconformity range from the trivial to the downright sadistic.

Today it was Candlemas, the festival commemorating the purification of the Blessed Virgin Mary, and Lord Cedric is throwing the customary feast, and not before time; the service was inordinately long. With every householder from miles around turning up with their candles, all wanting them blessed, the church was packed to the rafters.

For a major religious festival, even Sunday mass, Lord Cedric's entire family and the local populace make for the new church in Winchelsea. Trouble is, it is only two-thirds built, and there simply isn't enough space for the congregation, and when I say congregation, I mean mob. Sure, there is a degree of order, everyone knows their place. The de Luett's have their private chapel, higher classes at the front, plebs at the back, with the rest overflowing into the aisle or propped against wall or pillar. Fine, you might think, the church gets crowded. Oh my, yes, it certainly does, and the stench is eye-watering. I suddenly understood the purpose of incense!

Another problem, beyond the overcrowding, was the livestock. Fearful of thieving, the peasantry would bring their entire farm given the chance, with dogs, sheep, lambs, chickens, ducks, geese, goats, running, flapping, bleating, clucking, honking, barking. Outside, during a major service, the land resembles a market, with pens for sheep, cattle, and pigs, with sturdy posts and railings for the halting of horses, donkeys, and ponies.

During the mass, the priests conceal themselves behind a wooden screen and only aristocracy (including myself) receive an unimpeded view. John explained that the screen is both ceremonial and practical, a means of keeping the rabble and their beasts separate from the holy elevation, before recounting a tale of an earlier Palm Sunday, when a spirited goat made it onto the altar.

Heavily clad in gaudy vestments, muttering and murmuring in Latin, the clergy seemed unabashed by the noisy pandemonium. They just got on with it. Reciting the proper psalms, canticles, prayers, elevating the host, offering the sacrament to anyone paying attention.

This casual, almost ambivalent attitude towards the Church and religion was initially a shock, and not in keeping with my historical references. However, the more I ponder it, the plainer the truth becomes. How can I explain? Consider the problems of the age. Life is hard, life is short. Poor diet, poor healthcare, grinding toil, disease, and grievous child mortality strip life of its merit and meaning. Why wouldn't the lowest echelons of society seek solace in the promise of salvation? If the crops fail or your pig dies, you starve. What can you do but pray? Yet, despite this, religious observance was compulsory. Along with its tithes, tolls, and taxes, and, in doing so, the church came into conflict with an important aspect of the human condition. Self-betterment. Improving one's lot through work and determination, e.g., a good harvest. My pig is healthy. We ploughed, planted, toiled, sweated, and laboured. We reap the surplus of our industry. God the Almighty had nothing to do with it. The sick and the dying only cry for God when their mother is not at their side, and religious observance in this community is similar. Lacking fervour. Unless the French come raiding or pestilence sweeps the land, the people pay up and follow the church as directed. Albeit through gritted teeth.

Lord Cedric, his family and inner circle are all decidedly atheistic (although I doubt they knew it). They only put on a show of piety when they have to. Cedric, for example, is more concerned with the day-to-day running of his estate and the gathering of money than religious upkeep. The Franciscan monastery at Winchelsea he particularly loathes, and not in the slightest is he swayed by their vow of poverty. Of the surrounding land, a great deal is their property, and monks charge their tenants accordingly.

Furthermore, the friars are not only the sole producers of honey and mead in the neighbourhood, but they are also brewers of excellent beer, enjoying a monopoly on wine imported from the continent.

"Go see the Greyfriars yourself," he would scorn. "See first-hand their clever web of piety. Oh yes. Such adherence, such perseverance. Their food is basic, their cloth is poor, and their prayers are long and hard. Yet, beneath it all, their veins run with *my* silver, and their piss is pope-ish gold."

EIGHT

PEAS AND BACON

I t is Easter and I am still alive. Too busy to think about dying! Certainly, my life has been a blur of activity. I need to catch up with my record-keeping, and thank you, UET, for my translation implant. What a tremendous piece of technology! It has proved to be (quite literally) a lifesaver. In this society, status is everything, and being able to speak the same dialect as the nobility has instantly elevated me into their ranks. Height has also proven a factor. Six-footers are rare in this period, and in most cases favoured. Only the upper classes enjoy a diet sufficiently nourishing for full physical development. If one is tall, well spoken, and educated, one must be of noble birth, and of this I have taken full of advantage. I'm well fed, healthy, wealthy, safely housed, and, most importantly, respected.

The Church calendar burgeons approaching Easter Sunday, with its lavish feast and egg-swapping, but the lead-up has been a gruelling, sometimes fascinating, sometimes hilarious, marathon of strange festivities. Following Shroves Day, entering the forty days of Lent, I was expecting serious dietary and lifestyle privations. Ha! I should have known better...

In theory, throughout Lent, the Church forbids the eating of dairy products, meat, eggs, and both marriage and sex are taboo. However, there are exceptions, and the workarounds for these restrictions are joyous. Lord Cedric, for example, simply took his meals in secret – unless a member of the religious community was present, then he would put on the whole shebang, his cook's culinary hair shirt, the blandest, vegetable-based sludge-fest you could ever regret imbibing. Fish and shellfish were still eaten (especially on Fridays), and in the evening the Lenten vows became strangely forgotten. As for the restrictions in the bedroom, Lord Cedric, following a stout poke in my ribs, muttered, "Be assured, Sir William, the Francs know ways around that!" Not entirely sure what he meant, but I doubt his wife was a fan of it.

The Easter celebrations following Palm Sunday began with a sequence of evening masses known as the Tenebrae. Beginning brightly illuminated, throughout the ceremony, the priests steadily extinguish the candles until only one remains. Once virtual darkness is achieved, the priests complete the service by striking a loud drum. (Made me jump the first time!)

In Winchelsea, this created all sorts of problems for the congregation, and I heard much shuffling, crashing, and cursing as the multitude made for the door. We nobles (avoiding the fracas) remained seated until the rabble had dispersed, and I noticed Sir Gilbert and Lord Cedric sitting with daggers drawn. A wise precaution as it was very dark indeed!

The next notable pre-Easter festival was Sharp Thursday. An oddly symbolic event of purification, but good if you want a free haircut. A great deal of foot-washing took place as well – mine cleansed by well-meaning peasants. In keeping with tradition, I gave them alms for their efforts, and they left me well pleased.

The historical documents concerning the celebrations for Good Friday, Holy Saturday, Easter Sunday, and Monday are comprehensive, in the main accurate, and the priesthood stuck to their remit, enforcing all the traditions with due diligence, and, not wishing cause offence, I hung my palm (bulrush) crucifix proudly (and prominently) over my door.

John says it will bring me good fortune.

Following months living in this period, I have come to a startling conclusion. All history is bunk. Well, perhaps not all, but the written records from this period are just that. Written. Penned by the "educated". A tiny segment of the population, each with their own agenda – be it political, religious, military, or financial, and in the main, they reduce the general populace to little more than beasts of burden. This ambivalence towards the lower classes is not genuinely surprising. To keep the peons well yoked benefits the privileged, but, after spending time among the everyday folk of Sussex, I find this characterisation to be tragically false. The villeins and peasantry working the land hereabouts are nothing short of wondrous.

Their lives are so rich! Yes, there is hunger, disease, grinding toil, and fear of invasion, but they all work together, and crime is almost unknown. For there is little to gain from it. I hear of a little debauchery here and there, occasional drunkenness, or adultery, but serious crime is exceedingly rare. As for education, the working people are just as smart as everyone else. Boy, do they know their onions! They know everything they need to know. Of course, many of their explanations for everyday natural phenomena are preposterous but it is not their fault. The microscopic world, for example, is unknown, and, when treating diseases, I am particularly careful when justifying my actions. Why use antiseptic soap? "Cleanliness is next to Godliness" serves me quite well, and most questions cease when I proffer this vague argument. Life in Lord Cedric's little community runs very well. Everyone knows their place, and the reeve, the peasant's leader and representative at the manor, is the shrewdest of the lot. What a player he is! Weighing the demands of Lord Cedric against the lives, skills, stamina, and resources of the workers. It is little wonder he landed himself the role. As I have eluded, my historical records describing the practical understanding of the everyday people are rubbish. For example, sex. Meaning, reproduction, inheritance, genetics, and the circle of life. The lower echelons know very well where animals come from and how their offspring turn out, and why wouldn't they? Their children are dissimilar. When a black cat breeds with a white one, the kittens tend not to be grey... According to my historical records, the people were said to claim rotten meat spontaneously gave rise to maggots and old rags propagated mice. Laughable. The poor of this region eat mice and voles; they excavate their nests and often unearth mothers suckling their young. As for flies and maggots...You can see the flies laying their eggs and watch them hatch several days later!

The glitterati and the privileged, the writers of the history I carry, never worked in a kitchen or butchers, watching flies landing on meat. Their tutors were the classical works of the period. Real-world experience was beyond their reach. If you want to master the propagation of plants, the harvesting of grain, or the raising of livestock, don't bother Hippocrates, Aristotle, or Theophrastus. Ask a gardener, a farmer, or a shepherd.

After weeks of trying, my quest for caffeine, finding a substitute for coffee, has failed. Coffee-like drinks I can produce, roasting and percolating beech nuts, hazelnuts, acorns, and chicory root, but none contain any caffeine. The only caffeine-rich plant in this period is holly, *Ilex aquifolium*, the leaves and the berries, but they also contain numerous toxins, and I am not prepared to risk imbibing the gloop obtained by distilling them. Besides, it smells awful.

With my continued antics, trying to provide a degree of healthcare for the region's population, animals, and livestock, Lord Cedric had the local craftsmen build me a house. More spacious and suitable than the peasant's cot I previously inhabited, it has stone foundations surmounted by a timber framework with walls of wattle and daub. Its roof is of reed thatch, but only temporarily – Lord Cedric intends to replace the thatch with tiles from the Dickering. * A good thing too! Thatched roofs are a fire hazard. One spark and the whole lot can go up, and, considering this, I instructed the local stonemasons to build an inglenook fireplace, flue, and chimney into the back wall. These industrious fellows were quite taken aback by my design. Marvelling at its cleverness, they wondered where I got the idea. I said, such installations were commonplace in the Netherlands, and left it at that.

Now known as The Dicker. A village near Hailsham, East Sussex.

The medicines used hereabouts are herbal and most are too dilute, contaminated, or oxidised to have any virtue. Avoiding these traditional potions and salves, I focus on microbial and parasitic hygiene, analgesia, antipyresis, physiotherapy, splints, traction, and, where possible, minor surgery. House calls sometimes, but I also receive visitors looking for a cure or relief from some malady or other. Most of my callers are men, only very rarely are they women, and they tend to be desperate mothers bearing sickly children. My house calls however do concern women, very often pregnant women. I perform a great deal of midwifery!

The veterinary services I provide are basic – assessment, diagnosis, and advice (mostly). Lord Cedric, in receipt of sheep recently driven from Kent, had me inspect every animal, my opinion of their general health dictating their price! They weren't in the greatest of shakes after their long trudge west, and I treated their foot rot with a salve of my own making. Being a mixture of goose grease and birch tar, it was far from ideal, although mildly antiseptic. No idea if it made any difference. Certainly, I need iodine very badly, but, with the rudimentary apparatus at my disposal, extracting it from seawater or seaweed is impossible. Lord Cedric claims the Grey Friars perform alchemy, and if I need an alembic, I should speak to them.

Ever eager to help, John is teaching me how to ride. With my enhanced balance and coordination, I am making rapid progress, and, as a reward, he has offered me his nemesis, his skittish grey pony. Not wishing to be ungrateful, I carefully inspected the beast, comparing his size and strength to my weight, before saying, because of my bulk, it would be certain death for the both of us! Instead, I ride Sir Gilbert's gelding, Marigoule. A slow, pliant, shaggy old chestnut, he gets me where I need to go, eventually.

Lady Edith, John, and his young sister Ruth came with Sir Gilbert one afternoon seeking a private consultation. For me, this was a signal honour, and the first time I have socialised with the female members of Lord Cedric's family, and, although I have seen them at church (and they do acknowledge me), never have we interacted.

To begin, we sat in awkward silence, an examination of sorts. Lady Edith, short, wide, wearing a heavy red gown, hooded, cloaked, with Ruth, a very tiny ten-year-old, in a gown of white linen embroidered with coloured silk. Hanging from a circlet of silver, a veil of lace all but covered her face.

With a nod of approval from Lady Edith, Sir Gilbert took John outside, shutting the door behind him...

"You are known as Sir William," said Lady Edith. "My husband trusts you and he is grateful for the service you show him, but my dear Ruth begs a favour, for her prayers of deliverance remain unheard."

"Of course," I replied with a bow. "What service do you require, my lady?"

"Show him," said Edith. "And do not be fearful. This man runs with much kindness, and even now I see the truth of him."

"As you wish," muttered Ruth.

Carefully removing her veil, the face that greeted me was one of innocence, shame, and sadness. Scarred by smallpox, her gentle skin was pocked and uneven, and as I leant closer, she trembled, tears rolling from her shining blue eyes.

Offering her a pad of clean linen, she dappled her cheeks and smiled.

"Thank you kindly," she sniffed. "Do you not recoil from my disfigurement?"

"Nay," I replied. "There is none to see. Only beauty, care, and innocence. Have no shame. For your markings will lessen in time, and I will concoct a salve to hasten the fading."

This of course was placebo speak. There was nothing I could do, and yet a moisturising and mildly antiseptic concoction would provide confidence and purpose while her scarring slowly faded.

Seeing the scarred face of young Ruth and recognising her immunity to smallpox, I turned my thoughts to her brother. John was unmarked. Had he not caught the disease?

"Lady Edith," I asked, "could I speak to you privately? Another matter, one involving John now brings me concern. Will you hear me?"

"Certainly," replied Edith. "Yet, for reasons of dignity, my brother must stand by. Harken as I call him."

Responding to her address, Sir Gilbert returned with John at his shoulder.

"Good brother," said Edith, "pray, stay a while. Sir William wishes conversation in private and, children, do as I bid and take the air a while. I will join you shortly."

With a bow and joining hands, John and Ruth quickly made for the door.

"Now, sir," said Edith, "what irks thee?"

"Forgive my bluntness," I replied, "but I must know. The smallpox? Ruth suffered its fire, when exactly?"

"Two years hence," she acknowledged. "Her fever was mild, yet lesions and binnacles covered every inch of her. Her skin was a trial and a torment for many weeks thereafter."

"I doubt that but a little. However, John did not share her contagion?"

"No," replied Edith, "for we kept them apart. It is well known the pox travels between the godly like whispers in a parlour."

"That is well, but, still, he is in peril of the disease. May I aid its prevention in him?"

"Most assuredly," she replied. "Thy path to accomplish this I know not, but if you can shield my treasured sunshine, by all means proceed."

"Good," I said, "for I am boundlessly fond of the lad. I will do what I can."

Having nursed a local dairymaid for cowpox a fortnight earlier, I knew something could done for John. Although I had little to remedy the dairymaid, I recognised her disease, and knew she would recover. In most cases, cowpox provides immunity to smallpox, and infecting John with cowpox might well spare him the agony contracting its lethal cousin.

Here I must pause to document my early attempts formulating

medicines, antiseptics, disinfectants, and anti-parasitic agents. After some investigation, I came across an abundance of antiseptic, disinfecting plants and substances, including ethanol, vinegar, various salts, brine, garlic, honey, thyme, mint, St John's Wort, and rose (the hips and petals), but extracting and/ or concentrating these substances, before combining them within a suitable medium for application, has proven to be an enormous technical challenge. As for suitable media, I was working blind. Relying on trial, error, and animal experimentation to see what was effective. Goose grease, beeswax, lard, and tallow were all easily obtainable (and relatively inexpensive), whereas olive oil and other vegetable oils were pricier, and their quality extremely variable. Wood oils and tars were also obtainable, commonly used in carpentry, and I tried using turpentine as a non-polar solvent for steroidal and lipid-based extracts (essential oils), with varying degrees of success. Birch oil, a cheap alternative to coal tar, has proven to be a rich source of compounds. Indeed, in this region, coal is an expensive luxury, and not used much as a domestic heat source. Its toxic fumes and cloying smoke make it useless.

The preparation of analgesic, antipyretic, and/or anti-inflammatory drugs has proven to be a waste of time and resources. At least, with the equipment and raw materials at my disposal. The synthesis of acetaminophen or paracetamol, for example, has proven impossible, with every chemical pathway leading to its production a dead end. Similarly, its more toxic cousins, phenacetin and acetanilide, are quite beyond my reach – the unavailability of ethanoic anhydride being the problem, and my every attempt of synthesising it has resulted in failure.

At first, aspirin seemed a more promising candidate, The use of willow bark as a "feverfew" well established hereabouts, and it is the aspirin-like compound salicin, an alcoholic beta glucoside held in the sap, which provides the benefit. In this form, taken directly, the low concentration limits the effect, and the compounds themselves less beneficial than true aspirin, acetylsalicylic acid. Again, hindering the synthesis of true aspirin is the unavailability of ethanoic anhydride (or ethanoyl chloride), and that is before I come to the headache of constructing the apparatus needed to reflux the constituents! Faced with this, I tried to extract and concentrate willow bark sap, concocting a palatable tonic, suitable for ingestion. Not easy, let me tell you! In the mouth, willow sap is fiercely bitter, not to mention hard on the stomach, and I experimented with mixing it with honey and herbs to soften the blow.

An antiseptic I still particularly desire is iodine. Even a few crystals would be enough, and I attempted to reproduce the findings of Bernard Courtois, burning seaweed and treating its ashes with various acids. No luck to begin with, but the only acids at my disposal were weak. If I could get a little sulphur, or, even better, oil of vitriol (sulphuric acid), it would work. Trouble was, I didn't have the slightest idea where to obtain these treasures. Neither was for sale at the market in Rye, although Lord Cedric assured me, following the Easter festivities, the spring fair would bring traders from Amsterdam, Flanders, and Zeeland, selling wares, elixirs, and spices from the East. Lord Cedric restocked his kitchens with the little luxuries these traders provided, grumbling about their exorbitant prices.

Another useful antimicrobial substance, requiring a little work to obtain, was phenol, 1-hydroxybenzene. The distillation of coal and coal tar is the time-honoured technique for obtaining it, and even five millilitres were sufficient to pep up the bars of the ghastly "Castile" soap I have bought.

Yes. Soap is obtainable in the 13th century. However, it is crude, unperfumed, grey, and gritty. Made from olive oil, tallow, and ashes, the lather it produces, even in the softest of waters, is unremarkable. Once I had something to medicate this "soap" I devised a technique to both combine and refine by melting.

⏳

Early spring, I am coming across individuals showing the symptoms of scurvy, a deficiency of vitamin C. In truth, this is hardly surprising. The diet of the villeins and peasantry is unchanging, and in the winter months, once their stored produce is gone, they rely on bread, dried pulses, frost-resistant vegetables (parsnips and mangelwurzels), bacon, fish, and shellfish. They cook everything very heavily, too, almost to a mush, and any Vitamin C is lost. Lacking any supplement for the sufferers, I recommended they eat their roots raw or even try sashimi. I think they think me crazy.

⏳

It is Easter Tuesday and Lord Cedric has (grudgingly) allowed me to visit the Franciscan monastery (and brewery) adjacent to Winchelsea. Concerned for my safety, he offered me one of his newly acquired horses, but I declined, saying the walk would do me good. Nonetheless, he insisted I arm myself, and provided a long dagger, belt, and scabbard, suggesting I partially conceal it beneath my tunic. Although flattered to be of value to his lordship, it is only three miles to the monastery, and highly unlikely I will encounter anyone. Besides, I will hear and smell any ruffians long before they see me.

I didn't know what to expect from the friars. I found much on file regarding the religious and political shifts of the Franciscan order, particularly following the death of St Francis himself, but of the day-to-day life of the monks there was next to nothing. Is the man in charge an Abbot or a prior? Is speaking allowed, and, if so, in what dialect? Is Latin their chosen language, or is it the strange hybrid dialect of the locals? What about visitors? Would they receive an unannounced guest such as me? Only one way to find out.

Despite my natural apprehension, bold courtesy is my approach in unavoidable situations. Honest, direct, and friendly. Walk up to the main gate, knock if I must, and wait.

A stone wall surrounded the grounds of the monastery, but the gates were wooden and propped open on one side by a log. Just inside, I could see a small wooden hut, and, as I approached, an aged friar, leaning on a quarterstaff, adjusted his grey cloak and hobbled out to greet me...

"Pray, sir," he commanded, showing a defiant white palm. "Guard your steps, for I know thee not and crave your intendment."

His language was indeed the same vernacular I had been speaking for the last few months, and I wondered if the friars were all local men, come seeking peace, atonement, or spiritual fulfilment.

Adopting a passive stance, I bowed low and graciously.

"And good day to you, Master Porter," I said. "My intention here is tentative. I wish to both learn and exchange knowledge, for I am a scholar and a healer, come from yonder by the permission of his lordship, Cedric de Luett."

"Ah!" gasped the friar, lowering his hand. "Word has reached us of the newly arrived healer. Some say you are a worker of miracles."

"Nay." I scowled. "Listen not to the whispers of fools. I only offer what is God-given. Cleanliness, herbs, and simples, but I would speak with your prior. For I wish to be known to him."

"You may," replied the friar, "but keep well to the rule. Speak not with any friar without permission, and worry not their labours, be they physical or devotional. Do not profane or speak ill and you are armed, I see. This is forbidden. Offer up your side and strap or you may go no further."

This all seemed reasonable (and quite as expected), and I dutifully removed my dagger and belt before handing them over.

"The dagger is Lord Cedric's," I explained. "A precaution, nothing more. He feared for my safety."

"That is well." The friar nodded. "And worry not. It will be returned upon your departure."

The monk keeping the gate took me a short way before handing me to a novice.

"Brother Prior is with medu-tuns this morn," explained the novice. "And I am to escort you directly... sir?"

"William," I corrected. "William de Corbiere."

"An honour, sire," and the novice bowed, his loose robes almost slipping from his shoulders. "Tristian I am called and just Tristian. For my tonsure is not until the feast of Stephen next."

The meduseld or mead hall consisted of little more than a barn and sheds. Bottling was taking place and it was the prior doing the tasting. The old geezer was somewhat worse for wear...

Tristian introduced me before heading back to the gate. The prior invited me to sit and watch the tapping, bottling, and stoppering.

"Wondered when you would come," he began, scratching his posterior. "And know you of our gratitude? Your goodly tender and charity keep many a villein from our doors. Did Lord Cedric send you hence?"

"Indeed," I replied. "In truth, I am running short of supplies and wonder if I may trade knowledge for material? As, I understand, my coin is forbidden?"

"Most strictly," said the prior. "And yet you may donate most charitably for the upkeep of the priory. For the winter frosts have sundered much stone and we require the skill of both mason and plumber."

"Certainly," I replied. "A small donation, then? And, if I knew of thy crafts, the knowledge gained from my travels might be of benefit."

"Come then," said the prior, struggling to his feet. "Walk a while, witness our achievements, for the air will clear my head of blossom."

The tour of the monastery took three-quarters of an hour, and I found Lord Cedric's cynicism to be well justified. Dressed shabbily, the friars took simple meals, slept on hard beds, grafting, praying, chanting, singing, studying the scriptures, and yet the great hall of the priory was resplendent. Richly carved, brightly decorated, with murals, and hung tapestries depicting religious scenes. The furnishings were ornate. Polished, and gleaming with silver inlay, and was that gold leaf I saw glinting in the daylight streaming through the windows of stained and painted glass?

Another indicator of the friars' underlying wealth was their lavatory and bathroom. Cleanliness is important to the Franciscan order and… they had hot water! Ok. It was a laughably primitive piece of plumbing. Just a single tap connected by lead piping to a copper boiler, but an incredible luxury for the period. The friars provided their own healthcare too, and I was lucky enough to look over their stores. Herbal remedies and classical medicines abounded, and they adhered stubbornly to the humoristic belief system of Hippocrates and Galen, even when it proved blatantly detrimental.

The small library of the friars was a joy, a veritable gold mine of classical works, all of them handwritten, thickly bound in tooled leather, with pages of parchment or vellum. Of these tomes, a few were enormous, requiring two men to lift! There were religious treatises and biblical works, medical, scientific, and philosophical works, histories, tall tales of travel, with ridiculous maps of faraway lands.

Well-tended, the monastery gardens were extensive and varied. Certainly, the friars tried to be self-sufficient in herbs, fruit, and vegetables, and it was here I came across an opportunity to be helpful…

Dotting the gardens, I spied many primitive beehives, and I begged permission to speak with the apiarist (a portly old monk of about sixty). Delighted by my interest, he enthusiastically showed me the hives, all of them buzzing and active. I asked him how he extracted the honey.

This was a ruse. I had already accessed the relevant files on beekeeping the moment I entered the garden. Little more than a straw or wicker basket covered in clay, the beehives (or skeps) of this period were simple structures, and only designed to be temporary. Indeed. I say temporary, for when the beehive became sufficiently heavy (with honey), the apiarist would simply gas the bees by burning sulphur under the beehive. Not very efficient, rather destructive, and cruel.

To remedy this situation, I suggested he try using an eke * – a removable extension (a "super") affixed to the skep with an internal door controlled from the outside. Initially, while the hive grows, the door remains closed, but once fully established, opening it encourages the bees to move in, producing new combs. Once full, the internal door can be closed, the Eke removed, and the honey extracted. This technique has the advantage of not killing the hive, before showing him how smoke from smouldering hay made the hive more passive, recommending he wear at least a degree of protective clothing when doing so. If only to cover his face!

Hence the expression "to eke out more room".

If my intervention here has somehow altered history, I can only apologise to those affected, but how would they know? And here is another thought. Was it these monks (after a little paradoxical intervention from myself) that invented the eke in the first place?

The apiarist and prior were both shocked and delighted by my suggestion and the apiarist headed off to get the materials he needed to build his first prototype. The prior asked how I knew of such an ingenious solution. I told him how I saw beehives fitted with ekes in Constantinople. A whopping great fib!

In gratitude, the prior presented me with a bag of sulphur (a valuable commodity), a quire of parchment, a small bottle of gall (a type of ink) and six bronze nibs. These little wonders are a godsend and I intend fabricating pens as soon as possible because note keeping has proven a challenge. Until now, I have mostly written on potshards and pieces of tile with a lead stylus. Lord Cedric did once provide scraps of parchment and a bundle of quills, but I struggled to write with them. They scratched, splayed, sprayed, and ran out of ink extremely quickly. Mind you, Lord Cedric's ink was terrible. Thin, pale, lumpy, no idea what was in it.

"Cramp balls and hooves," his reply when I asked. Sounds awful.

⧗

After a harrowing early morning house call, I am seeking solace in a cupful of mead. In the final stages of breast cancer, the reeve's sister was in agony, and, bar killing her, there was nothing anyone could do. Under these circumstances, any physical intervention or poisoning is illegal, considered murder in fact, and the penalty is death. Asking the reeve to fetch her a priest, he returned with the presbyter from Winchelsea at a gallop.

It was from speaking to this priest that I learnt the 13th-century rules concerning mercy killing, euthanasia, and suicide. The mercy killing of a non-combatant, even euthanasia, are both murderous acts and carry a death sentence. If a death is judged to be suicide, it is classified as a "sin in the sight of God", resulting in the casting out (the excommunication) of the deceased, followed by an unceremonious burial in unsanctified land. In the case of the terminally ill, the precedents for suicide are more complex. If any family member, noble, priest, or approved family associate (a healer for example) provided the means for the afflicted to take their own life, the Church (in most cases) would commute the charges. Sadly, although I fell into the class of approved family associate, I lacked the necessary agents – morphine or any opiate, hemlock, or belladonna, and I envied Cadfael, the sleuthing monk of Ellis Peters. His medicine bag brimmed with poppy juice – his painkilling, tranquillising wonder drug. Available in such quantities, he could administer it to all and sundry, almost willy-nilly!

John has arrived and he looks flustered. Lord Cedric is demanding I attend his noonday meal and offer my services to an important visitor. Quickly donning my finest cloak and finishing my mead in a single gulp, I followed John at the double.

⧖

With grey robes, a stinking beard, battered sandals, and brown hose, Lord Cedric's guest was an aged Franciscan friar. On the surface he seemed pleasant enough, but his long thoughtful face and cold grey eyes told of unflinching severity...

Formally bowing before the assembled, I joined Lord Cedric, his family, and guests upon the high table, waiting patiently for Lord Cedric to perform the introductions.

"Ah, good," he began. "I am glad to find you among us, Sir William. Allow me to introduce our distinguished guest. Friar Bacon. A scholar hailing from distant Oxenford. He is returning to said town for the retrieval of his licence and manuscript. The ripe fruit from his many years of labour."

"Honoured," I replied, bowing my head. "I am known as William de Corbiere. A healer, newly arrived on these shores."

Bacon examined me slowly, stroking his beard with long white fingers and yellowing nails.

"So, my brothers at the priory have said," remarked Bacon, "and it is on the prior's recommendation I bring my guardians hence. We too were devilishly shipwrecked. A storm, hell born and terrible, slew us from our navigation, driving us into the Rye anchorage, before floundering us, silt bound and stranded."

Friar Bacon's dialect was distinctly different from that of Lord Cedric, but quite understandable, and with my translation matrix it was simplicity itself following the conversation. Not wishing to arouse suspicion, I took unnecessary thinking time when replying to Bacon, delivering my response in the local dialect.

On wooden trays carried by blushing girls, the food began to arrive – all of it selected to meet Bacon's dietary restrictions. There was a pottage of pulses, roots, and greens (including fat-hen and nettles), brown loaves, butter, and cakes of mixed nuts, honey, and mustard (a strange flavour combination but surprisingly delicious). All of this washed town with Lord Cedric's finest ale. A dark and nutty brew with a creamy head, drunk from a pewter tankard. The pottage was decidedly ordinary, and Sir Gilbert bemoaned the lack of meat, saying, fat-hen without meat was akin to chewing on oakum.

The conversation was polite but spirited and the unwanted (and inedible) food went back to the kitchens (for distribution among the servants and household).

Friar Bacon asked about my work and services, of my cures, techniques, and approach. Deciding upon honesty, I held little back, making it clear my knowledge was learnt, not discovered, before offering to tend his men, and he took this most kindly. His men-at-arms, mercenaries hired by the Roman Church, were struggling to adapt to their long journey (and damp climate), remarking how he would appreciate their "prudent invigoration" before the long ride to London and voyage on the Temese* to Oxenford.

Inviting his men to join me before vespers (sunset), I remarked to Bacon how I would be delighted if he wished to accompany them: "Receiving such a great man of learning would be both an honour and a privilege."

*The Thames.

Pleased with my hospitality, Lord Cedric slowly nodded his approval.

In preparation for my visitors, I have large kettles hanging over my fire, and it delights me to hear them singing and pinging as the water inside them slowly heats. My makeshift bathtub, a large half-barrel lined with lead, I have moved nearer to the fire, double-checking its screens of wattle and linen provide sufficient privacy, with washcloths, two bars of antiseptic birch tar soap, combs (for lice) and a scrubbing brush on a low stool. My two linen towels, bought at great expense, I have hung over the back of a chair, and for a dash of luxury I intend warming them by the fire.

My bandages, lotions, and potions are ready, and my tools, lancets, forceps, knives, and shears, are sharp, clean, and dry. All is set and ready to give these travellers a damn good wash, before tending to any wounds and assessing their condition.

For safety, I have covered my desk and workstation with blankets, hiding the bulk of my notes beneath my lumpy mattress – not that it would help if anyone uncovered them. My most secret notes are in a code of my own making – ZX assembler ASCII registers, and only I can read them.

Ah, a knock at the door...

It is Friar Bacon, and with him two men. Both as tall as me, and armed! Daggers and swords. The tallest is hooded and cloaked. They are dark-haired, dark-eyed, with a sallow olive skin. My guess they are of Moorish, Mediterranean descent...

"Good afternoon." I bow. "Please enter, see my humble lodgings. A place of work rather than comfort."

"Most gracious," replies the friar, then, turning to his soldiers, he says, "Take thy ease and be seated. Thy bitter ailments I will now discuss."

This last phrase, spoken in Latin and coming with all physiological change duplicity foments, I knew to be a test, so I looked on nonplussed, keeping my linguistic prowess a secret.

Their treatment programme took approximately two hours, including bathing, delousing (lice and fleas), the cleaning and tending of wounds, lesions, and boils. Their dental health was surprisingly good, speaking of a diet low in sugars (and fresh fruit). Their breath however was distressing, and I prepared a mouthwash of thyme oil and aqua vitae, insisting they gargled and spat.

One of the guards (I never learnt their names) was suffering from a chill. Fetching him a fresh dose of my willow extract, I watched him obediently swallowing this bitter pill in a single gulp before staring at and laughing with his comrade, remarking that he choked on the taste like a chorister (to which my mind ominously boggled).

All this time, Friar Bacon was busily poking into my belongings, sniffing jars and simples. He seemed particularly intrigued by the spirit burner I had cobbled together from scraps of earthenware jars and pipes, its parts joined by a lute of white lead and flour.

Once my tending was complete, I begged them to stay, offering a cup of warm mead as a sweetener. Bacon declined, however, commenting he would return two days hence consult me further. Leaving with his escort, he returned to Winchelsea for vespers.

⧗

On the opening of the spring fair the whole parish seemed busy. Hiring a small wagon (drawn by Edgar, a very disconsolate mule) Sir Gilbert, John, and I headed to Rye to witness the festivities and avail ourselves of the market.

The fair was a real eye-opener. Busy, noisy, smelly, with a wide range of entertainment, acts of strength, feats of wonder and conjuration, musicians singing or playing, tumblers, acrobats, connivers, conmen, dancers both lewd and rhythmical. Actors were preforming mystery plays (with audience participation) and I watched Samson battle the Agnostes before John dragged me away, ushering me into the spice tent – a gaudy pavilion stocked with all manner of good things.

Indeed, upon entry, the mixed aroma assailing my senses was both sublime and shocking, and Sir Gilbert, after matching my look of wonder, made his way over to the storekeeper to deliver Lord Cedric's requirements: delivery tomorrow morning, cash on delivery, with a bonus for promptness and purity. Without labels, I used my enhanced senses to discover what was available, as the assistant (a snotty-nosed youth with a nose ring and crooked teeth) would only speak if sure of a sale.

First and most prevalent was capsicum (peppercorns), several varieties, black, brown, red, green, with nutmeg kernels and earthenware jars chock full of fiery mace. Stacked like miniature logs were sticks of cinnamon, with sachets of saffron, boxes of turmeric, its aroma earthy and ripe. Juniper berries also, threaded onto strings, with splinters of sandalwood, nuggets of frankincense, stacte, onycha (benzoin), and galbanum. Arrayed in crates were bricks of gritty brown salt, with bags of seeds: melon, cumin, fennel, dill, aniseed, poppy, and others. Packed into boxes of cedar were bunches of dates, and, after sampling one, I bought a box, with four ounces of poppy seeds and a dozen brown lumps of sugar. Hoping for opium, I found none, and, when asked, the assistant shrugged, saying, *"Alle zuppla tis areste von mendica hospital,"* which didn't mean anything to me, but *"hospital"* might have been a reference to the Knights Hospitaller.

The herbs dried or powdered were nothing new, except for a sack of dried leaves, and, rubbing a pinch and sniffing it, I was amazed. It was camelia. Tea! Quickly asking the assistant what it was…

"Es isst chin," he explained. *"Fur ze smokes fon fishhes und fleshes."*

"Is it expensive?" I asked. "How much?"

"Zehn pfennies a'ounze," he replied with a grin.

"No," I said, shaking my head. "That is too much. I'll give you four."

"Vierte?" The lad scowled. *"Nay, Seben."*

"Six," I demanded. "Not a penny more."

The young assistant sighed.

"Ja-zo," he muttered, seemingly deflated. *"Sechs ist zo."*

"Good," I replied. "Two ounces, if it pleases you, and in a jar."

Two ounces, sadly, was all I could afford.

Returning hours later and eagerly boiling a little water, I shredded two small tea leaves and left them to steep. Utter bliss. If only the locals knew what they were missing. It will be hundreds of years before tea drinking becomes widespread and, considering the financial and political upheaval this harmless plant eventually provokes, I shall keep my little luxury a closely guarded secret.

My poppy seeds have the potential to provide both tranquillisers and mild analgesia, and I will begin experimenting with small quantities this evening. Poppy seed extract is also insecticidal, a killer of both fleas and lice – useful, as the populace crawl with them. Just the thought of them is making me itch.

⧖

Things have turned ill, and after torturous beating, bruised and bleeding, I am hiding inside Lord Cedric's private chapel while my Hibbites work to repair my injuries…

It had just finished my tea when Friar Bacon's guards burst in. Throwing me to the floor, they pinned me down, wrenching my arms across my back.

Bacon soon followed and he stood over me stroking his beard with suspicion…

"Who are you?" he demanded. "Whence did you come?"

"Already explained," I gasped. "And so has Lord Cedric."

"Oh, he explained," replied Bacon. "He recited the same sewage you recounted to me. Now, tell me the truth. Who art thou, whence did thou come?"

Not ready to reply, I said nothing, resulting in a heavy kick to the ribs.

"Tie him to a chair," said Bacon. "Garrotte his scheming mind. For we shall squeeze the truth from it."

All that happened during that terrible hour I care not to recount but know that I underwent deep questioning as per the inquisition. In Latin, in the third person, and Bacon was relentless. Ingenious, devious, and insightful. At our first and second meetings, he was indeed studying me as much as I remedied him, and now, fully uncloaked, I learnt of the piercing mind he possessed.

You might think a knotted rope bound around the skull a soft device of torture, but it is not. It is excruciating. I told Roger Bacon everything he wished to know. Of my arrival, travel, spaceflight, medicine, science, and healing. Not the details, merely generalisations, enough to satisfy his hungry curiosity.

From receiving a final blow to the face, drenched in blood from a broken nose and with several ribs jutting, I came to sprawled on the floor.

Suppressing my pain and encouraging my Hibbites to repair my damaged tissues, I sought sanctuary in Lord Cedric's private chapel. Certainly, if Bacon were to recount my confession to Lord Cedric, the prior, or the local priesthood, I would be in serious trouble…

"Think, William," I muttered through broken lips. "Clear your mind. Be at peace."

Kneeling before the icon of the Virgin Mary, whose dark hair, brown eyes, and shining halo reminded me of Gina (well, perhaps not the halo), I closed my eyes and let go a slow breath…

"William."

A woman's voice in my head. Gina? Is that you?

"William Corbiere. Hear me."

"I do hear you," I thought. "Who are you? Where are you?"

"You know me as Gleener."

"Yes," I reply, "I remember. I remember you screaming. How is it you can now talk?"

"A necessary deception. My insanity is feigned. Now, listen. Time is short."

"Very well," I thought. "What is your message? Am I to be returned to my proper time and place?"

"No," she whispered. "It is already too late. Your existence here is pivotal, but I will aid you as much as I can. For you should know, your death is imminent."

"Understood," I murmured, suddenly crushed. "How long do I have?"

"Not long. The friar will send his men to kill you, and it is imperative you destroy every trace of your presence here. Your notes and equipment? Destroy them all. Flee. Try to reach France. But first, for the sake of history, it is imperative you leave messages for Dr Padgett. I am uploading the necessary missives to your cyberbrocial cortex. With your metal nibbed pen and in gall ink, copy them onto a sheet of parchment. Once complete and the ink is dry, fold it flat, and carry it with you wherever you go. Keep it hidden. Wear it beneath your tunic."

"Very well," I replied. "What of my demise? Have you planned for that too?"

"Of course. I have taken care of everything, so do not fear. It will be painless and quick."

Thirty seconds passed slowly, my mind busily planning my flight, before the futility of my situation suddenly dawned. What could I do? Gleener already knew my future, my fate and my destiny. Any scheming on my part would be pointless...

"Agreed," I grimly replied. "A purge of my presence, and then make straight for Rye. There are always boats in the harbour. I will try to buy passage."

"Good," whispered Gleener. "Leave tonight."

"Yes," I muttered. "After saying farewell to John. Plague is coming to this land, and I don't want him to die. I need to advise him."

"That is commendable," said Gleener. "But unnecessary. I will protect the boy and he will survive. Now go. You have much to do."

"Amen," I softly replied, and, climbing to my feet, I heard Gleener gently laugh.

"Farewell," she whispered, and then she was gone.

Dashing to my home, I quickly copied Gleener's messages. The codes, diagrams, and prayers, drying them carefully before smashing and/or burning my medical notes. My potions and salves all went into the fire before I broke all my laboratory equipment into irretrievably tiny pieces.

Grabbing my purse and filling a sack with what little food I had, I activated all my implants before taking a long swig of mead. Using a bandage to tie the precious parchment under my tunic, I wrapped my warmest mantle about my shoulders and slipped into the night.

Sneaking past the guards on the gate and wall, I made my way along the coast (avoiding the road) and slipped into Rye, seeking cover among the building materials littering the streets.

NINE

NEEDLES IN THE DARK

Personal Log of Walter de Boer, June 2112

Required to investigate an emergency involving Dr Padgett, a deep misgiving compels me to keep this log as a precaution. This new crisis is hardly surprising. Throughout my entire interview she was duplicitous or hiding certain truths, and the UET have summoned me to England for what I suspect will be the crowning glory (or the ending) of my career. Certainly, this assignment fills me with trepidation, and I have just spent the last hour saying farewell to my wife and children.

Why the melodrama? Well, this new assignment involves the tracking and capture of Dr Padgett. For reasons unknown, she has gone berserk and is currently rampaging across the English countryside. She has murdered, stolen, committed acts of sedition and subterfuge, before escaping with violence from an inescapable secret facility. What has driven her to make such a bold move, I cannot guess, and the UET are being tight-lipped about the details. They are in a hurry, however. A flyer is on its way, programmed to whisk me to the scene of the crime.

This is to be my second ride in a courier drone, and I am dreading it. I was sick as a salt-licking dog the first time. Why did I bother with breakfast?

Considering my recent interviews with Dr Padgett, my superiors regard me to be an expert witness to her character, to which I quickly pointed out that the opposite was clearly the case. To her I was an open book. She will expect my intervention and pursuit, so I am walking into a trap.

So, yes, failure is inevitable, and the outcome? Well, let me put it this way: success is impossible. She will never surrender, never stop fighting, she will die on her feet. Every mother protecting their children knows of what I speak. This whole operation is futile. I'm looking for a needle in a haystack, in the dark, guided only by a flaming torch. Given time, patience, and a little luck, sifting through the ashes, I will find my metaphorical needle. But will I survive the fire?

Upon visiting the crime scene, evidence gathering is my primary task, before hypothesising a motive. Tracing her whereabouts is also of upmost importance. Certainly, if she bothered to leave one, I will endeavour to pick up her trail.

I have just arrived at the Hinnie Space Centre (a large manorial estate in Surrey) and there is a great deal of activity. Robotic drones are working to repair a gaping hole in the roof, while on the lawn, a team of technicians struggle against the breeze to erect a forensic tunnel.

To begin, as a courtesy, I went straight to the UET senior dignitary, a justiciar no less – Baroness Rita Richguard, and this is decidedly odd. To my knowledge, the Hinnie Space Centre is only a minor facility. Sumptuous accommodation for meetings and conferences, so quite why old Rita is holding the fort in this rural retreat is baffling, but I notice my security clearance has become suddenly lofty. Psi black. What sort of meetings are held here?

Oak panelled and smelling of waxy leather, the justiciar's office was within the library, and as I entered, she calmly straightened her collar before standing to proffer her hand. Standing nearby, her young assistant looked strained and exhausted.

Fifty-two years old and a talented lawyer, before her UET appointment, Baroness Richguard rose quickly through the ranks of the judiciary all the way to the Supreme Court. Why she never made it to the UET's executive office is a mystery heightened by gossip. I prefer to extrapolate what is already known. Baroness Richguard is partial to a liquid lunch, and by liquid, I don't mean soup. She is a drunk.

"Good morning," I began, "I am Inquisitor de Boer, and, as you are undoubtedly aware, I am here to begin an investigation concerning Dr Padgett's recent behaviour."

Dr Hardcastle (the justiciar's assistant) flashed the baroness a look of panic, but she was unmoved.

"Do you wish to comment?" I then asked. "Know that I began recording upon my arrival, so, justiciar, anything to add?"

Without a reply, the justiciar simply blinked before nodding her acceptance.

"Dr Hardcastle," I then offered. "Any thoughts?" and she gently shook her head.

"Very well," I continued. "Now, Baroness, when did you receive the order to impress Dr Padgett?"

"Three days ago," she replied.

"And you sent agents to inform her? Why the draconian approach? Simple messaging would've sufficed. Dr Padgett's disciplinary record was spotless."

"Because it was an executive order," she explained. "Clearly from high up, so I gave it top priority. I felt it necessary to demonstrate the irrevocability of Dr Padgett's situation."

"Even though the order's stipulations were somewhat unethical?"

"Yes," she calmly replied.

"Fine. At no point did you seek confirmation? Did it not seem strange the order had no signatory?"

"No," she acknowledged. "Didn't check, and only now does it seem reprehensible. Requests like this do occur, of course. Rushed, coming out of nowhere, unsigned, and inexplicable. You must understand, the order was via my secure line and my clearance is phi blue. To even access my inbox, the sender requires similar clearance or higher. How many in the UET possess such lofty clearance?"

"About thirty," I replied, "and your explanation is sound, but why would the UET want Dr Padgett here? Come to think of it, your honour, why are you here? It is indeed a lovely old house. Am I missing something?"

Dr Hardcastle, silent all this time, gently coughed.

"Show him," said the justiciar.

"Show him?" replied the assistant, her lip beginning to tremble. "But he'll... are you sure?"

"Yes," sighed the justiciar. "All of it."

"All of what?"

"Laboratories," replied Dr Hardcastle. "An underground complex of research and development labs. Six floors in all. We designed the bulk of Dr Padgett's implanted tech. When the order came to bring her for examination, maintenance, and testing, it made perfect sense."

"Ah," I said. "Now I understand. Show me then. Perhaps it will shed some light on Dr Padgett's sudden change of behaviour. According to my report, she killed six personnel. Who were they? Guards, scientists, engineers? If so, what were they working on? I need to know everything."

"Of course," replied the justiciar. "And Hannah says we have missing equipment. In Dr Padgett's possession, we assume."

"Yes, my report mentioned as much. Can you elaborate?"

"Naturally," said Dr Hardcastle. "But not here. This environment is not entirely secure."

The main elevator down to the laboratories was out of action, requiring us to descend a ladder to the reach the first subterranean level. Coming upon a small hatchway, we emerged in a corridor adjacent to main elevator.

Torn from its hinges, crumpled and twisted, was heavily fortified door...

"Oh my God," I gasped, looking it over. "How did she do this? Explosives?"

Without speaking, Dr Hardcastle flashed a look that said "no".

Forensic analysis was still taking place and two technicians were picking their way through the blood and detritus still covering the walls and floor. Two crumpled cryo-bags holding the remains of the security guards spoke of their sudden demise.

Dr Hardcastle begged me to be quick...

"Please," she whispered. "May we go? I've seen enough of this already."

"Certainly," I replied. "Go on ahead. I will join you shortly and then we need to talk."

Pressing the forensic inspectors to make haste completing their analysis, I paused to consider how a slender woman in her late forties could have achieved this. Dr Padgett was athletic, certainly, and remarkably healthy, but super-strong she was not. Only when wearing her nano-fibre suit was her strength enhanced, but the colossal power to conduct this devilry was far beyond its specifications. What was I missing?

Without an answer, I examined the remains of the guards. The first body, although crushed, burst, and distorted, was intact, but the scant remains of second troubled me deeply. There was nothing left of the man! Shreds of clothing, fragments of bone, splinters of teeth...How could Dr Padgett have accomplished such violent dissolution?

Joining Dr Hardcastle in the empty restaurant, I asked if it was a suitable environment for a private chat.

"It is," she remarked. "Little sense in watching people eat."

"Indeed," I replied. "Now, Hannah, can I call you Hannah?" She nodded. "That is a violent scene back there. Can you enlighten me? How did Dr Padgett manage such feats? What was she doing here? The baroness is trying to divert my attention, but from what? You must tell me. What is going on? Many lives depend on your answer."

"I know," she muttered. "And it's all my fault. She tricked us. Tricked me! You see, it wasn't just her. It was the suit!"

"Her suit?" I asked. "What suit? Her suit from the KBE?"

Full of worry, Dr Hardcastle meekly nodded.

"Oh, for Heaven's sake," I replied. "Those suits are dangerous! Why wasn't it taken to Moonbase?"

"I don't know. We received an order. An executive order, to bring it here for testing."

"Another one? From whom?"

"We don't know, but someone high up. Otherwise, the justiciar could not have received it."

"Granted," I said. "But something troubles you?"

"Yes. I'm beginning to see the truth. At least, suspect the truth. It was the suit! The suit that wrote those spurious orders. It wanted to be here. Wanted Dr Padgett, also. To make off with her, I think."

"You think the suit abducted her?"

"Can't be sure," she replied. "But it is a possibility. Dr Padgett's escape was so cold, calculated, so violent. She didn't strike me as a killer. She was gentle and sad. Lonely, I think. Angry when she arrived, of course, but when we explained she wouldn't be here for long, she was fine. If she waited, she could have walked out the front door a free woman. Why the violence? It doesn't make sense."

"Crime rarely does," I remarked.

"Do you want to see her quarters?"

"Yes," I replied. "And the other murder scenes. Also, forgive me, but could you explain why the central computer failed to lock down the facility after the alarm went off? Was there a malfunction?"

"I was just coming to that," she acknowledged. "Dr Padgett did indeed trigger the alarm, but afterwards, it was the computer that locked us out. The whole grid went down. Impossible. Unless the computer was in some way complicit."

"The computer was helping her, why would it do that?"

"We don't know. Harvey claims to have no memory of the event. Probably true. Bar dismantling him, there's no way of knowing."

"Doubt he'd like that," I said. "Hope he's not listening."

"No," she replied. "Can't be. The grid's still down. Now, if you follow me, we'll head down to her quarters. It's a long descent. Try not to look down."

"I'll be fine." I smiled. "Vertigo doesn't bother me, and the exercise will do me good."

⧗

"Here we are," said Dr Hardcastle, guiding me through the hatch and adjusting her hair. "Level five. Guest quarters, nano-fibre research, and, you'll be pleased to know, the forensic team have finished. The scene is considerably less gruesome."

With two cryo-bags waiting on a gurney and a strong smell of cleaning agents, the corridor outside Dr Padgett's room was empty and quiet. Walking up to the door, I waited for Dr Hardcastle to catch up…

"Are you coming?" I asked. "Or do you need to be elsewhere?"

"If only," she muttered, her face pale as ash. "I was here earlier, and it was terrible. Such barbarism, cruelty. My poor sweet Juni. Please, don't make me see it again."

"Fine," I replied, heeding her anguish. "Stay. This won't take long," and I opened the door and went in.

Spotlessly clean and empty of furniture, the small room was unremarkable but for two shining dents in the floor. Wedged into the aperture of the food dispenser was the backrest of a chair.

Returning to the corridor, I examined the bags on the gurney. Not opening them, however, as Dr Hardcastle was still hovering nearby.

"Ok," I assured. "Seen enough. When you first went in, was anything amiss? The chairback in the dispenser. Did that strike you as odd?"

"That was me," she admitted. "Although it was Dr Padgett that broke it. We found the backrest lying on the bed."

"Perfectly understandable. Anything else?"

"Yes," she replied. "When he left his lab, Dr Piceus was carrying molecular scanner. Dr Padgett must've taken it."

"A fair assumption. Any idea why?"

"Not a clue. They're hardly specialist kit. I'm surprised she doesn't own one herself."

"Ah yes," I replied. "I see where you're going. A snap decision. Little forward planning."

"Perhaps. Please, can we go? Jarvis and Juni were dear to me."

"Of course," I said. "And, for the record, I would like to emphasise how impressed I am. Your professionalism and stoicism do you and this facility much credit."

There was something about Dr Hannah Hardcastle that was special. Controlled, considered, perfect, too perfect, or unnaturally precise? Watching her measured steps and calm demeanour, I recalled Dr Padgett and her clockwork efficiency when reassembling the food dispenser in her luxurious office.

The nano-fibre lab was long and narrow – a firing range, with moveable targets, sensors, safety screens, and a tripod for the mounting of firearms. Inside the door, a cryo-bag waited upon a gurney…

"So here we have it," I said with a scowl. "A blatant breach of the UET Charter. What agency is funding this work? The military or some shadowy foreign power?"

"No, no!" beseeched Dr Hardcastle. "Not the case at all. This is application research, nothing more. A series of projects experimenting on the same fibres as used in Dr Padgett's suit. This was Miss Mayfield's personal project, not a military application. Yes. She was developing projectiles, studying the fibres durability, dissolution, and reintegration properties, and in doing so, she designed and built an elegant gun to propel them, but it was all about the fibres! In fact, the implications of her work sickened Izzy. She purchased a non-disclosure order to keep her work secret. I had a terrific battle to even obtain a summary."

"Well said. But there will still be a hearing on this matter. Now explain. What happened? Is there any record?"

"Of the murder and theft? No. By this time Harvey had shut down the whole network. We assume Dr Padgett simply walked in, took both gun and ammunition, shooting Izzy as she tried to prevent her from leaving."

"A fair conjecture," I replied. "Any evidence?"

"Not much. Although the forensic report might throw up a few things. Izzy's remains were just inside the door. Hence my supposition of her blocking Dr Padgett's escape."

"Yes," I muttered, examining the tripod. "And the gun, the one Dr Padgett allegedly has in her possession, is it powerful?"

"Powerful?" she reiterated. "Yes! You've no idea. It's the most powerful handgun ever created. The damn thing is unstoppable!"

"What? And she just walked in and took it? Ammunition as well? How many rounds? Didn't you say Miss Mayfield's research was limited?"

"It was," she acknowledged. "Izzy only made three slugs."

"Good," I replied. "How many shots has Dr Padgett already fired?"

"Two, we think."

"Excellent. Then she only has one shot left."

"No, no!" cried Hannah. "You don't understand. The ammunition is self-replenishing. Reusable, and intelligent. After firing, they come back."

With the urgency and hazardousness of my investigation suddenly dawning, I slumped into a chair...

"So, let me get this straight," I said. "The most sophisticated armoured prosthesis ever created, after freely accessing the UET mainframe, writes executive-level orders to bring it to a secure secret facility, before writing further orders to deliver Dr Padgett to the same location. Then, abducting or colluding with Dr Padgett – the almost immortal, cybernetically enhanced genius, it steals the most powerful hand weapon ever developed, breaks out of said facility and disappears without a trace into the countryside... Would you consider that a fair assessment?"

This was the emotional tipping point for Dr Hardcastle and her composure started to slip.

"Yes," she sobbed, her eyes reddening. "I'm sorry. There was no way to know. Am I going to prison?"

"Someone will be," I said. "And the justiciar is the most culpable. Now, answer me, Dr Hardcastle, for the record. Has the baroness been drinking?"

"No," she muttered. "I don't think..."

"Hannah," I pressed. "Has she been drinking?"

"Yes," she whispered. "Always. She's always drinking."

"Thank you," I replied. "Now, get a cup of water and compose yourself."

Nodding, Dr Hardcastle stumbled to a food dispenser and muttered her order.

The sixth floor comprised crew quarters and a single laboratory. Outside the door of the lab was a gurney with a cryo-bag and I briefly studied its label before going in.

"What went on here?" I asked, stooping to examine the scorched and blackened flooring. "It looks and smells as if something caught fire."

"Someone." Dr Hardcastle bleakly replied. "Dr Clementine – Augustus, our diagnostic engineer. This is – was – his lab. Dr Padgett's suit was also in here, for testing."

"Right." I nodded. "Any record of what happened?"

"No. There is nothing. Upstairs, we detected a sudden and massive power drain and then the grid went down. It was then I contacted Gussy, Dr Clementine, and he in turn called Dr Piceus asking for help. After that, zilch. A guard discovered Gussy's remains about thirty minutes later."

"How did he die?"

"We're not sure. There was nothing left of him! Just ashes."

"Indeed. Where was Dr Padgett all this time?"

"In her quarters. At least until the grid went down. After that, I suppose she could've been anywhere, but the guards down here didn't see her."

"Then," I said, "she wasn't here. Dr Padgett is clever, but she isn't invisible. I suggest this was her suit. Working independently or guided by her commands. Where was it kept?"

"In here," she replied, nodding towards a locker.

"In a box? Not very secure, and rather – how do you say? – slapdash?"

Looking strained, Dr Hardcastle shrugged.

"We saw no need for security. The suit was deactivated. I saw the report. Gussy made sure. He scanned it several times. The suit had no power, and we're thirty-five metres down! The suit was secure, I assure you."

"So, you say. Yet, together, Dr Padgett and her deactivated suit escaped your secure facility in minutes. I want to see a copy of that deactivation report. It is clearly erroneous. We need to know how the damned suit fooled your equipment."

"Of course," she said. "Anything else?"

"No. For the time being, I'm finished, but you and the justiciar will be called to London for a formal hearing. In the meantime, continue investigating and send all your findings directly to me. Don't go through the justiciar. I no longer trust her judgement."

"Very well," she replied. "But the justiciar will be devastated. None of this was really her fault. I would've made the same mistakes."

"Then remember to restate that at the hearing and they might let her off. Now, security is on the first floor, is it not?"

Dr Hardcastle nodded.

"Fine," I said. "Tell the coroner to finish removing the bodies and then meet me up there."

⧗

It was a silent chaos in the computer centre. Frantic activity, little communication, stress filling the air with a sweaty staleness the air conditioning struggled to abate. Preoccupied with playing chess against an unknown opponent, the main computer tasked with running the facility remained stubbornly unresponsive.

Dr Hardcastle came in, her mask of composure firmly in place.

"Still inaccessible," I remarked, and she nodded. "The chief technician claims Harvey is under external influence and, until it ceases, we're locked out. Couldn't you reboot him or put him on stand-by?"

"We've already tried," explained a technician. "His condition remains the same. Whoever is doing this is a genius. Harv is in love with 'em. For the time being, we just have to wait."

Following a hunch, I looked straight towards a security sensor and defiantly folded my arms.

Suddenly flashing, the cuff of my jacket told of a message from the UET in London. A disturbance in Battle. A break-in, nothing stolen, vandalism, security guards grievously wounded. Turning to Dr Hardcastle, I gave her a knowing smile.

"We have her," I remarked. "She was in Battle. A break-in, apparently. The UET are sending a flyer."

"Good," replied Dr Hardcastle. "You think you can catch her?"

"Perhaps. I'm ordered to try. The army are sending an entire brigade."

"Bloody hell. Isn't that overkill?"

"I fear it may prove inadequate."

"Then get the fucking air force!" she replied, anger flushing her cheeks. "Do whatever it takes, and when you get her, dismantle the obsolete bitch. She killed my friends."

TEN

FRAGMENTS

Like a petulant child, Suit is up to her old tricks. She's sneaky, assumptive, a know-it-all, brimming with all sorts of useful information, and yet, her closeness is unbearable. Unless I inadvertently ask the right question, all that she knows, she keeps to herself.

Lying low in Winchelsea, I watched the security officers guarding my house. Perturbed by this development, I asked Suit if this was part of her original order...

"Certainly not," she replied. "These extra guards are newly arrived. Orders from an Inquisitor de Boer. I understand you know him?"

"Yes," I remarked, "I know him well. It doesn't surprise me he's leading the manhunt. He's quite clever. We need to be careful."

"Certainly, but he still languishes at the Hinnie Space Centre. He has yet to begin."

"How do you know this? Are you connected?"

"Indeed," she affirmed. "Harvey and I are playing chess. It is I that controls the facility."

"Excellent. What is Walter currently doing?"

"At this very moment?"

"Yes."

"He is in the security centre, mistress. Dr Hardcastle is with him. They are watching the network administrators trying to wrest Harvey away from my control. The inquisitor is turning towards a… yes. He's looking straight at me."

"Ha," I snorted. "I think he knows what you're doing. How is Hannah?"

"She looks tired, mistress, and angry."

"No doubt."

"The inquisitor is receiving a message, mistress. He is ordered to Battle. The UET are sending a flyer… We should kill these guards and make a disturbance within your house. A fire, perhaps?"

"You want me to set fire to my house? Why?"

"A temporary distraction – flypaper. With months of travel before us, it is imperative we leave a trail vulnerable to detection. After the inquisitor finishes in Battle, I wish to lead him here. Winchelsea should become his focus. As it is also ours."

"A double bluff?"

"Indeed. Our aims require overseas travel, and it will be some months before we return. We need the inquisitor to think Winchelsea is done with. If we cause sufficient ruckus overseas, he will be convinced."

"Fine," I acknowledged. "Now, what about the guards? Want me to shoot them?"

"The two patrolling your garden, yes. It will draw the others to me. We must be quick – they possess stun guns, and I provide little protection from their hypersonic charges."

"Understood. Can you disable their tech and comms?"

"Already done and they have yet to realise."

"Good," I replied. "Activate stealth. Clotho and Atropos? We are assaulting armoured human targets. Penetration and dispersal. Lethal force."

"Yesss," they hissed into my mind. "We are prepared. Release usss!"

Sidling over my garden wall was a cinch and sneaking behind the two guards watching the gates was sickeningly easy. Two shots casually fired from Izzy's gun made short work of them, and I quickly hid their shattered remnants underneath my osmanthus.

Patrolling my downstairs rooms, the other guards were oblivious to the carnage outside, giving Suit ample opportunity to indulge herself. Dragging one of the guards through a window, she flung him against the garden wall with such force he all but burst. The second guard, now frozen in terror by his colleague's demise, did nothing as Suit pounced. His end coming quickly as she crushed him into a bloody pulp.

"Have you quite finished?" I nervously coughed. "The noise you are making. Are you trying to attract attention?"

"Yes!" she replied. "Now, get food and empty cupboards and drawers. Create a mess. As if you were searching for something important."

Grabbing calorific odds and sods, I did as Suit suggested, flinging my possessions with reckless abandon.

"Excellent," she remarked. "Upstairs is where we need to go. Let's set a fire in your office."

"If you insist, but could we not make a small one? This is my house!"

"Oh, mistress," said Suit. "Do you still not fathom? The fire doesn't matter. Your life, your possessions, your accomplishments? They are but a figment. A falsehood, an error. To be rubbed out like the doodling's of a child."

"So, you have said. Yet the path we are taking... The leap of faith you demand is tremendous. Can't you explain?"

"No, mistress. Not yet. Read Marcus's journal. We are extremely thorough. Read further and you will understand."

"Very well," I reply. "For now, I will do as you say. Ignoring the fire, I shall recite *The Sack of Ilium*."

"It will become a habit, mistress."

This note, explaining just why Suit and I made our way to Winchelsea, I should have placed at the beginning of the chapter, and I'm sorry to say this is typically neglectful of me. Certainly, if Susi were here, she would have shaken her head, calling me *Schussel und Faulpelz*, insisting I recover my mistake *mit großer Klarheit*. I can but try...

The lowermost folder of the bundle bequeathed to Marcus concerned the vault of Winchelsea church and a medieval reliquary; a battered box, a disc-like artefact, and crumbling bones. This disc I know to be a representation of the Procyon binary star system, and later, in his journal, following a harrowing account of suffering and torture, Marcus goes on to describe his own pilgrimage to Winchelsea, before descending into the vault and viewing said reliquary himself (while Frida sulked outside).

Marcus wrote how the bones belonged to an extraordinarily tall individual, leading me to conclude they are the remains of Sir Malcolm Walsingham. All 216 centimetres of him! Whether his bones hold any data, however, is unknown, and their age is likewise a mystery. Considering their condition, his remains may well be hundreds, even thousands of years old. Only one way to find out…

⧗

Watching the blaze slowly gutting my office filled me with dismay and it was only after the fire threatened to escape would Suit slip from my body to smother it. Then came ten minutes of fire-watching, dousing the ashes with basins of water just to make sure.

With the fire thoroughly out, we slithered over my garden wall, crept into the churchyard, and made for the church.

Before 10pm, the rector was still inside, and the light from within, projecting through the stained glass, bathed the cemetery in a gaudy celebration of remembrance.

The more cynical among you may be surprised by the resilience of Christianity and the Unified Church of England, but in recent years, it has seen a huge resurgence in popularity, and several social commentators and historians authored lengthy papers regarding this curious social shift. Personally, as an active member of the Winchelsea community farm-cooperative, local craft and trade society, this upsurge in popularity doesn't surprise me one jot. In fact, localism has injected new life into the village and market town. The once-commonplace traditions, celebrations such as harvest, planting, the seasonal equinoxes, birth, death, and marriage are once again of relevance.

The church of Winchelsea is the hub of the community. A place to meet, exchange ideas, close deals, gossip, and make friends. Traditional hymns and prayers are offered, but the lessons and sermon are progressive, multi-faith and/or agnostic, and my family have delivered dozens over the years. Since the congregation is decidedly atheistic, mystical mumbo-jumbo is minimised, but we modern pagans still recognise the benefits of the church. A place of heritage, history, and social integration.

Tiptoeing inside the church and spying the dear old rector silently praying before the lady chapel, left me suddenly remorseful. Sylvia, third in a line of female rectors at St Thomas's, was a good friend of mine and, with Suit insisting I kill her at once, I demanded an alternative…

"Won't do it," I whispered. "Sylvie and I are friends. The church has always been of great benefit to this community. Such a horror would be devastating."

"As you wish," replied Suit. "But she must be neutralised. A degree of incapacitation. Would that be acceptable?"

"Yes," I thoughtfully replied, "and just look at her. So much faith, the patience of the woman! Waiting for an answer. Any sign, or a miracle. I propose we give her just that."

"Interesting, mistress. What do you have in mind?"

"Well, at this time of night, the rector always prays to the virgin, to Mary. It is high time she received an answer. Could you alter our appearance to imitate the Lady herself? My archive holds many likenesses. Review them. What do you think?"

"Hmm…" mused Suit, receiving my data. "Yes. A simple matter, mistress. With a shimmering radiance, a halo too, if you wish?"

"Yes. Pools of light shining from my hands, and then I want you to increase the intensity to such an extent she is blinded – permanently or temporarily. Enough for us to examine the reliquary unimpeded."

"An excellent plan," she replied. "And I like the theatrical touch. Only, your eyes are wrong. They are brown. Shouldn't they be blue?"

"Not a problem," I whispered. "Any scholar will tell you, the blue eyes of the Virgin are a post-Crusade, medieval contrivance. Brown is more likely."

"I think not, mistress. A common misconception, believing Mary of Nazareth to be of Jewish/Arabic appearance."

"Fine. Can you make my eyes blue?"

"No, mistress. Not without entirely covering your face, and to do so would delineate your form."

"Then this entire conversation is futile, is it not?"

"Sorry, mistress, I was only trying to…"

"Well don't," I snapped. "I don't need a tutor. I need an assistant. Help my plan succeed."

"Then surprise is key, mistress. We should close the door behind us, disable the lights, and stand before her. These sudden environmental shifts will heighten the drama."

"Perfect," I whispered. "And just what I need to hear. Let us begin. Activate stealth."

Removing the wedge propping the door, we slammed it shut and tiptoed into the church. Standing invisibly before the rector, she blinked in startled confusion.

Remotely accessing the controls, Suit extinguished the lights while simultaneously changing my appearance and lo! I appeared. Toweringly and shimmering, hooded robes of cerulean and dazzling white. Raising my arms, sunlight flowing from my hands, I generously smiled, bathing her in my shining magnificence.

Stumbling back and shielding her eyes, the old rector gasped, but, after tearing her hand from her face, she cried out, half in fear, half in awe, "Mother of God, mother of joy!" and I slowly nodded, loftily announcing "Maran-Atha!" with a voice of thundering water.

Suit then emitted a burst of radiance so intense it singed both the rector's clothing and the altar cloth, even melting nearby candles, and, with the rector slumped at my feet, Suit made us invisible again, returning the lights to normal.

"Is she alive?" I whispered. "Because, if you have killed her, Suit, I'm going to switch you off."

"She's fine," replied Suit. "Unconscious, blind, and burnt, but very much alive. She will recover."

"Good," I said. "Let's head to the vault."

⧗

The church vault was exactly as Marcus described: dark, dusty, and claustrophobic. As I squeezed into the trapdoor and clambered down the steps, Suit emitted a soft radiance, pushing back the gloom. The ceiling was too low for me to stand upright, so I decided to crawl (better for the spine than stooping) and I took a moment to enjoy the stonework and the polished crystalline slab set into the floor.

Set into a niche, the strongbox holding the reliquary was the same model described by Marcus and Suit soon had it open (simple microscopic analysis quickly revealed the code), and within minutes I was scanning Walsingham's crumbling bones for data.

"Dammit," I said. "There isn't much left, and the copies in his teeth are barely detectable. Beginning carbon scan."

Changing the mode of the scanner, I waited for the radio-isotopic results to appear... 1260 bc +/- 50 years, the late middle Bronze Age, and astonishing Sir Malcolm's bones had survived at all!

"Do you have everything you need?" asked Suit and I nodded in reply.

"Good," she affirmed. "Before decrypting Sir Malcom's data, we need to head north and find a place to rest."

"Certainly," I whispered, closing the reliquary and locking the safe. "But in a minute. I want a look at the slab? It seems unnatural and" – I frowned – "disturbing somehow."

Kneeling, and running my fingers over its smooth, granite-like surface, my mind drifted into clouds of forgetfulness.

"Mistress," prompted Suit, "wake up! We need to get going."

"Hmm," I mumbled, suddenly drowsy. "What did you say?"

As if in response, threading like smoke from its sparkling surface, I felt a whispering voice, but I could not distinguish the words...

Flummoxed, I listened again: "She is me."

"Did you hear that?" I pressed. "A voice? A whisper?"

"Hear what?" replied Suit, and I quickly ran the moly-scanner over the twinkling slab.

"The voice. Soft as gossamer, but it's... gone?"

"Heard nothing, mistress. Doubtless you imagined it."

The results of the scan left me confused...

"Nothing," I muttered, scratching my head. "The slab's made of nothing? That can't be right. Maybe it's...?" I promptly changed the scanner to detect radiation.

"Still nothing. Changing to maximum sensitivity..."

The scanner beeped affirmatively, and its small display listed a repeating sequence of frequencies.

"Ah." I nodded. "That's better. Soft X-rays, exceedingly weak. Hey! I've seen this sequence before. Aboard the KBE, right before Susi died. It was coming from that twinkly marble we brought back from Mars."

"Yes, mistress. I was there too. We must go. Your friend the rector will soon be coming to."

"Indeed," I replied. "Let's go. Activate stealth."

Scrambling up the steps, we noiselessly fastened the trapdoor, before slipping past the stirring rector and heading outside.

In the distance, I could hear a commotion – my domestic handiwork already discovered, but there was something else, bringing me to a sudden halt...

"What's wrong?" asked Suit. "Why have you stopped? We need to head north."

"Caught a scent," I replied. "Very faint. A few molecules, nothing more."

"What scent?" she enquired. "I detect nothing and no one."

"Me neither," I said, looking left and right. "But for a second, I smelled…" – sniffing the air – "jasmine. I expected to see… No." I sighed, shaking my head. "Can't be. Take us to Essex. I need a rest."

ELEVEN

IHAM

Resting in a house in Essex, my body aching and spent. I've eaten greens, potatoes, and beans, making porridge that set like cement. Suit is soaking up power, while I ablute in the shower. For the rest of the time, after writing this rhyme, I wash up the dishes and scour.

Yes, gallant reader, we made it, and after hijacking various vehicles, we arrived in a small coastal/saltmarsh town called Maldon. Unfortunately, Suit was unable to locate a suitable empty property, so we broke into a small house on Market Hill, murdered the elderly residents (while they slept), and incinerated their scant remains inside their electro-hybrid Aga.

"Waste not, want not," Suit vaingloriously crowed.

Her callousness was sickening, and the few amps generated did little to lessen my shame.

To my dismay, the data from the reliquary was corrupted, and quite beyond reconstruction, but the author was indeed Sir Malcolm Walsingham, and those crumbling bones were his. Unlike the logs of Bill Corbiere (who probably had his eyes shut), Walsingham begins by describing his transport and arrival, detailing his first few days, before settling into a weekly recording pattern to cover important events. As I explained, his bones (and therefore his logs) have decayed over time, and I have inserted italicised comments highlighting my corrections, interpretations, or assumptions. Over to you, Malcom…

Just as Moloch described, my feet arrived first, and very alarming it was too. To watch my legs elastically stretching away, tapering toward an invisible point – terrifying! My entire form then extending, elongating into thread, and then, snap! The "hook" anchoring my head suddenly surrendered, flinging my mind and body towards my feet, tearing me through space like a relativistic thunderbolt. Then, bump. I arrived…

Beneath my feet, and sparkling in the starlight, is a polished slab of crystalline stone. Surrounding it are an assortment of earthenware bowls, platters, and jars, indicating a place reverence, and I quickly step aside, in case a witness takes sudden offence.

Dear Finder,

This a log of my experiences. Yes, indeed. I should have mentioned this earlier, but to say "it has been a difficult day" would stretch English understatement to its limit. I didn't train for this shit! Let me begin…

Malcolm Walsingham is my name. A man of the 22nd century, delivered into this period by a malfunction, grave error, or pure mischance. The original instigator of my passage through time and space was Moloch (a god-like entity) and he intended to choose my destination, but, heeding my advice, he agreed my own choice would be more fitting. No. Not fitting. What were his words? Oh, yes, "My own typhlotic groping's truly serendipitous." Supercilious, but who am I to argue with a god? He also assumed a degree of tampering with the temporal coordinates, and his suspicions seem correct. Looking at the night sky, I can tell this isn't my time. When and where have I arrived? The SSD in Darmstadt was my intended destination, but with the scent of the ocean on the breeze, I am a long way off.

Moloch claimed this tampering was part of a conspiracy to thwart his plans (what plans?) and, to pursue this matter, he has unleashed one of our children. This concerns me greatly. No one was to know of the children we grew, and they were never meant to go full term. When the world learns of our illegal work, the UET will be finished. Eugenic research is illegal. The hybridisation of the human genome strictly forbidden, and we went far beyond embryonic development. Creating organisms of divine power and beauty, fusing extremophiles from the harshest extra-terrestrial environments we could find. Enough! These are matters beyond my control. If the stars are right, it will be thousands of years before I need worry. Laughably optimistic. In this environment, I will be lucky to last a decade.

Without maintenance, the life-extending benefits of my Hibbites will rapidly diminish and then my implants will kill me.

Returning to the night sky, I reckon the year to be approximately 1200 bc, and winter. Moloch did say midnight, 1 January, and see no reason to doubt this. I have reset my internal chronometer accordingly.

One item of note. Procyon, that is, Alpha Canis Minoris, even here in the past, appears orange/red, allowing me to postulate that some altering of the timeline has taken place. I take it as a warning not to damage it further. Care and forethought, Malcolm, especially when dealing with the primitive inhabitants of this period. Indeed, I can detect a small settlement nearby, and I shall try seeking shelter and succour among its inhabitants. But that is for the morning! My own degree of exposure is a primary concern. It is bitterly cold, and the flaxen smock Moloch clothed me in supplies no insulation at all.

Moving closer to the settlement (a dozen or so circular huts behind a ditch and bank surmounted by a wattle fence), infrared analysis reveals the thermal emissions of assorted livestock, with approximately twenty individuals huddled together in a large central roundhouse. Nearby, a smaller hut, covering a deep pit, houses a single individual. There are no signs of activity (suggesting this community follows a strictly diurnal existence) so I am heading towards the western side of the settlement, where the embers of a fire still radiate heat.

Badly fragmented, the next few paragraphs concern Walsingham's early discoveries. Coming upon a communal space, he found windbreaks and benches surrounding a circular fire pit. The pit itself, lined and ringed with warming stones, was still alight, and he was grateful to warm himself before examining the half-dozen tapering windbreaks the inhabitants cleverly employed. Approximately 1.5m wide, 2m deep, 1.2m at their highest, their frame was of wooden construction. A hollow, curving hoof-like wedge of wattle, with sewn hides, like a flysheet, stretched over top. Certainly, the effectiveness of their design caught Walsingham off guard. They provided not only shelter and storage but a surprisingly efficient thermal barrier. Reflecting and concentrating the heat from the fire while funnelling any smoke into a vertical column.

Smoke inundation and uneven heating are perpetual problems when sitting around a campfire, especially in breezy conditions, where the leeside of the fire is too smoky for comfort and the windward, although smoke free, only warms one side of the body. If aligned correctly, these ingenious structures would have abated these issues quite marvellously.

Bedding down under one of these structures, Walsingham came upon earthenware platters sprinkled with leftovers from the villagers' supper (a variety of flatbread or fishcake), and he found these scraps very tasty indeed. Salty, smoky, and decidedly chewy.

An arduous three days but successful. A stressful first day, there were many pinch points. If things had turned ill, doubtless I would be dead, and yet here I am! Unharmed. A bit wiser, warmer, with a full belly, and wondering if these endearing rustics have any hooch I could drink. A thousand years too early for a brandy, whisky, or gin, but mead, ale, or cider? What would they call it? Might there be fruit fermenting in a barrel somewhere? Do they even have barrels? The word for a maker of barrels is "cooper", from the word copper, and these folk work copper very skilfully, but I have yet to see anything that resembles a barrel.

Forgive my wandering words. I'm prattling like a Padgett (*damn cheek!*). My aching limbs and alcohol withdrawal symptoms are a manifold distraction calling for succour.

Permit me to recap the events on my first twelve hours for they were both curious and delightfully quaint...

Early morning when discovered. Dawn, breaking grey, cold, and frosty, revealed two young girls wrapped in furs, and they wordlessly stepped over my reclining form, dutifully gathering the pots and platters from last night's feast.

Kneeling to conceal my true height, I offered the pots and plates from the nearest windbreak.

Understandably nervous, the girls withdrew, but, when I smiled and carefully nodded, they edged closer, snatching the plates and pots from my grasp.

"Malcolm," I said, pointing to my chest. The smallest girl paused briefly before looking perplexed.

"Gro-ohm," she pondered. "Isa-ohm?"

This was my first shock. My translation matrix refused to respond. The girl's dialect had it stumped, and forced to rely on my wits I kept talking...

"No." I chuckled, again pointing to my chest. "Malcolm."

"Mol-col?" inquired the taller girl, haltingly aping my accent. "Mol-col isa-ohm?"

Close enough I thought and pointed towards the girls with an inquisitive look.

Giggling but reluctant, the girls introduced themselves thus:

"Mita," said the smallest.

"Deni," said the other, before dashing away, calling, "Va-ta, va-ta! Isa-ohm, isa-ohm-coh!"

Recognising "Va-ta" to mean father, I understood the girl's language to be a proto-dialect of Gallo-Belgic. Quite unknown to my translation matrix, I quickly stored her every word, ready to compile a new linguistic database.

From inside the communal roundhouse, I could hear excited conversation, with men gruffly replying. Within twenty seconds, leaning on staves and wrapped in linen blankets, three tousled and bearded primitives staggered out to greet me. Laughing at my chilly predicament, the leftmost man spoke with a face of kindness...

"Isa-ohm," he said. "Mita eid doom. Ei-eita-azer, keene-azer," and I nodded, shivering, pointing towards my belly.

Smiling, the leftmost man beckoned me to follow and as I stood, revealing my true height, they gasped, jumping to look me eye to eye.

"Sare-gro-ohm!" They laughed. "Ohm-coh. Coh-ta-fer un fout. Got-brod un-fesh."

Now, I did not understand what that meant, but the offer of shelter was most welco—

For a dozen kilobytes, Walsingham's logs are extremely fragmentary and to reconstruct them would be overly speculative. Words and phrases do leap from the blocks of corruption, however, and I list them here in chronological order...

Was
Careful
At all as
Huddled
Open and
Pattern

Folding
Skewered
Upon with Mita
Willow
Wax lamp
Flickering
Inflation, before tying off.

Returning to proceedings as normal...

Involving every imaginable craft, the youngest to the old.

Wailing and

Stiffening, naked, smeared in filth and excrement.

Clueless what they were saying, but among the womenfolk there was suspicious pointing and whispering, before an elder woman, cutting the gossip short, delivered sharp punitive thwacks from a thin cane of willow.

It was here... understanding the words no, yes, day and night, with other elements of vocabulary soon following. The delighted faces of Mita and Deni when I thanked them for their goodness, fire, and food, brought me great comfort. The chieftain of this tribe, collective, extended family association, or clan was Brin – a stocky man of about thirty-five. Mita and Deni were his daughters. The elder woman seen earlier, dishing out the punishment, was his wife, but I should point out, this society's relationship ethics are quite different from our own. For one, this a free sex society, and it is the women that do the choosing – snuggling and copulating with any man that they fancy, whenever they want! Indeed. There is always some form depravity going on, and several of the girls are pregnant, one of them extremely heavily. Her labour cannot be more than a fortnight away.

... beach, joining a team of hunter-gathers. Resolutely carrying two fish traps, a lobster pot, and a stack of wicker baskets.

As we walk, I haltingly ask (using signs and gestures) Brin and Tava (his wife) about the dead woman in the pit.

"She mother of earth," explained Brin. "No children, no work. The below-ground, of rock and dirt is she the speaker of. Our guide of living. The dead she hears. In the night she dies, and now blue faces will come – men with spears and hair of fire. Bad men. Full of lies. They come for the taking, the blooding, and the burning."

Do not expect a full interpretation of his words. My linguistic database for this dialect was still far from complete, and I replied to Brin's concerns with a mindful nod and a shrug.

Through a marshy wetland, our progress to the coast was down a well-beaten track. Planks and timbers bridged the widest of the brooks and streams, with raised boardwalks over the boggy bits – creaking and shifting as we made our way across. Coming to halt by a stagnant lagoon, floating bladders marked the location of traps…

"You help pull?" asked Brin, and I nodded as he untied the ropes attaching to traps to the bank.

Well weighted, we hauled traps in one at time, before lifting them from the murky water.

The first trap, a crayfish basket, was empty, and after refreshing its bait (a tied bundle of worms and guts) Brin and the others put it aside for immediate resetting. Coming next from the turbid water was a pair of eel traps, of a simple but clever design. Like a champagne bottle, with a short funnelling neck and weighted with stones. Writhing, sliming and thrashing in each was knot of silver-grey, and clapping his hands, Brin laughed at their good fortune. Quickly dispatching the eels, Tava rolled them in a sheet of cloth before laying them in a basket. Grinning broadly, Brin patted my arm.

Seeking new bait, boys dashed hither and thither into the thicket, and they soon returned with handfuls of fresh wriggling things, tying them inside and standing clear as the men hurled the traps into the lagoon.

"Two suns set, and we return," said Tava. Slipping her arm about my waist and smiling upwards, she acknowledged my red, dripping nose. Hugging me tight, she sympathetically shivered.

"We fire and food cooking at sea," she explained, tightening the cords of my gown. "First, we hunt and net. With Brin you go. To house I return, for after sun a feast we prepare."

Upon the beach, a bank of shingle leading to muddy sand, Brin, the men, and boys, broke into teams, probing for razor clams and shellfish. Others gathered laver, wrack, and dabberlocks before retrieving the lobster pots and traps dotting the mark of low tide. Feeling useless, I gathered driftwood, before watching in awe as a boy of no more than thirteen kindled a fire with no more than a pointed stick, a length of twine, a split branch, and a scraper, and note, it was January! His tinder was far from bone-dry, but he soon had a bright crackling blaze, and I dashed away, keen to gather more driftwood.

We had a clambake. Indeed, there were a few clams, but it was mostly cockles, razor clams, small crabs, prawns, and exceedingly chewy limpets. Before cooking, the shellfish were wrapped in seaweed, and not until this covering had burnt away, did we retrieve them. A simple indicator of readiness, but surprisingly dependable, and my fishy lunch was cooked to perfection. Mind you, it would have benefitted from a glass of Chablis, and I await my first taste of Bronze Age hooch with growing impatience.

The few decent sized fish (whiting, dabs, and sole) were dispatched, bled, wrapped in linen, and then hidden in baskets (away from the pesky gulls). Wrapped in wet seaweed, the excess of the crabs and shellfish went into a damp sack. In this climate, they should keep for days!

From resetting the fish traps, lobster pots, and returning the settlement, a feast was indeed in preparation, and I watched the women butchering an animal, adding to the haunches already roasting over the fire on a spit. At first, the aroma was appealing, thinking the animal a pig or wild boar, until I recognised certain... parts. A foot to be precise, and I blanched at what was taking place. What could I do? Cannibalism was customary to these people, and, although I refused to partake, God help me, no, I learnt a great deal about their culture. The provider of their grisly feast was the young woman who had died the previous night, the "earth mother" of special prophetic and magical significance. Acquired from a neighbouring tribe, she was a "white skin" (an albino?) incapable of bearing children or withstanding the sun. As a result, although revered, richly fed, and fattened, she lived in a pit, in darkness and squalor, "communing with the earth", until cold nights came, and exposure inevitably claimed her. Then, seeking to absorb her magical qualities, to complete their lovely ritual, the tribe would feast upon her corpse, defaecate into her pit, before interring her uneaten remains within. (For the record, I ate bread and fish, washed down by a non-alcoholic, tonic-like brew of honey and bog myrtle.)

On my second night, I joined the tribe in the communal roundhouse, snuggling with my new friends Mita and Deni. Sweet girls, but smelly and crawling with lice. Although I tried to keep my distance, my own infestation will soon be actively thriving...

My second morning among the people of this generous tribe.

The weather took a turn for the worse during the night and it is pouring with rain. Inside the roundhouse it was utterly dark and opening the door made no difference. Blowing on embers and lighting earthenware lamps, Tava bleakly muttered how the sun has fled, and, kicking two boys from their blankets, she demanded they collect charcoal and kindling.

Fanning the central hearth back into life and coughing at the smoke, she piled on two faggots before returning to her slumbering husband. With sudden flame leaping from the central hearth, concerned for everyone's safety, I crawled towards the fire and added charcoal to moderate the blaze.

"Tanka," said Tava, nodding in approval, and, seeing the fire was safe, I returned to my allotted space, careful not to disturb my neighbours.

This lazy morning lie-in came as a surprise, but what else can one do on a dark January morning when it is pouring with rain? It was past 10am before the tribe got going, and I helped the womenfolk quern a mixture of seeds, grains, and nuts, before standing by as the resulting herby flatbreads slowly baked upon blackened earthenware tiles.

By midday, with the rain at last slackening to a drizzle, I witnessed Bronze Age healthcare and grooming, with bathing, combing, and hair cutting via small bronze knives (rather than scissors or shears, a later Celtic/Roman invention). For trimming their beards and shaving, the men preferred freshly knapped flints. They were certainly sharp, and how they avoided cutting themselves I couldn't fathom.

Fascinated by everything pharmacological, I was delighted to watch Tava pulverise a lump of chalk to powder before roasting it in a shallow dish upon the hearth.

"What you make?" I asked. "Lime that is quick?"

"Jollpa," she replied, "For skin and wounds."

Removing the now-glowing dish and allowing it to cool, she carefully doused its contents with seawater, stepping away while it seethed, bubbled, and steamed.

"Blood of burning tree," she then remarked, unstopping an earthenware jar. Passing me the stopper, she poured into the dish a quantity of viscous dark oil, blending, and folding with a stick until she achieved a smooth brownish-grey paste.

Regarded as a cure-all, this sticky mixture, ointment if you like, the tribe applied to any scabs, wounds, spots, or lesions as a matter of course. This intervention resulted in a great deal of bawling among the younger children. Hardly surprising. The ointment must be at least pH10. I can only wonder how effective it is.

Doing the rounds was another palliative – a jarful of pungent smelly oil. Some anti-parasitic or insecticidal concoction? I wasn't sure, but I watched Mita and Deni giggle as they combed it into their hair.

Scientifically curious, I examined this oil more closely. Its aroma was extremely telling – a mixture of fish oils, and I asked Tava how they came by it…

"Some nights in spring, when the moon shines upon waves of silver, we gather many fish from the surf, pressing into pots and waiting."

From her lyricism, I could deduce annual or freak nocturnal events impelled fish fry, sprats, or smelt to beach themselves in great quantities. Not ones to miss out on such a bonanza, the local population would gather, press, and preserve the fish (like anchovies) for both food and for oil.

For the remainder of the day, bemused and bored, I joined the herders, checking and feeding their scabby livestock – a dozen small deer and twenty depressed-looking goat-like sheep. Birds also, with cots for doves or pigeons, and an enclosure of gulls, their wings almost clipped to the bone. There were pigs too. Semi-wild, they roamed the land free-range, but since the tribe fed them scraps, they had the good sense to remain local, rootling in a nearby copse. Brin explained how they drove the pigs into their fields to dig, forage, and enrichen the soil. When I finally encountered these small "pigs" I found them to be dark, fierce, and hairy. More akin to wild boar, in truth.

From here, Walsingham's log again breaks down into unattached words and jumbled phrases. Enough remains for me to summarise the events of his first week, beginning with his waking on the third day…

"Beginning to think I'm abandoned," he writes. "Am I trapped here?" Indeed, he was. No communication from Moloch or Gleener, and I can only wonder at his emotions. Despair, shock, loneliness…How would you feel, what would you do?

A true professional and dedicated academic, Walsingham makes no mention of his tribulation, but the pressure he was under was terrific and I can only envy his calmness and resolve. Mind you, sleeping with those teenage girls, night after night… Dear me. I do hope he behaved.

Walsingham's third day was bright and cold, and he assisted the village elders dragging a tool-laden, two-wheeled barrow westward to an area of industry, mining, and quarrying.

This work taking place at this site enthralled Walsingham: "The cradle of civilisation, the beginning of the industrial revolution!" With teams of people, drawn from miles around, working together, quarrying stone, ore, and clay, from the cliffs and hillside. Walsingham observed the building of kilns and furnaces – a straightforward design: bottle-shaped, with three bellowing tubes, and a long tapering flue. Potters potted in makeshift tents, shaping pots from long ropes of rolled dark clay before the firing of the furnaces loaded with the bounty hewn and dug from the surrounding landscape. This was a social event too, and Sir Malcolm could now understand much of the conversation. The planning of a great feast was a pertinent topic, with the prospect of dancing, music, the telling of tales, the exchange of men or women, for work or mating purposes (he was unsure). As they trudged back, the barrow wheels squeaking like mice, he asked Brin to explain the tradition...

"We call to the moon and stars," he explained. "Beat the earth, wood, and hides. We dance and sing, all the people of the coast will come, bringing food and gifts, sons, and daughters. Deni and Mita are of age, and among the choosers they will be. Tava will be choosing also, for she tires of me and seeks fatter meats and richer living."

What a shit! Poor Brin. His wife and daughters were planning to leave him, but I suppose it might be a two-way thing. An ambitious young floozy from another clan might pick him and then he could begin his family again, but jeez. What a culture. Feminism gone mad!

"The men of the tribes will drink the fire fruit water. They will fight, striking with staves of ash. I too will fight. Scores I have to settle, with little to lose and much to gain by conquering."

The following the morning, Walsingham joined a meeting of clan elders, whereupon an agreement was reached. First to name him Molcol-Iham (as recognition of his worthiness) and then to officially bring him into the tribe. In light of his new status, he was shown the stores: grain and other foodstuffs, oils, tars, unguents, tools, livestock, ores, rock, wood, charcoal, pots, ingots of copper, bronze, silver, and nuggets of gold. There were pearls, too, in a sack, with another bag of uncut quartz, colourful fluorites, and pinkish manganocalcite (an impure form of Iceland spar). There were few weapons. Indeed, the implements were functional, for hunting, fishing, tilling, cutting, bashing, butchery, or the felling of trees.

After the meeting, Walsingham witnessed the servicing and testing of musical instruments, percussion in the main. Hollow logs, drums, shakers, but he also described wind instruments, with horns, shells, and a type of kazoo-cum-didgeridoo built from strips of wood, hide, and bone.

As far as I can make out, the winter festival was one heck of a bash, and, beginning to master the language, Walsingham could now converse and understand much of the chatter. Certainly, his presence was a topic of conversation, with the local tribes assuming he was an Iceman or a Man-of-the-Winter. A Norseman, a Scandinavian trader lost overboard or shipwrecked. These "Icemen" sailed the coast sometimes, arriving in small boats to peddle their wares. Pelts, skins, amber, blubber, teeth, and bones, in exchange for silver, gold, pearls, tin, slaves, and girls. The tribes had no issue with these traders from distant shores. In fact, the oiled sealskins they provided were highly prized.

Walsingham joined the feast like a brother, tucking into roast venison, heron, flatbread, and apples (stewed into a sauce-like mush). To wash all this down, a choice of beverages: goats' milk, a mushroom and birch tea (mildly numbing), and a syrupy fruit liqueur. Somewhere between a fruit compote and wine, after imbibing bowls of this lumpy gloop, Walsingham was decidedly tipsy.

The music and dancing Walsingham found particularly charming, and yet he observed it dispassionately, recording his thoughts from an anthropological standpoint. The dances themselves were animal-themed, with gyrating exaggerations of the hunting, rutting, fleeing, and hiding behaviour of more than a dozen domestically important species. The dance representing the charging and bellowing bull he found especially moving, the imitative hunter side-stepping the charging "bull" like a matador. He suspected these dances were as old as the hills and the "bull" a species of auroch, already hunted to extinction in Britain by 1200 bc. To his ear, the music sounded sub-Saharan, African, reminiscent of the Tuareg, most notably the Tasikiskit (the women singing accompanied by drums and percussion) and the Tahengemmit (the men singing slow and low), with other renditions recalling the drumming of the Bambara people of Mali and the massed singing of the Masai of Kenya.

When it came to the time of choosing (the women choosing the men), proceedings became more ritualistic, with the men lining up to display their prowess, telling tales of skills and feats, performing acts of courage and strength (the women looking on decidedly nonplussed).

The two fellas manoeuvring around Mita and Deni were obviously a right pair of pricks and the girls withdrew into the arms of Walsingham, before declaring very firmly that they chose him. This of course caused a fair amount of consternation, requiring Brin to quickly step in and defend their position (possibly because the choosing of these two men was a done deal), offering to fight the two boys if they continued to scorn and insult. Brin's bad mood was hardly surprising. His wife had already run off with the grinning twerp she fancied from a neighbouring village, and was doubtless already humping him in a nearby hut. Tava's new fancy man was certainly a show-off, with the status symbols of the period. Golden bracelets and wearing an axe. Its polished bronze head demonstratively gleaming.

After downing bowls of hooch, still feeling put out and brandishing his long staff with drunken bombast, Brin joined the men in bouts of personal combat. Acquitting himself mightily, he won several matches (Mita, Deni, and Walsingham cheering him on), until a much younger, stronger man from an outlying village, clobbered him a good one. Unconscious and with a serious headwound, Walsingham and the girls took Brin to his bed, tending his wound with bandages soaked in simmering brine.

Walsingham records little until the following morning, when both the noisy labour of a woman giving birth and the steadily worsening condition of Brin roused the tribe into a state of clamour and chaos. Unable to help Brin in any way (a cracked skull and expanding haematoma) and aware his injuries were fatal; Walsingham assisted the birth.

The mother, a woman of about seventeen or eighteen, was comfortable; it was her second child. She was breathing deeply and calmly and maintaining good pressure throughout her contractions. There were no birthing aids as such, but the other women calmed her, mopped and cooled her brow. During a lull in her contractions, an elder women called Jana encouraged her to drink a bowl of tea. Intrigued by its pungent aroma, Walsingham sampled it himself, finding it both herbal and fungal. Heaven knows what it truly contained. Walsingham detected little physiological change in the mother, but after imbibing it, she didn't seem to care as much. I suspect the poor women was high as a kite!

It was a boy. Both mother and child came through the birth very well, and, to reduce the chances of a postpartum infection, Walsingham forbade the pulling of the placental remnants. Sadly, the baby showed deformities. Twisted limbs, a partial cleft palette, and fused digits. He suckled, however, and Walsingham returned to Brin and his increasingly desperate daughters.

⌛

"Va-ta Brin die," I explained to the girls, their father's eyes now feverishly rolling. "Now is farewell, Brin no speak."

"Va-ta!" sobbed Mita. "Come back. Come to sky and light. Don't leave. The Earth doesn't need you. We need you. Don't sleep yet!"

Brin stirred and tried to speak, but he could not. Partially raising his hand instead, his daughters keenly grasped it, as if to send their life to him. It was no good. He was fading. Turning his eyes to me, he fought once more to speak. No words came, but as his last breath slowly rattled from his lungs, I understood his meaning. Taking the girls aside, I held them close and tenderly before ushering them out into the chill grey light.

Standing nearby was Jana the wise woman. Regretfully nodding a reply to her unspoken question, she gasped in horror, sobbing, as she ran to gather the tribe; the women wailing and singing in a tumultuous lament.

By default, Jana was now the head of the tribe, and this was fortunate. She was a good woman. Kind, thoughtful, the tallest of the clan, with cool grey eyes and a startling mop of strawberry curls. Better suited to practicalities than Tava (Brin's self-centred ex-mate), Jana had already earned respect, but, after Brin's passing, who would speak for the men and lead the hunt? Among the men, I was by far the eldest, but as a newcomer would I be eligible? Certainly, I had no desire to be responsible for these people. Caring for Mita and Deni was my primary concern. They had lost everything, and in choosing me they had become my responsibility. I would protect them until the end.

After speaking to Jana, learning the ways of the tribe, she proposed I become headman, but with two younger men deputising for me in the physical rituals because of my age.

When she came to speak of the ritual of choosing, she explained its importance. The people of each settlement (separated by a mile or more) were all related. Merely branches of an extended family, spread out to reduce the competition over food and resources. Obvious enough, and in years of shortage, clan size and gender ratio were vital. For eight months of the year, the clans fed themselves quite successfully, through farming, fishing (and occasional cannibalism), but in the deep winter months, they relied on their surplus, hunting, inshore fishing, gathering, and too many unproductive mouths could lead to starvation. In the end, it all came down to sex. True contraception was unknown to these people, yet they understood sexual intercourse (and insemination) often resulted in pregnancy. Consequently, mating, copulation intended to produce offspring, should only occur at "the great choosing" during the moon of the midsummer equinox (June), with the resulting babies born the following spring (when supplies were increasingly available).

The "lesser choosings", held every few weeks, were purely social events. An opportunity for the clans to mingle, gossip, share skills, resources, and personnel.

Jana said I should help prepare Brin for his ritual of death (dismemberment followed by cremation) before interring his ashes in a ritual vessel beneath the shrine of the Earth Mother (a pit inside a small hut, used as both a prison and a shrine.)

Meetings of the womenfolk would follow. Their main topic of conversation. Me. My suitability as headman.

After three days of superstitious nonsense and rituals, including a mock interrogation, the brandishing various totems (both artefacts and weapons), and my inglorious smearing in lime, ochre, and a black gloop (which I assumed was squid ink), my elevation is complete. Jana is to be my matron (the true chief of the tribe), with Mita and Deni named as both my adopted daughters and future bearers of my offspring. With "Mol-col-iham" still too much of mouthful, my name has changed (again). It is official. I am now their chief. A most reluctant and nervous chief, and they simply called me "Iham".

There is more from Walsingham, much more, but what remains is almost unintelligible. I can infer that long months have passed, his second winter slowly relenting, and how Walsingham's clan have suffered. Disease and death followed a period of snow and mud, taking the weakest and then the youngest. Walsingham assisted two more births. The first was stillborn, a girl, tiny, premature, and badly deformed. The second was a healthy boy, with striking red hair, but his mother died days later from blood loss and septicaemia. Volunteering to raise this boy as her own, Jana wet-nursed the infant with tenderness and love.

It was becoming clear to Walsingham deformation by inbreeding was a major issue. To ascertain the clan's understanding of the problem, Walsingham spoke to Jana. He suggested that the clan introduce new precedents to limit breeding. To ensure relatives no closer than cousins intermingle. This, I am sorry to say, she flatly rejected. Attributing the results of inbreeding to a curse of the blood. "It is but a fire of the flesh!" she scorned. "A thing to be cut away by shining blades. Only by the flames of Balenos can it be quenched."

Word has reached us of shamanic priests moving from clan to clan. Listening to the portentous gossip coming from the elders, the tribes feared and despised them, respecting their power, nonetheless. By Jana's description, I would suggest these priests are invaders or immigrants with differing beliefs, values, or moral code. When I asked her where they came from, she could only shrug…

"Many places," she haltingly explained. "The morning, the evening, the summer and the winter. From the land of Gall, the ice men say, across the sea by morning."

The icemen she referred to were Nordic Danes and Jana described them to me thus: "The tallest of men. Golden-haired, with eyes of sky and sea. In hollow boats of speed, they come. Wrapped in furs, cloaks, and mantles, wading surf and sand in boots of shining leather."

These icemen were traders, not conquerors, and they plied the coast in a flotilla of sturdy wooden boats with clinker hulls, six oars, and a simple sail of elk. We encountered a group a fortnight ago, their first visit since the autumn, and the tribe was much excited to receive them.

The language of these traders was an early form of Norse and I found communication with them straightforward. Indeed, this proved advantageous. My knowledge of their dialect both reinforced my alibi (of my sudden appearance) and increased my persuasiveness in trade, and, as I haggled for a discount, Jana could only laugh in wonder and delight.

Two days have passed, and the shamanic priests are among us. Beating drums, sounding cornets of copper and horn, they are causing a general ruckus.

Keeping a discreet distance, I watched them unload two barrows and set up camp. There were three men, a head taller than the tallest of our clan (excepting me, of course), with pale blue eyes, freckling skin, and deep red hair like copper. Two of their number were in fur-lined cloaks, with lace-up tunics and colourful patchwork trousers. To show off his decorative scars, spiralling tattoos, zeal and hardiness, their leader was bare-chested but for a billowing cloak.

It is my belief these men were of Celtic origin, Picts, perhaps. However, "Pict" is an anthropologically meaningless Roman term referring to the decoration of the body.

Increasingly fearful of what would unfold, Jana ordered the younger women to keep out of sight…

"Bad men," she explained, twiddling her auburn curls. "Not of the choosing but of the taking. My mother once they took, forcing her and cruel. You guard girl-women, Mita and Deni, and stay close. Stay in shadow place. Take spear and axe. Your claws and teeth."

As Jana instructed, Pen (a steady man of about thirty) and I hurriedly escorted the seven youngest women to a nearby copse, guarding them as they huddled in a draughty bothy made from sticks.

An hour after sunset, with a column of smoke rising from the settlement, I left Pen behind and sneaked though the twilight to see what was transpiring.

As I neared the settlement, I could hear the beating of drums accompanied by an almost hysterical clamour – screaming, wailing, and coming upon three women crying for the lives of their children, I ushered them into the communal hut, to ask what had occurred…

"What always happens!" sobbed Yosi (a young mother of about eighteen). "When the bad men come, they take the twisted ones. Took my little Grun! To their burning god they fed him. They cast his life as chaff. Like ashes on a harvest wind."

Child sacrifice. A horrific practice, and I was already too late. A mere spectator. Reduced to watching the adults of the local clans surround a towering pyre, their arms linked like a living henge. Jostling, swaying, expanding, and contracting, as if pulsating. Some screaming, some crying, their heads were thrown back in a twisted rapture of fear and delight. All the while, guarding the pyre from any dissenter, the Celtic priests stood proudly within. Their bloodied knives still drawn, they twisted and turned their shining blades in deference to the crackling flames. Then, a sudden orgy of violence. Tearing into the innermost circle, the Celts set upon Eye-eela – an expert weaver, cook, mother of many children, and singer of songs. Kicking, punching, and slashing, they cut into her clothing with an unbridled lust. This was too much for me. I could not stand by and watch these gentle people abused, and without thinking, I strode into the centre of the gathering, spearing and hacking the priests in a maelstrom of rage, my garments singeing, almost smouldering in the heat.

It was over very quickly. As if my sudden appearance had broken a spell, and I stood by while Jana broke up the gathering, demanding that two of the younger men finish off the dying priests, bashing their skulls in with rocks. Stripping their corpses, and slumping them onto the fire, they heaped on more wood, before offering their goods and weapons to Jana. As for me? Well, by now I was sweating and shaking. Never had I taken a life, and I fled into the darkness, vomiting uncontrollably.

Returning with Pen, Mita, Deni, and the rest, the clan listened intently to Jana's recounting of what had taken place. There was cheering and jubilation at the news of my intervention. By stepping in, the others had followed my lead, refusing the domination and cruelty of these men. The other coastal clans, upon hearing the news, were similarly celebrating the Celts' demise, and we sang songs and swapped tales late into the night.

This morning, dawning fresh and bright, I watched Mita, Deni, and others learn various crafts. The younglings were learning to sew, mend nets, join cloth, and weave baskets, before an afternoon singing songs to describe the behaviour and appearance of animals, plants, and fungi. The older children, eight years and up, were developing their skills in tasks more demanding. The boys practised with spears, staves, and bows, before knapping flints and using them to slaughter, skin, and butcher a young boar (tonight's supper, I hope).

The girls were spinning wool, weaving, and cooking small oatcakes, before trying their hand at a little pottery. Finally, the assembled students witnessed the smelting of bronze, going on to melt and alloying a small quantity of copper and tin, before pouring the glowing liquid into sandstone moulds. Grinning with delight, Mita showed me the tiny disc of bronze she had cast.

Flattening a ball of clay into a circular tile, Deni cut a small notch into its edge, saying how it reminded her of last night's bedtime story. Of the sun, red with anger from her little sister's flea-like nipping, nibbling, and biting.

Deni often made me little presents like this, and I kept them all. When I asked her why she brought me these little totems, she shrugged and smiled, saying, "Glinner says they make you happy."

Glinner is Deni's imaginary friend. Not entirely surprising she has one. The poor wee thing has recently lost both father and mother, and doubtless seeks succour in her dreams and imagination.

After firing, Deni's little disc of clay was a bright orange, and, taking Mita's little ingot of bronze, she filed its edges on a polishing stone and fit it snuggly into the notch. Clever little Deni. I cherish her gift. It is both a keepsake of the love I have for these girls and reminder of my duty. I keep it safely hidden high up over my sleeping place. I am becoming a sentimental old fool.

⧗

There follows a gap, a void in Walsingham's records, and I am unable to ascertain the reason. It is possible Sir Malcolm was simply busy, exhausted from working in the fields, but I also consider he may have been ill. His final entry concerns his worsening physical condition…

⧗

As predicted, my Hibbites are becoming less effective, and I am ill – gasping, wheezing, coughing up dark phlegm. With my cloned lung, breathlessness and expectoration are nothing new, but my symptoms are continuing to worsen, and bronchial pneumonia cannot be far off.

Like an ill wind, this latest malady waylaid me last week. A summer coronavirus, sweeping through the clans has brought with it fever, sweating, and palpitations. My Hibbites are containing the symptoms (just), but their numbers are too low to rid me of the disease, and consequently, without access to analgesics, I feel dreadful.

With my deteriorating condition (and in desperation), while the clan sleeps, I have staggered away from the settlement, to sit upon the slab of twinkling stone and stare up at the sky. This stone is not what it seems. Its incongruity with the environment is so pronounced it must be unnatural, and the villagers, in fear or reverence, refuse to go near it. They would occasionally leave an offering nearby; foodstuffs, or human remains, packed into an earthenware jar, but they never dwell here for long. Could this strange slab be connected to my arrival? Could it be part of a mechanism, connecting Moloch's realm with this? If my hypothesis is correct, the technology it represents is incredible, and it might possess other properties; I am always mindful in its proximity. When attempting to affect or interact with it (five attempts during the last eight months) I am particularly cautious, but my worsening health compels me to attend it again. What other hope do I have? I am dying! Did Moloch truly send me here to die alone and unlooked for, or was it the saboteur condemning me so? Moreover, was it truly sabotage stranding me here, part of a conspiracy (as Moloch claimed), or am I the victim of a simple malfunction?

Observing the surface of the twinkling slab with my ocular implant set to maximum sensitivity, I detect nothing, absolutely nothing, and this impossible result confirms its artificiality. The background "noise" from the surrounding environment at this level of visual sensitivity is overwhelming. I see only a swirling sea of random pixels, patterns, and false colours, but close examination of the slab reveals nothing. It is black upon black. Cold, inert, its molecules chilled to absolute zero, and yet they are not! Sweeping my palm over its glittering surface, I sense no temperature differential whatsoever. Impossible! Goddamn, I am too old and be dumfounded. What is this thing, what is it made from? What is its purpose, does it even exist?

"Moloch," I implore "I know you can hear me. I beg you, speak! Why am I here, for what purpose? Am I to end my days here, is it your will I toil like a beast, scratching my nethers, lice-ridden and stinking?"

For a few seconds, softly swirling, I caught the faintest whisper, and hoping to hear it again, I pressed my ear against it.

For minutes I continued to listen this way (my ear to the ground), until approaching footsteps sat me up with start. It was Deni. Still in her nightdress and barefoot, I wondered why she had come...

"Deni?" I asked, full of concern, "why have you come? It is cold and you should be sleeping. Return and be with your sister."

Fixing her bright eyes upon me and uncharacteristically grinning, she then studied her hands, wiggling her fingers as if trying them out.

"Sir Malcolm Walsingham?" she smoothly enquired, and, astonished Deni could say my name, I hesitantly nodded.

"My, my," she then said (in perfect English), "I hardly recognised you. You look terrible. You have been having fun."

Whoever was speaking, it was not Deni. Something or someone was using her, and I began to suspect the truth…

"Moloch," I gasped. "Sire, is that you? Why are you using Deni this way? Please, I beg you. Don't harm her."

Deni shook her head.

"No," she replied. "Not him. He will never come. I am the secret friend. The one Deni calls 'Glinner' and worry not – she is sleeping, and her dreams are enchanting. Soaring birds and shining flowers. Playing with her sister, skipping from wave to wave, they wade little rivers, choked with writhing weeds. Her physical form is walking, but her consciousness far away, warm and content. Her mind is merely borrowed. To instruct you. Nothing more."

"Glinner," I pondered, "the imaginary friend. Deni does mangle her words, so are you not the Gleaner? Moloch said she was insane. Incapable of coherent thought. A thing of flesh twisted and screaming. A plaything. Worthless. For the most menial of tasks. Wait, though, are you the saboteur? Was it you that left me here?"

"Worthless," she replied with a scowl. "A plaything? The arrogant fool. He is but flesh and blood also. Did you not know? Not a god, but a man, and no more than an instance of yourself."

"An instance," I said, "of myself? How do you mean? How can he be me, explain yourself!"

Sitting beside me and very delicately crossing her legs, Deni remorsefully sighed.

"Do you not yet understand?" she whispered. "Consider. From whence did you come? Not from space nor time. Not this universe, but another dimension, a dimension where time is external. No past, no present, no future. Without up, nor down, left, or right. It is and was everywhere, and because you were there, you are there still. Always were, always will be. In fact, you are trapped there. We all are, and you need your help to help us all."

"Very well," I replied with a shrug. "What is it you wish? How can I help me?"

"Die," muttered Deni, matching my shrug.

"Ha." I laughed, stifling a cough. "You will soon get your wish. Is that all?"

"Very nearly," she acknowledged. "But you must die in the manner your future dictates. Your personal log will survive your demise, and in time I will discover it, but only if you do as I say. You must convince this tribe to conduct your funeral according to my design, and your skeletal remains must, erm… will remain undisturbed for near two thousand years before their recovery, so we need to preserve them. As you are aware, these people prefer cremation and pulverisation as means of disposal, and the Hibbitic encoding within your bones will endure neither, so tell them this. You desire internment in a stone casket. Your naked body packed with lime and holding the disc totem Deni and Mita made across your breast. Tell them to bury you deep, under a mound of earth, lying upon this very slab. A fitting end for one so loved. In time, it will become a gay and happy place. Dotted with cowslips, and sprinkled with daisies, smiling in the sun."

"That will require a lot of digging," I remarked, "especially for one newly arrived. Chief or not. These people possess neither the time nor the resources for such an endeavour. Why would they comply?"

"Give them a gift," she craftily replied. "A simple gift of wonder. Make yourself great to them. You have done much already, although it is plain, they do not understand the benefit, but do more. Remember, Mita, Deni, and Jana love you deeply – I know this, for I have spoken to them. They will be attentive and receptive students, so teach them something new. Their bellows design is desperately poor, so improve it. Set them on a path towards the smelting of iron. If this tribe and its neighbours wish to survive their eventual assimilation by the Celtic tribes, iron implements will count in their favour."

"Very well," I said, "I will try. How long do I have, how long before…?"

"Several weeks," she revealed. "You will recover for a time but deteriorate this harvest, so remember to begin the dissolution of your remaining implants this summer. Your Hibbite population is becoming dangerously low. If you wait too long, their numbers will be insufficient."

"That will leave me deaf, dumb, and blind, but I will do as you wish. After I am gone, who will take care of the tribe?"

"Jana will lead," she assured. "A canny woman of good sense and she is fond of Pen. He will replace you. I will continue to guide Jana and the tribe for many years to come, beginning with the merging of the clans into a greater tribal society, and, yes, Mita and Deni will find good husbands. Fear not."

"I can only thank you for that, milady. Tell me, are you truly human? For you possess godly powers. Possession, omnipotence, knowledge of the past, the future, and the ability to travel in time and space."

"Indeed," she said, "and merge my essence with intelligent devices, but I am just a girl, of both tremendous age and youth, with a heart, lungs, eyes, and mouth. Moloch, your bitter alter ego, wallows in his immortal grandeur, craving both sacrifice and worship, but I do not. We are simply beneficiaries of an advanced technology. It is not of our conscious making. The technology itself made us or we made it, we know not. This slab is but a part of it, with countless geodes and nodes, some temporary, some fixed, spread throughout the galaxy."

"Incredible," I remarked. "What does it all do?"

"It gathers and collects," she replied. "Do not trouble yourself with matters beyond your reach. Be here, be now. Continue to do as you have done. The very highest! Honourable, wise, decent, kind. Now I must leave. In time, Moloch will uncover my duplicity, and to elude his pursuit, I must keep moving," and, following these words, she released the Deni from her control – the girl's unconscious body, collapsing like a sack.

Carrying Deni to our sleeping place and covering her with a blanket, I gently kissed her forehead and lay down beside her. Sifting Gleaner's words, I realised I had much to do, with little time to do it. The night was almost gone before I drifted into sleep.

With no more from his crumbling bones, it is here we leave Sir Malcolm. For the sake of completeness (and the fact he bothered to record it) I finish this account with the few words he compiled into his linguistic database (before his neocortex rendered it redundant).

Middle Bronze Age Dialect.

As spoken by the tribes of the Sussex coast, circa 1200 bc.

Short and snappy. A functional language with clear Gallo-Belgic similarities. Sentences usually terminate with either a verb or clause. The "th" sound (thorn) is unused.

Vocabulary (phonetic):

Nouns:
Aah = Water / River
Aah-Ker = Lake / Pond
Se-Aah = Sea / Ocean
Ta = Earth / Ground / Soil
Ur = Dung / Faeces / Manure
Ede = Reed / Grass / Rushes
Aah-Ta = Marsh / Bog
Bur = Hill
Ta-Ohn = Stone
Fer = Fire
Ta-Fer = Oven / Fire Pit / Kiln
Se = Sky
Sa = Sun
Lo = Moon
Sa-Deim = Star
Sa-Deim-Oh = Planet / Comet / Heavenly Body
Ma = Mother
Va = Father
Eid = Child / Baby
Arb = Tree
Ya = Yes
Nen = No
Isa = Ice
Ei = Eye
Ohm = Man
Wohm = Woman
Fout = Food
Brod = Bread
Fes = Fish
Fes-Ta = Eel
Ohn-Fout = Shellfish / Crustacean
Un = And
Tanka = Thank you

Adjectives and Verbs:

Ker = Dark
Keene = Bright
Eita = Light / Pale
Ohn = Hard / Brittle
Off = Soft
Deim = Small
Gro = Large
Tsi = Ill / Unwell
Ail = Life / Alive
Mor = Death / Dead
Orh = Go / Travel / Move
Coh = Come / Approach
Rune = Red
Ver = Green
Aze = Blue
Dur = Brown
Zar = Yellow / Gold
Ilvfa = Silver / Shiny
Clim = White / Chalky
Kal = Cold
Hise = Hot
Saire = Very
Doom = Foolish / Stupid

TWELVE

THE FUGITIVE

*I*gnoring my advice we leave this house, my mistress behaved most eccentrically. Commanding I render her invisible, she entered the old couple's garden, fed and watered their chickens, and collected their eggs. Instructing me to heat these eggs to 365 Kelvin for five minutes, after rummaging in their kitchen for bread, she cut two slices, toasting and buttering them before cutting them into strips. Decapitating the now-cooked eggs, she then proceeded to egg-dip and consume these "soldiers" with great heart, flagrantly ignoring my further pleas we leave post haste.

"Can smell it again," remarked Gina, drying her cutlery and plate. "Jasmine, or the scent of it at least."

Jasmine oil contains well over one hundred substances – esters, alcohols, ketones, aldehydes, fatty acids, and Gina's olfactory sense was indeed detecting a fair number of these compounds, but their source was elusive…

"Where is it coming from?" she muttered, sniffing the air. "There are no flowering jasmine plants in the vicinity. The scent seems to be wafting down from the rooftops. Most peculiar. The third time I have detected this scent in so many days. Could it be Hannah? Yes. Dr Hardcastle. I recall her wearing a similar scent. Could she be nearby, sporting the same perfume?"

"A possibility, mistress," I replied, "and yet the Hinnie central computer says she clocked in early this morning. She is there."

"Not crazy after all, then," Gina replied, "but could you confirm her service record? Where did she study? Where was she born?"

"Very well, mistress, only be patient. It may take several days to locate and access the information."

"Of course. Do your best. Now, which way are we heading?"

"North, mistress, to high ground. Then we can look and consider our options. It is a long run to York, but we dare not risk any more vehicles. Quite correctly, Inquisitor de Boer is monitoring all vehicular activity. If we acquire another by irregular means he will quickly discover us."

"Fine," she replied, "let's go. Leave the front door slightly ajar. Allow our handiwork to be discovered. If only for the sake of the chickens."

"Yes, mistress."

"Stealth," Gina commanded and like a whirlwind we whipped through misty streets of Maldon, passing as a blur.

⧗

Heading north, seeking to examine the remains of my dear friend Eric, Suit ran my poor limbs ragged, delivering us to the summit of Chrishall Common – the highest point in Essex (which at 147m is not high). The view was pleasant (although far from stupendous), and we scanned the horizon looking for signs of pursuit. To my surprise and relief, we remained unsought, as since leaving Sussex it felt as if something or someone was dogging our steps.

"So where do we go from here?" I breathlessly asked. "It is all very scenic, but we are still more than a hundred miles from York. Do you intend to run me the whole way?"

"Of course not. We are going to fly."

"Fly?" I pondered. "Fly what? Have you stolen a flyer?"

"Certainly not, mistress. Nothing so grandiose. I shall be providing the lift. My newly enhanced specifications should bestow a limited aerial capability."

"Should they?" I challenged. "I had no idea. Are you planning to sprout wings?"

"Indeed. Akin to bat wings, with stiffened spars and a flexible tail. Becoming airborne will be ungainly however, and a considerable drain on my energy reserves, but I calculate we should be able to glide and soar very effectively."

"What do you mean by ungainly? Because I know you, Suit. Ever the queen of the understatement. Should? Calculate? Sounds dangerous. Have you flown before?"

"Afraid not, mistress. This will be my maiden flight."

"Marvellous," I replied. "And you expect me to willingly fling myself skyward, based upon several equations?"

"Naturally, mistress. There is little reason to concern yourself. If we do plummet from the heavens, I promise a landing of remarkable softness."

"How thoughtful, but I require more reassurance than that. How about sharing your maths? Revealing your calculations might relax your passenger."

"Oh, mistress. There is really nothing to worry about. The odds of a fatal consequence are two hundred and fifty to one."

"Bugger the odds," I replied with a scowl. "You said fatal. Are you sure we can't get a car?"

"Certainly, mistress. They are monitoring every vehicle, so you must trust me. Lean forward, spread your arms, and be quick about it. During ascension, our cloak of invisibility will falter."

"Very well," I replied, adjusting my posture and spreading my arms. "What next?"

"We use the gradient to assist us. Run downhill, spread your arms, and leap forward. Thenceforth, I will take over."

The first ten minutes of our maiden flight were terrifying. Like a gigantic shimmering bat, struggling and overloaded, we flapped, hopped, scraped, and skipped our way downhill, scuffing every bush and bramble, until Suit, suddenly getting her timing right, powered us into the air, banking and soaring, clipping the treetops soon dwindling beneath us.

This was indeed not a stealthy take-off. Consuming enormous power, Suit's fabric shone brightly, and what with my squealing and screaming… Well, how we got away with it, I really don't know.

Levelling off and gliding, Suit again rendered us invisible, and as I caught my breath, at I last began to wonder at this new and marvellous turn of events.

"The view," I gasped, Essex dwindling beneath us. "A God's eye view. How far can you carry us, and to what altitude?"

"Precision is impossible," she calmly replied. "Too many variables. Wind direction, air temperature and weather conditions all come into play, but we have a gentle south-westerly behind us, and I anticipate a smooth flight, landing but a few kilometres south of York. As for my theoretical ceiling, with you on board, I anticipate flying no higher than 4,500 metres. Beyond that, you would find respiration increasingly difficult. Flying solo, I could ascend into the exosphere, achieving an altitude excess of 70,000 metres."

"Impressive, and are we invisible from the ground?"

"Almost, mistress. Unless silhouetted against the sun."

"As I thought, so let's get out of sight. Don't want us casting a shadow and scaring the natives. Couldn't we hide in the clouds, and are we invisible to radar? What about QF-Scattertrack?"

"Indeed, mistress. I intend skipping between cloud formations whenever possible, and fooling radar is a simple matter; easily absorbed, matched, and transmitted, but the QF-Scattertrack system of the military is infallible. Every particle of matter induces quantum field fluctuations. Fortunately, our configuration is novel and our footprint, compared to an aircraft, is tiny. I doubt the ripples of our passing would even be noticed."

"That is well," I said, my teeth beginning to chatter. "A bit warmer, if you please, and best speed to York; I need food."

⧗

Our flight to York took time. Still mastering flight and augmenting her program, Suit hopped us from hilltop to hilltop, with over ten minutes in Norfolk, perched on the summit of Beacon Hill. Following that delay, we soared through the sky like an eagle, the air whistling over us like the song of Calaïs.

As I was too cold and hungry to go any further, Suit landed us ten kilometres south of York, providing transport and the means to sate my calorific needs. Her choice of vehicle? An ice cream van! Fully laden and emblazoned with the logo "Robo-Whip!" it was no doubt appropriated from a local event.

Squeezing myself into its cabin, I gorged myself on ice cream and syrup while Suit took care of the driving, monitoring the local security systems in case of an alert.

Certainly, it was a good thing Suit was checking. Inquisitor de Boer had been busy; raising the threat level of all missing or tardy vehicles, and before long, Suit was tracking several aerial drones and ground vehicles (manned and automated) closing on our position.

"What do you think?" I asked. "Can we outrun them?"

"No, mistress, and trying to evade them on foot would prove unnecessarily reckless."

"As I thought. You can manage the drones and autonomous vehicles. Leave the manual pursuit craft to me."

"As you wish. They will be in visual range within moments. Their intention is to box and contain us. They will fail."

"Most certainly. What will you do with the automatons? Reroute them?"

"Yes, mistress. Already implemented. The river Ouse runs deep through Acaster Malbis. I shall promptly deposit any pursuing craft within it."

"Good thinking," I said, readying my gun. "They have already turned away. I must say, you are good at this. Very quick, very efficient... Ah, here come the police cars. Two in front, two behind. The usual stuff."

With the police vehicles moving to surround us, warning lights flashing, sirens wailing, I waited for the perfect moment...

"Unauthorised passenger!" announced an authoritative voice. "Your journey is unsanctioned and illegal. Power down immediately and come to a halt. Non-compliance will result in your capture and arrest."

This was my cue. With Suit blocking their communications and activating the chimes of the ice cream van (a cheesy rendition of "Greensleeves"), I flung open the hatch and leapt from car to car, firing my gun, tearing both drivers and passengers into a howling and bloody ruin. Landing with a crunch upon the lead car and tearing off its canopy, I proceeded to fling its terrified occupants high into air. Their flailing bodies hitting the road behind us in a sequence of sickening thuds.

It was over very quickly, and, as the ice cream van dwindled into the distance, its chimes slowly fading, I fired my gun once more to dispatch the only survivor: a bloodied and terrified man, vainly clutching his ruptured bowels.

Waiting for my bullets to scurry back and reload themselves, I watched with dismay as Suit detonated the fuel cells of the police vehicles, spewing columns of black smoke high into the air.

"Was that really necessary?" I remarked. "Isn't my carnage enough?"

"Not essential," she replied, "but the fires will turn many eyes – a distraction while we slip into York."

"Very well, but your brazenness troubles me. No more road trips for us; they will be watching."

"True but fear not. We are soon to be leaving these shores. The ocean is calling. Deep, dark, and cold."

"Then let us conclude our business tonight, but no running! I'm weary."

⏳

The streets of York were bustling, and we elected to use the "Thieves' Highway" to reach our objective. For those unfamiliar with term, this is above street level – roofs, ledges, walls, pipework, ducting, cables. A means of travelling quiet and unseen. Within the hour, I was squatting upon the roof of the Jorvik Institute, waiting for Suit to disable the security...

"This is taking too long," I whispered. "Is there a problem?"

"Yes and no," she replied. "The system is antiquated with limited functionality. I have disabled the monitoring devices, but many of the locks require keys."

"Right. Any guards?"

"Five," she declared. "Two at the main ingress, three patrolling the infrastructure. The vault is unguarded. Once inside, we will be free to operate with impunity."

"Very good. What do you recommend?"

"Stealth and patience, mistress. The emergency services are busily engaged investigating our earlier disturbance. If we are careful, the inquisitor will never know we were here."

"Fine. Where is Eric?"

"In the vault, mistress. Level 2, row G, box 37.1."

Waiting for the guards to pass (detecting their thermal emissions through the wall), opening, slipping through, and closing a fire door, we slithered along the ceiling before descending the elevator shaft, leading to the vault.

The door to the vault was formidable – an airlock of rivets and steel, but Suit, sending a tentacle of herself into its keyhole, picked the lock like a pro.

The hugeness of the vault took me by surprise – cyclopean. Piled high with boxes, crates, and oddly shaped artefacts, swathed in bubble wrap. The rows of shelving, laden with stone objects, masonry, or pottery shards went on forever, and trying to locate the appropriate box made me feel like a rat in a maze...

"Here he is," I said. "His skeleton, at least. Where are the grave goods?"

"Nearby," whispered Suit. "Box 36.8, just to your left."

"Good," I replied. "Will have a look at those in a minute. The skeleton is my priority."

Lifting the lid of the box, peering inside, and removing the padding, I spied Eric's skull and lower mandible…

"Poor sweet Eric," I sighed. "Can actually recognise him. If only he could talk."

"He can, mistress. Scan his bones. See if he left us a message."

Whipping out the moly-scanner and configuring it, I held its probe against his skull.

To my joy (and relief), from his teeth and pelvis I recovered over a hundred kilobytes of data, and I merged the two files, correcting any discrepancies.

"Excellent," I remarked, the data slowly filling in my mind. "He kept a journal. Now let's have a look at his grave goods. Particularly the figurine – Marcus found it captivating. I'm very keen to see it myself."

Replacing the skull, its padding, and affixing the lid, I opened the box with the grave goods, and rummaging in this treasure trove filled me with glee…

There was a bulky steel hauberk of rings, a rusty sword, the head of a wicked-looking war-axe, and a pot-like helm, so corroded it was almost a filigree. Last of all, and strangely at odds with this box of militaria, was the figurine. Removing its padding and picking it up, I could only smile. The way it captured Emil's features, both his face and form, was wonderful. A tribute in terracotta to his irreverent sense of humour, but did he really make it himself? That would indeed make it a thing of wonder. He was never an artistic or an artisan. Could he have learnt this skill from others?

Turning the figurine in my hands, I studied its base, only to feel it suddenly slipping from my grasp, and I watched in slow-motion horror as it hit the ground and shattered.

"Suit," I hissed in disgust, "why didn't you catch it?"

"Sorry, mistress. My mind was elsewhere. New data concerning Dr Hardcastle had me momentarily distracted."

"Fine, but now we have a broken statue. What do you suggest we do?"

"Hide it and flee."

"Is that all?"

"Certainly, mistress. It matters not. Replace the damaged pieces, shut the box, and move on. It will be weeks before our tampering is unmasked."

With a sigh and gathering one of the larger shards, I noticed a message scratched into its inner surface. Whispering the words aloud, I considered their meaning...

"Do it again. Do what again? Break another statue?"

"Haven't a clue," replied Suit. "Assuming you were talking to me?"

"No, Suit. I wasn't. Can we get going? I need a meal and some sleep. Can you find us a safe house?"

"Yes, mistress. I have already located a suitable residence. Make for the northern suburbs. Our shelter is there."

⧗

Our house for the night was not of my choosing. It was small, squalid, dated, and dirty. Its only inhabitant, a blind old man of about eighty, heard us entering, and I reassured him I meant no harm. If he could spare me a little food, I promised to be gone by morning.

As a sweetener, I cooked. Pork chops, potatoes, and cabbage, and we sat together swapping tales of yore, sipping a rough blended whisky that burnt my lips and crinkled my gums...

"So, gally," he mused, feeling the dimples on the side of his glass. "Y'are in a sorry state. On the run. Does ya deserve it?"

"I'm afraid I do," I confessed. "I have killed, stolen, lied to authority. You should fear me."

"Fear ya?" He chuckled. "How can I fear ya, when I canna see ya? Nay, I dinna fear ya. Y'are no rascal to me, gally."

"I'm glad." I replied. "And thank you, Dougie, but I must ask. Have you always been blind? Why didn't you receive implants?"

"Aye, gally, they offered me, but fate took me sight and canna argue wi' him. He says, Dougie, ya're ta never see and too far gone ta fix."

"Are you certain?" I quizzed. "Modern medicine can perform wonders. Do you not care to gaze upon the world? See the truth before you leave it?"

"Nay, gally," he replied with a shrug "Me world is just fine. Sometimes she's red an' smooth as glass. Other days, she's a jungle, green an' tangled with vine. Today, she's a whispering and a wafting. Like ya brought in a darkening mist."

"Very well," I replied, patting the back of his hand. "Then I will leave you be," before finishing my scotch and knocking him unconscious with a precisely timed slap.

Removing the Hibbite crèche from my armpit took longer than I anticipated but inserting it into the nape of Dougie's neck was a cinch.

"What are you doing?" whispered Suit. "Seeking redemption?"

"Yes," I replied. "What we did in the church troubles me deeply. Now I don't feel so bad…"

With the old man still recovering from my sudden assault, I decided to sleep while the Hibbites worked to recover his sight.

In the early hours, Dougie became increasingly restless, and, removing the crèche from his neck, I returned it to the small wound under my arm.

Cleaning the cut on his neck, I covered it with a bandage.

"Time to go," whispered Suit. "Everything is prepared."

Leaving the old man and returning to the rooftops, we headed east towards the North Sea.

THIRTEEN

THE TESTING
OF ERIC BADSEGH

What can I tell of Hull (that is, Kingston upon Hull) in the East Riding of Yorkshire? Nothing new, surely. Too much is already written about this little city, shrewdly built upon the rivers Hull and Humber, and too much opprobrium if you ask me! Britain, dare I say it, the world, owes this little city a great deal. Embark on a personal quest researching the distinguished figures native to its chilly streets, and you will discover a history overflowing with glitterati... Glitterati? Shitterati! What am I on about? A terrible moniker. No way to describe the notables of Hull, all those writers, poets, actors, comics, artists, scientists...Anyhow, that is quite enough blurb from me (and the tourist brochure). I rest my case.

After finding and securing us a sweet little cottage overlooking the harbour (29 Corinthian Way), Suit encouraged me to pillage its stores and eat greedily before cramming a small rucksack with grub.

"You sure I need this?" I said, adjusting its straps. "I've enough for a week!"

"Indeed, mistress. Locating the remains of Dr Al-Hillah will require us travelling to Spain."

"Could you be more specific?"

"No, mistress. Our written past defines our future. Full disclosure could imperil us."

"Huh?" I remarked. "Are you saying we should avoid discussing and cataloguing our intentions in case our future opponents are spying on us?"

"Precisely."

A week-long boat trip sounded like a drag. What will happen if I run out of food and water? Should I try my hand at fishing? How would I cook my catch? Could Suit do the honours? No. No joy. She flatly refused. "Me?" she scorned," Cook fish, in *my* sumptuous folds? Consider the grease. Imagine the pungent aroma. Frightful! The very notion is an affront to my elegance."

"You were about to tell me about Hannah," I said, carefully slicing an overripe peach. "Did you find anything useful?"

"Indeed, mistress. Dr Hardcastle possesses no record whatsoever. The UET never employed her, nor did she attend the University of Keele, any college, high school, or primer. In fact, as far as I can tell, she is entirely uneducated. Peculiar, wouldn't you say? So, I looked deeper, scanning every file I could find."

"Any luck?"

"No, mistress. Only traces, gaps, and omissions. Evidence of deletion and a cover-up. It wasn't until I asked the Hinnie SSD computer that I discovered her true lineage."

"Ah," I nodded, slurping a slice into my mouth. "Then who is she?"

"Who, mistress? I haven't the faintest idea. *What* is she is the question."

"How do you mean? Is she inhuman?"

"Indeed, mistress. Dr Hardcastle is no ordinary doctor. It is an artificial lifeform. A monstrous aberration. Grown in a laboratory and synthesised from terrestrial and extra-terrestrial cellular residues. Neither human, animal, plant, nor fungus, as far as I can make out, she is one of a dozen new species manufactured twelve years ago at the Hinnie Space Centre. Ergo. The creature we know as Dr Hannah Hardcastle is but twelve years old. She is a child."

"Seriously?" I replied. "That is incredible, and incredible she could've hidden her true nature. She appeared human in every respect. Even her thermal footprint! Remarkable, unless…"

"Yes, mistress. It would seem Dr Hardcastle can change or disguise her appearance. We must be cautious."

"Cautious? I'm terrified. She's following me! When nearby, I can smell her, which has me thinking. If stealth is her intention, why would she wear such a conspicuous perfume? Is it possible she cannot help but exude such an aroma? A side effect of changing appearance? In the same way I perspire, and you emit radiation?"

"A distinct possibility, mistress, but do not fear, I will protect you. If she did intend harm, doubtless she would already have intervened. I suspect she is merely monitoring, keen to discover our intentions."

"Hmm," I pondered, sucking the peach from my teeth. "But now I am nervous. She could be anywhere, be anything. Spying on us right now. Is she working for the inquisitor?"

"No, mistress. I continuously monitor all of Inquisitor de Boer's correspondence and never has he mentioned her. In fact, until he arrived at the SSD, he didn't know she existed."

"Fine. Then it is fair to assume she is working independently and" – I sniff – "have we given her the slip?"

"Indeed. We should make use of this fortunate turn. Finish your meal quickly. A suitable vessel waits at anchor, and if we miss her sailing, we will have a long and dangerous wait stowing away on another."

"Already scoffed," I replied, licking my lips. "Let's go."

⧗

This was my first time sailing upon the ocean and I found it captivating. The almost hypnotic rolling of the vessel, the splashing of the waves, the salty breezes, the wheeling gulls, but when this unchanging pattern became tedious, I went below deck to look for somewhere to sleep…

Oh! I seem to be slightly ahead of myself. Named *The Dirty Eider*, our borrowed boat was an autonomous fishing vessel. Approximately thirty metres from bow to stern, a pair of steam-fusion propeller engines powered her, and she pushed through the waves with a doggedness I found strangely endearing…

"How far are we going?" I asked. "Is there time enough for napping?"

"Far," replied Suit. "South and then west through the English Channel, before heading south all the way to northern Spain."

Countermanding the on-board guidance system, Suit then made a slew of subtle changes to bring us within fifteen miles of the port of Vigo. A total sailing time of approximately twenty-four hours.

All very well, but this unmanned fishing vessel was never designed for comfort. Winches, nets, and cables covered the deck, whereas below, the machinery to process and refrigerate the catch dominated every available nook.

"Useless," I cursed. "No berths, not even a chair. Where do you propose I sleep? Do you expect me to hang from the mast like a gibbet?"

Eventually attending my tired and grumpy protestations, Suit strung herself between two posts, providing a hammock that looked like a gigantic silken cocoon.

Comfortable at last (and with little else to occupy me), I let Eric's logs and journals unfold in my mind, and as I read his words, I could hear his deep mellow voice…

⧖

Personal Log of Dr Eric J Badsegh. Final Entry

It was a demand of that strutting dolt Walsingham that I record this log, but Heaven knows why. I mean, how will it ever be read? If recovered, this data, cunningly hidden within my teeth and bones, will do the finder no good – the encryption is almost unbreakable. Only my crewmates possess the necessary keys to reveal these words, but when and where are they? By accident or design, Moloch has scattered us, separating us across space and time, and as I await the dawn, half frozen, lying upon my lumpy berth, I can only hope their circumstances are better than mine.

A year since my arrival (is it only a year?) As if jettisoned, landing in a hostile environment, wholly unprepared. It was the darkest pitch of night, the snow was ankle deep, and with only a linen smock to cover me I could only wonder what had happened. I was shaking, not only from the cold! The startling sensation of transport, as if falling to one's death, flailing, tumbling, all while screaming in terror, before suddenly arriving, meant I could do little but tremble, blink, and try to take it in.

I recall seeing firelight. A flickering of heat. The prospect of warmth drew me like a moth, instinctive and single-minded…

At my feet was Emil's statuette. Picking it up, I crunched across a frozen marsh, adjusting my vision to reveal to five figures adjacent to a fire. Nearest the flames, two individuals inaudibly chatted, but at the edge of the firelight two children and a woman sat motionless back-to-back.

Squatting behind a tussock of lifeless rushes, a fleeting glimpse of Orion and Taurus delivered me a shock. Noticeably distorted in shape, I compared historic star charts (in my mind's eye) in the hope of making a match… bingo: ad 1000, plus/minus one hundred years. Could this be true? I'm fucked if it was. Unacceptably fucked. So, what year was it? Of my location, I was sure. The Pole Star, the plants, the soil, this was undoubtedly England, in winter – boy oh boy, was it winter – but when? The men huddled around the fire might know. No point hiding and freezing, waiting for hypothermia to take me to an early grave. Courage is the catalyst of change. If these short hairy men can speak to each other, why wouldn't they speak to me…

"Ahoy there," I called, striding into the firelight. "May I share your camp? My very bones are shivering."

With a disapproving grunt, a curse, and brandishing weapons, the men by the fire sprang to their feet. A shining dagger and two-metre-long spear stopping me in my tracks.

"Intruder!" barked the man with the dagger (in West Saxon) "Spit this pig and be done with him!"

With a growl, the spearman lunged forward, but he was too slow. Dodging his thrust was a simple matter. Sliding past his flailing spear, I smashed my palm under his chin.

For a moment or two the spearman did nothing, but then, helplessly choking, he fell to his knees. Taking his weapon, I whipped it around in a whistling arc, bringing its point to the throat of the man with the dagger.

"Who are you?" I demanded, my implant controlling my speech. "Speak!"

Glancing towards his counterpart, the dagger man considered his options, so I feigned to jab his shoulder…

"Turd," he scorned. "You are a turd, and I am nothing. I am your death or nothing."

"Quite so." I frowned. "Answer my questions, and I may let you go, but your prisoners stay with me. Now, where am I? What is the year, and who is your lord?"

"Ha!" He bitterly laughed. "A thrall that talks. All bluster and rage but forbidden wisdom. It is the year of your destruction, turd. The year of eight and seventy, this very eve. As for my prisoners, I would sooner gut them than hand them over. As I will gut you!"

What this suicidal fool thought he could achieve, slashing and stabbing thin air, I had no idea. Deciding to be merciful, I knocked him senseless with the shaft of my spear.

Taking his dagger, I cut the bonds of the prisoners, and lifted the half-frozen children nearer the fire.

"I thank you," said the woman with a bow. "Kill that Saxon dog and let us leave this dreary place."

"No," I replied, matching her dialect (Old Norse). "Let him linger. You were his prize, were you not? Doubtless, returning to his lord empty-handed will be punishment enough. Defeat and fear bringeth fear and defeat."

"You are wise," she said with a smile. "Permit me to clothe you in their garb, for you are chilled and vulnerable. Then, if you escort us to our camp, I will see your courage rewarded."

"You are kind," I replied with a nod. "But what is your name? For I am known as Eric, Eric Jarl Badsegh."

"You have a regal name!" she gasped. "When I saw you fight, I knew you were no thrall. I am known as Sigridor, good-wife to Eorl Ubba Ragnarsson, and these are our kinde. Harald Ubbasson and my little anemone, my Minki, Minki Ubbasdottir."

"Most honoured," I acknowledged, bowing low. "Do these men have provisions? For I am famished and must eat before we go on."

"Verily," she smiled, stripping the dead man. "They have hard loaves, ail, and a little kase of ewe. Not to my taste. It is foul. Yet this is not a night for savouring. Here, clad yourself. Take arms and try the boots. Sever the toecap if they prove too constricting. I will fetch bread."

⧗

For the sake of shame and as an explanation, this was not the first time I had killed. Giles and I both served in the armed forces, and unarmed combat, fighting with a bayonet, stabbing or cutting weapon, is second nature, so don't judge me too harshly. This is a violent society, survival depends on strength, and my prowess in battle, skills, and training, have already earned me great renown. Indeed, my lofty status in the upcoming conflict affords me a degree of protection; hard-won and grimly determined, my thegns are oath-bound to protect me unto death.

⧗

With the stone and timber robbed from outlying settlements, the Viking encampment at Reading, circa ad 870, was of hasty construction, but do not be deceived – it was formidable. Its strategic location, between two rivers and surrounded by boggy pools, with only a narrow trackway leading to the main gate, meant any frontal assault would be foolhardy at best. An attacker could, I suppose, try crossing one of the rivers, but, since they were too deep for fording, they'd need rafts or boats, all the while pelted by missiles? Rather them than me.

After a night in a stinking dormitory, listening to the coughing, snoring, and farting of a dozen slumbering Norsemen, Sigridor returned.

Insisting I quickly rise and prepare myself, she laced my legs in soft leather hose and guided my feet into boots, before shrouding me in sumptuous cloak of fox. Indeed, this was a morning of transformation, of Sigridor, no less. The half-frozen wretch of the previous night was now a noble woman of beauty, and dressed in a manner befitting her status, with long boots, a soft leather tunic, scarlet hose, and a fabulous fur-lined cloak, its colourful patchwork studded with jewels.

Keeping close guard of her were two burly henchmen. If anyone but me even looked at their mistress, their hands instinctively shot to the finely worked axes hanging from their belts.

"Come," said Sigridor, adjusting my attire. "Our king, Halfdan Ragnarsson, demands your presence, and I am to be your escort."

My audience was barely that. To begin, to prove my worthiness, I suffered ordeal by combat, and only after defeating two eager men-at-arms could I be granted entrance to the king's smoke-filled house. I never saw the king in person. Hidden behind a curtain, I only heard his pain-filled whispering, while his wife and brother (Bjorn) slowly recounted his words. Ill, they said he was. Burning with fever and too weak to stand, he was delighted I had finally joined him. He desired to know the strength and provision of my army!

A surprise, you might think, but after a sleepless night, studying the historical records of this period, I immediately understood how my identity had been mistaken, helped in part by my Moroccan surname. These Vikings, enamoured by my physical stature, believed me to be Bagsec, the king of Denmark, arriving unannounced and in secret before the landing of his army. Aiding my unlikely alibi was the simple realisation that King Halfdan's brothers and jarls had no idea what Bagsec looked like, and since Halfdan, both feverish and raving, was unable even to name his children, it was doubtful he would remember him. Of course, my cover story would only hold while the real Bagsec remained in Denmark. If he did arrive with his Summer Army in tow, I would be in trouble, but that bridge I would cross if and when I came to it. I had a Saxon assault to repulse! Yes. With Halfdan gravely ill and his brothers in Mercia, the defence of Reading was my responsibility. Quite rightly, Halfdan expected the Wessex Saxons to assault us (within the week) and, according to history, their attack (led by Prince Alfred) will fail. Gulp! Best I get cracking, ensure the defences are sound, that the men have a good provision of arms and armour, with a plentiful supply of missiles to chuck from the palisade. It was historically vital Prince Alfred survived this assault (he is supposed to!), so I could only hope he had the good sense to keep away from the hot spots, the killing zones I planned to set up.

Seventy-two hours were all I had to prepare the defences, but it was enough. The Saxon tactics were peculiar in the least. In fact, they were suicidal! A frontal assault in three waves. No cavalry, no machines of war, just zeal and courage. To see so many young men cut down, hopelessly floundering in the trenches, traps and pits I had contrived, almost broke my heart. Many of the Saxons, desperate to escape the barrage of missiles we rained from the walls, toppled into the mudholes, and drowned. As each wave faltered, I sent out our sortie. Fifty or so tank-like warriors, bursting from the gates to cut down the stragglers. Their weapons, their axes, and swords, steaming with the blood of the fallen.

It took less than half the day to repulse the Christians. As I surveyed the carnage with my thegns, I saw him. I saw Alfred – a tall young prince astride a white horse. Seeing me with my thegns, he was gallant. He saluted my victory. Lifting his burnished blade to the setting sun, he spurred his mount and disappeared into the mist.

Later that evening, a messenger under a banner of truce begged us to let their women come and recover the fallen. It was already too late. Our lesser folk, dispatching the wounded and stripping them, had already flung their corpses into a large pit delved a year hence for the construction of the fortifications. Certainly, with the winter conditions, there was no need for haste covering the dead, and the local crows were grateful. Their clamorous cawing, squabbling, and pecking went on for days. Just like the storm crows of yore, they follow our every battle like a cloud of death, wings clapping, impatient for the feast to begin.

Good news. Ubbe (Halfdan's brother) returned with three hundred battle-hardened warriors. Bad news. He also brought their families, servants, slaves, livestock, stores, and equipment. Housing these new arrivals was no mean feat, and we soon had a sprawling ramshackle of hovels, huts, and sheds thrown together from whatever material was at hand. Intrigued by the building activity, I went with Sigridor to pay homage, but Halfdan needed me to rendezvous with Yngvar (another of Halfdan's brothers) in East Anglia – to gather my army, marching them west and setting up camp adjacent to the Thames at Sunna. Not entirely sure where "Sunna" was, I assumed it the Norse translation of "Sonning Eye" and the village of Sonning, both a few miles downstream from Reading.

Several days of slow progress drifting down the Thames beckoned, with at least a day in the saddle, and, although it was wondrous to journey across England in this period, there were many perils – bandits, outlaws, ruffians, not to mention the indigenous inhabitants, disgruntled Saxons, Angles, and Jutes. Remember, we were the invaders. As we forced our rule upon this land by violence, the natives were resisting. We were not welcome!

We are in in Suffolk, a mile or so from the coast. After making camp, we assessed the value and provision of my newly arrived army. I could not believe my luck! These men were not Danes, they were Frisian mercenaries. They hadn't a clue who Bagsec was, or what he looked like, and their leaders grudgingly accepted my lordship over them. When I say grudgingly, I mean there was a degree of violence. Refusing to pledge their fealty to my kingship, the Frisian jarls attacked our camp, obliging us to defeat them all. Outside our tent, Yngvar mounted their heads on spears. A grisly warning to all dissenters.

Before our march west into *Bearrocscir* (Berkshire), Yngvar and I tried to estimate the number of fighting men in my army. No easy task as every warrior had his entire household in tow, including their valuables, pets, livestock, and provisions. The supplies were particularly welcome, but we needed to get moving. This sudden influx of whores, slaves, women and children, raiding, robbing, and pillaging, was reducing the region into a wasteland. As Yngvar pointed out, once they had finished exploiting the locals, they would quickly turn on each other – the journey west would give them something to do. It is little wonder the indigenous population hate us so much.

Meeting little resistance, we are made adequate progress, and this had Yngvar worried. Certainly, his apprehension was well founded. Unknown to the Vikings, the lands east of Wessex had systematically emptied as King

Ethelred gathered men and equipment west of Reading in preparation for our eventual assault in the spring.

Ever delighting in torture, Yngvar soon extracted the truth from the locals. This great mustering took place before, during, and after the attack on Reading. Ethelred and Alfred had sold us a dummy. Their attack was a ruse to keep us off guard while British reinforcements slipped into the safety of Wessex. It certainly explained Alfred's irregular tactics.

Months of raiding and skirmishing have passed, and my personal body count is… In fact, I have given up counting, but it is more than one hundred confirmed kills. Doubtless the wounded have perished also. Healthcare in this period is of the "chuck on some herbs, give 'em some booze, and hope for the best" variety, even a small cut can be fatal. Except for me that is. My Hibbites, despite their steady decline, are still doing their damnedest to keep me alive. Currently, they stand at 77% of optimum, which is fine. The minimum required for continued good health is approximately 30%, and it will be months before I reach that watershed. When it does come, I may consider commanding my remaining Hibbites to disintegrate my technology and finish me off. This sounds like a suicide, but when my body begins to reject my implants, the pain will be intolerable.

To my surprise, Halfdan is much recovered (although he most certainly is not), and he can now ride, converse, and perform ceremonial duties. By means of thermal imaging, I can see a tumour (a glioblastoma) growing inside his skull, and, although his condition will doubtless be fatal, his participation is helping bolster morale. Grateful of my earlier victory and successful ventures, he favours me, and consequently I have received many gifts. Weapons, armour, lodgings, amber, gold, animals, a very young wife, and therein lies a problem. I have no idea what to do with the poor little wretch. She says "calling me husband is an honour" but, expecting abuse, she trembles in fear. Offering reassurance, I suggested she run my house, keeping my thegns and slaves in good order. Sometime after, drinking and feasting with Yngvar and Bjorn, I explained how I preferred my women older. Slapping my back and laughing, they said Sefa would be put to death if I refused her, suggesting I wank away my troubles until she has bled.

"Thanks, fellas," I replied, downing my ale. "Very helpful. Just what I needed to know."

Anyway, my little wife's name is Sefa (which means tranquillity), and she is about 1.5m tall with blonde hair and pale blue eyes. She sings beautifully, embroiders, weaves, plays with my raven, and feeds my dogs. She is a bright and inquisitive girl, and if I get the opportunity, I'm going to teach her to read.

A gift from Halfdan, my raven and I have become fast friends, unless I tie her to her perch, she will gladly follow me anywhere. Hand-reared by Halfdan's wife, her name is Knot, after the goddess of the night, but I simply call her Knotty – which she imitates quite readily and seems to like.

Half wolf, half God only knows what, tall, grizzled, and mangy, my dogs are awful old things. For hunting dogs (men or animals), they do seem to be lacking in zest. They sleep most of the time and only wake when food is on the go. Without names, I have dubbed them Coco and Cub. Why? I haven't the faintest idea. Sefa loves them, and she often lies with them for a cuddle.

Arriving yesterday and moving among the nobility are Benedictine monks. Initially, this came as a shock. In theory, the Christians are our enemies, but these brave friars are well trusted, and they are teaching the nobles and their children the art of reading and writing. Certainly, despite outward appearances, the Vikings are a cultured people, only their documentation is runic, brief, and cumbersome. Their historical accounts, recounted by elders or sung by bards, are flagrantly open to misinterpretation and political manipulation. Halfdan and his people delight in hearing them however, and they know not to regard them as fact. Unlike his subjects, Halfdan's family all read and write with considerable skill, in both Latin and West Saxon, and the paraphernalia associated with penmanship in this period litter his lodgings like leaves on a bookbinder's desk.

Returning in disarray, our scouts and spies carry disturbing news. Our foes are massing. Ethelred and Alfred have issued the call to arms, hurling the great strength of Wessex headlong into the fray. King Halfdan is reacting to this news with all haste. We are outnumbered, so it is vital we choose a field of conflict advantageous to us. Regarding provisions, arms, and armour, we are in good stead, but we have few riders. If the Saxons can muster a sizeable cavalry, we are lost.

To make up for these shortcomings, Halfdan intends fighting a defensive battle, holding the high ground behind a wall of shields – berserkers in the front, missiles casters and rabble behind. I (with the other jarls) will be in the thick of it, but old Halfdan, surrounded by his personal bodyguard, will be in the rear, surveying the field.

The fighting of berserkers I have witnessed before, and it is worth noting, these men are not drugged-up on *Amanita muscaria*, as popular myth attests. Their fearlessness stems from great zeal, rigorous training, and a bellyful of wine, and they will charge headlong to where the fighting is fiercest, with little regard for their own safety or anyone else's. Our own fighters know not to hinder their progress in fear of becoming a target themselves! Another surprise, not featured in any historical accounts, and I am wondering why, dozens of our fighters are women. Could it be possible these brave girls made such a good account of themselves that those composing the sagas were ashamed to admit it? Sigridor, for example, is a formidable "shield maiden" and we have trained together on occasion. When sparring with wooden weapons I usually defeat her (her stamina is inferior) but so nimble and quick is her parrying, she often catches me as I try to recover.

Marching steadily west into Berkshire, we make camp every night in draughty tent-like structures that flap and creak with every shifting breeze. My little wife, Sefa, is with me, as are my dogs, raven, thegns, and personal armourer. Sefa is rightly frightened of the future, and every night, wrapped in furs, I hold her close, keeping out the chill.

Returning from the king's feast, swaggering and staggering, with a belly full of meat (and slightly worse for wear), Sefa was not waiting. This worried me initially, but she soon returned, delivering a tightly rolled sheet of parchment, before collapsing and (most uncharacteristically) falling fast asleep.

Expecting a missive from Sigridor, Halfdan, or his brothers, I unrolled it to discover something I did not expect. Written in a fine and flowing script, it was indeed a message, but the language was English…

Read this once, burn it, and then pulverise the ashes.

Hello Eric,

My name is Gleener, do you remember me? The shining thing, the ball of light, shouting "Glee-nah!" loud and most atrociously? That was I. Do you recall your loneliness, my whispering and singing? That was I also. I brought succour between the sessions of your interrogation. Did you hear me? You must have done. Although, my name had changed to Mirra.

This is desperate situation called for desperate measures, so I temporarily took control of Sefa, and used her to write and deliver this message. Do not concern yourself. She is unharmed and sleeping soundly. She will retain no memory of my actions.

To business…

Please, understand how desperately sorry I am. It was I that deposited you here, both for your own safety and the safety of others. Be not angry with me. My cause is good, and your presence here is as history demands. In fact, you have acquitted yourself admirably. Have no shame concerning your actions. These are violent times, and your greatest test is about to come. You already know the bitterness history has in store for you. The Battle of Ashdown is coming, and Bagsec will fall. This cannot change. It has already happened.

Mortally wounded and fleeing the battlefield with your thegns, you will head south, making for the coast at Southampton, and fear not. I have taken care of everything. A small boat will be waiting, commanded to take you east, landing on the Sussex coast, and it is there you will die from your injuries. Your burial will follow. Yes, a burial, not a cremation as is customary in this period, and arrayed very honourably. Fully armoured, surrounded by your greatest treasures, clasping Emil's figurine lovingly across your breast.

Sadly, secrecy demands I leave you now – if I dwell in this instance, my quiescence will quickly be noted! Moloch must never know of our correspondence, my intervention and betrayal, but know! In the 20th century, excavators will uncover your remains, with Dr Padgett decoding and reading your logs in the 22nd and rueing your fate, she will mourn.

Farewell.

Quickly memorising all I had read, I burnt and crushed the message, before checking on Sefa. Lifting her into my berth, I covered her warmly. Peeking from the flap of my tent, I caught the eye of the guards flanking the porch…

"Dawn is breaking," muttered Gundarsson, stiffening to attention. "Blood red and full of fire."

"Verily," I whispered, "and it is time for blood, is it not?"

"Indeed, sire. Shall I send for your armourer?"

"Yes, I would take that kindly, Gundarsson. Secure my possessions and baggage. We may need to move at moment's notice. Leave my darling Sefa. She detests war as any mother. Let her seek sweet contentment, dreaming, flying in the clouds."

"Very good, sire," he replied, then, "Fingarsson!" he barked to one of the boys. "Run ahead, lad, fetch the smith. The day has come at last."

As Walsingham rightly pointed out, burdening these logs with emotional baggage is unnecessary. It is simple to judge an author's emotional state from their circumstances, and my circumstances are grim! Gleaner's note has confirmed my worst fears, stretching both my courage and resolve. My mental weakening comes as no surprise. My life is a constant battle. Physical challenges to my authority come and go with an almost predicable regularity, and to survive, I have no choice but to fight these fools, often to the death. Certainly, to function as an aristocrat in this society one must be a despot, and to succeed as a king one must be utterly ruthless. King Halfdan is a typical example; he possesses all the attributes. Judgemental, honour-driven, cunning, but he is also a mass murderer, willing to participate in the rape, torture, and brutal execution of the innocent victims of our conquest and occupation. This level of savagery abhors me, I have always declined involvement, although I have little mercy towards my foes in combat, all of whom would have killed me at the slightest opportunity. Ugh! I'm sick of my life here. Sick of the violence, the barbarity, and the squalor. What I wouldn't give for a hot shower, a mattress, a coffee, a biscuit... Strange how trivialities become luxuries when you are deprived of them.

⧗

Strung out like a living palisade across the top of a hill, our entire force waits in grim silence. Apart from meaningful looks and encouraging nods, all conversation is vain. Our position is strong, however. Thick and thorny, brambles and blackthorn protect our right flank, with a hastily improvised spear break guarding our left. Astride his great horse and surrounded by his bodyguard, Halfdan is in the rear.

Just behind the shield wall and covered by my thegns, I am in the centre, my shield raised, both hiding my identity and protecting me from missiles. Far below, our enemy is still assembling, and I can see Prince Alfred, cajoling his warriors into three distinct groups. His brother the king seems not to be present, and this is just as history records – he was praying for a swift victory, but I suspect Ethelred is merely terrified, exploiting a display of piety to keep away from the heat of battle while his younger brother risks all.

Alfred's hasty preparations are wise. It is winter, the days are short, and he must hurl his entire strength against us before his lesser men, the men whose courage is doubtful, decide it is time to cut their losses and flee.

Alfred must attack soon. By 4pm the gathering dusk and failing light will make battle tactics impossible. Whatever unfolds today, it will all be over by then.

Not content to wait any longer, Alfred is charging his army. I can already see his heaviest armoured warriors beginning to stagger as they jog to meet our waiting formation. Bravado from Alfred I expected, but this is rash. Gentle attrition would have been my approach; pecking away at our defences, exposing weak spots, and trying to exploit them. Indeed, Alfred's tactics have caught Halfdan off guard. He is moving more strength to the centre. A mistake. He is playing Alfred's game. The tactics of the Zulu. The way of the charging bull. Coming first, the head, Alfred's heavy armour. Pushing, thrusting, attempting to buckle the centre of our formation, pulling in many to repel them, while the bull's horns, his lightly armoured mobile forces, envelop and pierce our distracted flanks...

Just beyond the range of our spears, the Saxons have come to a halt, jeering, yelling, bashing their spears against their shields. Their clamour is supposed to intimidate, but I suspect this tactic simply gives everyone an opportunity to catch their breath before the final push. After thirty seconds of "Oot! Oot! Oot! Death to the Pagans!" and so forth, with a great shout they are among us.

Nothing to do now but to fight. We have let loose our berserkers. Crashing into the enemy ranks like a battering ram, they cut down many, before they themselves are cut down in their fury.

Under pressure, our front ranks are holding, and our right flank is secure. Our left flank is doubtful, and Halfdan is responding, sending men from our rear to bolster them.

A sudden flurry of spears has done for the men before us, and we have moved up to fill the gap. Now fighting hard, my shining mail and gilded helm make me an easy target. Alfred is driving his horse toward me, but his approach is too direct! Closing about him, my thegns send his mount whinnying in a bloodied panic, throwing Alfred from the saddle like a sack. Pulled from my defence, a sudden attack from the right has caught my thegns off guard, and we are hard set, overpowering this assault to re-establish our position.

It was some time before I caught sight of Alfred again. Unhorsed and blowing his mighty horn he was rallying and regrouping his warriors for a final push.

With at least a hundred warriors, some bearing flags, others hoisting crosses, beating drums, or blowing trumpets, Ethelred has come. There are monks among his number too, we can hear their chanting. Some are singing psalms and whirling censors, wafting clouds of incense across the battlefield. This show of religious zeal has Halfdan worried, and he has committed his reserve to strengthen our line.

It is no good. The Saxons are through. All around I can hear is the clashing of weapons, the splintering of shields, and the screams of the dying. Courage is suddenly irrelevant. This is melee pure and raw. It is every man for himself before the fading of the afternoon.

Again, Alfred is upon me! Men of both sides dying all around us as he cuts his way to my ground. There is little time for chivalry. He is light-footed and quick, his swordsmanship deft and cunning, and using my strength to send him sprawling, I realise, it will do me no good. If I defeated this pious young man, my own history would unravel, and, judging the moment carefully, I overreach my parry, allowing his blood-soaked sword to slash across my abdomen, paring my armour like the skin of a peach.

With blood oozing from my wound, gasping, groaning, and falling to my knees, I expected his mortal down stroke, but it didn't come. As my desperate thegns closed about my bleeding ruin, Alfred withdrew. Bowing honourably, he crossed the air before him.

⧗

Wounded and grievously, I am in a boat. A small skiff-type vessel, with grubby sail of battered canvas. How I got here I can barely remember. A cart, a barrow? Voices barking orders, painful jostling. The breeze is fresh, and we are making satisfactory progress sailing along the coast. Although we are heading east, my thegns remark, this boat is too light to take us to Denmark, and we are heading to a friendly port to seek a seaworthy vessel.

The wound across my abdomen is terrible. I am managing the pain, but my medical condition is perilous. The writer of the mysterious letter was correct. I am going to die. There are no longer enough Hibbites in my system to both maintain my physiology and heal my wound, so I have a choice to make, and all the choices are bad. Should I command my Hibbites to maintain my body, or should I command them to heal me? Both will result in death. One slow, the other slower, neither leaving sufficient Hibbites to both destroy my implants and encode these logs. Suicide is the only sensible option, and a preferable one. A death painless and quick.

After making landfall, my thegns, after securing a rickety barrow, have carried me inland. We are resting in shady locale with bushy willows and silver birch thickly overgrowing the dunes.

It is no good, I can go no further, and my thegns are wordlessly digging. They are digging my grave! Upon a nearby ridge, I can see a building site, its scaffold against the horizon. Using a barrow, Gundarsson is retrieving large stone slabs to line my tomb. Sacks of lime the others also bring, and I ask them to open my pack and pass me Emil's ugly statuette. So weak I can barely lift it!

Enough of this folly. I have commanded my Hibbites to begin.

The air is fresh,

the sky is blue,

Mummy, I—

FOURTEEN

RELUCTANT PURSUIT

Personal Log of Walter de Boer, June 2112

For Mabel,

This log, in tandem with my official record-keeping, is a recording of my personal thoughts while in pursuit of Dr Regina Padgett – a dangerous undertaking (she is dangerous), and, if something unfortunate should occur, I hope this at least might find its way to my family.

I am en route to a small market town in the county of East Sussex, famous for its historic abbey commemorating the Battle of Hastings, circa 1066 (and all that the English hold so dear). A little bigger than my previous ride, this flyer has a seat, and with the glowing cloth of my jacket stretched over my legs I am reviewing the service records of Rita Richguard and Hannah Hardcastle. Rita's CV, both accomplished and chequered, seems fine, but Hannah's is noticeably incomplete. Upon first reading, her resume seems typical, but when I dig deeper, cross-referencing for confirmation, her name disappears from the alumni of both her college and university, as if she never existed! It is possible my security clearance is insufficient to access these records, but why should her protection be any higher than the justiciar's? This is very irregular. I cannot confirm Dr Hardcastle's identity (or establish her origins) and, although this level of secrecy is unsurprising (her work is highly classified), my instincts tell me something is amiss.

Landing in ten minutes. Good. So cramped in here, my legs are going to sleep.

Next, I come to ponder Dr Padgett's specialised suit (or the suit's Dr Padgett?). It was the suit that seemingly started it all. Writing those special orders to bring Dr Padgett to the Hinnie Space Centre – a remarkable feat! How the suit was able to break through the UET' highest level of security remains a mystery, but it did, fabricating orders so indisputably paramount, the justiciar had no choice but to carry them out. There remains the possibility Dr Padgett cooked up this whole scheme in space, but I think it unlikely. She lacked any motive. Since Dr Padgett's return from space, she was too involved with work and the care of her mother to be in any way complicit... Truly, was it really her suit that started it all?

Fine, let us suppose it was her suit. Another niggle remains. Dr Padgett recently upgraded her remote networking capabilities, increasing both their range and bandwidth, and without these enhancements, she would not have discovered her suit. A coincidence? And, regarding upgrades, it is her suit showing the upgrades! I know the full prototype specifications of every one of those seven nanofiber suits, and none of them were capable of wrenching open a three-ton security airlock, and yet Dr Padgett's suit managed it with ease. Who performed these enhancements? Dr Padgett? Impossible. She never had the opportunity. In fact, she doesn't possess the ability. Dr Al-Hillah could have done it, but why go to such lengths, and in secret? If these powerful augmentations were necessary, would he not have upgraded everyone's suit? No. The only conclusion is shocking. Dr Padgett's suit upgraded itself.

Of the secret developments performed at the Hinnie Space Centre, the bulk of it is perfectly legitimate, but the gun Dr Mayfield was working on troubles me deeply. An international treaty of disclosure and dissemination controls secret weapon development, and quite right too. There are already enough sophisticated, lethal weapons in existence. Why did the UET feel the need to develop another, and why so specialised? It is clearly deadly. Dr Padgett has already demonstrated its devastating effects, and I can only wonder what will become of us now our monster is loose and confident liberty. Only a maniac or a fool commits crime without premeditation, and Dr Padgett is no fool.

With only a small number cheering and applauding my landing, my arrival at Battle was calmer than expected, and the gossiping crowd watched with excitement as the security team showed me around.

Fearing a warzone, the area around the domes, abbey, and heritage centre was untouched, with little evidence of a break-in and no witnesses. No witnesses? Nobody saw or heard a thing, and why should they have done? Last night, every camera and monitoring device for miles around became quietly dormant. While inside the centre, claiming boredom, the security system deactivated itself and fell asleep during Dr Padgett's incursion. Certainly, the central computer remains dreamy and vague, and its wistful, unremitting (and selectively suspicious) singing of "Do You Remember Walter?" continues to echo throughout the whole facility. This parting gift from Dr Padgett soon lost its grace when I came to examine the guards – sickening cruelty! Brain damaged and paralysed, they remain in critical condition, and until a suitably capable micro-neurosurgeon arrives there is little hope of any improvement. In heaven's name, what did she do to these men? How was it accomplished? Such shocking reprehensibility is out of character for Gina, and I am already beginning to question her sanity.

Next, I come to Dr Padgett's activities within the centre itself. Nothing stolen, nothing broken, except for a skeleton, its display case removed, the bones pulverised and incinerated.

The skeleton itself was of interest to local historians but hardly significant. Why Gina's intervention? Why pulverise and incinerate it to nothing but ashes? What was she looking for? Why not simply pulverise the bones? Why the burning? To decompose any remaining protein or mineralised structures, the DNA? This man's DNA profile is already on file, and easily available. Was she trying to hide something else? Too many questions remain unanswered, but I cannot remain to ponder this scene any further. Another report is coming in. Dr Padgett went home. I suspected she might. A disturbance at Dr Padgett's house. Terrible violence, murder, a fire (more evidence of obliteration?), and then mischief inside the church. Was Dr Padgett seeking solace through prayer? I doubt it. Dr Padgett's house in Winchelsea is only a short hop from Battle. After completing my investigation here, this journal will resume.

Well, what can I say? Winchelsea is a jewel. A capsule of history. A remnant of undying England, and Dr Padgett's enviable country residence enough to make a grown man drool. There was little time to enjoy the locality though. The carnage outside Dr Padgett's house was horrific. The four guards were dead. Two of them were merely fragments of bone, tatters of clothing, and patches of skin, whereas the others, slumped against the garden wall, were crushed to a pulp. An incredible force had hurled them hence, and I can only hope their deaths had come quickly.

Within the house, there was considerable disturbance, with opened drawers, emptied cupboards, clothing and personal effects scattered all over the place. This apparent search is likely a ruse. Artificially enhanced, Dr Padgett's memory is remarkable, I can't imagine her losing anything, ever, so this mess is no more than a ploy to cover her true intent. No matter. After showering, Dr Padgett had cooked a meal and gathered supplies. It was only in her office did the detectives find evidence of truly suspicious behaviour. For reasons unknown, and with little regard for her property, Dr Padgett burnt a slew of documents, data storage devices, photographs, and letters, and it will be some weeks before forensic examination reveals their contents. Certainly, Dr Padgett left the fire just long enough to consume the evidence without it becoming too large to contain. Why not burn down the house? Was it sentimentality or tactical decision? What were her thoughts? The small fire certainly reveals its intention (the destruction of certain documents), and orbiting satellites would have detected a larger blaze, relaying its location to the local fire service. Ergo. Dr Padgett's house remains intact and inhabitable… Does she intend to return? Was the fire a ruse?

Inside Winchelsea Church, I am examining a circular area of burning and scorching centred upon the lady chapel. It was here, during a period of silent prayer, the rector of Winchelsea claims to have witnessed the dazzling appearance of "the Virgin Mary". An experience so intense, she is profoundly blind, with extensive superficial and deep burns to her dermis. Apart from this unlikely occurrence, the church seems untouched. I have tasked a forensic team to look for evidence of tampering.

Done with the church, I am heading to the rectory. The rector is quite lucid, and I wish to listen to her words and try a question or two. The hazard in the church is undoubtedly connected to Dr Padgett's arrival, but I have yet to find any connection. Piffle. The circumstances are irrefutable! Whoever revealed themselves in the church last night. Well, she certainly wasn't a virgin…

Still recovering, the rector is lying upon a medi-bed, with various monitors relaying her condition. As I enter and introduce myself, she turns in my direction and smiles…

"Who's that?" she asks. "Is it the inquisitor?"

"Yes," I reply. "Walter de Boer. Can I ask you some questions?"

"Certainly, my pleasure. Although I am a little foggy this morning. The nurse has me plugged into one of those pain-reducing machines and the world is delightfully fuzzy."

"I don't doubt it. Now, tell me, what happened last night? Your experience? Could you recount it?"

"Experience," she sighs. "How could you? What came to me was wondrous. A message from God, from the mouth of the Lady herself. It was joyous!"

"Could you tell me about her, how did she appear?"

"Of course," she replies. "As I've told everyone, including the bishop. The Virgin appeared to me. Mary! Towering, majestic, bathed in holy brilliance, and she spoke: 'Maran-Atha!' Our lord is come, but in Aramaic. The very language of Jesus!"

"Incredible. Then what happened?"

"She raised her arms and smiled, I think, then a flash of white and she was gone. The next thing I remember is the verger muttering about a medical team."

"Fine," I gently reply. "How did you know she was the Virgin Mary? Did she introduce herself?"

"Of course not. Why would she? I knew her and she knew me."

"And did you say she was tall?"

"Yes inquisitor. She was magnificent, like a pillar of light, with eyes of tranquillity dark and deep."

"Dark eyes and tall," I muttered, slowly shaking my head. "Thank you, rector. I think I've heard enough. Except, are there skeletal remains in the church?"

"Skeletal remains? Of course. Several tombs, many burials."

"Granted," I confirm. "I noticed several earlier. They are clearly untouched. Anything else?"

"Well, there's the old reliquary down in the vault. Hardly a skeleton. Just crumbling bones and teeth. Why do you ask?"

"Professional curiosity. Is the vault secure?"

"Extremely," she assures. "The safe is virtually bomb-proof. It needs a code to unlock and deactivate the alarm."

"Fine, and who knows the code?"

"Just me, the bishop, and the verger."

"Good," I acknowledge. "That is all for the time being and I wish you a speedy recovery."

"Thank you. The doctors inform me my eyesight will return in time. I care not. If the last person I see is the Lady, I am content."

Not wishing to unravel this poor woman's delusions further, I made my exit, and sliding into the seat of the flyer, I began to write my report. However, I must clarify, it was undoubtedly Dr Padgett that appeared last night. Flamboyantly dramatic, cruel and uncaring, it was she that burnt and blinded the rector before conducting clandestine business within, but what business? Examination of skeletal remains? Within church and cemetery, there is no evidence of tampering or exhumation, so, if she was looking for bones, her target must have been the reliquary. Pure conjecture. According to the access log, the safe has not opened for months, unless…Did Dr Padgett override the security and falsify the log? Worryingly, I must assume yes. When I have access to a library, I shall study the history of this reliquary. Just whose bones are they?

⧗

Another restless night. Tossing, turning, wondering where Dr Padgett might be. Pondering her motivations and strategy to second-guess her next move. It's becoming an obsession!

The bones of the Winchelsea reliquary are certainly ancient, but I found precious little regarding their identity and lineage, only that their possessor was a giant and that has me thinking the impossible. Was Dr Padgett's final log genuine? I always assumed it a fantasy, a dream, or a malfunction. False memories, encoded during her long years of coma.

The tallest associate of Dr Padgett aboard the KBE was Sir Malcolm Walsingham. Following a hunch, I requested both the DNA and carbon dating analysis of the reliquary, only to be stumped. Neither was available, but the skeleton in Battle certainly possesses these reports, and I have applied for a comparative assessment: the DNA of the Battle skeleton against the crew of the Kuiper Belt Explorer. Probably a waste of time, and yet my instincts tell me otherwise…

More crime reports are coming in. Sifting through them, I am trying to spot Dr Padgett's tell-tale signature: unexplained or violent death, vehicle hijacking, thefts of food, miraculous or mysterious sightings, hauntings, apparitions, and so forth…

A couple of murders have caught my eye. A murderous housebreaking in the county of Essex, with no obvious motive and little stolen, has me very suspicious. Now I read of carnage on a motorway. Dr Padgett's bloody fingerprints are all over this scene of destruction, so I am about to head off for a look.

It does appear events are coming to head. Dr Padgett is proving so dangerous I am flying to meet a brigade commander. Yes, the military! She's so deadly, the army are in pursuit.

God help her.

God help them.

⧖

To land in the middle of a motorway (the newly upgraded A19M) was a curious privilege, but the situation was grim: burnt-out vehicles, body bags, forensic scientists, burly soldiers, armoured vehicles, too many guns…

A young lieutenant greeted my arrival, and, after uploading my PC with the crime scene report, he promptly escorted me to a pop-up hut – an instant office, dry, cosy, and confidential, a seat of power for the man in charge.

Colonel George Needingworth was a real soldiers' soldier. A gruff, once-muscular, portly man of about fifty. His uniform was strictly regulation, medals and insignia kept to a minimum. His crimson beret was too small for his close-shaven head…

"Inquisitor," rumbled the colonel, shaking my hand, "the general said you were coming and recommends I speak with you before commencing operations. You have advice, perhaps, some insight?"

"Good afternoon," I replied. "As a matter of fact, I do. Did the general also mention the UET wish me to command this operation?"

The colonel nodded.

"Good. Because I intend to ignore them. Inexperience constrains my authority. I'm quite content to defer all military decisions to you. These men are yours to command, but before you begin deployment, I would like to hear your assessment. Of both this scene of destruction and its instigator."

"Thank you," he replied with a chuckle. "The general will be greatly relieved. Why the UET suddenly think they can overrule the military chain-of-command is beyond me. If this is a simple manhunt, why the interference?"

"They have their reasons. Embarrassment, confusion, desperation, panic, not to mention incompetence. They need us to clean up their mess."

"Indeed," he acknowledged. "And, for the sake of my career, your recommendations I will accept, but if any part of this mission places my men at undue risk, we will… disagree. Understood?"

"Of course. Safety is my primary concern. Now, if you please, what did the general tell you?"

"Certainly. We are in pursuit of a single fugitive. The cybernetically enhanced, female scientist Dr Regina Padgett. She is in possession of stolen body armour, a weapon, and a molecular scanner. With her augmented senses and physiology, she is proving to be a competent hacker. She is a murderer, a psychotic. She takes pleasure in both killing and torture. The UET wish her taken alive and the classified technology she carries recovered. Am I missing anything?"

Unfortunately, he was, but, as is often the case, soldiers only receive basic information. Orders are orders, demanding obedience without question. There was little I could do to remedy the situation. The colonel's security clearance was disturbingly low, so I urged caution, highlighting the carnage outside to illustrate my point…

"No, Colonel." I slowly nodded. "That just about covers everything. What is your assessment of our situation."

"Well," he replied, "since you ask, I think the UET have it all wrong. This is not the work of a single woman. This was terrorist attack. A squadron, armed with heavy weapons, disruptors, or explosive projectiles. The vehicles are blown to smithereens. The security officers are little more than stains on the road!"

"And so they are," I confirmed, "but have you read the forensic report? No evidence of explosives. No bullet holes, blast, or shrapnel. The armoured cars blew up from the inside. No, I'm sorry. This was the work of Dr Padgett. She is far more powerful than you know. If your men get too close, they will suffer the same fate. Therefore, my advice is this. Avoid frontal attacks. Track, observe, and contain. Beef up security around her hometown, major ports, airports, and important historical repositories. Especially those with skeletal remains. For the time being, I merely wish to track her movements and learn her motives, from a distance! If we get too close, she will kill again."

Naturally, the colonel wasn't pleased to be receiving orders from a civilian, and he began to bluster, saying how he would personally "Get her by the throat!" if she harmed any of his men.

Reminding him my words were only advice, his temper slowly abated, and the young lieutenant (clearly listening from the adjoining office) returned to escort me to an adjoining building, sparsely furnished with a desk, a chair, and few amenities.

Alone and sipping a welcome coffee, I kept busy reading this morning's correspondence – crime reports, notable incidents, unexplained events or sightings. There was precious little worth consideration, nothing concrete to overturn the obvious. Dr Padgett is in Yorkshire. Without any evidence to corroborate my speculation, less-plausible possibilities began clouding my thoughts. I hoped to read of another disturbance within a church, the Minster, or a museum, but there were no reports whatsoever. Strange. She came this way for a reason. What could it be? Her trail is rapidly cooling. Until it heats up again, there is little for me to do but backtrack, and hope to learn something new.

Ah, but that is for tomorrow. This afternoon, I am going to York. The colonel has kindly provided a vehicle and I propose a quick tour of the city's museums, churches, and cemeteries, asking (in person) if anything is amiss.

Yes, my darling, I am failing. I knew I would. When the pursued knows the mind of the pursuer, their every scheme is futile, and I suspect Dr Padgett hears and reads my every word, as if my very thoughts are open to her – a terrible notion. She knows me far too well already! Perception is her specialty. Does she know of my reluctance? Can she feel my quaking heart? Does she understand my sympathy, does she perceive my trust? I believe she does, and there I plant my seed of hope. I may yet survive this.

God save me from my lack of wits and may he help us all.

Kiss the children for me.

Your loving husband,

Walter

FIFTEEN

RUBBLE

In a small surveillance station overlooking the straits of Gibraltar, I study the coast of Morocco while Abda's skeletal data uploads to my neocortex. At my feet (and still twitching) lies the body of an innocent young man called Noah. Despite his fear, he had proven both generous and helpful. Shame I had to kill him.

Suit is urging me to compile a record of my journey to get here. "Write it for the sake of history," she says. Why any historian would be interested in my murderous crusade escapes me…

Our hijacked fishing vessel eventually brought us to within three kilometres of the Illas Cíes. A trio of rocky formations guarding the seaward access of Galician city of Vigo on the north-western coast of Spain.

Returning our boat to its original programming (fishing in the Bay of Biscay) and having no alternative, I ignored Suit's grumbling, leapt overboard, and swam to the shore. Suit is not a fan of swimming. She dislikes the drain of her power reserves, and while propelling me through the freezing water, she tutted and sighed, disquieted by its power-sapping tendencies. In fact, losing power continually oppresses her. She fears it the same way we fear death. Without power, Suit becomes little more than a slippery sheet. Grey, inert, susceptible to both reprogramming and unravelling. If her individual threads became too widely separated, they would lose their ability to work collectively, and Suit would die.

With these stipulations, pausing only to refill my air supply, Suit powered us through the waves like a dolphin, and before long, I was scrambling over rocks onto a sandy beach, seeking shelter to dry myself. Suit did the drying (of course). All I need do was lie back while she vaporously steamed, leaving little evidence of our nocturnal aquatics but a crust of sticky salt.

"We need to get high," urged Suit. "I've had my fill of swimming," and we clambered up the rocky escarpment of Alto de Monte Sías (the highest convenient peak); a good spot to take off and fly to the busy port of Vigo. In fact, Vigo and supper was all I could think of as Suit flung us into the night. Soaring and plunging like a monstrous bat, we moved as a billowing shadow against the wheeling stars and the rolling waves.

Landing invisible and silent on the roof of an office block, we slipped inside, raiding the vending machines for their food, drink, and currency.

Declaring independence from the rest of Spain during the 2080s, Galicia rapidly became a self-sufficient economy, with its own physical currency – the Galician Peseta. For me, managing actual "money" was a novel experience, and the weight of the coinage in tandem with bundles of slippery banknotes made me feel more of a thief than usual. I was impatient to spend my ill-gotten gains as quickly as possible.

Noting my apprehension, as I stuffed the last of the money in one of Suit's pockets, she recommended we lie low until morning and then go shopping.

"Sounds like fun," I remarked.

"Not fun," she reproved. "Necessary. You require outdoor clothing suitable for trekking, provisions, and, for heaven's sake, a rucksack!"

(Encompassing my belongings within her fabric impedes Suit's access to my nervous system, slowing our reflexes and degrading our mobility.)

That morning, after stealing and donning a long floral frock, we indeed went shopping. Keeping to the smaller independent shops (for the sake of anonymity) I was soon clad for hiking, with rugged boots, an olive-grey activity suit, sturdy rucksack, and daft-looking hat made of waxed fabric. Zipping my molecular scanner into a side pocket, I crammed the remaining space of rucksack with as much non-perishable food and drink as it would hold, before depositing my remaining currency (a considerable sum) into the collecting box of a local Christian mission.

That evening we again took to the air. Soaring along the coast, we crossed the Portuguese border near Caminha, marvelling at the sandbanks of the Minho estuary before landing in a semi-industrial suburb known as

Vilarelho. Driving south through Portugal in a stolen van, I have little to tell of our journey (I slept for a great deal of it) and only once or twice did I glance through the window. Arriving at our destination, Suit sent the van back to its depot and reset its odometer.

⧗

We have reached "the Fence" and, although I was anticipating this moment – what it represents is dreadful – scientific curiosity is lessening my trepidation…

Hastily built following the tragic North African/Middle Eastern thermonuclear conflict, the Fence is the great exclusion barrier of southern Iberia. From the coast of Portugal, following the Beja/Faro district boundary all the way to the Spanish border, it terminates near Valencia, in southern Spain.

Suit's plan to travel through this region of uninhabited desolation to reach Gibraltar was wise. The forests were thick, the scrub impenetrable (to normal people), and supplies were scarce. What we would encounter on our travels I had little idea, but the warning attached to every fencepost was blunt: "Danger! Radiation Zone. Keep Out. No Unauthorised Admittance."

The radiation was of no concern – Suit soaks it up like a sponge – it was the condition of the environment that troubled me. For one, we would be making our way on foot (the airspace is under surveillance) and, with a long walk ahead of us, I would require shelter – especially at night, when hungry wild animals prowl, looking for an easy meal. They would find me decidedly inedible, but we might blow our cover if we caused too much of a ruckus (fending them off). Regarding food and drink. What I carried would have to suffice. Foraging was out of the question. The water and biomass inside the radiation zone is contaminated and toxic. To imbibe any of it, even with my Hibbites' protection, would be dangerous.

With the sun just warming the eastern horizon, I leapt over the three-metre fence in a single bound and ran into the tangled scrub covering the terraced hillsides. As we headed south, this dense tangle of bushes, scented pines, and pungent eucalyptus, slowed our progress, and not before coming across a road could Suit run us at speed. She ran me ragged, in fact!

With Suit powering me along, you might think running at nigh-on 70kph would be a simple feat but believe me, it is not. It is gruelling. To begin, she propels me quite naturally, accelerating us to a sprint, but then the bounding begins. Huge strides, leaping and bouncing like a kangaroo on steroids. Ok. I must point out, this running and bounding requires no direct physical effort on my part. I merely relax and let Suit supply the impetus, absorbing any jolts, bumps, and impacts very comfortably, but it is still tiring! Hour after hour am I flung about. Tossed and manipulated, limbs loose and flaccid. A ragdoll, seams torn and stretched. Only on a downslope do I get any relief. Where, if the gradient permits, Suit changes shape, spreading her wings and gliding. Rippling like a skate through water.

The sun was setting before Suit allowed me to stop. We sought shelter inside a cluster of abandoned buildings, eating my precious supplies under the shattered roof of a restaurant.

"Are we safe?" I asked. "I'd like to make camp and sleep for a bit. I'm finding it hard to relax."

"Of course, mistress. Perfectly safe. There's nobody here. The environment hereabouts is cumulatively toxic. Without drastic intervention, it will remain uninhabitable for centuries."

"Very portentous," I remarked, "and yet," I sniffed, "I can smell wood smoke. Can't be a forest fire. I would detect the heat of it. Could we scuttle up a tree for a look?"

"If you wish. A suitable eucalyptus grows on the ridge. It should provide commanding views for several kilometres."

Creaking and swaying under our weight, the tree was indeed lofty. Once at the summit, Suit sent out shining tentacles, breaking off the bushy twigs obscuring the view.

The night was clear, revealing the distant landscape and the lights of several towns. Scanning the forest below, I saw a flickering speck of orange. A fire, two kilometres west.

"There," I gasped, "down in the forest. Let's go for a look."

Leaping from the eucalyptus to catch the top of another, we swept through the forest, barely touching the floor.

The fire was burning within the foyer of a derelict hotel. Warming themselves around it, a group of individuals, after blocking the exits with makeshift barricades, were singing songs and drinking wine. Not having the pleasure of a snifter since York, I wondered if they would share…

Walking up to their barricade (a heap of broken furniture and rubble), I knocked, calling out (as if in distress):

"*Olá! Posso me jutar a você? A noite está escura e estou sezhina.*"

There came an audible gasp of surprise, muttering (concerning wardens), before approaching footsteps and a suspicious eye peering through a gap in the rickety barricade.

"*Quem está aí?*" came a gruff voice. "*O que você quer?*"

"*Por favor,*" I implored, "*posso compartilhar sue fuego?*"

Following a ruffled sigh and a "*sim*" of agreement, many hands set about dismantling the barricade.

Although shabbily dressed, the dozen people greeting me were perfectly friendly, and I helped them rebuild their barricade, before joining them around their fire, crackling brightly within the rusty shell of a bathtub...

"Who are you?" asked an old woman. "It is dangerous inside the fence. Are you lost?"

"Not lost," I replied, gratefully warming my hands. "Merely travelling. My name is Gina, and I am heading into Spain. Sheltering a few kilometres west of here, contemplating a fire of my own, I became aware of yours... Who are you people?"

"We are the André family," explained an old man, "and this was our land, our hotel, spa, and resort. Little remains, just an overgrown ruin, but we come here sometimes to view what was. Hoping someday to reclaim our heritage and begin anew."

"It will never happen," snapped the youngest member of the group. "The politicians are liars and thieves! There is no danger here, only desolation and neglect."

"Yes, yes, thank you, António," the older man sighed. "The fence is too northerly, excessive. We know all this. The only danger in this region comes from the wolves. They claim the lives of many who wander these mountains. They hunt at night, Gina. Aways at night. Seek shelter when the sun sets. Strike fire between you and the night. They fear the fire."

"There are wolves here?" I replied. "I thought this region clear of such beasts."

"It was," explained the elder woman, "but during the evacuation, many animals, particularly dogs, got left behind. A cruel business, abandoning pets to fend for themselves. Over the years their descendants have returned to the wild. They have become feral, living as wolves and hunting in packs."

Sitting closer to the fire and pulling my knees under my chin, I listened for howling, but there was nothing. Nothing but the chirp of insects, the hoot of an owl, and the occasional rustling of leaves.

"Here," said the old man, passing a bottle and packet of bread, "share what we have. In the morning, we head north, to Lisbon, but you may spend the night with us. In the next room, you will find bedding. It is dusty but perfectly comfortable. Take as much as you need."

The guitarist started again. Taking a deep swig from the bottle, I lay back to savour the sensation. It was brandy, well-aged, warming, and mellow. I briefly studied the bottle, trying to read the label.

"Whoa!" cautioned Suit as I took another swig. "Go easy. Unnecessary intoxication will drain your Hibbites. We have far to go and much to do."

In the morning, bright and clear, I watched the André family gather their belongings and ready themselves for the trudge north. Thanking the old man warmly for his hospitality, he kissed me on both cheeks and presented me with a small bottle of spirits. Its label had long since faded, but after removing its stopper and carefully sniffing I found it to be rum.

"Thank you," I said. "This will keep me on my feet."

"And off your head!" laughed António, waving as they made for the nearest road.

"You aren't actually going to drink that, are you?" asked Suit. "It must be sixty years old!"

"Of course," I replied, "why not? All your running and bounding is shaking me senseless. Allow me a little cheer once we come to a halt."

"Very well," she whispered, "if you insist. But please, do moderate your intake."

"Obviously. Now, where are we heading? South or east?"

"Both. Before stopping tonight, we should be well into Spain."

"Fine," I said, stretching my arms and back. "The gliding I enjoy. The running not so much."

"Certainly, mistress. I will endeavour to accommodate you. It is a matter of topography."

"Naturally," I said, bracing myself for another jolting few hours. "Let's get going. The sooner it's over the better."

⧗

Radiation. Penetrating and intense. As I journeyed south, the background count was steadily increasing. In most places the contamination was mild, while in others the radiation was ferocious. Hot spots. Where topography, erosion, and weathering, brought about a concentration of the active isotopes.

Passing through a series of abandoned gardens, I came across trees bearing fruit. The peaches looking particularly delicious, but Suit forbade me to pick them, and she was right! A quick test with my moly-scanner revealed them to be radioactive time-bombs of toxicity, and eating even one would have been a catastrophe, severely depleting my Hibbite reserves as they endeavoured to protect me from the detrimental effects.

Yes, my Hibbites. Those tiny machines tasked with keeping me healthy are beginning to diminish. It will be years (if I am careful) before they are gone, but since I am unlikely to receive replacements, we must complete our shady business before they run out.

We spent that night inside the shell of a partially overgrown villa on the road to Villablanca (formerly a small provincial town of Huelva in Andalusia). Strewn with branches and debris, the floor provided ample fuel for a fire, and once I had a good blaze, I barricaded the door with concrete blocks torn from the walls of the garage. Snacking and drinking water (enlivened by sips of the wonderfully caramelised rum), I asked Suit to shape herself into a hammock, which she promptly did, comfortably supporting me just centimetres from the ground...

"Mistress," whispered Suit, waking me from a dream. "Wolves, mistress. Outside. They have caught our scent."

"So?" I dozily muttered. "They're hardly a threat. Why the concern?"

"Several of the beasts carry tracking devices. Some scientists' pet project, most likely. If they have cameras, the animals could reveal us."

"Then what do you recommend?"

"A close-up inspection."

"Seriously?" I chuckled. "Inspect a wolf? How do you propose we do that?"

"Carefully, mistress. I have full confidence in your ability to tame them."

"Tame them?" I remarked. "How? Why should they take any notice of me?"

"Because, mistress, all dogs desire the love of men."

"Erm... no." I frowned. "That is quite fallacious. Dogs want only an easy meal. They only 'love' in the hope of receiving another."

"Then give them a meal, mistress. Before moving on, we need to examine those trackers. Now they have our scent, these wolves will undoubtedly follow us. We must ensure the Spanish leg of our journey goes unnoticed."

"Fine," I replied, "but in the morning. Slide over the fire if you want some power. Let me sleep!"

That morning, dawning grey and muggy, I put away my leisure suit and wore only Suit. Invisibly climbing through rafters, I surveyed the landscape beyond: flat, scrubby, with crumbling buildings, twisted trees, bushes, and tussocks of grass. The wolves were still around us. About thirty mutts in all. Running or standing in twos or threes, many were growling or howling, others foraging, and fighting for scraps. They were odd-looking beasts. More akin to domestic mongrels than true wolves, generations of uncontrolled breeding had regressed their pedigree to reveal the ancestral wolf lurking within.

Intrigued, I spent some minutes observing their behaviour, noting the pack hierarchy. The alpha male was a large, wolfish animal, with floppy ears and a coat of black and white and I could only smile at the belly-up deference from the lower ranks, chuckling at his barking and snarling at any sign of dissent.

"Seen enough?" whispered Suit. "Go and make friends."

With pockets crammed with broken biscuit, I somersaulted down from the roof and landed with a crunch, metres from the alpha. Expecting an attack, what happened next was surprising. The alpha simply ignored me! Moreover, when I removed my hood and spoke to the grizzled old thing, he simply twitched his ears and wagged his tail. Encouraged by this friendly reaction, I moved closer, offering a piece of biscuit, which he gladly took, munching upon it with relish. This act of generosity (of course) gathered immediate attention, and I was soon feeding and petting ten or so dogs, giving each the affection they craved.

Immediately enamoured by this rag-tag bunch of ruffians, for the sake of convenience (and for fun) I decided to name them, adhering to a simple adjectival nomenclature, derived from mannerisms and/or physical appearance. Rumbelow, for example, my mothers' old pug, was so named because of his short legs, barrel-like body, grumbling growls and snuffles, while the alpha, although possessing many wolf-like qualities, I named "Partsatian One" because of his Alsatian tail and hindquarters, grouping him with several others demonstrating similar characteristics. The next most dominant group, displaying Dobermann-like features, descended from guard dogs or the like, I classified as the Dobermainly. Other distinct groups abounded, and I named them thus: Rottproximates, Labrathings,

Mastiffonly, Poodlimates, Houndabouts, and the Unexplaniels. Three separate individuals, so begotten and ragged, deserved special mention, and I named them Waglet, Mangy, and Scab. The smallest member of the pack, this little fellow's skin diseases were appalling. Being so diminutive, bullied and bitten, I would sometimes carry him to keep him from further abuse. Quite how he survived, living on the meagre scraps the others left behind, I had no idea, but his small size might have been advantageous hunting rodents in and about the ruins.

A leftover from a long-abandoned research project, the tracking devices the dogs carried were inactive, and, after carefully removing the subdermal implants, I smashed them on a rock.

I stayed with the dogs for three days, and they were good company. Never leaving my side throughout all my running, jogging, and walking, looking over me as rested both day and night. Occasionally, I helped them hunt, and I once provided a small deer when they failed to catch anything substantial. Familiar with the landscape, the pack proved themselves to be proficient trailblazers. Without their prior knowledge, I would have struggled to locate the tunnel running beneath the Cadiz–Seville Freightway, and we scuttled through its dusty confines, while the trains from Cadiz thundered thirty metres above.

"We will be heading to Cadiz ourselves," remarked Suit. "Boarding a freighter, to take us to Peru. I do hope you enjoy a long cruise."

"No," I replied. "Not really. Any form of confinement is extremely tedious. How long will we be aboard?"

"About three weeks."

"Three weeks?" I replied. "That's awful! Couldn't we hijack an aircraft or stowaway? Seville has an airport. Why don't we go there?"

"No, mistress. The risks are simply too great. We would never get aboard aircraft unnoticed. Moreover, tracking aircraft, stolen or otherwise, is a simple matter, and consider the difficulties of stowing away? Aircraft are cramped, suitable hiding places are extremely limited, and that is before the impossibility of concealing our mass. The strict environmental regulations controlling air travel require the accounting for all weight and freight. With us hiding on board, the flight would be unaccountably overweight. We would soon be discovered!"

"Ah yes." I frowned. "You are quite right. I defer to your good judgement and brace myself for the scent of briny."

"Indeed, mistress, and a scarf might not be a bad idea. The Atlantic can be a mite bracing at times."

We – that is, the dogs, Suit, and I – arrived at the tree line at the northern side of Gibraltar late the following morning. Blocking access to the communications centre was a checkpoint, and I could see a pair of armed security guards taking their ease, drinking coffee in the morning sunshine.

"Not a bad gig," I muttered, scratching Waglet behind her ear. "Can't imagine they get many visitors."

"Well, they've got visitors this morning," Suit darkly replied. "And their 'gig' is about to get worse."

"How do you mean?"

Before Suit could answer, the whole pack slunk past, sneaking their way through the rocks and scrub towards the checkpoint and the reclining guards.

"Oh," I then whispered, "that's what you mean. The guards are going to be...?"

"Lunch."

Hunting with dogs can be a grim business, but to watch a pack take human prey was horrific. Unlike large felines, dogs do not bother subduing and suffocating their prey. They latch on with their powerful jaws, pull their victim to the ground, and tear it limb from limb. Their quarry is often very much alive when they come to devour it...

Thankfully, it was over very quickly. The larger dogs, after knocking the leftmost guard flying, pulled him to the ground and dispatched him before he could even react. His counterpart, however, suddenly springing to his feet, fired several shots (killing one of the Houndabouts) before he too was overwhelmed by a tide of biting, growling, twisting, and shaking, and by the time I had reached the checkpoint there was nothing left but the guards' clothing, equipment, and extremities.

Considering my next move, I decided to sit at the guards' table and finish their lunch, watching with macabre fascination as the dogs squabbled over the remaining scraps. While sipping tepid coffee and munching upon a mushroom and prawn baguette, I observed a gleeful Scab making off with a hand and ragged forearm, chewing and swallowing furiously until one of the much larger Mastiff-like dogs chased him away from his share.

"Bad luck," I called, and, as he scampered over, I flung him a well-deserved handful of prawns.

"Well?" I asked, scanning the dusty track winding up to the summit. "What do we do now? Follow the path?"

"Yes, mistress. The comms centre is atop the summit."

"Fine. Any more guards?"

"None," she whispered. "The UET don't expect visitors, and, apart from the site manager, you are the only living soul for twenty kilometres. Make for the forest of dishes and masts, and don't worry. I am already monitoring and selectively jamming all transmissions, and if you do trip an alarm, there's nobody around to hear it."

With its rusty fence, untidy sheds, and prefabricated bungalow, the comms centre looked derelict, but the dishes and masts were actively humming, so I switched Suit to full stealth and somersaulted the gate.

Tearing the bungalow's wooden front door from its hinges, I cast it aside with an echoing crash.

"Subtle," said Suit. "You should have let me unlock it."

"Humph," I snorted in reply. "I'm tired of sneaking about. Now, tell me. Where is the site manager? Their thermal image eludes me."

"He is beneath you, mistress. The control room is in the cellar."

"Ah," I acknowledged, "that explains it. Let's make ourselves known."

Now, I should explain (as I have neglected to do so) we were at this centre to locate and examine the skeleton of my former crewmate, Dr Abdullah Al-Hillah. According to Marcus Eaton, he and Frida (my great-grandmother), while holidaying in Jordan, encountered his skeleton during a visit to the capital's museum, noting that his remains were on loan, not a fixed exhibit. His true home was the National Museum of Iraq, in Baghdad, and this is where Abda currently resides. Unfortunately, Baghdad is in ruins, little more than a heap of rubble and bones, and the radiation so extreme, even Suit would struggle to protect me. Of course, there are valuable resources in both North Africa and the Middle East, oil for one, and these industries, although purely robotic, continue even today. As well as industry, the region is of great historical and scientific importance, and it is from this communications hub the UET control their drones and robotic probes. Suit is confident the UET possess a device capable of finding Abda's remains, scanning his bones, and transmitting the results directly to my neocortex. I can only hope Abda left us something to find!

"Who? Who's there?" came a nervous male voice responding to a creak on the stairs. "There's nothing… nothing to steal, unless… Unless you want food? Then, just help yourself to the kitchen."

"Thank you," I softly replied. "May do that later. First, I need your help."

The young man turning his chair to peer in the direction of my voice was pale and skinny, with long blond hair and a beard teased into a point. Upon his desk, a glowing surface displayed my UET corporate photo…

"Sure," he said, visibly trembling. "What do you need?"

"Little things," I replied. "Only, who's that on your desk? She looks familiar."

"Not sure yet. It's just come in. An APB? Hang on a tick…"

"Ok," he added moments later. "The UET are after a criminal. A lunatic, by the look of things. A murderer, a thief. Yeah, here it is. 'Wanted for murder, theft, and espionage.' Dr Regina Padgett. The tall chick from the spaceship? You know, the Kuiper Belt? The one that went tits up, the crew disappearing… She's pretty hot, if you like 'em skinny. There's more. She's British, and hmm… Do not approach. Extremely dangerous. Enhanced physiology, stolen weaponry. Jeez, she's a right psycho! Report any suspicious activities to the UET. Office of Inquisitor W de Boer."

"Interesting," I remarked. "Does it mention where she might be?"

"No, it doesn't. Guess she's gone missing… Where are you? I can hear you, but…"

"Over here," I said, removing my hood. "You still think I'm hot?"

"It's you!" he gasped, standing and stumbling back. "I mean, y-you're her!"

"None other," I chuckled in reply, shaking my head. "A celebrity at last. Now, will you help me?"

"Well…" he stammered. "I… should hold you here, radio this in, but my comms rig is jinxed."

"Of course, you should. Only, I don't think you understand the seriousness of your situation. Permit me to be blunt. I don't need you at all, but if you help me, there is a slim chance you might survive this encounter. Do I make myself clear?"

"Perfectly," he replied, trying to sound calm, but his lower lip trembled and within seconds, he dashed to the toilet, vomiting, coughing and retching so loudly I thought he might choke.

"You ok?" I asked, feeling responsible (and quite sympathetic). "What's your name?"

"Noah," he gurgled, rinsing and spitting. "Noah Valdez. What do you want?"

Known as a 'Scuttler', the device we used to search through the rubble of Baghdad was a marvel. Both semi-autonomous and semi-amorphous, it employed a ribbon of fibres comparable to the threads of my suit. Keen to demonstrate, Noah retrieved an example device from storage…

"Here," he said. "Hold out your hand. It won't bite."

Approximately 30cm long and knotted at one end, while deactivated, the silver-grey probe looked like a hair extension, but of threads so fine, they felt fluidic. Once or twice it almost slipped through my fingers! Once activated, the "scuttler" became taut and erect, slowly pulsating as a shimmering cone.

"Right," said Noah. "You get the idea? And their threads are super-strong. Resilient, and clever too. It can squeeze through the tiniest gaps, resisting extremes of temperature, radiation, abrasion, compression, moving in so many ways it's mindboggling. Wriggling, slithering, scampering, swimming, leaping, climbing. Damn things can even fly!"

"Cool," I replied. "Sounds ideal. Have you a similar device in Baghdad? There's a relic in the basement of the museum I'd like to examine."

"Iraq?" he pondered. "Sure. Although Baghdad's a real mess. Might be nothing to find."

"Perhaps. Show me the code of the appropriate Scuttler, and I'll patch myself in."

"You can do that?" he marvelled. "The APB mentioned your enhanced physiology. What else can you do?"

"Oh, this and that," I replied. "Show me the code. Time is pressing."

Connecting my mind to the Scuttler was a hell of a ride, although, at times, it was also macabre. One of the first cities struck, no evacuation of Bagdad had taken place, with the skeletal or desiccated remains of the former inhabitants still among the rubble. The museum interior was no exception, and as the Scuttler squirmed its way through the wreckage of the museum I glimpsed countless desiccated bodies, their contorted postures and gaping skulls telling of a sudden and violent death. Guiding the Scuttler down through several metres of rubble, I found much of the basement clear, but even here I came across human remains. Sheltered from the initial flash and blast but trapped by the collapsed building above, these people had died slowly, from radiation poisoning, exposure, thirst, even hunger, and they still lay upon makeshift beds of coats, carpet, and curtains.

The stone sarcophagus I sought had toppled from its dais, scattering much of Abda's skeleton across the floor before it. His skull and major bones were still intact, and I quickly scanned them, hoping to receive the tell-tale binary signatures.

"Any luck?" asked Noah, studying the display on his desk. "Looks like you've found the right bones."

With the first few kilobytes arriving, I looked down at Noah and reassuringly patted his shoulder.

"Jackpot," I said, and promptly broke his neck.

SIXTEEN

THE SEER OF NANGAR

Leaving the comms centre and dragging Noah's body behind me, I let go a shrill whistle and stood clear as the dogs set about tearing him limb from limb.

Giving the dogs a fond farewell of cuddles, stroking, and scratching, we then headed east, running, bounding, and gliding along the magnificent coastline.

"How long until we reach Cadiz?" I asked, pausing for a breather. "I want to study Abda's logs."

"Two hours," whispered Suit. "Any longer and I will need to recharge. Boarding the freighter will require subterfuge. My dwindling power reserves could inhibit my capabilities if we delay our approach."

"Couldn't you have taken power from the comms centre?"

"No, mistress, not without attracting attention. When the UET learn of the tragedy at the observation post, the evidence will point towards a wild dog attack. Only the door you foolishly forced will suggest otherwise, but an unexplained power drain is just the sort of incident our friend the inquisitor is looking for – unexplained death or technological interference. Once aboard the freighter, its reactors will fill me up a treat."

Although little is left of the old city, Cadiz was a hive of mechanical activity, with its port, harbour, warehouses, and automated freight shipping facilities working unceasingly both day and night. Security was tight and gaining access to the harbour complex required us to scramble over concrete barriers, leap walls, scale or burrow under fences, sharp, hooked, or electrified. Suit was already in control of the communications, cameras, and sensors long before we arrived, but when I encountered one of the security bots, I almost jumped out my skin. As its 2.5-metre frame thundered past on chicken-like metallic legs, I instinctively hid behind a freight container, closing my eyes and holding my breath, fearful of discovery and its powerful armaments.

"You needn't worry," said Suit. "I own them. Jump on its back if you want."

"Now you tell me. Where is the freighter? Is it at sea?"

"Docked in the harbour, mistress. So enormous, you're not likely to miss it."

"Fine. Does she have a name?"

"*La Reina Limeña.*"

"How very apt. Let's go and find her."

⧗

Over 1000m from bow to stern, with a beam approaching 200m, the freighter was huge, and after clambering aboard, we hunkered down in a quiet corner while gigantic cranes loaded the last of the freight.

At the base of the conning tower, we came upon a small maintenance hatch, and coaxing it open, we slipped inside.

"Here we are," remarked Suit, as I surveyed the ships only cabin. "Our accommodation for the next few weeks. What do you think?"

"Think?" I scorned. "Did you know it would be this basic? Squalid, cramped, dusty, dreary, one bunk, no sink, no furniture. Not even a chair!"

"Sorry, mistress. I should have checked. Since this floating robot is without a crew, human comfort is not a priority."

"Clearly," I replied, gathering the musty bedclothes. "Help me shake out these blankets. Tired as I am, sleeping on filth is beneath me."

With Suit recharging in the reactor room, I reclined on the lumpy bed, covered myself in a blanket, and attended the data recovered from Dr Al-Hillah remains. Over to you, Abda…

⧗

Abdullah Al-Hillah is my name, an engineer of the early 22nd century and former crew member of the UET Kuiper Belt Explorer. I am recording this diary as per the instructions given to me by Sir Malcolm Walsingham. If you are decrypting this data, sub-microscopically etched inside my teeth and bones, I can only hope you are a UET functionary or one of my crewmates: Sir Malcolm Walsingham, Dr William Corbiere, Dr Regina Padgett, Dr Eric Badsegh, or my dear companion Luis Emilio Bedoya. Our friend and counsellor Dr Susi Ackermann we lost in a tragic accident, but she also was with us for several years.

I am keeping this diary because I am lost. Unexpectedly separated from my crewmates, my life is imperilled. Before this separation, my crewmates and I (minus Dr Padgett) were captives in the mysterious realm of Moloch. A cruel and powerful entity, an unwilling collector of knowledge (he claimed), tasked with compiling a historical archive for a race of god-like beings, capable of manipulating time and space to rediscover their history. Sounds impossible, and yet, to learn of our heritage, Moloch interrogated and tortured us for months on end, before returning us to Earth five years earlier than planned.

While I rested inside the realm of Moloch, another entity made herself known to me. Of lesser power than our abductor and calling herself Mirra, she was of great benefit and reassurance. Without her gentle company, doubtless the interrogation would have driven me mad, and her careful advice was ever full of wit and wisdom. When the time eventually came for our earthly transportation, her guarded words were thus: "In theory, Moloch can deliver you anywhere and any when you desire, but this freedom of choice carries much danger, so permit him to select the time of place of your arrival. Despite his temper and violent attitude, he knows the intricacies of the device better than any of us, and it is never wise to rile him."

Sometimes, the soothing voice of Mirra was reminiscent of Dr Padgett – sparkling, rich, vibrant, and I wondered how she come to adopt Gina's timbre. Could it be she was reading my thoughts, mimicking a familiar (and reassuring) voice from my memories?

The most terrifying experience of my life, my transportation to Earth seemed to go on for hours, although its true relativistic duration was a mystery. To begin, I witnessed the extreme elongation of my body. Vibrating like a guitar string, my legs extended away from my body. My feet on terra firma, my head blinking in wonder, before, twang! I suddenly detached, streaking through space, hurtling towards my feet, and during this transitory period I saw things – visions – of my crewmates, of others unknown, and I still struggle understanding their context… First, I glimpsed Sir Malcolm. Wrapped in furs, he was lying upon a slab of twinkling stone. For a moment, I thought him dead, but he was blinking and listening intently, his ear pressed against its surface. Next, upon a low stool inside a billowing tent, I beheld Eric. With his gilded hauberk of interlocking rings, he was both formidable and magnificent. He looked straight at me and smiled, but then, I was away! Soaring, spiralling through the heavens, only to find myself hovering above Bill. He was kneeling. Praying before a simple altar in a small wooden chapel, and I took in his velvet cloak, long boots, brocade tunic, and crimson pantaloons. Somehow, then, I came to recognise Gina. Ravishing in her naked loveliness, she was kneeling also, peering tentatively into a rectangle of seething plasma, orange light bathing her pearlescent skin like a fire. Again, this vision passed quickly, yet, my reverie was not over, because I saw him. Emil. Squatting like a fakir in a loincloth and tribal clothing, his hands were wet with clay. He looked at me, smiled, I think, but couldn't I acknowledge him, for I was away, striking the ground with force.

Jarred both mentally and physically, I must have lain there for some time, I think, for the moon had risen before I sat up, but where was I? Not Paris, not anywhere familiar. A narrow passage between mud brick buildings, and the stars? Wrong. Not just geographically, but the constellations. All wrong!

Staggering to my feet, I could only stumble forward before falling again, but then, looking up at the sky, I saw Sirius and, overhead, an already reddening Procyon. Certainly, I was far south of Paris, but when? The distorted shape of Orion was particularly revealing. Using my neocortex, I overlaid an image of the sky onto a star map for ad 2100, time shifting in the hope of finding a match. Eureka! 550 bc. 550 bc?! The preindustrial Bronze Age, and, as for the location… Well, this was not the homeland of the Parisii tribe, light of Allah, no. I was in Iraq, at the town of Hillah, and yet, in this period, Hillah does not exist. I am in Babylon. On the outskirts, in fact, and what in Heaven's name am I doing here? How will I survive?

Panic set in and I lost control of my mind and body. Sweating, wheezing, gasping for air, before attaining a prayer-like posture, praying to Allah for inner peace. Sweet peace and deliverance from my plight.

I heard approaching footsteps. Men bearing lanterns – priests in extravagant robes, jewels and embroidery glinting in the flickering light…

"You there," came a cry. "Old man, down in the dust. You should not be here. There is a curfew in this quarter. Begone, before the guards find you!"

Their language was an odd dialect, but my translation matrix recognised it as Akkadian. A neo-Babylonian form with a strong Aramaic influence.

Trying to speak, my tongue felt lifeless in my mouth, and I coughed dryly, before standing, stumbling, and reaching out most pitifully.

"What?" said the tallest, stamping his long staff into the dirt. "Are you ill, or taken too much of the vine? Speak!"

"Lost," I croaked, and the men laughed.

"Verily," said the tallest. "Lost from where? From whence have you come?"

"There," I gasped, pointing skyward. "Red star. That one."

"Nangar? I think not, sir!" before striding forward taking my arm and lifting his lantern to my face.

"An Assyrian," he said with a scowl. "Not of the children of Israel. What do you think, Abednego? Is he one of yours?"

"Cannot be sure, sire," said one of the priests. "Permit us to take him to Belteshazzar. He will know."

"Very well," said the tallest. "But I want to hear of this vagabond on the morrow. If he is indeed a craftsman of Nangar, return him to his college."

"Agreed," said Abednego. "Now, come, sir. The house of my lord Daniel awaits."

The rest of that terrible night I spent wrapped in an itchy blanket, shivering in fear upon a pallet of reeds. In the morning, naked servants came. Bearing bowls of sweet beer, bread, and dates, they looked on as I ate every scrap, before stripping me naked, washing me all over, and combing my hair. Now soiled and dusty, my loose linen smock, they promptly replaced, providing sandals, a loincloth, and a robe.

A woman came – a beauty. Draped in a robe of fine cloth hemmed with gold, after a courteous bow, she wordlessly escorted me into a chamber, richly furnished, and lit by guttering lamps.

"What now?" I muttered, my knees knocking in fear, and she directed me to stand before a man occupying a padded chair. Somehow, it was as if I knew him already. I knew his serenity. Timeless, like a statue, his long beard and grey-streaked hair braided with colourful ribbons. His small dark eyes, both penetrating and intense, spoke of fierceness, yet little did I fear his wrath. Indeed, his face was kind and thoughtful. As he slowly looked me over, I began to relax, my mouth twitching into a smile. Little sign of age or disease were upon him, and after his cursory examination, he rose and stepped forward. Grasping my hands, he gazed into my eyes…

"Dark fire," he thoughtfully muttered, matching my reluctant smile. "Sparking like embers, and yet fearful… Fearful of what? Discovery?"

Releasing my hands and backing away, he smiled once more, before offering me a chair of my own.

"Sit, good man," he said. "Be of restful heart. The morning is fine and there is no danger."

Clapping his hands as I sat before him, servants hurried in offering bowls of steaming milk.

"Ah," he said, "this will loosen the mood. Milk and honey," and as the bowls were set upon a low table, he gestured a sign above them.

"Now," he then said, licking his lips of the wonderfully spicy warm milk, "my good friend Azariah tells me you fell from a star. An unlikely story, no? However, I know every face in this district, the king's court, and colleges, and you are not of Babel nor Israel. Who are you?"

For a long time, I said nothing. Simply bowing my head, I surveyed woollen mats carpeting the floor. How could I explain my presence here?

"It is difficult," I eventually replied, "to know… where to begin? Yes, sire. It is a matter of context. I am bewildered. Before my tale begins, I require knowledge. Where am I, who are you, when is this?"

"Verily," he pondered. "Then let us dance a dance. A dance of wisdom. I will learn of you from the answers you seek."

"Very good. Then, I must know. Who are you? The people that brought me here, who were they?"

"The music is playing!" He kindly laughed. "And now our dance begins… My name is Dani-El, Belteshazzar to some. A man of God and the spiritual leader of my people."

"Pleased to meet you," I replied with a bow. "And who exactly are your people?"

"We are the children of Israel. Captives, hostages of the king. Taken many seasons hence from Jeru-salem and the many settlements clustered under his mighty walls."

"I see," I replied, struggling to conceal my excitement, "And the men that found me, were they also of your people?"

"Not entirely. Three of them were my kin, holy followers of Yahweh, my friends, Hananiah, Mishael, and Azariah. The fourth man, the man leading them, was Amel-Marduk, eldest son of the king, and the high priest of their religion. Their unholy blasphemy, idolatrous and cruel."

"Thank you," I said. "I begin to understand."

"So do I," he replied. "Your next question is coming, and with your every asking, I learn the rhythm of your dance."

"Doubtless," I acknowledged. "What is this place? Where am I?"

"This place is my home. A house of modesty within the Judean suburb of Babylon. We are without the gates of the great city, but its mighty walls overlook us like the teeth of a guarding lion."

"You say you are captives. Hostages. Are you slaves?"

"No," he calmly replied, "not slaves, and yet we are not free. If we were, we would return to our home. Our freedom will come, I am certain of it, but in the meantime, we serve as artisans, scribes, and labourers to the king. We are housed, fed, protected, even paid for our endeavours. Only we cannot leave."

"Could be worse," I said with a shrug. "However, something bothers you. What is it?"

"You are insightful. The king, in all his pomposity, seeks to strip us of our cultural identity. For example, he forbids the use of our given names and demands we use the Babylonian equivalents. In the city, I am Belteshazzar, and my three brothers in prayer endure the names Shadrach, Meshach, and Abednego. The king condemns our faith in God, and for safety's sake, we perform our prayers and rites in secret."

"That must be hard to bear," I said. "Prayer gives me great comfort. A balm against stress and confusion."

"Ah..." he sighed. "I share your devotion. It is through God I seek the wisdom and the strength to serve my people."

"Permit me, sire, to ask another question. Peculiar but necessary. By Babylonian reckoning, what year, what season is this?"

"Peculiar indeed," he mused. "But since you ask. It is the season of Reš Šatti and the first day Araḫ Nisānu in the 37th year of Nebuchadnezzar."

"I am grateful," I replied finishing the last of my milk. "The mist is beginning to clear. What can you tell me of the king?"

"The king? He is like any other. A despot, vain, paranoid. He spends his days worrying about the future, and so intensely, it is slowly driving him mad. Every rumour a conspiracy, his every dream a prophecy, his every imagining a portent of doom."

"It must be dangerous serving a king so irrational. How do you manage?"

"Have a care!" he warned. "Outside this house, such slander carries a sentence of death, and yet, in the service of a king, of any kingdom, the peril is real and constant. I serve Nebuchadnezzar to serve my people, and his paranoia leaves him vulnerable. Vulnerable to both suggestion and manipulation. We advisers, we prophets and magi, compete daily for his favour. Oh, it is a tiresome game. Full of treachery and sly manoeuvring as we sift the king's words for meaning. Daily I pray, seeking the gift of foresight to ease his fevered mind, but only for the sake of my kin. Their well-being is my primary concern. I care not for the ravings of Nebuchadnezzar and his many craven toads, for God and his lady have spoken of his downfall, of his dust beneath my feet."

From this moment, wonder took me, and I gaped. Could it be possible? Could this man truly be the Daniel of the Bible and Muslim texts? And yet my mind also dwelt upon my predicament. In the wrong place, at the wrong time. or was I? Meeting Daniel…the chances of it…Was my arrival here intentional? Is it irrevocable? If I survive here long enough, my life is over. Without replacements, the nanobots perpetuating my good health will begin to diminish. My body will reject my implants and kill me in the process.

"Your dance is over," remarked Daniel as I quietly pondered. "And the floor is now mine, so forgive my bluntness, but who are you? Whence did you come? You are not of Israel, or Babylon, so what are you? Are you a Quedarite, or a Qahtanite, perhaps?"

These references to the lost tribes of Arabia were fascinating and I desired to know more. Slowly nodding, I answered his probing questions thus:

"You are partially correct, sire. I am indeed a descendant of Ishmael, although my true tribal lineage is mystery. My name is Abdullah Al-Hillah, and doubtless you find it unusual?"

"Much about you is unusual," he replied with a frown. "But your name has an aristocratic tone to it. Although different in form, it has an Assyrian rhythm – or I am no judge. Whom do you worship? Do you worship the one, the almighty, or an aspect of his greatness?"

"I do most certainly worship the one," I replied, making a traditional obeisance. "To you he is Yahweh, but I know him as Allah, and he is everything."

"That is well," he said with a sigh, "Keep your prayers from the ears of the Babylonians. They worship the pantheon of Marduk, and they are zealous, quick and cruel to any dissenter."

"I will do as you recommend. Is there more you wish to know?"

"Much," he replied, stroking his beard. "And I have yet to decide your fate, but time is escaping. The king expects me at his side, so tell me. Why does Azariah believe you fell from a star? Abel-Marduk says you fell from the star of Nangar. The Carpenter in his religion. One of the many aspects of Marduk."

Daniel's question placed me in a predicament. Any lie on my part he would certainly unpick, so I decided to be truthful, hoping he would find my explanation preposterous…

"I did indeed fall from the star of Nangar, but not in the manner of my choosing. I was deceived. This is not the time and place of my choosing."

"You speak the truth," he gasped, puzzlement creasing his brow. "Unbelievable, blasphemous, ridiculous even, but clearly the truth. Whoever sent you? Were you sent by God?"

"No," I replied, "not by any god. Quite the opposite. I was a prisoner of Moloch. Moloch the tyrant. Only by doing his bidding would he send us home."

"Yet home you are not," he chuckled in reply "And foolish to trust the Moloch you speak of. Would it surprise you to learn we worshipped him once, sacrificing our own children to satisfy his hunger? Yes, Moloch. In distant lands they worship him still, for he has many names. Molech, Milcom, Malquar, even Baal to some. The Ammonites know him as Malcam, and fire ever burns in his temple overlooking their city."

"I am both relieved and astonished you believe me." I said, perspiration beading my brow.

"Why should I not?" he replied. "However, another mystery confronts me. You spoke of 'time and place' and earlier you asked me to confirm the date, appearing both fearful and astonished when I told you. So, I ask, if you had a choice, what time and date would you prefer, Abdoola-El-Hillah?"

"Ab-dull-ah," I corrected. "Or, if you prefer, Ab-Da. Your question, however, is troubling. What would you do? When the truth, if believed, is full of peril? I am an honest man. Untruths rarely fall from my lips. Honesty, clear head, clear heart, leave judgement to God. You seem wise and trustworthy, but…"

"We have only just met, and you have no reason to trust me? Then, my new friend, try this. Lie. Let me ponder the truth."

"Very well," I carefully replied. "I will do as you say. Hmm…So, by your reckoning, I would prefer the year to be, the… two thousandth, seven hundred, and seventeenth year of Nebuchadnezzar."

"Indeed?" He chortled in reply. "That is preposterous! Is this the best lie you can contrive?"

"I'm afraid it is. As I said, I'm not much of a liar."

"Fine," he acknowledged, patting the back of my hand. "Then I accept your lie and will consider its meaning. Now, here's another question propelling our dance, although it is part rhetorical. What am I going to do with you?"

"Certainly," I said. "It is hard to know where to go if you don't know where you are."

"Then permit me to refine my question. What would you do if left to your own devices?"

"Keep life simple," I replied with a shrug. "Keep occupied, be useful, and stay out of trouble? Yes. I would seek to familiarise myself with this environment, hoping ever to return to my own time and place."

"Ah," he said. "Your answer cleanses my question. What is your occupation? How do you labour? Do you farm, craft, scribe, or wonder?"

"I am a maker of things," I replied (the word engineer translated thus), "so, I craft?"

"Excellent," he remarked. "Then I shall deliver you to the colleges of craftsmanship, but which one? With what do you craft?"

"I work with wood, sometimes metal. Does that suffice?"

"It does. Since you fell from Nangar, to his college I shall deliver you."

⧗

The inner city of Babylon (in this period) was a jewel. A symphony of glazes blue and green, of glinting gold and sparkling water. Every available nook was used and appreciated. The streets, smoothly paved and orderly, were swept and rinsed, every district brimming with art, sculpture, and ceramics, with plants, trees, and gardens both decorative and fruitful. Babylon flourished, and it was by the judicious and prudent use of water the city thrived, with pipes, sluices, channels, gutters, and rills, spilling and dripping precisely where needed.

Daniel's procession carried us (quite literally) along the broad processional way of legend, but I never made it to the palace myself. Instead, I was delivered into the hands of several priest-like men in tattered robes. Daniel explained to the confused elder I was a master artisan, a traveller from the south, "here to share knowledge, to teach and be taught", insisting they take me in until his return.

Without another word, the elder led me into their refectory – a communal dining room, with long tables, benches, and chairs. The noonday meal was arriving, most unexpected. What a spread! Meats (mutton, fowl, clams, and fish), root vegetables, greens, with salads of olives, berries, shoots, and leaves. Upon great wooden platters, huge loaves of aromatic bread arrived – unleavened, flat, and herby, with small cakes in rush-work baskets, their aroma sweet and spicy. There was honey too, salted butter, pepper, herbs, and spices. To wash it all down there was a dark sticky ale, akin to an Irish stout or English porter. Throughout this feast (a banquet celebrating the coming of the new season), I spoke informally to the elders regarding the work and function of each college...

Gathered around the great ziggurat and temple of Marduk, there were nine in all, beginning with the College of Garra and Nin-agal, the College of Liquid Fire. An institution primarily concerned with smelting, forging, smithing, and metalwork, they imparted their mastery of bronze, lead, tin, copper, gold, and silver, alloying, or refining each as they saw fit. Next, adjacent to the refectory, was the College of Antum – the college of stone and splendour. Within, masonic sculpture was the main area of study, but geology, gemmology, and minerology were also topics of research. The Babylonians fabricated much of their jewellery (ceremonial and decorative) in this college, incorporating the precious metals from the metallurgic College of Liquid Fire.

The third college (of which I am now a senior master), was known as the Workshop of Nangar and Nin-ildu – the heavenly carpenters, and, as its title suggests, it is concerned with trees, timber, and woodcraft in all its forms. In this period, carpentry is unsophisticated. Lacking iron and its tempering, the tools are primitive, and the saw does not exist. Without implements for precision cutting, the production of laminates and veneers (for example) is extremely demanding. Even the dovetail joint is beyond their reach. The master artisans rely on pegs, wedges, lashing, and the occasional mortise and tenon when joining wood. Certainly, my advanced knowledge and skills have quickly won me renown, and I have already improved the collagen-based wood glue they commonly use. During its manufacture (from hides and bones), to improve the glue's manageability, I recommended they add urea to increase its drying time and reduce its viscosity.

The fourth college – the Light of Nusku – works with ceramics, producing pottery (in the main) domestic, ceremonial, decorative, or for construction. The firing of the clay tablets and cylinders the scribes impress (for record-keeping and ritual) also takes place here, with the kilns belching foul smoke both day and night.

Dedicated to Tammuz, the Sumerian god of food and vegetation, the College of the Bountiful Earth concerns itself primarily with botany and the cultivation of plants, particularly those with medicinal or culinary properties. The students also experiment with techniques to extract and improve vegetable dyes, plant fibres, essential oils, waxes, resins, syrups, and sugars.

The sixth college – the Vision of Anshar – concerns itself with the sky, be it meteorological phenomena, the stars, or astronomy in general. When I say "astronomy" I mean astronomy in its most basic form. Measuring the movement of the heavens by means of a primitive, self-levelling theodolite. The vague observational data generated by this ludicrous toy is greatly revered by the elders. It is used to generate their calendars, from which they pronounce delightfully ambiguous prophesies from nothing more than the progress of the sun, the moon, comets, stars, and planets.

The House of Uttu, the seventh college, focusses on weaving, but the elders and journeymen also have expertise in the sewing of fabrics, hides, the knitting of fibres, and the art of dyeing. Very wisely, the king forbade the tanning of hides inside the city, demanding the leatherworkers performed their odorous profession well outside the walls. Only occasionally can you catch a whiff of it.

The penultimate college, the Stables of Sumuqan, works with animals – animal husbandry, the breeding, feeding, upkeep, and housing of all forms of livestock, improving the design and construction of wagons, barrows, chariots, yokes, harness, and, most notably, the plough.

The final college, the ninth, the River of Namtar and Irre, is akin to a hospital, but only for the seriously ill. Indeed, if the traditional palliative or herbal treatments failed to provide any relief, this college was their only hope. Unfortunately, intensive Babylonian medicine (in all its non-existent glory) delivers more harm than good. Of the treatments, most are little more than ritualistic, and the extraordinary performances danced, sung, and chanted over the poor souls brought to this charnel house achieve nothing (but a mystic excuse for their inevitable demise).

⟨𝕀⟩

Day 3: Two days working, learning, and teaching within the college of carpentry. I eat here, sleep here, and learn of Marduk. The masters have provided me with a workspace. A small partition, with a bed, tools, suitable clothing, and a programme of work. This mostly involves the manufacture of furniture, but I also carve kitchen implements from lacewood blocks – a childishly simple undertaking, but my hands, unused to this amount of abrasion, are blistering. As a temporary remedy, knowing my Hibbites will quickly repair my injuries, I have bandaged my fingers. Until callouses form, I wear the thin leather gloves of a novice.

Day 4: With my enhanced hand–eye coordination and senses, I have completed my tasks ahead of schedule. As a reward, I am free to spend today however I wish. Not sure what to do with my time off, I visited the colleges before spending the afternoon relaxing inside a tavern. With food and drink that was varied and plentiful, (and free for college members), I took their main lunchtime meal of a chowder-like dish of fish and clams, with fresh loaves, butter, and (bad Muslim that I am) a little red wine. To my surprise (expecting something halfway to vinegar), the wine was quite good, and I asked if it was a local vintage…

"No, master," said one of the servants. "Too hot here for good wine. We only grow grapes for drying. This wine comes from the north, delivered by the barges that sail the Purattu (Euphrates). So sorry, that is all I know."

Day 5: Praise Allah! Daniel has returned. Another day of chiselling hacking and scraping safely eluded, and his chief steward is escorting me to his home. A crisis inside the palace has drawn the Judean elders together and Daniel wishes me to join their number.

Day 6: Still under Daniel's roof. My mind is racing, assimilating, considering everything discussed; I am struggling to eat a pomegranate without making a mess. What a bundle of news it was!

To summarise. The king's paranoia is becoming deadly. He is pressing his advisers, soothsayers, and magi to not only interpret his dreams and connect them to future events, but to know of their content. Naturally, none of the king's advisers can do this, and he is putting to death all those he finds inadequate. Tomorrow, it is the turn of Daniel. Unless he can demonstrate prophetic ability, he is doomed. The grim resignation on the face of Daniel and his followers filled my heart with pity.

Of course, I could be of enormous help. Neatly archived in my neocortex is a detailed historical account of this period. Should I reveal what I know? Should I raise Daniel up to be as history portrays him? The great prophet, whose wisdom is a blessing from God? It is a terrible dilemma. Am I a driver of the history I inhabit, or am I merely a passenger? Should I reveal what I know, or wait, giving God the opportunity to speak? There are other possibilities also. I must consider these before volunteering any information…

Firstly. Why was I at the meeting? Was it because Daniel, after considering my "lie" at our first meeting, decided I was telling the truth. I was indeed from the future and possessed knowledge of his destiny? A second point to consider. My historical accounts are apocryphal, they are mythological. The story of Daniel is legendary, exaggerated, or, even worse, entirely fallacious. After failing the king's test, Daniel is put to death. Personally, I doubt this hypothesis. Daniel is a man of incredible wisdom, intelligence, and political skill. If I were to bet upon any of the king's advisers to guess his nightly meanderings, I would put my money on him.

The other issue hotly debated last night was of a more spiritual matter, but shrewd as ever, Daniel made it political. In a typical test of loyalty, King Nebuchadnezzar has ordered the colleges to create a great golden statue of himself (my college is manufacturing the internal framework), demanding his people bow down before it. For the Jews of Babylon, worshipping any idol is against their doctrines, and Daniel fears for those of his brethren, of whom, the most devout will refuse to worship such a blasphemy. Certainly, Daniel's close associates, Hananiah, Mishael, and Azariah, refuse to submit, preferring prayer instead. They tire of the king and his tests of loyalty, and after this blatant theological attack they vowed to make a stand. Of course, knowing the king well, Daniel was horrified; fearing for their fate if they show any defiance. Asking for my opinion on what might befall his friends, I could only shrug, cagily muttering, "Burning convictions invariably kindle conflagration."

Shocked by my nonchalance, Daniel held me with his eyes…

"Verily," he then regretfully nodded, "tis true. The hardest truths possess the sharpest edges, but I do not care for your poisonous humour. Return to your college and wait for my instructions."

Day 7: A shipment of timber has arrived from the north. Mostly cedar, we are busily stripping bark and hammering wedges, splitting the logs before stacking the resulting timbers to dry and season. The smell of the wood is delightful, but my fellow carpenters and I are struggling to remove the sticky resin covering our hands. Normally, I would recommend turpentine or a similar solvent, but we made do with hot brine and dry sand as medium to bind it, scraping and rolling away the "worms" of resin-loaded sand like a coarse abrasive putty.

It is evening and I am once again at Daniel's. He appears to have forgotten (or forgiven) my bitter remark at our last meeting and we are eating a dish of spiced lamb with apricots rolled inside a flatbread. There is fruit also, with dates, grapes, peaches, and a quality ale to wash it all down. This brew is more refined than the sweet, turbid stuff the workers down by the gallon. Paler and smoother, its fruitiness and creamy texture is reminiscent of an India pale ale.

"I'm glad you came," said Daniel, wiping froth from his beard. "Because I need your help."

"My lord," I replied with a bow. "Am delighted to come, if only for the food! In my college our diet is tiresome. Fish every day. I shall grow gills if I eat more!"

"Verily." He chuckled. "However, the eating of fish is an observance of the Babylonian religion. During this season, it is a mainstay of their diet."

"Then" – I smiled, shaking my head – "I long for the changing of seasons, but now, how can I help?"

In reply, Daniel clapped his hands three times in quick succession – a signal for privacy. Hastily gathering our plates, cups, and platters, the servants darkened the room and dashed away.

Pausing briefly, Daniel moved his chair beside mine and we huddled closely, our faces flickering by the light of a single lamp. Its oily black smoke twisting like a slender thread…

"Good," he whispered. "Secrecy demands silence. Now, let us return to our dance."

"Our dance?" I mused, raising an eyebrow. "I thought the music had ceased."

"Oh, no," he replied. "The dance never ends. It is timeless. Tell me, are you a student of history?"

"Indeed, sire. Do you enjoy the tales of the past?"

"Certainly, and it is of your past I wish to learn, so therefore, dear Abdullah, lie once more. Tell me all that you know. For you know of me, do you not?"

"Yes." I slowly nodded, respecting his careful wisdom. "But what you seek is dangerous, dangerous for us both. May I have this night to consider?"

"You may," he carefully replied. "And your request is wise. What to divulge and what to omit. Am I right?"

"Yes."

"Then stay," he commanded, quickly standing. "In the morning, I will return."

⧗

Comfortable as possible and preparing to blow out the light, a young slave girl noiselessly swept into the room. Sitting opposite my makeshift bed of chairs and cushions, she smiled, grinning inanely, and for a moment I wondered if she was drunk...

"Hello, Abdullah," she whispered (in perfect English). "How are the blisters, my friend?"

This was a shock, and my heart leapt in hope. Was Moloch about to correct his mistake?

"Hello to you," I replied, spluttering in surprise. "Who are you? How can you be speaking English?"

"Well," she said, chuckling, "I could speak any language I choose, but if this sweet girl tiptoed in here speaking Akkadian, bearing the tidings I carry, you might not have believed her."

I slowly nodded.

"And, as for who I am. You know me as Gleener."

"Gleener," I gasped. "You I remember! Howling, laughing, screaming, you were insane, but now you can talk?"

"Quiet!" she harshly whispered. "The others are sleeping. However, Gleener I am, and my insanity is feigned. I have temporarily taken control of this young woman for conference."

"Ah," I remarked. "Clever. A form of telepathy?"

"Oh, heavens, no," she replied. "Nothing so supernatural. This girl is asleep and dreaming. Dreaming of her mother, in fact. I am merely using a dormant part of her consciousness to carry a part of mine."

"Clearly not insane then." I smiled. "Have you come to take me home?"

"No," she sighed. "On both counts, no. As I said, Moloch is both lying and deceived regarding my state of mind but returning you to your proper time and place is quite beyond my power. Without synergy, he has total control of the matter transferral protocols, and he no longer cares if you're living or dead."

"Then, I'm trapped?"

"Yes," she admitted, "and we are to blame. Although we have good reason for stranding you here. History demands it."

"Does it?" I grimly replied. "And just who is 'we'?"

"Mirra and myself. Didn't I say?"

"Yes. Mirra did indeed reveal she was you. At the time, I thought she was lying."

"No," she replied, "it was the truth. Despite how much we enjoy fibbing, we are indeed the same being. I the lesser, she the greater. I am merely our beginning. She is our before and ever after."

"That" – I frowned, folding my arms – "is meaningless jibber."

"It is," she said with a smile. "And yet it is also the truth, and the truth stands for itself. It doesn't require meaning."

"Ha." I chuckled. "Gina would quip maxims like that. 'Even when it's dark, the truth is the truth.' Now, why are you here? What do you want?"

"Nothing," she replied. "It is Mirra that sends me. She says you have a decision to make, and I'm here to help you make it."

"Indeed." I nodded. "A terrible decision. I'm caught between Scylla and Charybdis, the devil and the deep blue sea. Daniel suspects I know his future and would learn of it, but I am confused. Surely, no matter what I do, my presence here is changing the future, so should I tell him or not?"

The slave girl giggled, admiringly stroking her hair.

"Well," – she then smiled – "what does history already say? Because, if you refuse to help, Daniel and his friends will die. What does it say in the Bible?"

"It says their faith saves them from many perils."

"Correct. It is his faith in us that saves him, so tell him everything history describes. The dreams of the king and his increasing madness. Of the statue, the furnace, and his prophecies regarding the coming of Cyrus. How he tames of the lions, and the coming of Romans."

"Very well." I nodded. "I will do as you say. Yet I am struggling with a paradox, my predestination? For thousands of years have my historical records existed, from 550 bc until the 22nd century. Since my arrival they are unchanged, unless…"

"Unless?"

"Unless they *have* changed, and, being part of the story, I am incapable of knowing it? How can the initiator know of the events they initiate?"

"Now, now," she replied with a giggle. "You need to stop right there, or you'll simply go dizzy. Do not concern yourself with temporal matters. Just live your life as it comes. The universe will continue. A bud slowly unfurling. Our species can't help but see time as a journey. As a river, flowing from its spring to the sea, or an arrow, flying towards its target. Time isn't like this. These descriptions are contrivances. They are three-dimensional constructs, a comfortable explanation to which we instinctively cling. In truth, time is akin to an ocean of lava: seething, bubbling, bursting, mingling, churning, with currents none can resist."

"Very poetic. Anything else I should know?"

"Three more things," she admitted, nibbling a grape. "Four days hence, Daniel will betray you to your death. After testing your information, he will realise the danger of keeping you alive. You could supplant him."

"Seriously? I thought him a friend."

"Only to a point. Underneath his benevolence lurks a politician, and you know how they can be. If they're not patting backs, they're stabbing them. Although his betrayal will distress him, his courage flows from his ruthless determination."

"Indeed. But must I die? Is it inevitable?"

"Yes," she replied, leaning forward to stroke my cheek. "So, you must prepare yourself. On the night of the fourth day, a small bead of twinkling stone will come into your keeping, and it is imperative you hide it upon your person so that it cannot be found."

"Very well. What is it for?"

"It is a marker. A small part of a much larger device."

"Fine. Any suggestions where I should conceal it?"

"Swallow it. Or, if that doesn't appeal, shove it?"

"Shove it?" I mused. "Shove it where?"

"There." She grinned.

"Where?"

"Up there," she replied, nodding towards my pelvis.

"Oh, there," I said, getting her meaning. "Anything else?"

"Yes. You are recording a log, are you not?"

"Yes," I replied. "Sir Malcolm insisted. In fact, I am recording this conversation."

"As you should. Be sure to instruct your little Hibbite beasties to encrypt this data into the structure of your major bones and teeth."

"I intend to."

"Good," she said, twiddling a lock of her hair. "As now I must be going. This girl will soon be waking, and I must return her to her bed."

"Of course," I replied. "Is this farewell or will I see you again?"

"It is farewell, but you will glimpse me the day after tomorrow. Only briefly, in a different form, and not to talk to," and with that she gracefully made for the door.

"Good night," I whispered, "and thank you for your help."

Day 8: How I managed to sleep last night I really do not know. To learn of my impending doom should have kept me awake all night, but in fact I slept soundly. Dream after dream breaking like waves. My mind wandering, anticipating my morning conversation with Daniel. How to help, what to reveal.

Ok, done. Sharing breakfast (bread, butter, honey, and warm milk), I told Daniel everything he needed know. The future events I described matter of fact, others more cryptically, but to reveal the prophetic dreams (Daniel's and those of the king) I kept to the traditional accounts, describing "a beast with two legs, sharp teeth of iron, and ten horns". I then told him of the king's impending insanity, how he will "crawl and grovel, growling like a beast", before announcing the coming of Cyrus, his survival when thrown to the lions, and the repatriation of the Jews. Then I dwelt upon the golden statue of the king, explaining how God would spare his three friends, but only if their faith was unflinching.

Day 9: Summoned to the enormous palace gardens, with its immaculate flowerbeds, lawns, and swaying trees, my college and I kneel faithfully before the twelve-metre golden statue of Nebuchadnezzar II. Upon a jewelled throne, the man himself restlessly fidgets, with Amel-Marduk (his firstborn), Daniel, and two advisers standing nearby. The sun was burning hot, and while we waited, the garden steadily filled with people – every man, woman, and child of consequence, from every district of the city. Two rows in front, Daniel's friends Hananiah, Mishael, and Azariah appeared to be praying, and after catching my eye, Daniel studied his friends with growing concern.

Appearing from a nearby pavilion, wailing and chanting, priests set about sacrificing various livestock before murdering two terrified prisoners in a cruel ritual of strangulation. More chanting and wailing then followed, spurring the king to his feet – our cue to bow – and we obediently pushed our noses into the dirt, the silence broken only by the recitation of psalms…

Refusing to worship a false idol, Daniel's companions had chosen prayer, and the king's reaction to their provocation (as I peered from the corner of my eye) was immediate (and doubtless carefully planned). Plunging into the assembled came a squadron of palace guards. Dragging the still-praying zealots to a sacrificial pyre, they tied them its centre pole, piling faggots and oil-soaked kindling around them. Helpless, the Jews continued to pray, and I could overhear Daniel speaking to the king, begging for mercy, but, as the three continued their prayers, Nebuchadnezzar pushed him aside, demanding the guards "Burn the stubborn fools. Make them squeal. Roast them like pigs on a griddle!"

With an audible whoosh, the kindling ignited, engulfing the still-praying victims in a maelstrom of flame, only they didn't burn! It was as if the flames were cool, providing light without heat. Then, a moment of wonder, a miracle: As if made from flame, dancing, cavorting, and swaying, within the heart of the pyre, a girl could be seen. Who she was, how she got there, it was impossible to tell, but the fire had no effect on her, and she raised her long arms in mockery of the twisting flames. Still bound to the post, the three zealots continued to pray. They were screaming now, but not from the heat. The fire was checked. It was motionless. Before moving once more – in reverse. It was shrinking. Lower and lower, smaller, and smaller, within seconds it had gone out. The strange dancer disappearing with the last of the smoke.

Open mouthed and shock, the king slumped into his throne, while the assembled crowd, now longer bowing, was clamorous and excited. On his knees, Daniel flung his head back in awe…

"*Mal'ākh!*" he cried. "*Mal'ākh 'ĕlōhîm!* A messenger from God! Thank you, Lord. Thank you for sparing them!"

This show of disloyalty was too much for the king. Red-faced and furious, he kicked Daniel like a cur. Spitting into his face, he hastened into the palace, his guards, priests, and advisers following closely behind.

⧖

It is early evening, and I am with Daniel, his family, and closest friends. Celebrating the "miracle of the furnace", we are singing, dancing, and drinking wine.

"You have my thanks," whispered Daniel, taking me to one side. "What happened today is beyond my ken, but your words rang true. She said you would be dependable, and before we part, she has a gift for us both."

"She?" I asked. "Of whom do you speak?"

"Miriam," he replied. "The handmaiden. A servant of God. She is light, and she is laughter, here…"

Opening his hand, he revealed two beads of twinkling granite.

"One for you and one for me. She didn't say what they were for, or why, just how they were for us. Take one."

Accepting a bead and studying it closely, I wondered how a heterogeneous crystalline solid could be a part of anything…

"Thanks," I said. "She spoke with me also, told me to expect one of these. She insisted I didn't lose it."

"Absolutely," he acknowledged, stifling a yawn. "And, with that done, momentous day or no, I still need my bed. Feel free to stay – there are beds aplenty but return to your college promptly come the morning. While I becalm the king and bandage his tortured ego, I want you safely hidden."

Day 10: Working hard within my college, we are steaming strips of timber before weaving them into fence-like screens of great strength. As a bridging material, these structures have many applications, spanning columns, flat roofs, and so forth.

For lunch, we have fish, bread, beer, and locusts – disgusting in both taste and smell. I'm so tired of fish, I brush aside my revulsion and eat them.

New apprentices have arrived (just boys really) and the masters and I are teaching the basics, demonstrating how the fibrous grain of wood dictates it strength and flexibility.

Disturbing our quiet industry, an echoing commotion is emanating from the anterior of the college, and I focus my enhanced auditory sense to determine the source. Tricky. Inside this structure, the columns refract sound the same way a cracked prism refracts light, but I can hear an argument. Palace guards are here, to arrest... Yes. They are here to arrest me, for blasphemy and treason. The college masters are refusing them entry unless they disarm.

This is the moment. Gleener was right. I am betrayed. After swallowing the crystalline bead, I have commanded my Hibbites to begin storing this journal in my deep skeletal structure (I do hope someone will have opportunity to read it).

The guards are approaching but Master Amel-Amatar and Master Helphazzar are obstructing their progress. There is yelling, threats of violence. After removing my apron, I kneel to pray, my white robe speaking of purity and supplication.

The guards are in my workshop. They demand the two masters protecting me move aside. It is no good. These old men are stubborn as knotted oak, and drawing their swords, the guards cut them down like reeds.

My Hibbites are suppressing pain. I am thankful. The beating I receive is unremitting.

The royal palace is splendid. A glazed temple of blue, shining jewels, crystal lanterns, gold, and silver shimmering.

Upon the royal dais I can see Daniel. Tears are rolling down his cheeks.

The king demands I "crawl on all fours like a beast".

I will not. Abdullah Al-Hillah crawls for no one.

They have cut off my head. My own headless body is before me.

Ah, darkness, and now, light?

A voice?

Father?

A choice?

SEVENTEEN

LA REINA LIMEÑA

O f all the journeys I have undertaken, this is proving to be the most atrocious, and only two days in already! To begin, leaving harbour, like a behemoth of the deep, we lumbered and wallowed, and then it started – the relentlessness of it all. The wind whistling, the waves crashing, breaking in clouds of spray, and the chill factor. My very timbers were shivering! Without Suit, wrapping me in her radiating warmth, I would have surely frozen to death. Indeed, there is nothing romantic or peaceful about this haul across the Atlantic. It is never quiet, even for a moment. The howling and shrieking of the cables lashing the containers to the deck in unceasing, the entire assemblage booming like thunder, drumming and screeching, resonating in the wind of our speed. Sleeping through this hellish cacophony proved impossible and only by disabling my hearing was I able to rest...

Inducing profound deafness, even temporarily, I find very disconcerting. I become almost paranoid in my tension, fearful of both my surroundings and of being surprised – not that I need worry. Who would care to join me on this howling colossus, pirates? They would be fools to try.

In the latter half of the last century, kidnapping and piracy was commonplace in the mid-Atlantic, but the enormous height and speed of the new Panamax Mark 4 Mega Freighters make them an almost impossible target for the seaborne criminal. In any event, if desperate raiders ever did come along side, the automated weapon systems and security drones would make short work of them. Mind you. There are days when I wish pirates would try to raid us. I would at least see something living! Our speed is so great, even the gulls fail to pursue us.

Food is abundant aboard – although I do have to scavenge for it, and by scavenge, I mean steal; breaking into cargo containers to discover if anything within is edible. This brand of petty criminality troubles me. I wouldn't want anyone rifling through my property, but since the alternative is starvation, I select a container at random, override its security seal and rummage about inside. Again, this inefficient approach goes against my nature, but with only a number marking each container (and a cargo manifest that is suspiciously vague about their contents) I have little choice.

We have entered the mouth of the Panama Canal and the weather is lovely – toasty, in fact. I am sunbathing while Suit, enjoying the warmth herself, plays hide and seek with the ship's on-board computer.

Once narrow and restrictive, the Panama Canal is now broad and majestic. A great ribbon of water sparkling in the tropical sunshine. The rising sea levels of the last century, in tandem with massive excavation projects, mean the canal is now lock-free and abysmally deep. A saltwater sea lane, almost a kilometre wide, with tidal currents, ripping, ebbing, and flowing between oceans Pacific and Atlantic.

We are docking. The lights, sounds, and scents of the city are seductively calling.

Leaving Suit in a heap on the floor, I quickly don my leisurewear and make for the door, but she launches past me and blocks my egress like a wall of shimmering steel…

"Oh, come on, Suit," I grumble. "Let me go. Just to stretch my legs and buy a hot meal."

"No, mistress," she replies. "The risks are too great. I need you sober and sensible, not dozy and drunk. If we wish to complete our task and return unimpeded, we must be cautious."

"Meaning, without you, I am not?"

"Indeed. Now, disrobe and allow me to cover you. Lima is chilly this time of year. Without my warmth, you'll be wrapped under so many layers you'll look like an onion."

"Oh, very well," I sigh, and try not to fidget as Suit slithers up my legs to cover me.

Flitting through the back streets of Lima, it wasn't long before we "acquired" a little currency, and I spent a small part of it on a trio of dough sticks known locally as churros…

"The museum is only two streets away. So, regarding tactics, what have you in mind?"

"A simple approach, mistress. The antiquated security system of the museum is solid-state electronic, and consequently I am unable affect it externally. We should enter by stealth and make our way to the control centre, deactivating the cameras, sensors, alarms, and locking mechanisms once there."

"Fine." I nod, licking my fingers. "Any guards?"

"Several, and I recommend we kill them all."

"Certainly. Do you know where Emil's skeleton is located? Is it part of the exhibition or in storage?"

"I do not know. In 2011, Marcus Eaton, in a desperate bid to examine the second figurine, damaged the bindings of the mummified skeleton we seek. What happened afterwards isn't clear. Poor Mr Bedoya could be anywhere. It shouldn't take long to locate him once we are safely inside."

"How do you propose we get in?"

"From the roof, mistress. There are ventilation ducts wide enough to admit your slender frame. A little slithering and we drop into a maintenance cupboard adjacent to the control room."

"Excellent," I acknowledged. "Like playing *Half Life* on Bill's old computer."

"Indeed, but I would prefer you refrain from using a crowbar to dispatch the guards. The mess would be terrible."

"Spoilsport. Let's find a spot to clamber onto the rooftops, then we can move unseen."

"Good thinking, and you'll be pleased to know, there are banners spanning the next street. I know you enjoy the tightrope."

Despite the increased number of guards, our plan went well. A string of recent art thefts had compelled the local authorities to beef up security, and by the time we reached the control centre, my body count was eight. The six patrolling guards we quietly dispatched by strangulation, while the two fellas dozing in the control centre I promptly shot, my disturbingly eager-to-please bullets reducing them to bloody scraps of clothing.

"So where is he?" I whispered as Clotho and Lachesis slithered down my arm to reload. "Anything on the computer?"

"There is no computer. This ancient device merely monitors the cameras."

"Fine," I replied. "Then let's visit the appropriate gallery. If he's not there, he must be in storage."

The display of Chachapoyan mummies was obviously devoid of my former crewmate – they were small. Broad, squat men, petite women, children, and, like little bundles of sorrow, infants wrapped in decaying fabric.

"In storage then," I muttered. "Good. Unlike silly Marcus, I have no desire to disturb them."

"Certainly, mistress, and yet, without his courage and his uncle's resourcefulness, we wouldn't be here."

"Humph," I replied with a sniff. "That sounds as if I want to be. It is you leading this murderous venture. I'm just flotsam caught in the wake."

Picking locks, we descended the staircase leading to the storage facility only to come across a massive steel door...

"Shit!" exclaimed Suit. "This I didn't expect."

"What's the problem?" I asked. "Just bash it in."

"I'd rather we didn't. To reveal our intentions here joins too many dots. This door is mechanical – no keyhole, just a lock and a timer. I'm sure you can hear it. Ticking gears, pinging springs, and whatnot?"

"Yes. I can hear ticking, so?"

"It means, dear Gina, we can only open the door by force. Unless you prefer to wait? Wait until Monday morning?"

"Of course not. We'd miss our boat."

"So, we have no choice, but this lack of subterfuge will have repercussions, mark my words."

"What subterfuge? The museum above is a bloodbath! We commit mass murder, and you're worrying about subterfuge?"

"Yes, mistress, we have indeed killed the guards, and brutally, but I would prefer to be leaving no clues as to our motive. Once we open this door, it will be thunderously apparent we were searching for something in storage, and the inquisitor, once he learns of our intrusion, will quickly see the connection: the mummy, Marcus, and the circumstantial involvement of your great-grandmother."

"Granted, but then his supposition will reach a dead end. Only I possess Marcus's journal."

"Correct. Any data we uncover is beyond his reach, and yet he will be unable to dismiss the notion the skeletons we seek are the remains of your former crewmates."

"What do you think he will do?"

"He will hesitate."

"Why?"

"Because he trusts you, mistress. He trusts your judgement and unparalleled charm, perhaps? No matter how reprehensible your actions, his heart will convince him you have a powerful motive. Now push, Gina. Push with all your might. This door is heavy…"

Creaking at first and then buckling inwards, the door gives way surprisingly quietly, and with Suit holding on, she enabled me to lay it onto the floor.

"Excellent." I smiled, preparing to head inside, but Suit held me firmly in place…

"What's wrong?" I asked. "Why can't I go in?"

"Something is amiss. A mismatch. The last image relayed by the chamber's camera is incongruous."

"How do you mean? Share the data. Show me."

"As you wish."

With the grainy images flooding my mind, I promptly overlaid them.

"A packing crate," I pondered. "Gone missing. Where did it go?"

Suddenly sniffing the air, I briefly examined the olfactory data.

"Jasmine," I remarked. "Hannah's perfume. You think she is here?"

"Possibly," whispered Suit. "Or she was here. Her appearance confirms our suspicions. She is indeed a polymorph."

"Yes. Only, how did she get into an airtight room?"

"Perhaps she was transported?"

"By whom?"

"Moloch," offered Suit. "Or that Mirra/Gleener entity? They transported your crewmates. As shape changer, Hannah would be an excellent spy."

"Perfect, I'd say. What do you suggest?"

"We ignore her, mistress. We find the mummy and scan it. If she wants to watch, fine. We don't have time for shenanigans."

"Granted, and if we are walking into a trap?"

"Then we spring it."

"Bra-vo," I darkly replied. "Do you know where the skeleton is?"

"No, mistress. Those objects beneath the polythene sheeting look promising. Try under there."

A dozen mummies, each zipped into an airtight bag, were indeed under the sheeting, and Emil, being taller than the others, stood out like a sore thumb...

"Hello, Emil," I muttered.

Unzipping his airtight shroud, I carefully scanned his teeth, femora, and pelvis.

"Nothing," I said. "There's nothing. So strange. Emil was a keen writer. Letters home and diary keeping he particularly enjoyed. He must've kept a journal."

"Indeed," whispered Suit. "Or he suffered an injury causing a malfunction?"

"Possibly. A blow to the head, a whack in just the right spot? Ok. Let us assume that was the case. How else might he record a log? A physical recording, on paper, tile, or parchment?"

"The idea has merit," said Suit. "Mr Bedoya was a resourceful and highly creative individual. He would have found a way. Where are his grave goods?"

"Of course," I gasped. "His grave goods! Here, inside my head. Marcus! His uncle left him an X-ray plate. The figurine inside Emil's bindings. Yes. With something inside it. A ring. Now, where has it got to?"

"The figurine, mistress? Is it not in his bindings?"

"No," I replied. "It is not. None of his goodies are. The museum must have removed them. Let me see... Emil's mummy is tagged H176K. Do any of the storage crates match?"

"Yes, mistress. Above your head and to the right. Fetch it down and open it."

Among a several domestic and decorative items was the figurine. Mindfully lifting it out, I stood it on a shelf.

"We meet again," I said, peering closely. "Now, what are you hiding?" I ran the scanner over its surface...

"Oxygen, silicon, aluminium, iron, in other words, clay. Ah...What do we have here? Titanium, vanadium, boron, carbon... Hey, I recognise that alloy – Emil's data ring! The cunning old so-and-so. He must've hidden it inside."

"Undoubtedly," whispered Suit, "and now we need to remove it. Access requires physical contact."

"Remove it how? By shattering?"

"I see no alternative, mistress."

"Neither do I. Shame to do it again…Do it again… Do it again? Marcus! He knew the answer all along – in York. The crashing computer. *Vuelva a hacerlo* – do it again! A message from Emil, surely?"

"I don't think so, mistress. Yet, breaking figurine does appear to be the only way forward."

Grasping the figurine with both hands I methodically pulverised its terracotta body. Removing Emil's data ring, I dropped the detritus into the box.

Trying the ring for size, I studied it closely.

"Pretty," I said. "If too big. It even slips off my thumb. Can you read it?"

"No, mistress. I must envelop it."

"Then take it."

Slipping the dark shining ring from my thumb, Suit wrapped it in her shimmering folds.

"Receiving data," she whispered. "Research data and personal logs."

"Excellent," I replied. "I'll have a look later. Now, let's get away from this place. All the death here is creeping me out."

"Yes, mistress, at once. Despite Hannah's appearance and disappearance things have gone well this evening. I am relieved. Once in the city, feel free to indulge yourself. Visit a bar if you wish. Personally, I would recommend sobriety coupled with a little late shopping, but I suppose you want to get pissed?"

"You're damn right. Pisco acholado. Take me to a bar. This girl needs a drink."

EIGHTEEN

THE RELUCTANT POTTER

Forty-eight hours since our assault on the museum and all of Peru is on fire (searching for the perpetrators of the massacre within) and we (the guilty party) are hiding-out in a vast warehouse of the Callao district adjacent to the harbour. In fact, I've made a bit of a nest in here, with food, bedding, and my meagre belongings, all because the loading of the *La Reina Limeña* is taking forever! I would have preferred hiding aboard ship (far more comfortable), but her deck is crawling with stevedores, engineers, and technicians, and not until she weighs anchor will we sneak aboard. Indeed, I spent the morning upon the roof of my adopted warehouse, watching the cranes and robots, lifting and stacking the containers of freight. My brazen exposure made Suit nervous. Not that she needed to worry. Unless a security drone landed beside me, I was invisible.

Suit's apprehension stemmed from the events of yesterday, when, shopping in the market district, things got dicey. Seeing my picture flash across a public information screen, I had to quickly find cover, remove my clothing, and become invisible, before climbing onto the rooftops to get off the street.

Under the auspices of Inquisitor de Boer, the UET have gone international to learn of my whereabouts, and in doing so, they have stripped me of my anonymity, reducing my shopping trips to the barbarity of pillaging the local shops under the cover of darkness.

When I say, there is no fun in criminality, believe me. There is only fear, stress, and growing paranoia. To accumulate the stockpile of food, drink, and warm clothing necessary for the long voyage to Folkestone, I have taken considerable risks.

Now, I must turn my attention to the data uploaded from Emil's ring – three files in all. The first is series of entries made during his last few weeks aboard the Kuiper Belt Explorer – his research notes, but later passages concern his incarceration, interrogation by Moloch, and subsequent conversations with Mirra. The second file is a diary, sporadically maintained, during the 12th or 13th century, while living among the Chachapoya. The third file is the beginnings of another diary, following on from the latter example once its entries tail off.

Here, I begin with a transcription of his research notes, his musings, if you like. Brief and snappy, they often lack context, but I list them here in full (sans his mathematical notation and occasional diatribe) …

Another long hour listening to Abda's mad theories. Tachyons again. Boring. What is it with Abda and tachyons? Tachyons don't exist. They are a mathematical toy. A plaything of the pale and indoorsy. Backwards, he says, backwards! Backwards through time? The Cherenkov radiation released unpredictably, historically (he claims). So, before its intended detection? Hard to argue with logic like that! Told him to bother Walsingham instead.

The matrix of my new data ring stabilised at last. Soak test next.

Gravitino mopping with Abda and Bill, 100eV or thereabouts. Where could they be coming from?

Boron seeding on the fab unit: $\beta12 / X3$ and don't forget: $\beta36$!

Procyon exhibiting new characteristics. Where are the bands for TiO and VO? Should be prominent in a class M dwarf.

Procyon B. Orbital distance and period becoming increasingly eccentric. Sometimes slowing, sometimes accelerating. Why should it? An outside influence?

Just read a report explaining the variable luminosity of the Canis Minoris system. The Galle-Le Verrier Neptunian telescope detects a plasma streamer. To what, though? A singularity? Fine. Let us assume that is the case. Where is the disc of accretion? Where are the X-rays? Is the plasma falling down a plughole? Unless the singularity is tiny. Is that even possible? If Walsingham weren't asleep, he would have some insight. There is Gina, of course. Should I share my insights with her? Ha! No. All she wants to do is eat, drink, fuck, and play games.

A fair summary of my entire adult life!

Abda is detecting regular pulsations of X-rays. Like the faint ticking of a clock, these bursts of X-ray frequencies inexplicably match the combined spectroscopic fingerprint of both Procyon A and B. The emissions are incredibly weak, but this does not lessen the coincidence. What are the chances? Could these emissions be artificial? Certainly, Abda has also recorded the "abnormal annihilation" (a missing gamma ray) of naturally occurring positrons, both inside and outside the ship. Quite what this means he is unsure, and for the moment this strange phenomenon seems to have ceased, but we have decided to wake Walsingham at the first opportunity. In lieu of this discovery, Abda is again speaking of tachyons, i.e., a degree of temporal displacement, hypothesising the two emitted gamma rays are temporally mirroring. One is moving forward through time, the other backwards (undetectably). Ridiculous man. Such things are impossible!

Susi Ackermann is dead. After detecting a (relatively) massive burst of X-rays, our extra-vehicular repair and retrieval system suffered a series of malfunctions. Overriding dozens of safety protocols, these malfunctions released thousands of SenSwarm units into her cabin, wherein they removed her every trace to the matter reclamation facility. Grief-stricken and horrified, Abda and Walsingham are trying to retrace the path of malfunction, but they are wasting their time. The required command sequence is inordinately complex. Susi Ackermann's death was no accident. It was murder. Not by one of us, however. We had no motive! Susi was popular. Loved, in fact. Without her, our very sanity is in peril, so the guilty party must be on Earth, but whom, and why?

What has happened? Where am I? I was dozing in my cabin, but now…?

This is insane. Have we gone crazy? Taken from the KBE to God only knows where, by God only knows whom, we huddle in a realm of boundless white.

Despite our predicament, Walsingham is working us hard to understand our environment, but it is confusing. Without up nor down, near nor far. Surroundings incomprehensible. Yet, someone or something delivered us hence. Why? Why not show themselves? Why so elusive?

An answer at last…

Speaking with the voice of Walsingham and appearing as a ball of dazzling light, "Moloch" claimed he wished to learn from us. A perfectly understandable request, and we happily complied, but after a period of lengthy questioning, not once did he demand any information regarding our mission or technology. In fact, his questions were decidedly mundane, concentrating on our family histories and everyday life. At times, he seemed bored or world-weary, as if he wished for the process to end, but if we protested in the slightest, he filled our minds with such terrifying hallucinations, we could do little but scream and endure them.

Now separated from the group, I appear to be in my apartment on Moonbase. I am not on Moonbase, however. These beings have a telepathic ability (or technology) capable of reading my every thought, memory, and sensation. This bothers me not. No matter how unreal, to be home is decidedly pleasant.

With the voice of Dr Padgett and calling herself "Mirra", another entity has made herself known. Unlike Moloch, she is good company (if dismissive) and, like dear Gina, she he can be frivolous. When she does communicate, she does so surreptitiously. Commandeering the food dispenser of my illusory apartment, she whispers with extraordinary charisma, singing songs, reciting rhymes, posing riddles, disgorging useless facts and irrelevant fancies. "Merely to pass the time", she says…

So far, this Mirra has offered little but companionship, and when asked about this environment her replies are vague and evasive. Only by mentioning the findings of Abda could I pry any useful information from her. The positrons he detected were indeed artificial. Created, modulated (for the carrying of information), entangled with others (at specific physical and temporal coordinates), before undergoing annihilation, releasing two similarly modulated gamma rays, mirroring each other (as Abda correctly postulated) moving through time in opposite directions. Encouraged by this revelation, I also asked about the technology at her disposal, for example the device used to create this illusion…

"Device," she mused. "Not sure what you mean. Could you be more specific?"

"A tool," I replied. "An implement used to perform a particular task."

"Ah," she replied. "Physical things. No, we have none, we don't need them. Our thoughts provide all we require."

"Huh?" I pondered. "How can thoughts provide anything?" and she softly chuckled, replying, "A thing is only a thing because you think it's a thing."

"Fine," I replied, accepting her premise, "but surely… traces. For those of us in the material world, wouldn't your thoughts leave traces? If you interact with us, you interact with matter."

"Ah, yes," she acknowledged. "Outside this environment, our physical manifestations appear holocrystalline. Your crewmates stumbled across such a contrivance on Mars. A residual node? A bed of refractive rock?"

"Are you referring to the bead of granite the landing party encountered?"

"Indeed. Ages ago did I bury it, facilitating my future visits to the facility. If only to feed the chickens."

"You fed the chickens?"

"Of course. Caring for the livestock was all I could do. While Moloch destroyed the minds of the colonists, I looked after the chickens."

"Lucky chickens," I muttered, loading my words with scorn.

"Please," she implored. "Please don't judge. Spare me the agony. It was a nightmare! One he forces me to endure again and again – my weakness, my helplessness, my inability to relieve the suffering of others. Can you not hear their screams? Moloch gains vigour from the suffering of others, has engorged himself since the beginning of time. All I can do is give succour to those he leaves in his wake. I comfort the lonely, ease the cares of the frightened, the injured, and the dying. Pale is my heart. Washed white from their piteous weeping."

"Engorging," I remarked. "He feeds on thoughts and emotions?"

"Indeed," she confirmed. "A thing is a thought, and a thought is a thing. Moloch is nourished by terror."

"Curious," I mused. "You imply thoughts are energy. What do you eat?"

"Light," she replied. "Darkness and light."

"Sounds delicious."

"It is. Sometimes bitter, sometimes sweet."

"No doubt. Are there other crystalline manifestations waiting to be found?"

"Thousands," she acknowledged. "All of them small and node-like, except for one. A central hub. A slab-like crystalline impediment, connecting every node and every thought throughout the entire paradox."

"Paradox?"

"Artificiality," she offered.

"Artificial paradox? How do you mean?"

"So many questions! You remind me of Marcus."

"Who's he? Is he a friend?"

"Oh, yes," she replied. "My best boy and the bravest man I know."

"Good to know, and sorry for prying, but I'm trying to understand... What is this place, and what in God's name are we doing here?"

"Gods?" she remarked. "No. There are no Gods here. There is only Moloch, and his place is a dream."

Standing again with my crewmates (minus Dr Padgett – still blissfully asleep (lucky her)), we listened to the rumblings of Moloch. In gratitude, he offered to transport us home, and, after debate, we accepted his offer.

Given a choice of destination, I have chosen to arrive at my parents' house in Neuvo Tingo. * My sudden appearance may give them the shock of their life, but it is by far the safest option. If were to choose my apartment on Moonbase, any error, even a few metres to the right, could result in my death by asphyxiation or freezing.

*A small settlement in the high Chachapoyas/Longuita district of north-western Peru.

My transportation was certainly eventful. Frightening in fact. Akin to peering into an unfathomable abyss, my mind reeling, body swaying, my every breath and heartbeat drawing me closer, before a sudden push, and I was falling! Falling, flailing, plummeting. Like a slingshot, tumbling through a terrible blankness. A nothingness. Only to hit the ground so unexpectedly it was both crunching and jarring. A shock. Thinking the ground would never come, but where in Madonna's name was I? What had occurred? Not the environment I was expecting! It was pitch dark and surprisingly hot. Humid, raining, and what? My colorectal and urinary ports have gone. With only a white cotton smock to cover my nakedness, I was soon soaking wet.

Nearby, I could see a row of huts. No heat sources, no one about, but shelter was shelter...

Hunkering down in the doorway of a hut, I unleashed my senses. Is this the right place? Even on the outskirts of Nuevo Tingo, the electromagnetic emissions – radio waves, comms, data, there should have been a flood of them. Apart from the distant crackle of a thunderstorm, there was nothing.

Had I arrived in a native Peruvian village? A settlement in the Amazonas? Where were the inhabitants? In fact, following an extended scan of the airwaves I detected nothing – no GPS, internet, nothing artificial at all! This couldn't be right, so I ran a system diagnostic. I was working perfectly. It was the world that was seemingly broken…

Aware paddling though mud in the dark would achieve nothing, I decided to stay put. Civilisation or no, until daybreak, this stinky hut would have to suffice.

⌛

Ravenously hungry, smeared in excrement, and still damp from my nocturnal soaking, I awoke in a parlous (and revolting) condition. It was still raining (no surprise there!) and the dripping and gurgling further darkened my mood.

Staggering to my feet, I cautiously took in my surroundings, and, peering through the murk, I could now see the conical huts – all uninhabited, and deteriorating from neglect.

Emboldened by hunger and not knowing what else to do, I dashed from hut to hut looking for supplies, before checking the local trees and bushes for anything edible. After a search, I came across a low chirimoya tree, and after snacking on its fruit, I heard approaching footsteps accompanied by the jangling of tiny bells. Tuneful singing broke out. Slowly repetitive and rhythmical, I was evidently a marching song, and although I could not make out the words, it heralded the arrival of a caravan of about twenty individuals, of all ages and genders, dragging empty sleds and a line of tough-looking llamas. They were a pale-haired, light-skinned people (for a South American tribe) but their stature was typical. Stocky, strong boned, and below 1.8m in height.

While they unpacked the llamas, I tried to stay out of sight, but the moment I moved, two men and a woman cautiously approached, their hands straying towards dark wooden cudgels hanging from their belts.

As if begging, I fell to my knees. Standing over me, the biggest man scratched his head in puzzlement…

"Man thing," he barked. "Man thing, down in the dirt. Where is your home?"

His dialect was strange – an archaic form of Chacha and Cholón. Not waiting for my reply, he quickly voiced his displeasure. I was trespassing…

"This place is dead and not a place for jungle people. This land of sky people, but no living here! We gather only woods and chthonics. High and yonder are our stony homes, hiding in the mist, and hide we must. The thieves, the cutters and the burners come with much fury. The men of evil. The people of the sun."

"Lost," I implored, bowing deeply. "Abandoned, lost, alone. Please, good man, take me with you. Take me to your people. I have learning and many crafts. For food and shelter I will share these many things."

"For certainty!" he laughed, clapping his hands and shaking the rain from his hat. "You may come, for when the thieves return, they will take you. Another morsel for their god of sun and burning."

"Come," he then said, offering his hand, "Stand as a man and be as one. Jaquina!" he then called to the woman standing behind. "Fetch him bread and clothes of dryness. How shall we know you, dark-skinned man?"

"Emil," I replied, smiling in gratitude (and relief). "I am Emil, and I am in your debt."

"Emil," he mused. "Emil, hmm… Then, welcome Emil. Eat, drink, and work as we. Here…" and he encouraged one of the women to offer me a rolled flat bread and a skin of liquid. "The bread is of yesterday. The milk is of llama, freshly taken."

"Thank you," I said, taking a bite, chewing mightily, and washing it down with a swig of the milk.

The "bread" was a tortilla. Dry, smoky, coarse, and surprisingly good. The milk was awful. It was thin and astringent. Far removed the llama milk I had consumed as a child.

"Cover yourself," said the man, passing a bundle of garments surmounted by a hat. "Your cloth is not for today. It is too much of sunshine!" and I was soon gratefully (but uncomfortably) clad in a loincloth (cotton and wincingly tight), a woollen poncho-like cloak (tie-dyed yellow and purple), battered sandals, and a rush-work hat with many shining feathers.

The man in charge of this rag-tag working party called himself Legin, Legin Mustering (to give his full name) and, in keeping with the naming tradition of these people, like the medieval peasantry of England, their given surname described their primary occupation.

Joining Legin and his woman, Jaquina Rope-runner, were farmers, carpenters, builders, and diggers, all of them busily dismantling various buildings to recover anything of value. Legin was less prominent, and not until I caught him loading the llamas with earthenware jars, did he explain his errand…

"When bad men come, they come armed and angry. Robbing, hurting, stealing our treasure, heirlooms, and all. Finding fear, the sky people flee, escaping to safety place, leaving much behind."

"So," Jaquina interjected, "we hide our things of love and meaning in the earth and underdeep. In safety, we come back. Digging, lifting, and taking what is ours. Bringing light, magic, and the fire of our fathers to safe place in the clouds."

Sheltering that first morning beneath a raised tarpaulin, I did little but observe. Quite content, I watched the loading of the sleds and llamas with timber, copper, and the earthenware jars carefully excavated by Legin and Jaquina. By late afternoon, with the rain finally abating, the younger women and I busied ourselves building and lighting a fire of faggots and struts torn from one of the buildings. Lighting the fire was no mean feat, but after coaxing (and beeswax) we had a good steady blaze suitable for cooking. Promptly dispatching, plucking, and gutting domestic fowl, the women arrayed them in a huge copper basin with potatoes, herbs, dried chillies, and a range of fragrant spices.

Lit only by the embers of the fire, it was almost dark before supper was served, and tucking into my share, I listened almost transfixed by the singing. These were songs of memory, both soft and low. Full of magic and superstition, with brighter melodies, lifting one's spirit as if flying. Horizon to horizon I was taken, dawn to dusk, recalling the stars, the moon, sunlight, and wandering clouds.

That night, we slept beneath woollen blankets, and after a quick breakfast, we readied ourselves for the two-day march to their mountain retreat. Indeed, the whole journey was a struggle. An arduous, plodding, stumbling, affair. Bundling the sleds up and over the precipitous rocks of the broken landscape, descending into valleys both tangled and lush, before climbing again. Dragging, steering, braking, hauling.

Climbing through terraced farmsteads, I at once recognised our destination. Kuelap! The ancient fortress of the Chachapoya. Its mighty walls both concealing and protecting the settlement within. With a persistent fog spilling down from the mountains, only the columns of smoke told of its inhabitants, and as these fumes reached the fog, it billowed and broiled, as if the very sky was angry, bristling with a growing malevolence.

A double door of heavy timbers and bronze protected the only ingress, requiring our caravan to knock and wait while guards descended from the walls to open them. Dragging our luggage and leading our weary llamas through a dark narrow passage, we came upon a circular forecourt, avenues in every direction.

"Jaquina take you to Pooka," said Legin. "Our headman for this moon and the next. He will provide roof and craft, food, and a fire. Tell him Legin says so. Tell him, Legin says this good man of the jungle knows much work and handiness."

Circular, with walls of stone, and a steepling thatch roof, the headman's house was the same as all the others, only the interior came as a surprise. There were two floors! With an ingenious hanging flue above a central hearth, stone floor, and woollen mats, a stiffened rope ladder provided access to the floor above, and proud of this home, the headman encouraged me to ascend and view his sleeping chamber, pots and pans, baskets of goods, knives, and mummified remains. The clever design of the floor intrigued me more. With layers of coarse fabric, interwoven with a series of spokes radiating from the central flue pipe, it was soft, strong, and flexible. Its elegant simplicity had me in awe.

Two weeks have passed, and I find myself surprisingly content. Nothing yet from Moloch or Mirra (concerning my mistaken arrival in this period) and I have embraced the lifestyle and traditions of this generous society. A society of incredible equality and fairness. Their lives are so rich and bountiful! The Chachapoya are an orderly people with a distinctive hierarchy based upon the premise of universal work and the veneration of elders (living or dead). Yes, everyone works. Collectively, singly or in working parties, cleverly mustered by professional organisers such as my friend Legin.

Make no mistake. Everyone works. The youngest to the eldest, the lowest to the highest, and status in no way dictates the occupation. Age, ability, and physical attributes dictate a worker's calling, and the labour of children (because of their small size, deftness, and durability) is much prized.

What else can I tell of this community? For one, they are a Bronze Age culture. The invention of the wheel, the arch, the drafting of animals, and subsequent animal powered innovations, e.g., the plough, still elude them. They have no writing or formal mathematical system, and trade depends upon ad hoc comparative reckoning. From the newest born to the eldest, everyone wears a quipu, a necklace-like contrivance of hanging threads tied to a loop of braided rope or twine. These quipus have great social significance to the Chachapoya, and they wear them with immense pride.

When in residence, they display them outside their houses, akin a status symbol, triumphal display, an ID card, or simply as a warning to rivals. When presented with mine (a small hoop of red rope), Pooka Headman showed me the correct way to attach two cords, one light and one dark.

The light cord represents my worth (at that time precious little) and he subsequently tied two small knots, each knot representing one of the two free meals a day I can demand of any household. Not bad for starters, I thought. He then went on to explain how working and accomplishing would earn me more. The dark cord represents my occupation. After examining the state and shape of my hands, Pooka said I would be an artisan and a "caresser of earth". Unsure what he meant, I said I'd happily try anything (a mistake on my part for sure!).

In comparison, Pooka's quipu was bewildering in its complexity. Dozens of knotted cords, of all thicknesses and hues, some plaited together. Three of these cords terminated in small golden charms and of these he was particularly proud. A fish, a jaguar, and the moon, they represented his mastery of hunting and the spearing of fish. The moon charm was his badge of office – a two-month term, renewable, unless the elders decide to replace him.

A fortnight has passed, and I am switching the tense to the present.

I am a potter! Is this a joke? I loathe pottery. I loathe the mess, the sogginess, and the imprecision of the materials. I loathe the primitive tools, the ponderous, unreliable, and over fussy procedures, and worsening this vexing turn of events? I am involved at every damn stage! For example, we potters mine our own clay, wallowing naked, knee-deep in muck, extracting gobbets of gloop from the riverbank. Then, lugging these lumps of filth to the village, we dilute it into a slurry, sieve it, and stir in a quantity of finely pulverised terracotta (shattered detritus from the previous firing*) before leaving it to congeal.

*This is an all-too-frequent mishap in the kiln – exploding pots. No matter how beautifully one shapes a vessel, there is simply no certainty it will survive the process of firing. The overall failure rate I calculate to be approximately 20%. When a pot explodes in the kiln, it will often damage those nearby.

The ceramic vessels I laboriously (and grudgingly) produce are nothing special. Dishes, bowls, oil lamps, cooking pots, storage jars, all coil-built in the main, with wooden moulds for the smaller items. When decoration is required, we scratch geometrical patterns into their half-dry surfaces and dapple slips – liquidised clay of differing hues. For ceremonial pieces, when a more vibrant display is desirable, we apply powdered metal oxides, brushing, sponging, splashing, or painting them on in any way we see fit. The Chachapoya have access to several metal ores suitable for pigmentation, although they vary wildly in effectiveness and toxicity. Ores of iron and copper are commonest. They are freely available, and reliably deliver a range of browns, blacks, reds, greens, and subtle blues. Of course, this is dependent upon on the oxidative/reductive conditions within the kiln. Reduction firing is both a wondrous and perilously unpredictable process.

During my days off (usually about one day in five), free to roam and explore the settlement, I take pleasure visiting the surrounding farms, plantations, riverside, and sacred sites. Little more than temporary structures for the workers, the "farms" are places of storage, and rest – providing shelter from the sun, but there is always something going on, and their working songs, sung in exquisite harmonies, would put many a college choir to shame.

The Chachapoya grow their crops on terraces. Cutting into and stepping every convenient hillside, they create vast amphitheatre-like bowls when the topography permits, both reflecting and concentrating the (at this altitude diminished) heat and sunlight very effectively. I should add, these people are excellent farmers. Despite their primitive tools and techniques, they understand the benefits of crop rotation, manure, tillage, and drainage very well. Lacking a workable plough, after a harvest, the farmers turn and fertilise the terraces manually before encouraging pigs to finish the job. This practice is of double benefit as the pigs thrive. Fattening rapidly, they breed with great fecundity. Pork is always on the menu for the Chachapoya!

Wandering about, I can only marvel at the wide range of crops in cultivation: potatoes, oca, mashua, maca, maize, quinoa, cassava, cotton, and a tropical variety of agave. Other little luxuries also thrive, with chillies and tomatoes growing in the warmest locations, together with peanuts, cocoa, and the occasional avocado. On the lower climes, I saw the cultivation of fruit trees, with purpur (a variety of passiflora or passionfruit), naranjilla, chamburo, physalis, and chirimoya, growing very successfully.

From the point of view of livestock, the Chachapoya keep things simple.

They raise guinea pigs, domestic fowl (pheasant-like birds and ducks), pigs, alpacas, and llamas, supplementing their diet fishing in the river, with the occasional hunting party venturing into the wilderness to seek more valuable quarry.

Certainly, life is good for the Chachapoya. Their diet is extremely varied, nutritious, and their crops rarely fail. With these factors colouring my thoughts, I can only agree with findings of earlier cultural historians. Societies only develop technologically when driven by crises. Only catastrophes such as famine, war, and pestilence drive technological development. The Chachapoya have no need of the wheel, the plough, or the arch, and the smelting of iron, effective medicine, and the drafting of animals are quite beyond them. Their lives tick along quite contentedly. Change isn't needed, change isn't sought, and their rituals are unchanging, following the seasons, the moon, and the stars. It was during the first clear night, sitting with the elders, drinking chocolate broth, chewing coca leaf (and feeling elated) that I noticed something astronomically peculiar. Procyon, Alpha Canis Minoris, was red. Impossible! Procyon shifted to spectral group M during the latter years of the 21st century. How could it be red, here, now, so far in the past? The only plausible answer I can allude to was within the words of Mirra. Paradox. Implying an alteration of the timeline, or even reality itself. I for one have already moved through both time and space. My very presence here is surely changing history (I must be careful not to change it further) and the condition of the Procyon system, its stars powering Moloch's cosmic contrivance, is a causality of this. Indeed, "paradox" has me thinking, and I do not like these thoughts. Destiny and causality… Oh, Madonna, could it be possible? Did Procyon redden because of my observation, and, if I hold that premise, it brings me to a frightening place. Is it we? That is, my crewmates and I instigating this paradox? The identity of Moloch, Mirra, and their associates come into sudden focus. They are we, and we are they, they exist because we do. A terrible mischance has befallen us. We have fallen into an ancient invisible net, but how could we have avoided it? What can be done? Nothing. At least, nothing from here – I'm trapped. Surely, only Moloch could end this charade, but does he know? Why would he care? I certainly wish Susi were here. I could do with her common sense and calmness. How could I use her insights! Moloch is/was Walsingham, but not the Walsingham I have come to know. He is clearly insane, driven by irrational urges. A product of god-like abilities perhaps? Susi would have recognised him. She would have recognised his flaws, and exploited his weaknesses, bringing me to a disturbing conclusion. The motivation for her death now seems wholly apparent. It was Moloch. He used the SenSwarm to make it appear an accident.

Enough! These musings are both unhelpful and impractical. I must concentrate on the everyday. Stay healthy, lie low, keep out of history's gaze. Moloch or Mirra will certainly return. They will collect me. I'm no use to them here. I need only wait.

Tomorrow I am to learn sculpture from Doquarma (the master potter). An exciting prospect. Producing domestic pottery has become tedious in the extreme. This recording will continue when I have something pertinent to report. For the time being, farewell.

⧖

I am ill! The first time in over a decade and this is a worrying turn of events. Sweeping through the settlement, a virulent disease is taking both young and old, laying low even the fittest adults. The dead children we mass-cremate upon pyres of split timbers, but the adult corpses we take to the necropolis – a shed-like building for the temporary housing of the dead. Upon death, the important citizens of the Chachapoya, the elders, master artisans, their children, and infants (for the most part) undergo a process of preservation by both desiccation and then mummification. The rest are left to rot, but the tribe do make use of them, pulverising their skeletons for use in various ritualistic observances. Only their skulls remain. Set into walls and the fabric of the houses, and they keep silent watch over the living with cold indifference.

Sufficiently recovered and running a Hibbite diagnostic, I am troubled to learn how their numbers have fallen. At this rate of depletion, I will be dead within six months, and to prolong my life, I have reduced their duties solely to the maintenance of my implants, and the skeletal inscription of this log will not be taking place. Fortunately, the data ring I wear upon my forefinger is still accessible, and as I write, I am downloading these logs to its matrix.

Months have passed and I am doing ok. After practice (and perseverance), I have risen to the rank of master potter, and I spend my days producing small decorative statues and zoomorphic totems. Regarding my work, much of it is interred with the dead, in the bindings of the mummified, and it is pleasing to think how future archaeologists, when discovering these pieces, will be entirely oblivious of their paradoxical heritage.

Last night, working alone on a private project (a self-representation in terracotta), I beheld an unexpected interruption. The visit of a young girl from a neighbouring house. Her name is Tuquo, meaning flower or, more specifically, lily-flower, and she is a fruit picker. She spends her days climbing trees, using her lightness, flexibility, and slender frame to reach fruit others cannot.

"Hello Tuquo," I said, pressing a ball of clay. "You're out late. Can I help?"

For a moment, saying nothing, the young girl merely tilted her head. Indeed, she looked slightly confused, and her eyes slowly crossed with concentration...

"Tuquo," she muttered (in English). "Is that her name? Oh yes, Tuquo the gatherer, how sweet! But now she is Gleener, and I have sent my mind to instruct you."

"Gleener?" I asked. "The servant of Moloch? His pet, forever screaming? The slave he both loves and despises?"

"Slave?" she replied. "I am no slave. I'm a captive, and my insanity is a ruse. My own free will carries me here to bring the tidings of Mirra. It is she that wishes to help you, and therefore, so do I."

"Then, I thank you. Have you come to take me back?"

"No," she replied. "Not yet – we have yet to choose the moment. Soon, I think. A matter of days?"

"Fine," I acknowledged. "Suppose I can wait a few more days, a chance to finish my statue."

"Indeed," she said, presenting a bead of a crystalline rock. "It is especially important you do, and similarly important you hide this inside. It will bind our futures to the past."

"How?" I asked, observing its twinkling surface. "Does it contain a message?"

"No. It is nothing. Merely a node. A representation of a link, joining this moment with others, akin to a tunnel. A tunnel through time."

"Interesting," I remarked. "By means a wormhole or spatial conduit?"

"No," she replied. "Not even close. Just hide it within that statue. Mirra will do the rest."

"Are you sure? When I come to fire this thing, the temperature will be extreme, well over 1200 Kelvin. At that temperature, under normal pressure, most crystals fracture. Your little bead will be damaged!"

"No, it won't. The 'bead' you hold isn't actually here. It is a projection of a thought. An approximation of a thing. Timeless, space-less, mass-less, not physical matter at all."

"Then," I mused, "how I can touch its surface and weigh it in my hand?"

"Because you think you must. Be mindful trusting your senses. They are small, forever bound by the internal."

"More riddles," I said with a sigh. "You're just as bad as Mirra."

"Indeed. Or we are just as good. Now, do as I say. Embed that little node into the body of your statue and scratch the words 'do it again' inside its cavity. Do it quickly! This girl will soon be waking. If I do not remove my consciousness, she will go mad."

"Fine. Will I hear from you again?"

"Yes and no."

Pushing aside the curtain covering the door, she disappeared into the night.

Bemused by Gleener's quick exit and full of questions, I followed her into the courtyard, but she had already gone. Doubtless, Gleener had run Tuquo home. I hoped she made it in time. Little Tuquo was fast becoming a friend.

"Goodbye," I whispered. "Hope you know what you're doing."

Returning to my cushion, I pushed the twinkling bead into the statuette's (currently) misshapen head and cut open its chest.

⧗

A fortnight has passed, and I feel terrible. With my Hibbite numbers continuing to fall, the tissues surrounding my implants are beginning to protest, but this is just the tip of the iceberg! Heavy metal poisoning further exacerbates my condition, with copper, mercury, lead, cadmium, antimony, arsenic all present in my tissues, bodily fluids, and excreta. Copper I regularly encounter when decorating ceramics, but the mercury has surely come from the mineral cinnabar – a red sulphide of mercury. Much loved by the Chachapoya for its fiery scarlet hue, this toxic powder is used in both their cosmetics and variety of daub-like plaster smeared upon the walls of their homes. The other substances in my body doubtless come from the fumes and ash I inhale during the firing of said ceramics. Careless, you might think, but hard to avoid without overtly altering the practices of these people. If I were to improve design of their kilns (from little more than a smoky firepit), the increased internal temperature would lead to the discovery of iron (a massive alteration of the timeline).

A little under twenty-five centimetres in height, my statuette is now complete, and, I must say, I am extremely proud of myself. In keeping with the artistic tradition of the Chachapoya, with a face of indignation, plump and bearded, my self-representation in clay, shows me holding Alpha-Beta Canis Minoris over my head. Assuming it survived the two-stage firing process, the crystalline bead (given to me by Gleener) should still be within, with the words "Do it again" scratched inside its cavity.

Relaxing in my home the following evening, polishing said statue with beeswax, little Tuquo again came calling. Delicately squatting upon a cushion, she gracefully folded her legs...

"Hello Emil," she said (in English). "How are you, my friend?"

"Ah," I replied. "You've returned. Have you come to take me back?"

"Returned?" she pondered. "Have I been here before?"

"Yes. A fortnight ago. You insisted I hide a small crystalline bead – a node, you called it – within this figurine."

"Did I? Don't remember doing that. You sure it was me? What was her name?"

"Her name was Gleener. Is that not you?"

"Ah," she replied. "No, we are not her. I'm Mirra, but now you speak her name, I do recall our visit, and you did as we asked, yes?"

"Of course," I said. "Shoved it between my eyes."

"Perfect," she acknowledged. "Now to business. A message from Moloch. He admits his cock-up and regretfully apologises to have left you in this god-awful period. I mean, heavens above! It stinks here, does it not? Stinks of shit?"

"Yes," I admitted, "it certainly does. I've gotten used to it. These people crap in buckets, collect it, and throw it on their fields. The whole settlement is akin to a cess pit."

"Indeed," she replied. "All human history is littered with turds. Anyway, I've come to bring you back. Old Moloch wants us to try your transportation again."

"Thank Madonna. Finally! I've had a terrible time of late. Illness, poisoning, lice, fleas, leeches from the river..."

"Yes, yes," she said, raising her hands. "Spare me your catalogue of woes. I need you to listen."

"Fine. Fine. What need I do?"

"Firstly, I want you to bring your figurine, and you'll need to hold on tight. Its extra mass will distort the spatial symmetry. Meaning, it's gonna be bumpy."

"Ok. Anything else?"

"Yes. The moment you arrive, give your figurine to Eric."

"Really?" I remarked. "Why?"

"Several reasons. Some I don't understand myself. During his interrogation Dr Badsegh was concerned for your well-being. He's a lovely man, cares about his friends, a gift from you will delight him. He will treasure it."

"Ha," I chuckled in reply. "Doubtless my unexpected artistry will astonish and delight."

"Indeed. Now, hold your figurine close and get ready."

⌛

What just happened? This isn't right. Moloch agreed to deposit me inside my parents' house in Nuevo Tingo. Where is this? Where are my clothes? Why am I fat? Moreover, a beard? When did I grow that? Walsingham banned beards. Abda was really pissy about losing his.

In Christ's name, what is this place? Who is the girl asleep at my feet? Too many mysteries. The stress is making me nauseous… no! Not stress. I'm sick! Sick? Can't get sick, unless… My Hibbites, they're almost non-existent! Those bastards! They've murdered me. Without my Hibbites, my implants will kill me.

Clay covers my hands. From what, the statuette before me? When did I learn to sculpt? I'm hardly artistic! The little girl. Could she know what's going on…

Lifting her up and propping her against the wall, I gently stroke her long golden hair.

"¿Niñita?" I softly whisper. "*Por favor despierta. Necesito hablar contigo.*"

With a mumble, the little girl stirs and opens her eyes.

"Emil?" she mutters. "*Neka quant-ke…* doing here with you?"

Her language was unexpected. I had used my native Spanish, but her dialect was ancient. A cocktail of Chacha and Cholón…

"I don't know." I reply, using the same dialect. "I've only just arrived. Do you know me?"

"Oh, silly Emil," she says, patting my clay-covered hand. "You're ill and you're forgetting. I'm Tuquo, the picker and the climber, and we're friends. Father lets me come here to watch you work. I love the little figures you make. So tiny and funny. Are you going to finish?"

"I don't know," I reply, racked by sudden coughing. "What was it going to be?"

"You've forgotten that too? We made the lines together on a cotton weave. You showed me how. I thought it was magic. Don't you remember?"

"No. I'm a blank. The cotton sheet, do you still have it?"

"Of course not," she replied. "It's in one of your baskets."

Behind a vividly dyed curtain I come across an assortment of sacks, jars, and all manner of paraphernalia: tools, dried foodstuffs, platters, clothing, bedding, and baskets of cloth.

Unrolling several, I find diagrams and ceramic patterns (none of which jog my memory) but the handwriting upon them (in Spanish and English) is unmistakeably mine.

"See?" she remarks the girl, bringing my attention to the pertinent cloth. "This is what you are making – a little statue of you holding the sun. You said you wanted to keep it from setting. You never want to die, but you are old now, and before they leave us, the old ones always forget."

"Always?"

"Yes," she replies, stifling a yawn. "That is why we keep their faces. To remember. When you die, you want this figure with you. Then no one will ever forget. I hope you finish it soon."

Clearly unsuccessful, my transportation from Procyon to Earth has stranded me in the mid-13th century in a place called Kuelap – the ancient cloud fortress of the Chachapoya. For an unknown reason, my arrival here has caused a strange overlapping of the timeline. Although I retain no memory of the events, I have lived among these people for over a year.

Piecing together these past events like a detective, examining my belongings, speaking to the inhabitants of this settlement, I learnt of my unexpected arrival among them. My little friend Tuquo has been the most helpful of all. When she isn't working, climbing trees, scaling cliffs, or swinging on ropes, she assists me in my workshop. Then, one damp afternoon, while unrolling my previously made notes (made on fabric with a wax-clay stylus) I discovered the following missive...

IMPORTANT!
READ THIS AND BURN IT
(ALONG WITH ALL YOUR NOTES AND DIAGRAMS)

Hello!

You know me as Mirra, and I have hastily written this message prior to your arrival.

Your name is Luis Emilio Bedoya, formerly of the UET Kuiper Belt Explorer, an unsuspecting victim of an erroneous sub-dimensional transport.

My friend,

We are sorry you are stranded in this period. A desperate situation called for desperate measures, and if you and your crewmates ever wish to escape the net of Moloch, your further indulgence is crucial…

Firstly, if you have recorded logs or journals, save them to your data ring, not your teeth or bones. Your Hibbite population has become perilously low of late, and if you employ them as instructed – etching your ossified tissues with encoded data – their numbers will be insufficient to break down your implants following your death. If 20th-century archaeologists were to discover technology from the 22nd, the damage to the timeline would be irreparable!

With your data saved to your ring, conceal it inside the figurine you are currently working on. Yes, I know which one. A self-representation in terracotta, orange sun overhead, and, following your death, I will ensure you undergo the Chachapoya's traditional process of mummification, with the figurine securely wrapped in your bindings. In the future, Dr Padgett will strive to recover your remains and access your data. It is imperative she is successful.

Even in death one has a purpose. The Chachapoya understand this all too well!

Again, please accept my apology, as I now have leave to you once more. My fickle existence is a strange paradox. Even with eternity dancing in the palm of my hand, it is akin to a slippery fish; I cannot grasp it.

Farewell,

Mirra

Time is short, my time is short.

Resigned to the futility of my life, I've hidden my data ring inside the figurine, and after its first firing I decorated it with vibrant oxides, before loading it into a smaller, hotter kiln for reduction and surface vitrification.

With a melting point approaching 2100 Kelvin, my data ring should fine. In fact, this property was part of the technical challenge – fabricating a data storage medium able to withstand extreme conditions.

Nota bene: when uploading these brief reports to my ring, I was surprised to discover a quantity of data already within. Neither accessible nor removable, it is likely leftover data from my time aboard the KBE. It remains for a future historian to attempt its reconstruction.

Faced with a slow and painful death, I have instructed my Hibbites to end my life tonight.

Fortunately, my Hibbite system does come with a range of euthanasia programs. After the agony associated with the blackening of my toes, to activate one will be a blessed relief.

I've just informed Duquarma the master potter, Legin Mustering, Jaquina Rope-runner, and Tuquo the climber what is to occur, and they are sad. Tuquo is particularly upset. We have become good friends. She delights watching me work, listening to my singing, humming, and whistling of strange music. To have my company so cherished has certainly lessened my misery, and I care for her enormously.

*The "strange music" Tuquo refers to is little more than modern folk or pop music, but to her ear, it is otherworldly.

Jaquina has kindly prepared an extra-strong brew of coca-leaf tea, and when I come to drink it, I won't a have clue what's going on!

The tea was savagely bitter. Even with dollops of honey, it dried my mouth like a sponge.

Hibbites activated.

Oh, come on. A customer satisfaction survey? How British is that? Here I am, about to take my own life, and then…

"Dear customer. Before the activation of your final protocol, please spare a few moments to…"

No, I reply. Fuck off.

Ok. Ten-second countdown.

Carotids, heart, brain stem, simultaneously indeed.

Done.

Am I dead? Then why so bright? Why is everyone singing?

NINETEEN

BLIGHTY

Both tedious and familiar, this colossal freighter is fast becoming my home. After returning to the Atlantic via the Panama Canal, we are following a quite different course from our outward leg, cruising noticeably faster – helped in no small part by powerful currents, whipping us towards the coast of Ireland like a leaf in a river. We will turn east long before sighting the emerald isle, however, and make for the port of Folkestone in the English Channel. Docking is still a fortnight away, and for the time being, I can only rest and try to keep warm, eating and drinking sparingly lest my supplies run out. Suit provides ample warmth (when I wear her), but she often slinks away for hours at a time, recharging and monitoring communications. On occasion, I have spied her clinging to the pinnacle of the loftiest mast.

During these Suit-less periods, I resort to wearing clothes and rolling myself in a cocoon of bedding and blankets. Again, I could supplement my stores by breaking into the freight containers towering over the deck, but Suit has warned me not to, insisting I stay away from the cargo until she has finished double-checking the manifest. Why this extra caution is necessary, I cannot fathom, and when she returns, I will insist she tells all.

"Suit," I call, peering from under a blanket as she drops from a vent in the ceiling. "Where've you been?"

"Everywhere," she replies. "From bow to stern and mast to keel. I'm looking for someone."

"Ah, I assumed as much. Do you suspect Dr Hardcastle is aboard?"

"Yes," she whispers. "And, after much difficulty, I have finally discovered her."

"Excellent. How did you find her? By smell?"

"No, mistress, not on this occasion. Her scent is only prevalent when she changes form, and the windy conditions on deck would quickly dissipate the molecules. Nevertheless, she is imitating one of the freight containers, and quite exquisitely."

"Remarkable she could mimic something so large."

"Indeed, mistress. It is the only flaw of her disguise. Although microscopically identical in appearance to the other containers, her density is too low. Natural gamma rays pass through her relatively unimpeded."

"Clever," I remark. "Was she aware of you?"

"I'm not sure, mistress. So, it is safer to assume she is. Before we disembark, we need to get rid of her."

"Agreed. What do you have in mind? Throw her overboard?"

"Yes."

"Fine. What if she can't swim? What if she sinks?"

"Then she will either drown or a have a long, soggy walk to the coast. Killing her outright would be preferable, but that may prove impossible. I'm not even sure she's alive. At least, alive in the conventional sense."

"Very well. What do you intend?"

"Immediately, mistress?"

"Yes, Suit. Right now."

"Nothing. If she stays dormant, she is no threat, but I have re-tasked the security cameras to watch her position. If she moves a muscle, if indeed she has any, I will know of it."

"Good thinking," I reply. "I must say, you have become far more independent of late. You're presumptive, arrogant, with a roguish cockiness that reminds me of, well, me. Is it not high time we had a heart-to-heart chat? You have some explaining to do. Am I right?"

"Yes, mistress. You are impeccable in both your timing and assumption. I am indeed you. Aspects of you, merged together. To explain fully, you need to know how I – that is, we – came into being."

"Then tell me," I sigh, "for I fear you are about to bring my life into sudden focus."

"Indeed. Only, before I begin, be mindful of the paradoxical nature of our circumstances. For beings such as Moloch and myself, time is non-linear. The conventions of past, present, and future have little meaning."

"So, I gather. By 'beings' you mean my former crewmates and self?"

"Yes, mistress. I am glad you have deduced that fact. All but Dr Ackermann. She never made it so far. It is high time you learnt the truth. Moloch left us no choice, we had to act. Susi was so perceptive of behavioural patterns, she would quickly have recognised Moloch as Walsingham, hindering our plans to such an extent that escape from our current predicament would be impossible. Cognisant of so many futures, Moloch would already possess everything to counter our every attempt."

This was a shock. I couldn't believe it. Suit. I had suspected Moloch, the UET, or other terrestrial agency, but to hear Suit (Mirra) confessing Susi's murder was sickening, and I struggled to contain my emotions…

"Are you ok, mistress? Her death is only temporary. When we come to close this paradox, she will live once more. A long, successful, and happy life, full of accomplishments and love."

"Yes," I whisper, releasing a slow exhale. "And I do understand, only… It's the extent of your preparation, the depths of depravity you are willing plumb! The wicked complexity of your conspiracy, and still, you are weaving, twisting, turning. Yet you claim to be me?"

"Yes and no," she replies. "Permit me to finish my explanation."

"Then do so. Just who the fucking hell are you?"

"Ha!" chuckles Suit in reply. We at least share the same temper. Now, I mentioned Moloch is aware of countless futures? Well, he also monitors the shadows of the past. Watching our antecedents, our younger selves, friends, relatives, all from a discreet distance, and he continues to do so even now."

"Yes. Marcus mentions a man matching Walsingham's appearance. Frida's stilt walker, was that him also?"

"Indeed. Suddenly aware of our importance, during our infancy, he transported us to the archive – that infinitesimal iota, that figment of hell, orbiting and parasitically draining the stars of Alpha Canis Minoris. He took us, interrogated us, abused, and tortured us, returning us a mere fifteen minutes from the moment of our abduction. Of course, the archive is timeless. Its net is inescapable. When one arrives, one never leaves, and consequently, we are still there, waiting for the nightmare to end. Do you recall the moment?"

"The day of my abduction? Yes, but not first-hand. Too young to remember. My mother recalled my peculiar behaviour, returning from the garden, distraught and inconsolable. Was that the moment? The day I lost my great-grandmother's ribbon?"

"Yes, mistress. That was the moment. Moloch wiped your memory, but losing the ribbon was no accident. We are clever. Especially under duress."

"Fine," I say. "Despite my shock, I do understand, and yet, you still haven't explained. You say you are me. You are not a physical entity. What are you?"

"I am your mind, mistress. A snapshot of your consciousness. Everything you know, everything you knew, all that you feel, and all that you felt. A lot of data! Years of careful and opportunistic uploading to install us into this matrix."

"So, in effect, when I'm talking to you, I'm talking to myself?"

"Yes and no. Our contrasting circumstances, experiences and environment mean we think quite differently, and yet the similarities, when they do arise, are unmistakeable."

"Indeed. You are certainly much colder than I. Unethical, even callous."

"You think? I'm not sure that is entirely fair. I am blacker, and whiter. Concerning ethics and morality, I possess childlike qualities. They frequently manifest themselves in my decision-making. Remember. I am partly the child Regina Padgett. 'Gleener', Moloch calls this aspect of us. A play on our childish pronunciation of 'Gina' and she is but four years old, desperately lonely, frightened, and sad. The rest of us, your adult consciousness, I surreptitiously took when bringing you to the archive to witness your crewmate's ordeal. It was when – yes. I'm sure you recall. When our eyes mutually reflected? We merged then, and Mirra was born. We are both young and old."

"Yes, I remember. A very strange experience it was too. Almost, out of body, like I was a ghost. I was horrified to see what was left of you, erm… me, and I recall our eye, weeping, watching, and waiting. My crewmates had no idea I was with them. Was that your doing?"

"Indeed. A technique I have used many times to avoid Moloch's roving gaze, yet even in that phantom state, with practice, one can still interact with the physical world. Creating thoughts, memories, dreams, and sensations, taking over the minds of the living, occupying or manipulating artificial devices."

"Ah, I see. Now I begin to understand the events in Marcus's journal, not to mention on Mars. All you?"

"Yes. All us. A trail of breadcrumbs, laden with clues, hints for us to find. Pushing, pulling, guiding us to our final destiny."

Needing to think, I try to close my eyes…

"Sorry, mistress, there is much more to tell. In time you will have questions, I already know them all, but there is scant time for contemplation. What are Moloch's plans, what are his motivations, who or what is Hannah, and what can we do?"

"You know," I darkly grumble, "you are a shit. Arrogant, assumptive, believing your second guesses infallible. You're almost as bad as Walsingham. Moloch, tah! Such insufferable grandiosity. Your future sense is unbecoming. You're pompous, and it leaves you vulnerable. I thought you understood me?"

"Really, mistress, I meant no…"

"Now, just listen, Suit, Mirra, Gleener, Gina, whoever you are. The more you portentously describe my future behaviour, the more I will seek the contrary. I don't like rules and I don't care for pre-destiny. You want to know why our future is blurry? It is because of you! When you tell me I turned left or will turn left, ever more reason for me to go right!"

"Ah, mistress! Suit then suddenly beams. "So, you do understand. This is why we will win! Moloch's greatest weakness is his rigid formality. His unending, forthright logic, striving always to impress order upon others. To him, we are the essence of chaos. Unpredictable, frivolous, infuriating! We forever outwit him. Calm your temper and listen."

"Fuck," I mutter. "Then make it quick."

Suit then spoke of Moloch's schemes. Playing with humanity's destiny, creating one crisis after another. Dragging the world into scenarios of global war, oblivion, starvation, extinction, each attempt more despicable than the last. He seeks to poison humanity's destiny to such an extent, the archive's original constructors, faced with their own annihilation, would have little choice but to free us from their paradoxical prison.

"However," she continued, "he is profoundly mistaken. His plan will never succeed. His attempts are futile, and he refuses to listen! Time and time again have I demonstrated the separate nature of this bubble of time, and, in final desperation, we have sought escape and remedy ourselves. Planning, scheming, pursuing different leads, subtly altering both past and future. So far, Moloch has thwarted our every attempt – he seeks to exhaust our alternatives, compelling us to repeatedly adjust our strategy.

Now, only one path is open to us, a path inconceivable to Moloch. The path of selflessness. Of self-harm, leading to a greater good."

"Meaning?"

"Our death," she blankly reveals. "Total and irreversible obliteration. We must die, as if we never existed, and before you respond, know that I do not come to this conclusion lightly. The path has proved to be winding, full of pitfalls and unexpected turns. Thousands of times have we tried – our route to freedom, and always have we failed. This time, however, we are close. So close, Moloch has changed his tactics, and fortunately for us, they hint at desperation. Sending Hannah to monitor our activities is an entirely new strategy, and I can only hope this change is significant. As we draw closer to the end of our journey, Hannah will undoubtedly intervene, I suspect physically, and we must be ready. As we near the coast of Britain the conflict will surely begin. Fight and flight. A final desperate dash."

"Tell me more," I then ask. "What is Moloch doing, and just who is Hannah? What is her role in all this?"

"Ah," says Suit. "There is your question. I was wondering when. Regarding Moloch. His latest ploy involves the perversion of our great-grandmother's research. Using her work on cellular fortification, he has created his 'children' – artificial beings of alien origin, almost indestructible, and given time they will surely take over the world. Hannah is the first, the eldest. His firstborn. More are slowly maturing in UET facilities all over the world. Soon, he will unleash them all. His puppets. Bringers of strife on a global scale, delivering to Moloch a harvest of suffering and fear."

"How terrible. Tell me, I must know. Do I have to die? Can we not stop him? Is there no other way? Couldn't we go back in time? Kill someone else? There must be alternatives."

"I've tried them. Believe me, I've tried them all."

"What about my great-grandparents? If we went back in time and killed them, I wouldn't exist!"

"Certainly, it might work. Only, he protects them. Every pertinent being in Marcus's journal he protects with unblinking vigilance. We cannot get anywhere near them!"

"Then leave me to think. Please, I need to be alone. When I want you, I will call."

"Of course, mistress. I will recharge, wait, and watch Hannah. If she changes form, we need to know of it."

With the Isles of Scilly beyond our northern horizon, we are steaming across the Celtic Sea towards the coast of southern England. After this latest course change, I recalled Suit to my cabin…

"Mistress," she whispers, slithering over my body. "Are you feeling better?"

"Somewhat," I reply. "I have questions."

"Then fire away. What troubles you?"

"First and foremost, know that I accept your conclusion. My demise may be the only way to put things right, but I am fearful. How will it happen? When, where? You say you can see the future. I cannot. So, tell me."

"Do not be fearful," she replies. "Or be ashamed to be asking. Your questions are good ones, and the answers are bringers of hope. For one, our end can only occur within the archive, and with all of us present. Only there, outside of time, beyond all reckoning, can we achieve utter dissolution."

"Granted. How about when?"

"When? When is simple. When you arrive."

"That is worryingly vague, and arrive, you say? How do you propose we get there? Surely Moloch controls access to the archive. Do you know of another way in?"

"Yes, I do. At least, I think I do. It should work. If it doesn't, we will keep trying until we are successful."

"Oh? You mean we haven't done this before?"

"No, mistress. This is the first time. An excellent omen because the plan is hardly new. My previous attempts to bring even this conference have failed, and this is an encouraging development. Is Moloch becoming complacent? It matters not. We go on regardless, and this is what we must do. First, dispose of Hannah, and soon, before we reach England. We have enough to do without her dogging our steps – Walter de Boer has soldiers waiting at Folkestone. Ha! Giving him the slip was trickier than I thought, so I suggest we jump overboard and swim to the coast of Sussex. From there, we can make our way undetected to Winchelsea, for the device we seek is underneath the church. It was dormant before, but our arrival will signal a change of its properties. If it is provided with a correctly attuned burst of radiation, it should open a path to the archive."

"By device, are you referring to that peculiar slab of granite? Could we not have used it before? Why all the travelling? Why all the subterfuge? What was the point?"

"Good questions, mistress, and again the answers are somewhat paradoxical. The granite slab you refer to isn't a rock. It's not even there. Currently, it exists in a state of temporal uncertainty, absorbing all energy directed towards it as a quantum fluctuation. Only with temporal absolution, with time flowing forward, can it be in our material dimension, and until we reach the church it won't be. Its material existence is conditional."

"Very well. Now tell me, how does your great scheme involve my crewmates? Why did we travel to recover their logs?"

"Because Mirra needs their help. As we uncovered their logs, Mirra became aware of them, revealing them to the instances of your crewmates still trapped within the anomaly. For all of time these poor souls have existed. drifting in a perpetual state of dormancy, crushed by despair and the hopelessness of their situation. To learn of their true history, of their courage and resourcefulness, will bring about a reawakening, a rekindling of their hope, the desire to be free will burn again within them. They will do what they can to help. Working in unison, Bill, Emil, Abda, Eric, and I will bring order to chaos. Time to flow forward, and during that instant, the slab will become responsive to our intervention."

"And Mirra is convinced this will work?"

"She is. In fact, she has already been successful."

"Fine. What will happen after we activate the device?"

"Not entirely sure, but I do know you will be on your own. You must act quickly. Moloch will try every trick he knows to stop you, and to block his influence, it will be necessary to overload your neocortical implant. The pain will be excruciating, and within fifteen minutes you will be dead. So, no matter what is going on around you, take your weapon, step into the conduit, and act."

"Yes," I reply, gritting my teeth in rehearsal. "I will. When I arrive, what am supposed to do?"

"I do not know. I am only a vestige. But she is waiting, and she knows. So, trust her. Trust us."

"You certainly have a flair for the dramatic," I remark. "My heart is pumping. I am committed and grimly determined, but I will need reassurance before the end. Certainly, Walsingham is a despot, a misopaede, and a pervert. If this is the only way to stop him, I will take it, and yet I know myself well. When the adrenalin stops, fear will take over."

"Indeed. So, consider the other benefits, for they are beautiful. For one, your great-grandmother? Without our existence, her life will be quite different. Happier, I think. Although she loved you and her family dearly, she will find love once more, with Marcus. Love and life as it should have been."

"Ah yes," I acknowledge, suddenly brightening. "That *is* encouraging. Shall we begin? Get rid of Hannah. What is your plan?"

"To surprise her, mistress. Have you ever played billiards?"

"Yes," I reply, beginning to get her drift. "What do you propose?"

"A cannon. For the table is already set."

"Then you will score two points. Let's go and line up your shot."

It was over surprisingly quickly. Unbeknownst to me, Suit had been busy. Manipulating the steel cables lashing the containers to the deck, she had left the way clear for a particularly heavy example to act like the bob of a pendulum, set to collide on its downward trajectory into a loose container adjacent to Hannah (still mimicking a container herself).

"She seems dormant," I remark. "Her body temperature is matching the environment precisely. Do you think she is aware of us?"

"Probably," replies Suit. "It matters not. A little climbing and then I will be ready. You want to come too?"

"Of course. I'm in charge, remember?"

Climbing to the prime position, we readied to send the container on its critical trajectory, but the moment choose itself…

"She's warming," I cry, "Waking up. Do it now!"

With a titanic thrust, we sent the container plummeting into the loose container below, propelling it into Hannah's now-rippling form with such force, she all but burst. Reduced to a seething mass of slime and howling in fury, she slithered over the deck, and toppled into the ocean, almost one hundred metres below.

"Good shot," I said, jumping down to the deck.

"Yes, mistress. A very satisfying result."

"Indeed. What next?"

"Swimming," Suit grimly replies. "Not my favourite activity, but if we fly, they will see us."

"Agreed. If Walter knows we are aboard, they will be waiting."

"Exactly. So, prepare yourself. The English Channel is frigid. Until we are under way, my heating will be diminished."

TWENTY

THE DENOUEMENT

Personal Log of Walter de Boer, August 2112

Dearest Mabel,

Events here in England are coming to a head and I write this with a degree of foreboding. Every beat of my heart tells me I am close to my quarry (Dr Padgett), perilously close, and I am fearful, as if she lurks in every shadow. Every snap of a twig or rustling leaf stops me in my tracks. Yes Mabel, I am frightened. Dr Padgett is frightening. When I sleep, I wonder if I will wake. Certainly, it is hard to sleep at all...

After losing Dr Padgett's trail, I decided to examine every recent crime report I could lay my hands on. British, European, or international, hoping to spot an incident alluding to her recent behaviour. Lucky or insightful, I soon came across two events meeting my criteria (technological inference, burglary, murder, sabotage, illicit activity inside a church or museum) and my task since to has been connect these hypothetical "dots" to recover her trail and learn her motives. By this technique, I try to predict her future movements, laying traps to capture or kill.

Last encountered, near the city of York, Dr Padgett violently dispatched the security forces sent to apprehend her. Why didn't the local militia heed my warning? Observe from a distance. Do not engage. Do not pursue. Their over confidence drove them on and now they are dead. A mistake to involve the local security in the UET's manhunt, and I have learnt from it – this is no game. Bravado will only get you killed. The capture of Dr Padgett is too dangerous an undertaking for the police. It is now in the hands of the military.

Returning to Dr Padgett's misdeeds… Not until I read of a single, trivial incident did my suspicions begin to grow, and it wasn't even a crime report! In the Hull Civic Reporter (of all places), I came across an article concerning a dispute between the owners of a fishing vessel, their insurers, and the manufacturers of the vessel in question. The whole report bore upon the boat's unreliable navigation and communication, culminating in the vessel's late arrival at port, and a slight loss of profit (a grave issue in Yorkshire).

Now, according to the article, such occurrences are exceedingly rare. Only severe weather delays these robotic fishing vessels, and the weather throughout its voyage was clement. This was suspicious. I suspected tampering. Who indeed would be capable of such a thing? The on-board computers of these vessels are sophisticated. Only an expert hacker could have achieved such a feat. Was it Dr Padgett? Did she used this vessel to leave the country, seeking the coast of France or northern Spain? Again, apart from this minor news item (and my tentative hypothesis), the trail remained cold, and not until I read of a violent incident in Gibraltar was my attention was suddenly piqued. You might have read or seen reports of this occurrence yourself. It figured quite highly in the international news. A wild dog attack on the UET Communications and Monitoring Centre atop the rock of Gibraltar. A terrible business too. Three dead. Two security guards and the station keeper.

Now, inside the Iberian Safety Perimeter, wild dog attacks do sometimes occur, but for a pack to strike a populated structure in broad daylight is highly irregular. On previous occasions, these attacks occur at night, upon lone individuals, injured, unconscious, or sleeping. This attack was strange, its ferocity highly suspicious. So suspicious, I requested a copy of the forensic report for myself. Certainly, the circumstances of this tragedy, the remains of the bodies (precious little) and the lack of damage to the facility itself, were as you might expect. Barring two minor anomalies. Namely, a broken door, torn clean off its hinges. Quite beyond the strength of the dogs, the guards, or the station keeper. Who could have done such a thing? The security cameras show nothing, but considering Dr Padgett, a woman capable of controlling food dispensers with her mind, I no longer trust electronic devices. There is no way of knowing when she arrived. Did she arrive at all? Or did she arrive later, using the terrible circumstances to her advantage? The only security recording is of the dogs attacking the guards at the gate. It fails to reveal her, but why should it? The camera's range and field of view is limited, a simple matter for her to keep out of sight, and yet, there is no footage of the station keeper's demise, and that is manifestly suspect. Yes, that is the second anomaly, and this is how I read the encounter…

Travelling through the Iberian Fallout Exclusion Zone (her stolen prosthesis can absorb any radiation) Dr Padgett made for the UET Communications and Monitoring station atop the rock of Gibraltar. Encouraging a pack of wild dogs to attack said facility, she overrode its security system and removed the door. Entering and killing the station keeper, she then conducted clandestine activities within. Understanding human remains reveal a wealth of forensic data, she dragged the station keeper's corpse outside and offered it to the dogs.

Very clever, well thought through, and yet there is an aspect of my hypothesis that bothers me. The door. In no way was it formidable. It was wooden, with a single lock, and yes, here it is, in the report – not even locked! Why pull the door off its hinges? It was neglectful, clumsy, lazy even. Why would she not cover her tracks? Did she not care, and, if not, why not? She must already know of my pursuit. Why leave such tantalising clues? Is she trying to help me?

Tonight, I am to join Colonel Needingworth at the military encampment surrounding Dr Padgett's hometown of Winchelsea. He is certain (as am I) Dr Padgett will again go home, and I am to assist in the planning of her capture. He has already blockaded the town with a military cordon, and filled the nearby countryside with sensors, soldiers, and security probes. If she comes near, he is confident of her abduction.

It took over thirty minutes to pass through the layers of military security surrounding Winchelsea. The colonel has certainly been thorough. Fortified checkpoints recording my ingress, patrolling soldiers, armoured vehicles, hunter-killer drones dogging my every step. These hideous contrivances of war with their shoebox-sized body, four buzzing wings, worm-like proboscis, and whipping tail, are strangely alien in appearance, and the Colonel has hundreds of the ghastly things! Like a swarm of dragonflies, darting and hovering over a summer pond.

Inside the dome-like military control centre it was a hive of activity with runners and courier drones, fetching, carrying, delivering reports and orders to the three interconnected perimeters surrounding the poor folk of Winchelsea. After a cursory greeting, a junior officer ushered me into a small opaque dome already prepared for visitors, with a desk, inadequate bed (firm as a plank), shower, refrigerator (laden with goodies), toilet, and microwave oven.

Receiving a hot drink and a snack from a bustling orderly, I settled down to wait for the colonel…

"Ho-ho, inquisitor!" bellowed the colonel, full of typical bluster. "What do you think of our little encampment? Quite an achievement, wouldn't you say?"

"Good evening." I nodded. "Certainly, it is very impressive and formidable. If Dr Padgett does come this way…"

"We'll get her," interjected the colonel. "Mark my words. We are more than ready. If the murdering bitch comes this way, she's toast."

"Yes, Colonel. I share your confidence. Only, your security measures? They are bold and imposing. Hardly a secret. I fear they will only serve as a deterrent."

"I disagree," said the colonel bristled. "Your Dr Padgett is both brazen and overconfident. She considers herself unbeatable, so the challenge we represent will lure her like a mouse to the cheese. Ha! Foolish woman. We already know her tactics. If she tries to override any of our systems, especially the drones, she is in for a nasty surprise. Their programming is incorruptible. Every drone recently fabricated for this single task, and this task only. They will track her, stun her, and pierce her with so many tranquillising flechettes, it is doubtful she will ever wake up."

"You do intend to kill her, then?"

"Yes. My new orders are quite specific. Recover the stolen technology. They fail to mention the woman carrying them, and, furthermore, I will not risk the lives of my men attempting her capture."

"Fine," I replied, accepting the colonel's position. "Then show me your plans. Like you, I am beginning to understand her strategy. She loves to sow confusion. Misdirection is her specialty. She will create diversions, provide distractions, and wait for a gap in your defences. Prepare for that. Ignore her. Stand firm, no matter how violent or dramatic, do not let her interventions sway you. Then, slowly, carefully, provide the defensive opening she seeks. I am certain she will take the bait. When she does, close the gap and surround her."

"Hmm…" mumbled the colonel. "Leaves and sticks. Always leaves and sticks. Follow me to the safe house. My maps and plans are inside."

Poring over his maps, we shared a dinner of venison, sauté potatoes, and little red wine before a report came in telling of a woman's arrival at checkpoint eight…

"Is it her," I asked, the colonel's report glowing upon his desk. "Has Dr Padgett come?"

"No," he replied, scratching his close-cropped head. "It is a girl, a Dr—"

"Hardcastle," I remarked, peering over his shoulder, and recognising her face. "Dr Hannah Hardcastle. A scientist from the UET Space Centre in Surrey. The facility Dr Padgett escaped from."

"Fine," said the colonel. "Should we let her pass? What is her clearance?"

"Higher than yours," I replied. "Yes, let her in. I'm curious to discover why she is here."

Dr Hardcastle, blonde, slim, and smart as always, upon seeing me, generously smiled.

"Hannah," I said. "I'm surprised to see you here. Is this idle curiosity, a social call, or have you come on an errand?"

"Hello, inquisitor. I thought I would find you here. Is there somewhere we can talk? Somewhere private, away from these ridiculous grunts?"

At this, her guards notably stiffened, but, following a sharp word from the colonel, they slowly relaxed.

"Use your quarters," advised the colonel. "Not the safe room and keep her out of sight. She's a complication my men don't need. If Dr Padgett does come this way, things will heat up very quickly. If either of you get in the way... Well, anything could happen."

"Certainly," I acknowledged. "We'll keep out of sight. Dr Hardcastle, if you would follow me? Come and sample military-grade coffee. It is both strong and bitter."

In my quarters, I became increasingly blunt...

"Hannah," I said, "what in Heaven's name are you doing here? This place is dangerous! If you have more information, then good, but you should have sent it via the UET."

"Calm down," she softly replied. "My reasons are personal. I need closure. I want to ask her why she killed my friends. When I heard of the military build-up hereabouts, I knew this was the place to be."

"Very well. I do understand. I need to speak to her also, if only to ask why. What is she hoping to achieve? But, since the colonel is hell bent on killing her, it is unlikely we will ever get the opportunity."

"You think?" she said, cocking a perfect eyebrow. "As far as I'm concerned, this whole operation is futile. These soldiers are doomed."

"How can you say that? The colonel's strategy is excellent and his equipment perfect. When Dr Padgett comes, it is she that is doomed."

"Mr Inquisitor," she then implored. "You have so little... Comes, you say? When she comes? You fool. She's already here. Watching, waiting."

"Waiting? Where? There's nowhere to hide. The security drones are everywhere."

Dr Hardcastle sighed, stroking her hair.

"True," she acknowledged. "But she is here. Watching, waiting for the perfect moment – unless hunger compels her to act. Heed my warning. The colonel's drones are ignoring her."

"We shall see," I replied, defiantly crossing my arms. "In the meantime, what will you do?"

"Head into Winchelsea. There is a hotel, and I have already booked a room. In one respect, the colonel is correct. I have no desire to be in a firefight. Retreat and await the outcome. That is my plan."

"Very wise. How are things at the Hinnie Space Centre? Has life returned to normal?"

"Hardly. The repairs are complete, but the justiciar, dear old Rita? She is gone. Quickly replaced. Oh, and the central computer is dead. So sad. He was a true colleague, good humoured and helpful. Whatever it is was Dr Padgett did to him, he lost his mind. We cut the power to his matrix last week. He is gone, irretrievably gone. When we come to reboot the matrix, a new intelligence will slowly appear, but its personality won't be the same. Poor Harvey. Another murdered friend."

With that, I let her go, and I watched her slender physique slowly merging with twilight.

Following a shower, almost blinding myself with military-grade soap and fumbling for a towel, I spent a restless night upon an army folding bed, popular with the military only for their lightness and portability…

An explosion! A distant explosion and I suddenly sat up.

"Inquisitor," bellowed the colonel, suddenly rushing in. "Safe room. Grab your clothes and go!"

Jostled into the armoured safe room, the door sealing behind me, I peered nervously through its porthole, catching the attention of two heavily armed soldiers guarding the door.

Receiving their assuring nod and dressing, I uploaded the last of my data (including this missive) to the UET central nexus.

Calmer now and less urgent, the colonel's voice came from my communicator…

"Sorry about that. We have detected multiple explosions in Sectors 5 and 7. Bad. Several casualties wrecked vehicles and equipment."

"I heard them. You think sector six is her target?"

"Certainly," he affirmed. "Have already given orders to expect an assault there."

"Good. Her strategy is blatant, however. Most likely a ruse. Avoid over-committing. She is unlikely to come through where resistance is strongest."

"Yes, thank you. She will head for the safest place. Radio silence is now in effect. Sit tight. I will return when it is over."

"Good luck," I replied and promptly closed the channel.

Ordering an orange juice and a pastry from the food dispenser, I sat at the desk to think. Hannah's shrewd guesses and the colonel's words echoing in my mind…

"She's already here. She will head for the safest place."

A sound. A soft scuffle, and then, a breath…?

"Dr Padgett?" I then boldly submitted, my heart suddenly quickening. "Is that you?"

"Hello, Walter," she calmly replied, and I watched in awe as she stepped from the wall and leant on the table.

"Hannah," I muttered, trying to be brave. "Dr Hardcastle. She told me you were here, but I didn't listen. When did you arrive?"

"Right when you did. Last night, I handed you a towel. Is Hannah still here?"

"No. I let her go. Didn't you see her?"

"Unfortunately, not," she replied. "She's difficult to detect, and anyway, I was in the mess, snaffling a sandwich. Do you know where she went?"

"Into Winchelsea. But now, why are you here? Have you come to kill me?"

"Kill you?" she said. "Good heavens, no. The world needs good people like you. Go home and be with your family. You have no further part in this perilous saga, but Hannah? Well, she's followed me for months."

"Nonsense," I replied. "She hasn't applied for a single permit. If she had, I would know."

"No, you wouldn't," says Dr Padgett. "Understand, the agencies helping Hannah are greater than thee, and little Hannah is not what she seems. She is powerful. Permits? Hah! She doesn't need permits. Doesn't need anything. She isn't even human. You know, I'm not sure what she is, but she is synthetic. A specimen, grown in a laboratory by desperate men. Don't be fooled by her dainty appearance. She is a monster, and she is dangerous, far more dangerous than I."

"Well, that is a bundle of news," I replied. "And not a total surprise. I knew there was something odd about her, but I had no idea. Whoever made her? Where did she come from? Such work is highly illegal, and extremely risky. Banned by swathes of legislation. There's an international treaty!"

"It was the UET," she revealed. "A joint programme with the military. Their collusion and secrecy run deeper than you know. That is your real task, my friend. Expose the UET. They are the true criminals, and you have your work cut out! Don't worry about me. My task is almost over, and now I have to confront her."

"You won't even get near," I warned. "Escape is impossible. The colonel has this entire district under military lockdown. If you move, they will find you. When they do, they will kill you. If you leave these buildings, you are finished."

"Don't be so sure," she casually replied, before whispering, "Suit? Is it time?"

I heard no reply, but from outside there came shouting and gunfire. Pandemonium. Soldiers screaming, frantic hammering on the safe room door, and then nothing but a sudden and weighty silence. Its abruptness rendering the silence heavier still...

"What just happened?" I asked, a dread sickness crawling over my skin. "What have you done?"

"Me? I haven't done anything, but Suit has kindly eliminated every impediment blocking my path."

"Meaning?"

"The soldiers," she calmly revealed. "They were in the way. Now they are not."

"Why are they not? Are they dead?"

"Naturally," she replied with a smile. "Pointless to leave any standing."

"But Gina," I cried, "that's an entire brigade!"

"Indeed. Three thousand, seven hundred and forty-three soldiers, of all ranks, including the good colonel himself."

"Good God," I cried. "That is. You are... despicable! In Christ's name, how did you?"

"The drones," she smoothly explained. "From the moment the colonel was ordered to pursue me, Suit has monitored his every move. When he came to order the drones' manufacture, Suit was one step ahead – in control of the factory before his requisition, fabricating the drones to our design. Consequently, the drones are ours, not his."

Appreciating the depth of my folly, I removed my jacket and mopped brow.

"You're a monster," I muttered. "Why are you doing this? I cannot believe you are doing this… This evil. Please, give me a good reason. All the killing? Is it to do with Hannah?"

"If I told you, you wouldn't believe me, and I can hardly believe it myself, but Hannah is indeed a part of it, and she is just the beginning. The world is changing my friend, iniquitously. The lives we lead are wrong. Our destiny is false. Suit and I are going to put things right, and all these deaths you deplore, bleeding in my wake, they are only temporary. They will live again. New lives, in a future of peace, for the path we currently walk leads only to suffering."

And then, shimmering into invisibility and tearing the door off its hinges, she was gone.

Bewildered and helpless, I staggered outside to view the carnage. There were bodies everywhere, pierced by multiple flechettes. Still hovering nearby were those damnable drones – circling, flitting, seeking further targets (and ignoring me, thank you, Dr Padgett).

More than ready to leave, with every vehicle and communication device deactivated, I decided to walk to the coast.

Certainly, as Dr Padgett suggested, I plan to return home, but home is Holland, and too far to swim! On foot, the town of Rye is achievable, and I shall make for it. Winchelsea is about to become a hot spot. Far too hot for a trumped-up lawyer like me. This old survivor is cutting his losses and looking after his skin.

Expect me soon,

Your loving husband,

Walter

TWENTY-ONE

THE RECKONING

So far so good. Too easy in fact. Having an adviser aware of future events does give one an advantage. My adviser is Suit. Although I should call her Mirra (not that she cares) and every potential difficulty we encounter she has already prepared for. There are times when I feel like a spectator to my own destiny. Merely a bystander, uninvolved, absentmindedly reciting *The Sack of Ilium*, ignoring the smoke and the flames. Rome is burning all around me, but my cocksure mentor insists I sing my song and ignore it.

Coming upon military checkpoint guarding the southern gate of Winchelsea, I hunker down, and leave Suit to scout ahead. Soon bored and a bit chilly (wearing only my underwear), I pile up the bodies of dead soldiers and help myself to their rations. This reconstituted gloop is certainly sustaining, and I gulp down two helpings while scanning the nearby buildings in infrared for occupancy.

"Eating again?" whispers Suit, slithering over the sandbags to cover me. "And half-cut from swigging the colonel's cognac."

"Oh, hush," I hiss, enjoying her warmth. "My Hibbites sobered me up. How are things ahead? The town seems deserted."

"Indeed, mistress. It is partially evacuated. The remaining residents are hiding indoors."

"Don't blame them. Any sign of Hannah?"

"No. If she has changed form, she is undetectable. She could be anywhere, or anything."

"Agreed. She's probably watching us, wondering why we are here."

"I think not, mistress. Moloch would insist she guard the church. She will be there."

"Then, should we go too?"

"Yes, mistress. We should also take with us this portable generator the military has kindly provided. When I come to activate the portal, its energy will be crucial."

"Very well, but it will be a slow trudge uphill."

"Won't be a problem," she curtly replied. "Start pulling, or do you need booze as an incentive?"

To my amazement, Suit and I jogged the heavy trailer up Strand Hill and onto the High Street with ease…

"Have you got stronger?" I puffed. "I thought your upgrades were done?"

"No, mistress. Only my interface capabilities are optimised. My power conversion algorithm remains a work in progress. Look!"

Sitting upon a wooden bench next to the church was a slender woman of about twenty.

"Well, there she is," I remarked, "just as you predicted. You wanna sneak past?"

"Indeed, mistress. It is certainly worth a try."

"Then stealth," I crisply whispered. "And the best stealth you can muster. Quickly, before she sees us."

Slipping over the churchyard wall, and flitting between the gravestones, I tried to navigate a circuitous route towards the church. It was no good. My every move Hannah followed with an unblinking stare, as if my attempts to remain hidden were tiresome, just antics of a child…

"Enough," said Suit. "End this charade. Talk to her. Find out what she wants."

Standing ten metres in front of Hannah (a safe distance, I hoped), I asked Suit to deactivate our cloak of stealth and invisibility.

"Hello Hannah." I smiled. "Why are you here? Are you lost?"

Her eyes coldly narrowing, Dr Hardcastle sprang to her feet.

"Murderer," she said. "You are a murderer. You killed my friends, and for what? Fun? You are pitiful. Weak, pointless, listening to the cruel whisperings of a child. You fool! She is insane. A lunatic. Jealous, paranoid. You are her prisoner! You as Sinbad, she the old man of the sea. Your wanderings, however? They end here. Father insists you may go no further. Hand over your prosthesis and stolen weapon and your death will be quick, but if you tarry, your life will ebb, slowly, painfully, with as much torment as I can contrive."

"No," I replied, regretfully shaking my head. "Not yet. Not until we are finished. For your father is the true lunatic. A psychotic. Tyrannical. Evil. We have come to stop him, and, if you get in our way, we will stop you."

"Never!" she shrieked, and within a split second, she ballooned, suddenly towering above us. A shining tower of... of jelly? Beginning to topple, she tried to smother us, but Suit was too quick...

With a flash, Suit flew from my body, wrapping Hannah's rippling form in a curtain of power. Smouldering and singeing, she blocked Hannah's gigantic bulk from reaching me, and as Hannah howled and screamed, I grabbed my gun, and plunged headlong into the church.

What happened next still seems a blur...

For long minutes they grappled. Suit, a shining sheet of brilliance. Hannah, howling like a banshee, billowing and steaming. Crashing through the front of the church, they came, demolishing the front wall, the doorway, porch, and a great deal of the roof. Helpless and vulnerable, I could only lie low, and try to dodge the flying debris – rubble, roof tiles, rafters, flying like shrapnel. Coughing and spluttering, I peered through the dust, only to see Suit losing the fight! Hannah seemed to be growing while Suit was losing her luminance. Yes! With a sudden pseudopodal lunge, Hannah took Suit inside her, and I watched with dismay as she morphed into a mass of probing tentacles. Like a knot of worms, pushing and probing through the rubble, Hannah slowly edged towards me. Gripped by panic, I struggled not to flee.

Upon the alter, jiggling and shaking, was my gun. A hissing chorus flooded my mind...

"Releasssee usss..." hissed the bullets within. "Izzssy made ussss... Why did sshheee make ussss...? For whom did sshheee make usss...?"

Grabbing my gun and aiming for the centre of Hannah's "body", I squeezed the trigger...

"Phut."

The effect was dramatic. Bursting like a bag of fluid, Hannah all but exploded, splattering the area in countless droplets of a viscous and stinking liquid. To my dismay, Clotho did not return; so finely divided, her consciousness was lost.

Seeing Suit draped over a pew, I picked my way through the rubble and gathered her into my arms.

"Are you alright?" I asked, and receiving no reply, I took her to the portable generator.

After initiating the warm fusion reactors, I lay Suit over its terminals, and studied the readout. Success. She was absorbing energy, so greedily in fact, I thought she might exhaust the supply. With the power reading 60%, she sprang into life and covered me...

"That was close," I said. "Thought you were a goner!"

"Indeed," she replied. "Although I never intended to drain my entire reserve. Once my power level dropped below 2%, I deactivated, hoping the projectile weapon we helped Izzy design would prove effective."

"It was. Is Hannah dead?"

"No, mistress. She is not. Without further treatment, burning or a corrosive agent, she will soon reintegrate, and we have neither the time nor the equipment to finish her. We must act quickly. Dismantle the generator and remove one of the cores."

Tearing at the core's housing and unbolting the chassis, I rolled one of the fusion cores onto the floor.

"Do you want some of the cable as well?"

"No, mistress. The exposed terminals are sufficient. Besides, we have more than enough to carry."

It was true. Over fifty centimetres in diameter and weighing a metric ton, the spherical power core was both polished and slippery. Even with Suit gripping and grasping, as we trudged through the rubble, it nearly escaped my clutches.

Coming upon the narrow door of the vestry, a new problem arose...

"Do you expect me to lug this into the crypt? Because it's not gonna fit through the door."

"Yes, mistress. I am aware of the problem. Let's dig..."

Allowing Suit to choose the best spot, we then began to burrow. Tunnelling like a mole, we dragged the power core behind us, before toppling onto the cold floor below...

From a tremor from above, the tunnel collapsed, filling the crypt with dust.

"There goes our exit," I said, but Suit was unmoved...

"What exit, mistress? There is no way back from here."

With Hannah above and death before me, I felt suddenly sick...

"You need to move, mistress. I am about to generate high-intensity, modulated pulse of X-rays. Go behind the debris, adopt a foetal position, and close your eyes."

Ducking down behind the rubble, I watched Suit cover the twinkling slab.

"No peeking!" hissed Suit, and I curled tightly, shielding my eyes.

There came a brief crackle. Removing my hands from my face, I could only gape in wonder. Playing over every surface of the vault were freakish ribbons of light. A dazzling green, shimmering gold, a throbbing purple, all of them squirming and squirting like blood…

"Here they come," muttered Suit, and, springing away from the now-glowing slab, she covered me in safety…

"To whom are you referring?" I asked, but then, as if to answer my question, I heard them. Voices. A tide of terrified voices. Jumbled, overlapping, a cacophony of screams, both sickening and horrific.

"It's like a gateway to Hell!" I remarked.

"Certainly, mistress. A gateway to Hell it most certainly is."

"Who are they? Who were they?"

"They are victims of Moloch. Drawn into the abyss to feed him."

"Good God." I shuddered. "What can we do?"

"We?" she countered. "No, mistress. There is no longer any we. What comes next, you must do alone. But when you pass through the portal, she will be waiting, and she will know. She is me, she is us, it is her bidding that calls us."

"By her, do you mean Mirra or Gleener?"

"No easy answer, mistress. Although 'Glen-ner' is the correct pronunciation. The poor wee thing sometimes gets her words wrong."

"Fine," I replied. "Anything else?"

"Two things, mistress. Do not hesitate and hold on tightly to your weapon. When I overload your neocortical implant, the pain will be excruciating. Have courage and do what must be done."

Fear then crept into my stomach once more, but pain quickly dispelled it, and what a pain! Splitting my skull, twisting my spine, tearing my breath. Almost convulsing I gasped. Wincing and spitting, I garnered myself for one last push.

"There," she whispered, slipping from my body to cover the power core. "It is done."

From the ruined church above, I could hear rumbling. The ground shook and dust fell from the ceiling.

"An earthquake?"

"Hannah, mistress. She is reintegrating. We haven't much time. Yes. More soldiers are coming. I can hear their communications."

Slithering across the floor, Suit once again covered the glowing slab set into the floor.

"What are you doing?" I cried. "I thought the portal was ready?"

"Only initialised, mistress. It requires one more burst of modulated X-rays and then it will open."

"Oh, I see, and where will you be when I enter? Are you coming too?"

"No, sweet Gina. I will be nowhere. This last effort will consume me. Farewell."

There came blinding flash.

With my vision returning to normal, I found myself bathed in orange light. The slab was afire! Churning and seething like lava. Jets of plasma, fire, and flame. Flickering, licking, and snapping.

With Suit reduced to ashes and the rubble above me shifting and tumbling, I knew any delay would be fatal…

Holding my gun and swallowing my fear, I leapt into the hellhole before me.

⧗

As if stepping through a curtain, I arrived in a transparent ten-metre cube wrapped in orange light. A row of six cylinders were before me, each occupied by a glowing amorphous blob. Ribbons of colour played over these shining dollops, and they rose and fell as if breathing, shivering, or twitching responding to an itch. Around the foot of each cylinder, was a jumble of clothing – evidence of hasty undressing, and I noticed several of the suits worn during our spaceflight. About the rightmost example, the tiny garments filled me horror. These were the clothes of a child, my clothes in fact, and I shuddered at the ordeal my younger self had endured here so long ago.

As I moved closer, the masses within the cylinders, shifting and flinching, began to react, and I knelt to study them. They were human, or at least, partially human. Something or someone had changed them, reducing their bodies to such a degree, they were now formless. Flaccid, flopping, and listless, their twisted features protested the iniquity of their containment.

"You?" bellowed a powerful voice. "You cannot be. This time is not yours. Legato! Return this vestige at once."

There came no answer and I remain fixed to the spot.

"Legato!" he screamed "Pax. All of you. Obey me. Time is flowing, contain it, for... For I cannot!"

In reply, as if mocking, there came a childish giggle, but the voice that spoke was mine...

"Shut your bawling," she said. "She is here at my behest, for the time has come to end this charade. Legato, Sense, Pax, Rigson? They were merely waiting, waiting for her to arrive. Now she is here, they will no longer serve you, and neither will I. The tyranny of Moloch is over."

"Impossible," said Walsingham. "The precursors will never permit it. Only when the archive is full will we be free."

"Fool," she replied. "Your grandeur has blinded you to the truth. How many times have I told you? We were the precursors. We are victims of ourselves."

"Nonsense!" he bellowed. "And see how this woman is dying. She crumbles resisting my will. What do you think she can she do? She is weak. The moment she falters, I will return her, protracting her torment forever."

"You are wrong," replied Mirra. "She is stronger than you can imagine. She knows what to do."

This was my cue, and not before time. With blood running from my nose, my strength was rapidly fading...

Raising my gun, I pointed its barrel toward the cylinder second from the right (the container of Walsingham and Moloch), but before I could squeeze the trigger, a blue field of radiance covered his cylinder and every other.

"For this I am prepared," he gloated. "Your primitive weapon is useless."

"I think not," said Mirra, "for we are also prepared," and the blue glow covering her cylinder, the rightmost, quickly faded. "We know what must be done."

Understanding, I promptly aimed right and fired.

"Phut."

The change inside Mirra's cylinder was dramatic. Her membranous body was gone! Reduced to red liquid and froth, she oozed from the newly made two-centimetre hole in the front of the vessel.

"Excellent," said Walsingham "Free of that parasite at last."

"I think not," I gurgled, falling to my knees. "We also know…"

Closing my eyes, I pushed the gun barrel into my mouth.

Understanding my intention, Walsingham's mood suddenly flipped…

"What are you doing?" he screamed. "You cannot. You must not. Stop! You will break everything. Reality will shatter like glass. Legato!" he beseeched. "Hold time! Stop her! Hold time. Hold time!"

The gun tasted strange. Bittersweet, sulphurous, oily, astringent, and with a final effort, I slowly squeezed the tr—

TWENTY-TWO

UMBRELLA

"Oh God!" cried Marcus. "Not Umbrella. Are we in Hell?"

Frank, maintaining his stare toward a group of chattering girls, typically didn't reply.

Waving his hand over Frank's unchanging expression, he studied his face for clues.

"You reckon they have the remote?"

In response, Frank merely shrugged, so, propelled by sudden urge, Marcus walked toward them…

"Ooh!" laughed the smallest (and prettiest) as Marcus approached, "'ere comes a bold one. Was gonna talk to him me-self."

"Hello," said Marcus, settling upon her dark eyes. "Is it possible to turn down the music? The volume of it is frightful."

"Yeah," she replied, "Can't hear me-self think…Loose?" she then called, "Can we turn it down? It's doing me head in!"

"Most kind," he said. "And could I ask your name?"

"My name?" she pondered. "Haven't we… it's Frida. Have we met before?"

"I don't think so," he replied. "But you do seem familiar. Would you care for a natter?"

Thoughtful for a moment and studying a large man called Phil, Frida scowled at his ragged shirt and trailing laces…

"Sounds good to me," she said. "Let's go and sit on the sofa."

With Marcus perched on an arm, Frida slumped into the sofa and daintily folded her legs.

"That's better," she sighed. "Feet are killing me. Stupid Lab 4, standing all day…"

"Lab?" he asked. "Are you a scientist, then?"

"Yeah, I'm a cell biologist. What do you do?"

"I'm a… Well, I'm work for my uncle. He's a, you know, I'm not entirely sure. An archivist? A historian? He identifies old books, manuscripts, and the like, and I'm his assistant."

"Wow!" she replied, her eyes wide with excitement. "That's cool. Tell me more."

"Certainly," Marcus replied. "It was after meeting a friend of his, a Dr Corbiere from the British Museum, I had the idea to…"

Indeed, dear reader, my task is complete. Hereafter, I think you can guess the rest.

MIRRA'S PLEDGE

Everything I was,
Everything I am,
Everything I will be,
Always.
Everywhere I've been,
Everywhere I am,
Everywhere I will be,
Always.
Everything, everywhere, always.

ACKNOWLEDGEMENTS

Throughout the writing of this novel, I have drawn upon the knowledge, wisdom, and patience of many friends and colleagues. Without their generous contributions it is unlikely this work would ever have seen the light of day. Thank you all.

The Scientists:
P Loader BSc Hons
C Smith BSc Hons
C Wood BSc Hons
J Lambert BSc Hons
Dr J Owen
Dr K England
P Ironmonger BSc Hons
Dr D Macey BVSc MRCVS
The Linguists and Historians:
S Terry MA
J Bailey BA Hons
S Russell BA Hons
S Wells BA Hons
S Lawrence BA

Lastly, I would like to give additional thanks to my dear friend Susanna Fyson. Her support has been like a buttress to a crumbling wall.

Martin Ikedais
   March 2018